JEAN SANTEUIL

Marcel Proust

TRANSLATED BY
Gerard Hopkins

WITH A PREFACE BY
André Maurois

SIMON AND SCHUSTER
NEW YORK
1956

LIBRARY OF CONGRESS CATALOG CARD NUMBER: 55-12297
MANUFACTURED IN THE UNITED STATES OF AMERICA
PRINTED BY MURRAY PRINTING COMPANY, WAKEFIELD, MASS.
BOUND BY RIVERSIDE PRESS, CAMBRIDGE, MASS.

Contents

Preface by André Maurois

When excerpts from *Jean Santeuil* first appeared in print, there were not a few readers who after a hurried glance were quick to voice a protest. "Why publish at all?" they said: "Proust himself decided to consign this version to oblivion, and it is for us to respect his wishes." I think, indeed I am sure, that they were wrong. There is really no connexion between the attitude towards his early drafts of a writer who later returned to the same subject with happier results, and the view taken of the "preliminary sketches for a masterpiece" by an admirer of the finished product. Because a painter decided to suppress the early studies which he made for a great picture, is that a reason why we should do the same? They have their own peculiar beauty, more casual than that of the achieved work, more adventurous, sometimes, even, more moving. It would of course, be wrong to present as final a text destroyed or completely recast by the author. But to publish a first attempt *as such*, to give the reader an opportunity to study the growing-pains of genius to set the earlier *Education Sentimentale* side by side with the second, or to compare *Les Misères* with *Les Misérables*, seems to me not only a useful but a praiseworthy enterprise.

I can say this with a clear conscience since I played no active part in the finding of the manuscript. When I was engaged on my book, *The Quest for Proust*, Madame Gérard Mante-Proust kindly put at my disposition a great many of her uncle's unpublished note-books. In these I found the early "states" of many scenes familiar to us in their finished form, a number of files, and some fragments of *Within a Budding Grove* written like *Swann in Love* in the third person, because, at that time, Proust had not had the courage to bring himself upon the stage. I knew that there still existed in the rue Alfred-Déhodenque house a great many papers which had not yet been even classified. When Bernard de Fallois, then a young literary graduate, told me that he was planning a thesis on Proust, I begged Madame Mante to give him access to her records with full liberty to make what use he liked of anything that he might find. She handed over to him not only the seventy note-books, of which he managed to make fair-copies, but also several boxes of torn and detached pages, which had been found in a wardrobe at the time of Marcel Proust's death. Neither Dr. Robert Proust, nor his daughter, had even thought that they might contain anything in the nature of a consecutive narrative. Bernard de Fallois took on the labour of garnering this abundant crop. His foresight, his tenacity, his pious and patient attention to detail, were amply rewarded. He found that he could piece together a complete novel—*Jean Santeuil*.

As an archaeologist, spade in hand, excavates from beneath a temple the traces of an older sanctuary, and, digging deeper still, an altar cut in the rock and dedicated to some prehistoric cult, this Proustian investigator found, behind the primitive *Swann* of whom I had chanced to get a glimpse, and sandwiched between *Les Plaisirs et les Jours* and *Remembrance of Things Past*, a novel consisting of a thousand pages, the existence of which nobody had so much as suspected. It was to be sure a matter of general knowledge that, in a dedication to Pierre Lavellée, dating from 1896, Proust had written: "I talk about MY book as though I were never to write another. You know that that is very far from the truth. Should I ever finish the one on which I am now engaged, I trust that you will not deprive me of the inspiration born of your affection, and the reward of your understanding. I beg that you will be tender to the faults which are the best of myself. Water them, and help them to grow"[1] ... Towards the end of September 1896, he said, in a letter to his mother: "I won't go so far as to say that I have as yet worked at my novel in the sense of being absorbed by it, or of seeing it as a whole. But I can at least declare that the exercise-book which I bought (several days before your departure)—incidentally, it represents only part of the work I have done, because, previous to that, I was writing on loose sheets—has now been completely filled, and it contains a hundred and ten large pages."[2] ... In 1899, he was still working at his novel. *To Marie Nordlinger, 5th December, 1899*: "For some considerable time now, I have been slaving away at a very long and exacting work, without, as yet, making much progress."[3] He was not speaking here of his translation of Ruskin, since he adds: "For the last fortnight I have been engaged on a minor work, something entirely different from what, for most of the time, I have been doing—an essay on Ruskin and Certain Cathedrals." It was round about 1900 that he started on his translations.

[1] Marcel Proust: *Correspondance Générale*, Volume IV, pp. 17–18.
[2] Letter quoted in *The Quest for Proust*, p. 114.
[3] Marcel Proust: *Lettres à une Amie*, pp. 5–6.

The novel was laid aside. It was long thought that these allusions to an earlier work referred to fragmentary and preliminary sketches for *Swann*. In a sense that was true, because *Jean Santeuil* is an anticipation of *Remembrance*, but so different from the completed work that a comparison of the two books cannot but provide a thrilling subject of study for literary historians and critics, while the especial beauties of the earlier book—of which only a part has been preserved in the reconstructed novel—will provide Proust addicts with fresh reasons for loving his masterpiece.

Not, I repeat, that we are here concerned with anything as perfect as *Remembrance of Things Past*. "I am writing at top speed: there is so much that I want to say." *Jean Santeuil*, written at top speed, was never revised by its author. Its repetition of words, the carelessness of its style, are obvious. The manuscript is an attempt to discover a technique for the novel which Proust had in mind. The process of transposition—so necessary to every novelist—is here little more than adumbrated. *Jean Santeuil* bears the marks of being much more naïvely autobiographical than *Remembrance*. The hero's mother and father are much more like the persons they actually were than are those of the final version. They had, in the interval, been sublimated by death, and we find in the bitter-loving quarrels of Jean Santeuil with his parents an echo, scarcely distorted, of the letters written by Proust as a young man. The accursed fires of Sodom and Gomorrha burn but feebly in the shadows, for the author dared not fan their flames during his mother's life-time. But the thing most to be noticed is that Proust had not yet found his true subject, which was later to give birth to the novel of novels—the progress from Time Lost to Time Regained. One cannot help thinking as one reads, of those early pictures by Cézanne and Van Gogh, which though far removed in manner from those painters' masterpieces, give us, because we know what was to come, the pleasure of recognizing the promise which they both so magnificently fulfilled.

*

What then *is Jean Santeuil*? "Should I call this book a novel?"—wrote Proust:—"it is something less, perhaps, and yet much more, the very essence of my life, with nothing extraneous added, as it developed through a long period of wretchedness. This book of mine has not been manufactured: it has been garnered." That is true. It was garnered, as chance dictated, by a man wandering through the bye-ways of time, who made no effort to follow a straight road, or to reach a definite objective. The characters appear and disappear as they do in real life, where successive layers of friends and familiars are laid bare, but never interpenetrate, and not at all as we are accustomed to find in novels, where the artist always sets himself to maintain a certain unity. So fearful too was Proust of identifying himself too closely with his hero, that he sets an even greater distance between the two by providing an Introduction in which he describes how, in a Breton farmhouse-hotel, he and a friend meet a famous writer, called C. whom the future author regards as the greatest novelist of his generation. The two young men make friends with C. who reads aloud to them the book on which he is working: "a long story, interrupted by passages of com-ment in which the author expressed his views on this and that in the manner of certain English novelists of whom at one time he had been very fond". The two friends learn from C. that the story on which he is engaged is strictly true, since he is incapable of writing about any-thing that he has not personally experienced. Numerous touches show that C. is Proust himself, obstinately though the fiction of the "second remove" is kept up. At the end of the Introduction, C. dies, and though the papers have said nothing of any novel being found among his manuscripts, the friends decide to publish the copy in their possession.

This long prefatory chapter seems to serve two purposes. It provides the familiar convention of a manuscript "found in a bottle" or com-municated by a stranger, and so allows the author to shift all responsi-bility on to an imaginary person, and it gives Marcel an opportunity to paint a first "portrait of the artist", since the methods of work which he attributes to C. closely resemble his own: C.'s love of the English novelists which corresponds closely to that felt by Proust for Dickens, Eliot, and Hardy, to whom he owed so much: his way of interspersing his reading with self-criticism designed to forestall that of his listeners, and, lastly (this more secret, more intimate), a certain sadism which the two friends are surprised to find in a man who seems to be so kind. Everything in this Introduction echoes what we know of Proust's own character.

It is at this point that the novel proper begins. The opening scene at once strikes a familiar note. It shows us the little Jean Santeuil suffering because his mother, who wants to bring him up to be manly, refuses one evening when a great doctor is paying a visit to her and her husband, to go upstairs when he is in bed, to give him a good-night kiss. It is clear that Proust's whole life was "milestoned" by a number of extremely powerful impressions, which provided the essential themes of all his work. His mother's kiss is one of these. It is not long before we are introduced to another—the terrible misery of being deprived of a daily meeting, in the Champs-Elysées, with a little girl who has become his first love. In *Swann* this little girl is Gilberte: here she is called Marie Kossichef, her Christian name being that of the "model" for both who, as is now known, was Marie Bernadaky. Jean is sent to a Lycée where he shines less brightly than might have been expected of a boy of his very considerable culture, because in his French compositions where what is required is a smooth and conventional style, he pours out his feelings of love and pity in too feverish a fashion, and adorns his writing with images borrowed from the poets. Jean's favourite reading is not the same as that of the Narrator in *Remembrance* (there is actually a space of ten years between the two books): they share it is true a passion for Balzac and Stendhal, but Jean Santeuil, like the Marcel of the letters to his mother, revels especially in Leconte de Lisle and Théophile Gautier. He will have nothing to do with the classical authors, finding them too rational. He likes to think with Leconte de Lisle—a philosopher with a special appeal for the young—that all life is lies and vanity, and that:

La vie antique est faite inépuisablement
De tourbillon sans fin des apparances vaines.

The second section takes us to Etreuilles, the first manifestation of Combray. The future Françoise appears as Ernestine. The great-aunt is there, a comic oddity. The magic-lantern projects the figures of Génevieve de Brabant and of Golo. Already the lilacs, the apple-trees, the hawthorns of Illiers are transmuted into things both magical and strange: the poppy flaunts an exquisite and scarlet flag at the end of its long stalk: the asparagus bring delight to Jean because of their tender tints of blue and rose. But these pictures entrancing though they are, have a summary quality. The Proust of *Remembrance* was to be a far greater landscape painter.

The third section shows us something quite new. We were not unaware that Darlu, his professor of philosophy, exercised a profound influence on Proust. *Jean Santeuil* introduces us into Darlu's class, and gives us a loving portrait of the man, here called Monsieur Beulier.

The scene in which he takes back his own New Year's gift, the description of his servant, are beautifully "done" and altogether absent from the greater novel. Meanwhile Jean has been introduced into the great world by one of his school-friends, Henri, son of the Duc de Réveillon, "the premier Duke of France", and by his own aunt, Madame Desroches. He discovers the "Guermantes Way". Visits to Réveillon, in Champagne, serve in the fourth section as an excuse for natural description and of portraiture. Much of the latter is excellent, but the curious feature of this portraiture is that the persons painted live scarcely longer than it takes the author to describe them, with the result that they move through the book more like the "Characters" of La Bruyère than the people of a Balzac novel.

The fifth section, and this again is peculiar to the earlier work, is closely bound up with two political events of the period—the Panama Scandal and the Dreyfus Affair. We witness the fall of a great Minister, Charles Marie. Proust was too much of a poet, and too fair-minded, not to see that there was something disturbing, something cowardly, in this execution by his own friends of a man who, though undoubtedly guilty, had yet like most human beings in a similar position, a deal of fundamental innocence in his make-up. There is matter enough in this episode to serve for a whole novel by Balzac—or by Proust himself— which might well have been intensely interesting but, in fact, was never worked out. At a later stage we are given the opportunity to be present at the session of the *Cour de Cassation* which revised the sentence passed on Dreyfus. Colonel Picquart and General de Boisdeffre are presented in a series of impressionist touches, and with remarkable honesty, for in spite of his pro-Dreyfus sympathies, Proust had the courage to show Picquart in a disappointing light, and Boisdeffre as an impressive figure. Very little of this material was used in *Remembrance*, and where used at all, was not amplified. In the later book, Proust very wisely dealt with the "Affair", not by bringing the chief actors on to the stage, but by showing events only as they were reflected in the minds of Saint-Loup, Bloch, and the Guermantes.

The sixth section moves to Begmeil in Brittany. It contains a superb description of a storm: "Tempest at Penmarch", and ends with the first appearance of the linked feelings of present experience and remembered past, a theme which in *Remembrance* is bound up with the episode of the "madeleine", and serves as a prelude to the whole work. In *Jean Santeuil* it appears as no more than a short passage on the violin,

which becomes quickly submerged. But for us who know the greater
Proust there is genuine pleasure in this "first state" which gives us
the theme in a more modest and ephemeral form. The seventh section
introduces us to army life at Provins—a foretaste of the later passages
dealing with Saint-Loup. But this part of the manuscript contains in
addition to a number of fine landscape-pieces, sketches of Réveillon in
Autumn and in Winter, a portrait of la Comtesse Gaspard de
Réveillon, in whom we at once recognize la Comtesse Mathieu de
Noailles, a great poet whose verses are sad but whose conversation is
witty and amusing, a contradiction which surprises Jean until he realizes
the poetry of la Comtesse Gaspard is very far from being insincere:
"On the contrary, they expressed something that went so deep in her,
that she could not even think, still less speak, of it, or define it, because
it was so different from her apparent self that to have revealed it in talk
would have seemed to her a sort of sacrilege. . . ."

Eighth section. Among a number of characters, destined never to
appear again, some of whom are spiteful enough to resent Jean's rapid
rise in the great world, he renews acquaintance with Marie Kossichef,
with whom as a child he had been so deeply in love, only to find that
this side of him is dead (first appearance of the theme of relativity in
love, and the withering away of feeling). It is to the subject of love and,
in particular, of the love felt by Jean for Madame S—— (Françoise)
that the ninth section is devoted. It bears a very close resemblance to
Swann, and the reader gets the impression that the author has matured
since the book was begun. He has experienced the agonies of jealousy.
He knows now that "When passions burst into bud on a full-grown
branch which has already known the burgeoning of many others, they
no more resemble the emotions felt in the dawning years of life, than the
hedgerose resembles the cultivated species . . ." The analysis of feeling is
here almost as subtle and profound as in *Remembrance*. The sole weakness of this part of the book is due to the fact that the personages live
only in terms of feeling. Françoise lacks the clear-cut characteristics
of Odette, as does Jean those of Swann. These abstract human
symbols belong to the world of the moralist rather than to that of the
writer of fiction. Still, the episode is in itself remarkable, and the "little
phrase"—here identified as a passage from the Saint-Saëns Sonata—
sheds upon it the light of that divine smile which as time passes and
it is no longer loved, becomes sad and disenchanted.

The final section concludes with some wonderful pages on the old age of Monsieur and Madame Santeuil. There is nothing comparable to that miraculous passage in which all the characters of the later book reappear "wearing the disguise of old age", for the author of *Jean Santeuil* was younger than the man who wrote *Remembrance*, and his contemporaries had not lived long enough to grow white hair. Nor does *Jean Santeuil* end with *Time Regained*, since Proust had not yet come to understand that the door of salvation through art was the only one through which he could pass. But the end of the earlier book is already filled with the poignant, yet consoling, sense of the irremediable, implacable, and continuous flight of Time. The tide of the years rises and engulfs the generations of men, who keep to their last gasp the ideas which were theirs in youth, but modified by age, blurred by disenchantment, and coloured by the reflection in themselves of their children. As a man of the seventeenth century, be he prince or artist, is seen by us essentially as a man of his time, so do Monsieur Santeuil and the Duc de Réveillon, in spite of social differences, show as representatives of the years round 1870 in which they grew to manhood, whereas both Jean Santeuil and Henri de Réveillon, born along on the following wave, belong to the group of those who "were twenty in 1890". This bird's-eye view of the lives of individuals brings out their poetry and their vanity, their humbleness and their grandeur. Madame Santeuil looks at her dozing husband, and sees that his sleep is already within measurable distance of death. The working of Time cannot be interrupted, and this sketch, finding its end in the idea of Time, marvellously heralds the much greater picture which the painter was now in a position to begin.

*

It should now be abundantly clear that *Jean Santeuil* is an entirely different book from *Remembrance of Things Past*, not only because it is unfinished, but because it lacks the master theme of the later work (the metamorphosis of a weak and nervous child into an artist); the continuity of the leading characters (Odette, Swann, Charlus, Legrandin, Norpois, Vinteuil, and many others are not yet born); the decision to write in the first person, and the courage to plunge into the sulphurous abyss of Sodom.

But no great writer is formed from nothing in middle life, and it is only to be expected that something of the author of *Remembrance* should be already apparent in the author of *Jean Santeuil*. Even in the earlier book there is an intuitive awareness of the nature of that substance from which all humanity is shaped, which never varies. The young Proust already has the equipment of a moralist who behind his observation of the individual can trace the general law. When he describes an old man Monsieur Sandré (Madame Santeuil's father), he is really describing all old men, "The expression on Monsieur Sandré's face might be dour, but, because he was old, it was also gentle. Old people do not love themselves, they love their children. They adore them, and must leave them. They suffer, not on their own account, but because they see their children failing to do what they ought to do. . . . They suffer from this knowledge but forgive those through whom they have gained it and go so far even as to admire what they condemn, because the severity of their judgment has lost its edge, so that they have become resigned to the inevitable and faults, just because they are their children's faults, are dear to them. . . ."

Everything serves him as a pretext for tracing unexpected resemblances between apparently diverse facts though in reality those facts, for all their seeming difference, are controlled by the same laws. Here is an example of what I mean. Jean at Etreuilles was far from blind to the cruelty of which Ernestine was guilty in her dealings with the kitchen-maids whom she tormented, and the animals she slaughtered. But in spite of his sensitiveness, he "could not help, at Etreuilles, taking sides with the only person who knew how to make his bed as he liked it, who produced all his favourite dishes and brought his coffee at exactly the right heat, and such beautifully smooth, not too thick, chocolate and cream. No matter how anxious we may be to act fairly and charitably towards others, our good will always goes to the barber who shaves us without drawing blood and can arrange our hair in such a way as to make us look our best. . . . At the risk of exposing him to a dressing-down from the proprietor of the shop and perhaps being sacked, we cannot bring ourselves to endure the attentions of the well-meaning assistant who . . . cuts our hair so that it looks like nothing on earth and, in his eagerness to show off, interlards his talk with pretentious phrases, and feel even less kindly towards him when, looking in the glass, we see ourselves becoming, minute by minute, less presentable under his innocent but clumsy ministrations."

It is borne in upon us how clearly Proust's sovereign intelligence realized that the truths of science must be general truths, though because that intelligence belonged to a poet, it never toppled over into the abstract. "Fortunately for the novelist there are fewer tastes and characters than there are human beings, or rather even the most highly individualized of human beings shares sufficiently in the tastes and characteristics of a very large number of his or her fellows to make it possible for me, when speaking of my friends, to surprise you by the deep knowledge I seem to have of yours, though I have never so much as seen one of them, so that like the simple-minded spectator of a card trick, you do not realize that the conjuror need not, by some miracle, have seen the card you drew in order to be able to tell you what it is, because the pack from which you made apparently a perfectly free choice was in fact composed of identical cards."

Proust was so well aware that the moralist and the novelist must go hand in hand, that he demands this double nature in his favourite authors, and is particularly happy when he comes on some comment in the course of their narrative which has nothing directly to do with the matter of the fiction. "For a writer whom we adore becomes for us a species of oracle whom we long to consult on a multiplicity of matters so that whenever he takes the stage and gives us his opinion, expresses some general idea . . . we are enchanted, and listen open-mouthed to the casually dropped maxim, disappointed only that it takes so short a time to utter. . . ." We no less than he experience this feeling in regard to Balzac and Stendhal, both of them writers who are unaffectedly prone to make aphorisms, and even more in regard to himself, for the long chapter on Madame S—— contains a complete essay "*On Love*". No philosopher has ever analysed the emotion of hatred with greater penetration than Proust displayed in the following passage. "Of this nature is the hatred which compounds from the lives of our enemies a fiction which is wholly false. We attribute to them not that state of normal human happiness shot through with the common sorrows of mankind which should move us to entertain for them a feeling of kindly sympathy, but a species of arrogant delight which merely pours oil upon the furnace of our rage. It transfigures people no less than does desire. . . . On the other hand, since it can find satisfaction only in destroying that delight, it imagines it, it believes it to be, it sees it, in a perpetual condition of destruction. No more than love does it concern itself with reason, but goes through life with eyes fixed on an unconquerable hope. . . ."

And so he appears to us as a moralist, and a man animated by a high nobility of feeling. Proust was brought up by parents whose strictness

and narrowness of outlook sometimes wounded him, though they
taught him by the example of their lives to have a sense of honour and
of loyalty. He may have come to see sexual love as a relative emotion,
but he never for a moment entertained a doubt of the purity of mother-
love, of tenderness in friendship, of the duty of goodness, of devotion
to beauty whether in nature or in art. The asceticism of the creative
artist could not be described in *Jean Santeuil*—which was conceived
during Proust's worldly phase—as it was later in *Time Regained*, though
a certain solemnity of tone more than once foreshadows it, as in music
we hear announced by an impressive pause, the march or hymn which
in a moment or two will fill the listeners with a sense of enthusiasm or
piety. After the worst moments of hot injustices his heroes become
once again responsive to the sweet influences of a calm and friendly
scene, to the happiness to be found in an exchange of smiles, to the
gentle rustlings of a lovely evening. Often, when Jean is alone in his
room his spirit, freed from all restraint, gives to objects a life not of this
world and he becomes aware of the presence of humble and fraternal
gods. When he finds himself, with his mother or with Monsieur
Beulier, in the presence of generosity of mind pure and undefiled, he
feels an emotion which far from being a merely self-indulgent surrender to sensitiveness, is on the contrary laced through with humour.
"If we really seek to discover the effect of true grandeur upon us, it is
too imprecise to call it just respect, rather is it a sort of familiarity. We
become aware of what is best, of what is most sympathetic in us, and
in others, and we laugh at those others as we laugh at ourselves. . . ."
That is Proust at his best, and it makes us realize incidentally, why he
was so fond of Dickens.

*

The second important thing that strikes us about the author of *Jean
Santeuil*, when the author of *Remembrance* looks through the still mal-
leable mask of his precursor, is that he is a poet. "The truth of the matter
is," he says, "that what happens in a man's life is without interest so long
as it is stripped of the feelings which make that life a poem." From the
very first moment that the earlier book was started, he knew instinctively that truth begins only when the artist "takes two different things,
establishes the relationship between them, and imprisons them within
the necessary construction of a beautiful style". *Jean Santeuil* swarms
with comparisons. More than ever in this achievement of his youth, do

we realize how spontaneously and naturally Proust thought in images. Here are a few examples taken at random. Madame Gaspard de Réveillon finding something to laugh at in everything, and showing by her temperamental response that "gaiety is a basic element in everything, which we can disengage from all that comes our way, without having to look for it, just as carbon is proved by chemical analysis to be not something which we need go to the moon to find but a quality that is present in all bodies which we find around us, needing only to be freed": the Vice-Principal of the Lycée greeting the school dunce with the "timid and protective smile of a Minister meeting the Leader of the Opposition": the dying fire (in the Réveillon mansion) which seems to be in need of fuel, and now and again emits a tiny squeak, "like a cat asking for milk": Jean Santeuil casting a veil over his father's feeble conversation "much as a charming woman will tirelessly labour to set to rights her husband's blunders, or as a painter will envelop the badly drawn portions of his picture in deep shadow": Jean in love "like a hen, not knowing whether she is hatching a chicken or a snake, but, driven by nature to give life to the egg, he brooded over the unknown future and his doubting hopes with all the untiring warmth of an expectant heart": "Life is beautiful only when seen from a distance. Fundamentally it promises nothing more than that can be contained in the most boring of all the hours a schoolboy may spend in form. By 'getting through it somehow' he will have lived all life in advance, as in a small sample of material we can see the whole piece which, after all, is no more than a repetition of the same threads similarly woven": the portrait of General de Boisdeffre, "Though he still gave the impression of youthfulness his cheeks were covered by a delicate red and purple mottling such as one sees on garden walls in autumn when they are clothed in Virginia Creeper."

For Proust knew even then that the second term of comparison, that which is seen through as it were the transparent window of reality, must be brought in juxtaposition with an elementary sensation, or with some spectacle offered by Nature. In *Jean Santeuil* he speaks of the poetry of trees, of wind, of sea, better, young though he was, than any author of his time, and as a man who had tried with something of a mystic's fervour, to achieve communion with things seen, and as a reader who had sought and found the secrets of Chateaubriand and perhaps of Stendhal, too. Take for instance, this passage from the opening pages of the Introduction, "And there in that truly sublime spot he followed with his eyes the movement of the clouds, observed the flight of birds above the sea, listened to the wind, and scanned the sky like an Augur of the ancient world, not so much to draw from these sights a presage of the future, as, so far as I could see, to find in them a memory of the past: for the first drops of falling rain, the sudden piercing of a sunbeam through the murk, sufficed to bring back into his mind rainy autumns of an earlier day, and sunlit summers; whole periods of his life and forgotten states of consciousness which now grew bright again in the intoxicating glow of poetry and of recollection." The high place, the "truly sublime spot", remind us of Stendhal, but the rest of the passage, the description of the natural scene impregnated with human feeling, the whole long and melancholy phrase, belongs to the Proust to be and to be nobody else.

Between the style of *Remembrance* and that of *Jean Santeuil* there are to be sure notable differences. This novel of his youth, this first "state", was written at full speed, and without any of that patient retouching, that smoothing and polishing, which we know from the evidence of the note-books was lavished on his text by the full-blown writer. It is rich as we have just seen in innumerable comparisons, but it is rare to find in it any of those long-drawn-out metaphors, brought up over long distances, their coming announced very quietly by an adjective sent on ahead, then suddenly invading a whole paragraph in close order, like the famous image of the Opéra seen as an aquarium. In *Jean Santeuil* there is less artifice, but also less art.

All the same there is no lack of felicitous resemblances between the two books. We find the same adroit alternation of aphorisms or of elaborately composed periods with extremely simple commonplaces: "This is what I call really hot—a storm would be welcome"—"*I* know someone who's going to enjoy his bed", effects which Proust doubtless borrowed from Anatole France, whose books were his favourite reading at that time. It was from France too that he borrowed the trick of bringing together two dissonant and contradictory adjectives. Not that he often employed it, for he had already developed an especial liking for hedging a substantive within three or more adjectives, the rays of which he directed upon some very precisely delineated subtlety of meaning—"Marie's sparkling, sweet and mocking smile." Though by and large, the phrases are less carefully modelled, there are some, even in the early pages of *Jean Santeuil* which succeed in achieving the masterly precision for which later he was to have so marked a preference—"He mixed his strawberries now and again with small quantities of cream-cheese, with all the accumulated experience of a colourist and the intuition of an epicure."—"A menu may be as informative as a communiqué, but it is also as exciting as a programme."—"'It's my little Christmas celebration' he told his mother with the restraint of a philosopher and the tenderness of a poet."

To sum up: in this work so miraculously saved from oblivion, we find almost all the elements which went to the making of the poetry, at once intellectual, poignant and tender of *Remembrance of Things Past*. Almost but not quite all, for some part of Proust's genius had not yet emerged from limbo. This was largely owing to the fact that, at the time the earlier book was written, he had not embarked on the translation of Ruskin. We can see from a comparison between the style of *Jean Santeuil* (especially that of the first part) and the style of *Swann* how much Marcel was to owe to *The Bible of Amiens*. Painting and music play a less marked role in it. There are no images borrowed from Carpaccio and Mantegna: no references to Zephorax, the daughter of Jethro: no angelic musicians, no warriors leaning on their lances. It was Ruskin who taught Proust to give to his periods the slow movement of breaking waves, or the form of twined curls to be seen in Florentine paintings; to encrust with amethyst and coral the simplest description of flowers, of light reflected on water, of a dish of braised beef. When he wrote *Jean Santeuil* Marcel was still under the influence of Flaubert in whom he was so deeply read, whom he could parody so well. Many pages of this book are written in the imperfect tense beloved of Flaubert, that same imperfect which Proust likened to a moving staircase, and thickly sown with the collective "on": "Tout de même, c'était bien bon quand, commençant à avoir froid, à avoir faim, on retraversait le village et qu'on apercevait derrière les arbres du parc les lampes dans le salon, et qu'anticipant par l'imagination sur ce qui était déja là à attendre, mais qu'on ne trouverait que dans deux minutes, on se sentait près du feu, puis à table sous la lampe, devant la soupe chaude que l'on versait dans votre assiette et qu'on allait a manger."[1]

*

I return to the point which I made when I began. These precious papers were rescued by a combination of luck and intelligent detective

[1] I must apologize to the English reader. There is no form of the English imperfect which could provide an equivalent for Flaubert's (and Proust's) use of that grammatical subtlety. The printing of this passage in French has, therefore, seemed unavoidable.—G.H.

work. Can it seriously be maintained that they should have been left in obscurity? Even to ask that question is to expose it as nonsensical. The friends of Proust, who form an immense society of the spirit scattered through all the countries of the world, will find in *Jean Santeuil* autobiographical details which it is impossible to read unmoved, scenes and characters as yet unknown to them (a political novel, a philosophy class, a lecture on Political Science, a hospital common-room) and early variants of many essential themes. Already the hero has discovered the unreality of life, the emptiness of sorrow caused by the loss of love or friendship, or forced on us when we have to leave places to which we have become attached—an emptiness the full extent of which we realize when other persons and other places inspire us with similar feelings. Only when that happens do we understand that love and attraction are not properties of people or of places, but only of ourselves. The image of the magic-lantern beams in which the objects of our successive love are transformed, does not occur in *Jean Santeuil*, but it is prefigured and announced as, too, is scattered through the book, that moral grandeur and supreme gift of pity which in Proust's work, have the power to purify even immorality. In short the addicts will find here the Proust of their devotion, but younger, sometimes maladroit, often a great artist. They will discover too a Proust whom up till now, they had never known. Who can arrogate to himself the right to deprive them of so much treasure, such a deal of delight? Who, now that the buried ingots have been revealed by a chance blow of the pick-axe, could bring himself to seal the entrance to the magic cave?

ANDRÉ MAUROIS
de l'Académie Française

Translator's Note

English-speaking readers, those of them especially who make their first acquaintance with Proust in the pages of *Jean Santeuil*, may find much of it confusing and confused. In fairness to myself I would point out that not the whole responsibility is mine, but that some part of the burden must be carried by Marcel's ghost. This book was never revised for publication. There was no proof-stage and that, in the case of an author who was the greatest "proof addict" of all literary history, meant the absence of an essential process in the production of a finished work. Instances of carelessness were left uncorrected, and the difficulty of reading Proust's crabbed handwriting has resulted in the creation of additional difficulties of which the author was innocent.

Jean Santeuil was an experiment in both style and method. The long, unrolling, undulating periods, interspersed with parentheses and commas, were here being "tried out", and it is not surprising that as they flowed from Proust's pen, they should sometimes have lost their way. By the time he had mastered this complicated method of writing, the vast sweep of these tremendous sentences had acquired a beauty and a perfection which, once one has come under the spell, are irresistible. Proust did ultimately achieve a sureness of phrasing, and a sense of direction which enabled him to give shape to no matter how elaborately contrived and entwined a pattern. But in his 'prentice days this sureness was lacking, and there are in *Jean Santeuil* many pages in which the writer became quite plainly syntactically lost. This looseness, this uncertainty of drive, is closely bound up with the search for an adequate technique in the telling of the story. *Jean Santeuil* begins as a novel narrated in the first person. But very soon (though only on occasion) the convention is abandoned, and a paragraph which begins with "il" as subject, will be found to progress through "on" to a finally devastating and revealing "je". Names too play the traitor. Etreuilles soon, and without explanation or transition, turns into Illiers—that village near Chartres which later entered into immortality as Combray. Persons too are mentioned —notably in the section entitled "Sunday at Etreuilles" who confuse the reader by their strangeness, and remain unaccounted for. But it is, perhaps, in "Portrait of a Friend" that the most interesting shift of nomenclature occurs. In that chapter the author sets himself to describe Jean's greatest friend—Henri de Réveillon, whom lovers of Proust will at once recognize as a first sketch of Saint-Loup. At once however *Bertrand* is substituted for *Henri,* and it becomes immediately clear that Proust, remembering no less vividly than he was creating, had in mind that Bertrand de Fénelon, on whose character he drew for the complete and ultimate Saint-Loup.

So many are the inconsistencies that I have thought it unnecessary to employ the pedantry, save on rare occasions, of notes, and improper to make the obvious changes. Colonel Picquart is described on the same page as wearing "his sky-blue uniform" and "civilian clothes". Two "Florentines" become "two Venetians". The Réveillon mansion is situated in the rue de Varennes, but an incident occurring in Place de la Concorde is visible from its windows.

But *Jean Santeuil* is more than a projector which throws light upon its infinitely greater successor. It has, as Monsieur Maurois points out, many beauties of its own, as well as a great deal of matter omitted from *A La Recherche du Temps Perdu.* Enthusiasts for that book will find this "first state" wholly fascinating, and so too it is to be hoped, will readers who have not yet been made free of the Proustian world.

As Proust himself points out, a book later to be loved may at first reading seem only to be difficult and exhausting. It is begun, it is abandoned, it is returned half-read to the shelves. Then a day comes when it is taken down again. The labour of the earlier reading will be found to have vanished, and the former feeling of repulsion to have matured into adoration.

GERARD HOPKINS

INTRODUCTION

Should I call this book a novel? It is something less, perhaps, and yet much more, the very essence of my life, with nothing extraneous added, as it developed through a long period of wretchedness. This book of mine has not been manufactured: it has been garnered.

Introduction

I had gone to spend the month of September with a friend at Kerengrimen, which in those days (1895) was a farm tucked away among
apple orchards on the Bay of Concarneau, miles from any village.
A great many Parisians and English people were in the habit of
going there for the summer and using the house as an hotel. But the
owner old Père Buzaret still called it a farm, and was at pains to see that
it should look like one. This he had done on the advice of several
painters who once they had discovered the place returned to it year
after year, staying till the season was well advanced, leaving pictures
behind them when they could not settle their bills, and enjoying his
friendship to a far greater extent than did his other visitors. They
flattered themselves that by teaching him "taste" they had put him well
on the way to make a fortune. Until such a time as the weather broke
—when dinner was served in a well-heated room—meals, worthy of
the marble splendour of the great Swiss hotels, were eaten in the open
air, off rough farm tables, facing the sea. We are often surprised
to meet in the flesh what we have always thought to be an abstraction:
to see with our very eyes the golden-hearted prostitute whom, scout-
ing literary convention, we had imagined to be worse precisely as
novel-reading had taught us to expect, and so too other stock figures,
such as the gardener who loves his flowers and talks of them in a
language rich with picturesque allusions, as well as the rural scene
with all its charms of farm and meadow unspoiled by vulgar embell-
ishments. A painter is as much astonished to discover a sensibility akin
to his own in a ploughman or a sailor, as we are when we come
upon a delicacy worthy of our own refined sensibilities (which those
of our own world so often lack) in the letter of a laundress telling of
the death of her son. The language of our own day striking at us from
a passage of the *Iliad*, some crisis in the history of Egypt revealing a
similarity with an event in our own humdrum lives—such things serve
to show how the basic substance of humanity, often invisible and

3

as though intermitted, is still a living reality to be found where least we expect it.

*

One afternoon when I was chatting with the landlord I learned that the guest, sitting not far from us at one of the big tables, whom to my shame be it said I had not much remarked, was none other than C. the man whom I and several of my friends held to be the greatest of living writers. My companion had gone fishing. Impatiently I awaited his return that I might communicate this piece of news. At last he appeared, and to my joy immediately realized the importance of my discovery. Not much time was left to us before dinner. We spent it in drafting a number of letters, all of which we burned though when dinner-time arrived we decided to make do with the last, though at the moment it seemed to us to be so much the worst of the lot that we regretted having destroyed the others. Had we waited twenty-four hours we might have done better, but we could not bear to wait, nor to think that C. should be left for a single hour in ignorance of the fact—an ignorance which did not seem to have disturbed him so far—that he was within close range of two of his most fervent admirers. Realizing that our names, which then were and have since remained completely unknown, would mean nothing to him, and wishing to avoid the charge of being mere vulgar busybodies, as well as to enhance the value of our enthusiasm, we carelessly made mention of a duchess of our acquaintance who had told us that she knew him well. We felt that without actually lying we might add that we had seen him for the first time in her house. My friend then gave the letter to one of the maids who promised to deliver it as soon as C. came in.

While he was engaged in these preliminaries my heart was thumping. Naturally, we were even more on edge when we reached our table, and remained in that state until we had convinced ourselves that he had not yet come down to dinner. Each time the door opened we were prepared to receive either an embrace or a challenge. We were only too conscious of our letter's infelicities. At last our man appeared: he seemed to be very gay, very muddy, and took his place in high good humour between two English ladies with whom he was, it appeared, on the best of terms. Suddenly the maid brought him a letter. From that moment we concentrated our attention on the food before us, keeping our eyes on our plates and trembling each time we heard anybody get up. At long last he left the room with his two English companions. By that time we felt sure that letters such as ours were a daily event for him and that he paid no attention to them. We were hopelessly diminished in our own esteem. Self-assurance is as vulnerable as any other human faculty. The winning of a school prize brings confidence; the failure to pass an examination produces self-doubt. Still, our letter contained passages which more than passed muster.

C. returned. We made ready to rise. But no, he had come back only to get a cigar. That done, he turned about, and we saw that he was coming in our direction. We concocted no plan of campaign but got up and went to meet him. Nothing we said to him was what we wanted to say, and much of what we did say seemed to us later to have been extremely stupid. He made no reference to the Duchess. We found out afterwards that she had confused him with somebody else, and that he had never been to her house. Nothing we thought could have been better calculated to awaken his suspicions. However he showed none, and almost certainly felt none, so little weight actually attaches to things that we are inclined to see as important. We questioned him on many matters which at that time lay close to our hearts, some especially which concerned the country in which we found ourselves. We snatched from his conversation the names of several places which became for us the objectives of many expeditions, and these took on for us a quality almost of pilgrimage. When he spoke of things that he had found particularly charming, employing some more than usually careful phrase to explain the nature of a taste which at once assumed great prestige in our eyes, it had the effect of making more definite, thoughts hitherto vague which the sincerity of his words awakened in us. In the manner of young people in the presence of an admired master, we asked him about things that he had mentioned in his books. As time went on, and other residents at the Inn left, we saw more of him, and when at last the two English ladies whom he accompanied as far as Quimper, departed in their turn, we became his close neighbours in the dining-room, though we rarely ate with him, because he always turned up late and after the other guests had finished their dinner.

By dint of putting many questions to him, and to others about him, we finally discovered when he did his work. He look long walks along the cliffs, climbing all the while, and doubtless working himself into a fever of thought, for from below we could see him going faster and faster, occasionally breaking into a run and shaking his head, until he arrived at the lighthouse-keeper's cottage which stood in a place where no one ever went. And there in that truly sublime spot he followed with his eyes the movement of the clouds, observed the flight of birds above the sea, listened to the wind, and scanned the sky like an Augur of the ancient world, not so much to draw from these sights a presage of the future, as, so far as I could see, to find in them a memory of the past: for the first drops of falling rain, the sudden piercing of a sunbeam through the murk, sufficed to bring back into his mind rainy autumns of an earlier day, and sunlit summers; whole periods of his life and forgotten states of consciousness which now grew bright again in the intoxicating glow of poetry and of recollection. Many a time did we watch him thus, my friend and I. He seemed to us to be gazing at something which he found a difficulty in understanding. Every firm and sensitive movement of his body, in particular of his hands which he clenched each time he raised his head, appeared to be an outward expression of the concentrated effort of his thought. And then all of a sudden, it was as though he were filled with happiness and ready to sit down and write. At such times he would go into the lighthouse-keeper's cottage, where once he had taken shelter from the rain, and now went almost daily. On leaving he would give his host a small sum of money—though large by local standards—which at first the man seemed shy about accepting. This confirmed us in the idea that C. was moved by an impulse of generosity which so I thought sprang not only from his desire to give pleasure, but from an ignorance in money matters and because he wanted others to think well of him. He often stayed there many hours writing. The lighthouse-keeper and his wife would go into another room so as not to disturb him. Sometimes when the moment came for him to leave, her husband being absent in his boat, the wife would run into the lane to call back her geese which the barking of the dog had sent fluttering seawards, so that quite often some of them were drowned, so badly did they swim. On one occasion my friend and I, spying from behind a rock on C.'s hours of work, saw him, as soon as he was sure that the lighthouse-keeper and his wife were out of sight, amusing himself by chasing the geese to the water's edge. When the woman came back and not seeing the geese, began to call them, he pretended that he had not noticed their absence. But he must have been laughing to himself which proves that he was not so kindly as these people thought him. The woman was terribly put out when she found that the geese had got away, for she could not recover all of them. The sea being rough that day, two were drowned, and a third dashed by the waves against a rock.

Nor was that all. A couple who were staying at Kerengrimen—this was their second visit—told us a great deal to the detriment of C.'s character. They had met him for the first time the year before, when they had taken all their meals in his company and in addition been in a position to do him a number of important services. Once when he had had to make a brief visit to Paris, he had never so much as sought them out on his return, nor even answered two invitations which in spite of his rudeness they had sent him. They told us too that he was in the habit of sleeping with the servant-girl at the inn. I should perhaps explain that he once told me he never replied to purely social letters. He regarded such things as a species of lightning-conductor which diverted his personal electricity, thus preventing it from accumulating to the point at which it would release those storms of the spirit from which alone true genius can flash out, as a result of which the human word can amass the power which sets it echoing like thunder far and wide.

*

At the time of year when the Princess of X took up residence in her Château of Kercaradec—not far from Kerengrimen—with a numerous and brilliant concourse of her friends, we saw a very different C. He would set off smartly dressed for the château, and often would not return for several days. When at last he did so, he never had the satisfied look which he wore when he came back from the light-house-keeper's cottage. So marked was this change in him that once, when he was starting for the château, I plucked up courage to say, "You would do much better, sir, to go to the lighthouse, for as you must very well know you would return from it in a far happier mood, and would at least have written something fine." He made a face at that, like someone with a sore place which one has touched. All the same he went to the château, and for several days was more reserved in his manner to us. Then the time came for the Princess to leave Kercaradec, and after that he spent his days as follows.

In the morning when he had not been out all night, he would set off with a local boy who was his favourite companion to fish. Being physically very strong, C. had a particular liking for rough weather and often, stripping off his clothes, would plunge overboard and swim behind the boat for hours together. Frequently in the evening, he would send the servant-girl to wake the lad—who was already asleep in bed—with orders to get up at once and make the boat ready, which some thought very inconsiderate of him. For some reason or other, the state of the weather had appealed to him, either because there was a moon, or, on the contrary, because there was a storm blowing up. It was no rare thing with him on such occasions to stay out all night. He found it easier to sleep afloat than on shore, where he slept very lightly, so lightly indeed that he had given all the farm servants rope-soled slippers, so that they should not wake him when they were about their daily work. In the afternoon as I have explained, he would spend his time working in the lighthouse-keeper's cottage. The keeper must have been of a very placid nature, for his two predecessors had been driven mad by the winter storms which brought the waves breaking round the roof with a noise which, so it seemed, the human reason could with difficulty endure. Darkness came, but still C. wrote on though he could scarcely see the words upon the paper, so driven was he by the need to record the swiftness of his thought which at that time was at its full pitch. Making scarcely any noise, his host would come into the room to light the one poor lamp which it contained. C. unable to write so long as he was there, and wishing to show by his pausing that he must not stay too long, would lay aside his pen and turn on the intruder a pleased and happy gaze in which there was something of astonishment at seeing there before his eyes the lighthouse-keeper's red and tranquil face.

Sometimes a sailor would come in with a message for the man in charge of the semaphore, and touching his forelock would utter a breezy "good-day" which would cause C. to look up. When that happened the master of the house would get up and lead the visitor into another room where the two of them would sit smoking in silence, occasionally exchanging a few words in low voices, and there they would stay for hours together. C.'s behaviour at the Inn was much the same, and quite often it would happen that the landlord coming into the room would close the door again. Sometimes, while he was dressing, the maid who was putting things to rights, talking to him the while, would notice suddenly that he was answering in an absent-minded fashion, walking up and down the room, still holding in his hand a sponge or a pair of boots, but obviously thinking of something

else, and without the least idea what he wanted to do with them.
When that happened she would stop talking, continue with her work
of tidying what came first to hand and then noiselessly disappear. Sometimes he did not even hear her leave the room: at others, without
uttering a word, as though by opening his lips he might let some
thought take flight, he would smile his thanks. There were occasions
on the other hand when he had just finished working, or reading, or
waking up, when she entered. Then he would talk a great deal more
than was necessary to convey his needs, asking her, with much kindliness, how she had slept, or with deep solemnity what sort of a sermon
they had had that day in church, questioning her about the baker's law-
suit, about the cow's health, about last night's catch, seeming pleased to
mingle his private life with the lives of those who lived so close to him.
On these days she could feel that he wanted to talk, and would stay
there while he, often in bed, sipping his coffee and crumbling a roll into
the cup, would chat with her until suddenly she would remember the
stew simmering on the stove, or the cow she had forgotten to milk. It
was a great pleasure for C. to have her stay with him on these occasions,
just as I imagine on mornings when the sun, freeing its smiling face
from the early mist, addresses a long and loving welcome to all nature,
finding a pleasure in stroking the still empty sea, in warming the beaches,
in playing among the branches rustling in the dawn wind, and in letting
its friendly gaze rest on the sailor who has been afloat since the first light,
filling him with a sense of well-being and happiness, beading his forehead with sweat, or earlier still, to see its friendliness reflected in the
serene spaces of the sky all flooded by its radiance, and the little clouds
not seeking to resist its mood of sociability, not slipping away with
gloomy faces horizonwards as though called thither by more serious
concerns, or others, though unsummoned, trying to take the heavenly
defences by assault, diverting their guardians to other activities and so
forcing the sun to keep its glory to itself, hovering there in mid-sky,
drifting, maybe, but so slowly that like porpoises gambling among the
waves in perfect weather, they seem to float scarcely moving, as though
prepared to stay in the heavens indefinitely. And so it was that the one
thing the poet can ask of others, according to his mood of the moment
—to go away, leaving him alone in silence, or on the contrary to echo
his gaiety and respond to his friendliness—reactions which till then he
has sought in vain in the patronage of kings, in the adoration of the
world, in the society of his fellow poets, in the tenderness of family life,

C. had found quite naturally in this tiny Breton Inn. Not in the palaces which it adorns does the pearl take shape, but in an embryonic polyp, hundreds of miles beneath the sea's surface. Some such pleasure did I too feel, when I saw the fisherman, moved by a simple sense of reverence and a sure but natural instinct, tip-toe from the room where C. was working, or stay to talk when the mood for talk was on him, and so unconsciously help with his midwifery in bringing to delicate birth a work of which he would for ever remain in ignorance.

When the moment came for C. to leave he would say good night to the lighthouse-keeper and his wife as they sat at their evening meal in a room which contained nothing but a great compass mounted on a wooden base and a small, glowing kitchen range beside which they took their dinner at a little table. The light from the range and from a single candle did not extend to the whole of the room, but the patch of radiance which it focused on the wall was so eloquent of peace, so touched with the calmness of a quiet life as it shone upon the evening scene of undisturbed tranquillity when the day's work was over, that C. as he took his way down the cliff in wind and darkness would often turn his head for one last look at man and wife seated at their meal, and when he was too far off to distinguish them, he still could see the little point of light in which seemed to be concentrated the calm of all their daily avocations, the simplicity of their hearts, the comfort of their homely nook, the sweetness of their shared existence. And so he would set out for home, and conscious of being late and feeling cold would walk quickly and reach the Inn to find quite often, no one in the dining-room but myself and my friend, after, that is, the two English ladies had left. His face was expressive of satisfaction with what he had accomplished and he ate at a great pace, staring before him in a way that told of inner pre-occupation and often sat for minutes on end without speaking a word. Now and again he would take off his pince-nez, mop his forehead, pass his hand through his grizzled, reddish hair which was cut *en brosse* and laugh though never explaining why he did so. Close beside him, under an empty plate which served to keep them in order lay usually a number of sheets of paper, and these, we understood contained the sum total of his day's work. The bad weather having driven the other guests away, one after the other, until there was no one left at the Inn but he and our two selves, we asked him whether he would not after first giving us a summary of such parts of his book as we did not know already, read to us each evening what he had written in the course of the afternoon. After at first saying with some embarrassment that we should be bored, he promised to do as we wished, and after spending a whole afternoon telling us about the opening pages of the novel on which he was engaged, proceeded each evening when dinner was over, as had been agreed upon between us, to take the sheets from under the plate beside him, and start reading from them, after first indulging in a number of precautionary comments and interrupting his reading with a deal of self-criticism, designed to disarm his listeners —in the manner of all literary men—so that we were often compelled to call a halt and to ask him to go back to the beginning.

*

It often seemed to us that something the landlord had said, some humorous sally of the maid-of-all-work had been embodied in the substance of his fiction. But we never found in him a trace of that self-consciousness which so few writers, when they condescend to look down from the illustrious dwelling-place of genius to portray simple folk can resist the temptation to express, saying in fact though perhaps in not so many words, 'I need not point out that the honest toiler of the sea now silently employed in preparing the evening meal, would be much surprised could he know it was of him that I was speaking, that it was of *his* anonymous appearance, *his* humble labours, which, on these, the first pages of my Journal, would for a brief space hold the attention of the minister, the rich banker, the woman of the world, engaged in reading it.' Not once did I hear him say to the landlord, pointing to the scribbled pages, "You're there", and when Felicité said, "Since you write about so many things, why do you never say anything of Felicité and the tie she had to fasten round your neck, so's you shouldn't go out collarless? I'm sure that sort of thing would be much more likely to make people laugh than a deal of the stuff that gets printed", he would merely smile and answer: "I expect you are quite right." Indeed he could never have brought himself to say to anybody, or of anything, whether to the princess or Felicité, whether of his sleeplessness or the sea-shore: "You're in my book, that's in my book." For he knew well enough that they, as persons or as objects, counted for nothing in those moments of vision which had so often come to him in their presence. At most when he sat as he sometimes did at the landlord's kitchen table, an absent-minded, though very kindly look would come into his face. Then that he might not be disturbed, the landlord and the fisherman would stop their talking and sit drinking in silence, while the child played on the floor with the dog, and Felicité brought in the meal, as in that picture by Rembrandt which shows the Disciples at Emmaus. And at that moment the waters would be stirred, though in that stirring the people round him counted for nothing.

It is at such moments of profound illumination that the spirit drives deep into all things, and floods them with light, as when the sun sinks into the sea—the movements of a bare-armed girl idly twirling her racket as she waits for her tennis partner; the faint complaining of innumerable lilac leaves fluttering gently to the swaying of the languid tree; a man sitting in front of a café, waiting for his drink to be brought, seeking by a faint lift of the brows to express disdain of the company in which he finds himself, though actually making it clear what store he sets by the opinion of his neighbours—like those bad actors in a comedy, who, instead of the good lines of their parts, which they have forgotten, speak any sort of stupid nonsense—these things are stamped with enchantment for the observing eye seeing what formerly was shadow touched with a brighter light, or by the revealing stressing of a curve and realizing that they are no longer mere hieroglyphic signs but living facts expressive of the loveliest truth, and capable, by the simple fact of their existence, of providing an effortless intoxication such as other men seek in the absorption of noxious liquors, to be paid for later in terms of suffering, an intoxication no longer sterile and serving to show familiar things in a temporarily pleasing light, but revealing something quite different which lies beneath the fleeting vision. To all things that have helped and charmed him, the poet feels grateful, as the poor woman in labour feels grateful to the doctor for his great devotion, remembering with delight the freshness of the peach which soothed her parched throat, and the darting flight of swallows round her window at which she looked with such pleasure while within her womb the mysterious travail took its course. To that same doctor who first attended her, she will send a photograph of her baby, just as C. sent to the Inn-keeper a copy of the novel which he had written at Kerengrimen, or copied out in his own hand, for the Princess of X, some verses which he had composed during a solitary ramble in her park. Perhaps the woman will go so far, when the child

comes to be baptized, as to give him the name which holds the memory
of all those things which stood benevolently about him at his birth,
and later when she calls him Theodore, will think of the name as that
of the doctor, the kindly stranger, though it actually means Gift of God.
More than that she cannot do, knowing full well that his true self will
not be hers to dispose of; that though his smile, the colour of his eyes,
his gaiety, his courage, may have been derived alone from her who for
a brief moment was the source from which he drew his life, he will
hereafter be for all men, to whom in spite of herself she has given him,
to find both good and bad, she knows not which—for all those processes of nature to pour upon him their brightest rays, their most
noisome exhalations—subject to life in short, and eventually to death.
So, too, for C. was it with his book: he might dedicate it to a friend,
but he gave it to the world.

At times, however, when he had finished working, he would tell
Felicité of something in his book that came from her, the description
of her bonnet, a sentence from her talk. At such times she could not
believe her ears, but insisted on seeing for herself what he had written
and like someone looking at a picture for which she has posed, would
say, recognizing that it was indeed herself: "It's me right enough and
my bonnet, too! What will folks think! They'll be wanting to know
this Felicité you talk so much about, though often's the time I must say
you've driven me into a fine tantrum!"–"I'm very fond of you,
Felicité," C. would say, getting up and laying his manuscript aside. He
had done for it all that he could do: now it was time to return thanks
to gods and men. Then he would go downstairs to have a drink with
the landlord, with the fisherman, to take his relaxation, to shoot
sparrows, to joke with Felicité until luncheon should be ready. And so
it was that Felicité and the landlord liked most to remember how this
man of thought could laugh as loudly as another, how he was a jolly
fellow, speaking of him as they might speak of a reverend priest, saying
that he had no objection to good living, and knew a sound bottle of
wine when it came his way. And either because such odd intelligent
creatures, such noble characters seem to justify our humbler pleasures
by the mere fact of sharing in them and giving them the additional
charm of innocence, or because, since we are concerned only with the
spirit, be it ever so fine, so elevated, but do not know its material
envelope, we cannot tell to what species it truly belongs, whether it is
the same as our own, and vital, with something in it of greatness and

fineness which we may admire and can only cry aloud for joy when confronted with a complete and living reality.

One evening when we came home at dinner-time, we found C. in the garden busy correcting the French exercise of our landlord's little daughter. "I shall have nothing to read to you tonight," he said, "the weather was so lovely that I spent all day in the sea, and didn't write a line. Just look at this though and see how badly they teach the children French. Here's what this little girl has been given to learn by heart: *Un bon vieux père a douze enfants, ces douze en ont plus de trois cents, ces trois cents en ont plus de mille, ceux-ci sont blancs, ceux-la sont noirs. Quatre plats plats dans quatre plats creux, quatre plats creux dans quatre plats plats.* She's been told to read *Le Bourgeois Gentilhomme.* She doesn't understand it but has got to keep on at it just the same. She's been showing me where she's got to—it's the passage with all the Turkish words—*muphti, cadir, berir,* and she's reading it all very seriously, convinced that what she's learning are French words." But the little girl who had a great deal more confidence in her form-mistress's knowledge than in C.'s, did not seem much to relish this meddling with her work, and said to him in Breton, "You'd much better get on with writing what you have to write." Then after running about the garden, flinging her arms and body to right and left, while her pink ribbons fluttered in sympathy, she came back to us and began to recite her list of French words—"le avril, la biquette, la dure, la erreur, le messager, le monsieur, le toc-toc, le trisaïeul, le tuf, la vermine, le vilain, le vis-à-vis, le volé, le zèle, le zouave. . . ." Every now and again she stopped and looked at us, pleased to be able to give us her usual gentle smile, and glad not to be disturbed before again beginning to recite "le avril, la biquette" with all the ardour and serenity of faith.

We went upstairs for a moment to our room, and when we came down again C. was talking with much vivacity, in the Breton dialect, to the landlord and the fisherman. He was explaining that he had quarrelled with the new barber, whose charges he had found much too high. He was being very voluble, and obviously finding in his ability to joke in the local vernacular the same sort of pleasure that a child, who has just begun to master the art of swimming, will take in making some of the graceful movements which are the merest commonplaces of experienced swimmers. He seemed to be stressing the fact that he had spoken his mind to the barber, and was certainly not going to pay such prices, as if to imply that he would gladly have paid much more to the landlord and the fisherman because of the extreme friendliness and generosity which he felt when dealing with them. Indeed he had just ended the discussion by ordering a bottle of wine to be brought, when we reappeared upon the scene. We had played the traitor by bringing down with us, my friend, Balzac's *Curé de Village* and I, Stendhal's *Chartreuse de Parme*, since being half-way through these two works which we were reading with all the concentrated enthusiasm which any new and splendid book excites, especially when one has not finished it, we had minds for nothing else and were on fire to know C.'s opinion of them. Though there was no time to do any reading before dinner, we had brought them with us in the hope that he would ask us what they were. But we wanted first to ask him whether he had seen the sunset which had occupied the whole of our attention to the exclusion of *Le Curé de Village*, in my friend's case, and the *Chartreuse de Parme* in mine, and were filled with a hope that he might sum up his impression in a single word which would clarify our own, and make us more certain of what we had been feeling. But he said he had not seen it, being indoors at the time.

"So were we," said I, rather shyly, "but the colours in the sky were so lovely that we could not resist the temptation to go out and watch the effect over the sea. Colour," I finished up, "is always so superb!" I felt that in spite of myself I was talking like him, as though so to speak by humming the beginning of a tune I might put him in the mood to satisfy my curiosity about how it went on. "Douarnenez's the place for sunsets," he told us: "never seen finer anywhere." – "Is it easy to go there from here?" we asked. "I'll get all the details for you," he replied, and went to his room to look up the times of boats and trains. It made us feel embarrassed that he should go to all that trouble in order to supply us with information which we could have got from anybody, and disappointed that he should talk to us of matters which must be common knowledge. The disappointment was of the kind a neurotic patient feels who hopes to force from the doctor some deeply pondered verdict on his ailment, only to be told, "Put your hat on, please: you'll catch cold," or, "So long, and enjoy your dinner," or of that felt by a snob when a duchess sends him fruit from her garden instead of an invitation to her ball. While we were waiting for him we chatted to the landlord who was getting ready to go off on one of the large-scale

salmon catches which were just beginning and took place every night.
We had to admit that they would be too exacting for us, and that we
would not take the risk of going with him. "That's nothing but
natural," said the landlord, "and there's not many people as do, for the
most part. But that Monsieur C. he can't bear to miss one of 'em.
He'd be in a terrible taking if I didn't tell him in advance when the
season was due to start. He's been coming here for the last ten years,
eight months out of the twelve. A proper sailor he is." At this moment
C. came downstairs again, with the times of the boats which he read
to us. We pretended to take the information in just to please him.
Then we turned the talk to salmon-fishing. "Oh, it's a fine sport," he
said, "but even if it wasn't, I'd go just the same, because I've got into the
habit here of doing what everybody else does. If I'd taken a job as
professor of philosophy in some small provincial town—and it would
have suited me down to the ground—I'd have spent my evenings in the
local café, playing cards and swilling beer. I know that some people
regard that as one of the dangers of life in the provinces: they think it
undermines the character. Balzac has described that sort of existence as
the lowest state of degradation and sluggishness into which a man, who
might have had a brilliant career in Paris, can fall. He may be right, but
I don't agree with him. It would suit me—but I can speak only for
myself, though that is difficult enough in all conscience," the gentle
note which we found so charming had crept into his voice, "and I
certainly wouldn't presume to speak for others. There may be temperaments that need more intellectual stimulus—the theatre perhaps or the
society of their fellows, but that sort of distraction is no manner of use
to me—doesn't help me to see deep into things, just gives me a lot of
superficial feelings which stay with me the rest of the day, and produce
a mood of sterile excitement which gets in the way of my work. No, I
certainly can't complain of the way I live here." He stopped speaking
but kept on nodding his head with a vague look in his eyes, like a piano
which has just been played with the loud pedal on, so that when the
piece is finished there is no immediate return of silence, but a slow
fading away of sound which hangs about so persistently that even
though one can scarcely hear it, there would be immediate dissonance
should anyone attempt to play another tune.

After a brief pause my friend showed him his *Curé de Village*. "Have
you read it?" he asked. "Oh yes, but ages ago: fine, isn't it? Begins
if I remember with some terrible crimes committed in the heart of a

city, and then very gradually the characters become quite different people. They move into a land of hills, halt for a while in a village, and finish up at a great height in a sort of idyllic, Fénelon-like countryside, where the crimes of the heroine, who sets to work reclaiming the land and clearing away the poisonous growths, are ultimately pardoned. But I've forgotten a good deal of it." He broke off. "Won't you say some more about it?" asked my friend in shy but urgent tones. "I'm afraid I don't remember it well enough. There's nothing much I can tell you about Balzac. I know him very slightly. There are people who, when anybody asks them which of Balzac's books are the ones to read, reply, 'All!' It sounds rather simple-minded, but it's true. The full quality of Balzac is to be found not in this or that book, but in the whole lot. The individual novels read separately are not very good, though the characterization is always excellent. Strange, isn't it? I've never been able to hit on the explanation. The people you ought to get to talk about Balzac are those who know him well—and by that I don't necessarily mean literary blokes. No, the people I have in mind usually belong to a certain generation—retired Prefects, financiers who had a taste for reading when they were blessed with leisure, intelligent army men. For instance General de S. has a wonderful knowledge of Balzac. I sometimes hear fellows like that talking about him at the house of the Princess of T.—who also knows him well—and I love listening to what they have to say."–"But surely," said my friend, breaking in eagerly, "they can't have much literary taste?"–"I didn't say they had: obviously they haven't," replied C. "but they know their Balzac. There is something powerful about him, earthily powerful, but powerful all the same, which appeals to a great many people, though not very much to artists because few writers seem to work at a lower level. Still even artists have a weakness for him, which is odd. It's not by art that he produces his effects. The pleasure we get from him is, in some sort, adulterated. He wins us over, like life itself, by presenting us with an accumulation of badnesses. He is the very epitome of life."

*

He read to us as a rule in the dining-room, which was deliciously warm —the bad weather had made it impossible for us to go on taking our meals out of doors. When the reading went on too long, we would see the maid appear in the doorway, longing to clear away and go to bed. Then he would break off, and promise to finish soon. This he did because he wanted to get rid of her because he found her presence embarrassing. Often his narrative was interrupted by passages of comment in which the author expressed his views on this and that, in the manner of certain English novelists of whom at one time he had been very fond. These reflective asides, which some readers find tiresome, because they break the current of the narrative and destroy the illusion of life, were what we most liked to hear, so eager were we to know his personal thoughts, and resentful when they were concealed in one of his characters. We knew, for he had told us so, that what he wrote about was strictly true. He excused himself on these occasions by explaining that he lacked the gift of invention and could write only of what he had himself experienced—a funny sort of excuse, because the incidents of his novel are today so familiar, that even when they seem out of the ordinary, there is no need of the gift of invention to make them imaginatively true. But to what extent did he appear in what he wrote? Had he known the Duc de Réveillon, and could we if we visited the Marne see the mill of which he spoke, all covered with vines which had so tangled the wheel that it could no longer move? Then there was the problem of Jean, who has many of C.'s faults, but even more of his good qualities, his sensitiveness in particular and his warmth of heart, though unlike C. he is cursed with delicate health, has known much unhappiness, and is without talent for any of the arts. We dared not question him on these points, because once when we tried to do so, he had cut us short with a very brief comment. But they interested us more than anything else. We thought that a lifetime devoted to solving them would be well employed, because we should be led to the knowledge of matters which we loved above all else, and should learn what are the secret relations, the necessary metamorphoses, which exist between a writer's life and his work, between reality and art, or, rather, as we then thought, between appearance and reality—a reality which underlay all things and could be disengaged only by art.

But things which appear important to us at one period of our lives when it never occurs to us, so wrapped are we in illusions, that this importance can ever cease to obsess us till the day of our death, dwindle into nothingness with the passage of time. Early in November we were called back to Paris on important business and said good-bye to C. with whom we had recently been living in such close contact, and who since he had taken to reading to us every evening, had become for us a source of genuine interest. He seemed sorry to see us go, but did not accompany us as far as Quimper, as he had done the two English ladies. He himself was due back in Paris at the beginning of December. We promised to call upon him there, and felt both of us that time would drag until that moment came. But not once in the next four years did we go to see him, nor ever return to Kerengrimen, though we had planned to spend a holiday there in the following autumn. Seized with remorse, telling each other every evening that we really must do something about it, and then next morning forgetting our resolve, we ended by writing to him but no answer came. Once when we were within easy distance of Kerengrimen, we played with the idea of descending upon him, but so ashamed were we to think of the way in which our feelings towards him had changed, that we could not pluck up courage to show ourselves to the man who had witnessed the ecstasies of an affection which had proved in the event to be so little durable.

*

Last summer S. of whom I had seen nothing for several years (he was the friend with whom I had spent that holiday in Brittany) came to see me. "C. is dying," he said. "There is something he wants to tell us and has sent a message asking us to visit him together. He is at Saint-Cloud. The doctor who is attending him is downstairs." We learned on the way that C. was dying of galloping consumption but that his mind was perfectly clear. He had no illusions about his condition, nor was he in the least upset by the prospect of death. The goal of our journey was a small house with open windows giving on to a garden.

"I have made you come a long way, and knowing as you do, the nature of my ailment, this is the last sort of place in which you would expect to find me," he said with a smile, alluding to the fact that he suffered from what is generally known as hay-fever, and was therefore precluded from going to the country. "I have always had a passion for the country, but never thought it would be possible for me to live there: but now it seems I am immune to its ill effects. . . . All this has happened rather late in the day unfortunately but it is pleasant to think we have been reconciled, the country and I, before death takes me, as might be two persons who, born to understand one another, have been separated by a foolish misunderstanding. The country may have done

me a deal of harm in the past, but still more good, don't you think?
because I have so loved it. You used to say," he went on, turning to me,
"that you could find me a cure for hay-fever, and I always replied that
there was no such thing, but now you see me cured at the last by the
one doctor we had never thought of. You know the saying of the
Greeks, that Death is the greatest of all physicians, and can alone cure
us of our ills? I rather think that our doctors, from what I know of
their books, agree with them, at least in a pathological sense. And
Felicité (the maid who had always looked after him at the farm) agrees
with them, for she said to me this morning—you know how fond she
is of me, but also how much, like all women of the people, she loves to
disturb me, as though there were still something that might shake me
out of my longing for rest—'Up till just lately I still had hope, but
when I sees you here in the country, not sneezing nor fighting for
breath, I says to myself—this time I says it's the end—and it won't be
long now.'" And then he went on, "The time has come when death is
the only word that holds any truth for me. Since yesterday morning
the habits of a lifetime of which nothing could break me, have taken
flight, as birds moved by a premonition fly from the house of death.
They will I suppose never return. For the first time since I was twenty-
five, I can go to sleep without having the window open, and nature
in a flash, in a moment, has done what my mother, though she begged
and prayed me every day for twenty years, could never achieve. I have
always thought that the loveliest thing about Nature is the way in
which she can so easily both tie knots and untie them. I dreaded death,
because I always found it impossible, when things were going well
with me, to accept the fact that some day they might go ill, but Nature
has given death a kindly face, by sending on ahead those sorrows and
pains that are his ministers. So well have they prepared me that today
I long for death. Unaided I could never have reached that point. It is
Nature's power to bring about such changes in me that I most admire
in her. A day comes when one no longer suffers from a grief which
one had once thought inconsolable, when one finds oneself enduring,
with scarcely a thought, pains one used to think beyond one's power
to bear. Long ago I loved somebody who caused me torments of
jealousy. For two years I never set eyes on her, but those torments
never for one moment left me, day or night, until I became convinced
that the agony would rack me till my dying day. I was like a child who
thinks the night will never end. But by the time the second year was

almost over, I was cured and have never suffered in that way since. It is because of such cures that I am lost in admiration of Nature for they seem so miraculous and are so simple. Actually I believe that like doctors whose sedatives may all have different names, though the basis of each of them is opium, she too builds up her nostrums on forgetfulness, or rather on habit, which is the true name of her most potent drug, forgetfulness being only one of its variants. Whether there be pity deep hidden in these laws, which are so kindly-sweet in changing our condition, I do not know, but assuredly there is much of grandeur."

*

A few days later I saw in the papers the announcement of his death. Nothing was said about the novel, of which we had a copy, being found among his papers, and I decided, my friend being busy about other matters, to publish the version in my possession.

I

1. *Evenings at Saint-Germain*

The little garden door closed slowly behind Jean after the third time he had been to say good night to his mother and had been ill received. "I'm afraid he's rather miserable, Doctor," said Madame Santeuil gently, turning to Professor Surlande, meaning to excuse her son. "I have never, till this evening, missed going to see him in bed and saying good night and he is feeling upset. *Such* an impressionable little boy." – "He is what we should call a nervous subject," replied the Doctor with a smile, as though he had made a witticism. "I could tell as much from the look of him. I expect Doctor Marfeu is trying cold-water treatment?" – "*Cold* water?" said Madame Santeuil showing surprise: "dear me, no. Monsieur Marfeu has prescribed *warm* water: he insisted most strongly that it must be warm." – "*Warm* water?" said Monsieur Surlande with a laugh, "gracious goodness me, that is really very strange! Still, Marfeu is an excellent physician and you could not have chosen anyone better for your son. But I should not like to think," he added politely, "that I am the cause of your not saying good night to him." – "You mustn't think that!" exclaimed Madame Santeuil, "we don't want to mollycoddle him. We have had to give in to him far too long as it is—because of his delicate health you know—and being spoiled will make life very hard for him when he is older. My husband and I are so anxious that he should grow up to be a manly little fellow." "What are you planning to make of him?" asked the Doctor. "It's early days as yet to say," answered Madame Santeuil, "he is only seven. Nevertheless, we have several very definite ideas about his future, not that we should ever wish to go against our son: we want him to be perfectly free to choose, so long that is, as he sets his mind on a regular career, the Law for instance, or the Foreign Service." – "But I was under the impression," said the Doctor, "that he had strong leanings towards music and poetry?" – "But my dear Doctor," said Madame Santeuil brightly, "all parents think that their children are infant prodigies. They bring them up to do nothing, with the result that they think of themselves as being misunderstood geniuses when some little tune they've made up, which is applauded in the family circle and hailed as a masterpiece by their teachers, does not get played in public and accepted for publication. Music may be all right as a career for a Mozart or a Beethoven—but even so," added Madame Santeuil firmly, "I have no desire to see my son become an artist of genius. He has a good brain. With that, and his father's influential connexions, he could easily make for himself an important, well-paid and respected position in diplomacy or the higher reaches of the Civil Service which would really be so *very* much more satisfactory. Still, I must admit that I do my best to cultivate in him a taste for poetry." – "I suppose you have never thought of medicine?" asked the Professor. – "Oh no, Doctor. It's all very well"—this with a shy little outburst of enthusiasm —"when a man can attain to *your* eminence, but. . . ." – "It entails a lot of hard work," said the Doctor, and a reminiscent look came into his eyes. "Is that his room?" he went on, pointing to the only lighted window on the first floor of the darkened house-front. "Yes," said Madame Santeuil, "I don't let them keep the lights on in the other rooms, because if they did the midges might get into the house through the open windows." – "The aspect couldn't be better—due south," said the Doctor. "You're on clay, here, are you not?" Being insufficiently informed in the matter of soil, Madame Santeuil maintained a weighty silence. The light went out, and the window became merged in the general darkness.

"He's gone to bed," said Madame Santeuil glad of this diversion. "Sure you're not cold, Doctor? Wouldn't you like your overcoat? My husband and my father have just gone in to fetch theirs: they could easily bring yours too." – "No, I thank you, madame: the air is quite extraordinarily mild. What a charming garden you have, with a stream too, the water of which looks to me very clear and pure." – "It is a great comfort in hot weather," replied Madame Santeuil with becoming modesty; "and in a few years time when we are no longer here, it will be nice for Jean, if his health remains poor, to come from time to time for a breath of this good air." Monsieur Santeuil, having sat down, said nothing but looked tenderly at his wife, his mind carried back by those words "when we are no longer here" to the days when she had been fresh and lovely and to the long succession of years which had followed. With her head leaning back in her deck-chair Madame Santeuil, gazing upon the innumerable constellations of the sky, was lost in one of those vague reveries in which we indulge when looking at some immense spectacle, some brilliant but indecipherable inscription which we do not understand, trying to pick out in the vast expanses of the Milky Way her dear son's ruling star, no less vague, no less brilliant, no less distant. The Doctor bent on both of them a benevolent look. Monsieur Sandré, Madame Santeuil's father, his sullen old face leaning forward over his shabby, carefully brushed suit, sat smoking his pipe in silence.

They were shaken out of their silence by the living sound of the fountain and the smell of the rose-bushes which they noticed now almost as things unknown and new because, as they sat and dreamed, they had ceased to be aware of them. "How delicious it is here!" said the Doctor. –"Yes, isn't it?" replied Monsieur Santeuil. "It was simply and solely that I might be able to buy this garden at the very gates of Paris that I put up so long with a tiny flat and went without a carriage. No luxury could weigh in the scale with me against the pleasure of breathing the fresh air under these great chestnuts of an evening and of driving into Paris each morning through the forest in my little trap."–"I can see that you love Nature," said the Doctor. "I don't know," answered Monsieur Santeuil. "I certainly don't much care for art and I soon drop off to sleep when my wife reads the poems of Alfred de Vigny to me. But I certainly love this garden." Thus challenged, Madame Santeuil said nothing. For some moments now she had ceased listening to the conversation. Glancing up, she had seen the light come on again in her son's bedroom and felt a spurt of annoyance. A boy of seven *must* learn to go to sleep alone. Hoping that Jean would doze off again, she decided not to go up to him until she had seen the light once more disappear. In a very short while the window was pushed open. A small pale face showed above a white nightgown and a voice sounded in the darkness. "Mamma, I want you for a moment."–"Shut the window at once, Jean! you'll catch cold! What a little silly you are!" exclaimed Madame Santeuil rising from her chair in a panic. "Don't be so weak!" said Monsieur Sandré, "nice habits you're letting that boy get into, I must say!"–"Oh, leave her alone," said Monsieur Santeuil with a laugh, "If she doesn't go up he'll never get to sleep and we shall feel the disturbance much more in an hour's time."–"I shouldn't mind being disturbed," said Monsieur Sandré with weighty solemnity, "I'd put up with a deal of disturbance if only I could see that lad in better health. You'll never know a moment's peace of mind if you encourage your wife to break a rule." To this Monsieur Santeuil made no reply. "But Papa," said Madame Santeuil, "these prolonged nervous crises are the worst thing possible for his health. I'm sorry I've got to go up, but I must. I feel terribly ashamed, Doctor. I'm afraid you will have a very poor opinion of my son. He's not always as silly as this, but you see, he's so nervous: it's not altogether his fault."

Going to bed had assumed for Jean the proportions of tragedy and the horror that surrounded it was all the more frightening for being vague. As soon as it began to grow dark, and even before his lamp had been brought, he felt that the whole world was abandoning him and would have liked to cling to the daylight, to keep it from dying, or to take it with him into a shared death. But he could still find some respite from this deep, this indefinable, torment by going to the kitchen while talking to his mother. Very soon his big lamp would come, spreading a warm radiance, flooding his heart and his table with its powerful kindliness, laying a sweetness all about him. But when the actual moment of going to bed arrived the comfort he had found in activity and light was taken from him. No longer could he put off the saying of good nights, in other words, the leaving of the whole world for a whole night: he must give up all hope of talking to his mother if he felt miserable, of climbing on to her knee if he felt too lonely: even the wretched candle must be put out and he lie there, without moving, so that sleep might come while he lay abandoned, silent, motionless and blind, to the horrible, the shapeless suffering which, little by little, would grow as vast as solitude, as silence and as night. But always, until this evening, when undressing was done, he had called his mother knowing that she would come and kiss him when he was in bed. That kiss, that blest viaticum, was looked forward to with such feverish excitement that he kept himself from thinking of anything while he took his clothes off, that he might the sooner cross the space of time which separated him from it—the tender offering of cakes which the Greeks fastened about the necks of wives or friends, before laying them in the tomb, that they might accomplish without terror the sub-terranean journey and cross, without hungering, the Kingdom of the Shades. As such did Jean long to savour the fragrance of his mother's cheeks and the cool kiss laid like a compress on his hot and feverish forehead just where the golden fringe fell on the delicate skin, striking inwards to his small heart with the gift of peace. Then, and then only, could he sleep. This message at the day's end, brought to him in bed, awaited so impatiently, had magic in it and, like oil on a stormy sea, could calm his agitated spirit. It was that of which now he had been deprived, and would be on each succeeding night. But, in spite of his distress, he made, at first, a loyal attempt to capture sleep. He had blown out his candle as the doctor had noticed from the garden. But, try though he might to empty his mind of all thought, he could not help telling himself that his mother was harsh indeed to cause him so much pain. He could picture her, in imagination, talking with the doctor and his father and the scene which he conjured up made even more intolerable his lying there in an enforced immobility. At first the idea of calling to his mother came to him, but he drove it away, fearing lest he should displease her, and so, live for days in an agony of estrangement. To keep her son from yielding to such nervous fancies, Madame Santeuil had blamed his weakness as a fault, as something he ought to be ashamed of. It was the one thing about which she was severe with him. And he, still too young to be able to distinguish moral obliquity from physical distress, liberty from necessity, felt himself, in some vague way, to be responsible for all his agitation, his sadness and his tears though lacking the strength to master them. He could hear outside in the corridor, the footsteps of Augustin, the old servant, taking the washed-up dinner service back to the dining-room. He called to him. But Augustin, accustomed to Master Jean's nerves and having no-where to put down his load, pretended that he had not heard. Then Jean, with a sudden spurt of annoyance, and fearing that the old man, once in the dining-room would be out of earshot, called again more loudly, "Augustin, I may tell you in a moment to fetch Mamma." He did not dare to say, "If I ask you to fetch Mamma, will you?" because he might be met with a refusal to which he thought the other form of words would not expose him. Augustin, on his side, was careful not to say "no", but replied with kindliness and good-nature, "What, still awake, Master Jean? You ought to be asleep; it's late, and Madame can't be disturbed when she's with Doctor Surlande. That would be most impolite. She could not leave him suddenly and would scold me." – "She wouldn't scold you if it was I who had told you to go," Jean was quick to answer. "Most certainly I will not go," said Augustin. "You will, if I tell you to," Jean said angrily, "but for the time being I am not telling you. Go away, and let me try to get to sleep. Good night, Augustin." – "Good night, Master Jean." This final, friendly exchange did something to sweeten the bitterness with which Augustin's obstinacy had filled Jean's heart. By this time he was wide awake, and no longer wanted to sleep. He lay in the semi-darkness with his eyes open. He got up. He went to the window. He saw, quite close to him, his mother, his father, and the doctor. The moon, like a lamp set too low, shed its light upon them, though without enabling him to make them out distinctly, seeming to reveal and, at the same time, to conceal them. From their quiet movements he could guess the kindliness of their words which he could not hear. All of a sudden the guilty desire which had been haunting his loneliness, to call to his mother from the window, appeared to him in quite a different light, as something very simple and very natural. His mother was down there: she could be with him in a moment. He made up his mind. He felt calm and the sense of his calmness reassured him though he fully realized the gravity of what he was about to do. With a little twinge of fear he opened the window, called his message—as has already been described—ran quickly back to his bed, and snuggled down under the warm blankets with anxiety in his heart and his body shivering with cold. The anticipated pleasure of his mother's kiss no longer meant anything to him. He knew that she was angry. This evening, doubtless, so as not to agitate him still further, she would not let her face assume too severe an expression. But what about tomorrow? Why? Why should he not do what it made him happy to do? Why, later, as though it had not been done, should she not be as gentle with him as before?

His mother came and, in the warmth of her kiss, all his nervous agitation melted in sweetness and in tears. "Oh, Mamma, my head's hot and my feet are cold and I can't sleep." She took his feet in her hands and rubbed them, though not too softly for fear of tickling him. "Now I must go down again to Doctor Surlande, Jean." – "Good night, darling Mamma, and thank you." But, just as his mother was about to shut the door, Jean, feeling that her going was something irrevocable, that she was leaving him, that this time he could not make her come back, lost all control of himself and, jumping out of bed, ran after her, clung to her with such force that she all but fell and, torn between the seriousness of what he was doing and the despair which would follow her departure, burst into a fit of sobbing. This time his mother was really angry, determined to go, determined to scold him. His sobs redoubled. He let go of her and lay rolling about on his bed with a feeling of tightness in his chest, uttering little cries and using the violence which remorse was turning against himself to bring his misdemeanour to a head. Then he lay down again beneath the blankets and his mother, saddened by the sufferings of her son, by the feeling that she could do nothing to cure him, by this relapse on the very day when she had hoped that he would go to sleep without her, by the accumulated effect of all the years of his nervous ailments and vexed, too, at having to leave the doctor and her husband alone together, settled herself down beside his bed. Augustin, who had heard his mistress's footsteps and Jean's cries, judging by the very impropriety which he would have felt in disturbing her while the doctor was still there the importance she attached to Master Jean's sleeplessness because she had left the gentlemen in so precipitate a manner, Augustin, for whom Jean, from being a child whom he loved and teased, had all of a sudden become a person of importance whose moods could interrupt the most sacred duties of hospitality, Augustin, fearing to disturb his mistress, anxious to be of service to her, and, especially to see what Master Jean was up to now, Augustin, after waiting for a few moments, turned the handle of the door, and slipped on tip-toe into the room. His smile expressed shy curiosity, respectful familiarity, and extreme uncertainty. "Is there anything I can do for you, ma'am? I trust Master Jean is not ill?" Jean, who had wiped his eyes at the sound of the man's approach, glorying in the power he exercised over his mother, which Augustin seemed to have doubted, but which, for all that, was keeping her there, away from the doctor and his father, directed at the intruder a smile of happy triumph to which the feeling of dazzling and admitted superiority imparted a touch of affectionate good-will. "You see, Augustin, Master Jean does not know what is the matter with him, nor what he wants," said Madame Santeuil, sadly. "He is suffering from nerves."

Jean soon went to sleep and Madame Santeuil, moving very quietly so as not to wake him, returned to her husband and the doctor who was preparing to leave. "I am deeply distressed, Doctor, that you should have had to witness, even from a distance, this unfortunate display." – "I beg you, madame, not to disturb yourself on my account," replied the Doctor as he said good night. "I am sorry only that my presence should have kept you from staying with him longer. Fortunately," he added with a laugh, "unhappiness at his age is not a very serious matter."

It is, perhaps, permissible to hold that Jean was less wrong than the ironical doctor and did right to take his misery seriously. The strokes endured in those hours of childhood fell on the very metal of his heart, and the sounds they gave off might well reverberate with a fuller, a more cracked, or a deeper note as age set a harder crust upon his feelings. In the course of this story we shall have no occasion to say more about Jean's nervous sufferings at the moment of going to sleep. His life will lead us, as it led him, along more distant ways and no man, alas! can live twice over the years of childhood. The reader, however, would be much mistaken should he think that, even in so trivial a matter as has been described, Jean ever changed completely. Habit, the only one of all the ancient powers of this world which is stronger than suffering, might overcome, little by little, the cruel torments of which we have just been witnesses which, through all his early years he still endured whenever evening came. But each time, in youth, and even in maturity, that some circumstance occurred to suspend temporarily the anaesthetizing effects of habit, each time that he went to bed earlier or later than usual, each time that a light or an unaccustomed sound prevented him from unconsciously achieving the act of summoning sleep, he would feel deep down within himself, vague as a face that has been lost to sight, the awakening of a trouble old as his very life. When it was merely a light, an unaccustomed sound, or the lateness of the hour that kept him from unconsciously achieving the act of summoning sleep, the trouble remained slight and did not last. But whenever, in a country house or an hotel, he had to go to bed in a strange room, it was in vain that, while he read or brooded, he kept upon the table by his pillow Alexander at Penta,[1] familiarity with which made his own life and his own troubles dwindle in importance, and with the help of which he had long managed to conjure away their urgency, so that they showed as no more than a dust of corn-husks on the winnowing-floor of the centuries, in vain that he tried to break free from solitude and darkness by forcing his thoughts to dwell upon the morrow's morning, for always the feelings of the inconsolable little boy who could not go to sleep would flood back upon him and in his ears would echo the sound of that childish crying which once had been so muffled yet so piercing. Ever avoiding his attempts to catch and hold it, his earlier self would bump about the corners of the unfamiliar room like a bat, invisible and strange. And, mingled with those cries, would come

---

[1] Prolonged investigation has failed to identify the object referred to here as "Alexandre à Penta". The most plausible explanation has been advanced by Monsieur Maurois, who thinks that "Penta" is a misreading for "Pella"—Alexander's birthplace. It is just possible that there may be a statuette of Alexander at Pella, and that such a statuette, or a picture of it, was what Jean Santeuil kept on his bedside table.—G. H.

to him his mother's words when, on that distant and especial evening, replying to Augustin, she had sadly said, "You see, Augustin, Master Jean does not know what is the matter with him, nor what he wants: he is suffering from nerves"—those words to which we listened a while back and which had brought such happiness to Jean, because they had laid to the account of nerves, thereby absolving him from all responsibility, the sobs and screams which had caused him such feelings of remorse, which exercised so deep an influence upon his life. That new sense of irresponsibility which his mother then had publicly recognized in the presence of Augustin—as a nation recognizes a new government —had acted as a guarantee of his personal existence and assured his future. The cruel, the prolific struggles which, from earliest childhood, Jean had been ceaselessly waging against himself ceased altogether from the day when the nervous tension against which he had been trying to fight was recognized as something that, though unfortunate, was no longer criminal, so that instead of thinking that he must avoid feeling guilty of a fault he could realize that he was merely the victim of an illness. Not that in those days his will-power had been anything but weak. But, gradually, and as a result of constant effort, he did at last force it to get the upper hand of his nerves, constantly threatening though they were, so that it broke against them still, but with an ever-increasing strength and splendour, like sea-waves against a rock.

There is one last reason why we, no less than Jean himself, should take seriously those griefs and torments of his childhood and that is, that in spite of the doctor's smiles and his father's, he was never, in the years to come, to know any that were more lacerating. Later, indeed, whenever he felt depressed, interests, occupations, ideas and memories provided him with a ladder up which, once he could make up his mind to take the first step, he could climb, rung by rung, thought by thought, person by person, and so emerge into a place of hope where his spirit could disport itself at liberty like a colt let out to grass. But his childhood struggled desperately at the bottom of a well of wretchedness from which nothing could release him and which, as yet, no knowledge of the reasons for his gloom could illuminate. It was only much later that he learned the nature of its causes and then only of the secondary ones, for the basic cause seemed to him always to be so inseparable from himself that he could have got rid of it only by getting rid of his own personality. He could never get back into himself, after an absence more or less extended, without first seeing his suffering in the light of the old unease. But then joy came, joy that was half unhappiness and exercised strong rights upon him, being, as it was, his true self, though misted like sunlight resting for a moment on churned seas or the surface of a muddy river. . . . But it was older than such moments and had not been born of them. Sadness had reigned in undisputed sovereignty over his shadowed childhood.

2. *Evenings at Dieppe*

September came. Monsieur and Madame Santeuil made ready to leave Saint-Germain. Jean felt very sad at the thought of going away. As soon as it was six o'clock and the dusk had already fallen, he would more than once turn his head to look at the red sky which barred the dark entry to the forest, before going, with a sense of pleasure, into the dining-room which was filled with lamplight and the smell of soup from the tureen standing on the table. But go to Dieppe he must. The sea and the glistening sands hurt his eyes. He did not look at the setting sun. But, long after the sun had set, when night had fallen on a sea which had the blue-grey colour of a mackerel and looked so solid that the smacks seemed to cut it as with a knife, giving the impression of a great bank of sand, he would notice at the entry to the Forest of Arques the same red barrier that stood about the entry to the Forest of Saint-Germain and, turning up his little collar against the cold wind with its tang of salt, was pleased to go indoors and warm himself at the fire which already was lit for a while each evening.

"I think that Jean will have a feeling for poetry," said Madame Santeuil to her husband with the rather timid look upon her face which was occasioned by a fear, each time she began to say anything, that her humble, eager tenderness might bore her husband, might disturb his thoughts, his digestion and his rest. "Indeed," said Monsieur Santeuil, with complete lack of interest and, letting his arms subside on to his white waistcoat, resumed his study of the window-rail at which he stared with the dignified expression he had developed in the course of his public career and, especially, during his tenure of the post of Permanent Assistant Director of Letters and in the performance of his many honorary duties, though, in the bosom of his family, he was accustomed to give it a somewhat more casual and domestic colour. Then he lit a cigarette. Her husband's cigarettes had derived, from the Reports on which they had so often deposited a careless fall of ash, causing a faint spiral of smoke to rise from the paper, from the audiences which, for so long now, they had beguiled and scented and, more especially, from his incomparable gifts and official position—since he was forever raising them to his lips while he let drop the weighty words which were always listened to with attention and were sometimes decisive—an importance which she thought it her duty as an intelligent and devoted wife to respect and, if need be, to uphold. Even if Monsieur Santeuil had not been an excellent husband, filled with admiration for his wife's superior intelligence and tact, endlessly grateful for her passionate deference and devotion and had shown an inclination to seek doubtful pleasures away from home, Madame Santeuil would probably have sacrificed her own feelings to the need of ensuring her husband's happiness, and the efficiency and greatness of the State. Monsieur Santeuil, to be sure, had never yet been called to do much in the way of administration not having occupied the post of Minister, but as an ex-Senator for the Drôme, a man who had twice sat on the Budget Commission, had been Secretary of a Commission set up to enquire into social conditions in the suburbs, had once been Presiding Officer of the Court of Appeal, an intimate friend of the President of the Republic, a nephew of a former War Minister, and, for the last ten years an Officer of the Legion of Honour, he exercised considerable influence upon the course of events. If his position brought him honour, it was also a constant source of anxiety. No one was more frequently asked to exert his influence for persons anxious to have reserved carriages on the railways; no one was more often called upon to represent the Government at the funeral services of Marshals of France; no one was more persistently courted by those seeking promotion, decorations, licences to sell tobacco, or grand-stand seats for the Fourteenth of July Review. He kept all the requests for the latter in one pile on his desk and all the tickets at his disposal in another, and would scrupulously wait until the great day had dawned before making a final allocation. The way in which he tried to satisfy everybody, in spite of the many calls upon his time, impressed all with whom he came in contact. But it did more than impress his wife —it filled her with amazement. Much cleverer than he was, endowed with artistic taste, a wide-ranging intelligence, tact and a lively sensibility—qualities which he almost completely lacked—Madame Santeuil had remained convinced that these gifts must be trivial, seeing that so superior a man as her husband could get along very well without them.

She laughed at his complete inability to appreciate a work of art, his failure to deal competently with the problems of daily life, his lack of tact, the crudity with which he treated those who asked him embarrassing questions—with the affectionate tenderness that an artist's wife might show when tempted to tease him about his absent-mindedness or unpunctuality. As to his work, the judgments he pronounced with so much clarity, with so deep a knowledge of the law, and in so elegant a style, she was quite convinced that nobody with her kind of temperament could ever have shouldered such responsibilities which clearly demanded an intellectual equipment only to be found in rare, and decidedly remarkable, individuals.

Monsieur Santeuil now threw away his cigarette, and his wife accorded him that happy, fluttering attention which always awaited him when, having finished his work, he shut his ink-pot and joined her. She gave him a kiss and looked at him with a smile to which frankness and gaiety combined to impart a peculiar brightness. He opened the window. "That's the Newhaven boat just going out." Madame Santeuil leaned forward to look. The ship was growing smaller, but the gazer could still imagine from the shore the beat and thrust under the black hull of a powerful sea which was frothing like beer, looking, where it lay full in the sun, like a field in which green crops alternate with blue, with here and there a gleaming patch of snow and grey patches where the clouds made shadows. "If only I had not so much to do," said Monsieur Santeuil who could no longer see the ship on the horizon, "I should dearly like to have a little house at the seaside and spend many months of the year there." But since he found the sea without a ship upon it gloomy he shut the window and lit another cigarette. "How you *do* love Nature!" said Madame Santeuil who, all this while, had been savouring the look of happiness in her husband's eyes, "I really do believe that if Jean turns out to have a feeling for poetry it will be because he takes after you!"

"Poetry's something I could very well do without!" here interrupted Monsieur Sandré explosively. With his head drooping over his shabby, well-brushed coat he had been silently smoking his pipe in a corner, but now started to pace up and down the room with a sort of headlong slowness which eloquently expressed the struggle of the physical weakness of old age with a vehement temperament. "A fine thing it'd be," he went on ironically, "if that young fellow, instead of following in his father's footsteps, should take to consorting with idle scamps!" Monsieur Santeuil, who took a somewhat longer view, could not help smiling. "Don't be uneasy, there's plenty of time yet," he said with that amused refusal to be shaken out of his habitual calm which he liked to think of as being "philosophical". "Time! time! that's what they all say and then, before they know where they are, the years have gone by, nothing's been done in the way of discipline and one sees a young chap, son of an intelligent and successful father, with money to burn, dissipating a fortune that's been honourably amassed, dragging in the mud a name that's universally respected and ending up by starving to death, if not worse, among a scratch lot of good-for-nothing scribblers, the best of whom, those who aren't out and out scoundrels, are either spendthrifts like Lamartine or old skinflints like Victor Hugo. You'd do better to give him a length of rope and let him go hang himself!" –"Don't worry, Papa," said Madame Santeuil in whom, since she was of less tough metal and had been smoothed by much rubbing, her father's deeply etched ideas had been to some extent effaced, though they were still recognizably present. "Even if I wanted to make him a poet—which God forbid!—I am pretty sure that I should not succeed. I often read him poetic Meditations, Corneille's *Horace* and *Les Contemplations* because I believe that good books, even though he may not fully understand them at first, must, in the long run, provide food for his mind and refine his feelings. But he never listens for more than five minutes at a stretch!" To this Monsieur Sandré replied, "That only goes to show that he's blessed with a great deal more common sense than you and that you'd be much better employed in having him taught the calculus and modern history and in showing him how to make his own bed—though without a bolster, mind, because you might just as well give him a dose of poison right away as let him sleep with a bolster!" Monsieur Sandré sat down again and the present seemed to have vanished from his eyes in which all the past appeared to be gazing at all the future. He began to puff away at his pipe. "The new Foreign Minister has a high opinion of writers," said Monsieur Santeuil who had a natural tendency to regard as important only specific facts and the opinions of members of the Government. "He says they hold the future in their hands and that he would gladly see his daughter marry an author."–"That's what he says but I very much doubt whether he would really like it," said Madame Santeuil in a low voice, relieved to see that her father had not heard her husband's last remark, since it was her constant endeavour to keep them from quarrelling.

*

"Yes, I saw Madame Récamier right enough: it was way back in 1806. She was at the theatre with Chateaubriand and the Emperor was there—it's all of sixty years ago," said Monsieur Sandré. His eyes were fixed upon those living, breathing figures whom life had set before them long ago. Now that the life of that older day had turned to nothingness, the moving panorama of its prime, which nothing now could imitate—a gesture made by Madame Récamier, the Emperor arriving at the theatre—these things were still vivid in the old man's mind. And the vision that went to meet them was as bleared and feeble as a light which can reach the watcher's eyes only after piercing thick layers of night and darkness. Indeed, Monsieur Sandré needed to make no effort to recapture those pictures of a distant past for the time at which they had been painted was, for him, the present, whereas the happiness of his daughter seated there beside him, the career of his son-in-law opposite, the health of his grandson who had just been sent to bed and the interest which the Minister, Marie, sitting on his daughter's other side, showed in all of them, these threads that span the pattern of his life and of his happiness had, in that life, no place at all. They led already into that unknown future which, for our present life, is as though it were nothing, though, when it comes, we gladly sacrifice to it—as Monsieur Sandré did all his former existence and those friends of the old days now so long dead—the whole of that past life of which we alone can have a memory so vivid that it seems, to some extent, like a dream which we only can recall and is real for no one but ourselves. No, to see again those pictures of a far-away past, Monsieur Sandré needed to make no effort, had not to travel back along the dwindling road of half a century nor pass again through all the moments which, one by one, had led him from that distant time to the so different present with nothing in it of his former life except, maybe, a certain violence of temper, an outspokenness of which, even when he was young, his mistress or his mother might have had experience or the lawyer in whose office he had worked. No, Monsieur Sandré had not to make the passage of all those innumerable stages. The presiding genius of memory which, more quickly than any electric flash,

can make the circuit of the globe and, no less quickly, that of Time,
had set him back in the past without his noticing that so much as
a second had elapsed. Electricity does not take less time to bring to
the ear pressed to a telephone receiver the sound of a voice which, in
fact, is many miles distant, than does memory, that other powerful
element in nature which, like light or electricity, moving at a speed so
vertiginous that it seems almost to be its opposite, an absence of all
speed, a sort of omnipresence, is everywhere at once around the earth,
at the four corners of the world where its gigantic wings for ever
quiver like those of the angels which filled the imagination of the
Middle Ages. But, at the moment of hearing the beloved voice speaking to us from the receiver of the telephone, we seem to be conscious
of the distance which we have that moment overcome, though without
having been given time in which to realize it. In just such a way when
we wake from a brief sleep in a railway carriage we are aware, looking
out on the new scene now before our eyes, not so much of fatigue as
of the dizzy spin of distances through which, to serve our needs, the
engine has been rushing. In terms of time, a very few moments have
elapsed but, all the same, the sense is active in us of all that with
miraculous speed has been accomplished, of all that, unknown to us,
has changed. And so it was that those distant images presented themselves in a flash to Monsieur Sandré's eyes though the sense of the
extension in time of a great stretch of days instantaneously traversed
was, nevertheless, between those images and him. There was in the
quality of his gaze, as in the voice that reaches us over the telephone,
something that spoke of the fatigue occasioned by a passage through
the darkness of past time. What was visible in his eyes was a something
very far away so that it had the same property as stars which, when we
look at them, do not appear to be very distant from us. And, indeed, many of the things which were still radiating a present reality
in his mind—Madame Récamier, some movement she had made, the
Emperor, and the stir in the theatre as he entered—no longer existed
but were like those extinct stars whose light continues to reach us.

Without going so far as to recapitulate in detail the rapid and incalculable journey which Monsieur Sandré's thoughts must have been
compelled to make, his son-in-law and Marie, were, no doubt,
secretly reckoning its length in terms of years and thinking to themselves that Monsieur Sandré was certainly no longer young. But the
gaze that Madame Santeuil directed at her father was one of tenderness,

of pity and of admiration. She could think of the many years of his life only as she would have thought, for instance, of the weariness which ill-health had caused her son. It was they, after all, that, little by little, in spite of the way he had stood up to them, had combined to produce the person whom now she saw, exquisite, venerable and gay, but so fragile that the least shock might all at once demolish him. Her father was an old man! Never, for one single moment, did she forget that fact, but thought of it with terror, tenderness, timidity, always dreading lest, even by thinking, she might be guilty of brutality to a being so sacred and so feeble, never daring to let her imagination, save with a shuddering melancholy, play with the last terrible moments, from which anguish never kept her thoughts long absent, as, when we stand by the grave of someone we have loved, we keep our voices low and tread lightly, while with trembling hand, we drop the ritual earth upon the unresponsive coffin which hides from us the unhearing dead, because there is present all about us something so tender that the least sound might bruise it, so august that everything may be for it a cause of outrage. And her sense of pity grew as she thought that the evocation of the past, by reminding him how old he was, must be filling her father's mind with the sense of his great age and haunting him as she herself was haunted. Had it been her own death of which she was thinking she would have felt neither sorrow nor pain, but, though she knew her father to be even braver than herself and less concerned about his life, she thought with pity of this thing within his consciousness as of some pain which, if she could, she would have spared him. For it is the way of life to soften the sense of our own ills that we may the better bear them. But imagination leads us to dwell upon the ills of others in all their solitary desolation but does not let us see what makes those ills to them quite insignificant, and even sweet. It is on those ills, therefore, that pity makes us spend our tears while our own we do not even see. And so it was that the flickering and compassionate look which, at that moment, Madame Santeuil furtively directed at her father was also one of admiration. She thought of his memories as things that did him credit, much as when we speak of the age of the very old, we cannot keep the note of admiration from our voices.

The expression on Monsieur Sandré's face might be dour but, because he was old, it was also gentle. Old people do not love themselves, they love their children. They adore them, and must leave them. They suffer, not on their own account, but because they see their children failing to do what they ought to do and because life, seen in the persons of their children, brings to them an increasingly vivid realization—habits forming a substratum which, far from crumbling away with time, on the contrary becomes increasingly strong—of all that they used to blame in themselves and tried to eradicate. They suffer from this knowledge but forgive those through whom they have gained it and go so far even as to admire what they condemn, because the severity of their judgment has lost its edge, so that they have become resigned to the inevitable and faults, just because they are their children's faults, are dear to them. Thus it is that a father or a mother who once had high ambitions for their children, now feel only an immensity of love and show in the way they look, the way they move, in the expression on their faces, something that seems wholly detached from themselves, like a flower floating on the surface of a pond, something that is pure goodness, that shows in their eyes as though it had no root in the body, something infinite that gives itself and feels that there is not much time left in which to give itself. Even the way in which a father receives her guests is eloquent of the admiration he feels for his daughter and, in the look he gives her, there is no thought for himself. The theatre holds no more moving experience than the spectacle of an aging actress whose fragile body, dim eyes and faulty memory all betray her, though she forgives them for their dereliction, and lets the spirit play freely among the ruins of the flesh as it could never have done when youth, firm lips and flashing eyes bore witness to a love of life. It is then that one hears those tones in which the gift of self is absolute, in which one gives oneself, in the brief space of time in which it is still possible to give, to the daughter one adores, from whom one looks for no reward and when there is nothing left in the body to protest and cry—I want to live. In life (even more than in the theatre) there is something that defies description in the way a father or a mother looks, whose life is drawing to a point in which all that matters is to gaze with love and sadness at a daughter —sadness that is born not so much of the knowledge that soon the time of gazing will be over as because it is inevitable for one who loves another wholly for that other's sake and, being conscious of what is essential in his own life, is conscious, too, of sadness. And so it is that the way in which fathers and mothers look at a child, with tender criticism, silent admiration, melancholy love and an infinite but un-realized yearning for the happiness they wish her to have, is always, so

to speak, a vague gazing into space, sometimes accompanied by a
movement of the head which is partly the twitching of old age, partly
an attempt to express feelings for which there are no words and
expresses doubt, criticism, discouragement and uncertainty, though
the look in their eyes speaks only of love.

*

Madame Santeuil completely failed in her efforts to awaken in her son
a passion for *Les Contemplations* of Victor Hugo, or Corneille's *Horace*.
But her lack of success brought no comfort to her father who, if the
truth be told, needed no reasons for uneasiness since he was uneasy by
nature. Madame Santeuil, however, saw in it no cause for rejoicing
because, in her view, books, though totally unfitted to be a lifetime's
occupation, were admirably fitted to fill a man's leisure moments.
Hers was the attitude of those peasant-proprietors who, when they find
that a corner of their land is unsuitable for the growing of crops,
vegetables, or apples, turn it into a garden. She had been careful to
read to Jean verses which dealt with the noblest simplicities, summer
and wind, sunsets and church bells and the sea. . . . But, when they told
of bells, these poems said nothing to Jean, because, though the sound of
bells had already brought to him vague feelings of joy or suffering, he
had never, as yet, found in them the true beauty of happiness or
melancholy.

And so it was that he took no more pleasure in listening to a poem
about the sun or the wind than a river might have done, though a river
is far from being insensible to the glitter of sunlight when the beams
first touch it or to the wind which sets it rippling at the lightest touch,
or than the woods when fine weather dresses them in green and so
quickly thickens their foliage that they stand, in their massed solemnity,
for all the world like so many odes to the sun made visible. Jean was in
happy communion with sun and breeze, all redolent of woodland
scents, for both were slowly depositing scraps of their eternal life and
well-being in the rich soil of his days and waking in his heart a gaiety
which, sometimes, when the weather was particularly fine, could make
him forget his melancholy. Every day it was the first notes of the
Angelus, ringing from the distant countryside, that set him hurrying
home with his nurse so as not to be late for dinner. But poems that
spoke with ardours of the sweet sound of bells had no more effect upon

him than the most coldly chiselled of conventional allegories. And
though, not having noticed them, he never stopped to listen, for it had
not occurred to him that such music was sweet, they must, in some
vague way, have moved him. For, ten years later, his way of life having,
meanwhile, greatly changed, walking along a suburban street in Saint-
Germain, feeling a muffled burden occasioned by a sense of sadness and
indefinable regret for the lost years of his childhood which he would
never know again and the open-air existence which had been his in
those days, he was suddenly conscious of a faint and carefree sound
striking upon the membrane of his ear. First one note came, then
another and one by one the deep, sweet strokes of distant chapel bells
were borne to him upon the breeze.

Through gathering tears he could see again, between the lines of
growing corn touched by the setting sun, the path that led to his
father's garden, and before him moved a child's long shadow . . .
Absorbed by the light-winged flight of early years, like Prometheus
by that of the invisible Oceanides coming from no less far away to
murmur words of delicious comfort, in just such tones of sweet
solemnity, he listened to each tinkling note with a growing sense of
fear, as the sequence slowed, that each would be the last, only, a
moment later, to hear another thrill the air, so close to him and yet so
far away, that it was as though he could feel the heart that had been his
so long ago beat melodiously within his breast. To have had the power
to speak to him the words which suddenly awaken all a man's drowned
and hidden feelings, words which only those whom we most love, who
know us to our inmost being, can utter, they must, during those
homeward walks, as he hurried back with his nurse in the old days,
have caught and held the secrets of a heart already densely packed and
piously have hoarded them.

But, at the time when the bonds were being tied that were to hold
the sound of bells and Jean's life so closely bound to one another that
the ringing of quite other bells would later suffice to bring back all one
period of his life, at the time when the bells were taking charge of his
child's heart so that they might restore it to him when he felt the need
to steep his older, wearier heart in remembered freshness, their touch
was still too light for him to feel and those who tried to tell him of their
music spoke of something which, as yet, had no meaning for him.

3. *Marie Kossichef*

Some years before, Monsieur and Madame Santeuil had given a reception in honour of a visiting Highness who, insufficiently provided with introductions to the Faubourg Saint-Germain, and compelled to fall back upon the official world of the Capital, had charmed his hosts by his affability, out-distanced them in the liberalism of his views, and astonished them by the simplicity of his manners. This reception had been organized only after considerable resistance from Madame Santeuil who, speaking out of the pride she felt in the modest circumstances of her middle-class background, insisted more than once with a laugh that, "It, would have to be much too smart an affair for us to dream of," and from Monsieur Sandré who was suspicious of all great social occasions, and grumbled away to the effect that, "If he were really smart he wouldn't set foot in this house, just as he wouldn't have accepted the invitation sent him by the President's wife, or gone to the party given by the wife of the Prefect of the Seine. Besides, according to the *Figaro* he likes going to the Folies Bergères and dining first at Durand's at half-past eight, though I don't suppose he pays for the dinner . . ." Monsieur Santeuil, however, had more or less committed himself as the result of a rather annoying joke made by the Foreign Minister. His natural indolence had made it painful, and therefore impossible, for him to say no, and he now replied to Monsieur Sandré by enumerating the distinguished foreigner's connexions with certain royal and ducal families, the historical eminence of which he had learned long ago and which, by reminding him of his past, shed a radiant light upon his future.

In the course of the reception, at which Madame de Thèbes was one of the principal attractions, Monseigneur, whose good-humour remained unruffled, had as the result of a sudden whim introduced Jean—who petrified with shyness had spent the evening in a corner—to the famous fortune-teller, with a request that she should read his hand. She found in it a premonition of many dangers, about which she spoke confidentially to Madame Santeuil, telling her that, unless she

45

did something to counteract his ominous destiny, there was every probability that her son would "run upon the rocks". Madame Santeuil, whose only real faith was in the human reason, did not believe in palmistry. Nevertheless, she was as much frightened by these words as she would have been had she received a letter from an anarchist or a threat that her son would be killed. Shamefacedly, so long as she retained any authority over Jean, she was adamant in her refusal ever to let him travel by sea. Monsieur Sandré, true to the natural slant of his mind which led him to attribute all the rules and regulations of Christianity to hygienic precautions, persuaded his daughter that Madame de Thèbes, who was generally accounted a woman of great intelligence and much goodness of heart, having heard that the state of Jean's health was such as seriously to threaten his future, had intended by her use of this sombre symbol of "rocks" to warn his parents to look after him with exaggerated care.

This was the reason why he was not sent early to school, and why, when he was in Paris, he was made to spend every day in the Champs-Elysées—bare-legged, so that he might catch the sun—where the invitations of other little boys, the advances made to him by little girls, and the threats of his nurse, all equally failed to induce him to emerge from his terrified silence or to move away from the bench which was his place of refuge, and on which he obstinately remained with averted face. But a day arrived when a sudden change came over him. He made the acquaintance of a little Russian girl, with a mass of black hair, bright, mocking eyes and rosy cheeks, who was possessed of all the glowing vitality and joy of living which were so sadly lacking in Jean. As soon, now, as he awoke in the morning he began to think of nothing but the moment when he would see her laughing at her play. All the time she was present, he stayed close beside her, taking part in games of prisoners' base, hide-and-seek and sliding. When she arrived about three o'clock in the Champs-Elysées with her governess and her sister, his heart beat so fast that he almost fell down, and remained for a few moments with his face as white as a sheet before he could pull himself together. He measured his delight in seeing her by the immensity of his desire to do so and by the pain he felt when he saw her go away, for from her actual presence he derived but little pleasure. Too much agitated by the sight of her, he did not in any true sense see her at all, except when he woke in the morning or before he went to sleep at night. Whenever she spoke to him—as she spoke to all the

others—he hopped from side to side of the path in an ecstasy of joy,
feeling that he was loved. But he noticed, with sadness, that her kindness to him had nothing in common with his devotion to her, and that
she never felt any reluctance about saying: "If it rains tomorrow, I
shan't be here: see you again the day after." But, fortunately, it had
never yet rained once. Then a day came when it did. The storm broke
on a morning of fine weather about one o'clock, just as they were all
making ready to go home, and Jean realized that he would not see her
again that day. Without thinking to close the window, or to put an
overcoat across his shoulders, he stood for a long while crying, with
his contorted face turned towards the sky and wetted by the rain. The
great drops struck upon the bar of the window, splashed on to him and
seemed to summon others which followed hard on the heels of those
already falling from the dark canopy of heaven. Abandoning himself
entirely to the misery and cold which set him shivering, he took
account, as he might have done of somebody whose entrance he had
not noticed, and who had sat down sadly at his side, of the melancholy
aspect of a sky covered by a black pall of cloud in which every crack
of brightness was slowly vanishing so that it seemed as though no ray
of sun would ever again break through, nor in his heart a hope, to
dissipate the drops now falling as close-packed as his tears and seeming
as though they would never stop. You, reader, must have noticed that
he had but little skill in breaking free from sorrow. He could not then, as
much later on he could, when he was sad, take up a book or see a friend,
and cheat the miserable today by thinking on a glorious tomorrow.
But even in those days, and to the very end of his life, he could never
see rain without feeling that he was being deprived of a pleasure, though
it might no longer be keeping him from going to meet a little girl in
the Champs-Elysées. And whenever that happened he never ceased to
wonder that a sadness at his heart should so perfectly chime with the
tearfulness of heaven, as when, a child, he had been amazed to find that
the sky could share his sense, first of anxiety and then of desolation.

It was this year, though his mother had had no more success than in
the year preceding it with her attempts to make him feel a fondness for
Lamartine's *Le Lac*, that he read, over and over again until he had got
it by heart, the short poem by Verlaine which begins:

> Il pleure dans mon coeur
> Comme il pleut sur la ville

which he had found lying about on one of the tables. When he was older he ranked *Le Lac* much higher than this lyric which, at ten years of age, he had decided was the most beautiful poem in all the world. But children's intelligence and sensibility develop by fits and starts according to the chance flicker of a sunbeam or, still oftener, by the coming of a storm. And for that reason, their parents, even when they are as intelligent as Madame Santeuil, judging these things by their own formed and fixed standards of appreciation, are apt to feel bitter and inevitable disappointment at finding that their sons prefer, for instance, Verlaine to Lamartine.

*

When we are children each tomorrow resembles one of those cardboard boxes, as yet unopened which, on New Year's Day, await us in the drawing-room, piled under the lamp which, in defiance of the melancholy dawn outside the windows, seems to illuminate with an especial and delicious radiance the mysterious secrets with which the room is filled, some nestling together on the table, others, the larger ones, standing on the floor in a corner, which, at first unnoticed, will not for long conceal behind ample folds of paper the exciting promise of their curious shape and imposing size. If, in later years, you have enough of the child still left in you to take pleasure in a toy, you know that it is just another object, and no longer, however intricate its wrappings, does your heart throb with a thrilling impatience to know what this new something can be which has suddenly come into your life. Similarly, no matter how difficult you may have found it once to believe that Easter, New Year, Christmas, are just the same as other days you learn, through the long succession of the years, to see all days as so many tiny divisions marked by the minutes of your watch, small, empty pigeon-holes which this or that event will occupy or, more often than not, no event at all, though, apart from what they will prove to contain, none of them differs by a hair's breadth from its fellows. But no matter how often a child may be told that tomorrow will be merely a day, as today is a day, as yesterday was a day, he always thinks of each tomorrow as something utterly new, having no resemblance to today or yesterday, a mysterious world in which, beyond the shadow of a doubt, he will find happiness. The fact that today has been empty does not trouble him. Tomorrow is there while he sleeps, wrapped and corded like a mysterious present under the lamp on New Year's morning, with a card stuck under the string, waiting for him to be the first to undo the paper, to see, seize and carry off what it contains, and jump for joy. Tomorrow seems to him to be a world without end. Then, tomorrow becomes today. But a new morrow waits for him, a new world, and he plays with his worlds, breaks his worlds, but only the more impatiently looks forward to still others, and finds it hard to go to sleep, so full is his mind of tomorrow, so eagerly does he wonder what it will turn out that his aunt has given him, for the time ahead of him is an infinity, and for each day that he breaks in pieces—never having a moment in which to be bored, so tired out he feels and ready for sleep—a new day is given to him on which to start all over again, though to him it seems that he will start from nothing.

When we are in love we find again that lovely gift of childhood, so that each day becomes for us something feverishly looked forward to, the unknown goal of all our hopes. Each anticipated meeting, each letter hoped for, these are the things that fill our field of vision, while the limping, useless hours drag their slow length along, none with any comfort but that single one that counts and is so dilatory. Not till tomorrow shall we know it. God! what an age before it comes! How gladly would we leap into nothingness if only, by so doing, we could hasten the longed-for future. Why should it not be now? Why? Maybe she is not far from us. We leave the house, but all in vain. No, we must pass these twenty hours without her, with no touch of her presence. We must wait until tomorrow. Today is a world finished and done with a world with nothing left in it to arouse our interest. Let us forget about it. Ah! dear tomorrow, pressing so close upon me! How I despise today! with what melancholy disdain, with what a voluptuous sense of my own superiority, do I look back upon it, I, for whom tomorrow, for whom even the act of waiting, the thoughts that at this moment fill my mind, are things beyond the understanding of anybody else. Pitilessly, one after the other, I rub out the hours which this day has brought. Come night, and with thy massive walls encircle me, give to this passing day its last and timeless shape, and slowly let thy darkening flood wash over it!

*

"Jean, Jean dear, what are you thinking about?" asked Madame Santeuil. Monsieur Santeuil scolded Jean for dropping his glass. "How mannerless he is," thought Jean and felt inclined to cry and to laugh at the same time, so unimportant it all was. It seemed to him that he was suffering for Marie Kossichef, and the thought was sweet. "Why should I care whether tonight is more or less sad?—tomorrow I shall be happy." Each evening when he went to bed he thought: "To-morrow." Each morning when he woke he told himself: "I shall see her today." Waking once at one o'clock in the morning, he went to sleep again, smiling, for the thought had come to him: "Today is here." One morning when he woke, the world was hidden under snow. A power beyond his imagining had changed the face of the earth, making the roadways level with the pavements, obliterating the streets, setting a mute upon his hopes. Ceaselessly from the sky the snow swirled down and there was nothing he could do to hold it back, to stay the falling flakes, to force them back behind the clouds. When his nursemaid came in, she said: "No Champs-Elysées today, or not yet awhile, anyhow."

Towards noon the snow stopped. Jean's heart began to flutter. For hope, mingled though it was with dread, had once again taken possession of it and filled it with debate. Something in him said: "It will start again," and something else, "No, it's over." Madame Santeuil said: "There'll be nobody in the Champs-Elysées today." But the maid was not so sure. "One never knows." Madame Santeuil said to Jean: "In any case you may be sure Mademoiselle Kossichef won't be there, if that is why you are looking at the sky. She won't be allowed to dirty her pretty frock just for that." She spoke the words with a smile, as though they were not at all important. But to Jean they were in-finitely so and it seemed to him that his mother had divined his hidden misery and was laughing at it. He could have struck her and said: "I know she won't be there," and then sought for something hurtful to add so that he might make her pay for the wound her irony had caused him, for this disastrous news, the effect of which on him he did not want her to see. He went with the maid to the Champs-Elysées. It was true there was scarcely a soul there. The sun came out: the weather was lovely and on the shrubberies with their burden of snow the sun shone with a gentle light. A few of his little friends with their atten-dants, put in an appearance, one after the other. Then all the children began to slide in order to keep warm. The attendant maids agreed that they had better go home early for it would soon be dark. "Dark"— Jean hearing the word felt his cheeks go pale. The day would end without his seeing her. With his eyes fixed in the direction from which the Kossichef sisters would come, he joined in the game, running as hard as he could, the more easily to forget his grief. From time to time he wiped his face and found that tears were mingled with his sweat, but could not be sure that they had not been caused by the cold.

The expression of his face was suddenly transformed, but he did not move. The Kossichef sisters had come, swaddled in fur, and from under her fur-trimmed cap, Marie, her black hair hanging down, red-cheeked, blue-eyed, and laughing, shook hands with all of them. Their governess did not want them to play, but they persuaded her. Sliding began again, and snowballing. Jean now joined with them at playing with the snow, no longer oppressed by misery, stamping the pillaged garden with triumphant feet, the snow itself a dead thing, looking in the sunlight like fleece torn from the winter's body. Cold and heat meant nothing to him now: filled with a sense of happiness, he gathered the snow in armfuls and took it to Marie. He cheated so that she might win, and stuffed snow down the neck of a boy she did not like to give her pleasure. When she looked at him he forgot what it was he wanted. But always he wanted to be close to her, to be one of her "gang", to find an excuse for staying near her. But if as the result of some sudden chance they were alone together for a moment, he could think of nothing more to say to her. There had, all the time, to be something else for him to say, a game to go on with, an activity that could be saturated with his love and so seem delicious to him. But if there was no third term between them, no *thing* on which his love could play, then he put off speaking till the morrow—when he would have more time—thinking what he must say, when he was no longer with her. His love was like something he could hold in his hands, but only when it was contained in something else, which being absent, it would melt like the snow of their playtime. She paid no attention to him, but because she enjoyed the snow, made balls of it and threw them, laughing: and if it was at him she threw, he felt it was because she loved him. And he knew that the others knew that she loved him. And when he stood close to her and someone laughed, and someone else stared, and her sister said with sympathetic kindliness: "I'm going to pair you off with Marie," and Marie, choosing him for her side, laid a hand upon his shoulder and led him away in full view of the others, and they went together to collect more snow, or if the sun was in her eyes and she asked him to change positions with her, he would to please her, fulfil

her request with an enthusiasm that brought no answering thanks from
her—at such moments he was filled with the realization of his love, of
a love which, as though it were a reflected radiance which he might
not touch, but which the mocking laughter of some of his friends, her
sister's complicity, each "Look out!"–"'Ware!"–"Pax!" which he
had to shout at her, each stop, each ball of snow, each ray of sunlight,
seemed endlessly to shower upon him that he might grow the more
enchanted.

*

Monsieur and Madame Santeuil became seriously worried about the
constant state of over-excitement in which Jean seemed to be living.
He had never been asked to Mademoiselle Kossichef's home, for her
parents, who were far richer than Monsieur and Madame Santeuil,
lived in a world to which he had never penetrated. Marie's absence,
when she stopped coming to the Champs-Elysées, being intolerable to
him, he took to persuading the maid to go with him as far as the house
where her family lived, so that Marie might be the object of his walks
as well as of his thoughts. He would stop in front of it, finding peace of
mind in touching with his eyes and with his hands the door which she
pushed open and pulled to behind her several times a day, in staring at
her window, imagining her behind it, and feeling the distance which
separated them reduced to a few steps which he had only to take in
order to see her, after which he would go home less agitated, if not
happier. Everything that figured in the life of Mademoiselle Kossichef
found a place in his heart. He could not, without emotion, think of her
father, who saw her daily at luncheon and sometimes at dinner, who
could, should he wish to do so, have her with him all the time, even
during the holidays, those terrible holidays which would one day
separate them and so put an end not to his happiness, but to his very
life, on which he could not let his thoughts dwell for longer than
human beings can bear to think of death.

One day when a game of prisoners' base was being arranged on the
wide lawn of the Champs-Elysées, between the wooden horses and the
Ambassadeurs, Mademoiselle Nelly Kossichef, Marie's young sister,
picked sides. She touched each person on the arm, saying: "You're on
my side, you're on Marie's." When she came to Jean, who was always
afraid of hurting the feelings of somebody he did not care about by
showing a too obvious preference for somebody else, he moved

towards her, but she with a laugh said: "Oh, dear me, no! You belong
to Marie, I wouldn't spoil your pleasure for worlds!" "You belong to
Marie!" For a long while to come, in his moments of doubt, Jean
would hear the echo of those lovely words. Often when evening came
and he felt persuaded that in the day just over she had given proof of
her indifference to him, he remembered them: "You belong to Marie!"
and the sparkling, mischievous, kindly smile which had shown on
Marie's face when she heard them. If she did not love him a little, how
could she and her sister so publicly have recognized his love for her?
But he was to experience an even greater happiness. One day he went
home feeling definitely unwell and had to remain in bed for several
days. One of his little friends came to see him and told him that
Mademoiselle Kossichef had caught a bad cold and had been forbidden
by the doctor to stir out of the house during January and February
because of the severity of the winter weather. Thus, even when he himself should be well again, he would not see her for a whole month and,
not having anticipated this separation, he had not been able even to say
good-bye, or to speak the words which for so long now he had been
putting off from day to day. He spent two very gloomy days, not
being allowed up, not being allowed to drink or to read, telling himself
endlessly that he would never see her again, because, since they did not
visit at one another's home, they could meet only in the Champs-
Elysées, and she would not be there for two whole months. Again and
again, lost in the desert of his grief, he imagined her showing him a
delicious oasis, wanting to see him, sending her father to fetch him—
all of it a dream of impossible happiness which he soon tried to restate
in terms of reality—the desert being the necessity of their separation
and the fact of her indifference—which he now recognized as a mirage.
Then the morning would come, and with it the doctor saying that he
must not get up for yet another day. That scarcely irked him, so
quickly did everything sink beneath the waters of his misery and drop
so deep that no trace rose to the surface. About ten o'clock one morning
somebody came into his room. He did not even turn his face from the
wall against which he hid his tears. "There's a letter for Master Jean,"
said Augustin, smiling because of the importance of this event which
was rare in the life of a little boy of thirteen to whom no one ever
wrote. "Give it to me," replied Jean, not turning his head and, taking
the letter, laid it on the table which stood beside his bed. When
Augustin had gone, he opened it listlessly, since nothing now had the

power to awaken his curiosity. This is what he read. "My dear Jean, because it is so very cold and I've got a chill, I am not to be allowed to go back to the Champs-Elysées for two months. Mamma says you may come and have tea with me at five o'clock any day you like. We shall be able to play, though our games won't be such fun as in the open air, still it will be very nice to see you again for a little. Nelly and I send our love. Marie Kossichef."

The heavy pall of the sky which had been hanging over his head was torn suddenly to tatters. His sadly solemn admission that she did not care for him, the expectation of a miracle, which he had known to be absurd, as a result of which, by making it possible for him to go to her house, his life would suddenly have changed, in accordance with his dearest wishes, the dark necessities of life, those immense necessities which he could no more push away from him than he could have pushed a stranded ship upon the shore back into the sea, and which, lying like a wall across his future, would make of each tomorrow the sad continuation of today—it was they, he was at last, assured, that were the opposite of the truth, they that were errors light as straws, which he could blow away with a breath: it was the miracle, which he had thought could be realized only in dreams that had turned out to be the reality, the delicious, unhoped-for, triumphant reality! Jean had his mother fetched. Too much in a hurry to come in, she asked him from the door what it was he wanted. But he could not summon up the strength to tell her. Forgetting he was ill, he ran to her, waving the letter but unable to say a word. Then, worn out by this new delight which had fallen on him from the sky and, floating above his head, merely overwhelmed him the more, he dropped the letter from his nerveless fingers and collapsed in tears into his mother's arms. He was almost unconscious. His small body which for so long had been weighed down by shackles which even a strong and full-grown man would have found it hard to endure, could not but suffer severely when they were so suddenly removed.

4. *Separation*

The spring had now come and Monsieur and Madame Santeuil, who for months had been growing increasingly anxious about the persistent state of over-excitement in which Jean was living, decided at last on a policy of separation which the lucid good-sense of Madame Santeuil, vehemently seconded by Monsieur Sandré, had long been advocating as the only way of restoring her son's bodily health and peace of mind but which Monsieur Santeuil, in whose somewhat flabby heart love of his son lived on equal terms with love of his own ordered and placid existence, had constantly put off for fear of "causing the boy distress". One day Madame Santeuil who, as a rule, whenever Jean was disobedient or did something to annoy her, expressed the irritation she was feeling only by assuming an expression of somewhat insensitive severity, spoke gently to him of the grief she felt at the violence of a passion which could lead to nothing, because he was far too young to think of marrying Mademoiselle Kossichef, and merely had the effect of undermining his constitution. "In ten years' time you will feel quite differently"—that was the burden of her words, and of everybody else's, as though Jean's sense of his love as of something which had nothing to do with Time, were not blazing like fire before a high wind fanned by the fury of his despair. But now, whether as part of a deliberate plan or because she saw only too clearly the extent of its power over her son, she was careful not to speak slightingly of his attachment but talked to him, with gentle severity and with a sad look on her face, of what she was asking of him—to give up seeing Marie—as of a serious sacrifice. Jean, however, who as a rule was so submissive to her and could so easily be reduced to tears by a kind word, stared at her with dry eyes, or rather it was not at her at all that he was staring at that moment. For what he saw towering over him, so real, so appalling that it demanded on his part a hideous fixity of gaze, was the life and death threat which now confronted him. Even before he could begin the struggle for his own existence, he had got to come to terms with a reality which was far more serious and much bigger than simple unhappiness, that invisible yet undeniable fact which shows in Géricault's picture on the face of the cavalryman who, mortally wounded, still sits his horse and, before making up his mind either to pull himself together or to fall, looks steadily in the face that terrible unknown figure that is racking his body with all the torments of the final agony.

"Darling Mamma, it isn't my fault, and you mustn't be angry with me. I can't do what you ask, and I can't explain." – "There is no need for you to explain. I know what I am asking. You are not the first little boy who has fallen in love, and we all know what that means." To himself, Jean said: "How great is God who has made men in such a way that they can all love, and can understand what happens when others love, who know what loving means! How great is God!—how great is God!" he said over and over again in the silence of his heart, and the tears came into his eyes as his mother continued: "And that is the reason why, when one truly loves one's parents and does not want to cause them pain, one does difficult things to please them. Loving one's parents is more than just liking to hug them, than crying when one is separated from them. *That* is not loving, but something one does in spite of oneself, because one is sensitive and a victim of one's nerves. It has nothing to do with true goodness of heart." – "Nothing?" asked Jean. "No, nothing," replied Madame Santeuil: "even Nero could suffer from nerves." These words produced a profound impression on Jean, for, seeing only something very vague and shadowy when he thought about himself, he had no clear conviction about his moral worth, and accordingly, as in the book he happened to be reading at the moment certain of his faults were attributed to a criminal, and certain of his good qualities glorified, he would think of himself, turn and turn about, as Nero or as Saint Vincent de Paul.

"Loving one's parents means controlling oneself, exerting one's will, so as to give them pleasure. We are perfectly willing to let you see her occasionally, if only when you don't see her you will try not to think about her and brood. Will you promise me to do that?" said his mother. "Promise?—how can I promise what I can't do?" said Jean. "If one wants to do a thing hard enough," said his mother, "one can always do it." – "Can one *not* think?" said Jean with a forbearing smile. "One can always do what it depends upon one's will to do," replied Madame Santeuil. 'I promise to try," said Jean. "Then give me a kiss," said his mother, and let him see for the first time that there were tears in her eyes.

Madame Santeuil's grief moved Jean a great deal less now that he saw it, than when after some naughtiness he only imagined it. He felt ashamed at not feeling more than he did: there was nothing good in him except a sensitiveness that had nothing to do with his will. If the same could be said of Nero, then most certainly he was Nero. "You know perfectly well that we don't want to thwart you, but, quite apart from the fact that if you go on like this you will seriously annoy Monsieur Kossichef and will be acting very badly, your health will suffer. It is our duty, so long as you are young enough to obey us, to prevent you from doing things that are bad for you. Don't look so cross. Do realize how gentle I am being with you." – "But," said Jean eagerly, taking advantage of the hesitancy which he had noticed in his mother's voice, to make one more attempt to convince her, "if I don't see her I shall never stop thinking of her, and that will be much worse for me. Please! please!—you don't know what *is* bad for me. If you let me see her, I shall be happy. I shan't get all worked up, but shall be well and strong. I shan't go on thinking too much about her." He was perfectly sincere in proposing that he should be allowed to see her often, and so might not have to think of her too often. But he never saw her often enough to kill the desire in him to see her oftener still, or to keep him from thinking endlessly of the moment when he *would* see her. His condition of nervous excitement got worse, and an evening came when for the first time Madame Santeuil did not reproach him. For the next two days she avoided the subject. Jean was conscious of that uneasy feeling which comes in moments of a flat calm, when the storm seems to be gathering its forces.

*

Since Madame Kossichef never had time to look after her daughter, but let her go to the Champs-Elysées in charge of a governess, Monsieur and Madame Santeuil had no opportunity of seeing Monsieur and Madame Kossichef, who in all probability had never heard anybody speak of them. But the immense wealth of Monsieur and Madame Kossichef, the life of pleasure which they led, the husband's reputation for insolence and his wife's flightiness, aroused in the minds of Jean's eminently respectable parents a feeling of mistrust every bit as strong as the contempt which Marie's parents would undoubtedly have felt for them.

One Tuesday morning Jean had been thinking a good deal about his mother. It had occurred to him during the night that one day she would die, and that then there would be nothing left for him but to die too. He was now, in imagination, fondling the dear face which at times he had made so sad, and feeling it impossible to wait another moment without seeing her had gone downstairs to wait until she should come in for luncheon. He hid in the hall at the bottom of the stairs and waited. After a while, his mother appeared in the courtyard and went into the concierge's lodge. Afraid that she might scold him, he went back upstairs and from the landing called down, "Good morning, darling Mamma." – "I've just come back from seeing Monsieur Jacomier, Jean. I have been trying for a long time to persuade him to give you lessons, and now he has consented. He will be expecting you at two o'clock." – "Two o'clock!—but I can't: I'm going to the Champs-Elysées," said Jean, who had grasped the whole situation in a flash. "Then I'm afraid you won't be able to. It is quite time you started to do some work." – "Not go to the Champs-Elysées!" screamed Jean in a sudden burst of temper, "not go to the Champs-Elysées?—I *will* go, yes, I *will*! I don't give a straw for Monsieur Jacomier. If I ran into the horrible old monkey on the way, I'd kill him!—kill him. I tell you!" Madame Santeuil shut the front door behind her. Jean was still screaming. Monsieur Sandré came towards them, but Jean, who was fully aware of the part played by his grandfather in supporting the attitude adopted by his parents, pushed him violently away, saying: "As for you—I hate you!" – "If you go on like this, I shall call your father." – "Go on, call him then, I don't care!" shouted Jean, made bolder by the violent sound of his own voice: "I'll tell him what a horrible person his wife is, and that all she wants is to harm his son!" Then, snatching up the water-jug which was standing on the table ready for his luncheon, he dashed it to the floor where it broke in pieces. "André! André! Come here at once!" cried Madame Santeuil, "I think Jean has gone out of his mind!" Monsieur Santeuil, who was peaceable enough so long as his comfort was not threatened, was the more inclined to lose his temper when it was. "Papa, *dear* Papa," said Jean, falling to his knees, "they want to hurt me, mamma is persecuting me—you must protect me, you *must*!" – "Nonsense! your mother's perfectly right," said Monsieur Santeuil, not at all sure what he was going to say next. "This business of you and that girl is becoming intolerable. I can tell you this, you're not going to

see any more of her!" – "Not going to see any more of her?" screamed
Jean. "Brutes! that's what you are, all of you, brutes! No more of her!
—we'll soon see about that!" and Jean, as his father gave him a slap and
pushed him towards the gloomy study, collapsed in a violent attack of
nerves.

*

That same day Jean went for his first lesson with Monsieur Jacomier.
He cried all the way from the rue de l'Arcade, where he lived, to
Neuilly, without taking any notice of the passers-by, though as a rule
when they stared at him he was far too frightened to think of his own
troubles. When he saw a clock which marked the time when Mademoiselle Kossichef would be arriving at the Champs-Elysées, and
reckoned that he would still have time to see her, he stopped, stared at
his nursemaid for several seconds, seemed to hesitate, and then suddenly
went so pale that she had to support him. He let her take his hand and
walked on again, trembling. In the evening, when he was told that
dinner was ready, he did not hang back but hurried down to the
dining-room. Usually when he had been at loggerheads with his
parents, he found it an intolerable ordeal to sit opposite them at meal-
times. But, on this particular evening, though the words he had used
to them in the morning had exceeded in violence any he had ever
spoken in the worst of his nervous crises, his mind was so full of other
matters that he felt no embarrassment in their presence. As he entered
the warmly lit room, he said: "Good evening, Mamma, good evening,
Papa, good evening, Grandpapa," though he did not look at them,
knowing that he would get no answer. Much to his astonishment,
however, his grandfather, who was very much sterner with him than
either of his parents, was the only one of the three who returned his
greeting. All through the meal he thought he saw in his grandfather's
eyes something more than the rheumy moisture of old age. Monsieur
Sandré ate nothing, explaining that he had had a late tea and was not
hungry. Each time that Jean looked up he caught the old gentleman in
the act of hastily averting his gaze. When dinner was over, Monsieur
and Madame Santeuil withdrew to the study, but Monsieur Sandré sat
on for a while, his faded old eyes—which, when he looked straight
ahead seemed always to be focused on the far distance, or possibly on
something within himself—fixed on Jean, to whom he was as a rule
so harsh, whose most innocent fancies he was for ever thwarting, whom

he insisted on their sending to bed if they had forgotten the lateness of the hour, who for the last month had been constantly urging his daughter and son-in-law to separate the boy from Mademoiselle Kossichef, and though he never gave Jean a kiss, even on the 1st of January, now spoke gently to him, took him on his knee, and pressed to his cheek the dry old lips which nowadays were never parted except to utter reproaches and complaints and were salty with all the silent tears that they had drunk since morning. Through the door came the air from *Don Giovanni* which Madame Santeuil was playing to her husband. "Darling Grandpapa, Grandpapa darling," said Jean, clinging to the thin old neck, while his small body was racked with sobs.

By the time August came and the holidays, Jean had not failed, since that twentieth of March, to go, between two and four each day to Monsieur Jacomier's for his lesson. In spite of this regularity of attention, however, Madame Santeuil inferred from the nature of her son's holiday task, that he knew very little about Athens, Sparta and Thebes, though Monsieur Jacomier had spent every day discoursing on the history of those places. But she was delighted to see him happy and asked no more. He had just learned that we are no less imperfectly organized for pleasure than for pain, and that if our joys have shallower foundations than we think, our sorrows never last as long as we expect. That knowledge, thought Madame Santeuil, was quite enough for one year.

*

By this time Jean could manage to read *La Tristesse d'Olympio*, and other poems as well. The poets who had been the strangest to, the furthest removed from him now stood beside him while he read with seemingly a greater understanding than his years would warrant, helping him, as it were, to find words for something that had long been weighing on his heart, giving him the *right* words, understanding his vague, uncertain thoughts better than he did himself, and handing them back to him filled with light and power and with a depth of sadness and sweetness which, until then, he had found it impossible to express.

Nevertheless, Monsieur and Madame Santeuil, and even Jean himself, had passed within hail of Mademoiselle Kossichef without recognizing her for what she was. How should they have known that God had chosen her to reveal to Jean that bloodstained hill from the summit of which he would see this new star of the world arise, and that by continually turning upon him the churning magic of her gaze she would give to him the power to bear the necessary agonies? Our life is, at every moment, before us like a stranger in the night, and which of us knows what point he will reach on the morrow? We are incapable even of recognizing the Lord's anointed on the way, unlike Jeanne d'Arc who, passing over the courtier who she had been told was Charles VII, went straight to him who had received the sacred oil upon his forehead.

5. *Madame Lepic*

Every Sunday Monsieur and Madame Lepic dined at the Santeuil table. Edmée Lebon, before her marriage, had been a high-spirited, handsome young woman with a naturally gay temperament, a feeling for the arts and a longing for happiness. Madame Santeuil had known her at school and she had become her best friend. Then at twenty-two she had married Monsieur Lepic. He was a tall, thin man whose shrivelled face showed, as it were, the pallid reflection of a devouring inner fire of human charity, at once indefatigable and impotent. If in the course of the day Monsieur heard a child crying because its parents were beating it, it was all up with any hope of sleep for him that night. The memory of the child's cries were as nails driven into his flesh and would not let him rest. He was for ever on the look-out for cases of destitution to relieve, and his imagination was continually haunted by the wretched creatures whose lamentable lives he spent half his income in alleviating.

But admirable though he was as a human being, as a husband he was terrible. On the day after the wedding he locked his wife's piano, and it was never opened again. Not once during their life together did he let her go to a theatre, a concert, a museum, nor to read anything except *La Cuisinière Bourgeoise*, the only volume which, in his wife's hands, he did not regard as an abomination. Madame Lepic had to give up all her girlhood's friends, for not only did he forbid her to visit them, but he was adamant in refusing them admittance to his home. At the end of the first year of marriage, he did, it is true, relax this rule in favour of Monsieur and Madame Santeuil, but this was the only exception he would countenance. On the few occasions when Madame Lepic, who accepted the existence which he had mapped out for her with saintly resignation, plucked up sufficient courage to show a little gaiety, he could scarcely suppress a quick movement of anger and would tell her sharply to be silent. "There are people in the world suffering the extremes of misery," he would say "Injustice is rife everywhere, yet you, wretched woman that you are, can allow yourself to laugh," and could only with a great effort keep from striking

62

her. In the early days of their marriage he would wait until they were alone together before giving vent to his anger, but it was not long before he lost all power of self-control and would threaten her with physical violence in front of his friends. He stayed in bed late in the hope of repairing the ravages of his sleepless nights, and insisted on his wife and the servants observing the most complete silence until midday. After luncheon he worked on a Report he was writing on the poor of Paris and, since the least sound made him start, disturbed his train of thought and broke the continuity of his labours, his wife, to avoid provoking one of his terrifying displays of temper, dared not so much as lift a chair, for he insisted that she should remain in the next door room, which was separated from his own by only a thin partition, so that he might be sure that she was not receiving visitors. As well as being hypochondriacal he suffered from dyspepsia, and thought it essential to the proper functioning of his digestion that he should dine in the dark and go for a two-hours' walk after each meal. He did, however, permit the presence of a single lighted candle at dinner to enable them to distinguish the plates, the forks and the glasses. As soon as they rose from the table, to ensure that his digestive processes should not begin too soon, he dragged his wife with him on his two hours' tramp through rain, snow and wind, asserting that the deterioration in his health was entirely due to her, should she keep him waiting even for a minute. After three years of marriage, Madame Lepic had become ugly, melancholy and entirely turned in upon herself. Like an old gardener, whose body had been bent so long over the earth that he could no longer straighten it, her spirit violently subjected to a constant routine of household cares, was now incapable of standing upright. In the fourth year she became the victim of a species of nervous trouble which, each day, produced spasms of appalling pain. Monsieur Lepic, who dearly loved his wife, suffered agonies of grief. His nerves grew more exacerbated and his dyspepsia became worse. Madame Lepic's spasms were by this time more frequent. During the brief intervals between them she was so weak that she could do nothing but cry, and his pent-up irritability of a whole week used them as an occasion to burst its bounds.

But for the past twelve months Madame Lepic's health had been improving and, each time she came to the house, Madame Santeuil was delighted to see how much better she was looking. Then one morning, quite suddenly, Monsieur Lepic was found dead in his bed. He had broken a blood-vessel. Ten days later they buried Madame Lepic. She could not survive the abominable creature whom as a husband she had so sincerely adored. Doubtless, too, the atmosphere of continual storm in which she had existed, though at first it had nearly killed her, had later kept her alive. Like a cormorant, a seamew, or a gull caught by sailors and kept in captivity after a lifetime of skimming above the raging billows, she was not strong enough to endure the change from wild weather to calm, and so died.

The only person towards whom Monsieur Lepic in the whole course of his gloomy existence had been consistently affectionate and smiling, the only one on whom Madame Lepic had been able to lavish her affection without irritating her husband, had been Jean. There are some persons who, seemingly forbidden to share normally in human happiness, manage at times to do so in a strange and indirect manner. The happiness which Monsieur and Madame Lepic felt in Jean's company, because they loved him as they would have loved a son of their own had their sad union not been sterile, was the tender revenge taken by broken spirits and lives tragically grown askew. Jean returned their feeling for him. But he was so young when they died that he soon forgot them. Childless, friendless, Monsieur and Madame Lepic left nothing behind by which they might be remembered, and there will be no reason in the course of this narrative to refer to them again. If Jean had thought of them more often, he would, no doubt, when he grew older, have deeply regretted that they were not with him still, old, feeble, but alive. Nobody had known Madame Santeuil more intimately than Madame Lepic and, at a time when Jean was too young to foresee that a day would come when he would regret, more than anything else in the world, not being able to hear sincere and tender words spoken about his mother by lips which had so often kissed her cheeks. Madame Lepic had been for Madame Santeuil, the person whom she had most loved after her son, her husband and her father. But in those days it had never occurred to Jean that the people of whom, and the objects of which, the sight was to stir in him the tenderest emotions, and rouse the deepest movements of poetic feeling, would turn out to be, without his knowing it, precisely those that had witnessed the springtime of his life when thought and sensibility were taking shape in his mind and heart, and that, like altar-boys who, unaware of what they are doing, celebrate the most incomprehensible of mysteries, and consummate the greatest of all sacrifices, he was seeing more than he realized. A day might have come when Madame Lepic's trembling and suffering hands could have given back to him something of the feel of other hands—his mother's—in which they had so often lain when the unhappy woman had poured her confidences into sympathetic ears.

The persons who play a part in our ambitions and our sorrows when we are grown men, are no longer the same as those who leaned above us in the cradle and kissed our infant faces with faintly tremulous lips. The arms, still strong, or perhaps even then beginning to show signs of weakness, which lifted us, the eyes which sought in our features, as yet unformed, and our still innocent eyes, some loved memory of the past, some promise of the future's mystery, are not those that will meet the last ardent or feeble, and ever incomprehensible, message of our fading vision.

*

When Madame Lepic died, Jean was in his first term at school. Monsieur Santeuil's friends had foretold that a young man, who already had Alfred de Musset and Victor Hugo by heart, would most certainly come out top each year in French Recitation as a preliminary to carrying off eventually the prize of Rhetoric. Consequently, his parents were painfully disabused when they found that, in fact, Jean was being constantly punished for inattention, was bottom in Composition, and ended the year without any sort of prize or even an Honourable Mention. In each of his "set" French essays, in which the candidate was supposed to show up a short, correctly, if not elegantly, written exercise, he unbosomed himself on the motions of love and pity momentarily aroused in him by the character about whom he was supposed to be writing. He covered many pages, intoxicated by his own facility, with the expression of boundless and delicious melancholy suggested by the death of Jeanne d'Arc or the words of the Connétable de Bourbon, enriching them, to show the extent of his reading, with images borrowed from the poets. These efforts, conceived in tears, were listened to, when they were read to the class, with laughter. It would have been difficult to decide whether Jean who, so short a while ago had been in a constant state of hyper-sensitivity and filled with an ardent love of his fellow-creatures, had meanwhile grown egotistical and vain enough to relish the admiration of others. Was he suffering merely from the first blighting effects of the squalid, dank atmosphere of school? Was it that his over-responsive mind and body, exposed to the devastating attacks of life, were being forced to find protection by growing an impervious hide, something rough-surfaced, hard, abounding in coarse knots and scales, a skin that covered him because he needed it, as birds whose life is to be spent on water develop webbed feet? Or was it that a likeness to Monsieur Santeuil, whose inoffensive self-love we have already had occasion to record, unnoticed in the period of early childhood when characteristics are so unformed that even a boy's mother cannot say for certain whom he is going to "take after", had gradually been taking form and substance during his years of growth?

Seemingly, our true natures, which are concealed while we are very young, come more and more to the surface as we grow older and so influence our outward appearance that those who knew us once as a cherubic little angel in our mother's arms, see us, ten years later, in the guise of a business man with shifty eyes, of a conceited fop with all-conquering moustaches, of a debauchee with dark circles round his eyes, of a miser with the pinched lips of his father, of a fool whose speech and constant, irritating, laugh makes them feel embarrassed. But certain resemblances, certain physical or moral characteristics, weaknesses, faults, gifts or vices, do most certainly become visible at a particular stage in our growth, only later to vanish altogether, so that we become "changed men". I have a friend who at school was so like his mother's second husband that he might have been his son. Up till the time of his First Communion he was slim and good-looking. He is now Ovarot, the Banker, so ugly and so huge that he can scarcely walk. Horace, who has become a gymnast and a runner, was until he turned sixteen a consumptive boy whom the doctors had given up. My school friend, Léandre, who, after sampling self-indulgence in all its forms, became a seemingly incurable drug addict, is now a strong, sensible and healthy man, the kindest and most faithful of husbands. Finally, I had during my military service two friends, Julius and Phèdre. Both had quite exceptional gifts, one for music, the other for crime. But for the apathy of masters and the incompetence of the police there can be little doubt that the one would have composed a masterpiece and the other committed a murder. Since those early days, Julius has not written a note of music. Frightened by a life of pleasure, the muse has deserted him. He is now a half-wit. As to Phèdre, so strongly has repentance worked in him, that today he is more than just a decent fellow; he has become a saint.

Without in any way indulging in prophecy about Jean's future, I can safely say that Jean at school was distinctly vain. On one occasion he was asked to dinner by the headmaster. He felt it intolerable that his companions should remain in ignorance of this signal honour. One of them was rich and well-born. His marbles were of agate, and, young though he was, he sported long trousers, backed horses, expressed monarchist opinions and was an object of envy and admiration to Jean who very much wanted, by imparting this glorious news, to increase his own importance in his eyes. For a whole hour he considered how best he could tell it him, and at last, quite suddenly during a Livy lesson which had to do with Hannibal's crossing of the Alps, whispered in his ear, with a face which had gone as red as a cherry, and a delectable cherry at that, "I say, d'you know I've been to dinner with the head!" For a whole hour he had said nothing, and Fernay was not expecting this tremendous confidence. With a sudden start, forgetting where he was, he said in a loud voice: "What's that?" The master called them both up and threatened to keep them in unless they told him what they had been talking about, and Jean was almost ready to die of mingled pride and confusion, when Fernay said, in front of the whole class, "Santeuil was telling me that he had dined with the headmaster."

*

Jean was laughed at for his French essay, but he was punished for other tasks which he had copied from a friend's paper five minutes before class began, having spent the time since the subject was given out, in reading poetry or doing nothing. Each day he promised his mother that from then on he really would work, but when the next day came, a fit of even more intense laziness than that of the previous evening, when he had been allowed to lie fallow, resulted in his slamming his books shut and laying down his pen. "I know now what Jean's particular rock is," said Madame Santeuil one evening to her husband who, with his feet on the fire-dogs was staring happily into the flames, "it is not, as we used to think, his health, nor, thank God, is it a passionate temperament: still less is it, as his French master seems to think, excess of imagination, nor simple laziness, which is the explanation given by the physics master. No, the rock on which he seems likely to be wrecked is that lack of will-power which, when he was six, would have kept him from crying when he went to bed instead of falling asleep, which, last year, would have stopped him thinking all the time about Mademoiselle Kossichef, and which now would keep him in the right road when he is tempted to write nonsense, to think of nothing at all, to read novels and poetry, and to spend his time in confectioners' shops stuffing himself on pastry with the result that he has no appetite for dinner, as you may have noticed tonight, and, in the long run, will ruin his digestion altogether. This lack of will-power," said Madame Santeuil, "is a terrible rock indeed." – "Shocking," said Monsieur Santeuil, hurriedly removing his slippers, which had begun to smoke, from the fire-dogs: "I very nearly burned myself: why must you always insist on talking to me when I'm warming my feet?" Madame Santeuil was probably thinking, as her husband was, that by prolonging this conversation they were not likely to reach any solution of the difficult problem of how to provide Jean with a strong will and, leaning towards the grate where she could hear, though without understanding, the torrent of burning and dazzling promises which the fire was uttering through the smoke like the Sibyl, and gazing absently into the blaze which, among the logs and above a tumbled bed of glowing ashes, was roaring at the top of its voice like a rising wind blowing about a wood at sunset, here, in the shuttered room where the darkness was all a-quiver with the heat, and shadows showed upon the walls like windows of stained glass, and the flickering light gleamed ruby-like in the corners, she mingled her husband's silence with her own in one melodious harmony.

*

When Jean, instead of beginning his Latin verses, settled down to re-read *Ruth et Boas* or *La Nuit d'Octobre*, he felt far from comfortable, because a sense of duty was nagging at him, and, conscious of the pleasant satisfaction which knowledge of a task well done would have brought him, his delight in fine verse was less intense and less complete than it should have been. But, as between the bad verse he had to read, and the good verse he had just been reading, he was not, he felt, entitled to choose the good, because it was the bad that he was under an obligation to study. And so it was that when dinner was announced before he had begun to work, his scrupulous, but weak-willed conscience became a prey to the double bitterness of duty left undone and pleasure tasted. As a rule, however, this failure to do what he ought to have done was not due to the time he had spent in reading poetry, but to the way he had loitered on his way home from school, the way he had sat chatting in the kitchen, or had forgotten to warm his feet. Therefore, when darkness had fallen, when through the window's candid clarity he saw the sad and tender smile of the pink evening sky which seemed heavy with unuttered chiding, he bitterly repented having thrown away—as he might have thrown a pebble into water— God's lovely and mysterious gift, the whole of a day—a day which He gives us to use as we choose, filling it with sacred oil or with poison, a day which will never return, a day which, when we have emptied into it the very essence of ourselves, the lees of our weakness or the best of our efforts, will lie for ever broken among the scattered gleams of the oncoming night. "A day and then, another day," he said to himself, "that is my life, and I shall never have another. God has given me this one, and not another, that His will may be done." And now that he had reached the evening of his day, he could see himself already at the ending of his life, and, as a painter dissatisfied with his work may slash his canvas, furiously effacing the trivial image which he had inscribed upon it, though no other canvas was given him on which he might begin again. "This day only, and not another," he frequently said to himself before he went to sleep.

*

One evening, when the thought had come to him that the time might not be far distant when he would no longer be able to give pleasure to his mother, Jean had set to work in good earnest. With each day that passed since then another task had been completed and now, this morning, he had, with a feeling of joy, completed a set of Latin verses, already seeing in his mind's eye the end of the school year, and his mother's happy face at prize giving. He was feeling better, and was so satisfied, so pleased with life, that he could not refrain from smiling at the sun which was shining through the window and from making with his lips the sound of the kisses he would soon imprint upon his mother's cheeks. The set of verses was finished and he jumped in sheer exuberance of spirits. He meant to get started on an essay almost at once, but thought that he would go downstairs first for a breath of

fresh air and a moment's relaxation. In spite of the sun, the mild
breeze and a new smell in the air, he had sufficient determination to
break off his colloquy with these three lovely friends all tempting him
to play, in order to start work on his essay, and ran up to his room
again, drunk with the heady fumes of a resolution freely made. He
bumped into his father who, coming down and profoundly irritated
by his wife's nightly rehearsal of her woes, stopped him angrily.

"So this is what you do when you're supposed to be working,
that's what your fine promises are worth!" – "Let me explain, Papa,
you've got it all wrong," said Jean who, at his father's first words, had
seen the sun scurrying behind a cloud, and now stood trembling. "I
certainly have *not*: where have you been?—though it doesn't much
matter. There is nothing more to be said: your mother and I have
already decided that you shall leave your present school and go to
Henri IV." – "To Henri IV?" exclaimed Jean with a white face, "to
Henri IV?" – "You heard perfectly well what I said." – "I won't set
foot in the place!—and just when I was hoping you'd be pleased, too!
What a fool I've been!—that's the last set of verses I'll ever do!" – "We'll
soon see about that!" said Monsieur Santeuil. "And now," he added,
"go upstairs," with which words he began to resume his own way
down: "I really think you must be out of your wits." – "I'd say the
same about you, if I dared," mumbled Jean as he climbed the stairs,
torn between a fear that his father might have heard him and another
that he might not.

Jean had left the front door open so as to be able to get back into
the apartment without having to ring, but Monsieur Santeuil, not
knowing that he had gone out, had shut it. Jean, therefore, would have
had to ring, but felt too much overwhelmed with misery to face
Augustin's sharp eyes. He therefore went downstairs again, and sat in
the hall. The place reminded him of something. . . . Yes, it was here one
morning, when he had been no less overflowing with tenderness for
his mother than he had been today, that he had waited in hiding for
her return, only to be told that instead of going to the Champs-
Elysées he was to go to Monsieur Jacomier. The wretchedness of
having such cruel parents, parents who quite hopelessly failed to understand him, produced such a flood of self-pity that tears—which he
carefully kept on wiping away so that the concierge should not see
them if she happened to cross the yard—began to stream down his
cheeks. Then, though not ceasing to call down curses on his father's

head, he began to invent excuses for his mother who, on this morning already nearing its end, could not have guessed the tender affection which had overflowed his heart, nor that this very day a miracle had come about as a result of that same tenderness, and that an end had been made of the very laziness she had wished to punish, which now no longer existed. . . . 'If life is like this,' he said to himself, bowing his tear-stained face on his knees, and much struck by the thought of the impression that this gesture of humiliation would make on others, 'if human beings thus impose their decisions on those who have changed without their knowing it, while those decisions were in the making, if every moment is fraught with the danger of their being so far beside the mark, of their stifling a good intention, driving to despair those who love them and demoralizing those who are on the way to becoming good, then this world is too complicated a place for me, and life too hard a thing.' And from then on, in spite of his terror at being sent to Henri IV, like a child abandoned under a street-lamp still burning at dawn in a great city, in spite of the grief he felt at leaving his dearly-loved school, he made up his mind no longer to resist any of life's injustices, not even the most terrible, because the most immediate, one of all—imprisonment within the walls of Henri IV.

6. The Lycée Henri IV

Like his master, Xelnor, Jean held the view that Verlaine and Leconte de Lisle were the greatest among all the poets and, again like him, felt deadly bored when he read the classical authors. But, extending to the things of the mind the ceaseless anxiety of his scrupulous conscience, and mistrusting the value of his judgments no less than he did those of his actions, he kept on forcing himself to re-read *Phèdre*, *Cinna* and the *Fables* of Lafontaine with a fresh mind, in the hope that he would grow to love them as truly as he did *Les Poèmes antiques* and *Les Romances sans paroles* should they, that is, turn out to deserve his love. Having emptied his mind of all its former prejudices, he squarely faced those sphinxes of an earlier age who *ought* to have been able to say to him— see, now, how worth-while I am—though, in fact, after hours and hours of lonely colloquy, he found that they said precisely nothing. The poetic imagination which was spilling its dawn light in Jean's spirit from behind his still night-bound powers of reasoning, dazzled him with the brilliant glow that precedes the rising of the sun, and stimulated in him a desire to discover everywhere, in his daily tasks and in the books of others, the full splendour of its mysterious glory. The flashing images, the hectic style of the last of the Romantics worked him into a state of morning ardour which, chilled by the reading of *Britannicus* and *Cinna*, became more than ever a matter of excited search. But he had another reason for preferring not only Leconte de Lisle, but even J. J. Weiss, to Molière. His scruples, the discouragement produced in him by so many hot impulses which had resulted in only the weakest of weak results, his thousand and one dreams of tenderness and melancholy, the thousand and one discoveries revealed by those same dreams, all this had developed in him a habit of self-examination for which the study of philosophy had not provided the necessary food, and which, exhausting itself in an effort to keep hold of the elusive nature of his thoughts, had found, so far, its bearings and a natural nourishment in the exaltation produced in him by the reading of books which, no matter how superficially, gave him the sense of a philosophic

background. The subtle comments of Weiss which, as he was over-
joyed to find, echoed the feelings he had had when, alone in a garden,
he had invoked the sun, or on rainy days had sat pondering in his room,
the great spreading poems of Leconte de Lisle which juggled with
Time, and put into words of shattering power the conception of Life
as a dream, and the nothingness of things, were more alive for him,
more profound, more stimulating, than those classical works from
which such mental unease is absent. Ignorant though he was of
Micromégas, he had already measured the span of human existence
against the immensity, the eternity, of the stars, as well as the size of
his own body and of his father's house. He had lain for hours on end
motionless, convinced that any activity of poor, puny men must be
sheer mockery, then, feeling cold and hungry, had gone to dine, and
soon, feeling once again moved by a desire to write Parnassian verse,
had resigned himself to the necessity of living on vanity since it was
vanity to be alive. That he might not repeat the experience of dizziness
which had come to him when leaning above the great abyss and peer-
ing into infinite space, he decided that he would not speak of that in his
poems, but, on the first page of all his future writings, no matter how
purely "plastic" they might be, would write: "He whose book this is,
having reflected that France is a thousand times larger than himself, and
Europe a hundred times larger than France, the sun, etc.—he whose
book this is, knows that all is vanity, this book not excepted. Having
said this, seeing that a man must live and if he have imagination
write, he has resolved to continue." Then, having read these lines of
Leconte de Lisle:

> La vie antique est faite inépuisablement
> Du tourbillon sans fin des apparences vaines

he thought that may be he would put *them* at the beginning of his book
and under them add only: "The author of these pages knows that all is
vanity, but . . .", etc.

The poet Rustinlor, Director of Studies at the Lycée Henri IV, and
Monsieur Xelnor, his tutor, succeeded, however, in persuading him
that his scruples were unreasonable and that it was more intelligent to
read beautiful poetry, or even, added Monsieur Rustinlor, with a
great guffaw of laughter, and enunciating each word with careful
clarity, "To assume the horizontal position and enjoy the pleasure of

divine nirvana," than to elucidate the works of Horace and Ovid, who had, both of them, been "pretty poor fish". The general principles of Duty are difficult enough in all conscience, and more difficult than ever when it is necessary to apply them to particular cases. Monsieur Clodius Xelnor found it impossible to understand how it could be "bad" to read beautiful poetry, and "good" to elucidate inferior verse. His mind, accustomed to deciding by the application of very simple rules, whether any given poem was "execrable "or "amazing", could not, decent fellow though he was, imagine that for Jean there might be a moral good superior to aesthetic pleasure, or that he might attain to it by resisting the allurements of delight and doing his duty. Monsieur Clodius Xelnor (his name in the Registry of Births appeared as Claude Le Roux) did by slow degrees overcome Jean's sense of guilt, but it took him a long time to do so. We should, perhaps, blame the boy for surrendering, but we ought at least to give him credit for putting up so valiant a resistance. It was only later that he came to appreciate the value for the mind of exercises which, by forcing us to strip a thought of all conventional formulae, of the beauties of style we may have been taught to find in it, of all the academic aura with which, unconsciously, we have come to see it surrounded, compel us to get to grips with reality, to attain which has been the sole preoccupation of the works of all ages, whether it be that they deal with a Queen's love, the tale of a skylark, or the ambition of a soldier of fortune. Driving us to delve deep into the past in search of their origins, they equip us with a knowledge of, to turn perhaps later to respect for, the ancient splendours of our tongue. It was matter of small merit that Jean should, for a time, have been loyal to a duty which was so much in line with the development of his intellectual interests. It was only as he grew older, and became convinced that he was wasting time over niggling foolishness which he might have been enriching with the stuff of dreams, that he had to display strength of character by giving precedence to the former from a sheer sense of *duty*. For the past nine years Monsieur Clodius Xelnor had had the satisfaction of seeing his verses applauded in the *Revue Blanche*, the *Mercure de France* and the *Revue Indépendante*, and had dedicated one of his Ballades to Henri de Régnier—whose favour he enjoyed. But, in spite of all this evidence of glory (I, personally, should have felt most satisfaction in the last mentioned), one is led to the conclusion, taking ultimate truth as the yardstick, that such superficial splendours as newspaper articles, literary journals, and Latin inflexions are always much the same and count for little in the eyes of God, and that if a choice has to be made between Monsieur Clodius Xelnor and Jean, it is not Claude Le Roux who shows up best.

*

It was after a morning spent in eager study of *Les Contemplations* that Jean found himself demanding of poetry the key to the secrets of life, death and his own soul. It was while he was thus engaged that Monsieur Rustinlor came to fetch him for a walk. "What's that you're reading, Santeuil?" he asked. "*Les Contemplations,* sir."–"Hm, Hugo at his worst," said Monsieur Rustinlor, with a shake of the head, "much inferior to his plastic and wholly abstract compositions. If it comes to that, abstract poetry is always infinitely superior to poetry which sets out to *mean* something. Leconte de Lisle is superior to Daddy Hugo just because he is not overburdened with tiresome metaphysical considerations. Still, one can't help admiring the old man: when all's said, he was pretty terrific as a poet because, in the last analysis, he was a fool." Heaven and earth seemed to crash in ruins round the listening Jean. His education had not been conducted on a basis of religion, nor had he yet made the acquaintance of philosophy. Literature was his only creed and he had sought in it, with all the vigour of his intelligence, with all the conscientious seriousness of his nature, the key to Truth. "Victor Hugo was a great poet because he was a fool." He did not even try to give to Monsieur Rustinlor the smile which the antithetical form of this conclusion seemed to demand. So nearly had the preoccupations of his mind been threatened, that he could spare no thought for good manners. By this time Monsieur Rustinlor was well away: "Yes," he continued, "an old fool who could turn out dam' good poetry whereas all these scoundrels you're silly enough to admire, Weiss, Lemaître, and that fellow France—who at least has got a small dose of ingenuity in his make-up—all these intelligent chaps, even though their intelligence is more often than not just a pose, are quite incapable of producing a single poem correctly put together. As to sonnets, the less said about them the better. With the possible exception of France, who has not always lived in outer darkness, they don't even know the meaning of the word"—after which outburst Monsieur Rustinlor, laying a finger to his snub nose, laughed uproariously. "They've been your ruin," he went on, noticing the look of perplexity on Jean's face. "There has never been a poet (he pronounced it po-hett) who's loved anything in literature but plastic verse." – "Then I've been wrong in trying to develop a love of Racine?" asked Jean uneasily. "Racine was a pretty nasty bit of goods," said Monsieur Rustinlor, gathering his Olympian brows into a frown, "besides, it's always a mistake to *try* in these matters: one either loves, or one doesn't. Racine's tragedies are confoundedly boring, though in *Phèdre* there are one or two lines—for instance, *La fille de Minos et de Pasiphaé*—which Gautier maintained was the only good line he ever wrote." – "Really the only one?" asked Jean, making an unavailing effort to understand why that particular line was so beautiful. "The *only* one," replied Monsieur Rustinlor in a tone of triumphant irony, "and, damme, he was absolutely right, which is not surprising, seeing that Théo's one of the most wonderful old chaps there's ever been. He was terribly down on Racine—whose rhyming, incidentally, was despicable. There is, I admit, something to be said for his view of Jewish and Greek antiquity, but personally I put *Esther* well below two pages of Paul de Saint-Victor's about *Esther*, which are quite masterly, just as I rank very much higher than *Phèdre* a story by Pierre Louÿs which contains all Greece in a nutshell, and has the additional virtue of being exquisitely written."

Jean returned from his walk that evening haunted by a problem which it seemed to him quite impossible to solve, yet of so essential a nature, that he thought it almost immoral to go to sleep until he had reached some conclusion about it. If the noblest poetry was not that of which the subject-matter consisted of the great realities which hedged him round, which gazed upon him when he went walking, or sat working, saying: "Look us in the face, explain us, get to our very heart"—then poetry was nothing. Could it be, on the contrary, that it was Monsieur Rustinlor who was right, and that it was these realities that were nothing? If, for a moment, he escaped from the torment of his thoughts, *La fille de Minos et de Pasiphaé* brought them back into his mind with a cruelty worthy of those Immortals. Nevertheless, it was not without a certain feeling of pleasure that he repeated Gautier's sally to himself. He was not yet of an age to savour the lovely mythological sonorities of Racine's verse. But having, so far, been in the habit of valuing poetry as much for the richness of its meaning as for the brilliance of its imagery, he was conscious now, hearing somebody give supreme importance to a line which contained neither thought nor imagery, of that feeling of surprised delight which seizes upon us whenever an uttered word sets our world in a new light or changes, for us, the terms of an intellectual problem.

*

One day, Jean, having slept well, worked well, played well, feeling thoroughly contented, his conscience momentarily appeased, his mind at rest, his bodily faculties superbly tuned, was sitting with his head bent over his desk, quietly relishing the joy which comes from having solved the problems of existence, when one of the elder boys nudged him with his elbow and, with a sidelong look, said: "I say, Santeuil, what about coming on a woman hunt at four? Women are better by a long chalk than anything you can get out of books." Jean made some sort of an excuse, and promised he would go another day, though he registered a silent resolve never to do any such thing. But that evening, as he lay in bed with the light out—"What about looking for women at four this afternoon?—it's terrific fun"—those burning words set blazing furiously all the desires which had for so long lain repressed within his body, and it being impossible to get up now and go out, he lay between the sheets worked into a fever at the thought that it was not yet four o'clock, and that he could not there and then accept the exciting invitation.

Glorious daylight extinguished these evil thoughts, together with the night-light in the dormitory and the gas-lamps on the boulevards. Jean felt thoroughly ashamed of them and, conscious only of the happiness of being in perfect health and able to work, found it hard to understand how he could have indulged in such nocturnal broodings, the memory of which now faded until it was no more than a pallid presence in the general concourse of his dreams. But one day, in class, he repeated to himself the words spoken to him by the elder boy, or rather they echoed in his mind. He was on fire to make one in the proposed expedition. But on the chosen day the other boy was ill and absent from school. A little while later, however, he crossed the portals of No 6, rue Boudreau, accompanied by Jean, who was carefully hiding his feelings, like a young conscript who does not want the veteran at his side to see how frightened he is when, coming under fire for the first time, he feels the memories of childhood come back into his appalled and shattered mind to make more horrible still the torments that lie immediately ahead. They went up a not very dark staircase at the head of which there was a pay-box. But the daylight which brought a vague but friendly consolation to Jean even in moments of deepest melancholy, showed now as hostile and secretive on the squalid walls and insolent richness of the carpets.

"In there," said his companion, with the mechanical precision of a groom halting a horse at the entrance to the slaughterhouse, too ignorant of what may be passing through the animal's mind to feel either cruelty or compassion. To himself Jean said: "In a moment the door will have shut behind me, and I shan't be able to get downstairs again." He flung himself upon the bell, at the same time saying to his companion, "Will it really be fun?" and pulled it so violently that a vulgar voice could be heard exclaiming, to an accompaniment of laughter: "Doesn't want to waste much time, that bloke doesn't!" With a look of suspicion, which the sight of the bigger boy soon dissipated, she came to the door, showing a face which reminded Jean of a maid who had remained with Madame Santeuil only for two days, and of whom he had retained an odd and rather terrifying memory. She had been far better dressed than his mother, and had reeked of drink. When Madame Santeuil gave her notice, she had become abusive and, according to the cook, violent. Madame Santeuil had been ill for several days after she had left. They discovered later that the police had been on her track a considerable time. She was wanted for a double murder, and was sentenced to ten years hard labour. Such were the memories aroused in Jean at the sight of the face in the doorway. He found himself look with surprise at hard, cruel eyes beneath mascaraed lashes, and at cheeks mottled with eczema which a layer of rice-powder attempted, in vain, to conceal. The general impression was that of a gutter creature with something about her of the cunning of a card-sharper, the whole set in the showy tawdriness usually associated with women of the stage.

They went in. Jean found himself longing for the silence, the solitude and the charm of his own room so that he might collect his thoughts and still the sense of a nervousness that was new to him. Twelve women in wraps were seated in the "lounge" busily at work trimming hats. "What on earth are they doing?" asked the bigger boy, much to the astonishment of Jean who thought—though he did not know why—that this was what always went on in such places. "They're for the Sisters of Saint-John," cried twelve voices in unison. Jean took this for a vile joke. It was nothing of the sort. Old Mother Troncpoing (this was the name of the woman who had admitted them) had a sister who was a nun.

II

The House at Etreuilles · Lilac and Apple-blossom

The Streets · Ernestine · Mornings in the Park

Light Effects · Luncheon · Summer Music

The Cold · Le Capitaine Fracasse *· The Magic Lantern*

"Les Oublis" · Pink Hawthorn · Walks by the Loir

The Camelia · The Kingdom of the Sun · High Mass

Madame Sureau · The Bells · The Aigneaux Farm

1 . *Etreuilles*

Sometimes at Easter, when Monsieur Santeuil had not too much to do, he, his wife and his son made their first visit of the year to Etreuilles. But Monsieur Santeuil had said: "It won't be at all warm; Easter's early this year." On hearing this Madame Santeuil, who had plenty of taste in matters of literature, much practical good sense in the ordinary affairs of life, a fund of humour which found expression in the telling of even the simplest story, a gift of tact, warm affections and considerable skill in the running of a household; but was ignorant in matters of meteorology, geography, statistics and others of the sciences, was always amazed that Monsieur Santeuil should know that Easter would be early in any given year and found in this evident proof of his superiority yet one more reason for silently renewing her admiring praise and for reaffirming that vow of docile obedience which she had once registered in the secret places of her heart. In January Monsieur Santeuil had made an announcement: "The Commission will be sitting for the last time on the Wednesday in Easter week, which means that we shall be able to get away on the Thursday." Such distant plans, drawn up with precision by her husband, took on for Madame Santeuil something of the mystery of prophetic utterances and increased still more her wondering adoration. Easter did, in fact, come early and it was found possible to start on the Thursday,[1] just as Monsieur Santeuil had predicted. Though they took with them all the rugs and blankets on which they could lay hands there was only just enough of these to give protection against the cold and when they reached Etreuilles in freezing weather they stayed for a while warming their feet in the dining-room, where Jean's uncle kept rapping the barometer, hoping it might show that fine weather would soon return. That evening, when Jean went up to his room, he found a fire burning in the grate and, while he was undressing, heard a knock at the door. It was the cook with a spherical, stone hot-water bottle, known in that part of the country as a " blister", which she had hesitated to bring up

[1] The French text has *Mercredi*. I have not hesitated to correct so obvious an error.—G.H.

earlier because Madame Santeuil had told her to wait until Master Jean was ready to get into bed so that in this way it shouldn't have time to go cold.

May was a month that witnessed more things than the arrival at Etreuilles of old Monsieur Santeuil's son, daughter-in-law and grandson. There were few houses that did not contain in their gardens, no matter how small, planted against a wall or in front of the door, lilac bushes which sometimes shot up in a great spear of blossom, like a coloured steeple above the roof-top, at others spread a thick, gay tangle of flaring flowers over the tiles, or, yet again, clambered up the wall and hung over the street attracting by their smell the attention of the casual passer-by, even though he might be on the opposite pavement, and, when he had not noticed them already, compelling him to raise his eyes. And so it came about that, all through the month of May, each small house found itself dowered with an unexpected magnificence, a whole, silent household staff of young lilacs gathered about the door and filling the interior with sweet air and fragrant smells, a staff which could have been supplied in an Eastern tale only by a fairy gifted with poetical powers. But nothing could surpass the sight that met one's eyes, skirting the Cotte orchard, through the bars of the fence which ran for fifty yards, of espaliered apple-trees, all aligned at equal distances like a planned adornment of incomparable charm, their large white flowers all open with, here and there, little pink buttons turning to a blush, while below them, in unbroken profuseness, the leaves provided a background of that inimitable design which no other fruit tree can show. If one is so unfortunate as to go into the country at too late a season when the apple-trees have lost their bloom, the mere sight of that lovely leaf, when one knows the glittering glory which, in the full moment of its beauty the apple-tree can bear, fills one with a feeling of regret so poignant that no other flower, however lovely, can bring consolation and the mere spectacle of the fine patterned filaments of the pistils which, in blossom time, lie at the heart of each bloom like an obscure, mysterious choir hidden away in a gleaming basilica, can awaken such regret, so much pleasure, or start in us so great a love as no show of the most beautiful flowers in all the world can ever do. And this infinite pleasure which, as we skirt an orchard, comes to us at sight of the white blossoms of the apple-trees and the pink clusters of their button-blooms has in it something of a spiritual quality. The reason why neither the white pear-tree nor the pink of the Pennsylvania

rose can compare with them, lies deep in the heart. All of a sudden at
sight of that lovely leaf, about which there can be no mistake, of the
flowers larger than any other tree can show, more solidly massed in
gleaming clusters down the whole stretch of the espaliered stretch,
separated by the pink clumps of blushing button-buds, we feel in these
leaves, and in these delicious blossoms, something that speaks to us, as,
when walking in a sunken lane, we meet with a loved person who
smiles at us and says "Good day". We feel that there, beneath the
varnished greenness of the leaf and the satin whiteness of the flower,
some especial being lives, an individual whom we love, for whom no
one else in all the world can act as substitute. We feel we must not let
attention be arrested at the white satin surface of the flower, at the
varnished green of the leaf, that there is more hidden underneath, that
our pleasure is in something deeper all a-quiver there within, something we desire to seize and which holds an exquisite sweetness. It
seems that these white flowers which climb in unbroken profusion up
their supporting posts hold a message for the spirit, are, as it might be,
the very form and body of some period in our lives with which we
have just renewed a contact and can recognize. No longer is it, as with
other trees in flower. Each blossom and each leaf comes responsive to
some longing in ourselves. Moment by moment we think with happiness—"Yes, this is it!" What smiles upon us from out these clouds of
whiteness treading on one another's heels, spaced by their clusters of
pink buds, is something utterly different, a life unlike what we sometimes think of as life, the thought of losing which, though we may
find it needlessly intrusive, brings sadness. But then, contrariwise, our
happiness is such that we have no fear of losing it, no apprehension that
the fullness of its gift can be taken from us. For what in our pleasure is
so ravishing is something that we feel deep down, something more
than the mere passing moment for the sensation of an earlier time,
when we saw just such apple-trees in bloom, is there within us.

*

In the little town of Etreuilles the narrow streets were called by the
names of Saints—rue Saint-Hilaire, rue du Saint-Esprit. It was in the
rue du Saint-Esprit that they lived and to Jean it seemed strange that
their house should be an *address*, that their house, the house of the
doctor opposite, and, next to it, continuing the line, the window of the

grocer's shop, should, all together, make up the rue du Saint-Esprit, and that their house should have a number; for 5, rue du Saint-Esprit had the effect of something outside oneself, of something to which one could point and one's own house, seen thus from the outside, had an effect of strangeness. The Stationer lived in the rue de l'Oiseau, and, to reach the Square, one took the rue Saint-Hilaire. The town was dominated by its church, a place through which processions passed that was gay with the halting-stages of the carried Host; here lived the Curé, there the Sacristan, there the Nuns: it was a town filled with the sound of bells, thronged on days of High Mass by people walking by on their way to church and sweet with the smell of the cakes that were being baked for the meal that would follow the service. But its saints were a shade sombre, a trifle sad: it was a cold town with not much brightness for the eye: the nights there were long, the old folk complained of ailments, many of the children were sickly and all its inhabitants were solemn-faced and slow of speech: the Curé was often called to the bedsides of the dying and the bells tolled often for the dead. There were other streets, too, that bore the names of things familiar and of different living creatures—rue de l'Oiseau, rue Plat-à-Barbe, for in this town there was no lack of knives, of pigeons, of wind, of shoeing-smiths.

*

There were in the small house at Etreuilles kitchen-maids and a gardener. But the ruling of the household and the right of access to the family was the jealously guarded preserve of Ernestine. Every year, when the visitors arrived, Madame Santeuil would say, "I needn't remind you, Ernestine, that Master Jean must have a bottle in his bed, not just hot water, but boiling, so that he can't bear his hands on it: or that the top end of the bed must be made very high, almost uncomfortable—I'm sure you remember that—so that he can't possibly lie flat even if he wants to, four pillows, if you can spare four; it can't be too high."—"Yes, ma'am," Ernestine would answer with a smile, for she was always as pleasant in her dealings with Madame Sureau's relatives as she was short with Madame Sureau herself. Long familiarity had done nothing to diminish their prestige in her eyes. She felt no spite against them, did not have to "break them in" to her ways, for she had never to live long with them. Their compliments went to her head: they came from Paris. When Madame Santeuil went upstairs to see whether

Jean's room was ready for him to go to bed she could always be sure of finding that the pillows were as high, the bottle as hot, as she could possibly have wished. "It really is astonishing how intelligent that woman is, and how completely she understands what one means," said Madame Santeuil. But Jean was still too young to realize that before a wonderful roast duck could be set upon the table, superbly limbed and shining with gravy so that his mouth watered with innocent desire, it had been necessary to catch a terrified creature, to struggle with it, to wring its neck and to drain away oceans of blood down the kitchen sink. When he heard cluckings and the flapping of frightened wings in the yard he still believed that it was only the cock being punished, but not hurt, for misbehaving with the hens. Similarly, he did not know that for all her smiling attentiveness when she was in the dining-room with the "family", Ernestine, in the kitchen and the pantry, could, and did, reduce the kitchen-maid to tears, lashing her, on the slightest pretext, with irony, contempt, insults and slanderous imputations, putting pepper in her drink and dirt in her food, and when, by chance, the girl had been to get fresh milk for Jean, setting sour milk in its place, forcing her, with threats, to commit all sorts of faults, complaining of her in front of her mistress, and making charges which the wretched, terrorized creature dared not rebut by revealing the truth.

Very soon, even at the risk of not finding another place, the maids all left, one after the other, without explaining why, so frightened were they of Ernestine. One, braver, perhaps, or more needy than the others, put up with the ordeal for a whole year. The rest departed after the first month of their employment. Thus it was that Ernestine need have no fear of seeing other influences arise in competition with her own. But it was in vain that the unhappy girls refused to say why they were going. Madame Sureau knew perfectly well the reason for their giving notice. Not that she ever found out the whole truth about any single incident, though none of them were ever wholly hidden from her. But she decided that discontented underlings were a small price to pay for Ernestine's "tremendously good qualities". And Madame Santeuil, easy in her mind so long as her mother-in-law had about her so intelligent, so devoted, a servant, one who looked after her so well, and to whom she had grown so used, urged her to endure the loss of all the "girls" the village could provide, rather than break with a retainer "the like of whom she would not find anywhere". Even Jean, though he could not sleep when, back in Paris, Monsieur Santeuil, indifferent like all his sex, to the illusions and sensibilities of the young, had answered without any beating about the bush when the boy asked him about Ernestine's relations with the kitchen staff, could not help, at Etreuilles, taking sides with the only person who knew how to make his bed as he liked it, who produced all his favourite dishes and brought his coffee at exactly the right heat, and such beautifully smooth, not too thick, chocolate and cream. No matter how anxious we may be to act fairly and charitably towards others, our good will always goes to the barber who shaves us without drawing blood and can arrange our hair in such a way as to make us look our best, or to the cab-driver whose vehicle is clean, who takes us at a gallop wherever we may have to go. At the risk of exposing him to a dressing down from the proprietor of the shop and perhaps being sacked, we cannot bring ourselves to endure the attentions of the well-meaning assistant who is bullied in the back-shop by his cleverer, but far less admirable fellows, but who slices bits out of our face, cuts our hair so that it looks like nothing on earth and, in his eagerness to show off, interlards his talk with pretentious phrases, and feel even less kindly towards him when, looking in the glass, we see ourselves becoming, minute by minute, less presentable under his innocent but clumsy ministrations. And so it is that the sheep, the chickens and the bullocks, whose agony we endure without giving it a second thought because it is necessary to our enjoyment, are not the only guileless victims who we daily allow to be sacrificed. Well-being, vanity, greed and superfluity are pleasant masters whose innumerable crimes, daily committed through the centuries and never punished, ensure the happiness of those who profit from them and guarantee their own continued dominance.

2. *Holidays*

About seven o'clock, when the weather was cold and Jean was still in bed, a servant came to light the fire. Snug and warm beneath the blankets, he watched the room grow gradually less chilly, lighter and more gay and, turning over to face the blaze, smiled as he thought of the increasing comfort that awaited him, the full measure of which he had not yet experienced. Motionless he watched, through half-closed eyes and from the very heart of his delicious ease, the thousand flickering twists which the flame made, like a gay and active housemaid who, while her young master is still resting, begins her task and causes the objects round him to shine and glitter. Often, on such days, if his uncle sent up to ask whether he would like to join him in a walk, he replied that he would not be going out till about ten and would join him somewhere in the Park near the canal bank. He wanted to stay by the fire till then, working. Very soon he saw the flame rise higher and higher on the hearth, shedding brightness and warmth, like the sun climbing up the sky. He jumped from his bed and, before dressing in the rather cold little washing alcove in a recess behind the bed, stood bare-footed on the carpet, warmed by the fire, rubbing his body down for a few brief moments in the heat, so that it should stay with him a little longer and keep him from feeling the cold in the alcove where he hurried into his clothes before the sense of comfort should be dissipated, eager to get back to the lovely blaze.

Through the open window of the alcove, which looked on to the little garden, he watched his uncle and his cousins starting out, setting the bell of the garden-door jingling as they passed armed with fishing-lines or spades and, sometimes, only with walking-sticks when they had planned a long tramp. But with his mind full of the marvellous adventures he would soon be reading by the hearth which would give him as good an appetite as any amount of exercise and, towards ten o'clock, make him feel that he would like to go into the Park, he did not for a single moment regret not having gone with them but looked happily at the fire, which by this time was filling the room with its radiance, and thought how it would purr gently at his feet while, cosy and comfortable in an armchair by the window, he would spend the time in reading. When ten o'clock drew near he went out sometimes with his book under his arm meaning to finish a chapter in the open air on a deck-chair by the canal. For by that time the air would already have lost its early chill and it would be delicious by the water. When he reached the Park he soon caught sight of his uncle who gave him a drawling, "Good morning. Ah, so you had work to do, and played the sluggard, eh?"–"Yes, Uncle," Jean would answer with a smile for, when life is happy, the simplest events project a kind of bliss much as on the unbroken surface of the canal the leaves of the tall poplars, the osier twigs of the little rustic bridge and Jean's stick were all reflected in the water, their images not vanishing but faintly disturbed by a light breeze or by the passage of a swan, to reappear entire a moment later. Jean's uncle would ask him how he had slept, and he, still glowing with the sense of freshness which stayed with him all day long when sleep, like deep, clear water had washed him clean, would smile his answer. "Chocolate and cream not lying heavy?"–"No."–"Have a lot of dreams?—I did." Jean could no more remember what he had dreamed than what had happened to him when he was two. But it made him happy to think that he *had* dreamed, that his uncle had dreamed, that at certain hours all men, imprisoned by an invincible power in dark, deep beds, within curtains smelling of lavender, all shared in a mysterious life in which the old were but little different from the very young, or from the superstitious inhabitants of the primitive world, and of which He, who had charge of them, was at pains to see that they should remember nothing.

"There are baked eggs for lunch today, filet of beef with béarnaise sauce and fried potatoes. Do you like *filet béarnaise?*"–"I should think I do, Uncle!"–"Good: and there may be gudgeon, too, if old David has brought any—but I can't be sure about that. Good heavens! It's a quarter past eleven, time to be getting home if we don't want the fry to be spoiled!" his uncle would say and call to the young cousins who hastily pulled in their lines and slung them round their necks. The spades they left because the gardener would be coming back, and, in any case, there was no one to steal them whereas the swans might have broken the lines. The order to start back had come at precisely the right moment for Jean who, with his mind set on baked eggs and *filet béarnaise*, was beginning to think that the velvety heads of the purple

irises on the surface of the water and the fragrant scent of Syrian roses
at the corners of the path provided insufficient provender for an
appetite sharpened by a morning's work, the passage of time and greed.
They would hurry back, the younger members of the party at a run
with the fishing-lines jumping about round their necks and getting all
tangled up so that they had to be straightened out before their owners
could catch up with their elders. By this time it would be very hot and
Uncle Jules would be mopping his forehead long before the village
was reached. Sometimes, as they crossed the Loir, where the gudgeon
dawdled and dreamed with their noses just above the surface in a lazy
manner that had nothing in it of suffering or infirmity, as was proved
when, at the slightest sound, they flickered away with a quick flash
of their tails, one of the children would noiselessly drop his line over
the bridge, hoping to catch one of the golden loiterers just as, gliding
with an appearance of sensuality among the glittering pebbles and the
water-weeds, they caught sight of some appetizing grub, a permitted
luxury on this glorious day and in the blue waters of a river where all
was happiness. But Uncle Jules, annoyed to find the youngsters falling
behind, would tell them sharply to come on. This summons they had
to obey and in no long time the party reached home. Jean's mother
would be sitting with a book in the dining-room, awaiting their return.
Then they would all take their places at the table and Jean's uncle,
fastening his napkin and settling into his chair, would say: "I don't
know about you, but I'm ravenous"—words which had a delicious
sound because they expressed a general feeling which, in a few
moments, as the heralding rattle of cold plates being changed for hot
ones bore witness, was soon to be satisfied. Then luncheon began.
Opposite the eaters lay the street where the sunlight never for a moment
ceased to glitter. By the time the fruit-course came, when the first
pangs of hunger had been appeased, and grapes and coffee were pointing a way to the less crude gastronomic pleasures, the postman would
arrive, and, with him, a new set of delightful longings made up of
curiosity, affection and human feelings.

★

Sometimes, when his uncle had planned a really long walk, Jean asked
to be awakened early. Monsieur Sureau had first to visit the Park in
order to give instructions to the gardener. It was the dawn hour when

all things, being as yet not touched by the sun, seemed dead. Quickly, they passed through the silent and deserted village which stood visible but shadowed, exposed neither to the slumber of the night nor yet to the light of day, like an uninhabited place on a planet from which all life has vanished. They reached the Park, the gate of which creaked as they opened it. They had no need of a key because the gardener was already there at work. He was hoeing a field which he would later sow. But the unillumined air, the silence that was almost like a wall, carried no sound to their ears. Such as there was seemed to break like a wave against it, stifled by its almost palpable softness. Monsieur Sureau gave a few orders to the gardener, after which he and Jean crossed the canal on their way to the lower road. The sun, now showing, touched the water which was not yet translucent but showed a surface of gold or of recognizable colours, mauve, pink, yellow, as at sunset. But very soon they would be lost, not in the creeping dusk of evening, but in the white glare of day. The sweetness of the hour was conducive rather to the joy of life than to silent meditation.

The stained-glass dyes which, at nightfall, follow one another on the water only when the dazzling gold has little by little lost its brilliance, would soon be swallowed in that different gold which marches on the heels of day, flooding down from the high Heavens. And the light, instead of slowly growing dimmer in a silence growing ever more immense, swelled, on the contrary, brighter and brighter, noisy with the mounting song of awakened birds, little by little merging into the dazzle of high day and full life, those magic colours which would distort for us, but for the speed with which they pass away, the appearances of things. And we regret their going. At evening we stand a long while trying to catch them on the water after they have vanished from the earth. And the glow of the domestic lamp, the sound of voices round the table, seem crude and coarse after the softness of those departing gleams, vulgar and workaday to one who has for a moment caught a glimpse of fairyland. Even more sharp is the sense of dis-illusionment when we pass from that world of dreams to a tranquillity which gradually wipes out regret, but also to activities and struggles with which the earlier experience has already disgusted us. At night, in bed, we give part of our thoughts to things impossible, forbidden. At night, hearing the breath drawn through our open mouths in measured rhythm, we can drink down draughts of sweet forgetfulness. But in the morning, no matter how relaxed we lie, there is no sinking back upon the pillows, no setting off again into that land where, perhaps, we may meet and even talk with those whom we can no longer see upon the earth, or, at least, we shall forget them.

Sometimes, all day long, the sun might shine but the eye not see it nor the blue of the sky for both would be concealed beneath a low and yellow layer of cloud. The canal would look yellow, too, luminous, but reflecting nothing. And suddenly the heat would be unendurable. There would be a heaviness in the air. But Jean, grumble though he might about the weather, would be conscious as they walked along a road which was all glare rather than sunlight, or in the fields at the far end of which the sun showed as a vague diffusion and the sky over beyond Etreuilles, for mile on mile, was darkened by a misty rain, or along the canal where carp and eels, not to be seen in the dull glitter of the warm, leaden, muddy water, leaped now and then, and the irises grew brighter moment by moment till they almost glistened, only to be plunged again in shadow—Jean would be conscious of a curious feeling that he was living simultaneously in the immediate presence of a particular day and in other similar days of long ago.

*

On fine mornings when Jean awoke—it was always rather late because he loved sleeping soundly, and his mother, glad of it, let him have his sleep out—he felt happy almost before he felt awake, his eye having caught sight of the sunlight's golden splashes on the table so that it was almost as though happiness were there to be snatched and held. There was happiness, too, by the window and in the garden, and everywhere a world of blue, nothing but blue, the deep blue of the sky, the blue reflected in the river which, in a short while, he would be crossing by the bridge with his rod and line. After smiling as he lay in bed and turning his face, for an instant, to the wall so as to give a final easing to his eyes which had over-taxed their strength by staring too suddenly at the golden sunlight which made no allowance for their weakness, he would get up and dress quickly, singing in sheer lightness of heart. Then he would go down to the garden and run to say good morning to the gardener who, with his straw hat tilted over his eyes, so blinding was the sun, would be perched on a ladder set against the trellised wall pruning nasturtium leaves. Both leaves and flowers were there, erect and burning in the shade, but with still about them the mildness of the

newborn sunlight in which for a few moments they had bathed, aglow
with that superabundance of life which we see in women coming from
the water when, dried and dressed, their cheeks look fresher, their eyes
brighter, their general air gayer than at other times. And so it was that,
intertwined among their leaves, the nasturtium flowers suspended
between heaven and earth, the white convolvulus with, at its heart, a
touch of fiercer colour like that of certain reflections of sunlight in the
sky, hanging over the river and sucking in the light which there broke
in a fine and luminous dust, the irises in neat procession all along the
little beds, the myosotis, side by side, lifting their little blossoms of
deepest blue, like scraps of the sky come down to earth—all these
flowers, in rows like the myosotis, or, like the sweet-peas, twined,
came from Heaven, it seemed, hard on the heels of the sun and, draped
over the trellis of the garden wall, had the appearance of an innumerable
host of Angels ranked on some Day of Days, like those depicted by the
great painters of the Renaissance; painted Angels, pink and blue and
vivid orange, some of them nasturtiums, sweet-peas, convolvulus
seeming to glide in a knit tangle to the earth upon the sweet air, others,
the violets and the shadowed pansies, looking as though they were
dozing or idling on the warm soil, some of them, two pansies, perhaps,
entwined and secreting in the shade the light's most wonderful colours,
others solitary, in every sort of posture but all aglow with happiness,
giving to all who saw them a sense of inexpressible delight, a feeling
that the gardener was a happy man indeed, that this garden was
Paradise itself, but seeming, unlike the painters' Angels, to be not so
much celebrating a religion of joy as to be keeping joy from decay,
to be participating in the glory. Nor from that general rapture was the
kindly tree excepted which endlessly dripped down on to the enchanted flowers about its feet, cowslips and violets and the simple grass,
now shadow and now light, nor the swan moving slowly on the river
bearing, he too, the gleam of light and happiness on his resplendent
body, plunging into a zone of shadow to emerge again in sunlight,
never, for a moment, disturbing the happiness about him, but showing
by his joyful mien that he, too, felt it though not by a jot changing his
slow, majestic progress, as a noble lady may watch with pleasure her
servants' happiness, and pass near to them, not despising.their gaiety,
not disturbing it, but taking in it no part herself save by a show of
gracious kindliness and by the presence of a charm shed by her dignity
on all around. Butterflies which, in the shadowed coolness, kept

undimmed the colouring of Heaven, fluttered from flower to flower, the very sign and symbol of fine weather, like women who saunter in a street dressed in their light and brilliant silks, only when the day is fair and the summer come. And all these butterflies, and more especially the small birds, frolicking in the air or perched in clusters on the trees brought, too, to mind the winged angels in those pictures of which I have already spoken, while, in the sky, thrown open to its azure depths, the sun sat all enthroned like God the Father, among his burning rays.

Behold! the Kingdom of the Blest—to which the play of sunlight, from Heaven to garden, from garden to our window, from our window to our life builds a ladder of glory and offers us its guidance as we climb. Behold! the Kingdom of the Blest, where is no obscuring secret, where sky is seen in river depths, and sun is bright upon the walls, and lovely butterflies beat silently their wings of blue, of white, of black studded with eyes of fire, coming we know not whence and fluttering among the flowers. All this was what Jean felt when he saw the sunbeams splashed upon his table.

Was that why he enjoyed so keen a sense of happiness? Why the live brilliance of the morning sun brings so much hope, the early frosts of winter so much gaiety, why the gold and level beams late in the afternoon even when they strike, during a boring hour of school, only on blackened desks scored by the penknives of innumerable boys, so charm us, we cannot say. But, so long as we are not tortured by too keen an anguish which deadens us to all impressions of sweetness and holds us motionless on a fine day of summer like a child in tears among his running, playing fellows, that charm can always exercise its power upon us. Thanks to it, and without having first to see in memory our games, the garden in which we played, the health, the hopes that then were ours, we can, for a moment, recover all the sweet loveliness of childhood. The colour of which we can say that it is truly beautiful, which, without having to exert our minds, we can fill with a sort of happy dream, is not that of gold, of rich stuffs, nor even of precious things, amethyst, gold or opal. No, it is that of all shadowed things, even of those that lurk in the corners of poor rooms, on which the sun shines and the brown, but inimitable, tint which, but for the sun we should not see at all, of the shadow cast by some object between us and the light. Thanks to that Jean, when he was quite old, expecting nothing more of life, making a hard living in a city which he never left, from which he could not even see the country, sleeping badly, waking miserably, without hope for the future, could recover the sweetness that he once had known, without really the memory of games and garden, health and the hopes of childhood. In those days to come he opened his eyes and saw the sunlight on the floor and it seemed, as of old, that happiness was something he could clutch and hold. He dressed quickly and, when he came back into the room, the sight of sunlight on the bed, of that lovely pale colour which the sun gives to sheets, would bring to his lips a smile of innocence. Smiling, he kissed his mother as when she was young and beautiful, embraced her as though they were together in the morning (when breakfast was over and all in readiness for the coming day) of a wonderful life that they would spend together, as though, side by side, they were about to begin this day of life. Lifting his hand he saw its shadow pass across the sheets and, in his power to make that darker blotch on the pale colour of the sheet in sunlight, seemed to feel the very essence of happiness. Work called him. He walked across the courtyard of the house but his smiling eyes were filled with a vision of the flower-decked past. He started for the Ministry, carrying his coat across his arm, for the day was growing warm, and humming a gay tune. He spent his morning copying letters but his face was as happy as though he were at play. The sun was hidden now and the sky grey. But the heat that drooped from it was as the heat of summer and even the light was summer's light making the waters of the Seine transparent. At such times, Jean knew so much happiness that he seemed about to faint. It was as though all life were standing still. The man who shared his room, feeling thirsty, had gone out for a drink. All was silence. From a distance came the sound of hammers. It seemed to Jean that he had just returned from a long walk after lunch at Etreuilles, that he had just entered the cool, fresh house. At those moments it only needed some-one to pass him a musty-smelling book, like one that had stood in the Curé's study, for his head to swim. The sun had reappeared and was shining so hot that the shutters had to be closed.

*

Often, when Jean came in from the paddock just before luncheon, he found the chairs already set about the table. No less punctually than the white noon glare lying still and motionless upon the roads, there, on the table, would be ranged the glittering, motionless, now fully mustered army of the plates with forks and spoons beside them, salt-cellars bringing up the rear, decanters, fewer in number, but taller, each in charge of a rank, and, supreme glory, by every plate a napkin twisted into the shape of a high cap, these being brought on parade by Ernestine only at the last moment, evidence that the hour of noon was close and that when the twelve strokes sounded the guests would wait no longer but take their places, so giving the signal to set in motion all the brilliant array of knives and forks and the procession of dishes which Ernestine, like a preoccupied Commanding Officer, led on, one after the other, a procession to be more than usually enjoyed when a bright sun set the wine in the decanters twinkling and played about the knives and forks. But on the days when Jean wanted to have a long interval before luncheon in which to read, what a delight it was for him, on entering the room, to find the chairs still ranged along the wall, and the round mahogany table quite bare in the middle of the floor, without so much as a sign of meal-time preparation. With happy content-ment he looked at the mahogany chairs still in their places by the wall on which the old china plates hung as bright as stars, not to be moved until half past eleven when Ernestine would take them down to do duty on the table. But previous to that Jean would have a good hour in which to read beside the hearth, for, judging by the coldness near the windows he could tell that the fire had been only recently lit. It still had got to heat the room and was already hard at work, from time to time letting a blazing log fall into the ashes, shedding a warm glow that flickered on the woodwork of the chairs and was never still. The clock, marking as yet no more than ten o'clock, seemed moved by the morning briskness to get on with its business, not skipping a single minute; of embarking on the journey which, like the sun, it must complete before midday.

There is, following an ample meal, a sort of pause in time, filled with a gentle slackening of thought and energy, when to sit doing nothing gives us a sense of life's richness and a feeling that the least effort would be intolerable. The melancholy we took with us to table has dis-appeared and, if we think of it at all it is only to smile, as at some black mood now past, its cause having gone. And with the melancholy, all scruple, all remorse departs from us. Should the opportunity occur we would do then what, in the morning, we had told ourselves we must not do, though the mere thought of it now sets our hearts pleasantly beating. But the first moment, after the meal has ended, is more innocent. For then each of those around the table has had his share of that high royalty of festival with which antiquity endowed the taking of food and does, in very fact, give the full sense of festival to all who have partaken. Then each, in his own way, observes the celebration, as one can see on entering the drawing-room for coffee before this special state of mind has settled on the company for, once it has, one feels that nobody must be disturbed. Look at them then: some immovable on the chairs on which they first sat down on entering and where they have remained so as not to have to make the effort of rising, others in places which habit, good manners or a sense of caution—for had they chosen a better there would always be a risk that they might be disturbed just when to move would be particularly unpleasant—have prompted them to choose. Each has laid upon some special pleasure, as on a docile slave, the task, without himself having to be troubled in his sense of well-being, of soothing him, of quickening his responses, of making him see with a more penetrating vision. One may be reclining in the posture of those who summon to their side their favourite animals, his much-loved pipe settled comfortable in the corner of his mouth, a thing of smoke and flame and stench for others, for him so sweet because it soothes with its warm, but not too warm, breath a palate rich with the fumes of food and drink. He breathes in the smoke and, as he does so, his chest gently rising and falling sets gently quivering, in its slow passage from up to down, the deepest chords of comfortable living. A glass of cognac stands beside him, near enough for him to sip and so to smooth his palate with a different, but not less powerful, flavour, without his having to move. Another, similarly stretched at length close to the great bay-window, which is all that stands between him and the shore and lets in the light and all the spectacle of the ocean without giving admittance to the wind which, at this moment, might be disagreeable, seems to be giving to his eyes, before which pass the sunlit colours of the green or azure sea, of white sails, of black steamboats, of smoke drifting across the sky, all the passive pleasure they are capable of absorbing. But the pleasure, entering through his eyes, spreads deeper and awakens in each sense yet other pleasures. Sunk in contentment every whit as deep as that the smoker feels, this other king of feasts dreams that he can sense the breeze which sets the fire crackling, wrinkles the ocean and inflates the sail. All about him sun and wind are partners in their play. He thinks that he can hear the cry of gulls above the jetty and can taste upon his lips the tang of salt. Then, though he has not risen from his seat, he feels the weight of happy listlessness and lets his eyelids droop upon his eyes like blinds which let us see the light, though not the objects, of the outside world. He is aware only of light striking his senses and not at all of solid objects. The light that reaches him is pink and white and golden so that he cannot distinguish what is the colour of his eyelids, what of the outer world, so that the world becomes for him like the sound of a seashell when we hold it to our ear, and do not know whether it lives within the shell or in ourselves. Yet another has drawn his chair up to the piano where, perched on a stool, a young man, more abstemious than his fellows, or for whom the exercise of his talent is so easy that it does not tire him and, maybe, is a necessary means of dissipating the no less troubling irksomeness that might oppress him should he not surrender to its call, is playing some delicious melody. He who has moved his chair towards the instrument has done so, probably, without rising more than enough to let him drag it behind him across the floor. If the piano is too far away he listens to it from where he sits and feels the tune to be the cause of all his happiness, yielding himself to it with so much comfortable response as he can summon up without emerging from his torpor. It carries him away, a willing victim, letting him tread a hundred times the self-same road, or wafts him to a distance with a sense of pleasure that is always new. Sometimes he joins his voice to the piano's notes feeling delight in its deep, vibrant tones and, in abandoning the passivity of simple auditor, is conscious of his own authority so that his mood of well-being increases though his tranquillity is not disturbed.

If, in that house of ease, a carriage is heard stopping before the door and expectant visitors are glimpsed waiting, before they get out, until they have the porter's answer to the inquiry they have made, though they do not doubt what it will be, then one notices how, with a speed of which one had not thought them capable, these wakened dozers flee like hares who have been interrupted in their nibbling and move a little farther off to where they can resume their meal, not without taking with them, one his cognac, another his pipe, a third his paper, preferring such sudden, sharp, disturbance to others threatening, feeling it to be the price that they must pay, once and for all, and without having to bother further, for the repose which will dispense them from having to offer their seats, from having to rise to show newcomers to the door, to sit comparatively upright on their chairs, to talk, to answer, to keep from making those grimaces, from indulging in those yawns, those stretchings, those rubbings of the eyes, which are the necessary accompaniments of a state of drowsy comfort, its almost physical and irresistible signs and symbols, the consummation of no matter what pleasurable sensation which spreads from the heart of slumber like the vanishing circles on the water of a pond which, without breaking its smooth mirror, die away after a stone has fallen.

Thus it is that a retrospective glance at the dining-room at Illiers where, on days of great heat, Jean and his cousins, unable to go for their usual walk, and having to let siesta take its place, sat for a few moments, their luncheon over, round the table before going up to their rooms, by waking in me other memories of other moments of post-prandial repose, has led me far from that little house in the country from which, as you will realize, no sea is visible but only a village street where, at midday, the passers-by are few. But, since I have made mention of crowned-heads of festival, it is my duty to point out that Jean's great-uncle, his uncles and his cousins though they, too, like those others, may have had their hours of blessed torpor and utter sovereignty, differed from the guests I have described though have not named since you, dear reader, are unlikely to have known them as I knew them (though, fortunately for the novelist there are fewer tastes and characters than there are human beings, or, rather, even the most highly individualized of human beings shares sufficiently in the tastes and characteristics of his or her fellows to make it possible for me, when speaking of my friends to surprise you by the deep knowledge I seem to have of yours though I have never so much as seen one of them, so that, like the simple-minded spectator of a card trick, you do not realize that the conjuror need not, by some miracle, have seen the card you drew in order to be able to tell you what it is, because the pack from which you made, apparently, a perfectly free choice, was, in fact, composed of identical cards) differed, indeed, from them as our modern kings differ from those of antiquity ,who were, so history tells us, as much farmers as kings, a belief which is strengthened by the portraits that have come down to us in which the simple attributes of a rustic existence bear witness to a more natural, and still innocent, sovereignty. They seem indeed never to have dismounted from their horses, never to have left those chariots in which they were carried to the fields, seated upon their cushioned thrones. And so it was that, at the moment which a while back I was describing, when the well-being that follows the first movements of digestion fills the whole of life, Monsieur Albert, his nephews, and his great nephew, sat firmly on their chairs, having merely finished the activity of eating and making no other movements. Monsieur Albert's vigour showed no abatement: he merely talked a little less, thereby giving proof that his faculties were being exercised at a slower pace. Each of those present sat motionless thinking of nothing and uttering scarcely a word.

One might include among the simple attributes of agricultural kingship the extremely complicated, because very primitive, piece of machinery which, at this point in the proceedings, the maid set before Monsieur Albert and in which he made the coffee by virtue of a prerogative which he would never have dreamed of sharing with anybody else. If, by chance, he happened to be away, visiting one of his farms, and did not get back for luncheon, "Who'll make the coffee?" became a question of almost national importance. Unless someone of outstanding importance, Monsieur Santeuil, for instance, was on the spot, this task was usually entrusted to the maid, who was looked upon as a kind of Secretary of State, so that the arbitrary appointment of a substitute was avoided. This machine was made of glass and so contrived that one could see the water coming to the boil, the steam permeating the coffee, and covering the sides of the container with blackish deposit, the water passing through a filter and falling back into a second cylinder from which it was then drawn off. Monsieur Albert listened to the water boiling and that music, though less sophisticated than the military tunes which serve to stimulate more distinguished digestions, but perfectly expressing the sense of wellbeing of which he was conscious, heralded the coming moment when the bubbling coffee would add to it an exquisite sensation of warmth, sweetness, liveliness and delicate savour and so complete his satisfaction. As for Jean, the very low degree of exercise which kept alive in him the modicum of activity which would enable him the more keenly to appreciate the comfortable process of digestion, consisted, as a rule, in keeping hidden in his mouth and, in moment of excitement shifting from his right cheek to his left a peach or cherry stone—a procedure which his mother solemnly forbade for fear lest he swallow it, though the doctor had told her that it would not harm him if he did, while Monsieur Santeuil shrugged his shoulders in such a way as to show his scorn of all such superstitious nonsense. Consequently, Jean was careful not to press it with his tongue too obviously against his cheek, lest his mother notice it. But the precaution was useless, because it was only long after he had spat out what remained and nobody was dreaming of calling him to task that Madame Santeuil, provoked by a suspicion as violent as it was unjustified, turned on him with a question, "What's that you've got in your mouth?" So long as he was still sucking the stone she had been free of all mistrust. But when he had got rid of it and no longer feared that his mother would give effect to her anger by sentencing him to a privation which now could not disturb him, he willingly admitted that the stone had been in his mouth all the time, either to baffle her, or because he felt a need to be honest, or because he did not wish her to remain in ignorance of the danger which he had so bravely run, she knowing what terrible consequences it might have had.

The only words ever spoken during this brief interval were: "It really is terribly hot: a storm would clear the air." – "I got in a proper sweat just coming up from the paddock, and had to change my shirt" – "Do you think we should be cooler if we opened the windows?" – "Oh, dear no: it's hotter outside than it is in." – "A hundred and four in the shade, even in the yard under the walnut." – "It won't be long before you go upstairs for a nap." – "It certainly won't, and my advice to you is to do the same." – "Not me! I'd rather walk ten miles than go to sleep in the daytime—it makes me feel feverish." – "That's odd, because I never feel well unless I've had forty winks—it's so refreshing." These last words were spoken by Monsieur Santeuil in reply to Monsieur Albert, a declared enemy of the siesta habit. There could be no denying, however, that when the others had all gone to lie down, he would retire into a small study, furnished in the "Oriental manner" with a hundred and one objects which he had brought back from Algeria—little mats on the stone floor, carved cocoanuts, and photographic views of mosques and palm-trees. It was situated in a small building separated from the main house, had no upper storey and looked directly on to the garden through windows glazed with small coloured panes. It made on Jean the curious impression of belonging to his uncle by virtue of some special privilege, as being, in some sort, a sign of superior social status and wealth not shared by the others, of being a house loaded with souvenirs, a sort of newly-constructed tomb, or an oasis, decorated after the manner of a Turkish bath and as dark inside as a church. Thither he would retire, safe from all interruption, for it was understood that he was engaged on some important work or that, maybe, he used it as a place in which to indulge in mysterious memories and, often, when he came from it, Jean saw him rubbing his eyes, emerging after replying in a startled voice to a summons from outside—which sometimes had to be repeated more than once—to come for a walk, and producing a general impression that sleep, in revenge for his abuse of siestas, had overtaken him in his wicker chaise-longue with a hookah within easy reach, just as he was about to start working, or rearranging his photographs.

Jean, on these occasions, went up to his room. The shutters were closed, but he drew his curtains as well, flung himself on his bed, and fell asleep almost immediately, starting now and again into wakefulness with a feeling of heaviness in his legs as though he had been walking, though it was of a kind to make him feel that he would like, in a moment or two, to shake it off by going for a stroll while he waited for the other members of the party, scattered like himself in various rooms in postures of relaxation, to reappear but, in the meantime, pressing against the cool linen of his pillow a face on which there showed the happy smile of one who has been deliciously awakened between two periods of slumber. From time to time the buzzing of a fly just quivering into motion took on a deeper and continuing tone. Then suddenly it stopped as the creature settled. Since it almost always advanced with band playing, he could tell from the sound how far from him it was and would wait until it was quite close before taking cover. But sometimes he was caught off his guard. It would alight upon his cheek, a bumbling, innocent object, a very sparrow among insects, with busy legs and brown, not particularly gauzy, wings. With a slap of the hand Jean would drive it away and smile to find himself again at peace after the not very violent movement he had had to make, which had pleasantly stretched his legs and body and had in it so much slumbering pleasure as would awake again at the smallest movement. But songs of a more celestial nature provide the special music of hot summer days out in the air and in the shadow of the trees where the birds singing in the choir fill all the Nave of Heaven with sweet sound. But the flies alone, perhaps accompanied by the noise of hammers heard in the street, thanks to the silence, and drawing from it on days of heat a particular harmony—not, perhaps, harmony in the strict musical sense, but harmony all the same, working in with all the other sounds and giving them a different quality—the humble flies alone, as I was saying, provide the chamber music of such torrid noons which have a special poetry of their own, cool in the darkness of drawn curtains, a poetry of silence behind the closed shutters in which nothing in the aura that it spreads has life except the chairs of wood and velvet, the linen-covered bed in its wooden frame, where the only flowers are those monotonously repeated in the pattern of the wallpaper, the mahogany chest of drawers where water does not flow over cushions of moss, but fills to the brim a noisy jug, where it is good, while the tiler hammers in the street, briefly to sleep with one's head upon the pillow. Those hot days have a poetry which holds a peculiar sweetness, less rich than that of the woods at the same hour, but more human, bringing perhaps a deeper sense of rest and, for that reason, deserving a music of its own.

In the years ahead there was more than one sad day, I know, when, compelled to stay in Paris at a season when the woods are at their best, scarcely conscious that summer had come and convinced that its poetry was something he would never know again, when, throwing himself down on his bed for a moment in the hope of forgetting the heat which was to him but an additional cause of weariness, Jean would suddenly hear close to him a noisy buzzing. It would grow louder. Then, all of a sudden, he would see a picture of that lovely Illiers time, with the apple-trees all blossom in the paddock, the tiler hammering in the street, when he had gone fishing in the lake, and he would feel grateful to the innocent musicians buzzing about him as though saying with noisy insistence that he ought to rejoice, that he was an exile neither from Nature nor from summer so long as they were there to tell, over and over again in monotonous song, the story of the season's everlasting glory. As, too, on some other day, in a street of that same Paris where not a single clematis thrusts through the chinks between the paving-stones the coloured, growing threadwork of its stalk to bear aloft the silky standard of its flower and wake in him a love of those streets, and to remind him that summer could come even there, he would notice, like some happy omen, a humble caterpillar in its brown velvet suit embroidered with green silk, at the foot of a warm and sunlit wall up which it was trying to achieve an arduous climb. With eyes fixed upon that sign, which it is not within the permitted scope of men to imitate, his heart filled with joy at the knowledge brought him by that visitor that Summer's God was truly there, he would long stand and gaze, conscious of a sense of pity and watch, not daring to lay a sacrilegious hand upon it, the favourite of that God, or rather, His very child, born

of Him perhaps that very morning and embarking without delay on
labours which would leave a long trail of silver slime to tell of its
passage on the earth, silently returning, again and again, to its task of
reaching an appointed goal no matter what might happen, suffering
blows without stopping to return them, moving for ever along its
destined road like one who some day would receive the recompense of
glory, buoyed by the promise of Heaven's infinite spaces.

We often maintain that music, heard once and in a different spot,
has the power to awaken in us the memory, the very charm, of the
time and place when first it struck upon our ears. For memory con-
serves the past without dismembering it, and what was once single in
reality remains single still, in recollection. But how surely does the
music of Nature, which, unlike the music of art, is not independent
of the time when it was heard, having nothing else to express, hold
vividly for us the charm of the very hour, the very season, the very
country scene in which it caught our attention. Nor is that charm, as
in man-made music, present only in the memory, but is truly part of
the music of Nature. An air of Schumann can recall for us the loved
voice which sang it years ago. We know, full well, it holds no trace of
one particular voice, that, since those distant days it has been sung by
others, that, like nature, it leaves to each of us the power of hiding in
its cadences our happiness, our memories, without concerning ourselves further, without being conscious of them, without preferring
one voice to another, because it belongs to all, expressing as it does,
an ideal that is beyond, superior to, the individual. We know that it
simply lends its beauty to adorn the illusions of memory that, an
indifferent messenger, it will carry its message to all and sundry, bearing
to each his dearest memory which it has not kept secreted, like those
woods which are so dense that they can hold as many secrets as they
have heard confessions and bury as much of happiness as they have
hidden loves. But the humbler music of Nature has a profound connexion, is in secret harmony with the season when it first was heard.
We may say that it is born of the essence of that time, that it shares,
quite simply, in its charm. Being born of it, of the cries of departing
swallows when the early frosts have come, of the buzzing of flies in
the heat of summer, it is but natural that those musicians should speak
of it to us, since, itself, it tells us of their songs. We do not need the
loved one to sing us Schumann's melody. She will sing it often for
others, for many others. But if summer did not come with its heat,

which nothing else can counterfeit, would not that spell, think you, the end of all the music of the flies? And so, when you hear it you have the right to recognize what you are hearing, to realize that the joyous welcome which your memory, its dear friend, extends is never likely to deceive.

*

Sometimes, in the high days of summer, a start would be made after luncheon and, since the plan was not to return until dinner-time, a snack was put up. If the sun was too fierce Madame Santeuil would lend her parasol to Jean. If the heat was really excessive, then, the party, by agreed consent, would walk as little as possible across the open fields but would follow the little paths along the hedgerows which grew above them on a bank of grass. The hedges, now completely green, no longer glowed with the tender colours of the hawthorn. The lilacs now exhibited only their dried and livid heads. The fruit trees, too, had lost their lovely robes of innocence. But, in their stead, the bright and scented flowers of innumerable cherries adorned the trees with a less airy, a darker show of jewels, vivid and pleasing.

Here and there, on the farther side of the bank, a poppy could be seen, born of the summer's heat, a visiting stranger among the tufted grasses and the luminous shadows, holding aloft on the stretched string of its green, thin stalk a blazing flower, so simple that it looked like one huge, scarlet petal. All alone it stood on the slope of the bank in an expanse of grass and, at moments, the breeze would make it bow its head and, in the shadow, set the red flower trembling, so light that the wind could play with it and yet too solidly attacked to be blown away. There, in the dark world of the grass, brought by no human hand and rarely seen by human eyes, it continued, through the passing hours, to blaze in the marvellous splendour of its scarlet and the simple monotony of its beauty, giving to the rare passer-by, glimpsing suddenly its high-held standard of bright red, the pleasure born of brief discovery, and that mysterious sense of something which flowers lose when they are planted out in gardens or gathered into bunches, but which they arouse in us so strongly when we see in a field, on the banks of a standing water or in a wood, the sudden isolated glory of a bloom or the inexplicable crowding of its like, giving the impression of some wonderful and delicate creature seeking solitude or wandering aloof

among the fields, or set against a rock without its rich and velvet head
suffering bruise or injury and even, when a train of periwinkles crowds
down to drink the freshness at the water's edge and hear the cool
silence, still standing there in solitude, no more troubled by the sound
of human feet than by the presence of a troup of young gazelles,
a heavenly vision which, with our eyes, we have surprised but not
disturbed.

*

When the days grew hotter, Jean, before luncheon, chose rather to fish
than to walk, keeping his energies for the early afternoon strolls or for
the longer expeditions that filled the time between four o'clock and
dinner. But sometimes, in the height of spring, a day, for all its
splendour, might be cold. Then, Jean would leave his lines, since, as his
uncle said, it was no weather for standing about, and they would go
together to a neighbouring farm a mile away or into the village on
some business of Monsieur Sureau's. Such times were pure enchantment
for the boy who found much to amuse him, warmed by the quick
walk with his uncle, his footsteps ringing loudly on the road, would
return the respectful greetings of the cottagers standing at their doors
and, while his uncle talked to the farmer or the wheelwright, would
stamp up and down or take a run with his hands in his pockets, saying,
in high good spirits, to the labourers or to the farmer's wife who was
listening at a distance to what Monsieur Sureau might have to discuss
with her husband: "It's certainly not warm today!" The same craving
for talk which drives us in a city to argue with our friends about
politics or our private concerns, finds satisfaction, in the country, in
talking to casual strangers, with the same air of solemn importance,
about the weather.

It is a joy for the city worker, when he goes quietly home, after a
hard day at the office for a quiet dinner with his family, to find
relaxation for his healthy weariness of mind and exercise for his tongue,
which for so long has been out of commission, during the brief interval
which must elapse before it finds more solid pleasure in contact with a
roasted chicken, to make some such remark as: "Not a lot of use
worrying—country's going to the dogs!" No less keen was Jean's
delight, revelling in the double warmth imparted to his body by racing
blood and a well-lined overcoat, in saying: "It's not exactly warm,
madame: the weather's all at sixes and sevens!"

When, about noon, he returned home with his uncle, how lovely it was, on opening the dining-room door, to see a blazing fire at which to toast his back agreeably as he sat at luncheon, Madame Santeuil fresh from her toilet and charmingly attired in her afternoon dress, reading her paper beside it, and to hear grandmamma Sureau say: "I thought a bit of a fire might be nice." Monsieur Santeuil, it is true, could have done without it, for, as Madame Sureau was fond of remarking, it would be difficult to find anyone as capable of keeping as warm as he did. Jean, for his part, was all eagerness to get as close to the fire as possible. "Anyhow, your son doesn't find it too hot," said Madame Sureau. One after the other, the remaining members of the party trooped into the room, each saying in turn to the old lady, "What weather, Grandmamma!—what weather, Aunt!" after which they all moved cheerfully over to the hearth. "Let me have a bit of the fire, Henri," said Jean. "You shall have my place in a moment." To each of them Madame Sureau made always the same reply: "Don't tell *me!* I've never known such a spring. One doesn't know where one is with it." She was one of those persons who, finding an almost physical pleasure in saying that everything going on around them is "extraordinary", end by finding it so, whether it be politics, drama in high life, changes of temperature or variations in the season—any of the small incidents, in fact, which go to make up life in the country. Had she lived all her life in a city, she would have found it too great a strain not to have put into words the distress which the misdeeds of the Government or the inconsequent behaviour of her friends caused her. Moreover, ever since a Radical mayor, who refused to raise his hat to the Curé, had been elected at Etreuilles, she had taken to regarding everything that occurred as a personal affront which caused her no sort of surprise, since she had foreseen it all. "In times like these, one should be surprised by nothing," she would say. She held the secular schools in some vague way responsible if business was bad or the season wet.

Sometimes the cold would continue for several days. In the evenings they all stayed chatting round the lamp since it was too chilly to go out. The cards were brought and Jean would feel the delicious oncoming of sleep and the comfortable warmth of the fire on his feet. "Listen to the wind," Monsieur Sureau would say, cocking an ear "No one'd think it was May. It wouldn't surprise me if we had winter back with us in a few days." The dread of such a disaster, the sense of the unforeseen events of travel, in such an eventuality combined with home comforts, made Jean laugh, and he went on with the game. "*I know someone who's going to enjoy his bed*," said his mother with a fond glance. He smiled happily. There she was, on the opposite side of the table, ensconced with her needlework in an armchair, her face brightly lit by the radiance of the lamp. "Aren't I right, old man? We'll be off upstairs in a few moments, both of us. I've told Ernestine to get your bottle ready." Then Jean, busy with his cards, would stretch his legs as though they were already twitching with pleasure at the soft feel of the deep, cold bed, and his feet fumbling for the hot-water bottle.

3. Reading

Since they started out for their walk immediately after luncheon, Jean quite often got back before three. He felt so tired that, in order not to have to move, he took over to the armchair everything that he might need, a paper-knife, the second volume of the novel he was reading and arranged them within easy reach of his hand. If it was cold and the maid came upstairs to light his fire he waited until the flames had caught, until she had raised the damper, until she had left the room for good and all, before curling up in his chair, there to enjoy, without having to move, the tremendous adventures of the heroes in his book and a delicious sense of bodily fatigue and mental liveliness. Every now and again he stretched his legs, sighed happily, glanced quickly round him, letting his eyes rest for a moment on all the various contents of the room, from the shell-splinter under a glass case on the mantelpiece to the photograph of the Châteaudun fire on the wall, as though to install himself once more in that happy world of solitude where nothing could prevent him from identifying himself with the doings of Captain Fracasse and the actors. Then he would start reading where he had left off. Sometimes, feeling the need of a little more relaxation, he would go over to the window which a branch of the Curé's pink chestnut could just reach, a huge branch which gave the impression that the tree was very much larger than, in fact, it was. All through the month of May it was a mass of blossom. Its innumerable little flowering turrets stood up stiff and close-packed above the spreading calm of leaves looking like a pink forest on the green slope of a mountain. And as each morning one may find a peacock's feather on the ground without his seeming to have one the less, so from that formidable and enchanting tree there fell, without its paying them the slightest attention, and without the watcher, proud of its fifty blushing towers, being aware of what had happened, so many blossoms that the veranda of the Curé's house looked as though it had been strewn with rose-petals. But it was not long before Jean returned to his reading and complete unmindfulness of his body. As a drop of wine taken on an empty stomach is enough to make a man drunk, the thread of melody which, beneath the window against which his chair was set, the nightingale who never left the chestnut sent soaring till it almost struck the pane, or, when leaning his elbow on the arm of the chair with his hand before his mouth, the fresh smell of his skin, was enough to intoxicate him with the sense of rest and happiness. Then, drawn little by little into the action of the story through which he followed with passionate excitement each several character, he lost, at times, all awareness of the outside world.

When it happened that his cousins outstayed him in the room below, sitting and chatting after their walk and before going upstairs to change their shoes and write their letters, and in doing so walked noisily down the corridor, Jean would break off his reading and pause uneasily, fearing interruption. But if one of them actually opened the door, he fixed his eyes once more upon the page, pretending to be absorbed. Then the intruders, fearing to break in upon so intense a moment of concentration, withdrew on tip-toe. When neighbours came to call his mother protected him, explaining that he was not available, that he was not feeling very well, that he had been ordered to rest. At times the danger assumed a more threatening shape and he would be forced to leave his room, feeling that someone might come upstairs to fetch him, and retreat into his uncle's study, one whole wall of which was covered with war maps of 1870 and a large-scale plan of the Department, determined to follow, no matter where, the heroes to whose adventures he was so closely bound. The study was on the floor above. From it he could hear the sound of people coming upstairs to the first landing, calling his name, knocking on all the doors, one after the other, opening them, and saying in loud voices—"He's not in here," while down below the maid explained that she had "seen him come in". Though he laughed to himself in the security of his hiding-place, he would willingly have wrung their necks. Then, hearing his uncle say to Pierre, the youngest of the cousins, "You've jolly well got to find him and tell him to come down," he would feel despairingly that he could not hold out much longer. When the main body of the search party had disappeared, Pierre would open the door of the lavatory, the window of which, kept permanently open, looked on to another great section of the fragrant chestnut which mingled its scent with the fainter odour given off by strings of orris bulbs hanging on the wall. These, Jean had recently learned, came from the irises growing by the swan canal in the Park, not far from the place where he did his fishing. Finding that the lavatory door opened without difficulty, Pierre could think of nowhere else to look for him, though sometimes he came upstairs as far as the study. When that happened, Jean, fearing that his cousin might be astonished at finding him there, and unable to endure the suspense of waiting for the door to open, would slip noiselessly out on to the landing and make a sign to Pierre, holding his finger to his lips which were puckered in readiness to utter a "Ssh!" and beckoning him to follow. Together they would go back into the study. Then Jean would shut the door as quietly as possible and, after listening so as to make sure that nobody had followed them, make it clear that he did not want to go down and that Pierre must explain to the others that he was not in the house.

Even when these terrible adventures did not come to spoil his pleasure in those of Captain Fracasse, even on days when there was no storm of rain—which always brought the maid hurrying upstairs and into his room where she laid towels on the floor to prevent the water, when it trickled down the window frame, from running over the parquet, Jean, when half past four struck, tired of reading and his body by this time, being fully awake, would shut his book and go down to tea. Drunk with the happiness he found in letting his mind relax into a state of indolence, and in moving his limbs, he would rush downstairs like a lunatic and run at full speed two or three times round the garden, tossing his head and cleaving the air with outstretched arms, mad with joy, and pretending to be a horse on the prairie or a gull skimming the waves. Later, and when he was still young, before his twentieth year, asthma and rheumatism made it impossible for him ever to run or jump or to let himself go completely. Sometimes, then, remembering with delight the sudden intoxication which, in that long ago, had sent him darting like a lightning flash through the wet flowers and branches of the lilac, shaking them with the violence of his passing, he would clamber with difficulty out of his chair and, with infinite caution, painfully put his foot to the ground, though never once did he think with bitterness of the strong boy he once had been and would never be again, nor envy him. Rather did he feel for him the tenderness a man might have for the sturdy son in whom he takes a tremendous pride and even more, perhaps, than he might do in the case of a son whom he could never know so intimately, reliving those times and drawing from their sweetness a melancholy sense of enchantment. After the first impulse was spent, he would go into the dining-room, the pleasant prospect of which had been wholly absent from his mind while he had been so deeply engaged in the adventures of Captain Fracasse. There, with its walls hung with plates, all of them modern and patterned with devices similar to those on the ones they ate off and which the diners amused themselves with comparing, his uncle, his cousins and his mother were often already seated. With the knowledge of a scientist and the unselfish attention of a father, his uncle would be keeping a watchful eye on the glass coffee-machine in which the water was already boiling. After first nibbling a pink biscuit, Jean would crush his strawberries into a portion of cream cheese until the resultant colour gave promise of the taste long dreamed of and now, in a moment or two, to become a reality. Meanwhile, he would add a few more strawberries and a scrap more cream, in carefully calculated proportion, pleasure fighting with concentration in his eyes, with all the accumulated experience of a colourist and the intuition of an epicure. From the Curé's pink chestnut, which was invisible from where he sat, so many blossoms had fallen that the threshold of the french windows looked as though somebody had scattered rose-petals upon it. The song of birds would drift in from the Curé's garden. Then the whole family would start out for a nice walk.

*

There was one day when Madame Santeuil had given Jean permission to stay at home all morning. Though she had advised him not to read too much, he, finding himself alone, was carried away by the thought that he would have time enough in which to read at least a hundred pages of the book he loved so well, *Le Capitaine Fracasse*. We often think what a pleasure it would be to talk about books, and other matters, to a very young and intelligent person. Actually, what we might read to him, what we might say, he would think extremely mediocre and, similarly, we should find nothing to interest us in his tastes. We often think that the object of our love flaunts its beauty, which to us is so adorable, on the surface for all to see. In reality, it is deep in ourselves that its beauty is displayed and if to gaze upon it ends by becoming a passion which we find it an agony not to be able to indulge more often, it frequently begins as a yoke the weight of which we find it hard to bear. Maybe when he first looked into *Le Capitaine*

Fracasse Jean had found some difficulty in accustoming himself to descriptions which had nothing in common with the things that *he* found beautiful (moonlight, bird song, and the Gods of Greece) but were wholly concerned with dusty tables and dirty walls, or filled with examples of the author's peculiar irony and his trick of indulging in asides to the reader—all of them things that Jean disliked intensely. It certainly does seem that after the first few pages he gave up all attempt to get interested in the book and returned it to the library, where it might have slept unnoticed for a very long while, like some-one with whom our first meeting has been a disappointment and has left no pleasant memory. But, then, one meets that someone again, and he is somehow different, so that the person who, at first, had struck us as being dry and pretentious becomes, as it were, a changed man whom we find it difficult to connect with the same individual. What chance it was that brought Captain Fracasse for a second time to Jean's notice, I cannot say. But the fact remains, that he had become a friend about whom the boy thought unceasingly, so that the hours he spent with him were filled with delight, no matter whether the day was one of rain, or snow, or sunlight.

In childhood it is not only love that we feel for a friend, but admira-tion, too. We think of him as being possessed of a supreme intelligence and omnipotence which we find in no one else. It was in this way that Jean thought of his book. What he found so enchanting was the in-exhaustible possibility of coming on the most beautiful phrases that anyone might hope to hear. Those phrases might, today, seem to him pretty poor stuff. At the time of which I am speaking, however, he could not help but be carried away, intoxicated, by certain turns of speech, like "thus it would appear that", certain rather old-fashioned expressions, such as "the good Homer", the use of rare words like "adonize", "Olympian", and periods at once so visual and so sonorous that he read them over and over in a sort of ecstasy and with tears in his eyes so that when he began a sentence containing some variant of "thus it would appear that," or some different version of "as Homer says," he was conscious of a sort of pent up agony of expectancy, all agog for the divine beauty to break again upon his ear, as a child runs to meet an incoming wave, without those phrases corresponding to any real beauty in the heart of the man who is reading, or, if you will, the adolescent's, though an adolescent who, at such times, is closer to Gautier than we are, and can better glimpse than we a beauty which no longer touches us. Each time he came, outside the general structure of the tale, on some comment, some phrase, which seemed to be wholly irrelevant to the movement of the story, he was more than usually delighted. For a writer whom we adore becomes for us a species of oracle whom we long to consult on a multiplicity of matters so that whenever he takes the stage and gives us his opinion, expresses some general idea, speaks of Homer or of the Gods we know, we are enchanted and listen open-mouthed to the casually dropped maxim, disappointed only that it takes so short a time to utter. And once the book is finished, when we can no longer take an interest in the life of Captain Fracasse, it being over and done with, and all that we thought of as being undetermined, thrilling and real, now that we know what "happened" has become insipid, an invention without life, we can always go back and re-read the passages on Homer, on "Messire Shakespeare, a poet well-known in England, and the protegé of Queen Elizabeth"— or some scrap of local colour which, to older folk, may seem somewhat stale, though it can turn the head of a young man to whom the most profound of Goethe's conversations on *Hamlet* may seem conventional and lacking the charm that he can find in repeating the magic phrase for the hundredth time, just as in music we never tire of a familiar air.

The characters, too, all seemed to him to be persons completely unrelated to anybody else and he would have been desperately disenchanted to learn that what he had been reading was just one book among many, a book like *Le Roman comique*, like *Wilhelm Meister*, like *Consuelo*, all of them works which he, no doubt, would have found excessively boring. All he wanted to read was something else by Théophile Gautier. He would have been horrified had he been told that *Wilhelm Meister* was better than *Le Capitaine Fracasse*, which, in his eyes, was something utterly unique, and not just simply a novel about actors. It may well be that he did even realize that it *was* a novel about actors, for so long as an author's genius holds us enchanted to such a pitch that we fall with rapture upon every comment inserted into the narrative on subjects already known to us but which his touch embellishes, thereby increasing our interest in everything he has to say, so, too, we see his characters as such living creatures that we should hate to think that they had just simply been contrived to provide the human interest of a purely artificial tale. Even at that age we are capable of feeling passionately about people in real life and people in books, without as yet knowing anything about life or understanding the nature of human relationships. We may, indeed, scarcely realize what actors are, and may have to wait until we are older to appreciate literary style. But, no, that is nonsense! We may, however young, be well able to feel the charm of style, yet so incapable of factual appreciation that, though we read a book with passionate attention, we may fail to grasp the details of a situation. Many things that we do not understand occur in books, as they occur in life, when we are young and we accept them as we might accept a dream many features of which are still obscure. But that does not mean that in the parts we do understand we are not able to feel far livelier emotions than we shall do later. About the characters in a novel which we read when very young there may be certain things imperfectly explained, but these merely add to the charm they have for us, and a power to attract, which if we read again that same book when we have grown to an age at which we understand more and feel less, we shall not find.

★

On some evenings, before dinner, there was a magic-lantern display in Jean's room. The chest of drawers with its load of books was pushed against the door, two chairs were brought in from Madame Santeuil's room, the curtains were drawn, the old workaday shade of green cardboard was taken from the lamp and replaced by a reflector, so that the light which, a moment before, had fallen quietly on the table, now, in the sudden darkness, produced a patch of concentrated brightness on the wall. And then, quite unexpectedly, upon that simple wall with its grey-patterned paper, above the old black sofa, a window, not an actual window of blue and red and violet glass, but the ghost of a window radiant with red and blue and violet, would come tremblingly into view, advancing and receding after the manner of phantoms or shimmering reflexions. Perhaps it was to these lovely colours, such as Jean had often admired on the pillars of churches when the windows shed on them a multicoloured and precious daylight, that Blue-Beard, Geneviève de Brabant, the traitor Golo, Sister Anne and the green plain stretching away from the castle keep, owed the fantastic poetry which his imagination found in them. Perhaps, on the other hand, it was because they belonged to Blue-Beard, that the azure beard and the scarlet robe were endowed with the prestige which was part of that particular legend.

But perhaps the most mysterious moment of all this fascinating experience was, for Jean, when, though he was still in his familiar room, neighboured by the washstand, the chest of drawers, the bed, he suddenly saw those marvellous shadow-forms take shape upon the grey-patterned wallpaper. For that was the moment when, the curtains having been carefully drawn, and the light of the lamp concentrated in a long beam moving obliquely across the wall to an unknown destination, his room seemed to be no longer his room, the lamp no longer his lamp. On that wall where formerly in a riot of fleeting colour, when a fallen log blazed suddenly in the darkness, a great light had flickered for an instant, and across which were now passing the marvellous dyes of church interiors and the characters of legend, Jean could see, a little below the mysterious band of light in which these apparitions were made visible (beyond it they vanished from view) the splash he had made that morning on the paper while he was washing. What, from behind that reflector in front of which strips of mystically coloured glass were slipped, projected the light upon the wall, what had burned his fingers when, in adjusting the reflector, he had touched the chimney, was his old familiar lamp which, in a little while now, when the chest of drawers should have been moved back into its usual place, when the chairs should have been carried away, when the reflector should have been dismounted and the shade replaced, would once again, as though roused gleefully from a fantastic dream, spread its globular, its soft and honest radiance on his book, leaving the wall in a half-light where the mysterious spot, the invisible trap-door whence ghosts had emerged to play their parts, should once more have merged in the general surface, a friendly half-light with which, one felt, phantoms, apparitions and the sliding movement as of impalpable windows of stained-glass had nothing to do, and in which, most certainly, they would not show themselves. Of such a kind was the only picture that adorned, and then but for a brief space, Jean's room. A spectral picture, composed of shadows; a phantom picture, a picture which did not last for long and, therefore, struck his imagination far more powerfully than would have done a motionless picture hung for him to look at all day long. Without the flavour of the pink biscuits which were handed round at Etreuilles after luncheon, but no less highly coloured though tasteless, was the story of Blue-Beard projected by the magic lantern. In memory Jean adored that living reality, as a collector in front of a picture, a father in the presence of his son, a man gazing on a precious fabric, another watching a dog, may be conscious of the presence of life before his very eyes, and strive to embrace it. But this was more: this was *his* life, this was the flavour which things have only for each one of us, and for us alone have kept it.

It is, perhaps, good for the human spirit to see in the whispering air, the sea, a piece of rock, things that are contemporary with creation and have survived the Flood. But there is, perhaps, for the mind a still greater emotional thrill in the sight, not of what *has* been, but of what has come into existence, of what life, though it may seem an ever-passing sequence yet is a definite *something*, has left behind it, has changed. These things which were created while our youth was slipping by, have a great power to touch the heart, the green crust which has slowly spread upon tree trunks in the Park, the green surface which has formed upon the pipes which supply water to the fountain, and which the very water, as an ancient mirror catches the colours of what it has reflected, takes on as well; or, if you are one of those who never go to the country, the dark tan which daily lighting-up time deposits on the chimney of your lamp. That thing, of all things the most precious, that irreparable something, which no object, however beautiful it be, however gifted with intelligence, can keep and render back, the thing that you have *felt*, the hours that you have *lived*, experiences that seem to be all spirit, immaterial, remembered—in them you have it, the slow and charming product of the old sweet hours, real and living, with those same green tones which, as the result of slow infiltration, have dripped from the bronze statue of Pan in the Park down over the marble pedestal. We gaze with love upon such relics of our past, as we might upon some priceless piece of needlework at which loved hands have laboured, soft green stuff in which there lie concealed the pipes of the fountain basin, stuff that scarcely existed at all when we were young, but today is so thickly worked, woven of the silent hours when we were dining or reading, when we lost our father, when we walked the roads at sunset, when we slept in old worn sheets, stuff that has been made by time, by *our* time, the time when Monsieur Grandi was still the Etreuilles lawyer, the time that comes back when we hear the name of the lawyer who married Monsieur Grandi's daughter and, later, made her so unhappy, the time when so great a coolness existed between the Radical Mayor of Etreuilles, who, nevertheless, was a great friend of my uncle and our own old friend the Curé; when we hear the name of the pastrycook which I can still see above his shop in the main street and catch my mother's voice saying: "We must hurry along to Mongeland's for a tart." That name still holds the sound of my mother's voice, the sense of time which even then was hurrying by, the memory of my schooldays, of the charm not of youth in general, but of *my* youth. I revere that name because it holds for me more of the divine, more of what will never come again, than could that of any artist or philosopher, more than a relic that might contain the blood of Christ. For that was *my* time. Even now I can recapture its midday warmth along the hawthorn path, the blinding light that lay along the uphill road on which we walked so slowly because the sun was hot, the smell of hawthorn trees, and of the tarts which I was carrying in a paper bag to eat when we should have come to Montjouvain.

It is said that nothing in our lives is ever lost, that nothing can prevent its having been. That is why, so very often the weight of the past lies ineluctably upon the present. But that is why it is so real in memory, so wholly itself, so far beyond replacement. And philosophers say, too, that no tiny scrap of recollected happiness, no simplest occurrence of the past, can be felt by others as it is by us, that we cannot enter into their way of feeling, nor they into ours—a thought which sometimes brings so sad a sense of loneliness to those who brood upon it, can, nevertheless, give to our past the unique character which turns our memories into a work of art which no other artist, however great, can hope to imitate, but can only flatter himself that he has inspired us to contemplate within ourselves.

*

Many other moments, too, were pleasant at Etreuilles. There was the one, for instance, when Jean would go, before dinner, to warm his feet in the cook's room, a sort of secondary kitchen communicating with the kitchen proper, where, tired of reading, he would listen to the cook's stories as she walked up and down cleaning the shoes. It was one of those tranquil moments when all things seem hedged about with the beauty to be found in mere existence, the charm of which is in the shadows at the far end of the room where the younger children's bed stands, in the soft light which turns the bed's bottom end to whiteness, in the ticking of the clock, in the lamplit face of the chattering cook, in the mysterious nooks and crannies of the kitchen lit by red reflections from the unseen range on which delicious things are happening, to be revealed only by the settling of a pot when the coals beneath it fall, or by the sound of something bubbling in the stove. At such moments, the sound of the cook's voice saying: "*I* should think those shoes of yours *are* wet!" is pleasant in your ears, because it is something that *exists*, as, too, the sight of the old chemist standing by his window, absorbed in the concoction of some mixture and brightly illumined by the lamp, is also full of charm because he *is*: the incessant babble of the fire is more agreeable even than that of the cook, because there is no need to answer it—though one feels it unnecessary to think about what one says to her, and in her eyes there shines something which is no less lively, no less fond, than the flame upon the hearth. It is delicious, too, to be able to talk when silence grows oppressive and one feels the need to break it with a trickle of words. Things then are lovely by being what they are and existence a tranquil beauty spread about them.

After dinner, one went, quite often, to the Festival of Mary's month. Dwarf hyacinths were piled in heaps upon the altar, mauve-coloured, curled, and tall columbines growing all the way up their stalks like a trimming of delicate and precious lace, of all the colours that one never sees on man-made things, in animals or cities, with the air, all of them, of having been born of those little clouds of heavenly tint which float for a moment after sunset in the sky, and tulips bright with all those glittering dyes which shutters make when they break up the strong glare of the sun. They stood in pots wrapped round with white foolscap paper. And nothing was more beautiful, emerging from the scroll of white and dazzling paper which hid it to the neck like a glowing shawl, than a great tree of Bengal roses, bearing not several roses on its stalk like pennants flying up the full extent of a mast, but bursting into one great scarlet bloom, a cup of dark and shining blood, from which unendingly were wafted, light and violet-sweet, invisible and unctuous, all the perfumes of Arabia.

Night came. How sad are those moments when rooms, as daylight flees, stay empty before those great reservoirs of warm radiance which men call lamps, have been opened! In the clear darkness, which grows deeper moment by moment, it is still possible to see the houses opposite from which the afternoon's bright colours have departed. They peer out with uneasy melancholy, like a troubled traveller arriving just as twilight falls at the strange street of an unknown city. Often then,

tip-toeing down the dark corridor and opening the kitchen door, Jean
would rejoice at the sudden vision in the darkness, raised at the far end
of the kitchen as though mysteriously supported in the air by a world
of shadows, of the spotless tile-work of the range all brightly lit, of a
red and unexpected glow, like a balcony with the unseen setting sun
still full upon it at a corner of a street already dark. A cloud of pink
smoke, doubtless suspended above a hot-water bottle by a jet of
invisible steam, hovered nearby while, like a sea-wave turned to
flashing diamond by the setting sun, the rhythmic puffing of a boiling
pot looked like flame. On its broad and shining breast the bottle caught
the hot reflection of the fire towards which it looked, though to Jean
it was invisible. With her eye firmly fixed upon the darkness which,
so suddenly, had filled her kitchen with red constellations, Ernestine
stood at her command post, skilfully controlling the fire with the tip
of her iron rake, now pulling a pot towards her, now pushing it away,
occasionally testing its contents with a wooden spoon, adjusting the
damper, seeing that all was going as it should, increasing or diminishing the colours of the glow which now was beating on a smaller pot
in which a chicken was cooking with soft and regular pulsations,
smothered in boiling butter and melted fat and giving off a sound of
spitting gravy; dimming with her ruthless rake, the red light upon the
wall by which Jean, on entering, had been so struck, because it seemed
to glow fantastically in the middle of the empty darkness, as though
deprived of material support—Ernestine was, for all the world, like one
of those technicians of the theatre attentive to their duty of regulating,
varying, and terminating, just at the right moment, the play of
coloured lights upon a scene of fairyland.

4. Le Jardin des Oublis

On the farther side of the town Monsieur Santeuil's father owned an immense garden, at first running level with the Loir but gradually mounting, here in slow ascents, there by a stone staircase giving access to an artificial grotto which stood at the same height as the wide plain where La Beauce began, to which a gate provided a way of entrance. This high point of the garden was of considerable width and was occupied by a magnificent asparagus bed and by a small contrived pond where a salamander slept clinging to the stone, motionless and covered with moss looking like the effigy of a water-god, but sometimes waking when Jean threw a stone, whereupon it would escape into deep water, leaving the feeling that it led a sort of supernatural existence, half ornament half goddess, and by a mechanical contraption which was worked by one of Monsieur Santeuil's father's horses and forced water up from the canal below where Jean, taking care to sit in the shade so as not to be seen by the fish, played his line for great carp which he soon had lying beside him on the grass among the buttercups at a spot where the swans, by reason of the lattice-work hanging from the rustic bridge, could not come. Rather than take the stony road which climbed beside the wall in full sunlight, Jean, when he wanted to reach the open country, would go by way of his grandfather's garden, being greeted at a distance by the gardener who was mowing and watering the lawn. As he passed he would draw towards him for a sniff the ravishing top of a lilac bush where the blossom rose from its leaves as from some silent, supple, sweet-smelling garment. He would catch sight of the delicately flowering tip of a young lilac lightly brushed with that indescribable freshness of colour which its scent conjures up before the eye with an extraordinary charm of which no amount of thought can ever plumb the secret. Then, making sure that none of the gardeners could see him, he would set his foot upon the carefully tended soil, put his arm around the bush and draw its scented head towards him. But, no matter how deeply he concentrated his senses upon smelling it, he always failed to discover the secret he was

122

seeking and, in point of fact, derived less pleasure from it than he had found, a while back, when, startled by the vision of the flowering lilac, he had ecstatically approached the living bush. By ceasing to hold its lovely face against his own and stepping backwards to the path, he restored it to its private world. But he could not keep from watching the graceful movement with which the light and much loved head sprang backwards and, still ravishing, still pure, and now quite motion-less, stood gracefully above the leaves surrounding it, like a decorative motif endlessly repeated, companions of inferior beauty, without colour or scent of their own, but none the less maintaining about them-selves a delicious freshness.

He returned to the path. And just as the hard, metalled surface of a road often brings joy to the traveller whose feet play thus their part in the sensation of healthy fatigue and in the feeling of natural, primitive life which country walking brings so abundantly, so was Jean con-scious of a sort of exaltation when he felt beneath him the subtle shifting of the path's innumerable pebbles, so tightly packed, so firm, that they scarcely moved, of the subtler and less healthy pleasure that came to him when he wandered by himself in the garden where, though there was no one but himself, the massed flowers in their abundance and their balanced symmetry, seemed to have been put there for the sole purpose of wakening in human hearts a deep delight. Paths where no trees stand, where all the pebbles are of equal size, seem to have been made by men, ingenious men, but far less simple than is Nature. But for whom did these skilled mortals intend such secrecies? Through all the centuries that have elapsed since their death, have not those trees, those waters, still as they were when they were first contrived, been awaiting the coming of the stranger for whom lilac has followed lilac, and the forget-me-nots have traced a thin blue line beside the tall red gillyflowers, scrupulously paired as in some meaningful design? But those paths lead now only to silent statues, where the flowers scattered about their heads by hands now vanished and the smile responding to an absent gesture, seem but the vestiges of days long past when those godlike activities were for ever interrupted in their task of making this spot a dwelling-place, only the plan of which, incomprehensible today, remains. Of such a kind, no doubt, was once that race of mortals or of goddesses.

Along those paths we come, now and then, only on statues and the ornamental lakes which swans inhabit. Climbing one of them, which looks as though it must lead to the master of this kingdom, or at least to the outlying dwellings of his dignitaries, at the very moment when the lilacs make a departing curve, when the pattern of the roses opens out to bound a wider space, when the loud hum of bees tells of a silence filled with a deeper sense of homage, we find that what, in fact, we have arrived at is but a bower smiling and silent as a brooding statue with a bench before it on which we can seat ourselves and rest. But we dare not break the silence, dare not disturb the brooding thoughts that fill the place, but must respect the silence and, if we speak, must keep our voices low, making no sound more violent than the murmuring of leaves in the light breeze.

Farther on there stand enormous chestnuts with branches bending very low like those of smaller trees, a race of young giants bearing upright on huge leaves tall blossoms looking like solid but delicately moulded towers. One such is close beside you, lifting each above each the superimposed tiers of bloom, motionless as the royal head of a bird exposing to the sun its vast, smooth, and sloping plumage of great leaves. Sometimes, by a bed, Jean saw a gardener weeding. But not, he felt, for such a race of men had these innumerable and magic gardens been contrived. The man was there only as a humble worker in some palace or cathedral. And Jean, too, finding between low-growing chestnuts, patches of hyacinths which he had come to water felt that they were his, yet not his, that the spot was like some tiny space of paving which one calls one's own, under the immense and sacred pillars of a small and wonderful chapel.

*

In the Park, close to the wall in a spot which Jean not often visited there lay, in a bare and treeless waste a stony amphitheatre with, at its centre, a post tethered to which, at times, were horses slowly moving in a circle at their task of pumping water. But when they were not there, only the post's shadow turned more slowly still about the arid place where no tree grew to give protection from the sun and once when he was walking with the boy, Jean's uncle had explained that it was in some sort a sundial. Downhill from the amphitheatre and joining with the Park, ran a growth of those immense yellow disks which are known as sunflowers and beyond the low wall stretched the nearby meadows which Jean, before first going to that spot, had never seen, lying full in the sun and serving as pasturage for herds of fat cows. He was at an age when the earth has not yet become something fully known and materially real, so that it would not have surprised him to find that this solid scene, planted with trees, and all so actual, where one could walk at will, opened directly into an unknown world. One day he had gone with his mother to a swimming-bath where, having been put to wait awhile in a cubicle apart, he had been allowed to see her bathing. Standing on a wooden raft that rose and fell to the movement of the water with, before him, an immense and liquid cavern that bellied outwards under plunging bodies which emerged again a little farther on and, though hedged about with other cubicles, seemed fathomless—he had felt, like those ancients who believed that in a spot not far from Pozzuoli was an entrance to the underworld, that here was the gateway to those icy seas whose limits lay within this narrow space, their angry potency surging between the piles through which they could be reached, though far below they opened into a strange and unknown world, a counterpart, perhaps, of the one with which he was familiar, but unvisited by any light of the sun. And seeing his mother splashing and laughing there, blowing him kisses and climbing again ashore, looking so lovely in her dripping rubber helmet, he would not have felt surprised had he been told that he was the son of a goddess and had been privileged to see the entrance to a world of fantasy unknown to ordinary folk, though lying close to the Concorde Bridge across which people daily passed without suspicion of its near- ness, as every day we walk above enormous navigable sewers to which there is no apparent entry, though the Prefect of Police and others have only to lift in the *Place* a stone, which looks for all the world like other stones and clamber down.

And you, reader, older though you are than Jean, have you not sometimes, gazing out from a garden wall built on a height, felt that what you saw stretching before your eyes was not just simply a pattern of different trees and different fields, but a strange country lying be- neath its own especial sun? The few trees reaching to the wall on which you lean are like those real trees which serve as a foreground to a painted panorama, a transition between what you know, the garden you are visiting, and that unreal, mysterious land spreading away in a vista of level plains richly diversified with valleys, basking in the light that bathes it in a changeless radiance, under a private sky where swim a host of glittering and tufted clouds. Around you are familiar things, the little rose-bush which, seen from below, seemed to block out all the view, to stand against the sky with its wire trellis and the little retaining wall which keeps the earth from crumbling. But climb to where the line of rose-trees ends, and suddenly, what lies beyond shows as a vast immensity of fields, chequered with light and shade and, farther still, green hills and, in the ultimate distance, yet other hills blue-tinted. You had thought you were in a garden and, walking down those lovely paths had never noticed that you were upon a hill-top in a tended, walled and builded place beyond which all was different, that the fair country, momentarily held in by enclosing walls and kept a prisoner there and all disguised, did, none the less, being true country, fade into the far, mysterious distance. In the Park of Versailles, which you know so well, objects are still real—the fountains as much a product of man's art as are the statues. There, as in this garden, you are, as it were, shut away from the world in a known place. But gazing from the terrace across the fountains and the statues and the follies, letting your eyes wander up staircase after staircase, beyond the last statues and the farthest fountains, you see—what?—a long canal shaded with Nature's poplars, the beginnings of a sort of lesser Holland, a mysterious country fading into the distance, and no longer real as where you stand is real. Such was the feeling that came vividly to Jean when, by chance (for he did not know the paths that led to it) he found himself on that high plateau full in the glare, where, he was told, the horses often circled and the sun in person marked the hours, where grew great sunflowers and—this best of all—which looked upon the sunlit fields he did not know (since, from the road, the Park concealed them) that seemed to him a strange, new land not to be found in the countryside of Illiers. And so he came to think of this bright amphitheatre as a place marking the entrance to some kingdom of the sun, where only sunflowers grew, and where, of choice, the sun came visiting with his mysterious horses. He knew, of course, that the sun's home was the sky: but might he not, too, come down to earth? Would that be any more surprising than that the great piles of a swimming-bath should open on to icy seas or than that, in his father's bathroom, there should be a great pool of living water, a place of wonder hidden within a well-warmed flat in a street than which none could well be farther from the Seine? Avid collector that he was of all books which made mention of the moon (and read without comprehension) when, in winter, his mother made him bring to the drawing-room, like some scientist without understanding of his science, or a magician, all his picture books about the moon, to show how many he had, did he not take with them a French grammar in which, under the word "Moon", there was a cut showing the moon with an eye in its middle and the vague outline of a nose? That eye, that nose, caused him a slight embarrassment as often did a touch of humour in descriptions by the poets (which was why he preferred Saintine's *Picciola* to Merimée's *Colomba* where, at any moment, a comic touch would spoil for him the ravishment of dreamy verse), and he would rather that the moon had been depicted round and full, riding in a cloudless sky. All the same, it was not only because he wanted to be admired by his mother's visitors that he took the grammar as well, or so that they might see five pictures of the moon instead of four. No, the fact was that he could not be absolutely certain that the moon might not, after all, be like that, and so, a book that was not really concerned with the moon at all, figured in his mind as belonging by right to his sidereal library of mystery, in which, like an astrologer, he thought that he could see the planet as it really was, a library where he spent so many hours of which, had he been asked, he could have given no account, leaving it only to show to lovely ladies in the drawing-room his different pictures of the moon and all the strangely assorted magic volumes which had made him free of that dark and motionless science beloved of old astrologers and little boys.

*

Almost at once, on opening the gate of the Park, one saw among the foliage of the spinney what the gardener told Jean were known as "snowballs", though when plucked, they did not melt but stayed as white and round as blossoms in the vases of the dining-room. Jean vaguely fancied he had reached a time when nothing any more would change, when his mother would stay eternally young, and he eternally free and gay in the fierce blaze of an unchanging sun. Beyond the first snowball thickets, the lilacs, here and there showed, among the dark green of their leaves, those blooms of dainty muslin starred with bright points, which, at a touch, would fall, crumbling to dust and distilling a sweet smell like that of a pastrycook's shop. All around, born of the earth, freed from their husks, floating upon the water, the languid creatures lived in the aura of their perfume and trailed enchanting colour. That lovely colour of pale mauve which, after rain, showing in a bow which looks so near yet cannot be approached, appears in the sky between the branches, metamorphosed into soft and delicate flowers which one can look at and approach, smelling an odour no less delicate than that upon the lilac boughs, can gather and take home. No people of the East could give more precious colour to their vases. It is the East that gave its life to the lovely lilacs, for the blood of Persia is in their veins, mauve or anise-white, slim Scheherazades motionless between the branches in all their nudity of precious fabrics, giving out the sweet fragrance of which they seem the visible embodiment, and which they powerfully exhale.

*

At two o'clock on hot afternoons Jean could be seen, followed by his cousins and sometimes by Madame Santeuil and Madame Serciers, whose children carried folding stools, going by way of the main street of Etreuilles and the rue de la Maladrerie, towards Les Oublis. Their road led them past the railings of the lawyer's garden. On either side of the path leading to the house one could see a line of elms, in springtime covered in dense green which lasted all the summer long turned golden by the sun for one hour every day and, now and then, set rustling by a breeze which, as it passed across the little sun-warmed leaves, sounded like the very whisper of their happiness, the gentle murmur of their smiling peace. At the gate a wall began, bounding the property and draped in clematis. An enormous pink hawthorn had topped this wall and fraternized with the tall lilacs in the Curé's patch next door. Their intermingled branches seemed to have made exchange of blossom, and it was as though a quantity of thick pink flowers had been given on loan to the Curé's garden into which they spilled, while a few clumps of purple bloom among the hawthorn growths appeared to be on a neighbourly visit to the lawyer's beds.

"Madame Leduc is not in her garden today, I see," said Monsieur Serciers. Yet one could not truly maintain that the garden was lacking in life. One had the impression that every single corner of it was a living dispensary where leaves were ever at work distilling balm, while all around the flowers gave off their heady perfume. Even at some distance from the railing one could catch a smell, so much more penetrating when gathered from the living plants by the breeze which rocked them, mingled them, composed them in a symphony, blew them apart and gathered them together, turn and turn about, than in the hot steam of infusions, or in a chemist's shop, the scent of lime flowers or acacia. Nature, too, was hard at work, taking advantage of the season and the time of day when every flying thing might go where it willed and the flowers lay open like palaces offering hospitality. One could see a bee, who had come from far away, enter the lawyer's garden, like a workman who has come to put something to rights, and whom, though his face is strange, one leaves to his task, realizing that he knows what he is doing, and understanding why he is there. A long task, too, it was, for it had much to carry off, and thrust deep into each blossom, plunging into the scarlet throats letting itself be covered wholly by the white veils of convolvulus, knowing well that when the moment came, it could withdraw, having the skill of its calling, as a surgeon knows how to undo a bandage, an army doctor how to extract a sword-point from a wound, a musician how properly to close a piano. Like workmen who are not distracted from their job by the arrival of guests, the butterflies brooked no interruption, but harnessed to their labours, poised on their chosen flowers, stayed there unflustered and did not damage them. The gardener, too, at moments joined his work to theirs, waging war against the orange-trees which, set at the entrance in large green tubs designed, before the footman should have put in an appearance, to offer welcome to the visitor with an ordered greeting as of vegetable statues, he stripped off their yellow flowers, packing them into a sack, intending to make a cordial of them which he later sold, thanks to the inexplicable tolerance of the lawyer, whom he robbed, but who, proud of his garden, agreed to everything his insolent gardener suggested and allowed himself to be persuaded that to let an orange-tree retain its flowers harmed its growth. And each evening, when he came back home, he felt a surge of pride and of admiration for his gardener, seeing beside the gate, high on the wall, superb geraniums flowering in little pots which did not shut them away from the universal germination all around, since it affected them too, so that, each day, above their enclosing pots they put forth new blossoms, red and smooth—and, after glancing at the rose-bushes and the wooden edging of his beds, would stop for a moment by the jetting fountain to listen to its splash and turn aside to watch a goldfish in the basin.

Next came the garden of the Curé who would often be seen silently reading his breviary beneath the trees and, looking up, would lift his hat with a smile to Madame Santeuil, Madame Serciers and the little boys. He appeared to be not wholly insensible to the immense release, exchange, intermingling, departure and arrival of the scents beneath his nose which, though he took a less active part in the procedure than did the bees and bumbling insects, he seemed to be enjoying no less deeply. When a petal, after exhaling all its contents, fell withered to the ground, he raised his head for a moment at the small sound it made, seeming conscious of the wealth of delight so silently released and giving to his eyes their share of pleasure by letting them follow the long ray of sunlight which had just penetrated beneath the foliage of the spreading oak, after which he resumed his reading. The heat was still intense when Madame Santeuil and Madame Serciers sat down with their needlework while Jean began to fish. Now and again they paused to talk. "I hope you will make an effort, Jean, to be in time for Mass tomorrow." – "If you're good, we'll have a game of draughts this evening." – "I have written to the bookshop ordering the second volume of *The Conquest of England by the Normans* for you." Or, maybe, she intended that to be a surprise, did not tell him that the book had come already, and then, when he was tired of fishing and wanted to rest, took it from her bag, producing in him an explosion of delighted gratitude which she answered with the smile of those who, meaning to keep something pleasant back, feel that the time for secrecy is past.

This small sound of voices by the lake, so distinct in the surrounding silence that it could be heard from the Park above, and anyone newly coming to the spot would say to himself, "There's somebody there, I can hear voices," took from these hours that were so glittering, so all-complete, so still, a quality of utter certainty. In the water, as above one's head, one could see the sky, looking, though inverted, so firmly fixed, so motionless, so solid, untouched by an unsettling breeze, untarnished by a cloud. The shadow of the grass might flicker in a tiny gust, but against a background of deep, unchanging blue, and if, occasionally, a ripple showed upon the surface of the lake, the blue remained unaltered, and it was as though it had been gathered into folds though its basic substance stayed the same. A swan might cast on it a passing darkness, but the sparkling blue remained essentially untouched: the swan's plumage did not hide the sun, but caught its beams diffused in the wide air before one saw them show upon the water, reflected first, it seemed, in the mirror of a feathered back. If it paused to drink, one heard the drinking and a sound like that of voices seemed caught in the same compacted silence, as though incised in something solid in a way that gave it clarity and limitation. Higher than this playground of the sun, there was a place still more mysterious, beyond the stone-rimmed pond from which the pumps drew water, where, at the bottom, the visible and tangled pipes no longer had the look of man-made things, for there, beneath the surface, turned to delicious green by invisible strands of water-moss which covered them, they lay in a knotted criss-cross, so firmly held by weed that it seemed they might at any moment crack, and actually, in one place, had been bent. The spot I have in mind was at the Park's highest point, a huge, flat spread of ground which was known as the "asparagus bed", ground as bare as all those places are, reserved for prodigies, before the magic spell has done its work, and which, in June, when he came into the country for Ascensiontide, showed to Jean's eyes as thick with ten thousand plants of succulent asparagus, standing upright, wild and free, as though it were not to be their fate, perhaps that very evening, to be served before him in a dish, for ever uprooted, hot, soft, but even so, looking as he had seen them where they grew. Or, rather, he had seen as living things what now he saw before him on the table, slim, long, some fatter than others, hard and pink, then fading into a faintish blue, with a soft and velvety head of green. At the far end of this asparagus bed there was a door, firmly bolted, which they opened often when they walked in the late afternoon. Then what lay ahead was field after field where lucerne grew, stretching into the infinite distance with here and there a poppy quivering in the breeze. Even before he reached the Park and was skirting the wall which, in the village street, when the last house was passed, marked the boundary of their garden, Jean would be brought frequently to a standstill by a strayed plume of lilac, or a great tree in flower, the one an ornament in simple taste, the other an arrogant monument spontaneously displayed or raised by the Genius of Nature, to the glory of the spring. Just as the white napkins laid by the pious women of the village in the open street, and spread with flowers, took on, at Corpus Christi, the character of altar-cloths so, too, did the wooden fence past which Jean was walking seem like a rustic altar raised to the glory of the spring by the piety of Nature, a sort of reredos, above which a lilac bush displayed its three-branched fan which scattered down a shower of delicate blossoms and laid upon the road which it had garlanded with new adornments the modest but exquisite tribute of its fragrance.

*

Farther on, in a shadowed spot, one of those places of mysterious coolness on hot, sun-drenched days, so like the dark places of a church, and which most it loved to haunt, gleamed a pink hawthorn, like some shrine in an obscure chapel, with all its rosary of lovely flowers, now of a flushed colour so vivid that it was almost red. Here and there an isolated bush of it stood like a monumental stone, the beautiful fretting of its leaves giving a passage to the sun, eloquent, in all its drooping nonchalance, of a mood of happiness, infinity, and charm. In the first years of these Etreuilles holidays, before his eyes had learned to observe and his mind was lazy, he had had no clear impression of Nature in the springtime, being conscious only of a confused sensation which made him want to shed his overcoat, go for walks, drink cream in farm-houses, sit in the shade and dabble his hands in the canal. It was then that from the many flowers about him which he neither properly saw nor loved, he had chosen as his own the pink hawthorn for which he developed a particular affection, of the shape of which he had a clear idea, and would beg a branch from the gardener, so that he might keep it in his room and, when he saw it at the far end of the garden, would stop to look filled with a craving for possession. Did the reason for this preference lie in the fact that the hawthorn is, indeed, more beautiful than other trees, that its spaced and coloured blooms look as though designed for festival, and that he had so often, during Mary's Month, in church, seen great sprays of it, cut and entire, standing in the altar vases? Was it that, having already seen white hawthorn, the sight of the red with blossoms no more simple but arranged with no less art, gave him that double sense of difference and likeness which can so profoundly affect the human spirit, though, no doubt, he had already seen the eglantine before ever setting eyes upon the rose and had never felt much love for either? Or was it that with the hawthorn, white and pink, he associated a memory of the white cream cheese into which, one day, he had crushed his strawberries, so that it flushed with an almost hawthorn colour and remained in recollection as the thing he most liked eating and was for ever begging of the cook? Perhaps the resemblance helped him to take notice of the pink hawthorn and to love it, because it held for him the treasure of that flavour in one imperishable memory of greed and hot days and radiant health. Did his affection for it date from the day when, lying ill, he had seen his mother come into his room, and heard her say, "The gardener has cut these sprays of hawthorn for you," and laid them on his bed, where, when she had gone and he was all alone, he had seen the bunch smiling with all its congregated flowers and spreading through the room the smell of all those roads on which he loved to run: was it then, that it had become charged for him with the glory and the loveliness of many other things which lay within the fragrance and the colour of its bloom? It remained within his consciousness not so much as the one flower of all flowers that he loved—it would never have occurred to him to say that—nor, indeed, as a flower at all, but as the concentrated essence of the spring, of springs now dead and gone, of the roads about Etreuilles, of dazzling days when he had been in a sweat, though never tired, and had gone home at three o'clock to resume the reading of *Le Capitaine Fracasse* in his shuttered room: the flower of Mary's Month.

*

Gradually, and at a later date, he came to know many flowers. An artist it was, who, with the prestige of his authority and the power to reveal beauty to unsuspecting eyes, gave him the *entrée* to their loveliness, as he did to that of many works by writers and by painters. For Jean's mind, as the years passed, was without companionship and needed direction. Often when he saw a flower in Monsieur de Montesquiou's button-hole, and remarked upon it, that consummate connoisseur of Nature, could, with a word, set him on fire with passion for the moss-rose, the deep blue of the gentian, and the rich pigmentation of the cineraria. There is something in us that lies more deep than aesthetic appreciation, something that is part of ourselves, something that is silently given back to us, embedded in a moment of the past which still lives on, intact and fresh, in some forgotten corner. A flower which an artist might consider vulgar was beautiful to him at an age when he could respond only to the verse of Déroulède, the prose of *Picciola*, a peasant's flower, a child's, the simple adornment of a village altar, so that he loved it for itself alone. And perhaps, in the days when he was less capable than later of seeing unaided something

that stood before his eyes which some friend taught him to love, that
friend was, as likely as not, the old farmer, his father's father, whose
reading never went beyond the newspaper and who had lost all hope
of seeing his dearest wish fulfilled, which was to go to Paris for the
Exhibition; or, maybe, the gardener, "on fire for" knowledge and
well-informed, who, when his day's work was done, would read the
novels of Montépin and historical works by Imbert and Saint-Amand.
Or, perhaps, his mother, when she had brought the spray which the
gardener had given her, and who, though she was filled with admiration
for any flowering thing that found its way into her drawing-room or
her bedroom—though they rarely came there—felt love for none of
them and was quite insensitive to the antics of animals or the form of
growing things, on that particular day, with one unthinking word,
had diverted to the benefit of the pink hawthorn the floods of love and
adoration which overflowed Jean's heart, though as yet he did not
know how to direct nor how to let them spread.

*

Sometimes, at the day's end, Jean's cousins would suggest a boating
expedition. On those occasions they all went down to the Loir, and
the boat would nose its way along the winding water-course into the
silent hiding-places whence the river drew its strength, to the ponds
in the deep shade where the unruffled surface of the stream seemed to
be waiting with a changeless expression of expectancy, like that upon
the face of a statue in a grove. The sound of the water dripping from
the oars seemed muted, that it might not interrupt the listening silence,
as a reader may quietly turn the pages of his book close to a friend who
is fishing. Sun and shade alternated on the river and in the greenery of
innumerable gum-trees which set a darkness in the deepest places,
while the liquid note of a hidden bird showed precisely where he sat
concealed, though in the vague expanse of trees, still unexplored, no
eye had seen him. All this seemed to give to the spot where the boat
lay drifting and not an oar was moved, the innocent look of a waiting
statue. Then they would rejoin the main stream on whose banks
buttercups in thousands grew in the grasses to the water's edge. An iris
would watch them pass, like a house soon lost to view. From the
hidden reeds, where he lived, a bird would shrill a greeting. They
would leave it far behind and still hear it singing from a distance until

its song subsided into silence. Sometimes, in a moored boat, they
would see a schoolboy with a girl. He had just discovered in himself
the marvellous secret of a happiness as new, as ravishing, as little touched
by all the common joys of life, as were the lilacs or the dark-com-
plexioned iris, a happiness which the sun's warmth seemed to increase,
which gave to life something eternally sweet, which, hitherto, it had
not had, like those snowballs which Jean had come on buried in the
thickets of the Park, and which, when plucked, did not melt in his
hand, but stayed, still white and fat, when transplanted to the dining-
room vases. Sometimes, Monsieur Santeuil would have them cut and
taken to the church for Mary's Month. And Jean, looking at them
there upon the altar, would dream of those that he would see tomorrow, when sun and sky would be a new discovery and he should
have found his way back to the Park. When Jean and his mother left
Etreuilles, Monsieur Sureau had gathered for them great box-
fuls of hawthorn and of snowballs which Madame Santeuil had not
the courage to refuse. But, as soon as Jean's uncle had gone home, she
threw them away, saying that they already had more than enough in
the way of luggage. And then Jean cried because he had been separated
from the darling creatures which he would have liked to take with
him to Paris, and because of his mother's naughtiness.

*

There was, in the Park, a tree of which Jean's uncle was very proud.
It was an immense camelia, twice the height of a man. But what gave
it its peculiar beauty was the way in which it spread from root to
summit, like an umbrella, so wide and so thick with shining leaves that
it was as though many bushes had combined to give it a girth which,
unaided, it could never have achieved. But so tall was it, as well as so
enormous, that it lost nothing of grace. All around it stretched a great
slope of bare earth, the new-turned sods empty of all vegetation, a
place where nothing grew, for, to the tree, as to a God, was dedicated
all the richness of the neighbouring soil. It was completely green without a flower and its motionless leaves, giving a smile to the visiting sun
and responding with a slight quiver to the spring breeze, seemed to be
guarding in secret a hidden splendour for the display of which the
moment had not come. One could feel that splendour concealed beneath
the gorgeous glitter of its leaves, under the proud self-satisfaction and

tranquillity which animated all the tree, under the calm strength and imposing silence from which the sun could force no more than a smile, the breeze no more than a quiver, but nothing of what in good time would appear.

One day Jean, who had been ill, paid his first visit in many days to the Park. As they climbed to the asparagus bed his uncle spoke. "Come and have a look at my camelia," he said, "it's in full flower." They changed direction, for the path they had been following would not have taken them past the tree, since it turned off towards the grotto where the garden tools, the spades and rakes, were stored. But because Jean had been far from well, he had been told only to read and fish. Consequently, there being nothing to take them to the grotto, they could go straight to the camelia. At a sudden turn in the path they saw it. Over the whole expanse of its vast umbrella long flowers were showing, red and pink, looking as though they had been fastened there in thousands by human hands. And the tree, full in the sun at this late hour of the morning, smiled at them seeming a little different because of all the lovely flowers which sprouted from it, as a woman in child seems slightly different, though the same. The leaves were as beautiful as ever, but everywhere among them great flowers of red or pink were now displayed. Jean had never seen, nor ever noticed, the tree before its flowering, nor any tree of any kind, bearing such innumerable blooms of red and pink, and he stood there all at gaze, as he might have done before an unknown woman, beautiful and exquisitely dressed, introduced to him by his uncle, smiling a welcome. All the more did this seem so, because things were never now for him mere things among others of their kind but persons whose equivalents did not exist. He never told himself that there were swans on the canal, but *the* swans, or, in a certain place, a camelia, but *the* camelia, all of them probably unique of their kind and, in any case beloved and known, like the swan who had tried to peck him, the tree now full of blossom to the left of the path leading to the grotto, persons with a distinctive character of their own, of whom, seemingly, there could be no double in the world, like his mother, his uncle, the gardener and the house at Etreuilles. But the person now before him was somebody quite new and he looked at it as he had looked at the beautiful lady whom he had met for the first time for the tree was also large and bright with new colours, smiling and slightly indifferent, like the lady who had smiled but who had not come to meet him with the same eagerness his cousins or his nursemaid would have shown, but had stood before him as upright, as majestic and as kindly as the tree.

And so it is with things that we shall later love the most. We meet them first as strangers who give us only a feeling of surprise. But it was not long before Jean was enamoured of the blossoming tree. When they returned for luncheon his uncle said to his mother, "We've been having a look at the camelia: it really is superb!" And to Ménard (the gardener) he never tired of saying, "Ménard, that really is a peach of a tree!"–"Yes," said Jean's mother, "it's very lovely."–"Oh, it's a wonderful tree, a grand tree," replied Jean's uncle: "but you shouldn't go to see it now, it's lost a good half of its blossom," he added, with the modesty and, especially, the self-satisfaction becoming the tree's owner, and with the exigence of those who are more knowledgeable in this or that than prone, merely, to love, who demand that Beethoven Symphonies be played by famous orchestras and think it not worth while to see Sarah Bernhardt in this or that part. But Jean so loved the tree that he could not think of it as being more beautiful on one day rather than another so long as it was still the same, so long as it still possessed its flowers. But, god though it was upon its own and sacred ground, the camelia was not the only god who presided over the Park. Through all the length of that place the exquisite and lacelike chapels of the hedges now were adorned, as befitted the Month of Mary, with garlands of pink hawthorn under the branches of white may, all mingled as in an offering beautifully woven with the eglantine. In certain corners of those little chapels set in the open air where, almost to excess, were piled great hawthorn branches starred along their length with dense white flowers, the fragrance was so strong that one felt almost giddy and, though the dome of green made a deep shade and a world of concentrated silence in which one could hear the great black bumble-bee at prayer in the tabernacle of the eglantine, though only his back was visible, the sun's rays managed still to penetrate as in a chapel where the windows are not filled with painted glass. As luncheon was drawing to a close, his uncle ordered the "stlawbellies" to be brought, naming them thus in imitation of his nephew, who had gathered them with him while they were in the Park. "They are exquisite," said Madame Santeuil, with the amiability of a guest and the eagerness of a connoisseur. "Yes, they're not bad: real wild'uns," replied Jean's uncle in the impartial tone of one who does justice to his children when they have been a success, or to his cook, when she has been especially clever with a dish, seeming to have uttered this considered opinion only because the evidence cannot be denied and thus enhances the value of his commendation.

*

That year one stayed very late at Les Oublis. About four o'clock in the afternoon the sinking sun, turning to full use the rich palette with which what remained of the autumn foliage supplied it, reds, greens, yellows and gold, made magical use of its resources and a sort of dawn was spread upon a sky of blue and pink, seen through brilliantly lit, fantastic leaves. It was as though someone were playing with a paint-box. All of a sudden, in a clearing at the far end of the avenue, the sky showed like a mass of flame as though reflecting an invisible conflagration. One hurried towards it, but the flames faded, and by the time one had reached the avenue darkness had all but come. One stood there with a sense of disappointment. The avenues led away into the night. A last gleam of the setting sun and, farther on, a first glint of the moon through evening mist in which fountains, steps and foliage mingled in a still confusion, lent mystery to the scene. One would have liked to go into the woods, but now that they were stripped of leaves it was as though they had been invaded, taken by force, conquered and swept bare. The nymphs who lived in them and had always made pretence that they were strong, now, like wild beasts and birds made prisoner in the forest who, when caged, go through the impotent gestures of those who would break free—the nymphs, chased and taken in the devastated woods were seen to be no more than statues, graceful still, but powerless, there at the entrance to the avenues where they had been set up, frozen in a pose of flight which never turned to action, making still a mere physical gesture of shooting. They had been allowed to keep their bows as captive boars in a great hunting lodge are allowed to keep their tusks, but could not now make use of them.

Now when the darkness fell, the park-keeper's lodge—a small building in the Louis XV style—was all lit up and, had one not seen the two keepers playing cards at the squalid kitchen table while the woman of the house cooked their supper at the range, from where one stood, looking at the tall windows which would have better graced a palace, drenched in a pale gold radiance with, occasionally (reflected from the fire, no doubt), a flare of red which spilled out on the branches of the copse, one might indeed have thought it a palace lit for festival, lovely in any case, and comforting to see in the black night where it was the sole repository of brightness, the only hiding-place of life, the one luminous vision which formed a link between the hurrying walker, uneasily conscious of the gloom, and an oasis of tranquillity flooded with human warmth, so that it caught at his imagination, not as a remembered dream, but as a lit interior snugly buried in the night.

5. *Sundays at Etreuilles*

Sunday seemed to Jean to be eminently a sun-day, perhaps because he was allowed to sleep late, and did not wake until the ten o'clock sun was in the sky, having for a long time shone upon the village, and having the appearance of a friend who has let you sleep, but, as soon as you open your eyes, looks as rosy and as red as somebody who has, for several hours, been sitting there beside you, working silently, with sunlight all about him and the sound of swinging church bells in his ears. The lovely, smiling sunshine on his chair, no less than the bells ringing to High Mass, told him which day it was. The weather might turn to rain later, but even when the streets were dark and the sky overcast, he always felt that the sun was hiding somewhere incognito, in the song of the bells, in his own late rising, in the throng that slowly moved along the pavements. There was something like the sun deep down within him, which, even if the rain were falling or a storm raging, made the rain less sad and the lowering sky less heavy. Their daily walk took place just the same and the ladies put their hats on just as usual. Whatever the weather they went to church, where the light entered through windows of red and green and yellow, so that one could not tell at all whether there was rain outside or sunshine. In any case, there was no rain in the church, at which Jean arrived very late, because he had dawdled in bed over his chocolate and because there was no need for men to hear the whole of the Mass. Not, of course, that he would imitate his father whom, sometimes on returning from the service, they would find at home reading, because he had got up late, or because the day was not fine, or because he had gone for a walk, and, catching sight of all the people coming out of church, had turned into a farm track so as not to meet anybody. Since he had set off on his walk as Jean was leaving for Mass, he had told him to tell his mother not to hang about talking when it was over but to come straight back at once, as otherwise she would be late for luncheon and Ernestine, who had been to the early celebration and, though she took great interest in her employers' salvation, took even more in her joint which must be eaten at once when it had been roasted to a turn, had issued orders to the effect that everybody must be home by noon if they expected to get anything worth eating. And, sheltered in the church from rain, Jean would sit down next his mother, though without saying "good morning" since that would not have been good manners in such a place.

But before starting for church he would go down into the kitchen where Ernestine, like Vulcan at his forge, would be stoking up the fire raking the glowing coals with an iron tringle, in an atmosphere of flame, and heat, and crackling which sounded like the mutterings of Hell. But on the range, as in a potter's workshop, and already exhaling clouds of white steam, would be standing a number of little receptacles, round-bellied saucepans and a vast copper, all of them bubbling away and exuding a creamy foam, brown, pink or violet, giving off a smell that was peculiarly their own and seeming to bear witness to the existence of a masterpiece which would later emerge from the violence of her art. The pots would be more numerous than usual, for Sunday was always the occasion for a multiplicity of dishes. On the table was a pile of peas already shelled, looking like small green marbles. At the risk of being late for Mass, Jean had made this visit so as to find out what they were to have for luncheon, as one who might have hastened there agog for news, news which had nothing Platonic about it and which, though it satisfied his curiosity, caused it to rise at once from its ashes, more sensual, more impatient, than ever for a menu may be as informative as a communiqué, but it is also as exciting as a programme. Then he would dart away happy in the knowledge that, during his time in church, the fire would be working enthusiastically in his service (Etreuilles as yet knew nothing of electricity—that other Power) a giant whom men had turned into a cook, that Ernestine, whose hands as coarse looking as those of certain sculptors, certain musicians, would be busy composing for him, with an infinity of gentle touches, a wonderfully finished work of art. Thus, once in church, and seated motionless upon his bench, with nothing to think about, he could brood at leisure on the joint which he had seen delivered to the tamed, industrious flames.

Nor had he said "good morning" to Madame Savinien, the lawyer's wife, tall and white in her black clothes and under her black curls. But she, seeing him arrive, would push her chair back, making it squeak on the stone flags, as a sign that she had noticed him, that being the only greeting she would permit herself to give in church. But there was nothing cold about that greeting, for Jean knew that after Mass, when the worshippers had reached the open doors where could be heard the encouraging sound of talk exchanged between those who had already reached the steps, all those who had shown their consciousness of one another's entry only by slightly moving back a chair so as to allow the arrival to push by, or silently shaking hands over their shoulders, they would embark, while umbrellas were being opened, or the carriage summoned which would take the great lady back to her estate, on all their belated greetings, all their stored-up conversations, all their adjourned good fellowship. This moment was now approaching. The church smelled good and Jean sniffed up, with perhaps even greater relish than the fragrance of incense and the scent of flowers, the delicious odour of the consecrated bun which had just been handed to him by Victor, the grocer's assistant, disguised as a verger, whom Jean pretended not to recognize, as, in a theatre, one does not bow to an actor on the stage whom one happens to know in ordinary life. He took the bun with an air of complete detachment as though the gift were not shortly to be offered to his appetite, like one who receives with a melancholy air an inheritance which he knows full well will be transformed, as soon as decency permits, into a pair of horses or a box at the opera.

The moment of departure came. Madame Santeuil said to her son, whom, until then, she had pretended not to recognize, "Put on your coat, or you'll catch cold," after which she addressed a few words to Madame Savinien, in a voice which she at first kept low, though it grew louder with every step she took, as a relative progressively, but very rapidly, puts off mourning once the reality of grief has ceased. As soon as they reached a point level with the pulpit, where the throng separated into two streams and Jean, out of politeness, stood back against the wooden staircase to make room for his acquaintances to pass—thus exasperating his mother who was a good deal further on— a buzz of conversation, as though a frontier had been reached, became distinctly audible. For though the leading worshippers were already outside the building and though the booming of the organ drifted through the doors, which those leaving the church kept continuously open, the voices of the people on the steps could clearly be heard and the feel of fresh air was on the faces of the departing congregation. Thus, in spite of a momentary return of solemnity in front of the Holy

Water stoup, the journey from the pulpit to the entrance was made in a buzz of conversation. "Don't tell me that Monsieur Santeuil has really turned up!" – "We were wondering whether you could bear to come over to Berceau one evening for a quiet little dinner?" – "We must hurry back because we're having those lovely hares you sent, for luncheon: they were beginning to smell delicious when I came away." – "You're much too kind: I must get my husband to shoot some more, since you're so fond of them." In the porch everyone drew delighted attention to the fact that it had stopped raining. The sky still looked purplish above the house-tops but there was a hint of sunshine in the Square, of that sunshine which, for Jean, was an integral part of Sunday, like the bells and the bun, a stormy sunshine on this particular day and rather too hot, like the bun, which Madame Santeuil, for that reason, found heavy and indigestible, like the array of cakes with crenellated tops of white icing covered with a sprinkling of pink sugar in the window of the large confectioner's shop on the Square, which Jean, since his mother never let him eat them, could only admire as he passed by, though they too, were an inseparable part of Sunday along with the sun, the bells, the bun, and the umbrella of Madame Savinien who walked back with them as far as the rue des Tréfossés, where she looked at her watch and turned back, saying: "I hope you'll enjoy your luncheon: I'm late, too; I'm sure to find that my husband has sat down without me."

Madame Savinien, as it happened, had not very far to go. From the corner of the rue des Tréfossés one could see the tufted trees in her garden peeping over the long stone wall. Then Madame Santeuil went on home with her son, both with their prayer-books in their hands. From the little window of the dining-room which looked on to the street and through which she could see everything that happened, Monsieur Santeuil's aunt had already caught sight of them and said to Ernestine, "You can dish up now." Sometimes, just as they reached the front door, Madame Santeuil, noticing a large black cloud over the weather-cock on the steeple of the church, would say: "There'll be rain before long," and then go into the house and kiss Madame Sureau whom she had not seen earlier, having been ready only just in time to start for church. The old lady was no longer able to go out and spent all her days in an armchair by the window, getting on a little with her needlework, reading the paper for a few moments but, for the most part, passing the time by adjusting her spectacles and watching through

the pane the various people who seemed only to be passing by, though,
for her, who had already seen them once that morning, or was
sufficiently conversant with their habits to know that she might have
seen them, provided conclusive evidence, by their exits and their
entrances, that nothing had changed in the routine of Etreuilles, or, on
the contrary, that something had, some occurrence which would affect
her as much as it did them, in short, that the familiar occupations of
the town were as usual, occupations to which some unexpected event
gave a touch of piquancy and which together formed that gentle
monotony which for her, as it is for all of us, was that most important
of all things—life. And to that she was deeply attached. Through her
window she could take account of all that happened, though she could
no longer play a part in it, except by accepting the message of her eyes
which, in spite of her eighty years, were still good. And so she sat
looking at everything that went on in the street and even beyond it.
She would say to herself: 'There's Monsieur Servan starting off to have
a look at his meadow,' as others might say, "It's late: nearly ten
o'clock!" Sometimes she would think: 'Surely, it can't be ten!' what
could be happening, 'But it *is*. The sun gets up so late these days, that it
seems as though one has only just left one's bed!' Sometimes, it really
wasn't ten. Maybe Monsieur Servan was expecting his children and had
gone into the town before they were due to arrive, on some errand of
his own. Then she would take council of Ernestine. No, this was the
day they were lifting the potato crop. "Oh, that's it, is it: he's getting
in his potatoes? Now I understand," she would say with an air of
satisfaction. "There's Monsieur Saurin just off to Vespers," Ernestine
would remark having caught sight of the grocer issuing from his house,
hatted and gloved, with his wife and their two little girls. "I expect
he's left Victor in charge of the shop, because, this being Sunday,
there'll be a deal of custom."–"You don't surprise me in the least,"
Madame Sureau would reply: "Only a few moments ago I saw
Monsieur Savinien go by with his little book. I *thought* he must be on
his way to Vespers. Heavens! it must be close on three! The sky's
clouding over. I shouldn't wonder if they got drenched before they
reach home. Of course, I know Madame Alexandre (Madame Santeuil) has taken her coat: but perhaps she hasn't started yet: perhaps
you'd better give her Alfred's umbrella." (Alfred was Jean's uncle).
"Not started yet! Didn't you see her waving to you through the
window?" Ernestine would answer with a roughness which always

gave much offence to Jean when he heard her talking like that to his
great-aunt, but in which Madame Sureau found none. Then, since it
was getting dark, Madame Sureau would draw aside the curtain so as
to be able to see better through the little window, and put some more
charcoal in her footwarmer. If Jean came into the room, she accepted
his kiss without returning it as though she had been some brightly
coloured reliquary. For, in the autumn of life her face had assumed the
red tint of a Virginia Creeper, and showed a network of veins. But she
scarcely ever moved. Then Jean would hurry out again. "I don't know
what's come over the weather: I'm positively freezing! Ernestine, give
me my coat," Madame Sureau would say conscious, in the stillness of
her dining-room, of the blustering wind outside. "Look, there's
Monsieur Savin just opening his umbrella. I knew from the way the
blood's been rushing to my head that it wouldn't be long before we
had rain. I've felt it coming on for the past two days." And indeed, red
in the face if it was going to rain, or with her coat over her shoulders
if the wind was getting up, Madame Sureau looked liked the little
monk hanging at the corner of the shop belonging to the optician who
gave Jean lessons in mathematics and, according to local gossip, had a
prosperously married daughter at Tours.

"Gracious! there's the doctor's gig come round for him again! What
a life that man leads! Fancy having to go out on a day like this! I
shouldn't wonder if there's somebody ill at the Dufoc place—I saw
young Dufoc going into the chemist's a while back."–"No," said
Ernestine, "his housekeeper told me he had a call from farther away
than that, it's somebody over at Les Berceaux." But Madame Sureau
who had never got as far as Les Bearceaux for the last twenty-five years
took no interest in what might be happening there except when
servant-girls were recruited at Etreuilles to help with a wedding or
when, in case of illness, they sent in for the doctor or the Curé. 'Ah!
there's my old friend Gigout getting into the trap,' reflected Madame
Sureau watching the doctor climb into the conveyance. 'Jeannot's got
to help him now: come to that, has it? Why, only two years ago he
could manage for himself. He's getting on. Well, we can't stay young
for ever. He must be rising eighty-six: not the man he was.'

Occasionally, somebody walking along the street would stop in
front of the three stone steps which led up to the front door. "A visitor
for you!" Ernestine would say. By this time the individual in question
would be out of sight. Then they would hear the thin tinkle of the bell

which, when the handle was pulled, always went on ringing for a while. Such visits were rare. People did, however, occasionally come, Madame Savinien, for instance, who was always very kind to Madame Sureau. Her hostess would ask her for the latest news. Then, "It's time for me to be off," her visitor would say. "It's no fun being old," said Madame Sureau, "my poor ribs keep me awake all night long and I can scarcely eat a thing nowadays." She complained about her life, but loved it and everything to do with it. If, when the day came round for Jean, her nephew, and Madame Santeuil to go back to Paris, she felt a little bit sad, she soon cheered up at the thought that she, at least, would be staying on at Etreuilles—with plenty to occupy her—ordering her meals, watching Monsieur Savinien go by and seeing the Saurins opposite sitting down to dinner. Sometimes she heard the passing bell, and thought to herself, 'Another of them gone.' Then she would send Ernestine to ask the grocer who it was. 'That was why I didn't see Monsieur Gigout come back.'

*

On Sundays she put on over her dress a tippet trimmed with bows of ribbon. She sent round to Monsieur Savinien for the Supplement of *Le Petit Journal* and when she heard the bells ringing for High Mass and saw everybody going to church, asked for her prayer-book, put on her spectacles, and, sitting all by herself and holding her book to the window so as to get a better light, read the prayers, as for sixty years she had done as one of the congregation in church, watched, as she walked thither, from their windows by old ladies who now had vanished as completely as a name above a shop which has changed owners, or as the books from the window of a bankrupt stationer's whose business has been taken over by a grocer.

Jean was singing as he walked: *Elle a dit de moi et ce qu'elle a dit est sincère*, but the happy gestures, the quickened pace, the energetic movements of the head, with which he accompanied the rather commonplace little tune showed clearly that its significance for him was much like that of certain simple words which come to us in moments of danger and, brought to the surface of our minds by some chance, mysterious, trick of memory, happen to be charged with the duty of playing the part which *should* be played by speech in our heroic adventure. It was in just such a mood that Jean, for the last half hour, had been singing

Elle a dit de moi et ce qu'elle a dit est sincère, without for a moment thinking what the words meant and in a tone of voice which was really only
an expression of the unconscious happiness which the bad weather was
producing in him, and his feeling that he was in tune with it, as he was
with the village grown suddenly dark and stormy because of the rain-
cloud overhead and the road which, a few moments back, had felt a
few eddies of dust and the rising wind playing in the grass, but was
now spotted with large drops. His was the kind of satisfaction one sees
visibly displayed on the face of any walker on the way home to change
his clothes, even though he may express it in some such words as,
"What a filthy day!" a phrase which is as little relevant to his true
feelings (which are shown by the gay tone in which he utters that
gloomy observation) as was the tune of *Elle a dit de moi*, feelings
which a growing sense of well-being and comfort drive away when,
instead of walking under the threatening sky, we go to the telephone
to ask a question, or, at the very least, set out in a cab drawn by a
spanking horse, from which we look with a superior air upon the
passers-by but from which, too, we can study the rain-charged clouds
as though they formed part of a stage-scene, as something, in fact,
which leaves us indifferent or prompts us to make to the friend beside
us some such pleasing comment as, "Just look at that sky—a perfect
Turner!"

A significant yawn or the coming of a gloomy thought are proof
enough that the growing sense of comfort has suppressed the happy
mood which we saw displayed upon Jean's face a moment back. But
you would have noticed that it long continued had you followed his
movements when, having taken off his boots and changed his clothes,
he went down to luncheon in the little Etreuilles dining-room where
his uncle had had the fire lit, the warmth of which drew from each
member of the party standing by it, a remark to the effect that it "really
was freezing", and where, by the window, Jean, parting the curtains,
looked out at the rain driving down with innumerable purplish lances
into the narrow rue de la Mercerie and was filled with the hope that it
would rain still harder, although his uncle had said that it would be the
ruin of the crops, with that ferocity of feeling which comes to us when,
faced by the spectacle of the unleashed elements, and transposing ourselves in imagination into the very heart of violence, we long for
the downpour to grow even fiercer, or when we feel disappointed that
the waves, during a storm at sea, are not as high as we had hoped they

would be, although we know that there are ships out there, or when, making ourselves one with the falling hail-stones, we become intoxicated by their mad rage and long for them to dash against the windows with still fiercer fury and to melt less quickly. It was a delicious drama to watch from the security of the little dining-room where a fire had been lit and the servant-girl had said, "It's so dark you'll almost be needing a lamp!" where everyone was as interested and contented as onlookers at some miraculous occurrence and Jean, his uncle having exclaimed, "There's poor Madame Levis without an umbrella—just look at her running!" rushed to the low window which was on a level with the street to catch the ravishing spectacle and saw the poor lady in her best black dress running so hard that she was constantly within an ace of falling down. "She must be coming back from Mass," he said, and waited impatiently for the moment when *their* cook, after seeing *her* cook, would be in a position to recount exactly to what extent her new dress had been spoiled. And then, how lovely when, the rain having stopped, the sun came out again and shone straight in through the windows. In a very short while one would be able to leave the house. But such natural dramas when witnessed from the depth of Gothic halls, where the daylight never shows in its true colours, where the watchers are protected even from the sound of the rain, and, looking into the Winter Garden, can see orchids growing in the depth of winter, lose their power to interest, and, at most, drive the blasé man-of-the-world to switch on the electric light with a bored look if it gets too dark and the weather is too bad, or, after a brief hesitation, to say to the coachman, "I shan't be going out today."

At Etreuilles, however, now that the rain had stopped and because it was Sunday, one could see the shopkeepers, one by one, putting up their shutters, the people in their Sunday best coming out into the Square and, from the windows of Monsieur Sandré's house, where luncheon would be late, ladies with handsome ribbons walking by and the Curé with two little boys who much intrigued Monsieur Sandré, until he discovered that they could only be the sons of the good man's sister, from which he concluded that they must all be feeling very happy and that undoubtedly Madame Torrèche must have arrived, which caused him to wonder why Monsieur Dieutourne, whom he had seen that morning, had said nothing about the approaching visit. "I must find out about that," he concluded. But since they were having luncheon

late, in spite of the fact that the street was beginning to fill with a
Sunday crowd, only the large apple tart was served, a tart that looked
as yellow as the door of the General Shop on the Square but covered in
a sauce as red as the flowers of the pink may which grew round
the porch of the church opposite the shop upon the Square. It was
definitely a Sunday tart, gazed at with admiration and eaten with relish
on those Sunday noons, with the narrow street outside on the same
level as the room and the sky purplish-blue when the weather was
stormy, or a-flicker with gold when the sun was shining. On that day
the company round the table was more numerous than usual because,
since the General Shop closed on Sundays, as did the other shops on the
sunshiny or rain-soaked Square, opposite the church which sparkled
with sunlight or looked purple when storm-clouds lowered, Jean's
cousins, a boy and a girl, came to luncheon, decked out in their best
clothes like all the folk of Illiers on a Sunday, with quiet voices and
pink faces which seemed to show the colours that went with the smells
of the shop, of the shelves loaded with stuffs, where Monsieur Clinteau
would summon Monsieur Fernand with a snap of the finger and thumb
—what exactly did that mean?—where the grocer entered without
embarrassment, and Monsieur Clinteau, in a neat black coat shook
hands with him though he sported only a blue smock, but as an actor
dressed as a middle-class character may shake hands on the stage with
somebody dressed as a peasant. Was not the grocer the nephew of the
Mayor, who had married Monsieur Clinteau's own cousin, that elderly
and markedly devout spinster who was following a little further down
the street with all her dogs and her maid, who was regarded as a social
equal, and on whom Madame Santeuil relied to look in on her mother-
in-law during the winter, and keep her amused, because they got on so
well and liked going to Mass together? So Monsieur Clinteau said to
the grocer, "How are you, Monsieur Saural, and how's your good
lady?" At these words, a malicious and ill-tempered look came into his
face, an expression which showed now and again when he was speaking, like a sort of nervous tic, and which he accompanied, both in the
shop and at his uncle's table, with a snapping of his finger and thumb.
He spoke slowly, picking his words in a dignified manner, and, when
the grocer asked him for a yard of cloth, directing his gaze from the top
of the ladder on which he was perched to the far end of the shop,
would say very slowly, "Be so good, Monsieur Fernand, to look out
some—cloth, you said, didn't you?—for Monsieur Saural—something

rather special, mind, and be quick about it!" but being incapable of actually framing a reproach for a fault which he could not specify, continued to fix his assistant with a majestic glare, while he slowly resumed, as though returning to calm waters, the task on which he had been engaged of looking through a stack of materials, bale by bale. In just such a way would Lieutenant Marengo, finding fault with one of his men, and saying "Diable!" (with great emphasis on the *a*), and in an effort to recover his own dignity as though he were the emperor in person at the head of his army, have looked at the fellow with a cold blue eye and a fixed stare which served to conceal his embarrassment, while continuing to give deliberate orders to the rest of the detachment, so as to produce the impression that his mind was still full of the reprimands to which he had avoided giving violent utterance.

But suddenly, out in the sunshiny Square, the clashing bells sent out a first summons, then a second after which, moment by moment, they indulged in a quick interchange, the first answering the second, the second the third, or according as one heard them, the third the fourth, the fourth the fifth, the last seeming to reply to the last but one, or calling up the next in succession—it all depended on how one caught the rhythm—and all together apparently engaged, with the superb and regular strokes into which they were putting every ounce of their strength, in battering down the tottering walls of silence. With all the accumulated force of their swift and rushing attack they seemed to be striking at the body of the quivering din without succeeding in breaking it while the sun as though set in motion by the ringer, looked for a moment as though it had gone into hiding only to shine out again with redoubled power on the window of the pastrycook's shop. But all the time that the bells were deafening the ears of the good folk of Illiers—awakening in their minds a feeling of familiarity since they all knew the ringer, but also of respect, because well before his day (this present ringer having held his position for only two years) the bells, for as long as they could remember, had sounded whenever anybody died (even when one had lost one's own mother) or whenever anybody got married (even on the occasion of one's own wedding, when they had summoned the neighbours) whenever one had to go to church, there to witness those very mysterious matters which always ended in the same well-known way when the altar-boy (the cobbler's apprentice) still swinging his censer signalled to Madame Clinteau that he would let her have her shoes back without fail that afternoon and especially when the bun which the priest had just blessed, while one kept one's eyes lowered and the sun shone into the church through windows of azure and blood-red, was handed round and an hour later, in the little dining-room with its white net curtains and the plates with their far from religious pictures adorning the walls, the prayer-books having been laid aside along with the fine Sunday hat and the sable muff, would be consumed like any ordinary bun—all the time that the bells, clashing together more and more quickly, seemed to set trembling the widening walls of silence and the great waves sent out their own particular din, the Square was filling up with ladies in their Sunday best and gentlemen carrying prayer-books, with the pastrycook appearing at the door of his shop, and going back for his cap lest he get a touch of the sun, and Monsieur Clinteau himself, abandoning the grocer who was still waiting for his length of cloth, walking across the shop to look out of the window where the blind cast a cool black shadow on the floor and bowing to his wife who smiled back at him as she passed with their little girl on the way to Mass—all this hurry and bustle of the good people of Illiers arriving at the church porch, this thronging of tradesmen at the doors of their shops or behind the windows, seemed, as the hands of the great clock drew nearer to the X of ten, to have been set in motion by the self-same operation that had started the bells a-clashing.

Little by little, as the bells swung more slowly the faithful became fewer, nearly all of them having disappeared into the church. But as a single isolated stroke rings out just when one thinks that the silence has returned to stay, Madame Sainters would be seen walking very quickly. "She's late, she's hurrying," Monsieur Clinteau would say. A considerable while later, Monsieur Grosier, making no more noise than a half-hour strike, would put in an appearance. "A fine time to go to Mass," Monsieur Clinteau would say to him, coming to the door and snapping his finger and thumb. But Monsieur Grosier laughed, for he had the reputation of being a man with an impish sense of humour, who loved to get to church just as the sermon was drawing to a close. At this moment the birds who had taken flight from the belfry when the faithful arrived and the bells sounded their final clash, all at two minutes past the hour returned to perch upon the tower, and were now busily engaged in hopping from one place to another and wheeling about the belfry. A gentle pigeon, looking as though it were cut out of zinc, had settled so motionless on the helmet of Jeanne d'Arc's statue, that it gave the appearance of an ornament, in perfect taste, added by the artist as an afterthought. Half past ten, and time for the shop to close. And so it was that Monsieur Clinteau, on that particular day with his wife and small daughter went to take luncheon in Madame Sureau's dining-room, where he embarked, with much snapping of finger and thumb, on the task of explaining to Jean the subjects depicted on the plates. But he was not sitting beside him, and had to pass the plates, many of which were sufficiently amusing by reason of the wording inscribed beneath the picture which he took as the starting-point of his humorous comments, through the connecting links provided by Monsieur Sandré or Jean's young cousin. For Monsieur Sandré was no longer as he once had been, put next to Jean. Jean had contrived this change after secret negotiations with his mother. For his uncle had been in the habit of tickling him as a joke, and this tickling had been such an agonizing experience for the boy that he would have preferred death to a life in which he was made to sit even if only once a week next to somebody who tickled him, all the more so since he had, on the subject of tickling, which his mother dreaded because of his nervous temperament, rather obscure ideas so that he regarded it as something that might be obscene and was certainly cruel. For two Sundays running Madame Santeuil had forgotten to make the change, and on those occasions life had seemed to Jean a thing of gloom and anxiety. It never occurred to him that a change of seats might be possible and saw before him an endless future darkened by terror. There are times when the weight of purely imaginary anxieties, and often the very real torment of genuine sufferings, could be shifted by a mere word which would cost nothing to the person capable of uttering it. But precisely because it does cost nothing, because it is a mere trivial incident in his life, the person in question puts it off to another day, and then forgets all about it, or decides that it is not a matter of urgency. What he does not know is that the lapse of time between now and tomorrow will be filled with a sleeplessness far worse than the pains *he* would consider important, and even if he does know, he regards the whole business as something not worth bothering about because he is aware that a word from him—which he will speak should the opportunity arise—will put an end to it as though by magic.

*

It was not only in Etreuilles that the tranquillizing influence of Sunday was felt. And as in spring the clematis in the chinks of the Curé's wall without any premeditated planning with the buttercups and poppies of the fields, the hawthorn and wild cherries in the hedgerows, undertook the job on feast days of decorating the walls and, at the critical moment having made themselves ready in silence, hoist their purple colours to flutter and glitter in the sun, so when Jean and his uncle at the end of an afternoon walk turned into the Aigneaux farm, they were sure to find Madame Laudet, whose person seemed to be composed of clogs, a fine figure in a white apron and regular and distinguished features, which for all their charm, inspired those who saw her with feelings of respect, offering to the entranced gaze of a great concourse of people seated round large wooden tables under the apple-trees the spectacle, beneath a naturally dignified face with neat hair arrange in complicated curls, of a superb bosom of green silk trimmed with black braid, green sleeves and a plum-coloured skirt. But in spite of the splendour of her toilet, since on that day of the week she was always desperately busy because of the crowds that came to the farm, she invariably retained her clogs. But this scrap of the broken chrysalis was no more unpleasing to the eye than would be the sight of Hector or Andromache in the wings, with their own hair plainly visible, waiting until the last moment before assuming their wigs, or of a hostess who not content with merely giving a party, but herself acting in the play which she is to present for her guests' entertainment, feels it incumbent upon her to mingle with the crowd in day clothes before appearing behind the footlights, since an evening dress would not be in keeping with the part she is to play. In just such a manner did Madame Laudet go from table to table, carrying a bowl of milk or a mug of cider, clad in the green dress which was but one among the many flowers in this gay social springtide, of this burgeoning of the happy human throng with its thousand different colours that go by the name of Sunday Best. The phrase, no doubt, would be spoken with a touch of disdain by a lady of fashion who had thought it more suitable to attend this sort of gathering in her simplest clothes, and with an irritability which would merely be the expression of her distaste, not deigning or not being able, to join in the general Sunday merriment, at having to expose herself to its influence, and, because she was conscious of a craving for and of the absence of a sense of pleasure in herself, feeling that there was something almost insulting in the pleasure of others.

All the tables being occupied, and fresh visitors arriving all the time, many had to wait for their orders to be attended to, in spite of the zeal showed by the little waitress who with her fair curly hair, her white frock and pink sash, was busy carrying trays as big as herself, with the rapidity and elegance of a dancer, standing when she was at rest, motionless and graceful, listening to the customers' requirements and answering in a low, shy voice which showed that she had been well brought up. Quite often, though there might be a number of customers waiting to be served, they scarcely ventured to remind the proprietress of their needs out of sheer politeness for Madame Laudet was respected as a very good sort of woman much superior to her position which in its turn was vastly superior to the life she led—seeing that she owned well-nigh all the farms in the neighbourhood of Etreuilles. All those present, moreover, were completely under the influence of her character and the charm of her appearance, and the chief reason for their going to the farm when they felt the need of a little refreshment was a wish to see her and to be in her home, much as some people may frequent certain restaurants, though the reason they give may be that the cider is better there than anywhere else or the cheese particularly good. But then do not people of fashion maintain that if they frequent one hostess rather than another, it is because she always provides choco-late biscuits and is the best maker of tea in town?

These "Madame Laudet Sundays" when the weather was fine reached their high point round about five o'clock. With the pleasure that she felt at seeing all the tables in the open air packed full, went the satisfaction of the shopkeeper whose business is thriving—was she, in that, so very different from a fashionable hostess?—and something like a modest pride at finding herself surrounded by so many kindly folk, and at being able to wield such power. The air would resound with compliments on her cider, on her appearance, on the number of her patrons—all of which constituted a little dig at the rival farm of Les Noyers where there was nobody. And all the while fresh arrivals would be turning up, and she was as much moved as though their presence had been a manifestation designed to do honour to the crown-ing of her life's work. Truth to tell in the simple-minded pleasure which she showed in listening to these compliments and accepting this homage she suffered far less from self-deception than does a hostess who just because her party has been well attended by guests who when they leave will grumble about how bored they have been and make jokes about the age of their hostess and her ridiculous mannerisms is as excited as any professor whose final lecture has been graced by a really impressive attendance. For in Etreuilles and the villages round about, the regular clients of Les Aigneaux spoke of Madame Laudet with the same warm feelings as sent them in droves to the farm on Sundays, and the same respect which they showed when compelled to wait uncomplainingly for the cup of milk or mug of cider which they had ordered. And as at certain parties one knows that one will get only tea and biscuits, and that one would be looked at very much askance if one asked for chocolate, so if a newcomer happened to order beer— "We don't serve beer," Madame Laudet would haughtily reply, and look with such disdain at the wretched man who did not know how to behave, that all those present would study him for a moment or two with ill-disguised curiosity and a deal of unpleasant sniggering.

Loyal to her ancient ways, Madame Laudet refused to enter into competition with many of the farms on the outskirts of holiday resorts, which followed in the steps of the local wine shops and offered for sale absinthe, vermouth and cherry-brandy. All she cared about was keeping up the reputation of her farm, and in this she much resembled those hostesses whose parties are known for good talk, and who refuse to provide their guests with music or private theatricals as some of their rivals do. "If they don't like it here, they can go somewhere else," said Madame Laudet, who was never one to entice new clients, but preferred to make access to her farm difficult, and was at pains to keep away customers whose insistence on absinthe—perhaps her dislike of it was due to the difficulty of serving it—inspired her with a feeling of mistrust, about which she would expatiate to her old regulars who had never in their lives asked her for such a thing. "I'd rather have nothing to do with people like that," she said. "I *choose* my customers. This isn't the sort of place where any Tom, Dick or Harry can come. Many would like to whom I won't have on the place. I serve only the folk I like." She was not alone in wanting to think of her house as something rather special.

1. *The Philosophy Class*

It was half past eight. The boys were waiting in the classroom, all of them rather restless and excited because their new philosophy Professor, Monsieur Beulier, whom they were to meet for the first time, had not yet turned up. Already several of the older pupils, ambitious of dealing directly with the authorities, and thinking that it would be rather grand to be seen walking back with them across the yard under the curious eyes of boys in the other rooms staring out with their noses pressed to the windows, were making ready to fetch the Headmaster and his Vice.

"Oh, stow it, you fools!" shouted Buffeteur, whose loud voice could always make itself heard and whose monstrous laziness had turned him into something of a hero not only in the eyes of the other boys and the school servants, but even in those of the Vice who when he said good morning to him did so with the timid and protective smile of a Minister meeting the Leader of the Opposition. The Headmaster himself when he visited the form to hear the results of the terminal essays, when the Professor announced as he always had done and always would do: "Bottom, Buffeteur," and Buffeteur, standing up in his place, called out with good-natured insolence: "Here, sir!" the Headmaster himself could not refrain from directing an ironical but friendly and unconsciously respectful smile at the great lout who moved throughout the year from bottom place to bottom place with the unfailing, unhesitating, unchanging regularity of a natural law. Jean was jerked violently out of his day-dreaming by Buffeteur's noisy interruption. He knew that Monsieur Beulier—in whose division there had at first been some hesitation in placing him—"We're afraid," Madame Santeuil had said, "that it may be the undoing of what little brain he has"—was a great philosopher, the profoundest mind with which even the most intelligent of his companions had ever come in contact, and he was trying, though without much success, in a mood of thrilled expectation and with high hopes that his sluggish temperament would derive great benefit from being trained in constant self-analysis, to imagine what the great man, so unaccountably late in turning up, would look like. "Yes, you nit-wits," went on Buffeteur, to an accompaniment of shouts and yells from the other boys who were now standing on the benches, "what on earth do you want to go and tell the Old Man for? Can't you get it into your thick heads that all we've got to do is shut the door as though the Prof were here, and carry on as we dam' well like?"

At this precise moment there appeared in the doorway a red-haired gentleman out of breath with running, having a silk scarf round his neck, a pair of pince-nez on his nose, and a brief-case under his arm. The boys, who were engaged in the dangerous occupation of clambering along the tops of the desks, like sailors on a ship clinging to girders, or balancing precariously on a couple of planks to an accompaniment of noises as various and as deafening as those of wind, straining rigging, and rough seas, made a hurried dash for their places. In so precipitous so headlong a manner had they carried through this manœuvre, that the professor on entering the room, saw them all there before him in their seats, like oarsmen at the thwarts, their faces still red, and their hair tousled by the wind, ready to obey orders. Jean could not really imagine what this philosophy class would be like, and had to fall back on the works of Renan and Barrès in an attempt to conjure up the right atmosphere of disillusioned charm. Then Monsieur Beulier began to speak. Jean was surprised to find that he had a marked Bordeaux accent. He said "phi-lo-so-phy", "fool-ish-ness", giving an equal weight to each of the syllables. His lively, ruddy face expressed neither scepticism, amateurishness, nor a desire to send his listeners to sleep. He spoke with a fluency which made Jean, who had never heard anything like it, feel so exhausted at the end of five minutes that he ceased to follow what was being said. Not once did the words "vanity of life" or "nirvana" come like a familiar and delightful refrain to recall his wandering attention. Never through the whole course of the lessons did there occur any of those sublime and sweet-scented images before which, throughout this headlong intellectual race, he might have paused for rest as at a flower-strewn wayside shrine. Nor was that all. He, who knew that there was no such thing as the "good" or the "true" was staggered to hear this man, about whose genius he had heard so much, speaking of goodness, truth and certainty, and amazed that he should refer, with obvious pleasure, to certain mechanical inventions, certain ways of growing flowers, which he had always thought could be of interest only to those who knew nothing about the world of the spirit. He had thought of the world of the spirit as of something superimposed on mere earthiness, in which there was no place for such material trivialities as scents, pity, corruption, melancholy, and cats. But chiefly he had thought of science as a form of knowledge which could appeal only to that barbarous race of beings, ignorant of the Muses and the Gods, whom the mathematics master thrilled each Monday morning with the new discoveries which emerged from the poisonous stenches and murderous explosions of experiments which always failed to come out as they should, and in the primitive and rasping music of chalk moving to and fro like a saw as he illustrated his horrible demonstrations on the blackboard. And so it was that Jean began to entertain doubts of the worth of his new professor, when he heard him calling the Law of Interferences "beautiful", and, referring to the labours of the bee, saying in a soft, sad voice: "There are times when I reflect how much happier than us are the scientists who know all about these matters. I have often thought how pleasant it must be for a very intelligent scientist or even for an ordinary man with a lively gift of curiosity, to have a thorough understanding of such things: there are moments when the wisdom of the printed word seems cold and lifeless in comparison with a bee's intense existence."

At this point, Jean gave up listening, and began to talk to the boys round him. Monsieur Beulier motioned to him to stop. A few moments later he started again. "You will take an hour's detention," said Monsieur Beulier, pointing at him, but in so calm a voice that Jean, accustomed to the violent outbursts of his other masters, concluded that what he was being given was not a real punishment at all but only a warning. Besides, when class was over, and Monsieur Beulier learned the name of the chatterbox against whom he had taken disciplinary measures, he would see that the offender was none other than the Santeuil who had been so warmly commended to him, and realize, that he had already looked over his holiday task. Of this effort Jean was excessively proud. In fact he was trembling with impatience, convinced that the work in question would give Monsieur Beulier a very high opinion of his abilities. Already, in imagination, he could hear him addressing the assembled class: "Gentlemen, you have in your midst one who is very much more than a schoolboy, one who is even now a poet and in time will be a great one." Seeing in his mind's eye the astonished expressions on the faces of his companions, tasting the sweet honey of those anticipated words, and each moment ringing the changes on that wonderful scene to come, he was working himself into a fever of impatience, calculating that a week could have been scarcely long enough to enable Monsieur Beulier to have read his work through and form a considered opinion of it, and realizing that being unaware of those signs of genius which marked him off so clearly from the rest of the class, Monsieur Beulier was probably still thinking of him as merely one of a crowd. Much to his surprise however fifteen minutes before the end of the hour, Monsieur Beulier pulled from his brief-case a pile of papers which Jean recognized as the holiday tasks. "I have decided to work through these before beginning my course, so as to waste as little time as possible," said Monsieur Beulier, and Jean's heart began to beat so violently that he thought it would burst. "None of these attempts are worth considering in detail," and Jean silently completed the sentence with, "but there are one or two which I have laid aside, because they are not, strictly speaking, school essays at all. . . . I won't go so far as to apply the word masterpieces to them, but I can already detect in their writers some premonitory flashes of the sacred fire." "They are pretty poor stuff," went on Monsieur Beulier, and his voice sounded very gentle, as he smilingly added, "but don't let that discourage you. No doubt, you were tired and had better things to do than work. I do not propose to judge you on the strength of these efforts: I shall merely make a few comments which may be useful to you." At last he reached the letter S. Having worked through a few other names, he said, "And now we come to Monsieur Santeuil. His is not one of the worst of these performances, though I can't go so far as to call it good. It is full" (like the others, of wildness and incoherence, said Santeuil to himself) "of all those current clichés, those literary bad manners, which you have picked up from newspapers and magazines. It is not your fault: you are not responsible. It would be foolish to expect you at your age to have settled standards of taste. A scrap of taste you certainly have: but it is only a scrap, a tiny flotsam of taste submerged in much that is bad. Still, it is there. You have a long way to go before you can hope to write" (a masterpiece, thought Santeuil) "a philosophical dissertation. You must learn to prune your style with infinite pains of all those metaphors, of all those images, which even if they were a good deal better, might appeal to a poet, but even so would be intolerable in a philosophical argument. But it is a mistake—even when the Professor of Literature is to be your audience—to raise your voice in order to utter banalities . . . *the scarlet flames of the setting sun*, indeed—how dare you write down such stuff! It's the kind of thing you might find in a small provincial newspaper— no, not even provincial, it would be truer to say, Colonial. Just conceivably, the editor of the *Mozambique Chronicle* might decorate one of his articles with such odds and ends of coloured glass and it is equally conceivable that the local ladies might hail him as a new Chateaubriand. But I'm making too much of such silliness—the truth is you wrote it without thinking. Again, why all this endless talk of exquisite odours and balmy fragrance? It conveys nothing whatever to the imagination, but is no more than the stock-in-trade of every little pedlar of literary confectionery. That's where things like this belong. No doubt you, like everybody else, have experienced the noble pleasure which certain scents can produce. It would be very much more interesting if you tried to indicate what the smells were. See how flabby and vague your phrases are. You say—*there one could breathe in heady odours from lilac and from heliotrope, rich with a wealth of obscure suggestions*. In the first place, leave *suggestions* alone, if all you can tell us about them is that they are *obscure*. If you can't throw any light upon them, you'd better say nothing at all. And don't mix up the scent of the lilac with the scent of the heliotrope. You must know that one catches the fresh smell of the lilac only after rain, whereas the heliotrope does not give the fullness of its scent—which is very subtle—except when the sun is on it. But it's not my job to give you all this good advice. I'm here for one purpose, and one purpose only, to teach you philosophy." The truth was that whenever Jean had been walking in a garden he had been reading poetry, and had never used his eyes nor smelled the flowers. All this discrimination meant nothing to him, and, in any case, he had found the professor's simple discourse curiously unattractive, since there had been nothing in it of those linguistic surprises, those imaginative purple passages which continually held, stormed and ravished his attention when he read even the less competent short stories printed in *Gil Blas* or the *Echo de Paris*. Though he felt no grudge against this man who had so suddenly, so violently, pricked the bubble of his self-esteem, he could not help thinking of him with a sense of timid and melancholy mistrust.

As soon as the class was dismissed, confident that Monsieur Beulier, on hearing his name, would be reminded of all the laudatory things he had heard about him, Jean said, with a smile, "I'm Santeuil, sir: the chap you punished just now." Monsier Beulier showed not the least astonishment. "I've come to ask you to let me off, sir." – "Let you off, young man?" asked Monsieur Beulier in his most honeyed tones: "Of course, it's all very tiresome for you, and, to tell the truth, I don't much like this detention system. It means you'll have to come along here tomorrow and spend an hour doing something which won't be of much use to you, when you would be much more sensibly employed in going for a walk to Versailles with a friend. You are perfectly right, I dislike this repressive system of punishment." – 'Well,' thought Santeuil, 'I've got off, even if the initiative *did* have to come from me.' – "Yes, indeed," continued the professor, "it's altogether a very stupid business"—and in the look he gave Santeuil there was an affectionate gleam of a kind that Jean had not so far noticed, "but how can I possibly let you off? No, I can't do that," he went on more briskly. "When I took this job on, I assumed the duty of making you all work, to the best of my ability, and I am responsible for the times when, as a result of talking to your neighbour, or of any other distraction, you don't work. It is not for me to change the disciplinary system of this school. Detention is one of its sanctions. You talked in class; I gave you fair warning, you went on talking, and now you've got to be punished. I can do nothing at all about it. But is there, perhaps, something behind this request of yours?—Some important duty you have to perform on Thursday?—that might make a difference?" – "No, sir," said Santeuil, going very red. "Then you will come in on Thursday, and do your hour—is that clear? But time's getting on, and I expect you want your lunch as much as I do," and hurriedly taking leave of Santeuil, Monsieur Beulier disappeared at a run.

2. *Henri de Réveillon*

"Mamma, Réveillon would love to come to lunch one day: when shall I ask him?"–"Well let us say Saturday, dear boy, if that suits you: your Aunt Louise is coming in to see me early in the afternoon and it might amuse your friend to meet her."–"That's a splendid idea!" Réveillon accepted the invitation, and, on the very same day, when Jean got home, he found that cards had been left. "Henri was dreadfully sorry not to find your mother in. Please make his appologies to her for not having yet called on her Day at Home, but you know how much he has to do." Jean took some of his savings, and at once went off to order a supply of cards. As soon as they were delivered, he left two on Madame de Réveillon, taking great care to turn the corners down. But what was his surprise when, next day, he found a card for him: LE DUC DE RÉVEILLON. He thought, at first, that something must have happened to Henri, and that his father had sent for him. Then it occurred to him that, if that had been the case, the Duke would have left a message. Besides, the concierge informed him that the card had been delivered by a footman. Since, therefore, he could think of no reason which would explain this attention, he concluded that it must be an exceptional favour generously accorded by an eminent man to a boy of seventeen who had always thought that men "of a certain age" left cards only on the heads of families or those who were engaged in a profession. Knowing no more of that tenderness, respect and kindness in others which his affectionate heart so badly craved than the pain of always being deprived of such manifestations, he felt an uprush of delicious pleasure which, immediately heightened by an emotion of gratitude, had after a few moments, developed into a sort of a love for the old Duke, into a passionate desire to show his devotion, to fling himself at his feet, and to die for his sake. His feelings were comparable to those of a young conscript whose ear Napoleon had tweaked, burning with a desire to cover with tears and kisses the hand which had so honoured him. But, on his way to the Réveillon mansion to leave word for the Duke, walking quickly, with a look of rapture on his

165

face, and the general appearance of a lunatic, he began once more to wonder whether the whole thing hadn't been just a mistake on the footman's part. Fortunately, he met his Aunt Louise who informed him that it was a generally understood courtesy for a husband to acknowledge a call made on him and his wife by leaving cards. There *were* fashionable folk who did not leave cards on young men but most of them did. If Jean for instance left cards on the Tonnereaus, whom he did not know, the probability was that on the following day he would find a card from the Marquis de Tonnereau. Jean thanked his aunt, and returned home thoroughly disappointed, and almost on the verge of tears, but pleased, all the same, to be able to tell his parents that the Duc de Réveillon had left a card on him. He did, however, wish that his father would leave a card on Henri de Réveillon, and was angry when his mother objected. "But his father left one on *me*." – "I don't know what people do in the world his father moves in, but in ours it would be considered quite ridiculous. I can't see your father, who is an extremely busy man, leaving a card on a boy of seventeen!" – "Why do you say seventeen? —Henri is six months older than I am." Finally, Madame Santeuil yielded to the representations made by her husband, and Jean gave his father a grateful hug. Still, he was somewhat bothered about whether the card would be left on the Duke at the same hour as the Duke had left his, and whether the formality could be carried through as well in the morning as the afternoon. But happy in this first victory he thought it wise not to press his advantage too far but to exploit his success with moderation. He was merciful to the enemy, and gave a magnanimous kiss to his mother who had stood her ground to the last, and had retreated only when Monsieur Santeuil had made it clear that he was on his son's side.

Before going further, I ought to say something about that Aunt Louise who was due to make Henri de Réveillon's acquaintance on "Saturday, round about two" and who had instructed Jean in the flattering but deceptive customs—almost all the customs of the great world are flattering but deceptive—pertaining to the use of what are generally known as visiting-cards. As the result of no mere chance, but because of deep-buried causes lying behind the phenomena of Society —so called—no less than behind phenomena of a more serious nature, behind social situations no less than behind historical events, the salon of Madame Antoine Desroches, before her marriage, Mademoiselle Grimaldi and Madame Santeuil's cousin, whom Jean knew as Aunt

Louise, had become, at about the time when Jean first met Henri de
Réveillon, and so remained until last year, one of the most sought-after
of all the brilliant salons of Paris. The chapter now to follow would
be just as worthy of a place in a psychological work dealing with
different varieties of human ambition or in an historical study of the
last years of the nineteenth century as in this far more modest story of
Jean Santeuil.

Poor, intelligent, ambitious and clever, Antoine Desroches had
during the period of his military service become the close friend of the
young Frédéric de Breslau Prince of Bremen who was the son of one
of the outstanding personalities of Imperial society and a member of
the Emperor's family. At the time of their first meeting Antoine had
already been awarded the *Médaille d'Honneur de l'École des Beaux-
Arts* and was shortly to go to Rome. He had staggered the young
Prince by the solid weight of his knowledge in all matters having to do
with the arts. On one of his leaves he went for the first time to the
Breslau mansion, where he astonished Frédéric's father and mother by
the way in which he discussed object by object the value of their
famous collection of pictures and other works of art in one case after
a cursory glance, raising a number of points, within the competence
only of a painter, which Baudry had not put forward until after a prolonged examination, countering his own conclusions with an argument
which had not so much as occurred to the expert who at the request of
the old Prince of Bremen had been called in to reassure Baudry about
the worth of a collection which had been called in question: in another,
proving on historical grounds that a certain attribution was without
foundation, and that an entry in the catalogue was erroneous. The old
Prince, having learned from Frédéric how poor his friend was, had
been anxious to give him some pecuniary assistance. Antoine, however,
had refused to take a penny, partly because he was naturally honest,
but partly because he was prompted by that obscure logic of ambitious
persons who will instinctively sacrifice immediate pleasure to the hope
of gaining a durable reputation for complete disinterestedness, a
reputation which is as valuable for the future of their passion, as the
temporary satisfaction of vanity and the desire for wealth, is fatal.
Antoine's father had all his life been a salaried worker. Antoine himself all through his years of childhood had had nothing from these
fashionable folk whose relations with his father were confined to

matters of business, but patronizing words. He was fated to be one of
those people to whom in exchange for services rendered one gives
theatre tickets, because one finds it impossible to invite them to the
house. His dearest wish was that they in their turn should creep and
crawl for an invitation to his table. There are human beings who long
for what they have never had, simply and solely because they see it
only in terms of their imagination, and look at it through rose-coloured
spectacles. The courtesan desires respectability or honest love. The
domestic servant independence, and many people life in the fashionable
world. It is for this reason that we so often see a butler who has been
treated with affection and thoroughly spoiled by his employers, whom
he might go on serving all his life with the certainty of coming into a
great deal of money after their death, leave them as soon as he has
saved up a competence, only to lose in a few months as proprietor of a
wine shop everything that he has put by during his years of service.
That, too, is why a successful actor finds his greatest satisfaction in
being "decorated" like any little Civil Servant, why the tart runs away
from the banker, who, though he may treat her like a street-walker
does at least give her two hundred thousand francs a year, with a young
spendthrift who behaves to her as though she were a woman of the
world, and by making her fall in love with him, persuades her that she
really is one. That is why so many young women or young men,
whose parents are looked down upon because of the way they make
their money, or because of their racial origins, abandon their friends,
compromise their happiness, risk their fortune, and, perhaps, even their
lives, in order to have an aristocrat as their second in a duel, or as a
guest at their table. It is worth noting that men of letters, who are often
the children of poor parents and see the great world only by light of
the glamour which their imagination casts upon it, often for the sake
of that world consent to a sacrifice which is more extreme for them
than it would be for others, since in addition to all the assets already
mentioned, they lay upon the altar of ambition things more important still, their love of solitude, the joy of self-sufficiency, the essential
integrity of their intelligence, the dignity of their position, and the
solidity of their fame.

But it is rare indeed to find men of letters who are quite such simple-
minded snobs, quite so deliberately ambitious, as we are led to believe,
and as they are often painted in works of fiction. Take, for instance,
the case of Lucien de Rubempré, the young poet who is the central

character of an immortal novel. The modern Rubempré—or, for that
matter, the Rubempré of any period—does not say to himself: 'I want
to arrive; I want to be a man of fashion, to be as much sought after,
as much feared, and as rich, as Maxime de Trailles or Ernest de Rastignac.' No, his secret thoughts are expressed differently: 'I want to have
experienced everything: I want to quench my parched brain, which
has been sucked dry by the labour of pure speculation, at the wells of
life: I want to *know* life, so as one day, to be able to show it as it is'
(a form of argument which does not urge him to experience poverty
or mediocrity, though they, just as much as opulence, are among the
various shapes that life assumes). He says to himself, 'Society can provide me with subjects, but I shall never be able to present them convincingly if I don't work from the model. How interesting for the
psychologist are those specialized growths to be found only in that
artificial segment of life and of the world which goes by the name of
the world, the most poisonous and the commonest of which is snobbery.'
Whether his perspicacity finds a certain pleasure in taking a cruel
revenge on others because he feels bitterly ashamed of the noxious
weed which he knows is sprouting in himself, or because by seeming
to flay the craving with words, he actually provides it with food and a
respectable exterior, the fact remains that the novelist who is also a
snob inevitably becomes the chosen writer of snobs. Sooner or later,
as a result of the influence exerted on the flabby by the perverted, and
the facile pleasures of the moment on the weak-willed, the world ends
by fashioning the poet in its own image, the more rapidly since by
gratifying his vanity and his laziness and accustoming him to live in
Society, it destroys the powers of resistance which he might have found
in solitude. Whereas, too, Rubempré quite deliberately looks upon
these people as enemies to be conquered, as embattled castles to be
taken by storm, what really happens is that the writer lays siege to
them not after long premeditation nor in any calculated fashion but
because he is under the influence of desire, because the operative force
at work in him, though he does not know this, is by no means the
accumulation of such dishonest arguments as I have enumerated, is not
even because his snobbery has persuaded him that they are more
powerful than other people; for what he really thinks is that they are
more charming, desire, in snobbery no less than in love, being the
cause and not the effect of admiration. He does not lose his heart to
duchesses because he has coolly and calmly decided that they are more

desirable than other women, but because being instinctively drawn to them he convinces himself that they must be desirable. Later he may tell himself, 'I deliberately chose this way of living in order to make my fortune' or 'I wanted, by getting myself treated as an equal by a prince, to restore to the socially despised writer the rank to which he is entitled.' We should be wrong to believe either in such an extreme degree of cynicism, or in so fine a fervour of disinterested endeavour; we should merely note as another example of such things, the ingenuity of those whom passion has persuaded that, by embarking on a career, whether it be noble or squalid, it is *they* who have taken the initiative, and that, instead of being slaves, they are masters.

But Rubempré has tempted me to wander. I must now return to Antoine Desroches, with a side-glance at Rastignac. The modern Rastignac, or, for that matter, the eternal Rastignac, does not say to Madame de Beauséant: "I need your protection and shall be deeply grateful if you will engineer for me an introduction to General de Canigliano." No, he makes believe that he stands in so little need of the protection she has offered, that he would find it inexpressibly boring to meet General de Canigliano. She has to insist on his accepting an introduction, and succeeds only after the second or third attempt. Far from abandoning his work in order to call every day on Madame de Nucingen or Madame de Beauséant, he, in fact, pays very few visits, letting it be understood that he is far too much absorbed in work which, according to him, is a great deal more interesting than the pleasures of the great world, thereby arousing the curiosity of the denizens of that world, and inspiring them with feelings of slightly bewildered respect for his unworldliness. He never speaks of the invitations he has received but always of the examinations for which he is studying and of his old friends of the Beaux-Arts. He says, "They may not be dukes, but I assure you that I would far rather spend five minutes in their company than five hours in that of Monsieur de Trailles" (for even while he is flaying the great he cannot refrain from interlarding his talk with their names). He does not say to Madame de Beauséant, "Thanks to you, Madame de Nucingen has asked me to go and see her" but "Have I really got to go and see Madame de Nucingen —what a frightful bore!" Or perhaps he does not say that in so many words so long as he feels sure that silence will make what he is thinking sufficiently clear, thus giving the impression that he has kept his views to himself out of consideration for Madame de Beauséant's feelings, and is a man who is used to doing his duty without complaining. The most he will permit himself is, just as he is leaving, to cast a backward and regretful glance from the threshold, and to say: "How pleasant it would be to stay here chatting by the fire." If he speaks highly of somebody's intelligence, the person in question is never a duchess, but always one of his middle-class hostesses who can do nothing for him. He makes it quite obvious that mere rank can never dazzle him, that he values only merit, and is happiest when that merit is obscure. If he praises a great man, it is as though he is doing so *in spite of* appearances, and only because personal experience has compelled him to overcome his natural prejudices. "No one I think could accuse me of having a weakness for those illustrious circles; still, one must admit that he is an excellent fellow and brimming over with intelligence." In the presence of great folk whom he does not know, he maintains an aloof and cold attitude: with those whom he does, he is frank, and even blunt. He does not conceal the truth about them, but tells them with brutal directness—all that they most like hearing. "What a lazy devil you are! what a complete rotter!" and when he is under the necessity of mentioning unpleasant facts, he hastily gilds the pill by adding a few affectionate words straight from the heart, and "in spite of himself". He will never wound, no matter how tactfully. He will never hesitate about taking Madame de Nucingen out if her dying father asks him to, for Antoine is not really bad at heart, but never, if he accompanies her to a ball, will he say, "It gives me an uncomfortable feeling to see you laughing with your poor father at his last gasp." Rather, he makes it possible for her to justify herself in her own eyes; "I know how much you hate coming to this party", he will say, "but it is one of those things you've *got* to do": and here, if need be, a tender note will creep into his usually rather rough voice: "Poor man," he will sigh, "it is your duty to do what he would tell you to do if you could ask his advice. You don't, do you, think that he would want you to stay, crying your eyes out and making yourself ill, in the fœtid atmosphere of a sick-room, and so miss, perhaps, the greatest success of your career? Besides, you are not strong enough for the duties of a nurse. It would be wrong to take advantage of the fact that he is too weak to protest, in order to do what he would most of all dislike." He will not say to Nathan: "How *can* you bring yourself to lick the boots of a dirty journalist who's not worth your little finger," but, "It's really rather funny to think that the obligations of life should force you into contact with men who are so far beneath you. You're perfectly right, though: it's one of those things one's got to do." Never, when in the company of dukes and princes would Antoine pretend not to recognize his old journalist friends. He would leave the side of a princess to shake one of them by the hand, knowing full well that by doing so he gained as much favour in the eyes of the princess as in those of the journalist. And so, grumpy and assiduous in his dealings with the great, affectionate and off-hand with the smaller fry, Antoine would have lived in a perpetual atmosphere of friendliness, had it not been for the existence of a species of mankind which he could not endure, which he was for ever decrying, because by so doing he could gain the double advantage of weakening his rivals and putting a spoke in the wheel of competition, and so keeping for himself the prey which they no less than he were after—a species he could smell a mile off, from whose tricks and operations he would brutally strip the veil, for whom he had neither pity nor indulgence—the snobs.

Antoine Desroches had flatly refused to take money from the Prince of Bremen: but, forbidden to offer his cash, the Prince employed his influence on his behalf. Instead of giving him a few hundred francs, he managed to get him appointed Assistant Director of the Beaux-Arts, Art Critic on the *Figaro*, and Inspector of Galleries, which employments brought in, together, something like sixty thousand francs a year. Antoine Desroches was like those so-called "respectable" women, who will never accept money from their lovers, but manage to cost them twenty times more than any little dancer would have done. Nor was that all. By refusing the Prince's gifts, he obliged the latter to treat him not as a protégé but as a friend. He was a frequent guest at his shooting-parties and his dinners. In this way he got to know several of the great personages of the Emperor's circle, and to them he rendered many important services by putting at their disposition his really first-rate knowledge in matters of art. By enabling them to make a lot of money, and by always refusing to touch a penny himself, he won their admiration and enjoyed their intimacy. At the age of thirty-three he married Céphise Grimaldi, the daughter of a great painter who, though he could not give her much in the way of a dowry, proved very helpful to his son-in-law when the latter submitted his candidature for election to the Académie des Beaux-Arts, of which Grimaldi was Permanent Secretary. It must be, however, admitted that what counted almost more than anything else with her husband was the fact that Céphise Grimaldi was one of the most beautiful women in Paris. To a keen intelligence she added a pair of green and liquid eyes. Antoine Desroches was deeply in love with her. It was a matter for great astonishment in the fashionable world that when he married the woman of whose good looks and quick wit he had long boasted, he made no attempt to introduce her into Society. Not but what the Princess of Bremen and several of his more intimate friends were eager to make her acquaintance, and invited her to their houses. He managed to evade these approaches, and was forced finally to explain that his wife was on intimate terms with all the eminent painters and sculptors of the day, in comparison with whom she found Society People cold and dead. He feared, he said, that he would never be able to induce her to play a part in the world of fashion. Nevertheless, he was voluble in praise of her charms and took particular pleasure in retailing a number of complimentary things that certain outstanding men had said about her, and this only whetted the curiosity of those who wanted to meet her. One day the Duc de Traves, the smartest man in all Paris, went to consult Desroches. "Ah, my wife is the person you ought to talk to about that," said Antoine, and, turning to the footman, added: "Ask Madame to come down, but don't tell her that I have got anybody with me. Otherwise," he explained, turning to the Duke, "she might not come." For the next few days the Duke could talk of nothing but the extraordinary charm and enchanting wit of Madame Desroches. One evening, when he was dining at the house of the Princess of Breslau, she said to him—giving the impression that she felt almost offended at not having been "considered worthy"—"I gather that you have actually met Madame Desroches?" A month later the Breslaus met the Desroches at "the waters".

Madame Desroches confessed too that there had been a time when she had felt slightly mistrustful, but that now the charm, the intelligence, and the kindness of the Princess had completely won her over. "Promise me that when we are all back in Paris you will sometimes come and dine with us," said the Princess of Breslau, feeling that she really could not do without Madame Desroches any longer. "She'll come, never fear: I give you my word for that," said Desroches in a low voice to the Princess, "but you must ask the pick of your friends to meet her, real charmers: you see, she has been so spoiled!" he added, looking affectionately across at his wife, who was out of earshot.

A month later Madame Desroches was "launched". The die was cast—to the advantage of Madame Desroches those said who, in the course of the next ten years, saw her name constantly in the papers as having been present at all the great dinner parties of the Faubourg Saint-Germain, and as having been seen sitting in the front row of so many Imperial and Royal boxes. To her disadvantage, others thought who, having admired the astonishing pastels which she had produced at the age of twenty, when she had been living untouched by ambition in the society of her father's old friends, were of the opinion that her worldly success had marked, not perhaps the decadence so much as the stopping short of her artistic activities, and the obliteration of those elegancies of mind which almost overnight, as at the touch of a bad fairy's wand, had been transformed into smart clothes, aristocratic friends and fine furniture. Who knows but that she may not often have regretted her inability to become again, as the result of a new metamorphosis, the Céphise of her earlier days, and have more than once tried to find the magic formula which might have summoned up a fairy, who, by a wave of her wand, could have turned the drawing-room of today into the studio of the past? Who knows but that the fairy may often have replied: "I will come to you when you have thrown overboard all this ballast of fine dresses, rich friends, grand carriages and have made yourself light enough to get up and follow me"? But at the point we have now reached in this story, tired of being ignored and at death's door as the result of being deprived by Céphise for so long of those day-dreams which are, for sprites and genii in general, the very staff of life, the little fairy had decided not to wear out what remained of her voice any longer in a vain attempt to give good advice. She may by this time even be dead. But, like a house inhabited by a woman of taste, those in whom a fairy has once dwelt never wholly lose a certain grace of mind which others do not have. Céphise never lost that look in her eyes which was like a darting flame, so that those who saw it could not but feel that they were in the presence of something charged with foreboding—the mouth which was like a magic talisman, the constant aura which hung about her of verbena with its gift of happiness, the rapid flow of words which played about those to whom she spoke like an enchantment, her wonderful power of bringing consolation to others, as though she, in her turn, had become a fairy now that her own fairy was dead, but a fairy who could do nothing to help herself.

The die, as I have said, had been cast, whether to her advantage or disadvantage each must decide for himself. But if she had loaded it, she had done so unwittingly, for she was perfectly sincere in her wish to preserve from the invasion of the great world that little society of painters and sculptors which once had been her joy. It is only fair, too, to point out that in all Desroches' calculations there was much love mixed with much ambition. He loved his wife so dearly that he wanted to be able to give her what he thought was the finest thing in all the world—a great position in Society—like the tumbler, whose simple-minded piety has been immortalized by Anatole France, thinking that the best way in which he could do honour to the Blessed Virgin, was by turning somersaults in front of Her altar.

But though Madame Desroches had indeed been launched it was only into the world of the Empire, or, more accurately, into one small coterie of the great world. If she could retain the eminence she had achieved, her fame would, after a while, spread through all the different regions of Bonapartist society, giving her the *entrée* to all the nobility of the Empire, and to the world or part of the world of high finance. But even that was not enough to satisfy Desroches. He dreamed of still higher conquests for his wife, and longed to see her shine among the stars of Parisian Society, to glitter in the most exclusively legitimist houses of the Faubourg Saint-Germain, among the great diplomatic hostesses, and to be received in those foreign royal families the conquest of which she has since achieved.

3. *Madame Desroches at Home*

It would be of no interest to the reader if I were to describe the house in which the Desroches lived. At a time when articles of furniture were collected piecemeal, because he who bought them found them useful, considered them beautiful, or knew that his relatives, his colleagues, the people who belonged to the same social class as he did, or who had about the same income, were accustomed to consider them beautiful and to acquire them, the shade of a curtain, the shape of a chair, the ornaments of a clock, were not matters of indifference because they gave the impression that they had, so to speak, been chosen by a definite individual so that the simplest chair took on a certain dignity because, from the very fact that its ample gesture had once supported the weak arm of a specific human being, it carried with it the whole atmosphere of an epoch. Gathered about any given family, the furniture seemed to surround it with the instruments of its pleasures, the reflection of its tastes, the symbols of its period. A house was merely another form of dress which the individual moulded to his own shape, and to the wider shape of the circle in which he moved. Furniture was a sort of tangible history in which, side by side, the individual, the profession which he exercised, the social class to which he belonged, were, as it might be, frozen, and perpetuated. It was the expression of its owner's dreams, and spread about him its accumulated memories. A Balzac could study a house as he might have studied old title-deeds and the dusty memorials of history, and so, from the shapes of the objects it contained, could decipher its meaning and bring to life the generations of human kind that had inhabited it.

But things are very different today, at least in that section of society which is generally known as Society with a big S. Just as a woman whose distinctive characteristic is not so much a particular cast of mind as membership of a particular "world", goes to the Lamoureux concerts several times a year, and to Bayreuth several times in the course of her life, without, for that matter, being any more musical than she is religious when she attends Mass on Sundays, so, too—provided she enjoys a certain income, or, more important, lives in a certain set, which contains within itself an infinity of sub-sets, she will inevitably have an "artistic" apartment, whether the style be Renaissance, Louis XIV, Louis XV, Louis XVI, Empire, or English. Should you call on the wife of a great doctor, a great banker, or a great aristocrat, you will find it impossible to tell from her house or her apartment what her husband is or does, and still less will you learn from its contents whether its mistress is intelligent or stupid, an idealist or a positivist, lazy or active, melancholy or gay. It will show to your inquiring eye only a number of "artistic" objects belonging to the period of Louis XIV, Louis XV, Louis XVI, Empire or "Maples". A woman who is completely ignorant of history will "work at" her house for two years, haunting sale rooms in the company of artists, or, if she knows none, relying on the advice of friends who are either misled by the dealers or let the dealers mislead her. Another, who has never read anything in her life, will display upon the table in her bedroom, a single volume, Turgot's *La Somme Royale*, for no better reason than because the decorative scheme is Louis XVI. A high-spirited little girl will be seen laughing and squirming in a high Louis XIV armchair. Madame S. is not particularly fond of pictures, but, because she is rich, will go out of her way to collect Watteaus or the paintings of Gustave Moreau's "first period". Madame X, the daughter of a Protestant or Jewish banker, if she insists on having pictures, might provide something interesting in the shape of portraits eternalizing the harsh or honest features of the defunct bankers who were the parents or ancestors of her own parents or her husband's. But not a bit of it. She lives in a house that once belonged to La Rochefoucauld, and consequently has in her bedroom a portrait of Madame de La Fayette. When will people learn that an artistic interior can be of interest only in the houses of artists because an artist's apartment, provided it is sincere and expressive, is just as likely to interest us as would that of a bourgeois, a noble, a magistrate or a banker, though it is permissible to think that the room of a poet, which is a sort of observatory where nothing should obstruct the view of the sky, or the activities of wind, storm or rain, should to some extent be stripped and bare, that the poet may not be distracted, but be able to concentrate his attention on every gleam, no matter how faint, of sunshine?

The house of an Edmond de Goncourt, an Anatole France, a Robert de Montesquiou is of interest to the novelist and can furnish him with the means of describing, or rather of resurrecting, the life that inhabits it. After long and tentative experiments with Watteau drawings, a Clodion statuette, a Hokusai print, these men have at last found the true corner-stone of the altar of God, and have enthroned it in the place waiting for it among those idols which had been assembled there as a result, not so much of unity of effect as of wayward enthusiasms. Madame Desroches's house, however, was, like the house of Solomon Accham, the house of Duferny, the house of the Marquise d'Ouessant or of Doctor Guénot, a museum for the use of those who are unfamiliar with museums, or so thoroughly familiar with them, that only private collections have anything new to show them. The sole difference was that the house of Madame Desroches was less beautiful because Madame Desroches was less rich. One has only to realize that the Réveillon family mansion, one of those rare aristocratic establishments which has not become just another example of the houses I have described, in other words, "smart" and utterly devoid of personality, was bare, icy, and almost as forbidding as a fortified castle, to understand why Henri de Réveillon, on the occasion of his first visit to Madame Desroches, had the same feeling of enchantment as might a young girl, brought up in the severe surroundings of a convent or a middle-class household, on suddenly finding herself in the company of easy-mannered Parisians whose conversation is brilliant, whose elegance of the most extreme refinement. So intoxicated was he by this new experience, that the most ordinary remarks on life or on history sounded in his ears like profoundly considered judgments. It came as a surprise to him that every wallpaper, every picture, every comfit-box might have something to tell him, though scrappy and vague perhaps, and that the smooth running commentary with which their exhibiting was accompanied, seemed to tell him more about the arts than he had ever thought there was to know. He listened with pleasure to these disquisitions, but could not have heard them to the end without being oppressed by a sense of weariness. At the same time he was deeply disturbed by a strong and heady perfume which met him on the threshold, and indicated that he was setting foot within some very special place which combined the pleasurable thrill of a chapel with the prestige that hangs about the dwelling of a courtesan.

4. *Mademoiselle Des Coulombes*

That same evening, in the great drawing-room of the hôtel de Réveillon, known as the "Salon des Adieux", because it was there that Saint-Louis, before leaving Paris, had said farewell to Geoffroy, Duc d'Aquitaine et de Réveillon, Henri, who had allowed himself fifteen minutes rest after dinner before going upstairs to make a fair copy of his Latin verses, was delighted to hear his mother singing the praises of Jean Santeuil, and the Duke echoing her sentiments in more solemn tones, so that the effect was that of a two-voice chant. Truth to tell, it was for the sole purpose of listening to this duet that Henri had decided to spend a quarter of an hour in the drawing-room, instead of going straight upstairs to enjoy a cigarette, it being too cold to smoke in the garden. But as it sometimes happens that an academic discourse may fall a prey to circumstances, or a respectable householder lose his way and wander into a riot, this eulogy had come within an ace of never being pronounced at all. The Duc de Réveillon, glancing through *Le Temps* while the Duchess was sugaring his coffee, had had his eye caught by a report of the majority accorded by the Chamber to the new Republican Government. Succumbing to a rush of blood to the head, he had exclaimed: "Scum!—no better than scum! If I had my way I'd shoot the lot of 'em, and in double quick time, too! d'Arenberg and Greffulhe actually voted with 'em! Here's the *Temps* praising 'em to the skies!—it really is the last straw! Enough to make a fellow pack his bags and clear out of the country! To think that dirty dog was sitting beside me at the Opéra-Comique the night the fire broke out! Can't for the life of me understand why God didn't let him frizzle!" But the only conflagrational satisfaction the Duke could get was by throwing the offending newspaper into the flames, at the same time calling down the curses of Heaven on the Government. "Scoundrels!" he shouted, and settled back into his armchair.

So he spoke, and it seemed as though God had heard his prayer. The fire, momentarily fed by the wretched sheet which it had received as an acceptable victim, a sacrificial offering, blazed more brightly,

seeming to body forth the divine anger as it turned and twisted for a
brief moment like a coil of infuriated snakes, after which exhausted by
its wrath it again subsided, loosing its hold on the humiliated journal
which, now no more than a tattered fragment of dusty ash, slipped
noiselessly into the grate, and then like a caterpillar transformed in a
flash into a butterfly, fled up the chimney in a train of sparks. Henri
looked at his watch, and seeing that he could stay in the drawing-room
for only ten minutes more, silently cursed the Republic and its new
masters for having prevented his parents from saying what they thought
of the friend he had presented to them that very morning, and feeling,
for all the world as a dramatist might have done whose first night had
coincided with the 2nd December, with the result that he never got
over his grudge against the Empire for keeping from his first performance a public more responsive to political excitements than to
theatrical novelties.

But the Duchesse de Réveillon, anxious to take her husband's mind
off a subject which invariably upset him, and not to deprive Henri of
the pleasure of hearing his friend commended, was also acting in
obedience to yet a third consideration when, turning to the Duke,
whose answer she could guess in advance, she said, "Anselme, you
haven't yet told me what you think of Henri's new friend?" The consideration in question had to do with the only other person who was
with the three of them on this particular evening in the drawing-room,
Mademoiselle des Coulombes, and was not wholly the product of
charitable feelings. Mademoiselle de Coulombes was an elderly and
impoverished friend of the Duchess for whom she occasionally acted as
"companion". Though her attitude to Henri was one of loyal friendship, she regarded him with that contempt which misunderstood and
poetically-minded spinsters feel towards well-regulated and un-
imaginative young males. Jean was everything that Mademoiselle des
Coulombes thought a young man ought to be, and her curiosity, no
less than her admiration had been aroused by all that Henri had said
about him, about his French essays and his love of reading, even before
she had met him in the flesh, and, in reply to the Duchess's remark that
she couldn't wish for a better friend for her son, had remarked: "Oh,
he'll never get on with Henri. You see, I *know* about these things from
having frequently met Monsieur Sully Prudhomme at the house of a
friend of mine in the country"; a comment which had made the
Duchess all the more anxious that Mademoiselle des Coulombes should

realize how great an impression Henri had made upon Jean Santeuil. Consequently it was doubly delightful for her to voice her praises of Jean. They sounded, however, less pleasantly in the ears of Mademoiselle des Coulombes who, as soon as she heard them, began to wonder whether she could have been right about a young man whom Henri was capable of making his friend.

The Duke who, since he had never fully realized the degree of disdain felt by Mademoiselle des Coulombes for his son, could scarcely be expected to understand his wife's malicious intention, now struck a mortal blow at the "Canoness" by saying: "What I like most about him is the quite extraordinary affection he seems to have for Henri. I get the impression, my boy, that he admires everything you say," he added, laying his hand on Henri's head, and secretly feeling that Jean's attitude was only right and proper. But Mademoiselle des Coulombes at once began to suspect that Jean might, after all, not be the poet she had presumed him to be when Henri had described his personal untidiness and his skill at French composition. The praises which she was hearing did not, therefore, particularly impress her, and she was now fully determined to wait until she had seen him before pronouncing judgment—a most unusual thing with her. If she could be with him, however, if only for a moment, she would at once know what to think. But it went very hard with her to renounce her dream of a young poet whom she herself had consecrated. Still, he had only to see her, to fall at once beneath her spell. From now on, in the hôtel de Réveillon she would have somebody to talk with of an evening. It would not be long before he came to see what a very second-rate person Henri was.

Meanwhile the Duchess, while working away at her embroidery, never ceased from sounding Jean's praises. She praised him because she had taken a liking to him, and the more she praised the more she liked. It was ever the custom of the ladies of the house of Dreux to believe that their noble lineage, the quality of their wine, their intelligence, their parties and their pregnancies were so much superior to those of other persons as to make of them beings of another species, and Anaïs de Réveillon had, up till now, been firmly convinced that Henri's horse was the most beautiful of all possible horses, and his hats quite unlike other hats. There was, in her eyes, something rather "special" even about his failures, and the regularity with which he came out bottom in French composition seemed to her actually to be a mark of originality and therefore a cause for rejoicing. It was, in any case, better than seeing him occupying the first place which, as everybody knew, was reserved for Jewish boys by Government-appointed teachers. If Henri had a friend, just the kind of friend, she thought—so anxious was she that her son should develop something resembling an enthusiasm for literature—that he ought to have, a friend whom he adored, whose simple, thoughtful, gentle nature had enchanted him at first sight, then, that friend must necessarily be superior to any friend that anybody else could have. Little by little she discovered in Jean all the qualities which she had laid by, like baby-clothes, for Henri's friend—should he ever have one.

Meanwhile, the fire, being no longer called upon to purge the earth of the monster, *Temps*, and having, for a while displayed a more than usually lively vigour and a gaiety which had been aroused in it by the noble deeds it had been called upon to perform, had once again grown quieter, and was now providing a discreet and soft accompaniment to the Duchess's words. The nimble flame hastily wove an ash more delicate than her embroidery. Then it sank down like a jet of water partially turned off at the main, which, in the very act of diminishing, still spouts upwards. Finally, it went out altogether until there was nothing to be seen but a glowing ember passing through the various stages of mysterious metamorphosis in a silence resembling that of forest undergrowth in autumn, when the only sound to be heard is made by a falling leaf or a chestnut dropping to the ground. Henri looked at his watch, and got up. "It's time I went upstairs and did some work." At this moment, the Duchess noticed that the dying fire which, now and again, like a cat asking for milk, was emitting a faint squeak, seemed to be in need of more wood. "Ask them, on your way upstairs, to bring some more logs, darling," said the Duchess, "but won't you stay with us a little while longer?"–"No, Mamma, it's time for me to go to my room."–"Time! time!" said Mademoiselle des Coulombes on a note of irony. "Would anything very terrible happen if you waited for another quarter of an hour? It is pleasant at any age, and especially at yours, to act on a whim. Only yesterday I was invited to dine at the house of the Marquis de Ribes—it was, as a matter of fact to meet Monsieur Sully Prudhomme. We had been asked for half past seven, but I was so deeply absorbed in my book that when I looked at the clock I saw that it was half past eight! You can imagine how *terrible* I felt, but glad, too, to think that I had not forgotten my engagement altogether, as I did last week when I was supposed to be dining with the Puybarons! It was only two days later that I remembered! Your cousin's always the same old scatterbrain," she added, simpering at the Duke. But, appalled by her own daring in having said "your cousin", she went scarlet to the ears, and would have embarked on a long and rambling excuse had not Henri, impatient to be gone, broken in with a "Good night". "You *will* introduce me to your friend Santfeuil, won't you?" she said. "*Santeuil*, Nasta!" exclaimed the Duke, "can't you ever get a name right?" – "Oh, do forgive me! I'm afraid my mind was wandering!" cried Anastasia with a laugh, while she timidly looked about her for a sign of encouragement. But the Duchess was busy with her embroidery, the Duke was poking the fire, Henri had just left the room, and Mademoiselle des Coulombes felt herself blushing hotly. She lowered her eyes, and to keep herself in countenance, passed a podgy hand over her face which momentarily disappeared, to emerge again like a red winter's sun briefly obscured by a dense cloud.

There were many such pleasantly monotonous evenings at the old hôtel de Réveillon. Human feelings, family connexions, social obligations, and other subjects of conversation are much the same in noble as in modest homes. Although the Duchess was the Emperor of Austria's cousin, her private life was not so very different from that of the middle classes, whose imagination it must seem so strange.

★

Some days later, Henri, who had always heard the "Canoness" most highly spoken of in the bosom of his family, though his mother detested the way in which she looked down her nose at people, as much as she respected her intelligence, said to Jean: "Wouldn't you like to know who it was said I should detest you?" – "Who was it?" – "No one you know: her name wouldn't mean a thing to you: Mademoiselle des Coulombes . . ." – "Oh, but my Aunt Desroches knows her: I gather she's a bit of a joke."

Hearing these words, Henri felt the whole edifice of his beliefs, opinions and admirations totter on its foundations. But, at the same time he was conscious that a great weight had been lifted from him. His admiration for Jean took an upward leap, strengthened as it was by the power he had so long attributed to the idol now so suddenly and so deftly overthrown. Truth to tell, Madame Desroches, whose intelligence was quick to seize on the ridiculous, and who detested nothing more than the absurdities bred of pedantry and pretentiousness, was only too ready to condemn as stupid anyone who, as she put it, "said stupid things". She had been to see Madame de Rivoli one day when Mademoiselle des Coulombes, surrounded by a number of old ladies who were listening to her with rapt attention, said to Monsieur Renan, "I sometimes find myself wondering whether Cicero was really sincere"—from which moment she stood condemned. On another occasion she had heard her mention "*Warvol*, that novel by Duns Scotus, you know"—though she had had the grace to blush, and had admitted that she was "getting things a bit mixed up". When one of the members of the higher aristocracy, who modelled his views on hers said, "I expect you admire Mademoiselle des Coulombes a great deal?" the reply had been, "She certainly is a wonderful specimen!" The irony which she put into the words, had about it something of the grandeur of that Divine Justice which gives to everyone his allotted place in the scheme of things. It may well be however that the pedantry, the awkwardness and the grimacings of Mademoiselle des Coulombes concealed higher aspirations, and a more sincere love of ideas, than did the always affable and subtle talk, the laughing lips, the fashionable clothes, and the perfect tact of Madame Desroches. Whether that was so, God will say at the Last Judgment. But in the meantime we live in a world where we are not judged for our intentions, and the day on which Jean met Mademoiselle des Coulombes at the Réveillons, he thought otherwise; that is to say, he agreed with his aunt. Consequently, that occasion did not at all come up to Mademoiselle des Coulombes' expectations and served to strengthen her opinion that Jean was by no means the poet she had thought him to be.

It was painful for her to have to admit that she had been, as she put it later, "deceived" in him. But that she had been was proved by two pieces of indisputable evidence—Jean's coldness towards her, and the pleasure he seemed to find in Henri's company. One of the causes of that pleasure was, it is only fair to say, the existence in Henri of certain matter-of-fact qualities which, though in the eyes of so romantic a person as Mademoiselle des Coulombes they were a sure mark of inferiority, we often find that poets value highly, and others seek who do not happen to possess them. When excitement sets the hand trembling as it writes—whether poetry, a woman's burning words of love, a man's proud rebuttal of hostile accusations—it always tries to find a pen that shall be free from all uncertainty, will not come to pieces in the fingers just when the perfect word is waiting to be put down on paper, never shakes provokingly, nor shows hesitation, lets the ink flow smoothly, and, unlike the thoughts of the writer, is unperturbed by whims—those humble whims of a pen which sometimes make it scratch the page without leaving upon it a visible trace, and sometimes lavish its contents in the form of blots that later have to be erased. For this reason, a poet never feels comfortable with a friend like Mademoiselle des Coulombes. He is perfectly capable of keeping his family waiting hours for dinner if he happens to be in the grip of inspiration when he ought to be going downstairs. On the other hand, if he is in a hurry to get through his meal in order to rush back to his writing, or to relax, he has no patience with the mild enthusiasms of a Mademoiselle des Coulombes, though they may perhaps be no less worthy of respect than his own, which express themselves in a fancy to look at some picture, to gaze at the sunset, or to hum *J'ai pardonné*, when she ought to be dressing, and result in her turning up at eight instead of at seven, thereby causing the poet an anxious hour, and driving him to call down impatient curses on her head because that hour has been stolen from his writing or his rest, and has had a bad effect upon his character and the functioning of his brain. The young poet tends to be hard on matter-of-fact qualities when they are those of a father who, obedient to a routine which means nothing in his own life, tears him roughly from sublime employments at the very moment when his imagination is soaring high above mundane matters simply in order to force upon him such trivial daily tasks as dressing, going down to dinner, performing his social duties, going to bed, or keeping an engagement. But later, when laziness, irregular habits, unpunctuality, and absent-mindedness have gradually turned his life into a heaven-hell, then it is that he feels the need of those sensible, disciplined characters in whom existence is peaceable and well-regulated, whose every movement has the sweet monotony of a clock.

Mademoiselle des Coulombes's ineptitudes, her unnecessary flushings, her interminable and quite ineffectual attempts to excuse something she had just said, her trembling hands which dropped everything she touched, her infuriating delays, her involuntary accesses of confusion, her inexact information and irrelevant actions—these things sounded no doubt, to the ear of God—noting them in their due and proper place within the mighty whole—as a necessary and melodious contribution to the harmony of the spheres. But to Jean, who could hear sounds only in a time-sequence, Mademoiselle des Coulombes seemed to offend against every rule of music. If, on the contrary it was to Henri he put a question, or Henri whom he arranged to meet at some specific time and place, he could always be certain that the answer would be correct, the appointment kept. Henri never did anything he shouldn't do—though it is true that he had somewhat lax ideas on what he shouldn't do—and, consequently never wasted time in remorse. But then too since he did only what he thought he had a perfect right to do, he did not, like Jean, suffer from scruples of conscience. He talked a great deal less than Mademoiselle des Coulombes, but when he did talk what he said seemed very much to the point, and involved neither preparation nor apology. He was not lavish in protestations of friendship to all and sundry, but when he liked anybody, he proved his liking by doing things which left no doubt of his feelings in the mind either of him who inspired them or of anybody else. His fondness for his mother had nothing of Jean's ecstatic morbidity. He may not have feared so much to cause her pain, but did, in fact, cause her considerably less. He had a passion for life, but never let his thoughts dwell upon death. He liked his books to be neatly arranged, his fire to burn well, and his work to be finished punctually so that he might have time for pleasure, his carpenter's bench to be kept clean, his tools to be sharpened. And so it was that habit, that kind, blind guide which takes charge of our actions and sees to it that they keep always in the same path, spared him all anxiety, and arranged that he should be always happy, directing him each morning, when the sun rose, to the shelf where Quicherat's dictionary never failed to respond when he put his hand, with unfailing regularity, on its top edge to draw it out, and thrilled to feel its smooth leather binding against his palm, keeping far from him all temptation not to work, all uneasy speculation on what he should, or should not, do, all regret for the past, and all anxiety for the future.

Henri's existence was as pleasing to observe as a lamp that gives a steady light without flaring or getting choked with soot, as a fire that never smokes but spreads, with affectionate nonchalance, an agreeable and increasing warmth through all the room. He moved in a world of gaiety and good humour. In his relations with others he never made a false step, but was like a familiar and faithful tool which it is a joy to feel in one's hand, and always does what is asked of it. When his friends were attacked, he returned blow for blow with strength and accuracy. He had the charm of a perfect chord which brings delight to the ear, of one of those Italian churches which is neither mean nor florid, the beauty of which springs from the perfect suitability of every object to its purpose. He had that balanced orderliness of mind which, like a clock, can be relied upon to sound, with unfailing regularity, the hours for work, for sorrow and for joy, compared with which the undisciplined actions of the generality of mankind produce an uncomfortable feeling of wasted strength, of disproportionate effort, of inadequate results, of lack of control, of discord. There was about his life the poetry that is bred of days well filled and never allowed to run to waste, which is neither the sad poetry of yesterday nor the obscure poetry of tomorrow, but which, out in the country, or at the fireside, in Jean's imagination or in Henri's room, was redolent of a quiet loveliness.

5. *Monsieur Duroc*

Monsieur Santeuil came in to say good-bye to his wife. He was just off to the Ministry. "Are you going to walk, Papa?" asked Jean. "Yes," replied Monsieur Santeuil, and turning to Henri added—for he dearly loved to explain the reasons for his actions, "I find that walking provides healthy exercise, when not indulged in to excess, and is a good preparation for the day's work."–"My father," said Jean on a note of affectionate approval, "finds that he works better after a walk. Flaubert was of the same opinion." Whether from a motive of self-pride, or out of respect for his father, Jean drew a hasty veil across the triteness of the latter's conversation, much as a charming woman will tirelessly labour to set to rights her husband's blunders, or as a painter will envelop the badly drawn portions of his picture in deep shadow. Then, without a pause, fearing that his father might feel jealous of this new friendship of his with Henri, he said, "May we come with you?"

As the three of them were walking down the rue Royale, Monsieur Santeuil drew Jean's attention to a young man, well though not smartly dressed and good-looking though devoid of charm, who was just lighting a cigarette in a tobacconist's shop. "That's Duroc," he said. Jean set himself at once to study the stranger with curiosity. Monsieur Santeuil began at once to explain who this Duroc was. He had won all the highest honours at school, and, a year after leaving, had headed the list in the entrance examinations to the *École Normale* and the *École Polytechnique*. But he had proceeded to neither of those establishments, preferring to study medicine. He had won second place in his hospital examination, and, in the same year had had a piece on the subject of Regnard presented at the Théatre-Français, which had won the Academy prize. He had then sat for the Foreign Office entrance and come out top. He was now *chef du cabinet* to the Minister, though this did not prevent him from making a good deal of money at the Bar, and winning most of the big bicycle races.

So remarkable a combination of gifts, so unusual a power of application, and the ability to organize his life on so encyclopædic a

scale filled both Henri and Jean with amazement. They were extremely
anxious to make the prodigy's acquaintance. "You will find," said
Monsieur Santeuil, "that in spite of all he has to do he never gives the
impression of being wrapped up in his work—I mean, Jean," he added,
turning to his son, who was frequently absent-minded, "that he is of a
most equable disposition. He finds time to read everything, dines out
every night, and is so punctual in answering letters and keeping
appointments that I don't know what your mother would say who
thinks it extraordinary that I can manage to get through all my
correspondence in the course of a week, whereas you who have nothing
to do can never find the time to write a letter. It so happens that I had
to send him a note this morning on a matter of business. I have no
doubt that he will find it waiting for him at the Ministry, and am quite
sure that I shall have his reply tomorrow morning. And, in spite of all
he has to get through, his letters are always to the point, and admirably
phrased."

Monsieur Duroc had just finished buying some stamps, and was
emerging from the shop with an expression on his face of mingled
gravity and gaiety, when Monsieur Santeuil came to a halt in front of
him, and held out his hand, saying with the happy air of somebody
who has just unexpectedly run into a friend, "Why, if it isn't Duroc!"
Jean was conscious of a slight thrill of excitement at the prospect of
meeting a man whose life, all disciplined control and intellectual
harmony, realized an ideal which had always seemed to him to be
unattainable and in comparison with which his own feeble good
intentions and limited gifts seemed to grovel in outer darkness. Monsieur Duroc at once raised his hat, and Jean felt proud to think that his
father was so highly considered by a man of such distinction. "Allow
me to introduce my son and Monsieur de Réveillon." Monsieur Duroc
saluted the two young men with that pleasing amiability which
implies a consciousness of superiority in the man making it, combined
with a respectful attitude towards those to whom it is addressed with
so easy an air of condescension. It differed completely from the salutations of young doctors, Republican deputies, or recently appointed
magistrates, all of which are marked by a crude heartiness, designed to
create a sense of equality, or by a timidity which shows only too
clearly, by reason of its back-slapping, hail-fellow-well-met air, or an
expression of servile embarrassment, that no such equality, in fact,
exists. It displayed, at one and the same time, the affability of a public

servant and the stiffness of a Republican; it acknowledged the graces of social intercourse without itself being graceful, like a party given by the brilliant wife of a Keeper of the Seals with moderate views, conducted with a good deal of artistic pretentiousness, but no art, in the spacious and handsome rooms of the Ministry.

"And what may be *your* chosen career, young man?" inquired Monsieur Duroc of Jean. Jean turned bright red, like an examination candidate who has been questioned about something to which he does not know the answer, and wants to suggest to the examiner the vast complication of views and anxieties to which it has given rise in his mind, and which a simple "I don't know" would not suffice to convey. But Monsieur Santeuil answered for him. "I intended him for the Foreign Service, but the young rascal is determined to be a poet—of all things! Hanotaux thinks highly of his work," he added hastily. Monsieur Duroc, while bowing to his chief's considered opinion, remarked in a kindly tone: "Speaking for myself, I cannot help regretting that Monsieur Santeuil should have turned his back on the Foreign Office, where it would have been a great pleasure for me to have had him as a colleague, and I must confess that I do not see why an official career should interfere with his literary ambitions. A gift of that kind is a very useful thing to have, not only when sitting for an examination but afterwards. It is to some extent true to say that our best diplomats are those who can write the best reports and once one has reached the rank of secretary, there is much opportunity in the documents designed to come directly under the eye of the Minister, for the display of an elegant style. Happy the man who has to read what you write, and who, generally speaking, can do a great deal to further your promotion, if you are able to instil into naturally dull subjects a certain degree of charm and imaginative grasp." As he uttered those last words, Monsieur Duroc exhaled the smoke of his cigarette, which he seemed in some miraculous way to be able to hold in suspension between his nose and his throat. "That is precisely what I told him," exclaimed Monsieur Santeuil, delighted to hear the point made with so much good sense and grace. Jean was an excellent son, but his father could not help feeling rather sorry that he was not in some vague way a little more like Monsieur Duroc. Jean who had never regarded poetry as some sort of a seasoning to be added at will to matters of business, but convinced all the same that Monsieur Duroc was omniscient, now said with all the sincerity he would have shown in a personal interview with God, knowing that his every word, his every silence, was going to be understood immediately by a mind which could find no difficulty in reading his: "I am afraid, sir, that I am already only too much inclined to enjoy the pleasures of society, and I mean as soon as may be to turn my back on everything of that sort. The career you suggest would make it necessary for me to go a great deal into the world and would destroy any scruple I might have about doing so. Work with me is not something that I can do a great deal of at a time. If such small efforts as I can make were all to be directed to matters outside myself, then—do, please forgive me, in your case, you see, things are so very different—the effect on me would be one of, well of *desiccation*. What I need is an opportunity of concentrating my mind, of digging deep into myself, of trying to find out the truth of things, of expressing the whole of myself, of occupying myself with what is genuine, and not, like what you have been describing, essentially futile."—"A noble ideal," said Monsieur Duroc with a smile, "but I confess that to me your view of poetry is somewhat vague, somewhat confused. What you need, believe me, is to clarify your mind. You fear the world. But success in the eyes of the world is what, really, we all of us seek, whether our work lie in the sphere of thought or in action. You should try to make others aware of your value. For what have all the great scholars, all the capable and far-seeing statesmen worked at, if not, some day, to win the admiring smiles of the ladies? Your mind, I can see, is scrupulous—perhaps too scrupulous: you want to work not for your personal, but for the general, good. Well, then, has it never occurred to you that a diplomatic training could supply you with as many noble ends and various interests as the curiosity of your intelligence or the ambition of your father could desire? You feel that you have a gift for poetry. Have you never thought that as a young Attaché in Rome, the Eternal City, in the Metropolis of our neigh- bours across the Channel among the marvels of Piccadilly, perhaps even in Constantinople, hard by that Bosphorous which has seen the birth of so many wonders and where I first had the honour of meeting your father at Monsieur Cambon's table, you would find beauties of many different kinds capable, provided you can appreciate what you see, of furnishing the setting—to be discreetly used, I need hardly point out, but for that very reason to be the more appreciated—of numberless reports drafted with a feeling for the poetry of your sur- roundings? Your father tells me that you are fond of philosophy. Are not the pilgrimages to Mecca primarily a philosophic subject, involving as they do the problem of the individual conscience at odds with individual risk, of body and soul, faith and science?"

Monsieur Santeuil was listening with the greatest admiration to Monsieur Duroc. With precisely such subjects he had had to deal. It was matter for regret that he had not heard this little speech earlier for it would have furnished him with just those philosophical phrases he required to serve as preface and conclusion to his own disquisitions. But Jean was made miserable by the thought of how much energy he would have to expend in argument with his father before he could destroy the ill effects of so much specious reasoning, and show that if he went into diplomacy it would mean the impoverishment of his life and the starving of his intelligence which, already, owing to laziness, he was inclined to deprive of its necessary sustenance, that his poetic gifts would not find sufficient opportunity of exercise in the compilation of stylishly worded despatches, nor his hunger for philosophy be satisfied by the study of monetary problems or the question of the Mecca pilgrimages. "But," he went on, "I very much want to live near my mother, and life is so short. If I enter the Foreign Service, I shall have to begin by spending two years abroad." – "That is perfectly true," replied Monsieur Duroc, drawing in another mouthful of smoke from his cigarette, "but a mother's love becomes finer and more virile when she sees the son, who was little more than a child when he left her, grown to man's estate, not because he can show hair on his chin, but because she feels that necessary sacrifices have given him a more determined character." Monsieur Santeuil was filled with admiration of the masterly way in which Monsieur Duroc had formulated the very reproaches which he himself had more than once addressed to his wife when criticizing the foolish way she had of petting Jean. "You say," continued Monsieur Duroc, "that you want to express your soul. Does that really mean very much?" Monsieur Santeuil laughed loudly at this sally, and Jean blushed, thinking how foolish he must seem. "You will realize the justice of my question, when I remind you of this talk of our's in, say ten years time," added Monsieur Duroc. "I have not, myself, made a deep study of physiology," he said with becoming modesty, "but ask Monsieur Marfeu, who is a friend of your father, what precisely the soul *is*. I am very much afraid that when you do so he will laugh in your face," he added with an abruptness which was in disagreeable contrast to the polite manner of his recent greeting. "Besides, I entirely fail to understand why a particular occupation should stand in the way of a man having other interests. The truly gifted are those who can turn their hands to many things. Read what Carlyle has to say on the matter. Boccaccio was a first-rate diplomat, and Shakespeare might have been as great a monarch as he was a poet." Jean, who for some minutes had been in a condition of complete intellectual prostration, all of a sudden at this mention of Carlyle, felt his mind beginning to function again, as though he had been given a cup of strong coffee, and was momentarily drawn to Monsieur Duroc, as one is when a stranger unexpectedly reveals the fact that he knows somebody whom one loves and venerates.

"That is true," he said slowly, his eyes fixed on a point in front of him, as though his thoughts had assumed visible form. "Still, Baudelaire habitually failed in his examinations . . ."–" . . . Which is why his poetry has so strongly morbid a strain, and is, if I may say so, ridiculously over-valued by our young decadents." The word *decadents* set Monsieur Santeuil laughing loudly, and caused Jean to grind his teeth as though certain words, quite independently of the connexion in which they were used and according to the person who used them, were either intelligent or stupid. By this time they had reached the Concorde bridge. A crowd had gathered, and they stopped to watch. A soldier was quarrelling with a cabman, and, all of a sudden, with a quick movement, sent his antagonist reeling backwards against a lamp-post.

"Good for you, Tommy!" cried Monsieur Duroc. Jean, hearing him, was conscious of an indescribable sense of discomfort, followed by a feeling of delicious contentment. Monsieur Duroc might be all he was, might know all he knew, but he had just said something which neither Jean, nor any really intelligent person, would ever have said. This emotion, however, was still vague, when Henri whispered with a nod of the head in the direction of Monsieur Duroc: "Put a sock in it!" It was as though lightning had flashed from a sky for some time obscured by a dark mass of cloud. Jean burst out laughing, and pressed Henri's hand in sheer gratitude at having been released from an oppressive sense of self-doubt, and at the same time from the need of admiring Monsieur Duroc.

★

"Shall I be seeing you tomorrow, Sunday?" Jean said to Henri. "Not tomorrow, I'm afraid: I've got to go with my mother and father to

call on Monsieur d'Utraine." Jean had heard a great deal about
Monsieur d'Utraine's house, about his wit, about his suits, about his
painting. He said, with simple-minded effusiveness, "Oh dear! how
I wish I knew him!" If anybody else had said that, Henri would have
at once replied: "Why not join us? That is to say, if it wouldn't bore
you," like a man who gives his purse to the first person he meets, at the
same time apologizing for loading him with such a responsibility, from
fear of hurting his feelings by seeming to oblige him. But Henri, whenever something that he said involved ratification by his mother,
became at once "pure Réveillon", that is to say somebody for whom
Jean, in other words, a little middle-class nobody, took rank as a casual
acquaintance, a "foreigner", something like the "hostis" of the
Romans. Though the hereditary social code of the Réveillons was
more or less silent on the subject of the "hostis", and contained little
or nothing which might regulate their behaviour towards him,
because the problem of their relations with members of the middle class
had never seriously been considered, nevertheless, a sort of makeshift
set of rules, necessitated by a few exceptional cases such as the family
doctor, the children's tutor etc. had given to such relations a character
of extreme wariness and it was only under great pressure that a
decision was ever reached when it was a question of a Réveillon
including the hostis of another noble house in the complex pattern of
such exceptional cases, as it is only under pressure that a deputy is
"included" in legal proceedings. Have the itch in the privacy of your
own home if you like but don't give it to other people's children—
that, in a few words, serves to sum up the general attitude of their
world in matters of this kind.

When it was necessary to take a "line" and to opt for "inclusion",
it was done with high magnificence, but in a manner which made it
sufficiently clear that it was not to be understood as establishing a
precedent. To give but a single instance: one day the Duchesse de
Réveillon happened to meet, at the house of her niece, the Marquise
de Réveillon-Bouchage, Monsieur Calpin, an artist who had painted
a portrait of the Marquise. Madame de Réveillon-Bouchage was loud
in his praises when she introduced him to her aunt. (She felt more than
usually pleased at being able to make this polite gesture, since she hoped
that it would be taken as an expression of her gratitude. In fact, the
thought came to her that the amethyst tie-pin which she had intended
to give the painter, might well be changed into a quite simple little

ornament in rhinestone, the difference in value being more than made up by this presentation to the Duchess. She even thought that if she could arrange for him to dine, just once, with the Duke, there need be no question of her giving him anything at all.) The Duchess, who was standing at a small table, in the act of choosing a sweet biscuit, began a rocking movement consisting of two distinct phases. The first of these brought her a step forward to greet the painter in a manner which seemed to him nothing less than prodigious, he being accustomed to the rather off-hand politeness of the middle-class ladies of his acquaintance. But, at the very moment when her body seemed about to touch Monsieur Calpin, so that apparently, there would be nothing left for him but to take her in his arms, she withdrew quickly, moving like a mechanical toy, while her back, well behind her centre of gravity, in the likeness of the pendulum of a clock, executed a movement of retreat no less expansive than the earlier gesture of greeting had been. It was quite obvious that the whole complicated manœuvre was intended to convey, "You may look at the lovely flowers, my dear sir, but be pleased to remember that they are not for you."

For the next three months, whenever the Duchess met Monsieur Calpin at the house of her niece, she repeated the same form of salutation, while her eyes expressed the greatest astonishment, not that she failed to recognize him, but in order to make it quite clear that she did not know him. At the end of that time, Monsieur Calpin having once on the occasion of a call, made a sketch of Henri, her greeting gave it to be understood that she did, at least, know who he was, as one may know who the man is who once came to lay the carpet, or the plumber who has been to the house on several occasions to mend the taps in the dressing-room. There were even days when with seeming hesitation, she held out her hand to him, in precisely the same way as she might have offered him a shilling, thinking to herself, 'I don't believe I tipped him last time.' But poor Monsieur Calpin was completely taken in by the good manners of the Duke, who, from the very first moment of introduction always seemed to recognize him, and shook hands as though with an old friend, but shouting in so loud a voice that the windows shook, and as though to make sure that the Heavens should hear, and bear witness to his politeness, "How-de-do, my dear sir!"

It so happened that Calpin, when dining one evening at the house of the Marquise de Réveillon-Bouchage (by that time all hope of the tie-pin had faded, and he was merely being invited to his hostess's charity bazaars) found himself sitting next to the Duc de Réveillon, who had Madame Desroches on his other side. Perhaps with the intention of giving Madame Desroches, as well as Calpin, an object lesson in the "politeness of dukes", the Duc de Réveillon, who had just asked Madame Desroches what she had thought of the performance of *Don Giovanni* at the opera, lowered his voice, though it was still far from being inaudible to the other guests, and said: "Tell me, who is this feller?" Madame Desroches conveyed Calpin's name in a whisper, and her opinion of *Don Giovanni*—which she thought had been much better performed at the Opéra-Comique—quite loudly. "Were you there, my dear chap?" inquired the Duke, turning to Calpin as though to a bosom companion. That was all. Calpin, envisaging a flood of invitations to bazaars organized by the Marquise (Bethlehem Club) thought himself entitled to ask her to bring the Duchesse de Réveillon to his studio. "I am sure she would love to come," said the Marquise, and smiled, as though ravished by so entrancing a prospect. But the Duchess never took advantage of the invitation. It occurred to Calpin that perhaps the Marquise had forgotten to pass it on. After a few months he repeated it. The Marquise smiled precisely as she had done the first time, and with even greater deliberation. But she never mentioned the subject again. Finally, at the end of the year, she appeared in Calpin's studio with her children's tutor, who having successfully coached her son for his *baccalauréat*, was being rewarded for his hard work by being taken to the studio of a "worth-while" painter by a distinguished marquise.

Henri was perfectly well aware that his parents in no way treated Jean as a "hostis", far from it, in fact. Besides, there had been a time when Monsieur d'Utraine must, himself, have been one. But, as the lover of Madame d'Aubergin-Crillot, and Vice-President of the Jockey Club, he had been granted the "freedom of the city"—with all the advantages which went with it. Still, Henri thought that it would be wrong to give a definite answer without first consulting his superior in the hierarchy, namely his father. It cost him nothing to refrain from replying to Jean, "You must go with me." There was no doubt at all that he was very fond of Jean, would have liked to share everything with him, to please him on all possible occasions, and to make it quite clear that it was his dearest wish to please him. But this tenderness, and the warmth of fellow-feeling which it had kindled in him and was now at its extreme of intensity, as when the sun breaks through for a brief space on winter days, could not change the well-balanced solidity of his nature. Feeling quite certain that his mother would agree to Jean going with them, he was not impatient, as Jean would have been, to show that he wanted nothing better than for Jean to be of the party. He knew that there is a time for everything, and, for the moment could think of nothing to say except; "He really is a charming fellow, you know."

When he had left them, Monsieur Duroc asked, "Which d'Utraine were you talking about?"—adding, with a smile, as though the name were in some sort a witticism, "Frédéric, I suppose?"–"Yes," said Monsieur Santeuil, grasping the point of the joke, "I wouldn't for the world have said so in front of anyone who seems to know him so well as the gentleman who has just parted from us, but my own opinion is that the man's a perfect freak—quite mad, you know." This comment had the effect of making Jean feel all the more sure that he would like Monsieur d'Utraine. Now that he no longer thought of the ideal man as somebody who had passed every examination for which he had ever sat, he felt inclined to believe that he would find him in an individual whose overcoats were as original, as subtly coloured, as harmonously blended as his thoughts; who was as handome, as brave, as witty, as modest, as "smart" as he was gifted with intelligence and a talent for painting; who was a friend, not only of the Duchesse de Réveillon and the Princess of Wales, but of Anatole France, Tolstoy and Ibsen; who was a model landlord, and quite unbelievably gifted; who had been elected Vice-President of the Jockey Club and awarded the *Médaille d'honneur* of the Salon on one and the same day; whose house was no less a masterpiece than the pictures it contained; who had entertained for Mademoiselle de Guise a passion that was at once noble, ardent, exquisite, and melancholy, and, in short, truly reflected his character.

On that very same evening, Jean was handed by the servant a note from Henri, "Papa will be very pleased for you to go with us to see Monsieur d'Utraine."

6. *Portrait of a Friend*

There is one of Jean's friends whose nature and character I should like to put on record. Even had I not had a great fondness for him, I should still wish to do so. Doubtless, we have better things to do than to record details of character, no matter how generalized, nor how individual they may be. It is, however, but rarely that nature vouchsafes us those revelations which we feel compelled to commit to paper without bothering to think whether by so doing we are likely to display our intelligence or our brilliance in a flattering light, indeed, on the contrary, feeling a strong disinclination to make concessions to either. But between such moments of true poetry and the simple observation of manners, there are other moments at which our fellows are revealed to us, or to one part of us, which though it may not lie at the deepest level, is not so superficial as the mere exercise of the observing eye.

This deeper form of observation is capable of suddenly confronting us with a quality in our fellow men which lies deeper than they themselves realize, which becomes the very mainspring of their being, of their reality. We see them as it were a little withdrawn from us, and suspended as in some delicate, intangible and gracious bubble.

*

Bertrand de Réveillon was one of those young aristocrats who, being endowed with a lively though by no means outstanding brain, are filled with a passion for intelligence, knowledge, talent, justice, progress and equality; who hold that mere nobility of birth is nothing and are even inclined, other things being equal, to believe so far as intelligence is concerned that an aristocrat is stupid because he is an aristocrat, a commoner intelligent because he is a commoner. At a slightly higher level of intelligence this attitude of complete detachment, where the question of birth plays a part, usually ceases. Such superior individuals, being of finer grain than many of their fellows, realize that there *are* members of the middle classes who suffer from stupidity, and not a few writers, statesmen and scholars as well. Discounting the outstandingly talented, they are only too pleased to find among those of their own world a number of persons whose gentleness, charm and good manners they know how to appreciate as qualities which have been denied to others, qualities which Bertrand de Réveillon, hungering and thirsting after truth and justice, consistently undervalued. Since in them intellectual interests are bound up with a more developed egotism, they find it easier to appreciate the advantages which a great position in the world can give, and are at pains to see that the source of such advantages shall not perish. The society of these gifted aristocrats is infinitely more agreeable than that of those of whom for me Bertrand de Réveillon has always been the type. Sharing many of the qualities of that middle-class society which produces most of the gifted and exceptionally charming individuals with whom they love to consort, but, at the same time, not cutting themselves off from the incomparably more gracious and attractive men and women of their own world, they enjoy a prestige, if only of strangeness, in the eyes of the vulgar. They live in what one may be allowed to call a society of exquisites. The nobility of their birth—which they very charmingly soft-pedal in their talk—their manners, their genuine interest in painting, philosophy, and literature, remain as it were relegated to the background of a life in which they exist in a framework of small red ducal coronets embossed upon their writing-paper, of armies of footmen who without their so much as noticing it, so strong is habit, consistently address them as Monsieur le Duc, or Madame la Duchesse, by pictures of their ancestors and of the châteaux which bear their names, and by an array of silver plate engraved with their heraldic blazons.

Bertrand de Réveillon had neither the depth of understanding to realize that those who wish to be free have other things to do than the changing of such trivialities, nor enough of that sensitiveness, or, perhaps I should say, aptitude, which a man who has saved himself from becoming engulfed in a universe of pure reason, can bring to the aesthetic enjoyment of such things, to the relishing of the small though definite charm that they can radiate, nor sufficient calculation to use them for the purpose of pleasing others and dominating them. If he had ever found pleasure in vanity—and most of us retain some remnant of vanity which, though it may change its form, never wholly disappears—it would have been that he had had a play put upon the stage, an article accepted for publication, an election won. But if the society of aristocrats who are intelligent only in the second degree is less enjoyable than that of those who are so in the first, it still has a certain charm which derives from their absolute lack of self-interest, and this, in the general hurly-burly of their middle-class friends—lawyers, young journalists, young artists—sets them apart by reason of a sort of moral attractiveness which is nothing less than the breeze of their spiritual purity. The young men who, in their own eyes, are the very embodiment of social justice, political equality, talent, and moral beauty, are so, in precisely the same way as Bertrand de Réveillon was the embodiment of Catholic youth—that is to say, in name. But in them, all those fine phrases conceal selfish ambitions, little though, perhaps, they realize it, for they are not sufficiently intelligent to see through the sophistries of the bombastic talk which they have learned from others, and repeat at café tables. Such phrases enshrine things all of which Réveillon wanted, but the reality of those things was not in the young men but in his own heart. What he most truly desired was to be forgiven for being an aristocrat. Fundamentally, these young men were flattered that someone of his sort should be their friend, but, not wishing to show that they were flattered, they rode his social superiority on a tight rein, though it stood in no need of restraint, and affected to treat him as an equal, as though he ever pretended to be anything else, or rather, if he did, it was only in so far as he thought of himself as being less important than they were but freed already from his aristocratic leading-strings and already almost one of them. The purity of his character was what constituted his charm. Consequently, they had not been able to exercise any very profound influence upon him. He had remained good in the midst of their covetousness, kindly in the midst of their back-biting, unalterably loyal in spite of their duplicities, simple where they were pretentious—except, perhaps, in matters of phraseology which he copied from them. These differences, clear at first sight to anyone with a gift for observation, became clearer still if, as the result of some sentimental crisis or some important happening you were brought into direct contact with his heart. When that happened it was like finding yourself stranded by a railway accident, and being made suddenly aware that you had stumbled into a hospitable and friendly village instead of being left on a possibly dangerous road where there would be little chance of finding shelter and a warm welcome.

But he stood out from among them, too, because of certain personal qualities which may have been the gift to him, essentially, of his aristocratic heritage. First and foremost was the sort of charming simplicity which one finds among people of his social standing (when, that is, they are not afflicted with family pride or caste prejudice) who have no reason to conceal a sense of inferiority beneath a show of brag and boasting, snobbery behind an abrupt manner, withering contempt for the neighbour who has lagged in the race for worldly success, or a sneaking admiration for those on a higher rung of the social ladder. Of all these ugly frustrations, your true aristocrat—by which I mean not a member of the petty nobility, but the bearer of a great name, and therefore innocent of all arrogance—is entirely free. About a man of the middle class—to which all of *us* belong—no matter how intelligent, how admirable, how simple he may be, there is always a little something, the ready-made phrase, the unpleasing gesture, which at once reveals to the quick-witted observer a suppressed wish to show that, for him, a prince is no different to anybody else, a way of saying "la Comtesse" with that particular inflexion which somehow indicates that he must really apologize for talking in so ridiculous a manner, a sort of general attitude which, in a genuinely superior being is almost non-existent, and which is often the legacy of the decent middle-class pride of a father or a grandmother who knew all about "keeping one's place", and who regarded titles and social ranks as mere vanity.

From what I have said it will be apparent to you that Bertrand de Réveillon had never, in the whole course of his life, been guilty of snobbery or condescension, had never felt the need to hide a feeling of snobbery, or the desire to express his condescension. His nature therefore had never been creased the wrong way. If he was kindly it was because his heart urged him to be so, or because he felt a liking for the person to whom he happened to be talking. For in his eyes that person was neither "better" than himself, someone with whom he must be careful not to be too easy-going, nor "worse", with the result that no hint of condescension came to mar a willingness to admit his attractiveness. And since our affections are but the expression of ourselves, they were in his case as pure as he was, which is why a friend could rely upon his devotion, an acquaintance on his good-will, those who confided in him on his discretion, and a friend in trouble on his certain and practical help.

There were qualities in him too that derived perhaps even more from his race than from his personal character. For to the freedom he enjoyed in the conduct of his life, which was the gift to him of noble birth, and made him a stranger to the calculating outlook of the ambitious, the contemptuous attitude of the self-made man, the bitterness of the humble and the unsuccessful, were added all those graces which he regarded as being of no importance, but which were part and parcel of himself and which he scattered with a generous hand among the vulgar boors with whom he chose to consort. He might disdain his aristocratic origins, but he could not get rid of the aristocratic elegance with which they had endowed him. He might surrender his hand into that of a lawyer, but that could not alter the fact that it was a delicate, long-fingered hand which, in responding to a greeting, had a free and easy movement and seemed pleased to remain for no inconsiderable time in the hand it grasped, this, I fully believe, being the expression of an unconscious memory of how his father, and others like him, always behaved when they wished to flatter an interlocutor by a seeming familiarity and an ignoring of social distinctions. The way in which he carried his head, his well-bred features, his appearance, his figure, his movements, all these things in him were marks of breeding. But they were all inherited from a distant past. Nearer in time was his childhood, which had been pre-eminently aristocratic and spent in activities which had made his body supple, and in a school of manners which had taught him a rhythmic grace which controlled his every movement—considerations which, for a young man of a certain social class, ensure that no matter what he does, whether it be entering a room, raising his hat, mounting a horse, taking a lady's arm, refusing to let anybody disturb himself by getting up at his appearance and motioning him to sit down again, doing, in fact, anything under any circumstances (so long as they do not carry an intellectual or moral significance), he will do in exactly the right way, at a ball, in a café, at the races, in any scene of the human comedy, without giving them a moment's thought, always adequate, always exquisite, always self-assured, and with an air of complete freedom, whereas, compared with him, a philosopher, a doctor, or a poet will be awkward, grotesque, embarrassed, over-emphatic, or, at the best—or worst—correct.

*

And so it was that one day when Bertrand de Réveillon, in order to reach me the more quickly, made his way across a crowded café by clambering over the tables and settees, that action of his roused in me something deeper than the pure spirit of observation, set him before my consciousness as something far more significant than a person merely seen, and filled me with a sort of happiness, thus scampering over the tables in obedience to instinctive influences of which he was not himself aware, so that the impression he made upon me was that of an apparition, unreal, gracious, charming.

I can never tire of saying that this ease of manner, this eloquence of kindliness, gives to friendship something special and without equal. Indeed, for these, in some sort sovereign folk, nothing counts, nothing arrests them, nothing exerts dominance over them but their own immediate need and that of their friend. And the friend never feels between himself and them that dreaded barrier of etiquette which is so much more to be feared than a friend's displeasure. We are separated by a wilderness of restaurant tables. I clamber on to them, and run across their tops. This I do with grace, so that I cause no laughter in those who witness the incident, but rather fill them with admiration: and this grace, this setting aside of the conventions, is all for you, who will thus arouse in other breasts feelings of envy and of admiration, as you sit there awaiting my hurried, my acrobatic approach, I shoulder aside conventions, I reduce them to ashes, I make of them a trophy which, with that grace of which I am wholly unaware, I lay at your feet. If you are tired, I am strong; if you are clumsy, I am dexterous, and every one of my actions is designed for you. There are many friends with me this evening, but they know that you are my heart's choice: they are of my world, a world in which men know that when one wishes to show a preference, a feeling of respect, there can be no question of "that sort of thing" not being "done", a world in which there is no fear, no dread of ridicule, no question of being formal and rather fearfully correct through an inability to *create* the correct form at any given moment. And so, I say to my friends, "Leave us together; I want to be alone with him"; or, "go and get him" this, that, or the other, for my friends are men of my world and will not feel humiliated.

I confess to a feeling of sadness when I think of Bertrand de Réveillon and recall how on that evening he clambered over the tables in order to reach me the more quickly, after dismissing his friends. For he who valued only intelligence, justice, talent, will be remembered because of something to which he attached no importance, of which he took no account, gradually ceasing to consort with those to whom it was a natural gift and seeking out those who did not possess it. And no doubt he would be right in his resentment. A man should not be judged for what he is by nature, for that in him which is not of his own making, for what is no more than a birthright and the fruit of education, and has nothing to do with that other "him", that character of later growth, which is the only part of him that counts.

But those somewhat deeper impressions which go further than a man's phenomenal self and bear within them a more than phenomenal truth, it is the duty of the artist to express, while leaving their profundity unexplored. All desire to please or to displease, still more, all concern to show respect, all fear of causing pain, even if those things involve what is most worthy of respect, or what is noblest, in an individual, and, as an object of portraiture, endow him with a phenomenal personality, tend, at once, to diminish all profundity of awareness in him on whom falls the task of giving reality to his impressions. It is therefore his duty to set such considerations aside. Bertrand de Réveillon, like all young men of his kind, was too much given to thinking that a purely individual impression—such as that of somebody clambering over settees in a café—which, to the eye of reason is of little importance, is without true value, and that the greatness of an impression is in proportion to its power of raising general ideas in the mind of the observer. Those men of second-rate intelligence who formulate theories or write books about anything in the world, are concerned to stress only some way of understanding the class-struggle or the influence exercised by love upon the active life. But when I once asked Henri de Régnier what he most liked in his favourite book, *Le Rouge et le Noir*, he answered: "I think the scene of the Review where Julien Sorel appears on horseback among all the military men"; and referring to a story much loved by Anatole France, "Yes, that terrace overlooking the sea is really very charming." Perhaps we should do well to realize that Bertrand de Réveillon, like any other single individual, was of no particular interest to Nature and if of any interest at all, only because he unconsciously expressed an essential truth that would long outlive him, which was why Nature had endowed with beauty an ephemeral impression, the significance of which was concealed, in order that a poet should be moved by it, should hold it fast, should plumb its depths, and disengage for others the truth it hid.

When you hastened towards me with so much agility and grace, it was not only the person you were in that passing moment whom your friend admired. No, what he felt was that all the free, alert, vigorous life of your childhood was there, in that instant, at your service, and that you dedicated it to his, as a generous host gives freely all he has. What joy then for the loving heart to feel all that separated him from a friend, all the distant past when we did not know one another, all the brilliance of an existence so far removed from my own obscure life, all the strength, so different from my own weakness, which seemed as though it must always be a barrier between us—to feel suddenly that the friend had said—the years that are dead and gone, the education so different from my own, are come again to me, or rather to us, that I may bind them in the suppleness of my limbs, so that running towards you, I can bear them as a gift, and so destroy all that might separate us.

Your greatness of spirit too, was made manifest in that act. For there is no graciousness unless we hold it to be worthless, unless it is an unconscious movement, unless it follows us when our thoughts are occupied with other matters. And your heart, no less, which gave the colour of affection to what, otherwise, was nothing more than a feat of human agility, which united the vigour which was the past's gift to you, with the alertness of mind present in that moment of our meeting, bringing them together in the natural effervescence of a desire to see me again, and finding ready to its hand a grace that was perfectly unaware of itself.

And so there was about that evening something infinitely refreshing, as are those moments when a person's charm dissipates all jealousy, all sadness, and concentrates into a single moment the whole of a life offered as a gift to friendship, so that restlessness of heart is thereby all wiped out. An enemy may have a beauty which makes it difficult for us to understand why we should hate him. A friend may have beauty which, alas, has nothing to do with our reasons for loving him. For such beauty is a truth of which the individual is merely the symbol, the carrier, and not the author. Whence it comes that the perception of a relationship like this, reaching us only through what is universal, can give nothing but happiness. Forgive me, Bertrand, for having on that day loved in you a beauty in which your self-esteem could take no pride, which could not in any way determine my affection.

7. Jean's Quarrel with his Parents

"What about having dinner with me this evening? I shall be all by myself," Réveillon had said to Jean as they parted at the gate of the Lycée. But Jean had not accepted the invitation. He had arranged to dine with Gantaud, Flubiste, and three girls, and did not intend to sleep at home. He knew that this would distress his mother, but, at the same time, he was sorely tempted. Besides, his mother would know nothing about it. For the last two years, on the pretext that it was better not to let his mother into the secrets of a young man's life, he had done many things without telling her, and had told her many things without doing them. The knowledge that this was so gave him pain. He made a great effort to pull himself together, and confronted the imagined joys of the promised dinner and the night that would follow it, with the prospect of a quiet meal with Henri, after which he would go home about eleven so as to spend an hour with his parents, sitting by the fire while his mother played the piano or read aloud. Or she too perhaps would sit doing nothing, and just talking about the people she had met during the day. And so it was that he sent an express letter to Henri to say that he *would* dine with him after all. Usually, when he had reached a decision, the alternative would immediately seem to him to be infinitely preferable. But this was not the case after he had sent his note to Henri. The idea of having dinner with him, and finishing the evening with his parents, had seemed to him, while he still had it in mind to dine with Gantaud and Flubiste, a tame sort of business. But now, and as though by winning the battle against his desires he had in some sort risen in his own esteem, he found charm in a prospect which it needed only a small effort on his part to turn into a reality, and was conscious of a lively happiness gushing up within him and inundating his whole being, so that it showed even in his face. He could feel that he was smiling, that his eyes were clear and innocent, that his mouth expressed goodness and a contented mind. Delighted at the thought that, thanks to this new arrangement, he would have an extra hour (he need not get to Henri's before eight) in which to work at the sketch he wanted to get done in time for his mother's birthday and determined to settle down to work in earnest, to see no more of Gantaud and Flubiste, but to come home every night at eleven, he slowly climbed the stairs, turned the key in the door, feeling in it, and even in his fingers, the friendliness, the happy tenderness which at this moment was flooding his whole body, and entered.

But unfortunately not everybody thinks the same thing at the same moment. Satisfaction at the idea of a good action on your part comes to full flower just precisely at the moment when you are perpetrating a bad one, while the anger caused by a fault bursts at the very moment when, aware of your own moral improvement, you have forgotten all about it and would be only too glad that others should have forgotten it too, ruled as you are by that absolute logic of the feelings for which all the pulsations of the vast world's enormous happiness are nothing but so many cries of intolerable anguish when the heart is sad, though if it is gay, it would gladly see as joyful bon-fires what are, in fact, the torches of vengeance and of death. Madame Santeuil was seated at her desk, writing, and did not notice Jean. Perhaps had she met his eyes and put her trust in what they were saying, just for a moment, she might have truly sounded his intentions, as, by throwing something into a river, one may learn in which direction the water is moving. Perhaps, if she had kissed him she could have made his happy hopefulness, his resolute optimism, flow into her-self. Especially had they had a few moments of talk together, she might have learned something of that noble strife of strong feelings at variance of which Jean's spirit had been the theatre, in which he had openly declared for the good and won the battle for it. Victories of that description were for Jean, of such rare occurrence that he could not but feel the need to give his mother a detailed account of the struggle in the hope of bringing balm to her bruised affections and of recovering her esteem. But Madame Santeuil was writing. She did not see Jean and heard only a quick footstep. She had just had a visit from Jean's professor who had told her that he was doing no work at all. Being a stern Republican he was only too glad to think that the nobly born had all the vices in the calendar, and, being ignorant of the fact that Réveillon was doing all he could to keep Jean from the evil influence of Gantaud and Flubiste, had accused him of flinging his friend into a life of debauch while himself holding back (for Réveillon was a worker) —a situation which seemed to him to be more than usually perverse.

"He thinks it fun to keep your son from working, a sort of a game, and can always dominate him, because Jean is cursed with a weak character." – "While he, you mean, because he is the stronger of the two, can stop before it is too late, and enjoy the little manœuvre without danger to himself?" concluded Madame Santeuil, justly incensed. She respected the teaching staff, and believed that the judgment of its members was infallible. In addition to this, in her, natural tendency, she had recently found out from the servants whom Jean had told of his intentions, that her son would probably not be home until the following morning. It was the first time that such a thing had happened, or the first time she had been told of it. She had been deeply hurt, but, after the initial effect had worn off, had said to herself: 'It may be all for the best: at least it has opened my eyes. I must now take definite steps: I must start the battle.' Then she had sought out her husband and told him that he must act—a thing Monsieur Santeuil never did except in the last extremity, realizing that action of any kind was not in his line, though once he had made up his mind he was apt to assert himself with immoderate violence, being convinced from the very moment of his first broadside that the enemy knew himself to be beaten and must now be reduced to powder.

Jean had entered with the feeling that he must get rid at once of what was pressing on his mind before he kissed his mother, and so, speaking from the little hall-way, said: "Mamma dear, I'm dining alone with Réveillon this evening," meaning to convey by his words that he was not to make one in the feverish and unhealthy excitements of a large dinner party, but, on the contrary, was to enjoy the innocent pleasure, the virtuous delight, of serious conversation with a dear friend. But Madame Santeuil, understanding the word *alone* to mean *without his parents, in the company of loose women, preparatory to a night of orgy*, felt the anger which she had been waiting to let loose on Jean, when the right moment should come, in reproaches and warnings, threats, prohibitions and orders, sweeping her off her feet, as water, intended for the making of tea, when it comes too soon to the boil, overflows on to the fire, and jets up into the face of the person in charge of the teapot. Without moving from her chair, she said in a hard voice: "Oh no, you're not: you're dining here with us! In my opinion you are seeing a great deal too much of Réveillon as it is. That has got to stop. Your father will have something to say to you about it."

No orchestral leader following up with a single sweep of his bow a gay andante in the major with a furious allegro in the minor could

have produced so sudden a change in the mood of an audience as did
Madame Santeuil's voice. Jean was staggered and his face showed it.
Where but a moment before had been a forest in all the glory of its
spring foliage under a morning sun, was now the darkness of eclipse,
the fury of a raging sea and roaring storm. It seemed to him that never
again would life and happiness, hope and radiance shine upon this
scene of devastation. His face went dead white, his eyes blazed out from
shadowed orbits. His legs which, so recently had climbed the stairs to
an imagined paradise, now trembled beneath him like those of a sick
lamb. Truth to tell, he could not yet grasp the full meaning of the words
his mother had just uttered, though their echo still reverberated in his
ears, vast and ominous, and sounding through the immensities of time,
as might the voice of an examiner announcing the subject of an essay
to a candidate who knows nothing about it, but feels that upon his
ability to make something of it will depend the whole future of his
life. He was not, for the moment, conscious of pain, but only of the
physical symptoms that herald pain, like a man who, in the grip of
sudden illness feels nothing but a shivering fit, and is still capable of
undressing himself and getting into the bed where he will lie for many
months—unable to leave it. The sight of Augustin near by, pretending
to be brushing Monsieur Santeuil's overcoat, but really engaged in
listening with intense interest to the progress of a scene from which he
could draw the satisfying knowledge that the position of the "son of
the house" was no more free from ups and downs than was that of the
family retainer—the knowledge that Augustin was within earshot, by
proving to Jean that his unhappiness was now matter for public
chatter, seemed to make of it something that was beyond mending.
At this very moment Monsieur Santeuil, hearing his wife's voice raised
in anger, and concluding that the battle must be at its fiercest, came out
of his study, a thing so unusual in itself that Augustin, dropping the
overcoat, stood staring with fear and anxiety clearly written on his
face at his master who interpreting the expresson as one of sympathy
with Jean, suddenly lost his temper. "If you don't want to work," he
shouted roughly, "you can do the other thing: you can get out!"
By this time Madame Santeuil had disappeared, leaving Jean alone
with his father, and feeling very sorry for her husband who, she persuaded herself, was of a very sensitive nature—no doubt in order to find
an excuse for his outbursts—and might, as a result of nervous
exhaustion, create a scene.

By the time five minutes had passed, the calm and sensible words which Jean had addressed to his father, had merely added to the latter's fury, and were being swept along as twigs and branches, thrown into the waters by dwellers on a river bank, as peace offerings to the angry gods, are swirled away on the bank-high current. "As to that rascally young Réveillon," Monsieur Santeuil was saying, "you will sit *down at once*, and send him a message to say that you will *not* be dining with him tonight." – "There is no need for Jean to write anything," said Madame Santeuil, who had just come back into the room. "I have already sent him word that Jean will not see him this evening, nor for many evenings to come." Up till then, Madame Santeuil had always considered it as due to her son that she should treat his friends with politeness. Even when she was angry with Jean, if one of them happened to put in an appearance, she at once resumed her conversation with him in the normal tones imposed, as it were, by a Truce of God. But now Jean felt himself overwhelmed by a sense of shame greater than he had ever known at the thought that he would have to blush for her in Henri's presence, that she had insulted him before Henri, and had insulted Henri too, and that the vexation which was now going to spoil the whole evening for him and which only Henri's company could have consoled, would now last for a very long time, and, for a very long time, would be a barrier between the two friends. He sprang forward with the intention of getting hold of the fatal letter, but his mother said: "It is no use your doing that: I have already sent it." He looked at his parents with fury in his eyes, thrust his hands in his pockets, stopped just long enough to say, "You've gone completely mad, both of you!" and then made a slow exit, slamming the door so violently behind him that the glass ornaments fixed to its panels (which had no idea that the damage inflicted upon them had nothing to do with doors) were shattered into fragments. Then, like a Roman withdrawing to the Capitoline Hill when the law had been violated, he retired to the privacy of his own room.

He was in a fever. His hands were trembling so that he found it difficult to turn the knob. He tried again, more violently, and banged the door behind him in a fury, instead of shutting it quietly. But, being hung on hinges older and less subject to disturbance than the young master whose hours of rest and play and dreaming it guarded, it came to a stop on the threshold and closed gently enough. He stumbled into the room blindly, bumped into the table and gave it a savage kick. He had meant to sit down in his armchair, but, finding it too hard and unyielding for his present mood of acute irritation, gave it a violent shake, accompanied by much cursing and fuming, as a man may round unjustly on the servant who, by mere chance, has been the witness of his shame or ill-temper. Then he began to calm down. He could feel his anger thudding with furious and powerless blows against his heart, like waves. Each blow was some new revenge contrived against his parents, some new insult mouthed and muttered and distinctly audible. And with each blow there came to him a momentary sense of relief, as, when we stand on the sea's edge our expectancy, strained by the slow building up, the gathering accumulation of strength, the toppling curve of each incoming roller, dissolves with a feeling of relief, when the wave breaks, only to form again when the process is repeated. He no longer even held it against his parents that they should have failed to realize the excellence of his intentions when they had punished him for the very faults he had determined never to repeat. For those intentions had been swept utterly from his mind. He could no longer remember a time when he had thought with tenderness of his parents, for such a thought at such a moment would have been intolerable to him. Hatred breeds hatred. He could see them, in imagination, having a furtive laugh together over the execution they had carried out, having coldly planned the whole manœuvre. He could hear them saying to each other, "A little fit of temper's not worth bothering about: I don't think we shall have any more trouble with *him*." And this concoction of imagined wrongs distorted his whole manner of feeling, justified his violence, provided fuel for his hatred, and spurred him on to thoughts of vengeance, so that again and again he said to himself: 'I'll show them! I'll show them!'

Roughly severed from his parents by his sense of their injustice, it was neither to Flubiste nor to Gantaud that his mind turned, nor to thoughts of pleasure. His mood of misery alienated him from those who would neither have understood it, nor have wished to give him consolation. The flood of his now unchannelled tenderness, diverted as it was from the family hearth, and feeling no wish to return to it, set strongly towards Henri. Grieving, he began to cry, and all his misery, and all his tears took the way that led to Henri, as, on sloping ground, the many rivulets obey its call, and end by merging. He wanted to go and live with Henri. The Duchess would be only too glad to give him a room. There his longings would at least be listened to,

his intentions understood, his happiness protected. Often, when we
have been the unwitting cause of a loved person being scolded and
grieved by those who are nearest to him, we feel, because of our own
scrupulous tenderness, or, perhaps, only because of his own discom-
fiture, that he must hold us to blame for what has happened, must be
annoyed with us, must love us less. You perhaps, who at that very
same moment might have felt yourself caught up in the worries or the
pain which, because of you, others had brought upon your mistress or
upon your friend, would have found some consolation in Jean's grief,
of which Henri was, really, the cause, realizing that his tenderness for
Henri, mingled with that grief and grown to double its size, was
seeking protection under Henri's wing and, perhaps, offering him his
own in return, as though it were mainly against Henri that his mother's
injustice had been directed. It was chiefly for Henri persecuted that he
wept. "*You* would not cause me pain, nor ever seek to do so!" he
murmured between sobs, hugging to his heart the image of the absent
Henri, whose frank and kindly eyes answered those words with just
the sympathy he wanted, as a dog, when his master, disillusioned in
all other loves, confides in him, seems without quitting his habitual
silence to agree with all that is said to him, and thus lays a flattering
unction to the afflicted heart. Then suddenly from thinking of Henri,
he began to think again of his parents and his fury grew. Nothing could
restrain it now that he had found for it a disinterested motive. It
burned to revenge itself, not for the pain that they had given him, but
for the wrong they had committed against his friend.

For a moment, thinking guiltily of the time that he had wasted,
dreading the torment of frayed nerves, the sleeplessness, which might
result from all this wild indulgence in emotion, he tried to concentrate
upon a book and to do some work. But even with the book lying open
before him, he was still conscious of the mutterings of anger, and felt
rather like a man trying to read with somebody making music close
beside him, or two men quarrelling within earshot, so that he cannot
keep himself from hearing the sound of singing or the bitter wrangling
of dispute, instead of taking in the meaning of the words on which he
is trying to concentrate his attention. He got to his feet, then settled
himself again squarely in his chair and stopped his ears as though the
rumblings of anger had a source somewhere outside himself. But it was
all in vain that, even by spelling out what was printed on the page, he
tried to find any sense in his reading. The waves of his fury kept

constantly crashing down until nothing was left but a castle of sand at the mercy of the incoming tide. More than once he started the process again, forcing himself to read the same sentence ten times over. But he grasped its meaning no better than a man who, lying in bed with a book, and his lamp beside him, feels that sleep is gaining on him, wiping out in its onward flow words that no longer make any sense, confusing one word with another word already swamped. So he closed his book and sat waiting, feeling his nervous exhaustion grow, and conscious that a headache was impending. He saw the moments flying by, one after the other, on spread wings, each carrying into oblivion the message with which it was charged, but which he lacked the energy to catch and understand as it hastened by. Then he felt so angry with himself that his anger with his parents grew to even greater proportions. And because his parents were the cause of his anguish, of his cruel inactivity, of his sobs, his headache and his sleeplessness, he longed to do them a hurt, or at least to see his mother come into the room so that he might—not fly out at her—but simply say that he had given up all attempts at working, and that every night now he would sleep away from home, that he thought his father stupid, and, if need be, invent some story of his having laughed at Monsieur Gambaud, alienated his good will, got himself expelled from the Lycée—and all this because he wanted to strike at her, to repay in words that should fall on her like blows, something of the harm that she had done to him. But these words, which he had no chance to utter, churned about inside him like some poisonous substance of which he could not get rid, which he could feel seizing upon his limbs, so that his feet and his hands began to tremble, to twitch as in a vacuum, seeking a prey they could not strike at. He got up and ran across to the fireplace. There was a terrible crash. He had just shattered the Venetian glass, given him by his mother, which had cost a hundred francs. But even the thought that his mother would be angry, would realize that she ought to have been more careful about tormenting him, that he was someone to be reckoned with, failed to calm him, for he was furious with himself for having broken a glass which he had thought beautiful, and which he had planned to exhibit for Henri's admiration the very next day. And, seeing in fragments what no amount of contrition could mend, put together again, and fuse once more into its ancient unity, he laid this fresh misfortune to his parents' charge.

Then his tears came once more, and feeling cold he went into his dressing-room to look for something to throw round his shoulders. But he had lost control of his hand so that it moved like a brainless creature and completely failed to carry out the small mathematical operation which consisted, because the inside of the wardrobe was dark, in fumbling a way through the different velvets, silks and satins of his mother's outmoded dresses which, since she had given up wearing them for many years, she had put away in this piece of furniture, until it could feel the wooden jamb, far back, which separated these garments from his own, and, on reaching the second rough-surfaced coat, to take it from the hanger from which it depended. Instead, it tore down the first piece of fabric it encountered. This happened to be a black velvet coat, trimmed with braid, and lined with cherry-coloured satin and ermine, which, mauled by the violence of his attack, he pulled into the room like a young maiden whom a con-queror has seized and dragged behind him by the hair. In just such a way did Jean now brandish it, but even before his eyes had sent their message to his brain, he was aware of an indefinable fragrance in the velvet, a fragrance that had greeted him when, at ten years old, he had run to kiss his mother—in those days still young, still brilliant and still happy—when she was all dressed up and ready to go out, and flung his arms about her waist, the velvet crushed within his hand, the braid tickling his cheeks, while his lips, pressed to her forehead, breathed in the glittering sense of all the happiness she seemed to hold in keeping for him. Deeply disturbed, he looked at the coat which, with its still fresh colours, its still soft, velvety texture, seemed the very messenger of all those years which now had ceased to have any meaning, to have been cut out of his life entirely, though in memory they had remained intact, unfaded. He raised the coat to his nose, felt the velvet yield, as of old, beneath his fingers, and could believe that once again he was kissing his mother on one of those evenings when, in the company of her husband, or of Monsieur Sandré, who was then still hale and hearty and quite untouched by sorrow and sickness, she was just about to set out for *Ma Camarade*—a play that was being given that winter—with the glow of anticipated pleasure on her face, sorry only that she must leave Jean behind, but treasuring in her heart the splendid and im-measurable hopes she entertained about his future, and setting upon his cheek, with lips which then were fresh and beautiful, a kiss as limpid as her faith and as her happiness.

He felt an irresistible desire to give his mother once again that old fond kiss. Seeing her in memory so sweet, so smiling, and so lovely, he forgot his present anger. But now she was not as she had been. The death of her father, Jean's laziness, sickness, and the passing of the years, had changed her. And since she never now wore that particular coat, which was too young for her age, too gay to go with her perpetual mourning, too tight for her spreading figure, too outmoded for a later fashion, he would never see her again as she had been. In a few more years he would not see her again even as she was now. He flung himself down on his knees at the foot of his bed, and his gushing tears tried to drain away his intolerable grief. He longed to be able to taste upon his mother's cheeks the last leavings of her youth and happiness, to hold prisoner for hours within his kiss the flying instants and the flow of life, all fading beauty and all fleeting hopes, the whole existence of that being in relation to whom he saw all things, who, one day, would be gone for ever into nothingness, never to be found again, leaving no trace, being as though she had not been at all.

But egotism or perhaps merely the demands of life keep us from thinking for too long about the death of those who are dear to us. Such thoughts are dangerous, are fatal, since, from sheer horror of that death they conjure it before its time, and spread a sadness all about the years still left to us for enjoyment and happiness, and so violent is the paroxysm of their onset, that we may be spared the thought of one day having ourselves to leave this world, they lead us on to leave it now, by suicide. So, as a man in the last stages of exhaustion ceases to think at all, and falls asleep, that portion of Jean's heart that had been drained by dwelling on the thought of death, lost the power to concentrate, and succumbed to a sort of torpor. He felt the reality of the present moment flood back upon him, and the sharp recollection of how unfair his mother had been to him at the very moment when he had been making so praiseworthy an effort to control his passions, of his father's stupid harshness, of the ironical manner in which their linked authorities had tried to sap his will, and this renewed sense of grievance stirred his anger into life once more, so that he remembered what it was he had made up his mind to do—to leave home, to write to the headmaster, explaining that he had decided not to continue at the Lycée, to announce these resolutions to his parents, and to remind them how wickedly they had humiliated him before Augustin.

But though the thoughts so recently aroused in him had been lulled to sleep, it was not within his power to treat them as though they had never been. He knew that the reason for his mother's nervous state was that she had had much cause for grief, and that for part of that grief he, himself, had been responsible. His anger flared again. Had not *she* been responsible for what *he* had suffered? He heard again the voice that she had used to him a while back (for anger brought into his mind, as jealousy into the mind of him who suffers it, the pictures that could cause the greatest pain). It gave him pleasure to think that she was to have his answer, she, and his father, too. How furious they would be!—furious, or perhaps, just sad. For was there really anything in the world that they loved better than they loved Jean? No, not even themselves. Madame Santeuil would gladly have given her life for her son, and if, after her father's death she had still clung to life, it was only because she knew that without her he would have been too intolerably oppressed by misery. Would Henri de Réveillon have done as much? At this present moment, perhaps, but probably not always. And even now Henri had his family. *Her* family for Madame Santeuil was just Jean. And for Monsieur Santeuil too. He knew that he was growing old, but went on working so as to have money to leave to Jean, a great deal of money, for Jean was a terrible spender, and Monsieur Santeuil was often worried to think what would become of his son when he should be no longer there. Yes, when he should be no longer there, when nothing any more should have the power to give him either pain or pleasure, when he should be beyond feeling tenderness or awakening it in his son (for Monsieur Santeuil was a materialist); when that time should come, it worried him to think whether Jean would, or would not, be happy. 'That's all very well, but though I may think these things, neither my father nor my mother are present while I think them. Their view of life is more down-to-earth than mine, and they believe that they have done no more than upset me. It would be a nasty awakening if I told them all this. And I will tell them. If I don't, they will think that they did right, that they have won a victory, that I truly am a fool, that I was frightened, that it was easy enough to get the better of me. . . .'

'. . . Yes, but things like that are not just a game. Every moment of our lives is serious, and our every action is rich with good or evil. I can cause my mother pain; no one can prevent me. But the fact remains that it will be pain, and that a day will come when I shall never again be able to give her pleasure. For we have only one life in which to love our parents, in which to give them pleasure, or to keep from grieving them. Soon it will be too late. And, just as there is only one life, and none other like it in which we can try again to do well what in it we did badly, so too our every day is unique and no day has its double. We leave on it a trace of happiness or pain given to others, and there can be no turning back the clock: that trace is there for all eternity. Yes, but papa said to me, "Get out!"' and he saw again his father's face made hateful by violence, and heard again the unspeakable things that his mother had said about Réveillon. All that was clear to him. He told himself that his parents would think they had intimidated him, that now at last his mind really was made up. His tears still flowed, but behind the storm of rain a new sun shone making all things bright and fair. From time to time he could hear his own breathing, like a man who, recovering his breath, still has happy confidence in his strength, or as, when a storm has passed, one hears an occasional drop falling from a tree which the sun already is beginning to dry. He leaned back in the old armchair which embraced him as gently as those who have been the witnesses of our extraordinary actions, and can stand surety for our moral grandeur. Farther off still, the table, the chairs ranged against the walls, the door, enclosed him in a circle of sympathy, like vassals filled with admiration, like servants more or less closely connected with him, who all felt proud to have such a master.

Lest all this tenderness should abandon him, and with no sort of shame at calling on the aid of something that had already done so much for him, he threw the little velvet coat about his shoulders. When he heard his father and his mother go into the dining-room for dinner, he waited until he felt sure that Augustin would be there, too. Then he joined them, trembling a little, but wholly master of himself. He went up to his mother, and in a low voice but loud enough for Augustin to hear, said: "Darling Mamma" (it was those words that cost him the greatest effort) "I have come to ask you to forgive me." He tried to put his arms about her. She turned away, but he said, "Please Mamma, I really am sorry: let me give you a kiss." And he did so. He was so near to tears that he burst out laughing. Then he went to his father who, at sight of him assumed a fierce and mulish look. He had to exert great strength of mind to say the same words to him. But he succeeded. "Papa, dear, I beg your pardon." He saw that Augustin was looking at him, but, nevertheless, touched his father's frowning brow with his lips. Weaker than his wife, more violent and yet softer, Monsieur Santeuil did not resist and Jean overcoming a slight feeling of repulsion, placed on the forehead which was still flushed with anger and ill-will a kiss of repentance. Then he sat down to table. His father noticed the coat he had about his shoulders which, as he raised his hand in eating, displayed its lining of pink satin. "It's ridiculous to swaddle yourself like that," said Monsieur Santeuil. "It's quite warm in here, and, in any case, that thing belongs to your mother. Take it off this minute!" Jean felt a surge of bitterness at finding himself so little understood, but took it off. His mother, however, looking at him with innocent eyes which seemed to grasp without the slightest difficulty all the thoughts that had been working in him for the past two hours, smiled. He grasped the meaning of her smile, saw that she had understood, that nothing that had happened was, for her, irreparable. Running to her, he flung his arms about her neck, burst into tears, and held her in a prolonged hug. But she, happy in the knowledge that she was loved, but not wishing that he should love her with an excess of passion which one day might cause him pain, said gently, in a tone of blessed common sense, and ceasing to smile: "Now, don't be a little silly: go back to your place, and let us get on with dinner." He could not bring himself to leave her, and told her in a low voice that he had broken the Venetian glass. He expected that she would scold him, and so revive in his mind the memory of their quarrel. But there was no cloud upon her tenderness. She gave him a kiss, and whispered in his ear: "It shall be, as in the Temple, the symbol of an indestructible union."[1]

---

[1] After this scene, Jean added a Codicil to his Will to the effect that the furniture of his room, and the little coat, should be kept by his father and his mother if they were still alive at the time of his death, and, in the event of their being dead, by Réveillon—at least the furniture, for it seemed to him a profanation that the coat should be so disposed of. But the idea that it might be sold was even worse. He did not know what to do. But, at the very moment when he was cudgelling his brain over the problem, his mother came into the room and suggested a walk. Then he stopped thinking about death, and turned instead to the enjoyment of life.—M.P.

8. *A Session of the Chamber*

The debate on the Armenian Massacres had just come to an end. It had been decided that France should take no action. Suddenly over on the extreme left a fattish man of about thirty, with crinkly black hair, who would have given the appearance, had you seen him, of being the victim of some indefinable emotional disturbance and looking as though he were hesitating to act in obedience to the prompting of some inner voice, stood swaying for a moment or two in his place, and then, raising his arm in a meaningless gesture, as though it were a necessary formality to be observed by those who wanted to address the House, made his way, rather unsteadily, and as though weighed down by the sense of his great responsibility towards the tribune. It was Couzon, who, ten years before, might have been seen working as a house physician at the Necker Hospital, and was now leader of the Parliamentary Socialist Party, having been simultaneously elected by the four great coal-producing Departments of France, and having chosen to sit for the most poverty-stricken, the gloomiest of them all, a constituency where there was little to distinguish the black and melancholy life above ground from working time in the Pits—the Department of the Nord. According to the Socialist, Anarchist, and Anti-Semite journals, he was the only genuine orator to be found in France, and the equal of any in the past: while the Government, Monarchist, Opportunist, and even Radical organs, described him as nothing but a demagogue who had turned a gift of facile speech to bad uses, in short, a windbag.

Jean, to whom Couzon, though he had not intended to take part in the debate, had given a ticket, had noticed from his seat which was on a level with the tribune that his friend, who as a rule was so violent and so quick an asker of questions, had since the opening of the session, and for the last quarter of an hour, said nothing, not answering his friends when they spoke to him, not even seeming to hear them, but sitting with his eyes fixed before him, as though he were looking at a ghost which, though invisible to others, seemed to have the effect of concentrating all his faculties on some mysterious train of thought. Jean, who throughout the debate which had dealt only with the interests of the Government and its opponents, had been feeling in a vague sort of a way that a great many other things might have been mentioned, but had supposed that that it was not possible to talk about them in a Chamber filled with "practical" men. Now suddenly seeing his friend's eyes grow larger, his friend's hand pressed to his forehead as though to keep hold upon an idea which was difficult to focus, his friend hesitating, then saying a few words to his immediate neighbour which had the effect of turning all heads towards him without his seeming to see them, he understood that Couzon had been driven to speak by that sense of justice which sometimes took possession of the whole man, so that he seemed as one inspired. It was then that the "something" which he had vaguely felt had been left unsaid and which he had believed to be unworthy of the attention of the "practical", at once took on for him an enormous importance. It was the practical men who now seemed to him to be small and trivial. He felt deeply stirred. And so, when Couzon decided to raise his short, stubby arm above his head in the gesture demanded by convention, it was as though he were making a signal the meaning of which kept on ringing in Jean's heart. Seeing Couzon's short legs hurrying in ungainly fashion towards the tribune, he thought that never had human body expressed so much dignity and grandeur. There are, in Beethoven certain syncopated passages, which, though they lack nobility of theme, can never be heard without the hearer trembling.

But now, the majority of the Chamber, considering that everything which might conceivably be regarded as interesting and practical had been said, and guessing what Couzon was going to talk about and waste everybody's time, began to shout "Shut up!" to an accompaniment of slammed desk-lids. Jean was on tenterhooks lest Couzon should allow himself to be intimidated. He longed to cry out, "Scum!", to kill every one of the assembled wretches. One Deputy shrugged: several others yawned loudly. Somebody shouted, "Don't stay in that pulpit too long!" to which another replied, "Nobody warned us we were in for a sermon!" somebody else, "I'm going out for a breath of fresh air!" If sometimes Jean, not indeed in the presence of his parents whose hostility aroused in him an enthusiasm for all that Couzon did, but when he was alone, when he could think calmly, had wondered that Couzon should tolerate in his Party's newspapers, should himself utter in the House, violent, slanderous, and cruel attacks on certain members of the majority, he felt now that nothing could be bad enough for these odious fools, so ironical and so self-satisfied, who were making use of their numerical superiority and the sheer weight of their mental lumpishness, to try to stifle the thrilling, the almost incantatory voice of Justice. At this moment, driven by blind anger to give back, had he been able, blow for blow in defence of the weaker side, as had happened one day when he had learned that a thief had been betrayed, surrounded, and half-strangled by the police, and had wished that he were strong enough to murder every policeman he could lay strong hands on, without thinking for a moment that those same policemen whom he hated because they were the stronger and were having a good laugh over what they had done, might sometimes, too, be weak in the presence of a dead daughter, or under a thief's knife—Jean did not pause to reflect that these men who were shouting their views with such assurance, hooting at truth, and gagging the voice of Justice, might not really, perhaps, feel as strong as he thought they did, might sometimes wear upon their faces an expression that told of love, uneasiness, or a consciousness of defeat. Later, when he thought back to that moment when he would gladly have stoned those two hundred mocking deputies interrupting Couzon before he had begun to speak, banging the lids of their desks so as to drown his voice, he understood more clearly than ever before how it was that Couzon, seeing every day his ideas, his speeches, his suggested legislation, smothered by a triumphant majority, should go home with fury in his heart which made him see as devilish the faces made merely ugly by narrowness and pride.

There he was now, swaying on his feet, waiting, like a ship ready to set sail, but not yet loosed from its moorings, rolling to the movement of the waves, though not yet committed to the open sea. Once or twice he shouted, "Gentlemen!" His voice was strong, almost enormous, and some tremendous emotion had set it trembling. It was like a branch trailing over the side of a boat and quivering in the current. The other voices were feeble, almost inaudible, especially when they began to speak. There was something strange in those tones of his that might, it seemed, have been heard in a room twenty times as large—an insignificant detail, if you like, but when it has reference to a great man who has aroused your curiosity, not without interest: a material detail, no doubt, but not for that reason lacking in importance. It is rarely

that, when a very great man, even a great painter or a great musician
is under discussion, we are not informed that in the purely technical
side of his art he has done things which for anybody else would be
impossible. We laugh when we read of the Queen who said to Talma:
"What a memory!" but it is difficult, all the same, not to be interested
when we are informed that Sarah Bernhardt could learn a part in two
days, and that nobody else could compete with her in this. A detail of
that kind does not it is true exhaust the essence of her genius, but it
makes of it a living thing, like all else that has a bearing on it. At that
moment the President of the Chamber was saying with a smile: "May
I remind the honourable member that he is entitled to address the
House only on the motion, and in reply to the previous speaker." This
subtle allusion to the extravagance of Couzon's oratory and his
inability to "keep to the point" brought a great outburst of laughter
from the majority; it was as though each man were laughing not for
his own satisfaction but as though his mirth were, in some sort, an
expression of wit which deserved a hearing. Everyone said loudly,
"Very funny, that! Oh, very neat!"

"I know that I am entitled to do that and no more," Couzon said in
reply to the President, and in the same thunderous and thrilling tones
that he had used before. "I share that right," he added, "with my
colleagues in this place, and I swear to you, that even should it mean
my having to wait for a whole hour in order to get a hearing, I am in
no mood to surrender a jot or tittle of it, but am fully determined to
make use of every scrap." As quickly as the pressing of a trigger is
followed by the detonation, a frantic outburst of applause from the
extreme Left greeted this proud assertion. The rules forbad Jean to
join in it, but his heart beat with enthusiasm at Couzon's words. His
eyes were flashing. He leaned forward in Couzon's direction, and his
body was so tense that it trembled. But the majority responded only
by shouting " 'Vide! 'vide! 'vide!" The motion for an immediate
division was put to a show of hands, and carried. It was almost immediately followed by a vote in favour of the Government measure.
Weaponless, like a bound man who makes the gesture of striking a
blow with his manacled hands, Couzon, in a voice shaken by emotion,
cried: "You have just pronounced sentence of death on two hundred
thousand Christians!" His whole body was shaking, too, for he was the
first victim of those same blows which his words had been designed to
strike at the hearts of his listeners, and now set the emotions which had

dictated them tumbling within himself, as waves tumble pebbles and fling them on the beach. His voice was clearly audible above the clamour of the yelling, stamping members. The beating of his heart, tossed and tumbled in the tide of his eloquence, could almost be heard. Breathless, and wild with anger, he shouted: "You have just pronounced sentence of death on two hundred thousand Christians! The people shall know that, and the people whom you have trained in the use of arms will be avenged!" The tumult was indescribable. "No one's ever spoken such words in this Chamber!" yelled the Minister of Agriculture. "Disgraceful!" said the President of the Council, flinging himself about in a frenzy of righteous indignation. The men whose "political views are uninfluenced by sentiment" and who do not like "generalizations" are always the first to indulge in generalizations, and to exploit the sentiment of national dignity.

They could say what they liked. Couzon, bursting the barriers of his stormy spirit, had succeeded in delving deep into himself and bringing back the substance of his thought unmutilated. He was now as un-excited as a dog which, after swimming through the waves to bring back some object that has caught its eye, returns to the shore with no thought for the breakers drenching its steaming coat with icy spray. Jean, too, felt happy, and, with a smile on his lips, mopped his damp forehead. For all this while he had been with Couzon in the spirit, giving blow for blow, and now that this assembly which had so roused his anger had felt the lash, the tension of the last fifteen minutes lessened, and he found himself smiling for sheer happiness. Enthusiastic admirers were crowding round Couzon struggling to shake him by the hand. More than one of them had set his signature to articles which when he had first read them Jean had thought infamous, though now like Couzon himself he felt compelled to regard their authors as his friends, as when, attacked upon the highroad, a man will drink in a spirit of brotherhood with his rescuers, not too much concerned to wonder whether the fine fellows who have leaped to his defence may in fact, have done so, not because they hate his attackers totally, but for some different reason, and might, had the circumstances been different, have fallen upon him in their turn. Indeed, just as gentleness is more than usually prized by the strong, we are the more grateful for a display of friendliness by those who have a reputation for being violent and cruel. Perhaps too, their friendship, being armed at all points, is more worth having than mere disinterested feelings and powerless words. Not to prefer the latter shows, perhaps, a lack of generosity, but most men, and those, in particular, who pursue the career of politics, have good reason to suppress this conscientious scruple. Life and especially political life is a continual struggle, in which since the wicked are always armed, it is the duty of the just to be so too, if only that they may not see Justice perish from the earth. It may be objected that, though this figure of speech is common currency today, Justice is not, in fact, a person, and that when it perishes it does so just because it *is* armed, without much caring in what manner. But the answer to that is that if the great revolutionaries had been so fanatically scrupulous, Justice would never have triumphed.

9. *Monsieur Beulier*

Some days later the Duchesse de Réveillon's sister having been ill and needing to spend her period of convalescence in a milder climate, the two ladies started for the Azores where the Duke and his son later joined them. Their absence lasted for a whole year during which time Jean had no friends of his own age and several enemies. Among these latter there were three in particular, one of whom had a passion for the sea, brought with him into form books dealing with travel and science and could make the most marvellous ships out of match-stalks and string. The members of this trio scarcely ever said good morning to Jean, laughed at him if he addressed them, and when they met him in the school-yard or on the stairs, pushed him about or twirled him round in the hope that he might get giddy and fall down. He had felt much drawn to them by reason of their intelligence, was bitterly disappointed at their enmity, but bore no grudge. If, by chance, they were nice to him, he at once felt his old affection return, and was at pains to be nice, too. He did not realize that this need he felt for sympathy, this morbid hyper-sensibility, which made his affection overflow at the least sign of response, was regarded as mere hypocrisy or as a particularly irritating pose, by these young creatures whose colder temperaments went hand in hand with the callousness proper to their age. Ignorant of what had caused their antipathy, Jean whose sympathetic nature led him to think that everybody was like himself, and his modesty that they were probably his superiors, set himself scrupulously to examine his behaviour to these boys trying to discover whether some fault, some unintentional lack of consideration on his part, might have angered them. He talked to them; he wrote to them, but the only result of his efforts was to make still worse their attitude of heartless mockery. On one occasion he had written a letter so beautiful, so sincere, so eloquent, that the tears came into his eyes while he was composing it. When he saw that it had made no difference, he began to entertain doubts of the power which our affection can have on those who do not return it, of the influence which our thoughts and

our talents can exert on thoughts and talents which bear no resemblance
to our own. He repeated to himself the words that he had written, and
found them fine and persuasive.

Often when school was over he walked home with a boy named
Thénaud, the nephew of General Thénaud, whose parents stayed all
winter at their country place for the shooting, spent their money on
their own pleasures, and never sent any to him, nor even wrote. In
spite of his gloomy existence, Thénaud was habitually sweet-tempered
and gay. With Jean, whose professor had asked him to give the boy a
little private tuition, he was always very gentle, filled with admiration
of his superior gifts, and constantly making little jokes about his fads,
his nervousness, his tendency to exaggerate everything, his untidiness,
his excited way of talking, but always in so kindly a manner that Jean,
who was quite without vanity, accepted these comments as so many
rather amusing evidences of friendship.

*

Two years later Jean was walking one day along the Champs-Elysées
on his way home to luncheon, when he met one of the three "intelligent
boys" who had been at school with him, the one who had so persistently tormented him, and had been going into the Navy. But as
though their relationship as fellow-pupils had been, in some sort,
professional, obligatory, and temporary, like the relation of professor
to student, or corporal to private, so that one sees a professor shake
hands, when he meets him out, with the pupil whom during school
hours he has kept at a distance, or the corporal who in the regiment,
habitually gave the rough side of his tongue to a young man of good
family, respectfully raise his hat some years later when the two happen
to pass one another in the street, the corporal having in the interval,
reverted to his old employment of carter while the private has become
an engineer—the "intelligent" schoolfellow not only did not elbow
Jean aside, but greeted him in a forthcoming, though shy, fashion.
The likes and dislikes, the desires and the ideas, of youth change so
rapidly that a few years are enough to make them unrecognizable.
The intelligent schoolfellow had now nothing but the kindliest
feelings towards Jean. They stood chatting for a while, and it amazed
Jean to think that he should ever have been impressed by the other's
intelligence. He asked him for news about the other two who had been

his inseparable companions. "I ran into Fentel the other day just as I've run into you." Jean could not remember ever having known this Fentel, though the intelligent schoolfellow maintained that he had been in the same form with them. "Were you accepted for the Navy?" Jean asked. "The Navy?" replied the other with every mark of astonishment: "I never had any intention of going into the Navy—perhaps when I was very young I may have played with the idea, but never since then. I'm reading Law."–"So am I" said Jean. "Really, what lectures are you attending?"–"None."–"I go to them all, and it pretty well takes up the whole of my time." For a moment Jean tried hard to appreciate the fact that there did actually exist law students who spent the day going to lectures. But failing to do so and finding nothing else to talk about, he shook the other's hand with an affectionate smile to which the intelligent schoolfellow accorded an embarrassed acknowledgment.

*

Monsieur Beulier never engaged in thought except to speak the truth, and never spoke except to express his thought. Consequently Jean was at pains to provoke and garnered with respectful avidity Monsieur Beulier's views on everything under the sun. A profound intellect so completely convinces us that it holds within itself the laws of the universe, that Monsieur Beulier's hesitating replies seemed more certain than any dogmatic statement could have been, more filled with a true vision of the future, with meaning and with life than would have been the prophetic utterances of the oracles. Jean turned them over in his mind, and was never so happy as when he was remembering them. One day, a rather melancholy Christmas Eve, Monsieur Beulier began the lesson by saying to his pupils in a gentle voice: "Tomorrow is Christmas Day, we are going to celebrate it in our own manner. I am going to read you some stories." The Three Kings bringing nard, incense and myrrh, did not spread more fragrance about them than did these words in Jean's heart. Never until that moment would he have thought it rational to stop working on any one day rather than another. To celebrate Christmas had seemed to him mere childishness. All days were alike and therefore he found no pleasure in them. Through the medium of these simple words which, springing from the strictness of a mind obedient only to the promptings of reason, carried with them a sense of irresistible authority, Monsieur Beulier joined with an invisible thread the flat ordinary day that tomorrow might be, to that mysterious day on which Jesus had been born in a manger. The power of reason was freely admitting the right of fancy to play a part in work. It was as though a stream of poetry had been allowed to run into Jean's day-to-day existence, as though permission had been given him to open his imagination to a dream, to see to it that he should not be too much a slave to reason. Next morning Jean sent out for a copy of the *Echo de Paris* in which there was a story by Anatole France, and for a sprig of mistletoe which he stood in a glass upon his table. "It's my little Christmas celebration" he told his mother with the restraint of a philosopher and the tenderness of a poet.

*

A few days before the first of January, Jean, having gone to Monsieur Beulier for a tutorial, said with a blush that he had brought him a little New Year's present. It was a small Italian Renaissance bust of Hercules. Monsieur Beulier was delighted. He spoke to his pupil about Hercules, about how he stood for effort, for work. Then he rang for Mariette, his one and only servant, an honest countrywoman with a red fat face and grey hair, who, in addition to cooking and managing for Monsieur Beulier, also, when he did not want to interrupt his work, brought him the books and learned journals which he needed, and kept within her not very capacious head, which was as full of bumps and dents as a saucepan, not only the simple words which make up the vocabulary of stoking, laundering and the preparation of food, but those nobler, though for Mariette, just as familiar words, denoting a name, of Plato, Denis of Halicarnassus, and Hegel. Having come to be on good terms, from daily habit, with all his many volumes, she could pick them from the shelves without the slightest hesitation, and holding them gingerly but without any special show of respect, take them to her master. She would place them on the table, thus distinguishing them clearly in her mind, along with the ink-stand, the coffee-pot, and the tooth-pick, from the boots and shoes which she fetched in response to a rather vaguer system of identification—"the pair I was wearing yesterday"—from a less crowded row, and must stand against the chimney-piece in front of the table and always on the floor.

Mariette entered in response to Monsieur Beulier's summons. "Would you mind giving me," he said, "a yellow-bound book which you will find on the left-hand side of the bottom shelf of the bookcase. It has got *Bible de l'Humanité* printed on the back." Mariette, having often taken that same *Bible de l'Humanité* into her master's study, knew it well, in the same way that servants say they "know Monsieur le Duc de S——" from having frequently announced him. All those words therefore, "a yellow book on the back of which is printed, etc." were quite unnecessary. But Monsieur Beulier had clung to this ancient luxury of explanation, which dated from the time when Mariette had not yet "got the hang of the master's books" in which she maintained it took her longer to find her way about than among his underclothes. He had not been able to cure himself of this habit, or to keep pace with the growth of his servant's knowledge, so that he still said "a book with . . . written on the back" instead of a "book called . . ."—which, though a more abstract form of speech, she would easily have mastered. It was only with reference to the books in daily use that he had established himself on a simpler footing with her. Thus, he had grown accustomed to saying "Mariette the *Novum Organum*"–"Mariette the *Critique of Pure Reason*", and, if, while she was on her knees blowing away at the fire, she heard an early pupil asking Monsieur Beulier to explain something while he was finishing his coffee, and happened to catch the august but not unfamiliar name of Spinoza, she would say to her master, "Shall I fetch the *Ethics*, sir?"

Mariette appeared after a brief absence, carrying the *Bible de l'Humanité*, from which Monsieur Beulier read the striking passage in which Michelet sings the praises of work as personified by Hercules. While Monsieur Beulier was uttering the last words, "He has served me better than perhaps a better man might have done. I shall die, if not rich in works, rich at least in great intentions", the tears welled in Jean's eyes.

"Yes, such richness is beautiful indeed," said Monsieur Beulier, in a tone expressive of affection, "all the same, there is a charm, too, in simplicity." He rang again for Mariette, made her bring him the *Memorabilia* of Xenophon, read out the story of the family which, bored, finding life unsatisfactory, and being continually divided against itself, Socrates made, not only useful, but wise, happy and good by setting its members to work. After Michelet, the stripped-to-the-bone simplicity, the dryness, of this narrative seemed disappointing to Jean. But, "No," said Monsieur Beulier, "it is not a question of the other being better; they are two different things. Hang it all, there is room for all sorts, isn't there? Antiquity is not the nineteenth century. But this stuff of Xenophon's is, in its way, just as good. No one will ever write like that again. It is all so simple yet everything is said. That was a time when writers were not concerned to develop their ideas. They offered them for what they were worth without labouring them, without extracting from them all that they contained. The soft down upon them was preserved and the freshness." Where his master had sown but a single word, Jean, tending the soil with love, raised a fine crop of ideas. He found later, when he re-read it, more charm than he had suspected in that passage from Xenophon. He returned to it often in the years that followed, and, when he had about him intelligent friends who were not too pressed for time, unconsciously adopting the sing-song tones of Monsieur Beulier, he loved to tell them what he had found in it.

Being unable, in a narrative which must, inevitably, be a work of sentiment, to give a convincing picture of the essential Monsieur Beulier, I have confined my efforts to recalling some of Jean's memories of the man whom above all others he most admired throughout his life. Since he knew that the value of the human spirit cannot be precisely "placed"—I don't mean in terms of official recognition, but even in those of literary or philosophic reputation, which like every collective activity, is comprised quite as often of imitation, suggestions and more or less faked enthusiasms as of judgment, and is as much exposed to discussion in the world of Truth, as is the success of a First Night, or the monetary value of a picture in the world of Beauty, or the result of an election, or a legal judgment in that of Justice—he remained convinced that Monsieur Beulier was a greater man than either Monsieur Renan or Monsieur Taine, great though they undoubtedly were. If it is possible to see the cause in the effect, then Monsieur Beulier's genius is clearly visible in the talent of all the most outstanding of the young men of Jean's generation. But there can be no general agreement on this point, because Monsieur Beulier being free of all conceit, I won't say did not see clearly the result of his influence—for there was very little he did not see clearly—but thought that it was nothing to boast about, and should be, as far as possible, mentioned with caution. On one occasion he sincerely complimented a young man on some verses he had shown him, after which he advised him to burn them. "They are your first," he said, "and just look at what Leconte de Lisle's early attempts were like. Not that we know anything about his first poems, but even the second were pretty poor. Now, let us assume that you will succeed admirably in doing what it is in you to do: well then, if we give Leconte de Lisle—for whom, as it happens, I have no great liking—a mark approximating to a million, then you, roughly speaking, will be round about four or five—don't you agree?" Then, seeing the dejected expression on the poet's face, he added with great kindliness, "I'm exaggerating, of course: I think we might give you eight or nine—and that, you know, is not to be sneezed at."

*

No doubt the reader will complain that all this is merely slowing up the story. The fault lies with the youth of my hero, for there are moments when youth, before finally committing itself to the deep waters of love, of ambition, of the life of the senses, sometimes likes to call a halt while it expends itself on the passions of the intellect. I shall not from now on expose myself to this particular type of reproach. In a short while Jean's life will no longer be moving between his parent's house, Monsieur Beulier's lodgings, and school. There will be occasions, in the years before us, when he will visit Monsieur Beulier again, but those visits will be less and less frequent as well as shorter and shorter, and their stimulating effect will last for but a brief hour and be only indifferently remembered. At the moment when Destiny is about to take Jean roughly by the hand and make him change direction, while moment by moment the last hours of an existence which he had thought of as eternal, flit by, I should like to add one last memory to those I have recorded. In itself it is of but small importance, a mere adventure of the feelings, and as such so fluid, so intangible, that I may not perhaps succeed in fixing it in such a way as to communicate it to you. But I want at least to make an effort to recapture it before this short period of calm and sensitive awareness shall have passed for ever into the great void.

Jean had given the little bust to Monsieur Beulier a few days before the first of January. On New Year's Eve, Monsieur Beulier went to Jean's home to give him some tuition. "I, too," he said, "have got a present." It was a book by Joubert. For two hours he read it with Jean. When they had come to the end, and he had arranged to return that evening, so that they go on with the work which there had not been time to finish, Jean, looking at the book said, "No present has ever

given me so much pleasure." Monsieur Beulier took it from him, put
it away in his brief-case, and never brought it back. Having given to
Jean all its meaning, its very heart, and all it had to offer in the way of
moral support, it had given everything. It was in the spirit that the
incalculable value of the gift had lain. But the donor had given something
more precious still by thus adding to Jean's slender treasure of feelings
and ideas, a rare and charming novelty, a present that was wholly of the
spirit, a present that declared itself without modesty to be just what it
was, without the slightest hint of shamefaced oratory, a present that
had cost nothing, in which there was nothing either material or vulgar.
The simple way in which Monsieur Beulier had taken back the book
was to remain for ever in Jean's mind like the sweetness of those Gospel
words which not only declare disdain of riches and the unreality of
matter, but are stamped deeply with those teachings because they
exhale, like a perfume, a truth that is superior and far more delicate.
By this spiritual essence Monsieur Beulier seemed to be wholly per-
meated, as certain of Titian's figures seem to be enveloped in a beauty
that is not only the beauty of paint, but of life, so that looking at them,
we are conscious of great joy.

    And so it was that this man, whose clothes were worse than shabby,
who was ignorant of the niceties of social intercourse, who could not
even enter a room without betraying his awkwardness—could give
such sweetness and such authority to all he did as no prince, despite
his breeding could have equalled. He was neither handsome nor
ugly, but Jean, when he looked at his chubby face, his squat nose, and
the swollen veins on his hands, felt so great an uprush of affectionate
respect that, had not Monsieur Beulier's natural lack of effusiveness
kept him at a distance, he would have kissed them with the same tender
care he showed when he kissed the cheeks, the nose, the hands of his
mother. And so fresh does the spirit keep the body in which it dwells,
when that spirit is untouched by any trace of self-love, pretentiousness,
vice, or anything other than honest thought and warmth of heart, as a
grain of salt in a scrap of meat will keep it for a long time wholesome
and uncorrupted, that, whenever in the years to come, Jean went to
see Monsieur Beulier, though naturally he found him looking rather
older, there was always in the sudden pleasure which the senior felt at
sight of Jean, such gaiety, such affection, so completely disinterested a
wish to be of service, so obvious an absence of all personal ambition,
all desire to profit in enhanced prestige by doing what he could to help

his former pupil—a desire which often vitiates the behaviour of millions who have passed their twentieth year, that it seemed to Jean as though he were in the presence of a young man with all the bloom of childhood still upon him. His body might be aging like a worn-out dressing-gown, but the body was a very small part of the man. And though the spirit could not break altogether free from the flesh, it betrayed its presence, like a subterranean stream of pure water which is never far from the surface, in the sparkling mirrors of his eyes in which it ceaselessly gathered and overflowed.

IV

1. *Monsieur de Traves*

It was the season of the year when the lilacs, exhaling between green leaves the sweetest scents of Persia, were gracefully drooping, some their bright coronals of mauve, others their white flowers whose pellucid skin seemed still all glittering with the perfumes in which they had been steeped. One had the feeling that these exquisite creatures were foreign visitors come from those lands whither so often, when reading or planning, one has travelled in imagination, where everything not excepting the sunlight, is of a different colour from that of the French countryside. But these foreigners had hung above Jean ever since the days of his childhood when tired of games he had climbed the hill to take his rest in one of the thickets of the Park, and the day being hot, had walked slowly, brushing the branches from which the white and silky flowers with their bright and gleaming stamens showered ceaselessly down like a fluttering of torn muslin, or when he had accompanied his father on one of his tedious calls on the Mayor in his parlour where the flies, deep-toned and ever on the look-out for amusement, came constantly to plague the beams of sleepy sunlight, though they never succeeded in moving them from where they lay, and had to find consolation in exploring the map of the Department fastened to the wall, only to tire suddenly of that minute inspection and fly noisily off, for no apparent reason, or on the contrary prolong indefinitely their stay within a little copse on the green edge of which they seemed so happy to remain that it looked as though they would never make up their minds to move.

At such times as Jean climbed to the thicket with a book, he would hold his breath if he heard strangers approaching along another path for fear they might disturb him. Sometimes these intruders were people unknown to him who, glancing casually in his direction, continued on their way, drawing each other's attention to some plant, to some improvement made by his uncle, or saying "that'd be a nice shady spot for a picnic". During those long hours the lilacs had kept Jean company, and already, no doubt, he had found great sweetness in

237

their Eastern fragrance. It is said that with approaching age our sensations grow weaker. That may be so, but they carry with them the echo of an earlier time, like those great singers, past their prime, whose failing voices have to find support in the accompaniment of a concealed chorus. In just such a manner did the delicious scent of the lilacs, the anise-white of their skins or the brilliant mauve of their blossoms, touch in him a deeper chord than a simpler sensation would have done, no matter how delicious. The past opened its heart to the present, and the immediate moment became a world of the spirit in which he moved with a feeling of exquisite delight. The flowering lilacs, those strange and lovely visitors from afar, because they had leaned above his childhood, formed part for him of a private and especial universe, so that their scent awakened in him the very feel of the hot and peaceful summers of a younger day. Lovely was the white lilac with its lustreless anise-skin which seemed still limpid with the perfume from which it would appear, that very instant to have emerged, gleaming with all the beauty of the East. And lovely, too, were the soft veils of mauve floating motionless in the sun.

*

On one such day it was that Jean first made the acquaintance of Traves, the brilliant novelist who, for a brief period, was his fellow-guest at Réveillon. But not the visible aspect of Traves the man, not what he said in conversation, nor yet what Jean had been able to gather of his life, seemed to have anything to do with the strange magic of that private world into which the reader was transported on the very first page of one of his books, which, doubtless, was powerful in him while he worked, which he created while he wrote, which already in vague dreams revealed to him the precious matters, still as little solid as the Milky Way, that served him as the texture out of which he wove his tales. Fine though his eyes were, large and light-coloured, they seemed to be no more than windows opening on an empty room. Neither the circumstances of his life, nor his known habits, could in any way explain the mysterious way in which all his books resembled one another, how their highly specialized "type" seemed to be that of the single family to which they all belonged. That family must have had its dwelling in the skies, so little connexion did the actions of its sons seem to have with Traves's own life which appeared powerless to account for their peculiarities, though doubtless those who knew him well would recognize the use he had made in his fictions of this and that sweet or terrible circumstance which had come within the range of his own experience. For a man's life, no matter what its nature, is always the alphabet in which he learns to read so that whatever the phrases may be it matters little since they are always composed of the same letters.

Traves himself could probably never have said when precisely it was that he had acquired the habit of always recognizing the presence in his mind of certain thoughts by reason of a particular aura, an especial feeling of enthusiasm, which preceded their coming and gave to them a sort of added glory as of something real which he must make his own and endow, unchanged, with a quality of permanence. But quite certainly there was nothing in his life, nothing in his face, nothing even in his talk, which might have made it possible for others to extend their knowledge of those mysterious presences, and in all likelihood it was only through the precious crystal of his books that one could make a nearer approach to them. Those who would penetrate more deeply into the meaning of the mysterious nudes with lotus-braided hair who haunt with brooding eyes all the pictures painted by Gustave Moreau, or try to understand more fully those cliffs of his with statuettes on craggy outcrops, could never do so no matter how much detailed knowledge they might have of Gustave Moreau's life, how often they might have talked with him of art and life and death, or have dined daily in his company, could never succeed in delving further into the mystery of their origins and significance, nor, if it comes to that, could ever find out more about those beings who, like strange maidens of the sea, were like a precious cargo born to him on the thunderous tides of inspiration. All they can tell of them must be limited to the circumstances of their invention, the material elements which go to make them up (a landscape, perhaps, which he had seen, a vase he had admired) but never the hidden reason for the mysterious resemblance that they bear one to another, the essence of which, though it must have been inseparable from his inner life, since only so could he have given to it shape and form, since only so could it have kept pace with the movement of his inspiration and have freed him from the labour of creation, he, all the same, knew nothing about.

Traves's face was the face of a human being, as was his talk, in so far as it expressed ideas in words logically strung together, and, to that extent had something in it of reason, something, that is, which is common to all mankind. Not that his talk was other than remarkable (but no matter how beautiful the monstrance, it is only when one shuts one's eyes that one feels the presence of God) though it lacked Perrotin's brilliance. But Jean had noticed that with those whose art finds expression in writing, the spoken word is always very much simpler. They do not embellish it with the ingenuities and fantasies which bubble up when they sit pen in hand. When Traves and Perrotin were conversing, there was about the former a much simpler and less brilliant quality. He would constantly make use of the same words, seeming incapable of originality. He was marked by something that was almost *naïveté*, which led to his being taken in by the most obvious commonplaces of social intercouse (as when somebody said, "Here's Monsieur Gallé, who's come all the way from Nancy for the sole purpose of seeing you"). Nevertheless, remarkable though his talk might be, Jean found it unattractive and wearisome. If the truth must be told, he thought it rather inferior.

At this period of his life the idealistic theories associated with the profound intelligence of Monsieur Beulier had cleared his mind of the sophistical doctrines of sceptical materialism. He no longer took the slightest interest in sceptical or materialistic arguments, and refused to waste his time over something which, he thought, had been blown sky-high and was now generally recognized as false. Now Monsieur de Traves was deeply read in materialistic and sceptical philosophy, and showed for idealism a contempt which Jean regarded as indubitably shoddy. Views to which we have responded with fervent enthusiasm become for us the yardstick by which we measure everything. All that was best in Jean's mind had taken service under the banner of idealistic philosophy. It was in terms of that devotion that he judged others, and he found it impossible to admit that a materialist could be a man of intelligence. Books written to support the materialistic view were in his eyes so many scrawled pages of no manner of use to anyone, a mere wearisome collection of errors. Monsieur de Traves was for ever reading and quoting them. For them he reserved the full flood of his passion.

*

No matter what the point of view to which we have committed the best in ourselves, we find it impossible not to credit it with a sort of excellence, and to judge unfavourably those who adhere to its opposite. Even for the sceptic scepticism or rather a certain form of scepticism, becomes a species of faith, and every variant of dogma is regarded as pagan error. Jean secretly pitied all who believed in science and refused to admit the absolute validity of the self and the existence of God. That was his attitude to Monsieur de Traves. No matter what the subject under discussion might be, Monsieur de Traves championed all the views which left Jean so indifferent that he very soon ceased even to listen. Never once was the conversation concerned with those general ideas which Monsieur Beulier habitually developed, never did it issue in oracular statements about the soul or the intelligence. But in matters of fact such as the meaning a word had carried in former times, the usages from which it drew its derivation, the reason why it was impossible to argue that this or that writer had used it in this or that way, the attributing of "period" to an object on grounds of style and the comparing it with similar objects—in all such things Monsieur de Traves was an inexhaustible source of information. He found his greatest pleasure in arranging libraries and hunting for curios, occupations in which Jean never engaged, finding them boring in the extreme. In literature he had a fondness only for the works of the eighteenth century which Jean held to be utterly worthless, because unlike those of the nineteenth, they were not concerned to probe the mysterious truths which alone for him could provide the key to absolute truth. Any attempt to work down to the basis of Monsieur de Traves's talk —not its matter, but its form—must in the last analysis have struck on the ultimate and implicit assertion that Beauty has an objective reality. "Yes, that is beautiful, don't you see, because the word *Rome* is in itself a thing of beauty." – "*Lance*, I think you'll agree, is quite lovely."

2. *Days at Réveillon*

As a rule, when Jean rang for his breakfast to be brought, it would be late. He had it in bed while reading his letters. "Is Monsieur Henri up?" he would ask the footman. "Yes, sir: Monsieur Henri has been out riding, but he is back now and has several times inquired whether you were awake. I told him that you had rung, sir." A few moments later, as though to prove the accuracy of this statement, there would be a knock at the door, and in would come Henri. He wanted to make sure that Jean had not suffered from cold, to find out whether he would like an extra blanket. He brought with him the morning papers and asked his friend whether he would mind his having breakfast in his room. In that way they could chat while drinking their chocolate, Jean luxuriating in the delicious laziness of bed, Henri still more comfortably ensconced before the little table, fresh from his bath and his early morning ride. Then he would go off to finish dressing leaving Jean to read in peace. Sometimes a thought would occur to one of them which demanded the other's immediate approval, a joke which to be perfectly enjoyed needed the other's laughter, a piece of news in a letter which had to have astonished participation. Then, after first making sure that nobody was in the corridor—which was in the highest degree unlikely, since Henri and Jean were the only persons occupying rooms in that part of the house—Jean, wearing a plush dressing-gown, and carrying his tooth-glass in his hand, would venture as far as Henri's door. "I've come along to brush my teeth in your room, because you'll never guess who's engaged to be married!" or, since Henri was a good musician, "I've brought my shirt to warm in front of your lovely fire, but more especially because I want to ask you what tune this is." Then, Henri would sit down at the piano, and sing it, while Jean listened delightedly, his shirt hanging close to the fire, warming his legs: and all the time the footman would be knocking at the door of his room in vain to say that the others were in the dining-room. This news set Jean hurrying. He would hastily take from a drawer the new tie which "went" so perfectly with his face as to produce an

entirely different effect from that of the ones he had been wearing
recently, so that everyone felt quite convinced that it was a red tie
with a blue jacket, a white tie with a black suit, a beige tie with a light
coat, that made him look his best, each combination producing, as it
were, a new portrait of him, differently coloured, and creating a
different harmony. Sometimes a flower, taken from a bunch in Henri's
room, would add a note of richness, and intensify the general effect
of the colour scheme.

Henri, in order to spare his friend the embarrassment of entering the
dining-room alone, would be waiting for him, and, both of them being
late, they would run down the long galleries of marble, between the
busts of long defunct Réveillons, each standing on its separate pedestal
along the walls on either side, where portraits hung. Jean would think
that he had reached his goal, only to find another gallery opening
before him. They took a different staircase from the one they generally
used. Without Henri he would have been lost. The other members of
the family were only just going into the dining-room. At each of the
four corners of the table bunches of blue-green maidenhair fern, and
in the middle zinnias, red, yellow and mauve, snapdragons and African
marigolds, gathered by Mademoiselle de Réveillon in the course of her
morning walk in the Park, all freshly plucked, showed the full brightness of their tints on which lay a patina of dew as yet not dried, and
caught the gay beams of sunlight which, from the depths of the Park,
had pursued them into the confines of the room, imparting to them
that especial subtlety of tone which made them look like painted
flowers upon the surface of the porcelain stands in which they were
arranged, carnations stiff and upright, or violets blooming on their
green and rounded stalks, so that reflected on the white-panelled walls,
they produced the impression of motionless designs, as blue as hyacinths,
as red as roses. But already eggs were steaming between the fresh tints
of the flowers. Chairs were pulled to the table, napkins spread on waiting knees, napkins as fresh and innocent as the joy sparkling in every
eye and now enhanced by the discovery, between the golden waves
of scrambled eggs, of little fleets of bacon, half drowned and barely
visible, which those, now seated, began with a will to rescue from the
wreck. This, to be accurate, was no surprise to the Duchesse de
Réveillon who that very morning had conceived the idea and imparted
it to the cook. But, though the pleasure of discovery was not for her, and
perhaps because consciousness of success brought its own satisfaction,

she seemed to be far from displeased. The author of a successful play cannot share the thrill of gratified curiosity which the audience feels, being still ignorant of what is to happen on the stage. But applause gives him a different variant of delight which is not to be despised. The Duke and Henri mingled their pleasure with Jean's. This was not for them, as it was for him, the first time that they had eaten scrambled eggs and bacon. But the joys of habit are often more to be relished than those of novelty. A dish of hot lobster, set in readiness for Mademoiselle de Réveillon who never ate eggs, added to the pleasing smell of zinnias and snapdragon a fragrance which was not, as was theirs, an end in itself, but was destined to add the finishing touch to an anticipated, and more material, form of possession. But already the talk had turned upon what had happened in the night, a trivial incident which in the world of the Great House assumed the importance of an event.

"My poor dear friend," said the Duchess to Jean as he entered the room. "I am afraid you must have spent a dreadful night. What a storm!—a most unpleasant introduction to the country!"–"I assure you, Madame, that it did not trouble me, I heard nothing but the faint sound of rain," said Jean, who vaguely remembered that he had been awakened for a moment, had realized that a storm was raging, and then had settled down into the snug warmth of his bed and immediately gone to sleep again with his face to the wall and the blankets pulled up to his chin; or, on other occasions, had heard nothing at all, though the footman, when he brought his chocolate, had in the course of one of those conversations in which he knew well how to combine idle chatter with interesting information, not failing in his duty to his employers, but providing just sufficient news to save the guest from blundering into an untruth which would have been too patent when he met the Duchess later in the morning. Sometimes, however, when the word "storm" was mentioned he would take a chance and reply, "Yes, I heard the thunder, but soon went to sleep again," whereas he had in fact, heard no thunder at all. "What you heard was hail!" exclaimed the Duchess, delighted to think that her hail had been thus promoted. "It does not in the least surprise me that you should have taken it for thunder. Once or twice I nearly made the same mistake, and the noise got me out of bed!" To visiting friends that afternoon, or, sometimes, not waiting so long, to the servant entering with the next course, she would say: "It was so violent that Monsieur Santeuil really thought it was thunder!"–"He might well have done,

Madame," the servant would reply from his place near the door, with the frightened air of one who finds himself momentarily divorced from his normal function. "The postman told me that during the whole two years he has been in the district, he has never heard such violent hail, not even in winter." – "Do you hear that, Astolphe," the Duchess would say to the Duke who was busy with his letters. "The postman says it was the worst storm he has known for two years," while the footman stood motionless, seemingly honoured by this display of familiarity, and embarrassed because he felt that perhaps he might be expected to say more.

The storm, on such occasions, was the sole subject of conversation. It had begun while Jean was still in bed, and before luncheon, while the Duchess sat in the drawing-room with her embroidery, whenever anyone came in, she would say, "My poor, dear friend! what a night! what a storm!" Still earlier, when she had gone into her bedroom, the longing to talk to her maid of what had happened, had overcome her natural reserve. The storm was, as it were, a bond between them. But if the events of the night made the women more talkative, it made the Duke and Henri more active. It was an excuse for them to have their horses saddled, so that they might ride off to see whether the harvest had been ruined, to make sure that the windows were in good repair, to give an order for additional wood for the fires, to get out their heaviest overcoats in preparation for bad weather, and in short to take such precautions as are necessitated by an impending journey, to accustom themselves to new habits as though they had suddenly discovered that they were in a strange country. Everyone was at great pains to discover what really *had* happened. The Duke had been awakened by the first claps of thunder round about two o'clock. It was only later that the rain had started. "It was earlier than that," said the Duchess, "you did not wake up at once." – "You can't have looked at the time," replied the Duke, who would never admit that others slept more lightly than he did.

*

Jean and Henri would leave the Duke and the Duchess to pay calls in the neighbourhood, or simply to go driving, while they for their part set off to tramp the countryside. Sometimes a storm would take them by surprise, and when that happened, they would shelter under a thick-leaved apple-tree, and watch the falling rain, convinced that it would not last long. Before them lay dark green and melancholy fields of clover, interspersed with innumerable apple-trees on which the deep red fruit gave evidence that the season had reached its moment of maturity. Along the hedgerows the close-packed, delicate hawthorns which in springtime dressed the world in white, had only recently given place to the more sustained decoration of scarlet berries, while poppies, trembling in the breeze on their long green stems, looked like red pennons fluttering mast-high among fields of corn already turning pale. Beside the roads the tiny bells of Dyer's weed, the endless tracery of meadow-sweet, spread a tangled growth between huge pyramids of reaped hay waiting to be carted. Every caprice of Nature's colouring and all her passing thoughts, each birth of springtime, each finished work of summer, all things inseparable from warm and sunlit air beneath blue skies were there to show that neither sun nor blue sky had gone for ever but would at any moment come back again, and that between them and what remained of summer the rain had but for a moment spread its coarsely woven net to catch the luscious orchards and the red fruit on which, till recently, in colours ripened by the sun, the promise of summertime's return had lingered. Later, as the year wore on, it would no longer be so firmly fastened to the boughs, but would long have all been gathered in the barns or left to rot upon the roads. And indeed before long the shelterers could come out again, and as they walked could see, like some altar raised to the summer's glory, backed by a still dark sky, an immense pyramid of yellow straw on which in no long while descended Heaven's benison, the strong, delicious archway of a rainbow. They continued then upon their way, venturing sufficiently far to see the beginnings of a new country, a land more sombre than the one they had just left, and with a quite different personality which could not but impress itself, no less profoundly, on the minds of those who had seen it, if only once. The roads ran now through woodland. The mysterious smell of leaves and mould-encumbered earth rapidly supplanted the fresh scent of grass, the sweet fragrance, thinned by passing breezes, of buttercups and cornflowers. The season here seemed to be different from, less advanced than, that at Réveillon. It was from Réveillon each year that spring first moved in this direction, making a little progress every day, still wooing the eglantines to blossom in the hedgerows, where already, at Réveillon, they had withered. When those native to this spot, whose hay was not yet cut, might have occasion to go to Réveillon, they would meet, once Montoirs had been passed, oncoming carts piled high with straw, as from some land the ways of which were foreign, its summer earlier. Still farther on the land was even wilder and the soil less good.

*

There were times when Jean, having woken earlier than usual, or having not been visited by Henri, would make his way downstairs a full hour before the second breakfast was ready. He would find the Duchess in the drawing-room absorbed in the *Revue des Deux Mondes* and she would say good morning, without however moving from her chair, or asking him to stay with her, or offering to go with him, but determined to continue with her reading as though he were not a guest beneath her roof. When a visitor has been for a few days in a country house, the room he has been given, which even his host and hostess would not dream of entering without first knocking, where he can have a fire when he likes, and close the shutters when he wants to, comes to seem so much his own that he feels himself to be no longer a stranger. He is at home when there and the drawing-room becomes a No-Man's-Land where his hostess does not so much receive her guests as meet with persons happening to share the house with her, persons whose habits are their own, and different from hers. Often at these moments of the morning greeting, the Duchess would break to Jean items of bad news in quite indifferent tones, saying, for instance, "I rather fancy that you won't find Henri: I think he has gone to Etreuilles with his father." But as time wore on they found an increasing pleasure in being together.

*

One day, when she had gone out with a handkerchief tied round her head and a loaf of bread in her hand, Jean met her. "I am just off to feed my peacocks: won't you come with me?" she said in a somewhat absent-minded voice which, though it did not imply a hope that he would stay where he was, could certainly not be understood as expressing any real eagerness for his company, but to be merely stating a fact. He couldn't, surely, find any amusement in the prospect of feeding a lot of fowls: what an idea! But Jean in the absence of Henri went with her. They entered the great court which lies behind the Château.

The spot is completely open to the sky, and on this particular morning the ancient flagstones lay smiling and golden-tinted in the sunlight. Once, perhaps, they had found life less easy, but in the lifetime of the last two generations of the family, they had been concerned only to echo the sounds of the bailiff's trap each morning, after which their work was over for the day. The bailiff's little house was whitewashed, and showed no more than two quite simple windows, but across their balconies Virginia Creeper and a riot of yellow roses had laid a pattern, and hung from them in exquisitely delicate and airy swags. At this moment a peacock perched upon the roof, displaying its glittering colours, just as a hundred miles away the sea must be doing under a no less radiant sun, providing the richest and most marvellous ornament imaginable.

3. *Visitors*

Rainy days, which meant staying indoors, reading by the fire, and, when that grew wearisome, going down to the drawing-room at five o'clock, though usually one kept away from it until dinner was just about to be announced, to chat with the Duchess, to see the lamps brought in and the post arrive, to glance at the papers and hear the words, "Put another log on the fire, we've still half an hour to dinner," had a peculiar charm. Often there were visitors present, the Saint-Sauves ladies, for example, whom nothing could daunt. Such visitors were almost always those who, one had told oneself that morning, would be pretty sure to come—and what a bore that would be! Nevertheless, the Duchess scarcely ever failed to welcome them with the same form of words, "Oh, what a lovely surprise!" Circumstances did much to aid the conversation: the rain was an excuse for saying, "It must have needed a deal of courage to come out in weather like this! my dears, you must be soaked!"–"Oh no, indeed: we came in the closed carriage—besides, I do so think that girls ought to be brought up not to mind a little rain," Madame de Saint-Sauves would say, who did everything on principle. At this remark there would be much whispering among the young ladies, who appeared to be protesting under their breath. "*I* know somebody who does not share that view," Madame de Réveillon would reply, kind but percipient.

The particular daughter concerned sometimes summoned up enough courage to repeat in her ordinary voice what she had just been whispering, and what everyone pretended to be full of eagerness to hear. It was, as a rule, something like, "Rain is never very pleasant." Then all those who had thought the carriage would be bogged down in the lane, and that they would be brought to a dead stop, immediately joined in the conversation. This was the moment, usually, when Jean, tired of reading, entered the drawing-room, and was surprised to find company present. On the occasion of their first call during his visit, the Duchess had said, "Henri, introduce Monsieur Santeuil to your cousins." The girls had expressed amazement when they learned that

Jean played no instrument. Since Henri never went to their meets, their paper-chases, or their balls, the Duchess had grown into the habit of explaining these social lapses by remarking that he was "deep in his music". They, for their part, hearing that Henri had a close friend who was not at all "smart", had assumed that he was a musician. "You must bring your friend to see us, Henri," they said, "he says he'd love to come, so this time you won't have any excuse. Do you realize it's two years since you last paid a visit to your cousins at Saint-Sauves!" – "We'll all of us come," said the Duchess. "Oh, how wonderful that will be, but I simply *daren't* say a word to Mamma first, because it might positively make her ill," declared the eldest—who professed to have a passion for her aunt—with exaggerated enthusiasm.

Madame de Fontanges, who came regularly each week, always went into ecstasies over the view, as though she had never seen it before. When the Duchess left the room to make tea, saying, "Those who would like some of *my* tea had better come too," as though her tea was a commodity supplied under letters patent, a delicious and forbidden pleasure, a sort of a test by which to separate the sheep from the goats—Madame de Fontanges skipped after her, drawing out her watch after first raising her veil, assuming for the occasion a childish voice, and saying, "It's wery, wery naughty to have tea at six o'clock" —after which she went through a pantomime intended to convey that she just couldn't resist the temptation. "I shan't be able to *touch* my dinner—still, a visit to Réveillon doesn't come *every* day," though she frequently went there several times a week! Each of those present asked the Duchess in turn for a cup of "her" tea, accompanying the request with a smile the intention of which was to make it abundantly clear that she was well aware what it was she was asking. The Duchess for her part was careful to make enough to satisfy all possible demands, and was lavish in her supply of the precious fluid. Monsieur de Vidaine expressed himself as being deeply touched that his hostess should have had a mind to his grog, and the Baronne de Sainte-Euphémie that she should have remembered her particular preference for tea *without* milk —*one* piece of sugar only, and just *two* squeezes of lemon. Then the conversation would take a new turn. The various ways of passing the time at different country houses were compared. At Fontanges, the gentlemen were enthusiasts for fishing. "Oh, no one fishes here!" declared the Duchess. "Henri has never shown any liking for it. As a matter of fact," she added with no very great show of interest, "I am not at all sure that there *are* any fish here." – "No fish? What nonsense, my dear," intervened the Duke who could never bring himself to admit that Fontanges had any advantage over Réveillon, "your son may take no interest in catching them, but there are more fish at Réveillon than any-where else. Don't you know where your favourite pike come from?"

Madame Exel, a new and immensely rich country neighbour who had bought the Montmorency shooting, and was not exactly a wel-come guest at Réveillon, could talk about nothing but the Duchesse de Bourgogne's theatricals to which she was going, and waxed eloquent on the subject of all the friends of hers who would be present. "I think it most unlikely that we shall go," said the Duchess. "Sophie was kind enough to drop me a line, but we don't much like being social when we're down here. My own opinion is that the country should be a place of rest, though for a young woman, who has not yet gone out much, it is, of course, quite different." That night, at dinner, Jean was given the life histories of the various visitors. The general opinion was that this or that grand-uncle—who happened to be dead—would have amused him, or that somebody's niece, who might or might not turn up in a fortnight's time, would almost certainly appeal to him.

*

Once, when Jean was walking in the woods at Réveillon, he met a cyclist who stopped at sight of him, and appeared to be most effusive. It was Monsieur Rustinlor. He shook hands warmly, and his initial almost instinctive greeting was uttered in a throaty voice, his eyes fixed with a friendly look upon his interlocutor, his manner somewhat awkward. But the tone in which he spoke again a moment later was quite different—almost drawling, and accompanied by an ironical smile and a general "poetic" attitude. The resultant impression being that the *first* Rustinlor, which had vanished almost as soon as it had appeared, was his natural self, something that he had inherited directly from his father or his mother, something he had been born with, something that if he had not had a taste for literature but had been an honest grocer like his uncle, would still have been his. Jean asked whether he "was at work on anything". Monsieur Rustinlor replied that poetry with him was a thing of the past, that the matters which were now occupying his attention were a great deal more real and exciting, these, he added sententiously, drawing his brows together in a mocking grimace at once condescending and ferocious, raising his finger, and laughing, being "politics, immorality and cycling". According to him those were what really mattered, and not literature, which merely sought to imitate the true emotions which *they* provided. "I still have a warm feeling for old daddy Hugo," he said, "but there is more genuine poetry in a brisk walk through the Forest of Vincennes in good thirsty weather, provided one's in form, or in the bed of a certain young lady, who shall remain nameless, living behind La Trinité, than in all *Les Contemplations* or *Les Feuilles d'Automne*. As to the historians and the dramatists, that fellow Tacitus, that chap called Shakespeare, or Messire Balzac, they never painted anything half so thrilling as what is happening at this moment. Go to the Palais de Justice, my dear man, go to the Chamber, take a look at Esterhazy, make a study of all that business, Lanevois, Picquart. If human nature's what you're after, take my word for it, you'll find it there, in the raw, passion in all its manifestations, and so on and so on."

All the while that Jean was listening to him, he was vaguely conscious that what gives literature its reality is the result of work accomplished by the human spirit, no matter what the material facts that may have stimulated it (a walk, a night of love, a social drama), of a sort of discovery in the world of the spirit, of the emotions, made by the human intelligence, so that the value of a book is never in the material presented by the writer, but in the nature of the operation he performs upon it. It was only, he felt, because of some crude misunderstanding, of ignorance about what constitutes genuine intellectual labour, that people who begin by writing poetry persuade themselves that they can find an analogous form of truth in reading newspaper paragraphs, in travelling, in making love, in gambling, in mingling with the world of speculators or politicians, that they can, in such ways, attain to a life which, according to them, is at bottom far more literary than literature, and what is more, within the reach of everyone, an experience which has the effect of making many young men who once busied themselves in the writing of bad verse, or of none at all, and spent their time, like Monsieur Rustinlor, in reciting the verse of others and discussing literary theories in cafés, realize that they are eminently suited to sleep with women, to play at cards, to applaud their favourite orators, to shout "Shame!" or "Sheer Balzac!" to read the papers, to make money and to spend it, in short, to get to know the true poetry of life. In doing these things moreover they enjoy the

pleasant feeling that they have abandoned the shadow for the substance. From the moment, indeed, that they cease to feel that there is
another sort of prey, a more real prey, in poetry, they consider it their
duty to acquire the possession of *things*, in other words to devote their
energies to possessing what they can never have (it being possible to
possess things only through the operations of the mind) namely,
material objects. But Jean had but a confused view of these matters,
and thought it more polite not to insist. But he did instinctively feel
that Monsieur Rustinlor had not, by the look of things, gained in intelligence (impossible to deny of course that he was what would be called
an "intelligent" man: what Jean really meant was that his intelligence
had not reached a higher level than the one on which it had lived hitherto) and it seemed to him surprising that true poetry should be the per-
quisite of men like him, that one shouldn't, in some way, have to *deserve*
it, that it was something within the reach of all and sundry, and could be
found in leaves touched by the morning sun, or on a woman's lips.

  "By the by, I don't suppose you've heard, have you, that I've
become a married man?" He had taken to wife the daughter of an anti-
Boulangist lawyer who had suffered a good deal of inconvenience as a
result of the Boulangist movement. All the same he need hardly remind
Jean that he had always been an enemy of the "established order", that
he had always wished to "live dangerously", that more especially he
had always looked on literature as an activity standing outside and
above all consideration of Party, and even of the respectability of its
practitioners, "I shouldn't admire *La Légende* any the less if Ravachol
had produced it, quite apart from the fact," he added ironically," that
I have a good deal of sympathy" (much playful-ferocious business with
the eyebrows, voice rising to a shriller note) "with what Ravachol did
in fact produce."[1] When Jean mentioned the name of Barrès with
admiration, he said, "A nasty piece of work, and that goes for his books,
too. There's nothing much I don't know about Boulangism. My father-
in-law, who, though he mayn't be much of a dab at literature, is as
shrewd as you make 'em when it comes to business, and an altogether
delightful fellow" (in point of fact he was the sort of man to whom
before his marriage, he would have referred—and probably still did—
as one of the lowest of the low, brainless, cunning, colourless, and in
general a social menace) "would open your eyes a bit if he cared to tell
you what Barrès has written about him—dragging in personal matters

[1] Ravachol was an anarchist who threw a bomb into a crowded Paris café.—G.H.

where they don't belong. You know, none better, that I pride myself on being impartial, especially in literary matters, but also that I'm not one to mince my words." Jean, feeling that the father-in-law's private affairs were in question, thought he could not very well press for details without seeming rude. All this talk about "impartiality" which Rustinlor quite clearly imagined that he was now showing, amused him. What amused him still more was that when he took his old acquaintance back to dine at Réveillon, that fire-breathing eater of aristocrats who made no bones about wanting them all sent to the scaffold, waxed enthusiastic as a result of the hospitable welcome extended to him at the Great House, declared that his hosts were "quite charming", that there was about them the "true poetry of the Middle Ages", that in short they were "utterly delightful and the salt of the earth".

Being entirely devoid of those intellectual scruples which are part and parcel of the genuinely intelligent, he never attempted to discuss his impressions, to analyse the nature of the attraction which certain people exercised upon him, or the instinctive reaction which he made to a show of good manners. To his father-in-law, as to the Réveillons he applied the blanket term "delicious" giving it to be understood that he ranked such deliciousness far above poetic gifts, thereby breaking with everything he had always formerly maintained. The fact of the matter was that he knew nothing whatever of that "life" the glories of which he sang so loudly, and had accepted uncritically all its ready-made ideas ("intelligence and honesty are stupid") with the result that they had struck no real roots in him, and inevitably disappeared at his very first contact with the intelligent and the honest. Besides, he had always admitted certain exceptions—for example in the case of his own father who according to him was a "perfect marvel", and in that of an old notary who had always been "kind" to him, and whose deep knowledge of the law he had much admired, though in the latter instance he had come to terms with his conscience by saying that the man had a profound acquaintance with "certain legal texts of the seventeenth century which if the truth be told contain more true poetry than all the rational colourless lucubrations of Messires Boileau, Racine and Molière".

*

Next day a young diplomatic attaché, who was spending a holiday in the neighbourhood, dined at Réveillon. He was a great friend of Jean,

who had asked the Duke whether he might ask him over. The guest
proved to be endowed with a high degree of intelligence. He was
thought well of in the Service, and "knew all about" philosophy,
archaeology, music, and the reading of character from handwriting.
His conversation was adorned with a pretty turn of wit not uncommon
at that time in the Foreign Office or at least among his contemporaries
there. It took the form of retailing psychological anecdotes which
usually ended up with some such comment as, "Don't you think that's
really rather charming?"–"It seems to me that, coming from so-and-
so, that's pretty good."–"There you have the man in a nutshell."–
"Almost worthy of La Bruyère, isn't it?" But to these anecdotes,
which others would have retailed with an easy laugh, or in an off-hand
manner, Expert-Foutin imparted something of his own personal
character, which was compounded of an extreme susceptibility to this
particular kind of intellectual enjoyment, of artlessness, and an admiration for those of his friends who had told him all these "gorgeous"
stories. In short, he gave to his performance all the simple-minded
sweetness of his nature, accompanying it with bursts of irrepressible
merriment which caused him frequently to break off in the middle of
what he was saying, and usually brought tears into his eyes. But he was
just as willing to engage in erudite exchanges, packed with general
ideas and personal views, about, say, Beethoven's music which, to his
mind "was typical of its period, and the complement, one might say,
of its political outlook" or the architecture of Flemish cathedrals
"which, mark you, was developed among a constitutionally lazy race
of Walloon extraction".

Another pronounced feature of his talk, deriving from the deliberately
moral tone which he gave to it, was an expressed horror of men of
letters, critics and "pure" artists. He spoke so often about the danger of
intelligence or of aesthetic sense divorced from all moral considerations,
saying that personally he "infinitely preferred decent young fellows
who have never read a word of Flaubert etc." that he seemed to be
giving utterance to some personal grudge, so much so that Jean could
not help feeling that he must at some time have been supplanted in the
affections of a young woman by some novelist whose real defects as a
literary man he had detested. Perhaps however it was actually no more
than one of his innumerable theories, the one of them all that best
expressed his attitude to life, and, unknown to himself, that ideal
of solid, respectable domesticity which had influenced his early

upbringing. In his view Jean was the possessor of a first-rate mind:
far from holding that he had limited abilities, he believed that only
laziness stood in the way of his becoming an administrator or a sociolo-
gist of distinction. Since Jean, as a friend, had never been other than
charming, he saw in him none of the defects which he held to be
inseparable from the profession of letters. "With you," he said, "it's
quite a different kettle of fish." He was by nature an upright man
though tending to dryness and because of the pleasure he took in
applying intellectual standards to everything, was for ever involved in
crises of conscience, finding it impossible even to advise a friend to take
a journey without worrying himself sick over the moral responsibility
he would incur by committing himself either for or against.

When therefore the Dreyfus case came under discussion, Jean was
appalled at hearing him say that if Dreyfus were innocent it would still
be the duty, however painful, of the Government to conceal that fact,
and to declare him guilty in the interests of the greater number. It was
terrible to think that he might one day be a Minister, and a wise and
honest one at that! Pondering these things, Jean felt that his whole
belief in intelligence and the power of reason had collapsed in ruins,
that philosophy, sociology and psychology no longer had any meaning.
The less higher education there was, the better. His thoughts turned, by
contrast, to an old friend of his father's, a decent, elderly man who,
though he never used his mind, and was devoted only to the Opéra-
Comique and the novels of Delpit, was extremely good-hearted and
sensitive. When his daughters were ill, he would spend whole nights
watching beside them, and was almost out of his mind with anxiety.
His kindliness was the talk of the neighbourhood. 'What a shame,'
thought Jean, 'that *he* isn't a Minister—all the more so since I happen
to know that he believes in Dreyfus's innocence!'

Yesterday's newspapers had been delayed, and arrived with those of
the current date. Letourneur had become President of the Council,
and had announced in the Chamber that he was determined to prevent
any revision of the Dreyfus trial, in support of which attitude he had
been supported by a large majority.

*

"I have just had a line from Perrotin: he says may he come to dinner,"
said Madame de Réveillon delightedly to her husband. She ordered a

very special menu, gave instructions for flowers to be cut, and devoted all her energies to arranging the drawing-room, since Perrotin, who frequented the houses of many Jewish and American hostesses was on intimate terms with Berthe (the Duchess of Penn) and a constant visitor at Ilisgamault, had strong views on comfort and display. He was the possessor of a sharp tongue, and it was a matter of prestige with Madame de Réveillon to see that her house should not be thought lacking. "He'll be with us for one night only," said the Duchess: "I expect he's off to his Spaniard's." This was the way in which she habitually referred to the excellent woman who had accepted him as her lover in order to advance herself in the Great World. As a matter of fact all the ladies of the Vicomte de Perrotin's circle, the Duchess de Bellegarde and the Princess d'Arretoiles among others, received her. So far, the Duchesse de Réveillon had not made her acquaintance. She went out of her way to explain this lapse. "There's nothing *I* can do about it: he has never suggested that I should. I have not met her, and couldn't for the life of me tell you whether she is dark or fair." But she let it be understood that she had no objection on principle, and that it was merely a question of time before the meeting would take place. It was said moreover that his daughter would have an immense dowry, and might well make a marriage which would leave the Réveillons far behind. Not that the Duchess was thinking of her for Henri, and it seemed better therefore that things should remain in statu quo. "On the whole, I think it would be better if we *didn't* meet. That doesn't mean that I'm not very fond of Perrotin, because I am. But I am also very fond of Julie (the Vicomtesse de Perrotin), who was my poor sister Saint-Point's best friend, and wouldn't for the world do any-thing that might cause her pain. Between ourselves, I believe he'll be tactful enough not to raise the question." And indeed, though he regularly took Madame Torreno to see the Sipièges, the Cévoiles, and the Prisieux, he had never so much as presented her to Madame de Réveillon. She felt touched by this show of consideration, happy, and perhaps slightly annoyed.

The weather was appalling, and this worried Madame de Réveillon because it meant that Perrotin would be in no mood to make allow-ances. He arrived wearing a soft felt hat, a raincoat, and gumboots. Since he was Perrotin, it occurred to nobody to wonder whether such a get-up were "quite the thing". On the contrary, the general opinion was that it was "*just* the thing" and that in point of fact the whole arrangement was extremely ingenious and very daring—a choice of clothes that would be excessively warm in case of rain, excessively light in case of heat, and adaptable to any vagary of the climate. It was a case of a work of art being imposed upon an audience by the sheer prestige of the artist, and not having to pass through the measuring gauge of endless private discussion which would never reach any conclusion unaided, of something that was thoroughly sensible in itself, which the spectator was asked only to admire. To approving comments Perrotin modestly replied, "It's convenient, you know: good in rain and good in heat."

Perrotin, who was small and hideous, set great store on deceiving his wife because he had a reputation for "smartness". His ugliness, his huge nose, his unhealthy complexion, his skimpy legs, gave the impression that they had been made for him, like his gumboots and his large soft hat. Though his manners were those of high Society, his features indicated an essentially low nature, and the foolish curve of his nose, the shifty expression of his eyes, the pimples on his face, produced a frankly disgusting effect. Though he was stupid, he was considered in Society to be a man of staggering wit because he was always to be seen sending little actresses into fits of the giggles, and was in the habit of telling stories—many of them pretty "steep"—with a bored air and a complete absence of any sort of "style". He acted for elderly dowagers as an intermediary between them and vice, as other men might perform the same service between them and learning, because they were supposed to have read every sort of book, whereas he was supposed to have had every sort of woman. They would look at him and say to themselves: "There's no experience that man hasn't had," as one might say of an explorer, "Only to think that man's been to the Pole." All through dinner he told stories in his toneless and affected voice. Like an actor, he said things designed to provoke laughter by exploiting the element of surprise. "O.K., that's all right by me—oh no you don't!" then, suddenly switching, and becoming a member of the public, laughing loudly and tying himself into knots, with expressive glances at all and sundry. "Do you realize, Perrotin, that it's all of forty years since we first got to know each other?" – "True enough, way back in 1849 it must have been, at the house of that old Lacets hag who was own sister to the Duc d'Etoille, God bless my soul! I don't wish to conceal from you, dear friend," he went on to the Duchess, "that this husband of yours infinitely preferred to the

Marquise de Saint-Lieuvin, or Athénais, if I may so express myself, seeing that that was her name, and I can't say it wasn't, not even to please you, though I don't suppose you care any more than I do, or—" —addressing himself to Jean, "you either, eh?—So *that's* all right. . ." (Pause for laughter). "Well, as I was saying, your husband, though he wasn't your husband then—infinitely preferred to Athénais her ash-blonde maid—no use concealing from you that in those days he had a passion for ash-blondes—whom I shouldn't be far wrong in describing as a golden lioness. Well, this lion of yours, your husband I mean, for he *was* a lion and no mistake—don't protest, Madame—as near a lion as no matter—as Athénais very well knows, eh, Justin, old man," with a glance at the Duke, "you must forgive me, Madame: I know that your husband does not, as the concierges say, go by the name of Justin, any more than I do, or you, for that matter, madame la Duchess" (much laughter on the part of the narrator who, at this point, took the hand of the Duchess on whose right he was sitting, and patted it "Ah, *dear* Duchess!"). Then he switched to art and spoke of a play by Monsieur Donnay, of Monsieur Lemaître and Monsieur Pailleron, for, as a well-brought-up man he always said "Monsieur" when speaking of people he did not know, thereby almost, though not quite, giving them a standing as men in Society—not quite, because though one might know their names, one did not know *them*—as one says, when talking about a wedding: "What sort of a fellow is this Monsieur Hutchinson who's marrying Berthe's daughter? I'm told he's everything he should be, though I can't say I've ever met him: but Saint-Pieds came across him at Mathilde's, and formed a very good opinion of him." Then he began to criticize a play having to do with high Society. The philosophy of a man of the world can be more or less summed up in some such statement as the following: "I've no doubt these gentlemen have a great deal of wit and imagination, but the fact remains that they talk about matters of which they know nothing. Some Tom, Dick, or Harry has the impertinence to introduce us into the house of a duchess, though it is only too clear that he has never been in one. The great novelists were great novelists maybe because they had great gifts, but also because they were the sort of men who would have been accepted everywhere. I remember perfectly well how, when I was a boy, meeting Balzac at my Aunt Célestine's. He painted a wonderful picture of the Society of his day because he knew it from the inside. The same holds true of Delacroix, who was on intimate terms with my Uncle Fitz-James. Say what you like, there is no short-cut for the man who wants to write about Society; he's got to know it at first-hand. Nothing will change my opinion on that point. Personally, I see nothing against Monsieur Lavedan going to the Moulin-Rouge, if that sort of thing amuses him. But he mustn't turn round afterwards and say that he's been showing us a duchess's drawing-room. That really is going too far!" Jean felt stupid in the presence of Monsieur de Perrotin, reflecting that he would never enjoy a reputation for wit, and doing his best to take Perrotin as a model, though without success.

4. *Walks*

Sometimes it had rained all night and continued to do so all through the morning. But after luncheon the rain would stop, though frequently the sun did not appear, and Jean and Henri would set out along the road. The only sound to be heard was that of the vain Virginia Creeper at her toilet, drying her scarlet leaves, and now and again letting fall a drop of water which struck the flags with a pleasing "plop" very different from the noise made by the first onset of a heavy shower, since it heralded the return of fine weather, and the renewal of life spent in the open air. To this very soon was added the small chirping of birds, who, as at dawn, before committing themselves to the dangers of flight and full song, were prudently testing the sonority of the atmosphere, and waiting until they could be sure of the weather. But no sooner had they passed beyond the wall of the estate, and found themselves in the wide silence of the empty road—field-work having been made impossible by the rain—than they heard, coming from the farms, now silent and as though wrapped in sleep, the notes of a bolder challenge, the fanfare of cocks heralding the new day at ease in their yard, from which they issued over a circumference of many miles their ringing proclamations which, like bugles sounding the reveille, summoned those around to start for market, and urged both men and women to begin those labours in which they, personally, would play no part.

Henri, as has already been mentioned, was much interested in botany. The study of that science and the collecting of specimens, satisfied both his love of order, the need he felt to do a lot of walking, and his taste for all that was charming. He loved a countryside where there are concealed caves among the rocks and lonely valleys between the mountains (into which perhaps no human foot has ever ventured, for to reach them one must clamber down a short distance from the entangled slopes, and then work one's way along the faces of enormous boulders, ultimately arriving at a bottom which leads nowhere except to a sheer mountain wall, so that one has to retrace the same path when the time comes to turn back) always wet with the spray of torrents and scarcely ever dried by the sun, in which growing things unknown elsewhere thrust upwards with surprising vigour, and colours show in the damp earth with a special brilliance. Often, when they reached their goal and no sound came to them, Henri would set off to look for some particular plant which he wanted for his collection, Jean would settle down in one or other of the tremendous clefts, retreats seeming the more remote since silence reigned there at the heart of solitude and a wooded shoulder hid from view the farther parts of the valley, where quiet was so complete that he could almost hear the breathing of a butterfly poised on a flower. From where he was he could no longer see Henri. Alone in the sweet valley he stayed, lost in wonder at sight of the slender stalk of a violet digitalis, a noiseless brilliant dweller in that spot, with for companions, only a few snapdragons in family groups of four or five. He would ponder on the nature of such places, hidden corners of the earth which one may pass unseeing, though they have been there all the time, at the foot of a rock, on the brink of a torrent, secret worlds cut off from all outside them. He was in one of them at this moment, a living sentient being, though he could not but feel that he should be lying dead beneath the digitalis and the snapdragons that knew no world beyond. The place where he had been born was more than far away. It was a different universe. One spot in all the earth is just itself. No matter how peopled it may be it stretches only so far, and no farther, than the dwindling view of appletrees, just so far as the sea-breeze carries. Beyond are other places, no less separated from the rest of the world, from things their trees will never see beyond their own horizon, places where night falls on different things, places where a passing thought of Nature seems to have become frozen and left in ignorance of all beyond, but having too a face, in some sort the air, of a living person, an individual face with which some may grow so familiar that they feel for it a certain friendliness, a feeling that is more than friendliness, while others see it as a stranger, and only for a moment, the face of one who cannot follow when they turn away, who cannot move, but stays in its appointed station waiting for the dusk, its own especial dusk unshared by others, the ice-cold shadow of the mountain, the wind from the ocean, and having seen it thus, they will perhaps be never able to forget, so that the chance resemblance of some other spot of earth will, of a sudden, bring it back again, filling their hearts with a great longing though probably they know that never more will they set eyes on it. Yes, far far away some other place will bear a likeness to it, thus proving that the other had indeed its own and individual face, though often it is impossible to tell why the remembrance has arisen, as when the presence of one person brings to mind another. But never will it be indeed the same, resemblance merely serving to accentuate the fact of absence. 'If someone else resembles me,' thought Jean, 'the reason must be that there is something about me that is individual.' And he gazed upon the digitalis. He would have to leave it, and it would never have anything to look at but the three snapdragons and this little cleft between the rocks, never having known a flower on which sea winds had blown, nor a living creature that had been in Italy. And places nearer still were just as far, since it knew neither far nor near, but lived separated from all the rest of the world knowing only the three snap-dragons. He felt a sudden longing to take it away with him. What matter if it meant uprooting it? He would have liked to have taken the whole valley away, to snatch it from the isolation which had given him for the first time the feeling of something which was wholly itself, which was wholly outside all other things and would never be able to draw near to them, was something with which only silence could share its solitude. But he dared not do so. One fears to touch what is so wholly itself. How could he take the digitalis without the snap-dragons? He would have to take all or nothing—the form of the cleft, the unique quality of the solitude, the very form and feature of its silence. The time had come for him to rejoin Henri. He said to him: "Come back a little way with me. I want to show you a lovely digitalis, but you must promise to leave it where it is": then, not going back into the cleft, but standing at its entrance, he pointed the plant out to his friend. "Oh! that's not worth taking!" said Henri, "just *digitalea corrunbea*, I've got one of those already, they're as common as dirt, you can find them everywhere—in France, in other parts of Europe, in America—or so the books say," he added with a laugh.

These words sounded a solemn note in Jean's mind, and he looked now at the digitalis without sadness, seeing it, not as a lonely, perishable flower, but as a type, in life a vast and spreading presence, in Nature an imperishable thought. 'I, too,' he reflected, 'have often felt isolated from the rest of the world, just like this poor growing thing. But at other times I have felt that the world is filled with thoughts similar to mine which have existed from the far distant past, and that others will be born in times still to come with thoughts no different, others for whom I have sometimes dreamed of leaving, as a token of friendship, in a book that should be myself, thoughts that would have a similarity to theirs.'

Then they started back, and Henri seeing from Jean's eyes that he was deeply pondering, walked on ahead, silent so as not to disturb him. But little by little Jean's ideas pressed less vigorously upon him. The reason no doubt was that he had brought clarity into what had been working within him, and now, wearied by so strict a concentration, let his mind at last turn happily towards his friend. He watched him moving there in front of him, and understood the tact which had led him to set a distance between them and to keep silent. With a little spurt of affection he linked his arm in Henri's, and said, "Dear Henri, I am so happy, so very happy, to have you." – "It's getting late," replied his friend, "and now that you've finished thinking, let's walk more quickly," but he gave Jean's cheek a friendly pat just to make clear that if he had limited himself to an answer so little in tune with the other's outburst, it was not that he wished to imply an adverse criticism of Jean's emotion, but only that, though he had found the words sweet, he could not answer them in kind, and, instead, with a friendship no less warm, he could offer in exchange, not the sovereign remedy of an equal exchange for which he could find no words, but intelligent sympathy in return for genius, calm common sense for nervous excitability, and for his person the whole of himself with all that it implied—his life.

★

Jean loved to saunter in the garden at Réveillon, hatless, and walking slowly down the gravel paths with their bordering of flowers. A white rose-bush would greet him, bearing on each branch an enormous cluster of white blooms, pressed close together, as in the old days, they had overflowed the vases in his uncle's drawing-room which were filled on Sunday mornings with flowers from the garden, so that the room was sweet with the same soft fragrance as met him when he passed the bush. The pleasure which he tasted then was as much in himself as in the flowering shrub. Henri, at such times, could guess what he was thinking, and would move away that his friend might the better seek within himself the meaning of that scent. There are moments in life when, in front of some painting by Van Dyck, we feel that there can be nothing more delicious on which to expend our love. At other times that feeling comes to us at sight of a white rose-bush. What joy then to see—as in these flower-beds at Réveillon—all the masterpieces of the world of roses blooming in one long procession of decked trees, offering to the heart on fire, more than would seem possible, with love for the first white bloom, for another of deep scarlet, for a mass of small pink flowers like shallow bowls, for a simple crimson petals like those upon the eglantine—a whole gallery of rose-trees, each one of which seems lovelier than the last, each still a rose-tree as can be seen by its swelling and voluptuous glory, but each holding the enchantment of a differently imagined beauty, here rich in crimson splendour, there draped in the purity of white unsullied petals, so that we feel as in the presence of an artist's work whose every canvas demands a new love for a new dream, each setting new freshness on each new invention. The patron, enchanted to have thus before his eyes so rich a collection, is overcome with amazement at the in-exhaustible fecundity of the painter whose separate conceptions are all so original and fresh, though each expresses the glorious fulfilment, without admixture, of all his splendid and enamoured self.

But as one can love but one painter, so one can love but one flower. At the roots of the rose-trees was a multitude of geraniums, pink and red, of zinnias, of roses, of golden marigolds and violets, all that riot of violet, bronze and red which, in childhood, we were used to see running unchecked in those gardens where we felt no love for them, though now, in other gardens, we rejoice to see them crown the beds, filling them with colours of enchantment, ravishing, intense, and scented colours, which bring to us the lasting glory of an older day, telling us that the flowers which then were gay and living are not dead but persist in creatures which have no memory of us, these mad nasturtiums, these rose-trees motionless, these fuchsias with their eyes fixed on the ground, so that it is as though the world were not, as we had thought it, a continuing sequence of pictures which do not come again, as though the years that are past still live, as though the flower-beds of an earlier time have lasted on, as though the spirit of those days still floats in these gardens that resemble those which we remember, where at the same hot hour the butterflies pursued each other madly.

After luncheon, when the days were fine and the weather "just right" for a walk, as the footman had said that morning when he called him, Jean liked nothing so well as to spend a little time with the

Réveillons, doing nothing at all, sometimes ensconced in a rocking-chair, sometimes stretched at full length upon the ground. The lawn, over the whole of its extent was drenched in sunlight, not merely bleached or gilded by the sun, but penetrated through and through with heat, soaked in sunlight, nourished on sunlight, as a woman who has slept too long seems to be nourished on sleep, sunlight for a moment made visible at the glittering tip of a grass blade. "If you don't put your hat over your eyes you will get sunstroke," said the Duchess. Pigeons were strutting on the lawn with slow and leisured steps as though engaged in cautious exploration, while hopping sparrows seemed to be occupied in a process of rapid auscultation, as though convinced that the place was suited to some sacred rite or knowledgeable excavation, this sun-gorged spot of earth seeming indeed to be a patch of ground that must be crammed with works of art since upon its surface was scattered a mystery of pigeons carved from some precious metal with the grey sheen of old silver though of a more tender substance, so solemn in their silence that in each burst of frolic flight they seemed to be engaged in ritual dancing, their chiselled shapes so exquisite, down to the delicate adornment of their beaks, that whenever they alighted, they gave the impression of completing for a fleeting instant the perfection of the object they had chosen for their momentary dwelling-place. Sometimes fluttering within the great silvery antique vase at one corner of the lawn, they seemed to show how deep and vast it was, how full to overflowing with those things one so often forgets it had to offer, which the bird appeared to be seeking; sometimes coming to rest upon the head of a statue of Minerva, and so endowing her visibly with one of her attributes, giving her a sudden headdress designed for great occasions, all throbbing and alive, or motionless and radiant with bright tints, adding to the statue a touch of extra colour borrowed from Nature such as delights us in certain sculptured figures of the ancient world, sometimes strutting slowly on the grass which, though golden, aroused thought of only ordinary pleasures—heat and laziness and sleep—grass beautified, grass dedicated to fair forms, where walked the mysterious birds of silver-grey, and stood, her limbs in harmony with the general scene and greenly draped, the statue of Minerva, crowned with a pigeon and holding out her daughter to receive the benediction of the sun which drowned her in its golden flood.

But lovelier even than the pigeons—for they were the very heart-cry of the glittering day which gave to all things their extreme perfection, where nothing came to mute the light, so that their shadows passed black across the ground, brilliant in their very blackness and seeming like the hinder side of universal radiance, so that every moving thing upon the ground could do no more than hide it for a moment and then let it shine out again, since like a hidden god, its presence was everywhere. On this day the sun had come down to earth, and a man might, as once did Joshua, tell it to stay in its course. When in the Great House which stood full in its eye, somebody closed a window, or in the game-keeper's little cottage, the sun, repulsed, bounded away for a moment, only to return again, when as the Duke's carriage drove across the bridge that spanned the Loing, could be seen like a morsel of live silver dropping and drowning, the flash of its window scurrying upon the water, and lower down upon the Loing itself, nosing the stonework turned green by the passing years, now golden in this sunlit hour, the little boat, which, like all else, was revelling in the day's delicious torpor, lay afloat upon the surface where it rocked as in a hammock, letting itself be voluptuously lifted by the gentle swell, the square of woodwork of its stern all patterned by an impalpable and flickering net of silver made from the flash of sunlight on the top of tiny waves.

*

On such fine days which one greets with the thought, 'If only there were less wind how lovely it would be,' the Duke suffered a good deal because wind brought on his neuralgia. But the Duchess, even while she was saying to Jean when she met him on her way back from feeding the hens, clutching the flying ribbons of her bonnet, "Do you like this weather? I don't know how to cope with it: I've only been feeding the hens and just look at my hair!" would, as did Jean and Henri, look as happy as the woods and vines, blown by the wind but glittering in the sun. On the roof of the game-keeper's cottage, letting the sun play upon its blue neck and green tail, and as much aglow with those two colours as the sea on such days of wind and sunshine, was perched a peacock, completely motionless save for a few twitched feathers which the wind had caught, as though he had been frozen into immobility so that nothing stirred on all his body except what the wind had set in motion, to the gusts of which he could offer no resistance.

"What are you planning to do?" Henri had got to work for his science *baccalauréat* and Jean wanted to read. "Take my advice," said the Duchess, "and explore the little pine-wood—I don't think you've been there yet, but Henri can show you the way. You'll be protected from the wind, and if you don't want to come back for tea there's a convenient farmhouse quite near, among the vines." While she talked she unbuttoned her jacket, because merely to stand still for a few moments chatting in the sun, made one feel hot. What she had said was perfectly true. No sooner had they reached the little wood than Jean and Henri were out of the wind. They settled down far enough from one another not to be disturbing or disturbed. At the end of a few minutes Henri had lost all sense of where he was. Jean had not yet started to read, but was still looking about for a comfortable spot. They could hear, although they could feel nothing but a gentle breeze, a continuous murmuring, as though of the sea. Whenever Jean raised his eyes he could see in front of him a great spread of sky like a shoreless ocean, blue and calm to the horizon in spite of the susurration close at hand, though that was weaker now because, as often happened in the afternoon, the wind had dropped. Filmy white clouds were moving across the sky with a scarcely perceptible motion, like homing sails. Sometimes they passed close, moving quickly, with others hard upon their heels. But in the midst of all the calm immensity a few seemed to hang motionless, like fishing-boats at anchor. Jean resumed his reading and then when he felt tired, laid aside his book, letting the sun beat upon him and illuminate the thoughts which his reading had set afloat within his mind, one by one, while the wind, with that faint stir it gave to everything, quickened their movement without his having to make the slightest effort. He could feel them drifting by. He would have liked to talk to Henri, and felt disappointed to find that he was absorbed in his reading, so hard is it for us to understand that the moment of happiness, the time for rest, does not come simultaneously to ourselves and others, and that what for us is bright and shining has not yet reached another's consciousness. When after a period of fruitful work we hurry along a street wild with happiness, quite often the sight of us merely affects a passer-by deep sunk in gloom with a sense of mistrustful irritation, and when we meet a friend, just when we feel most warmly towards him, he often chooses that selfsame moment to remember angrily that we greeted him coldly when we were feeling less cordial, at a time when filled with yearning affection, he had been conscious in us of nothing but a lukewarm sympathy. But at last Henri closed his book, and they started for home together.

They went by way of the vines which, glittering in the sun, seemed flooded with a joy not less than Jean's. They reached the farm where the stones before the door seemed stroked by the sun, giving back smile for smile. They sat down to drink beneath the apple-trees which were now full of ripe fruit, having long lost their springtime blossom, though they still retained in the tangled tracery of their delicate branches something of their former charm with its memories of youth. Wild grasses on the wall were carelessly confiding to the wind. Not now did Jean, as once he had done when saying good-bye to Mademoiselle Kossichef, wonder whether he would ever know happiness since nothing ever seemed to give him a pleasure that was whole and perfect, but always fell short of expectation, and no matter how lovely this or that might be, never chimed perfectly with his yearning heart, but made him feel misunderstood and impotent, a prey to misery and despair. Now however in his walks and in his dreaming everything seemed to outstrip the pleasure that he felt within himself and to answer it. The woods, the vines, the very stones, were at one with the brightness of the sun and the unblemished sky, and even when the sky grew overcast, the multitude of leaves, as in a sudden change of tone, the earth of the roads, the roofs of the town, seemed as though caught up in the unity of a brand-new world. And all that Jean was feeling seemed without effort to chime with the surrounding one-ness, and he was conscious of the perfect joy which is the gift of harmony.

5. *Evenings at Réveillon*

There were evenings when Jean got back just as dinner was being announced so that he had no time in which to make a complete change. Hurriedly then he opened the door of his bedroom, felt his way along the wall to where right and left of him he was conscious of an obstruction as though he had reached the end of the room, though in fact there was a wide and empty space in the middle into which he penetrated without actually leaving the room at all, since there was no door, and found himself in the dressing-alcove. There he struck a match and lit a candle so as to waste no time in finding the things he needed after which he blew it out and withdrew. So short a time did he spend there that quite often the candle had no opportunity to get fully alight before he had extinguished it, and was already half-way down the stairs. Thus it was that while he was snatching up a handkerchief or a tie, the feeble flame, which was not yet strong enough to light the whole of the alcove but only the narrow area of the chest-of-drawers, produced by its own unaided efforts, no sense of gaiety. But already in imagination Jean could see the dining-room brilliantly illuminated under the lamp, his friends assembled, dinner on the table, and a letter waiting for him under his white napkin, so that as soon as he had blown the candle out he ran down the long corridors and descended the stairs. He almost felt it necessary to pause for a moment before opening the dining-room door so as not to be dazzled and suffocated by the great wave of light and warmth and delicious smells which suddenly broke over him. But even while he was still in his dressing-alcove in front of the chest-of-drawers on which the flame of the candle, which was taking so long in asserting itself and seemed to be hovering on the confines of light, and was not to be given sufficient time in which to bring to completion its attempts to achieve a perfect radiance, arrested at the last stage of cold before finding warmth, of hunger before dining, of solitude before company, of darkness before emerging into illumination, the tiny trembling flame brought him the same joy as dawn before full daylight comes.

In those moments of pure delight when desire already anticipates satiety, when he hastily took everything he needed from the drawers and made sure that he would not have to come back for something that he had forgotten, there were none to see the gleam of happiness in his eyes, revealed by the flickering candle-light, except the small dormer windows of the alcove with their muslin curtains, through which each morning when he woke he looked to see what the weather was like, and to glance down over the fields and woods. This happiness was for the moment confined within, diffused throughout, the little dressing-place, though in a few minutes now he would be leaping along the corridors, setting impatient feet upon the stairs, imparting to the treads down which he dashed four at a time the weight of his delight, and to the short length of staircase which led to the dining-room, up which he moved as though he had put his foot in the stirrup and felt his energy renewed—this happiness of expectation was now spread about the alcove like a fine dust of pollen, drenching, soaking, caressing, flicking with delighted vision there, in the topmost drawer which was so difficult to open because the key no longer fitted, the soft white pile of handkerchiefs on which the light lay like milk. Ah! tables bumped against in passing, flick of sheer joy given to curtains hastily pulled to, door slamming as though blown by the winds of hope. Ah! all that happiness left by her son behind him in his room, and to be found again, to be breathed in like a soft breeze of joy, when bed-time comes—if only Madame Santeuil could have come to drink her fill of it within those eyeless shadowed silent walls—what radiance would it have brought her mother's heart—the heart that beats in every mother's breast which on its high course through the heavens is powerless as the planets are to light itself, but waits eternally for light to come, when her son's happiness, that star of destiny so long looked for, brings her no gleam.

*

So now you can all of you see what life Jean led at Réveillon and know the happiness it gave him. That, according to the Princesse de Durheim whose house near by offered very different diversions, just showed the kind of young man he was. She lived in a Château with an enormous hall filled with white fur rugs and English furniture where, after dinner, she played upon the organ. Guided by an exquisite taste

she always carried with her those pictures by Claude Monet and
Pissaro from which she could least bear to be separated and without in
any way clashing with the period style of her interior, reflected best
the feel of the surrounding countryside. She always had artists staying
with her, and instead of playing foolish games the guests were set to
write each his own variant on a given theme or to record in paint the
beautiful effects of nature. They enjoyed going to Mass at Réveillon,
for nothing is more delightful than a village church, though the
Princess had begged the Curé to train his choir in singing Bach instead
of the detestable music in which, before her coming, it had indulged,
though the Duke and Duchess would have willingly endured it all their
lives since they were too little musical to suffer from it. Among the
Princess's chosen friends walks were as frequent as at Réveillon, but
not as there indulged in for such simple reasons as to go fishing, to pay
visits, or to do errands in the village. Walks for her meant admiring
scenery under some especial quality of light, to listen to church bells
in the distance, and to return home with a new sensation or a sketch.
When the weather was bad at Réveillon one sat snugly by the fire, or
if one feared to get a headache, went down to the village or payed a
call on some neighbouring house. At Durheim such days were held to
possess an especial charm and one got one's feet wet for the sole
purpose of sampling the weather. No one there would have dreamed
as at Réveillon of sacrificing moonlight after dinner to a game of
cards.

Life at Réveillon differed too from life at Soulanges, where lived the
Marquis de Porterolles, a man of the world with little feeling for art
(the Princesse de Durheim held him to be little better than an imbecile)
but who loved to surround himself with "intelligent people", and
maintained that he would be bored to death unless he had about him
women of wit and at least one man reputed for his conversation who
could hold his own against them. He was fond of entertaining writers,
though writers whom the members of the Durheim set looked on as
nonentities, well-known literary figures with a liking for Society.
"How bored they must all be at Réveillon," the Marquis would say,
reflecting that his ducal neighbours never at their table heard the
brilliant talk of famous persons, nor the delightful sallies of pretty
women with a gift of wit. And other people too would have felt contempt for life as it was lived at Réveillon, where the land was not
farmed, where no one bothered his head about harvesting or sowing,

where paying visits in the neighbourhood was looked on as a tiresome duty, and a game of chess as a most important occupation, where Jean never did anything more tiring than to go for a country stroll before dinner or in the morning to accompany the Duchess when she went to feed her hens.

But lazy though that life might be, it must have been enjoyable since as you now know it gave such happiness to Jean—a happiness much greater than he could have found in Paris among those famous men and pretty women whom the Marquis de Porterolles found so necessary, though Jean endured their absence without a qualm. Many a time after listening to them, hoping to remember what they said so as to retail it later to quite other listeners, he had gone home feeling glum and miserable, with the taste of dust and ashes in his mouth. The only way in which he could break free of the thought that he had spent a wasted evening was to say to himself, 'Well, anyhow, I did hear the celebrated S—— and saw the lovely Madame T——. When all's said and done it is interesting to have met them and will be something to remember.' He sought consolation for his boredom and his gloom in the fact that he had "met them" and this, it was essential to believe, would have an interest in the future which he could most certainly not find in it now. It was as though the springs of life had dried up in him. Whenever he had a moment to himself, he rehearsed what S——, or Madame T—— had said, finding that he had nothing else to think about. How different the afternoons at Réveillon had been when thoughts flowed in him with so strong a tide that Henri, seeing him staring seemingly into a great gulf, had walked ahead so as not to disturb him. He had gone once with the Princesse de Durheim to look at a sunset and she had been full of fine phrases. "It is a perfect Monet," she had said, "Oh, what a sky!" But when he got back he had had to admit that he had felt none of the pleasure he had hoped to find, that the sky had looked cold and glittering and as boring as a woman's dress, and with no more depth in it than that. There might, he had felt, be a whole succession of skies, blue and pink and green, to look at which would give him no more pleasure than the changes in the Princess's wardrobe through the cold round of her fashionable days. Life, Society, he thought of as nothing but cold and glitter like the Princess's conversation, producing the same sense of boredom that he felt when he was with her, its quality as tedious and as empty as her water-colours. The dear old Duc de Réveillon never noticed the sky. When there was bright moonlight, he would say: "My word, it's cold! We'd better not hang about." When there was one of those mists so dear to the heart of the Princess, he would remark, "If you're thinking of stretching your legs, you'd better take a coat: there's a devil of a fog!" and if the day gave him some sort of pleasure, he innocently attributed the feeling to some quite other cause, saying, "Good walking weather and fine for the time of year. How light it is! you'd never think it was close on five!" When it was windy he would say, "When there's nothing special to keep one out, home's the best place on a day like this." But when he had to leave the house for some unavoidable reason, he made the best of it. "'Pon my word, I rather like walking in this sort of weather," and if it began to rain, would turn up the collar of his coat and seem to enjoy the downpour in his face. Indeed, on such occasions he looked a great deal happier than the Princesse de Durheim, for all her affected ecstacies and well-turned phrases.

The fact is, Nature would be a poor sort of thing were it to be regarded merely as a sequence of fine pictures, by admiring which we may give evidence of taste. She cannot be separated from our lives, neither in the present when if we look upon her with detachment she gives us nothing, nor in the future when once we have come to love her. It needs but a dismal autumn day when the sun sets unseen, a road drying after rain, or the coming of the earliest winter chills, to make us drunk on the remembered beauty of the past and the primal substance of our lives.

6. *Going Home*

During the last days of his visit Jean learned much to his delight, to row upon the Marne, and also took a great liking to the son of the Réveillon schoolmaster. He never ceased to regret that he had discovered these two pleasures so late, almost at the moment of his departure, for had he known them earlier, they would, he thought, have given an infinite charm to his stay at Réveillon. In this he may have been wrong. Perhaps he delighted in them as he did because he knew that he would lose them so soon. A day came when his mother wrote telling him that his grandfather had been very ill, though he was much better now, and that that was the reason why for the past month her letters had been so short, why she had left off pressing him to return, and why his father had not made the trip to Belgium which he had been planning. The explanation she had given in her letters was that bad weather was keeping him in Paris, though she had feared that this must seem very improbable to Jean, since Monsieur Santeuil was not likely to be influenced by such considerations. She had been careful when writing to her son to conceal her anxiety, going so far as to take a supply of her own letter paper with her so that he should not see that she was staying with her father. Such precautions were as it turned out completely unnecessary for Jean had suspected nothing. When the Duchess asked him for news of his family, he had replied, "Mother's last letter is very short. She has a great deal to do: Papa is staying on in Paris because of the bad weather." As a result of egotism, or of an insufficient gift of observation, he noticed very little of what was going on around him, and never thought of finding out the reason for the absence of one person or the arrival of another. He accepted without question the explanation given him. He was glad to know that his grandfather was well, and that his mother was no longer anxious. He set out the more happily on a boating expedition with the schoolmaster's son for knowing that, had his mother been a different sort of woman, he might have had to abandon Réveillon, return in haste to Paris, and exchange the life he was now living for a gloomy sick-room existence. He felt extremely grateful to his mother for behaving as she had done.

He wrote to her each day, describing what he had been doing, the people who had come to dinner, and asking her to send the clothes he needed. He sent her news of the Duke's gout which at first had rather spoiled his pleasure since the Duchess had not come down to meals. The dining table had had an impermanent look about it and he had been in constant fear lest Henri should have to stay with his father. But very soon the gout had shown signs of improvement though since the patient had to take things easily, the Duke and Duchess had both got into the habit of not coming down, though their absence no longer meant that he need worry or live in a constant state of eagerness for news. He soon came to find his meals alone with Henri so pleasant, though at first there had been something melancholy about them, that when at last he was told that his host and hostess would be resuming their accustomed places at the luncheon table, he could not help feeling as much disappointed as one does when the time comes to leave a place where one has been happy, to terminate a way of life to which one has become accustomed and will never know again.

Inevitably his stay drew to an end, and an evening came at last when having been driven to the station by the Duke and Henri he took the train for Paris. He planned to buy a boat as soon as he should get home, to go for daily rows, and on the very first Sunday after his return, to visit Soissons where the schoolmaster's son had just started on his military service: in fact he deluded himself into thinking that he could transport lock, stock and barrel from Réveillon to Paris all his recently acquired habits and the wish to continue in them. He had not announced the hour of his arrival; consequently, there was nobody at the station to meet him. Night had fallen, but not the silent Réveillon night, where the fields lay silent under the stars, and the glow of lighted windows in the Château showed pale in the darkness. Here city houses hid the sky, electric street-lamps the night, crowds of carriages and hurrying pedestrians overlay the silence. To make his way at all he had to push and fight, keeping a watchful eye on traffic all the while; no one it seemed to him walked here for walking's sake, as they do on country roads, but only in order to reach some definite destination. He thought of all the places where, by walking fast or taking a cab, he might get to. A multitude of desires to which he had for long been a stranger, awakened in him, intersecting in his mind as rapidly, and with varied lights as strangely coloured as the traffic in the streets was huddled and confused, and pressed in upon his heart with a no less phrenetic movement. In ten minutes he could be at the house of Madame Desroches or again since it was opera night, could dine and dress, though if that was his intention he would have to hurry and to arrange with the barber to come and shave him. He found himself passing a number of theatrical posters, each of a colour that was strange to him, and all bearing the names of plays he had not seen, and of his favourite performers, so that he was conscious of an anticipatory thrill, seeming to catch the very smell of the auditorium, and the sight of the rising curtain. It would be amusing to run across this or that friend again. At this very moment he was passing Sourcier's house. The shutters were open: the rooms were lighted. He must be back from the country, what luck! He stopped for a moment to verify his assumption at the concierge's lodge. "Oh, yes, sir: they returned three weeks ago." – "Is he in?" – "Yes, sir," the man replied and, turning to his wife. "Mr. Paul's in, isn't he?" – "He most certainly is, and told me he wouldn't be going out again this evening, and that I could send up anyone who called." – 'That's that, then,' thought Jean. 'I'll come round again after dinner.'

The nearer he got to the boulevards the lighter grew the streets. The lamps seemed to be in a rare state of excitement to think that they were shining down on something thrilling, something artificial, something attractively unhealthy. The cab turned into the rue des Saints-Pères. Jean thought how surprised his parents would be, his mother how excited. He could see them in imagination; was already eager to fling his arms round their necks; could hear himself answering their questions and the way in which they would press dinner upon him. Already he was with them in thought, impatient to think that he was still some distance from them in the flesh. When the cabby reached the rue Bonaparte, but instead of turning into it continued along by the river, thereby lengthening the drive, Jean put his head out of the window, meaning to say, "Hi! you've gone wrong!" and then decided that he would let himself be taken on down the rue de l'Université, and so get home the sooner. But because he could not sufficiently vent his disappointment by upbraiding the man from inside the vehicle, where he knew his voice would not be heard, he kept on repeating to himself out aloud, "What a fool the fellow is, what an ass!" and when at last he paid him off, told him what he thought, though by that time it could not do the slightest good. He summoned the concierge, told him to take his luggage in, and asked for news of everybody. He reached the front door of the apartment at last, rang the bell and stood there deeply moved by the sound of the tinkling sound which he new would draw from his mother the surprised inquiry, "Who *can* that be as late as this?", and from his father, "Whoever it is, say I'm not at home!" followed by the servant's startled withdrawal. He was conscious of a sense of oppression in his chest, either because he was being kept unduly waiting, or because, without noticing it, he had taken the last three flights at a rush.

"Are my father and mother still at dinner? Is everyone well?" – "No, sir: Monsieur and Madame have finished dinner, and are taking coffee in the drawing-room." Since the carpet had not yet been put down again, he could hear, with a little catch at his heart, the sound of his footsteps as he made for the drawing-room door. He turned the handle. Now was the moment when his parents would get that little shock of surprise which, for the last hour, he had been so happily anticipating. What he had been awaiting so impatiently had come. He threw himself into his mother's arms, and then his father's. His mother thought that he was looking well, drew him to the lamp, decided that after all he didn't look too good, and affectionately reproached her husband for not being sufficiently excited. She asked after the Duke's gout, wondered whether the schoolmaster's son had been able to see him off at the station, whether in spite of the weather, he had managed to get his row that morning. "It wasn't raining at Réveillon: but I had my packing to do." To find himself thus confronted by his two lives simultaneously, amazed Jean; to hear his parents talking of people they did not know, people whom, for the past two months, he had loved so dearly, in whose company he no longer was. He said, "I'll tell you everything later: do you think they could get me something to eat?" – "My poor darling, *don't* tell me you haven't had any dinner!" Hastily he announced that he would dine and sleep at home, that he really had come back, happy to say all these simple things, happy in the knowledge that his return was quite an event for the servants, filling them with surprise and joy. Then he went back to his parents. Madame Santeuil was reading an article aloud to her husband, who asked him jokingly please to allow her to finish. The moment for which Jean had waited so eagerly had come. But the happy emotions which it is so great a delight for us to provoke and to feel, at such times, take no deep root, do not become the substance of our lives which go on precisely as on the days we have left behind us. Not without a certain sense of disappointment do we take up the old familiar existence, even though for an instant it has turned out to be precisely as we had expected that it would be.

"Come over to the light," said Madame Santeuil to her son. "Gracious, how shabby that jacket looks! D'you mean to say you've been wearing it at Réveillon? I must send it to the tailor without fail tomorrow morning." At these words Jean became suddenly conscious that the doors of his parents' home had closed upon him, that an infinite distance now separated him from Réveillon, a distance which he could never hope to cross again. Ah! if only by some miracle now that he had embraced his mother and his father, he could find himself in the great drawing-room, with the Park and the distant countryside beyond the windows! He stamped with his foot upon the ground from which he would so dearly have loved to flee. But he could not hear the sound of this protest which was stifled by the drawing-room carpet, which had recently been relaid, and seemed to him like those "Leads" in Venice which separated prisoners from the outside world. He sat down to table, but the meal was a poor thing compared with the dinners he had eaten at Réveillon. All the same his mother grumbled at him for eating so much fruit, saying that it would upset his stomach. When he had satisfied his appetite, she suggested that he had better go to bed. Monsieur Santeuil was one stage ahead, having appeared in his night-cap, with a candle in his hand. "You two can stay talking as long as you like," he said, "*I'm* off to bed." All these familiar, time-worn habits were at war in Jean with those newer ones he had so recently acquired— so that even the sweetness of his mother's voice when she said, "I don't want to spoil your first evening with serious matters, but tomorrow we must have a good talk: I won't say anything now, because this isn't like an ordinary evening," irritated him profoundly, because she seemed to be presenting as a moment of supreme happiness and suspen-sion this cruel hour which was filled for him with a task far harder than the mere resumption of work and duty—the renewal of old habits. The wretchedness of ordinary life, endured so gaily when it is part of our normal existence, is made far worse when it comes as something new, and is exaggerated by the working of imagination. When Jean got into bed he had no longer round him the great corridors and endless galleries of Réveillon. From his father's room he was separated only by a wall so thin that he could hear him turning in his bed. It seemed to him as though he were spying on the sleep of his gaoler, though what good that would do or how it might help him to escape from prison, he did not know. At last he managed to fall asleep without a gleam of hope and a feeling that tomorrow's sun would never rise.

V

The Marie Scandal · A Great Minister

The Young Edouard Marie · A Warning

Marie's Success and Fall · Jean Intervenes

with Couzon, the Socialist Deputy · Early Days

of the Dreyfus Affair: The Fifteen Counsellors

Jean and Durrieux · General de Boisdeffre

Rustinlor and Politics · Colonel Picquart

From the Opéra-Comique to the Palais de Justice

The Deposition of Monsieur Meyer · The Affair and

"The Figaro" · The Truth of the Matter

1. *The Marie Scandal: The Young Edouard Marie and His Mother*

In those far distant days of which I am now speaking, dear reader, when Monsieur Santeuil was a gentleman with a black beard, and Madame Santeuil a young smiling fair-haired woman in a fantastic velvet dress, whom you might have seen, while Jean was still alive, in his photograph album, before they had become a sort of glittering indistinct irrevocable and melancholy dream with about as much connexion with the Monsieur and Madame Santeuil of thirty years later and with Jean too as the faded pictures in which Jean found it as difficult to believe that he had played a part as would have done had they been recorded when his father and his mother were first engaged—days which in fact had been as unremarkable and as solemn as those of the present moment when we have work to do and desires to gratify, days which we think of as important and real, when we do not feel for those with whom we live the respectful solicitude for persons who will not be with us always, whom one day we shall no longer be able to treat with adoration—in those distant days, which were just ordinary common-or-garden days, Charles Marie, Santeuil's oldest friend, at that time a Deputy, a former Minister and the most influential member of Parliament alive, used often to turn up unexpectedly to dine with the Santeuils. Although Madame Santeuil never failed to apologize for the unsatisfactory nature of the meal, which was more than usually exiguous because as she would explain, she had not even been sure that her husband would be in, the fact was, however, that as soon as Monsieur Marie appeared, she had hurriedly sent the maid, much to the latter's annoyance, round to the confectioner, the cooked-meat shop and the ice-cream merchant. As the result of a knuckle of ham, a *paté*, a strawberry *mousse*—which gave to the Santeuil table an appearance of unusual richness—the bonds of the old friendship between Marie and Santeuil were destined to be drawn tighter because Marie who was greedy, was always so delighted that he promised to come again and Monsieur Santeuil was conscious of a feeling of warm satisfaction to think that his friends, even when they appeared unannounced, could always be sure of being entertained in a manner which did credit both to his wife and to himself.

Marie had always odds and ends of political news to impart in which Santeuil took a keen interest as did also, it must be confessed, Augustin, who on those occasions always arranged for the cook to bring the dishes as far as the dining-room door and so spare him the disappointment of losing a single word of what the guest might have to say. And since Marie who looked on Augustin as an old friend (he was a thoroughly decent sort and a generous visitor who never failed to give Augustin a tip and had procured for his brother a good situation in the City Administration) never made any bones about speaking in front of him, Augustin had the glorious privilege while handing round the sauce-boat, of hearing a number of State Secrets which he almost felt had been intended for his own particular ear. "I ran into the Minister of Agriculture just now, but was careful not to tell *him* what I am telling *you*." When such words fell from the lips of the distinguished guest, you may well imagine how proud Augustin felt to think that he was more "up in" the secrets of the Government than even the Minister of Agriculture.

Augustin's satisfaction had probably nothing to do with the pleasure felt by Madame Santeuil each time she saw Monsieur Marie arrive—even though his presence *did* send up the household bills. Nor had she the slightest curiosity about politics, for like one of those planets which receive light only from a star, she was incapable of enjoying any pleasure which she did not share so that she was never conscious of it until it had irradiated the face of someone whom she loved. Nothing ever really brought her happiness unless it had done good to her father, her husband or her son, and had given them pleasure. Now she knew that her husband took a great interest in Marie's conversation and it pleased her to think that she had been able to make pleasant for him one of those simple family meals, from which out of sheer kindness of heart he was never absent. Besides, though she would have thought it strange to have a stray affection for any woman friend outside her own family circle, it seemed natural enough to her to have

a fondness for Marie, who was devoted to her husband, had done him
more than one service, and might some day take her son under his
wing, and liked to spend his evenings in their small world. Marie was
a model of good nature, simplicity and unaffectedness. He was generous
and always ready to help his friends. For many of the unfortunates in
whom Madame Santeuil took an interest, but would not bore her
husband with, he had obtained Public Assistance, or, when this was
impossible, had, in the simplest possible manner, helped them out of his
own purse, because he had a kind heart and cared nothing about
money. He found jobs for all her protégés and set up the widows
of Santeuil's former colleagues in tobacco kiosks. But there was
yet another and even stronger bond between Marie and Madame
Santeuil.

This woman who would have thought it very wrong to give any
considerable portion of her heart to anyone other than her father, her
husband or her child, feeling as she did that they were her appointed
responsibility and the persons whom God had put in her charge so
that she might keep them good, happy and strong, had had one great
woman friend—perhaps because Santeuil's affection for that woman's
husband did in some sort sanction her devotion. That woman was
Madame Marie, an exquisite creature, ravishing and intelligent, a
wonderful wife and mother who had died of consumption at the age
of thirty. She had been a Jewess and only the irresistible effect of her
charm and an intimate knowledge of her virtues had made it possible
for Madame Santeuil, who came of a family in which a dislike of Jews
had been prevalent, to regard her as it were as a sister. But on any human
being who is blessed with real goodness of heart, great intelligence
and sweetness of nature combined with unusual charm is bound to
have an effect. Confronted by persons possessing such qualities we can
have feelings only of adoration. Even a bigoted peasant girl would have
felt that the soul of so perfect a Jewess must be more pleasing to the
Lord than all the Christians, Curés and Saints in the world. Just before
she died, she had committed her husband and her son into the hands
of Monsieur and Madame Santeuil. To Madame Santeuil she had said
"No matter what may happen—and I sincerely hope that nothing ever
will happen which might weaken the bonds between Charles and your
husband—I beg that the memory of me may prevail upon you never
to abandon him, and I dearly hope that the friendship between him and
your husband may never grow less. Please believe me when I say that

Charles is the soul of goodness. If he should ever act wrongly, it would only be, *could* only be, that his heart had run away with his judgment, and that he had acted out of affection for persons who perhaps had not been worthy of his love. Keep an eye too I implore you, on my poor Edouard. It frightens me to think that at fifteen he knows next to nothing about life."

In that she was not far wrong. Edouard's outlook was very strange. Thanks to his father's connexions what might have been impossible for anybody else was never impossible for him. If a school division was so full that there was no vacancy for anybody, his father could always, under the very noses of other pupils, manage to get a place for his son. If no seats were available for a play which Edouard particularly wanted to see and it was impossible to get even standing room no matter how much one was prepared to pay, his father always succeeded in squeezing him into the Minister's box. If he had a headache, he was given antipyrine, and he looked on the small ailments for which he was entirely responsible, having left his muffler off, or got over-excited at a party, as so many rather long "detentions" which his father's influence could have spared him. When, being of a weak and nervous disposition, he had expressed fears about military service, his father had smilingly observed, "I have had a word with the Minister for War: don't worry, everything will be all right." As a result of all this, it had become impossible for him to believe that any unpleasantness could threaten him which his father could not dissipate with a snap of the fingers. When therefore his mother fell dangerously ill, it never occurred to him that she might die. He looked on death as he looked on military service: it was just a misfortune which might come to others, but not to the wife of a man who could always "arrange" matters, who knew all the most famous doctors, and could at any moment enlist for his wife the assistance of all the Ministers, the whole of the Chamber, the President of the Republic, and the King of Italy. When in fact she did die, he spent an evening weeping beside her body, calling to her, wanting her to speak to him. While on the floor below the Ministers, the President's aide-de-camp, and the Italian Ambassador were signing the visitor's book, he stopped crying and felt suddenly that he was in the presence of some strange and unknown Power, a Power over which no testimonial, no amount of influence, no authority could prevail, against the great surge of which such things counted as nothing, were broken in pieces without the enemy having to exert the slightest effort.

For the first time he realized that there was something stronger than his father, something that was not, like his father, prepared to satisfy his every whim: and once again he burst into tears.

*

The only fault that Madame Santeuil and even Santeuil himself could find in Charles Marie, was the pleasure he took in advertising through the medium of the public Press the names of the famous persons whom he called his friends and who dined at his table. Not that Santeuil was ignorant of the fact that Marie's honour had been called in question by certain persons, but this he regarded as the price one paid for being in politics and was only too ready to overlook in Charles Marie the very natural weakness which made him want to make sure that the two or three persons who, claiming to know for certain that he had been guilty of a dishonourable action, had harshly blamed him, should learn from the papers of the triumph of the man whom they had thought it possible to humiliate. Are we to believe that Madame Marie in the whole course of her brief life had held the same good opinion of her husband as that which we have seen was shared, at the time when this story opens, not only by the Santeuils, but by almost all the great political personages belonging to the influential majority of the French Republic? It is never possible to be sure to what uncertain and wavering degree the blindness of extreme affection can co-exist with clear-sightedness. It is perfectly possible to believe in something and yet to doubt it at the same time—even death. Things which occasion deep feeling in us are to that extent like life itself, which is the object of faith and of love. We believe in the continuance of love but doubt it too. We believe in, but doubt, life everlasting. We believe in the fidelity of the woman we love, yet doubt it. It is difficult to suppose that the mother or the sister who loves us unconditionally should be blind to the potentialities—even the bad ones—of our character, and difficult also to believe that essential love should not pardon those detestable elements which may be inseparable from the object of it. It may well be that Charles Marie's wife both believed in and doubted his moral qualities. Perhaps we ought to hold that when, on her death-bed, she said to Madame Santeuil that should her husband ever be found to have done wrong it would be because he had been led away by his kind heart, she meant her remark to be regarded as a piece of wild talk to which no importance should be attached, a comment on something which she had no reason to think would ever happen, but *also* as a toned-down expression of what she knew to be true in her husband's case, of what she foresaw *would* happen, a sort of sorrowful lie by which she hoped to persuade others, if they remembered it, not to judge her husband too harshly, not to abandon one who for all his unworthiness she had loved devotedly, should a time come when, his bad tendencies having changed little by little into disastrous realities, he might only too probably be abandoned by his friends.

For all we know Marie too when he was not actually with his wife, may have thought that her opinion of him was compounded both of faith and doubt. Not knowing whether charity or uprightness was the strongest element in her character, he could not perhaps be certain whether, if she had got wind of certain matters, she would have spoken to him about them, or kept silent. The probability is that he did not often trouble his head on that score, for though he was good-hearted, intelligent, hard-working, generous, and always anxious to help others, he was neither a dreamer nor prone to melancholy brooding. He loved his work, he loved power, he loved display, and such other simpler pleasures as he found in the Santeuils' affection for him, the unpretentiousness of their lives, the warmth of their esteem, the open-armed welcome which they always extended to him. Only later did it become known that he had also enjoyed dabbling almost daily in a number of decidedly shady concerns and that there was nothing he would not do to make money. Until then nobody had thought it particularly surprising that he should frequent the company of two or three rather doubtful bankers, because after all a man who had once been Minister of Finance, and might be again, must feel it necessary to keep in touch with people of that kidney. Several who have since disappeared— one committed suicide, another is now living in America, a third managed to keep on the right side of the law, but found that not many hats were raised, nor many hands stretched out to him in welcome—had awakened in Marie feelings of friendship which strange though it may seem were occasionally warm and cordial. It was not merely that these individuals were useful to him when he wanted to put through some financial deal which he was not anxious to acknowledge openly. It was more than that. They were the persons with whom he could talk freely about a side of his life which he was compelled to hide from the eyes of the public, from his colleagues, from his friends, and even from his wife. Any activity which absorbs some part of our powers gathers about itself curiosities and sympathies and makes us feel the need of confidences which are the more pleasurable when indulged in because, for most of our waking life, they have to be suppressed. A man who likes hunting invariably gets on well with those who share his passion; a man who loves to haunt bookshops can scarcely help being on good terms with booksellers, and a man who owns a motor-car with other enthusiasts of motoring, more especially if in his home circle he suffers from a temperamental and despotic wife who forbids him to talk about horses, old books or cars. We feel that in the company of such specialized friends we can take up with a part of our life from which we have been separated. I am pretty sure that there must, between the members of criminal gangs, be much amusing and cordial talk about cribs already cracked and those still to be attempted, which creates bonds of affection which are far less blameworthy than the shared activities which have created them, and moments of real affection from which tears, good-will, and disinterested friendship are by no means absent. You must take my word for it that a relationship of this kind did exist between Marie and his acolytes, whose own view was that they were not engaged in anything particularly wrong, that their activities served a political interest—and only temporarily at that, until such time as they should have amassed the fortune needed for the carrying out of their plans—so that it was easy for them not to suffer from qualms of conscience (which alone would have warned them that their conduct was illegal) by thinking of their enterprises in terms of prudence, fear, or the ill-will of others, and in the ordinary concerns of life were perfectly capable—as we can see in the case of Marie—of being good husbands, tender fathers, devoted and generous friends. I feel quite certain that if this narrative were not already over-loaded with irrelevant episodes, I could awaken in you a feeling almost of envy occasioned by a sense of well-being and comfort, by painting a picture of Marie and old Duclin sitting in a lilac-shaded arbour on a hot summer afternoon, with cigarettes between their lips under the motionless laburnums, with wasps bumbling round them, innocently enjoying the sun and smiling happily quite untormented by a sense of guilt. I might too succeed in touching your hearts by depicting the absolute trust which Marie had in Duclin's perfect delicacy, trust which was later proved to be well founded when Duclin, who after his arrest might have got off with a very much lighter sentence had he been willing to incriminate Marie, did nothing of the sort. On that occasion, though never again, Marie was safe and no hint of suspicion touched him. Still as a result of what had happened, he no longer felt quite so secure as he had done in the past.

2. *The Marie Scandal:*
Warning Shadows

You may feel no little surprise that for so many years Marie could have led the kind of life which meant that the shadow of catastrophe was daily hanging over him. But where the will to live and to gratify one's passions is strong, the only arithmetic is a calculation of probabilities, based on the assumption that as between two probables the pleasantest is the more likely. The debauchee who after a good dinner picks up a woman, knows perfectly well that he is taking risks. The traveller who books a passage to America is fully aware that liners do get wrecked or that when he gets home again he may find that his old mother or his weakling son has died during his absence. The idler who fails to write the book which might make for him an assured reputation or to draw up the Will which would give his children a fortune at the expense of the cousins whom he loaths, is not ignorant that the day which he has not turned to advantage may well be his last, since there is nothing unusual in a man falling a victim to a sudden attack of apoplexy or a runaway horse. The glutton usually realizes that gout is ever ready to pounce, and that alcohol is bad for him. But possible disaster weighs light in the scale against certain pleasure. The attraction exercised by a woman's arms, by the prospect of unknown seas, by the waiting sofa, the lazy cigarette and the anticipated saunter, works easily on a mind which is only too ready to conjure up the image of a pleasure which is so easily within reach that the heart beats at the mere thought of it. Few of us are prepared to sacrifice ephemeral delights to the knowledge that by yielding to the temptation of self-indulgence we may be risking irreparable unhappiness. And so it is that scarcely a day passes but we see the voluptuary hot on the heels of pleasure, the traveller travelling, the lazy persisting in his laziness, and the living enjoying life as it comes day by day without ever once thinking about death. It nevers occurs to the greedy man that the one more drink he is taking may make all the difference between gout and health.

Marie was no more mad than the men I have been speaking of and when on waking he read the letter summoning him to an interview with the examining magistrate, he found himself face to face with a situation about which he had often thought, although he had never really believed that it would ever arise—or not in this way. There is something noble about death and we find no difficulty in talking of it. Then one fine day we wake with so violent a pain in the side that we can scarcely breathe, with a sweating forehead, a trembling hand, and eyes that we can focus only with an effort. But the pain in the side which grows worse moment by moment has nothing in common with that idea of death which we can accept or put from us at will when life is smiling and we might be needlessly depressed by such a thought. The summons to attend on the examining magistrate was worded in the usual manner, and could be read as calmly as the symptoms of G.P.I. in a medical dictionary. But Marie, reading the words over and again, had the same sort of uncomfortably vague sensation as might afflict a sick man whose serious ailment suddenly becomes a silent night-mare, so that the clock with its pendulum and the blue vase on top of the chest-of-drawers assume the appearance of terrible monsters, more frightening and more eloquent of the unknown than in his moments of health the imagined torments of the damned could ever be. A heaviness in the head and the sight of the blue vase are the very form and substance of terror for the invalid, and he feels that the joy of life which once played in and out with the idea of death, like the sun shining between clouds on a radiant day, has gone for ever.

It will come as no surprise to you that the Palace of Justice being situated on the Quai de la Mégisserie, it was to his chambers on the Quai de la Mégisserie that Monsieur Croissin had summoned Marie. This simple detail which had nothing to do with life as he had lived it up till then, but was an essential fact in the new turn of events, seemed like an added pain, sharper than any which had preceded it, marking this new trouble, stressing the grip it had upon him. Silently, and with a sense of fear, he read the words "at his chambers on the Quai de la Mégisserie", the forerunners he felt of torments yet to come—much as a patient in a surgeon's waiting-room may hear a voice next door saying to somebody else that an operation will not be necessary. But his first thought was, 'Pretty good cheek, I must say, for this petty official to say he wants to see me. I could get him sacked without the slightest difficulty. I won't do that, though—just ask the Minister of Justice to give him a good dressing down.'

There was nothing particularly frightening about a visit to the Minister of Justice who was not only his friend, but to some extent his protégé as well. The prospect merely brought to mind the many dinners at which he had occupied the head of the table, the way in which he had always been ushered into the Minister's room while quite important personages were kept waiting outside. Thinking of these things he was reminded of his long life of honour and honours which was still unchanged and on a word from the Minister of Justice would remain unchanged until the day of his death. But no more business deals for him after this! He had had too narrow an escape. This summons to the Quai de la Mégisserie was something quite new in his experience.

He breathed again. The important thing at the moment, should he have to do a little explaining to the Minister of Justice—explaining which would end with an invitation to dinner—was to get hold as soon as possible of Voisin and Béziers, who had been his colleagues in that matter of Gisors sugar. With that in mind he sent a note to the Minister of Justice to the effect that he would like to have a word with him in the Chamber at two o'clock and another to Croissin saying that he could not manage to call on him today. Then he left the house with the intention of talking over with Voisin and Béziers the line of defence he intended to adopt. It was a warm day. He had the open carriage brought round and drove off smoking a cigarette and enjoying the fine weather. When he entered Voisin's room, he felt free to breathe again. He was in the presence of a friend from whom he need hide nothing and fear no moral sermonizing. One whole part of his life began at once to breathe more freely and to hold up its head. In the presence of this man to whom he could say, without any hedging or beating about the bush, "I touched two hundred thousand francs over that deal," without feeling humiliated or lessened in his own esteem, he was conscious of a sudden uprush of pleasure born of frankness and of pride. To refer to his business affairs and to discuss them openly was to know a satisfaction which was of long-standing and innocent to boot. By dint of denying what could not be proved, and of putting a different meaning on what could, together they drafted a defence much as he would have drafted a ministerial declaration.

He went home, ate a light luncheon, and started for the Chamber. The place was in an uproar. The Ministers had just demanded that judicial proceedings should be instituted against Marie. Only one friend greeted him, bluntly, and with that disagreeable violence of true affection which has been hurt by *your* hurt, and seems to be returning the blow which you have struck at it: "You must make a statement at once!" He mounted the tribune. A storm of cries rose from the noisy benches below. He felt as nervous as a man setting foot in a boat on a stormy sea. But there are moments when a man must risk his life, if only to show that he is not afraid, and with cold clammy hands, and head held high but trembling, he took his stand. He began to speak. But his words, if they were to sound convincing, needed the sympathetic background which only the thunder of public acclamation can provide. But that background now was lacking. He was listened to in silence, or with muttered disapproval, and the tone of his voice reflected his discomfort. Instead of being on terra firma with a friendly sea breaking at his feet, he was far from land, and though no waves broke over him he could see them forming. No longer were they magnificent to watch, but only terrifying to feel as they swelled beneath him. As a rule the power of his eloquence could be measured by the ebb and flow of approval in his audience. As a rule, when he was speaking, one could feel the words forming, building up, curling their crests, preparatory to crashing down with a resounding roar at the end of the sentence. Deprived of the enthusiastic reception which vested them with authority, and the background music which lent them harmony, his words sounded as false and as fragile as the unconvincing arguments of a guilty man, or as a mad woman's thin and wavering song. And because they could not break in a great climax of "bravos", he could no longer master that backward surge, that momentary ebb which was the usual preliminary to a renewed upward movement of his oratory. His gestures were no longer deliberate and weighty but abrupt and jerky like those of a man on a runaway horse. As when a human actor seems small and trivial when charged with some amazing role by destiny, and can only in our imagination appear equal to the task, so now, seeing Marie, a tiny figure against the seething of this vast assembly, those present began to wonder whether he was really a man fighting for his life, and not just an inferior performer miming the terror of Saint-Just in a badly mounted and produced scene of revolutionary violence, where on the stage the feeble muttering of a few "extras" completely fails to give a convincing representation of a tumultuous session of the Convention.

But by now the issue had taken on in Marie's mind an entirely different form which he was being driven to substitute for the appalling reality. He saw himself as the victim of dastardly cowardice on the part of Ministers who would rather sacrifice their oldest friends, men who had rendered tremendous services to the Republic, than risk their portfolios when suddenly threatened by an attack from a slanderous vindictive loud-mouthed and ferocious faction of the extreme Left. It is only fair to say that had he been in their position he would have acted very differently. He was one of those who know that in the affairs of life virtue is difficult, and so are indulgent towards their neighbours' faults, cannot bring themselves to be unkind, and cast the mantle of a resplendent friendship over the shortcomings of their friends, leaving to others who are more severe and sometimes more corrupt, the painful task of "turning a cold shoulder". Whoever you may be, dear reader, whether destiny has placed you in a village or a great metropolis, in the historical frame of a political or diplomatic career, or in similar circumstances of a more private nature where the full sun of publicity never beats upon them, I am quite sure that you will have to choose one of two camps—if only in the eye of God—that which contains the advocates of strict honesty and narrow puritanism, or that of tolerance and charity to all. Somebody, a girl perhaps whom you knew in your childhood, who has since been false to her marriage vows, or one of your closest friends, or some much publicized figure known for his parties, will give you an opportunity of showing to which group you temperamentally belong. Even though your unyielding attitude be inspired by a sincere horror of vice, it will be bound to appear cruel to someone close to you who in similar circumstances has acted differently and in these days when moral sanctions have been relaxed and nervous sensibility is more than usually marked, maintains that cruelty is the only vice which we are justified in condemning. True, this laxer attitude, even though it may be due to no more than a tender and indulgent pity for others is wholly compatible with more severe standards observed by critics in their own behaviour, or may have made them swerve from the strait and narrow way simply owing to the difficulty of remaining censorious and at the same time feeling indulgent to others. This may seem to you to be merely the sign of a corrupt nature or perhaps dictated by material considerations such as the pleasure of remaining on friendly terms with the lady in question who though she may be much to blame is both witty and charming and *does* give the most delightful dinners. For the trivialities and the dramas of history, so thrilling when seen from a distance, are composed of the same elements as make up our more humble lives, and form the very substance of the universe. History resembles astronomical analysis, that science which can reveal the composition of the most distant stars because they contain the same elements, the same gasses, as the road along which we daily walk, as the body in which we live and the bones which one day will lie beside our mother's.

*

On two or three occasions already Marie had tasted the joy, after feeling convinced that *this* time he really *was* going to be caught, of knowing that he was not even under suspicion, of feeling that the future lay still intact before him, that all the wrong things he had so far done were as though they had never been, that he had only to turn over a new leaf now to make it possible for life to flow on untroubled, happy, and glorious. For we think that what we have not done as yet, what we have not so far even decided to do, can be fashioned according to our will, and turned into something which will be in our best interest or set our conscience at rest. Seated in his armchair beside the fire, opening the letters which came to him every day from all the greatest persons in the land, Marie had the comfortable feeling that he would do what he wanted to do, and was the undisputed master of his actions. Unfortunately however as soon as he felt the need of money, as soon as the desire to make money got a hold on him, he at once persuaded himself that he had already made the necessary decision, not to be sure to embark upon a life of shame which could lead only to dishonour, but to do just one little thing which could not possibly have any unwelcome consequences and could not be really wrong because the most honourable people in all Paris were coming to dine with him that evening. True he would not have liked to tell them what he was planning, but after all of which of them could it be said with any certainty that he had not got secrets which he would not willingly confide to others? Ever since his childhood and more especially since the death of his wife, Marie had been reasonably pious. But far from disturbing his conscience religion pacified it. Does it not din into our ears, in every sermon commonplace, in the formulae of prayers, in its very dogmas and sacraments, that even the best of us is living in a state of sin? The thoughts that troubled his conscience became less difficult to face, less painful, were indeed rather pleasantly appealing, so soon as he realized that they were part and parcel of religion. He felt more comfortable when he realized that none of his familiar acquaintances was in a position to cast stones, but ought rather to be beating his breast in repentance for misdeeds which were no different from his own. The fact that he went to church, that he declared before God and the congregation that he was "a miserable sinner", seemed to him to constitute a confession sufficient to make it unnecessary for him to go into more precise and painful details. He was left with the illusion that so far as his fellow-men were concerned he was not living a lie.

Alone with himself and face to face with his conscience he no longer said, "I have stolen twenty-five thousand francs", words which he would have found it extremely disagreeable to hear, since they would have damaged him in his own eyes—but, "Oh God, I am a miserable sinner", a statement which was productive of a rather pleasurable emotion. And because for some time past subsuming under the vague words "sin" and "fault" certain more specific sins and faults, as— "I have been taking money to which I was not entitled", "I have been guilty of misappropriation", etc.—the words "money to which I was not entitled" and "misappropriation" emerged less and less into the light, their place being taken by the more general terms "sin" and "fault". Since the facts that most separate us from our fellow-men never make us *not* want to be like them, of equal value with them or on terms of intimacy with them, these two words had the enormous advantage that they diminished the space that divided him from others, seeing that they made him feel that he was participating in the common wretchedness of mankind and was smirched, if smirched at all, by the curse of original sin.

Meanwhile his position in the world of politics had been growing in importance year by year. Few members of the Chamber were his equals in intelligence, more generous-minded, more sincerely concerned for the general welfare of the State. The good he did was not confined to steering through the House a number of excellent enactments which relieved the poorer classes of a good deal of taxation without in any way embarrassing the Budget, and negotiating several international treaties which are today admitted to have been largely instrumental in assuring the national security. You will not find in any book the record of his benefactions. They are enshrined in the hearts of many in his Department who thanks to him have known greater happiness than ever before—in memories of help given from his own pocket when a husband was ill or a son out of work, of daughters placed in good employment, in the knowledge that his door was never shut against those who came to him for advice, that food and warmth could always be found in his kitchen, that his woods were free to all and a lift in his carriage always forthcoming when there was room, in daily additions to the meagre tables of the poor, in the right accorded to all and sundry to collect firewood from his estate in winter, and the certainty that small gifts of money would go with it, in the fact that roads were kept clear of snow so that the local Deputy could ride comfortably in bad weather, and, more than anything else in that sense of human dignity which brings sweetness to the lives of humble men and women when they find themselves treated by the rich in a manner that is only too often reserved for their dealings with the rich—consideration, cordiality, and the chance of talking as man to man.

And now knowing all this when you see in the papers that the electors of the Somme are represented in Parliament by the admirable Jules Craveil who is ardent in defending the cause of the People against that wealthy class whose privileges Marie upheld, who has never dirtied his hands in financial deals, of whom it can be said that he has never called a stockbroker his friend—when you learn from those same papers that the electors of the Somme have never ceased to regret Marie, even though he *was* found guilty in a magistrate's court, and though even at the height of his power he consistently voted against the Socialists and the Income Tax—you will not, I think, attribute those regrets entirely to local corruption.

As Jean grew older, Marie came more and more to realize that in him heart was more highly developed than intelligence. Although this man of politics had no great feeling for poetry, except for the patriotic verses of Déroulède which had at least "something to say" and performed a "useful service": although he had little leisure in which to read anything but the endless documents which supplied as it were the raw material of his excellently-worded reports and the admirable pieces of legislation which embodied the essential qualities of his mind—he was on the other hand a devoted student of history. It gave him confidence in his political labours because it hallowed the efforts of those great men of the past who had worked in the same field. He basked in the indulgent smile accorded by history to the memory of men whose faults it glossed over, regarding them as those of spoiled children, even when they were as startling as the peculations of which a Mazarin, a Gort-chakoff, or a Richelieu had been guilty. The verdict of history allowed him to see his own faults as in some sort the results of necessity, not of that necessity which is inseparable from erring human nature—against which religion tells us it is our duty to struggle, hard though the struggle may be—but of a necessity inherent in the nature of great men, a necessity which has an interest for the mind, which forms part of the easy charm of an *élite*, a necessity which, in short, we should accept. If religion was the ascetic principle of his inner life, plunging it into morbidity, history was the stimulus which by restoring him to health made him look on life as something that grew increasingly attractive, and was there to be enjoyed.

*

It happened that shortly before Marie much to everybody's surprise was arrested as the result of the unexpected discovery of certain com-promising documents which had remained hidden for many years, young Edouard Marie, then just twenty-five, having left a theatre on a night of high wind, returned home feeling thoroughly chilled. We know very little about the effects of wind, about fever, or generally speaking about nature and life. There seems, however, to be some reason to suppose that this particular wind and the particular fever to which it gave rise, must have been more than usually pernicious, because the chill turned to inflammation of the lungs which in the space of a few days brought death in its train. In this way did Edouard Marie leave the world without ever having been undeceived about the purity of his father's character and the everlasting nature of his father's power. Destiny had taken care to remove in the nick of time one from whom certain matters should for ever have been concealed. In doing so it resembled a man who, having a number of very harsh things to say to a friend, is restrained by feelings of delicacy from broaching the subject in the presence of his child. Nature acts in this way because she knows that the grave has neither eyes nor ears. Eyes that once looked at us with love, respect and confidence, once closed for ever will never have cause to dilate with horror, or to brim with tears at the sight of something which at long last has been brought into the revealing light of day. The dark world of the dead and the world of the living lit by a pitiless sun, remain in complete ignorance of one another.

*

Hard-working young men always hope that when the moment of examination comes they will be asked just those things which they have taken such pains to learn, and that in a few precise answers they will be able to reveal the full extent of their knowledge to the examiner whose good opinion will then reward long hours of study. And so it is that no matter how brilliantly the candidate may have passed the test he always feels slightly disappointed when the examination is over. He may have got good marks, but only in subjects over which he has not taken much care. He realizes then that an hour's work instead of a year's would have sufficed to enable him to pass. It is no more reasonable in us to think that when a thief is brought to justice or a deserving case rewarded the Judge holds in his hand, and enumerates one after the other without omitting one, all the actions, good and bad, committed by the man before him, or that the man on trial has had them ever present to his mind during sleepless nights or periods of self-satisfaction. It is the least important of his thefts, the most casual and isolated, the one that has no really essential connexion with the general pattern of his criminal career, the one he has never dreamed will be brought up against him, of which, maybe, he is not even guilty, which turns out to have been the cause of his arrest. None of his other crimes will now weigh in the scale of his punishment, and must for ever remain unknown. But though the examination candidate who could not know what form the questions would take, and has been obliged to work for a whole year, though in fact the points with which he has to deal when the moment comes (though he did not know beforehand what they would be) prove to be those to which he has in fact given only the most cursory attention, the fact remains that his answers do provide a sort of cross-section of his mental equipment—as when we take a glass of water from a stream, it will serve to show whether the water is clean or contaminated, though it may show as clear in one spot, cloudy in another—sufficient to show whether his preparation has been serious or not. Just so, one single theft of the kind in which only a man of unscrupulous character could have been involved, will give sufficient grounds for the jury to decide against him, even though they may know nothing at all about his other derelictions.

As day followed day after the warrant had been issued, the whole of France came to know that Marie was a thief, though out of the whole tale of his malversations, one only was matter of common knowledge, the least important of them all, of which too it was not even certain that he was guilty. But the documents seized in his house proved beyond all shadow of a doubt that he had had dealings with a number of shady business associates, though the Judge, the Chamber, and the public at large entirely failed to grasp their true significance as pointers to others of Marie's operations, and were content to regard them as evidence of guilt in a matter with which as it happened they were entirely unconnected. But when a man has an open wound the material of his shirt though in itself quite harmless may act as a poisonous substance and so be the cause of gangrene setting in. To one in the grip of a morbid melancholy, those with whom he lives become dangerous enemies whose presence kills him. When a man is suffering from a serious disease the most innocent secretions of his body, the air he exhales when he breathes, the water that he passes, provide all the evidence the doctor needs, because in them he can read the terrible truth. The servant who reveals to him, unknowingly, the existence of an ailment of long standing merely by saying that his master has for many years been in the habit of getting up in the night and opening the window so as to breathe more easily, has an exact counterpart in the servant who, called upon to answer questions in court, frightened by all the panoply of justice, and though suspecting that his master is in danger does not know what that danger may be, fails to realize the damage he is doing when he admits that Monsieur Marie made a point of seeing Graveil every day.

3. The Marie Scandal:
Jean Intervenes with Couzon

Since it was the Party of capitalists and opportunists against which the Party of the poor, or the Socialists, had to wage relentless battle, Marie's ruin was for them a positive godsend which must be turned to the best account and not allowed to be hushed up by an unscrupulous opponent. In this fact is to be found the explanation of the daily newspaper articles which brought despair to Marie and the abuse levelled at him during debates in the Chamber, from which he suffered as from successive apoplectic strokes, though to those who uttered them, or let them pass unquestioned, they sounded as no more than the cries of outraged justice intent on castigating vice, and like the screaming of swallows devouring noxious insects in the damp dawn hours, serving to herald the coming of a purer and more equitable day. The fury of the extreme Left against Marie redoubled when a judgment of "not proven" deprived them of the sentence which was to set the seal upon their triumph, and brand as with a red-hot iron for all to see that whole class of traitors with which a final break must be made. This "not proven" was the more exasperating perhaps in that it had been brought about by Santeuil who happened to be a close friend of the Judge, and was the only person who had stuck to Marie from the beginning. A campaign of more than usual violence was started against him in the organs of the extreme Left, more particularly in *l'Ere Nouvelle*, which was an out and out supporter of Couzon's politics. Every morning Santeuil was accused of having profited from Marie's peculations. There were loud demands that he should be removed from his post in the Civil Service. His private life was made the object of the most horrible slanders. Consequently Couzon was not surprised when he was told that Jean had called and was asking to see him. Since it was the hour of the morning at which he was in the habit of receiving visitors, and since several other persons were waiting who would in due course be accorded an interview, he realized that the meeting, highly embarrassing and tiresome though it would be, could not be avoided.

Many years had passed since the days when Couzon would have blushed at the thought of shaking hands with a dishonest man or attacking an honest one. His passion for integrity and the difficulty of bringing off a political victory had compelled him to identify his conduct with that of the Party. A Party is far stronger than a single man's unaided efforts, and in exchange for its support he had had to sacrifice all personal considerations in its interest. For a long time now he had shuddered at the idea of figuring as a traitor in the eyes of his followers, of incurring the enmity of those who fought for him, merely in order to take up the cudgels on behalf of a "Moderate" who had fallen unjustly under suspicion—a useless piece of quixotism in any case since a single voice raised in protest could have done no good. For some years now—and the passage of time has much the same effect on all of us— his ideals had coarsened. He had become absorbed into a routine of behaviour which though it might be directed to the attainment of less pure ends had a solid backing and of this routine he was now more or less a prisoner. For some years now he had lost that generosity of mind which had marked him in his younger days when without the faintest qualm he would have been prepared to do himself grave injury if he had thought he could be useful to someone who had never been other than hurtful to him. He no longer fought for anybody but himself— though it is only fair to point out that for him that word "self" included his ideas of justice and social equality—with the result that, life being quite full enough of personal struggles, he never let himself look beyond them. If we add to all this that for some years now he had got into the habit, fond though he was of Jean, of regarding Santeuil as a thoroughly wicked man, not only because he persistently refused to take Couzon seriously, but because he was a supporter of all that the Left Wing considered vile, was in fact one of those persons whose removal would be of lasting benefit to society, and whose conviction at the bar of popular justice would merely bear out the tenets of radical philosophy, it is not difficult to understand how it came about that Couzon should regard the slanders now being circulated as so many well-founded probabilities, or more strictly speaking as truths which if they had not yet been proved very soon would be. And so having made up his mind for the various reasons already stated, not even to try to exercise a moderating influence on the hostile section of the

Press, he no longer felt himself to be even guilty of an act of cowardice from which in any case he would not have recoiled. He held that it was impossible for him to interfere on personal grounds with the processes of justice, no matter what the ways and means chosen by God for its manifestation might be. Nevertheless Jean's visit was a painful though long-foreseen ordeal. He sent word that he would certainly see the young man if that was what he wished though he would very much prefer that the interview should be postponed until later. To this Jean replied that he would like to speak to him at once. Couzon therefore gave orders that he was to be shown in immediately.

During the few moments of waiting he felt more than usually agitated. His memory of Jean's unfailing admiration of him in the past, and still more—though it had less power to soften his determination, but more bitter to the taste and wiped out the relative tenderness of that recollection—the thought that the young man had once regarded him as the yardstick of justice, disturbed him profoundly. Tears came into his eyes as he considered all the sacrifices which his position as a Party leader forced upon him. As soon however as he heard the sound of Jean's approaching footsteps, the second of those two thoughts, that Jean would no longer look him in the face with an expression of respect and confidence, but would regard him as a man who had like a false god taken advantage of his simple-minded faith—which was manifestly unfair since for over a week now his father had been screening a series of the most abominable actions—stopped the tears from flowing. When the door at last opened and Jean appeared, he was red in the face and almost trembling. But contrary to what he had expected there was nothing violent, contemptuous or aggressive in Jean's attitude. His natural kindliness combined with feelings of admiration which were of too ancient a date to be wiped out in a moment, enabled him to realize not only the reasons which had led Couzon to behave in this way but also those which had prompted his own initiative in the matter. He pitied the man because he realized the full nature of the sacrifice that was being asked of him. Truth to tell had he been left to himself he would merely have treated the attacks on his father with contempt. But for his mother's insistence that he should beard the lion, and her implied reproach that if he did not he would be behaving as an undutiful son, he would have taken no steps at all. He felt ashamed of asking Couzon to do for him and his family something which as he very well knew would put him in bad odour with his Party.

Consequently it was in the gentle tones of an old friend prepared to forget the recent state of war which had developed as a result of the Press campaign that he now took upon himself the disagreeable task of speaking the first words. "I hope you will forgive me for making a nuisance of myself and coming here with a request that you use on my behalf the influence which should be at the service of others. But where else could I have found . . ." and, suddenly conscious of his isolation in the presence of this good and brilliant man, he had to exercise all his self-control to keep from flinging himself into the other's arms.

★

"I apologize for bringing up personal matters at a time when you are so busy," Jean went on, "but it seemed to me that I had no right, just because I did not want to bother you, to leave untried anything that might save those who are dear to me from great unhappiness." Couzon shook his proffered hand warmly and asked him to sit down. Which of us at moments of high seriousness in the presence of one who has it in his power to bring us much grief or boundless happiness, is not aware of the deep solemnity that sounds in such purely conventional words as those in which he is asked to take a seat, words of which normally we are scarcely aware? Their sudden significance may arise from the fact that the most trivial details of tremendously important interviews serve to keep the occasion long in our memories, or because at a moment when conventional expressions seem out of place, when we are about to speak frankly in an effort to win over an adversary or to perish in the attempt, conventional expressions make a more than ordinary impact upon us, so that we are eager to take them not as the common coin of an inbred habit but as the sincere expression of genuine feeling. At such times the tiniest thing has an ominous significance. Through the open door of the room where we are waiting for an interview with a surgeon, we see a maid laying the table and little flecks of sunshine touching the surface of the dishes. In a short time, we tell ourselves, the surgeon will be resuming the agreeable routine of happy joyful meals. The consultation we shall have had with him, the little operation he will have performed, will be for him no more than purely speculative activities, prosaic dreams serving to exercise his mental faculties, and put an edge on his appetite. By time evening comes and he has set off with his daughter to some fashionable

reception, he will have forgotten all about them. Why should it not
have the same unimportance for us? An event which is so trivial to him,
which is soon to be buried under the silt of a thousand similar events,
may well be no more serious for his patient, may not really disturb the
essential preoccupations of that patient's life, may not tear through the
close-woven network of his varied pleasures ranging from the delicious
warmth of golden eggs served between jugs of cold beer to the glittering Balls at which he will be received with smiles and deferential words.
With the same passionate intensity we cling to conventional formulae,
striving to find beneath words which have been too long dead to have
any meaning the promise of something we most urgently desire to
happen. A mistress may have written to her lover saying that she does
not love him, but the phrase she uses is "dear friend"; what she says is
that she has a "fondness" for him, and he finds no difficulty in making
those words, like a willing bawd, say precisely what he wants to hear.

Jean sat down close to Couzon, with perhaps a more than usually
strong feeling of affection. The power which certain persons have at
times to influence our future, gives them in our eyes an importance and
a charm the effects of which we quite naturally and without conscious
duplicity, allow to show upon our faces. Our overwrought nerves set
us searching for subtleties which at other times would pass undetected,
and make us thrill deliciously to the simplest act of politeness, to a
gratifying appearance of interest, to a response which we think is
eloquent of a kindly concern. "Have you read the articles which
l'Ere Nouvelle has been devoting to my father over the past few days—
no, that's not quite accurate, in their issues of yesterday and the day
before? One of them was certainly published two days ago," said Jean.
The detail of date was of no importance whatever. But when we have
things to say which mean a great deal to us, we cling to every tiny fact
because it relieves us if only for the moment of the effort to find words
for what we feel it so difficult to talk about. "Yes," replied Couzon,
"and when I was told you were here, I at once assumed that you had
come about those articles." – "You were perfectly right," said Jean, "it
is precisely about them that I have come to see you," and waited for
a second or two in the hope that Couzon would utter without further
prompting the words he wanted to hear and so save him the necessity
of asking for an assurance. "But I find it hard to believe," Couzon
continued after a brief silence, "that your father can have been seriously
disturbed by those attacks. Their very violence deprives them of any

significance they might otherwise have had." Hearing this Jean went very red in the face. He felt that he had been brought up short by the kind of hypocrisy of which he would never have thought that Couzon could be capable. "If that's what you think, you're very much mistaken," he said sharply. "My father has been made extremely unhappy, and if you could see my mother you would be shocked." Couzon shook his head sadly as though to express the regret which the whole business was causing him. "Politics are the very devil. With the best intentions in the world . . ."–"I don't suppose you speak like that to the journalist who wrote them," said Jean with a sudden spurt of anger. "If my father has been guilty of anything it is of loyalty to a friend and a feeling of sympathy for an unhappy fellow-creature: but that's no reason for inventing slanderous statements."–"We'll talk about that later," said Couzon who knew that by keeping a number of questions apart one can sometimes wriggle out of having to answer all of them. "The important thing, as I see it, is for you to calm your father down, as much for the sake of his health as of his honour, which ought to be well outside the reach of that kind of imputation. You must make him see these things in their proper proportions, which are those of a newspaper campaign, painful perhaps, but really quite unimportant."

Jean looked at him for a moment or two with an expression of contempt. Then in calmer tones, "Couzon," he said, "you're just laughing at me. You must know perfectly well that I didn't come here to be fobbed off with that sort of nonsense which I could have thought out for myself without taking up your time. I've known you too long not to realize that you can do better than that. You're not the sort of man who thinks that he can help somebody by disguising his refusal to do anything of the kind under a lot of platitudes and then send his visitor away feeling so grateful that he daren't admit even to himself that he is disappointed. You're not that type. I suppose you think my father *is* guilty?"–"No, that's not true," said Couzon.–"You're in no position to pass judgment on my father", replied Jean. "He may have certain faults which you find particularly unpleasant, but that doesn't alter the fact that he is a big-hearted man. You must know that he has done what he has for Monsieur Marie fully realizing what the consequences would be to himself and that knowledge should have left you in no doubt about his heart. I can tell you this, that if you came out in defence of my father against *l'Ere Nouvelle*, you would be doing a far less

courageous thing than he has done in standing up for Marie. It is your
duty to do that, because you are perfectly well aware that my father is
innocent, whereas there was good reason why my father should think
Marie guilty."–"Give me a moment to think things over," said
Couzon, whose expression for the last few minutes had made it quite
clear that he was engaged in a tussle with his conscience.

Jean stopped speaking. Couzon was deep in thought. He knew that
there was a good chance that he might be able to put a stop to the
campaign but he knew also that by doing so he would run the risk of
discrediting himself. He did not feel moved in this matter by the
generous almost lyrical emotion to which, as a rule, he was obedient.
"Honestly," he said briskly, "I don't see what I can do," at the same
time trying to give the impression that he was still thinking hard. "Am
I to send you along with a letter of introduction to the editor
of *l'Ere Nouvelle*, is that what you want?"–"A letter of introduction! You must be mad!" said Jean explosively. "A pistol'd be more to
the point."–"Yes, I suppose you're right. I really don't know . . ."
–"What d'you mean, don't know?" said Jean with violence. "You
must know perfectly well that if you told the editor point-blank that
unless he stops his attacks you will speak for my father in the event of
his taking action against the paper—which he certainly will do, and if
in the meantime you wrote a letter dissociating yourself from his
activities, and saying that you regard his wretched hirelings as the
lowest sort of slanderers—you must know perfectly well that if you
did any or all of these things the whole campaign would crumble!"–
"In the first place I'm not at all sure that it would and anyhow I couldn't
do it. Unfortunately you see I am not my own master. I am committed to the ideas which I have sworn to promote and defend and I
can't, just when your father has been guilty of an action which I condemn, by sacrificing in the interests of personal friendship some part
of the integrity which should inform the behaviour of all public
servants, I can't, as I should be doing, take a page out of his book, and
indeed go further than him in evil doing by sacrificing to private
motives the general good which if it is to be upheld needs the cham-
pionship of all those with whom you want me to break for ever . . ."
–"I know nothing about the general good: all I know is that these
scribblers have destroyed the happiness, certainly of one person, perhaps of three persons. I don't believe it is God's will that people should
deliberately behave like that in order to promote the general good. I

know your ideas: they are built on a concern for justice. You were the
first person to open my eyes politically. Now you've got the chance
to show that justice is not a vague conception, an empty word: you
have got the chance of serving the cause of justice in a practical manner
—and you refuse!"

"You don't understand, Jean. I am refusing because I don't feel that
I have any right to give priority to your father's happiness, and your's
too just because I happen to know you. There is something closer to
my heart—the well-being of millions of human beings who have just
as much right to happiness as you have, who have put their trust in
me, whose claims I cannot successfully champion without the help of
those with whom you want me to break."

"What you are doing is to sacrifice the good of all, not in the cause
of private friendship, but of one overriding interest—your own
political career. Yes, I say the good of all and I mean it, because by
being unjust to my father the journalists of *l'Ere Nouvelle* are not only
themselves guilty of injustice, but sow injustice in the minds of all who
read them. They make them bad. They have roused in them a desire
to see in tomorrow's paper that one of their fellow-men, who was
thought to be good is wicked, that somebody whose only desire is for
a quiet life has been ruined. If they think it helps their case they will
lead the public to hope that he will be arrested and will do their best
to see that he is, thereby making the Government itself unjust. A day
is coming when the Party which those journalists represent will be in
the saddle—about that I have no illusions, and when that day does
come, their reign will be the reign of injustice. And while they are waiting for the Government to become unjust, for the laws to become
unjust, for injustice to become the master of us all, they go about
preparing for that happy future by seeing to it that slander, the love of
scandal, and cruelty shall be seated on the throne in every man's heart.
By attacking my father they have done far worse than make three
people unhappy—my father, my mother, and me: they have turned a
great many of the people who read them into evil creatures—and that
perhaps is worse!"

4. *The Marie Scandal (Conclusion)*

There were plenty of persons in Paris who could not bear the thought of Marie's prosperity: Gustave Pointelin whose Ministry he had over-turned as the result of a famous speech and of the vote which had followed it: Gaillon, against whom when he was Minister of the Interior he had waged bitter warfare: Rustinlor who had served under him at the Beaux-Arts, of whose verses he had made fun, treating them as unimportant trivialities: Victurnien, whose wife Madame Marie had consistently refused to receive: some because he had not obliged them, others because he had. Certain men, because Marie's friends had kept them at arm's length, had assumed that he had spoken ill of them. All in short who believed that he enjoyed being a Minister, attacked him now, because the thought of that enjoyment was odious to them. One might have believed, to hear them that during the previous ten years—the period of Marie's glory—unrelieved despair had been the lot of Marie's enemies. Such in fact was very far from being the case. Hatred like love lives on lies. The papers might report that Marie's recent visit to the Department of the Nord had been a triumphal progress. But Gustave Pointelin had certain knowledge that the truth was very differ-ent, "That even in his native village there were children who threw stones at him."–"Stones, Gustave!" exclaimed Pointelin's mother-in-law in her broad peasant brogue, rolling her r's, and with an expression of naïve astonishment: "If you ask me I'd r-rather have a deal fewer decor-rations and not be insulted by the childr-ren of my own village: poor little innocents!"–"Yes, stones!" said Pointelin with the air of a thoroughly well-informed person: "You can take my word that it was far from being roses, roses all the way"—savouring the first drop of pleasure—"it must have been a nasty shock for him!"– "Gr-racious! stones aren't at all nice, that they aren't: what a way to be welcomed!" murmured the old lady in a ecstasy of delight.

"But that wasn't all," went on Pointelin. "What do you mean, Gustave? Was there something else?"–"Things'll go from bad to worse, believe me. He's been pretty badly snubbed, and I don't mind

telling you I wouldn't be in his place for all the portfolios in the world!
I know for a fact that the Sub-Prefect refused to be present at a banquet
which was given in his honour at the Prefecture. Actually *nobody*
turned up. The Prefect's lady sent word that she was unwell and
wouldn't so much as go downstairs until the Minister of the Interior
ordered her to do so. All the same she refused to shake Marie's hand!
That must have put a pretty wet blanket on the proceedings!
I gather that he looked about as cheerful as a death's head! It
can't be much fun to know that those one meets are only there under
compulsion! I know that if *I'd* been treated like that I'd have scrapped
the whole tour. It'll do him a lot of damage in the country." Of such
a nature is hatred which compounds from the lives of our enemies
a fiction which is wholly false. Instead of thinking of them as ordinary
human beings knowing ordinary human happiness and occasionally
exposed to the sorrows which afflict all mankind and ought to arouse
in us a feeling of kindly sympathy, we attribute to them an attitude of
arrogant self-satisfaction which pours oil upon the flames of our anger.
For hatred transfigures individuals no less than does desire and like
desire sets us thirsting for human blood. On the other hand since it can
find satisfaction only in the destruction of the supposed self-satisfaction
which so irritates us, we imagine that self-satisfaction, see it, believe it
to be in a perpetual process of disintegration. No more than love does
hatred follow the dictates of reason, but goes through life with eyes
fixed on an unconquerable hope. Just as Jean used to go to sleep each
night hugging the thought that Mademoiselle Kossichef would come
to him next day and say, "I love you", so too did Marie's enemies
set a date for his ruin which they believed could not be long
delayed.

But, like the Jews they had to wait a very long while for the day of
their deliverance. Pointelin died without seeing the promised dawn,
though firmly convinced that it would come, and left behind for the
enlightenment of his friends an account of the history of his times
which differed very considerably from the generally accepted version.
He believed that those in power were already on the very brink of
collapse, and that those who so far had played no part in events were
marked out to be the future's Men of Destiny. Some more fortunate
were present at that session of the Chamber in person or if not in
person, then at second hand through the medium of newspaper photographs, when as the result of the turn of Fortune's wheel which sooner

or later makes every possibility actual—it being the fate of all men and
of all human institutions to decay—Marie and his Party fell as resound-
ingly as the most fantastic hatred could have desired. For since the
human spirit is compounded of the same elements as Nature there is
not a dream which the course of events does not, in the long run, make
real. The dreamer finds that the tyrant who now holds him in subjection was once the smiling child of his own fantasy. Is there anyone
in the world who cannot, on some winter evening, say to us, "I, too,
was there: I, too, had a part to play in a novel of real life?" or who does
not hide in the secret places of his memory the material for a novel
which he does not want to narrate and will probably never write?
For the other actor now lies beneath a distant tombstone, or lives on
still in a foreign land among many thousands who know nothing of
his secret, where you are unlikely ever to find him. But is it altogether
true to say that the novel will never be written? For it has been from all
eternity in some man's mind, has been already set down in thought's
invisible ink. Is not that what you mean, dear reader, when you assure
me that if only you *liked* you could merely by telling the truth write
the most dramatic, the most incredible, the most romantic of novels?
But novels lose their power to charm when they become real. And so
it happened that as soon as curiosity and hatred were satisfied the public
faced by the novel of real life which Marie's fate had become, were
conscious of a sort of disappointment, the disappointment and even
boredom which we feel when at long last we are confronted by the
landscape which in imagination was so enchanting, or recognize in the
face of some illustrious but very ordinary-looking man the features
we devoured with our eyes when we saw them displayed in a photo-
grapher's window.

Marie received no sentence but he had to resign his seat. For the past
ten years no one could have more thoroughly enjoyed than he did
reading the daily papers, where the sight of his name each morning,
accompanied by such flattering epithets as, the Eloquent Statesman,
the Brilliant Financier, the Great Figure of our National Life, had like
a delicious breeze wafted to him the admiration and the distant envy
of thousands of fascinated readers. But now that the headlines read
"The Malversations of Monsieur Marie" or "A Thief Caught Red-
Handed" try though he might not to open the sheets, he knew each
day a subtle torment because those words in staring type seemed to
speak to him of the scorn of a thousand gloating eyes, the drunken

frenzy of a million hatreds, the insults of a million enemies, and as
jealousy borrows from the delights of love its implements of torture,
had a horrible resemblance to what once had made him happy, was no
less public, just as undiscriminating, and struck as deeply into his heart.
And as in the days when he had lain innocently in his bed—when the
sun, his first morning visitor, brought the first instalment of praise and
adulation—revelling in the thought of his rivals' envy, of his enemies'
fury, he had felt himself to be invincible to all attacks, so now, confronted by the base and cowardly abuse of his foes, he knew that he
was weaponless. Once indeed when like a prisoner who tries to strike
at the mocking passers-by who spit at him, but impeded by his hand-
cuffs, is knocked to the ground by his warder and hears the insults and
the laughter grow louder, Marie had issued a writ against one of the
offending papers, the judgment went against him and he had to pay
the costs of the action. Since that incident not one day had passed but
some vile article appeared which not seldom contained the most revolt-
ing slanders at the expense of his wife and son.

I do not know what Monsieur Santeuil might have done if his
wife had not been at his side to guide him. For some years now she had
managed to re-awaken in him the generous sweetness of which few
men can boast, though in the old days before his marriage it had
seemed to be part of his nature. She had never concealed from him the
promise she had made to Madame Marie and now with that humble
authority, that inflexible gentleness in which her power lay, she compelled him to adopt the only right attitude. On the very day that the
summons was issued, they went the two of them together to see Marie.
But he would not receive them. He had always when addressing his
colleagues in the Chamber flayed politicians who were in the habit of
dabbling in Big Business, and now silently all day long and in the
watches of the night, kept on saying not to them but to himself: 'What
an abominable libel! You'll never get anybody to believe it!' But he
feared that people would believe it, and was ill at ease in the company
of others. He could have felt comfortable only with Cerpin and
Vieuxdons, who did not consider that he had done anything wrong.
He was worn out and did not feel strong enough to endure the
questions which Santeuil would put to him, or more especially to go
on saying as he had done all his life, "I am an honest man!" He
felt that before he could speak those words again he had to shift
the heavy weight of conviction in those who had turned against

him. He thanked God he had been spared the shame he would have felt had his wife lived to witness his downfall.

*

As a magic door which watches, like a guard with the gift of thought, the entrance to some enchanted palace, the eyelids, under a too fierce glare close of themselves upon the fragile nerve within and thus protect it from an attack too fierce for it to bear. No less delicate, no less tough are those organs of our sensibility which calling upon such aids as fainting-fits or dizziness, sleep or fever, enclose it in a thin but impenetrable envelope when too great a pain is threatening. At the height of the battle, when the situation was becoming really dangerous, a god seized Ajax by the hair and hid him from his enemies in a cloud. Just such a cloud had hung for several days about Marie's consciousness until the agony began to lose its initial force and he could once again stand up to it. The noon heat was intolerable to him and he waited for the evening with the same impatience that a sick man feels when he waits for the doctor in whom he has confidence but who is long in coming because he has other patients to attend to first and other sufferers. But at last it came, laying a cool compress on Marie's forehead, giving him a fresher air to breathe, and some hope with which to face the morrow. One evening when he had opened the window to let in the coolness of the dusk, and was lying on the sofa which he rarely left, Nature plunged him into sleep like a showman who before producing shadows on a screen must first darken the room. And while he slept a gentle breeze began to blow on him, touching his face with soft fingers. "Marthe, Marthe," said Marie in his sleep, "come close to me. But of course, you don't know, do you?" His wife only put her arms about him and looked at him with loving eyes. Then more urgently compelled to lie to her than to others he said: "Isn't what they're doing to me abominable? Don't you, too, detest these wicked men?"

Since she asked no questions and had come to him with so much sweetness in her face, he thought that she knew nothing and trembling with fear at the prospect of telling all, would have sent her away but she took his hands as though begging him to let her stay, and it was then he realized that all his suffering was known to her. She turned her tear-dimmed gaze upon him and smiled encouragement. Most certainly

he did not fear that she suspected him, but all the same he wished to
say to her, as he had said to others, "You do well to pity me, for I have
been made the victim of much calumny." For some time he had got
into the habit of lying, but to lie now seemed to him more than usually
painful. Then she, taking his hand in hers, said with a smile, "You must
not let it worry you. What you did was never really wrong, because
you have been always kind to others, generous and compassionate. All
honest men will take you to their hearts; it is only the evil-minded who
are against you. But in a few days everything will change. Don't you
agree with me, Santeuil, that what he has done is not worth so much
suffering and that we have forgiven him?" Then Marie saw Santeuil,
whom so far he had not noticed, standing beside his wife. "Come now,
get ready; he has come to take you for a walk. Try to make him forget
his troubles," she said, taking Santeuil by the hand, "I leave him in your
charge. Why such a melancholy look?" she added, kissing her husband
on the forehead: "A day will come when you will be amazed to think
that you should have made yourself so miserable for so little." Then
Marie went out with Santeuil, feeling that he never wanted to leave
him more. For the first time he was conscious of the unbelievable
sweetness of knowing that he had won the forgiveness of an honest
man, not by lying, but because his friend knew the whole of the truth.
Faced by this miracle, he was overwhelmed, like a man haunted by the
memory of an irreparable calamity who realizes suddenly that he has
been dreaming, and that now, at last awakened, he has close to him
what he thought he had lost for ever.

When Marie came out of his sleep the feeling of happiness was still
with him. But he felt separated from Santeuil, felt that he must see him
at once. For the first time he left the house, and had himself driven to
Santeuil, to the man who did indeed know everything, but through
the intercession of a dead woman and because of his own generosity of
heart, had forgiven him. He took to lunching or dining with Santeuil
every day. Once again he knew the pleasure of not being sure beforehand what he was going to eat or of being sure only a few seconds
before the steaming dishes made their appearance; of looking at his old
friends with eyes that were bright with a sense of well-being and
sympathy. Gradually the dark days withdrew, ceased to lie upon him
with the deadweight of their gloom, living on in his memory only like
those dead and gone persons whose statues powerless to harm, are all
that is left for us to look upon. But that was not the sole source of his

happiness. What he wanted was to see come true his wife's prediction that a day would dawn when everything would be changed. He could afford to wait for the time when he should once again recover his position of power, and see his enemies confounded. There was no sign as yet that it was on the way. His name was still a storm-centre. Scarcely anybody in the Chamber spoke kindly to him. He could not have addressed the House on any matter however insignificant without loosing a clamour of hostile voices. But he knew that life is full of strange reversals and took comfort in that refuge of the unfortunate. His twenty years of politics seemed to prove it. There was nothing he could do to hasten the coming of his ultimate triumph, but come it would, of that he was sure. So he waited with impatience. He did not let his mind dwell upon the successes of his enemies, did not try to do them harm, because he knew that it was not worth the trouble, that soon they would be snared, and that meanwhile they could see that he was happy.

Because he was proud and not bad at heart, that was all the vengeance that he wanted, but he wanted it to be complete. Time passed and as a man who, seated in a boat motionless upon the waters, gazes at the small waves and little by little, caught in a daze, comes to believe that they are in a conspiracy to push him forward and that the boat really is moving, he watched time pass and it seemed to him that the day for which he was waiting was already being prepared. For a while Gaillardi's Ministry could be sure of commanding a crushing majority. But since it was Marie's view that in the conduct of foreign affairs, finance and agriculture, it was leading France to disaster he denounced, in unsigned articles, its fatal policy, and knew that very soon now the country at present blind and daily applauding those who were leading it to the edge of the precipice, would have its eyes opened at last and would pull itself together. Each time that the Government's majority fell, he had a feeling that the electorate was growing weary, that soon a new era would begin. And when it seemed to be recovering its popularity, he told himself that from excess of evil good would come, and be perhaps more durable; that it was better that the cup of bitterness should be drained and nothing left. Circumstances would never be wanting in a state of affairs which seemed to be confirming the most pessimistic opinions.

On one occasion war seemed imminent. On another a strike outlasted its normal term. In two Departments Socialist deputies were

elected. There was a mob manifestation against the Chamber. In all
these things Marie saw the symptoms of approaching ruin. Meanwhile
the world continued to revolve, to be happy, to pursue its various
ambitions, and to satisfy them. And then at last the Government fell.
Since a long time elapsed before another could be formed, Marie, like
those young girls whose constant reading of novels falsifies their sense
of reality, saw the event as constituting a revolutionary situation,
something quite unlike anything seen so far. He interpreted a change
of personnel at the German Embassy as indicating a contempt for
Europe, a routine piece of business in the Chamber, such as the replacement of a Judge, as heralding things to come worse than the most bloody
actions of the Convention. His agitation and his hopes were confirmed,
not only by these incidents, but by others invented by the newspapers
which he for his part believed to be true. The new Ministry was composed in part of his friends, in part of men who had shown generosity
to him in the days of his misfortune. But their interest lay in avoiding
anything that might give the Opposition a handle against them.
Nothing from this point of view would have been more dangerous
than a move in favour of Marie. They could find excuses for their
pusillanimity by arguing that any such attempt would injure them and
do him no good. From that moment he regarded them as the scum of
the earth, hated them more bitterly than he had their predecessors,
longed for their downfall, and was all agog for the first signs of dis-
affection in the country. In the Chamber he no longer greeted them,
and listened to all that went on in a ferocious silence, taking notes, and
making his plans for the day when he should once more be a Minister.

His hair was by this time completely white. He was a broken man
and prematurely old. He despaired now of ever returning to power, but
was too proud to admit that this was the root cause of his gloom. He
still believed that a day of glory and rehabilitation would dawn for
him, but began to wonder whether it might not come in the form of
the Presidency of the Senate, or of the Republic as had been the case
with Ferry—in other words, a tranquil glory, and not as he had hoped,
a chance to realize his ideas. Perhaps it would be better like that. A
leisurely apotheosis would be more in keeping with his age than a
fighting future, and his successors would follow his political line and
give him the honour. He would be revenged, even if only after he was
dead. History often makes amends for what has gone wrong in a man's
lifetime and in the very act of snuffing him out, takes his heritage upon

itself. But judging by the way things were going, he would not now
have long to wait. The men who had replaced him were one after the
other thrown on the scrap-heap. Resort was had again to former
colleagues. Every morning, every afternoon, when he took his daily
walk, he kept on repeating to himself the names which he would choose
when the moment came for him to form a Ministry, and the words of
his manifesto which he could see in imagination as they would look
in the newspapers, together with an account of the enthusiasm with
which they had been greeted in the Chamber. Public anger wore itself
out. The *Revue des Deux Mondes* accepted his *Memoirs* for publication.
In moments of crisis the Opposition organs more than once printed
interviews with him. He was asked to take the chair at a banquet
organized for the schoolmasters of his Department. On leaving he
caught a cold and died two days later of pneumonia. In obedience to
his wishes there were no funeral orations, no officials wreaths. He was
buried beside his wife and son under the violets of Beauceronges.

5. The Early Days of the Dreyfus Affair

Captain Dreyfus was arrested on a charge of communicating to a foreign Power certain documents bearing on National Security, was tried *in camera*, condemned on the strength of a number of exhibits which he was never shown, and sent to Cayenne. The proofs of his guilt were however gradually made public. Since they seemed to be far from satisfactory, an inquiry was opened by the Cour de Cassation with a view to deciding whether grounds existed for setting in motion a complete revision of his trial. The sittings began each day at noon. In a not very large room on raised benches at the far end and along the two side walls, wearing high caps, swathed in their official robes and quite motionless—looking like portraits of long-dead magistrates painted in their traditional costumes and with the very faces of their period—sat the fifteen Counsellors listening to the depositions about the value of which they had to decide. Their fantastic headdresses covered brains so highly specialized that had their owners expressed views on literature and painting or ventured on some original remark in conversation or written correspondence, the probability is that an artist, no matter how willing he might be to listen to the opinions of men trained in a school so completely different from his own, would have felt hopelessly at sea. When the weather was fine and the sky blue above the Palace, the walls of which changed from gold to pink as though the colours of cathedral windows were flooding the heavens and spilling over the city, they went on foot to their court. Sometimes when the sun shone full in their faces, one or other might be seen in the course of the session shielding his eyes with his order-paper. At other times it rained so hard that lamps were called for very early in the proceedings. On such days the Counsellors came by omnibus, frequently meeting a colleague on the way, and chatting with him. When at last they were all settled on their benches—the oldest among them giving the impression that they were asleep and then by a sudden word showing that they had woken up, for when we have to do with old gentlemen silently listening, we often feel as though we are in the presence of white-headed, bleary-eyed and elderly seals in a cage at the zoo with whose habits we are unfamiliar, so that we find ourselves wondering whether they are dozing when in fact they are merely motionless—they forthwith applied themselves to the task of extracting the truth from the facts laid before them.

★

Every evening now when Henri wanted to see Jean, he had to go to a café where he would be sure to come on him with Durrieux, for not an evening passed but Jean was eager to be with Durrieux. For a month past his whole way of life had changed. Every morning he started early from home so as to arrive in good time for the Zola trial at the Cour d'Assises, taking with him no more than a few sandwiches and a small flask of coffee, and there he stayed, fasting, excited, emotionally on edge, till five o'clock at which hour he returned to the centre of the city—in a crowd of persons who were not as he was in that pleasing condition of men whose whole lives have been changed as the result of some special stimulus—feeling lonely and melancholy because the excitement was over. To go out again after dinner for a meeting with Durrieux, who had fetched him in the morning and gone with him to the court, who had stayed there with him standing through the long hours hearing the same things, applauding at the same moments, rushing away to watch the arrival of the same actor in the same drama, having as he had done noted the peculiar inflexion in a barrister's voice, some movement in the public galleries, the expression on the face of some influential spectator—was for him in some sort a proof that this experience of thrills and emotions was not insubstantial, not just a private dream, but had been lived through by others, was to plunge once more into the events of the day just past, to remember, to argue, to go to the heart of the matter, to give an enduring quality to all he had been feeling. And because death once it has come is absolute, so that everything to do with life, our schoolfriends and the scenes of former days, seem meaningless, and little more than a buzzing in the ears—we fear its approach because we want nothing we have known to die, and cling to every detail which might keep life from vanishing into nothingness. That is why we so eagerly treasure letters and memories, old friendships that once united companions in arms, the warm affection of former fellow-travellers, school comradeships, and the prolonged intimacy of colleagues. In shared sorrows and shared joys we find a basis for healthy fondness and happy talk. No life that is in any degree feverish can ever be wholly exempt from those periods of calm which follow on the heels of excitement, when we feel, as we look at the expressions of lively satisfaction and tranquil happiness on the faces of those who sit talking about nothing in particular over a modest glass of beer, that something greater than them is present, which has brought them together and smiles upon them.

Let me take as an example of what I mean two comrades who have just passed the same examination after long months of poring over books which no doubt were extremely tedious. The life they lived in one another's company had had its moments of quiet happiness when they would stop working for a moment on spring days to listen to a nightingale singing in the tree outside the window, or to look at the motionless lilac with its tier on tier of soft, delicate pyramids of purple bloom rising in the bright air like a perfumed altar. How tender its colour! How delicious the scent must be! Jean—for it is of him that I am thinking in the days when he was working with Henri for the *baccalauréat*, always wanted to go out for a sniff. But no, there was work to be done. Should they open the window?—but that would mean letting heat into the room, besides, the twittering of birds and the noises of the street would be sure to distract their attention. In winter after dark had come and dinner was over, there had been long hours of work in front of a roaring fire in a place of quiet privacy and reading, protected by the flickering flames, which soon Jean would exchange for a place smaller and deeper still, his bed. But first he must go out for a breath of air. How cold it was, and what a noise the wind was making in the chimney! But Henri would go with him. For was not Henri his one and only friend, if by friend we mean one from whose face *our* life, and not a stranger's, our own, true life, secret and radiating happiness, smiles out at us? Then later when the examination had begun, Henri came to fetch Jean every morning at six o'clock almost before it was light. Each of them had his supply of paper, his bottle of ink, his sandwiches. No sooner had they reached the examination hall than they heard their names called from the roll just as they were swallowing a mouthful of black coffee from the flasks they had brought with them, which now they would hurriedly slip back into their pockets. The fatal moment had come when a folded slip of paper was handed to the Professor which he would open, a simple sealed and folded slip which contained the subject of the essay, till then unknown, just a plain piece of white paper which the Professor standing there in full view of the candidates tore open. Within it lurked a power that would determine their future—which for the moment was all they cared about—the full power of all the ineluctable immensity of fate, there at that very instant, to become real though still invisible, a power that might spare or glorify our past, a tiny slip of paper with, in it, what might turn out to be a sentence of death or a few days of reprieve. The solemnity, the tingling excitement, of that instant was still, for Jean, embodied in the presence there with him of Henri, who had shared his feelings. Life had bound them together in the stringency of that experience, and they felt closer to one another than to anybody else. Thus too you might see soldiers in a bivouac, laughing, talking, smiling at life and staring at the sky, or opposing Seconds after a duel, or each evening Durrieux and Jean at their café table after the day's hearing of the Zola trial.

*

And so it was that in those days when passions burned at fever heat, there was never any lack of calm and cordial scenes, long interludes of talk and laughter, the happiness of friend with friend, each smiling at the same life, each seeing the other smile. And so it was that Jean, after taking a bath, changing, and dining at home, went to meet Durrieux at their café where after mingling all afternoon with the feverish excitement of that Renaissance Palace which goes by the name of the Palais de Justice, with its immense marble staircases and its long galleries looking on the river, caught up in the agitation of public affairs like two Florentines of the fifteenth century or two Athenians or any of those whose burning preoccupation it is to play a part in the thrilling events of their city, they came together to discuss the day's excitements, endlessly arguing, eagerly speculating on the morrow's session, enjoying the peace of the evening like those two men of Venice, those two Athenians we have imagined, conscious of no passion more lively than that of feverish discussion, no pride more sweet, no relaxation more delicious, than to think that they had both been involved in the general swirl and to talk of it as they sat side by side after dinner under the trees.

In just such a way on that particular evening did Jean and Durrieux sit and talk, draining their beer to which the tranquillity of the hour and their happiness gave an added flavour. At last the time came when they must part—though not for long. "You'll come for me in the morning, won't you? Between now and then I must put the finishing touches to the notes which I've got to make for Labori."

By half past eight as usual Jean was up and dressed. Durrieux, punctual to the minute, came to fetch him. Nine o'clock. "We'd better hurry, this is the day General de Pellieux is to give evidence: the place'll be crowded and we may not get in." Jean, fresh from his bath and on his toes, took his packet of sandwiches and together they hurried downstairs. "Hi! Cabby, Palais de Justice!" At noon they rushed out for a quick lunch. When they got back they were greeted with an extraordinary piece of news. General de Boisdeffre, who so far had made no statement, had been sent for. A heated argument had started between two generals and since everybody realized that there was nothing he did not know, he had been asked to attend the Court—he, the Chief of the General Staff of the Army, who, had he wished, could have been President of the Republic or even Emperor. What would he say?—anything he liked, secure in the knowledge that France would at once obey. The Court had been adjourned, pending his arrival. An aide-de-camp had gone off at a run to find him. All the curious, all the privileged, agog with excitement about affairs of State, who had managed to penetrate into the Galerie de Harlay, though not into the Courtroom itself, were waiting for news, and each time that an eyewitness of the proceedings appeared, coming from the narrow passage which led from the gallery to the Court, he was at once the centre of a dense and noisy throng. "General Goix has taken the stand: he says there is definite proof of guilt. It's expected that General X will say that the proof is false. There's been a very sharp passage of arms between Counsel and the President." A similar throng, no less noisy, would now and again gather round two barristers engaged in fisticuffs. All these privileged and curious citizens, sauntering and down the Galerie de Harlay, had seen the aide-de-camp emerge at a run, but before they could intercept him, he had jumped into a cab and been driven off.

There were fresh arrivals from the Courtroom: "Two generals are going at it hammer and tongs: one of them has just said he knows what General de Boisdeffre's opinion is, and the President has sent for him."

There was a rush for the door. A crowd formed at the top of the stair-case to see the general arrive. "Twenty past twelve: it'll take a bit of time to get to the Ministry: he can't be here in less than fifteen minutes. What's he going to say? It's been the general opinion for some time that he wanted to testify. This time the Minister can't refuse per-mission. No one's been warned. They won't have had time to brief him. What's he going to say? The end's in sight now. Everything depends upon the line he takes. If he says one thing, then Dreyfus'll be back in a week from Devil's Island, if another, well then old chap, it's all over. No one will ever be able to say a word in his favour again!" There they all were on tenterhooks. Some were hatless having come straight from the Court. All and sundry were crowded at the head of the stairs and all the way down them. There was a touch of sun on the great flight. The sky was showing white with patches of blue. It was that stationary time of the day when the afternoon seems to hang motionless in the sky above our heads, laying upon the town or on the fields here sunlight, there shadow, here peace and quiet, there the regular rhythm of hard work—a crane handling steel girders, a plough-man driving his horses, but seemingly outside time, all sharing in the same slowing down which gives to the afternoon a sense of life in some hidden place, moving slowly and without noise so that each tiny sound is audible, as when a wave withdraws from the shore and there is utter silence so that we feel as though the tide had paused and can hear distinctly the ripple of the water and the sound of sand and shells being dragged backwards.

A cab drew up. An officer got out accompanied by a gentleman in civilian clothes. "That's not him." – "Yes, it is" – "Nonsense, that's not Boisdeffre." – "It is, I tell you." The gentleman in civilian clothes was very tall. The most noticeable thing about him was a very high top-hat tilted at an angle. Listening apparently to the officer beside him with close attention, he moved forward slowly with a stiff motion of the legs, as though he were very tired. Every now and again he came to a halt. Though he still gave the impression of youthfulness his cheeks were covered by a delicate red and purple mottling such as one sees on garden walls in autumn when they are clothed in Virginia Creeper. There was a look of concentrated attention in his eyes but from time to time they blinked with a sort of nervous tic and now and again he plucked at his moustache with an ungloved hand. In the other he held a piece of paper and a pencil and these he stuffed into the pocket of his overcoat which looked very shabby and gaped at the neck, where the top button was undone. He seemed very calm and completely unhurried. The impression produced was that the nervous tic which set his eyes blinking, and the hand tugging at his moustache, as well as the red embroidery of his cheeks, the shabbiness of his overcoat, and the stiffness of his leg, which must often have been broken in falls from his horse were, all of them, the special characteristics which together made up that august object known to all as "General de Boisdeffre", part and parcel of his grandeur because they were his own private property, were never separated from him. It was with those blinking eyes that he looked out upon the world: it was as a result of smoking cigars and drinking brandy after long days of exacting work that his cheeks had acquired that veined and purple look. As he passed the onlookers raised their hats and he returned the salutation politely like a man of very high rank, some Prince of the Church, who, knowing that he may excite envy, is at pains to disarm it by the perfection of his manners. All the same when the First President came by and he like everybody else had to uncover, it was obvious from the rather self-conscious way in which he raised his hat, from the nervous blink with which he completed the salute, that in spite of everything, he felt it distinctly odd that he should be living at a time when General de Boisdeffre must join in showing deference to the President of the Municipal Council who was a mere nobody. But he made his bow all the same, aware of what must be done, and did it better than anybody else, and with a more perfect graciousness. With the same courtesy he acknowledged the raised hats of the bystanders, but without seeming to notice them, always deep in thought, occasionally blinking his eyes, moving his stiff leg, fingering his moustache, and passing his hand over his reddish cheek, as though he were stroking the muzzle of an old charger which he had ridden till it dropped. And while he climbed the stairs, preoccupied and stiff, with the aide-de-camp at his heels, there was not an onlooker but was anxiously wondering what he was going to say. Those ruddy cheeks, those blinking eyes, even the gaping overcoat and the enormous top-hat cocked at an angle, those common-or-garden gestures and objects were all of them charged with an irresistible emotional appeal which was reflected in the watching faces of those who would not have dared approach him save in the most deferential manner, feeling themselves to be under the influence of an immense, a European, a universal personality. As he turned for the last time to face the staring multitude, he gave a final blink as though to mark the crucial moment of his mental concentration, of that thought still unknown to any but himself, though already formed and ready, which suddenly would burst from the privacy of his consciousness, and change not only the life of one man and one family, but the whole course of European affairs.

As the general entered the Galerie de Harlay and made his way towards the narrow passage leading to the Court, with his eyes on the ground, his mind still busy with the secret thought which no one now could stop him from putting into words (the Minister had not yet been told that the Chief of the General Staff had been summoned by the Court), imprisoned in a lanky body, in a not very strong agglomeration of flesh and bone which anybody could have killed but which nobody dared to approach, a man who had not so much as a stick with which to defend himself, holding nothing in his hand but a slip of paper and a pencil, and wearing a gaping overcoat with the top button undone— at that very moment he was brought to a standstill by a group of persons emerging from the narrow passage he was just about to enter. It was some seconds—so much courage did it need to acquaint him with what must seem like an unheard-of breach of manners towards the Chief of the General Staff of the Army who had been brought all that way for nothing—before he learned what had happened. The President, who, no doubt fearful of possible diplomatic complications should the Chief of Staff make a statement before the Government had been informed of what was in the wind, in all probability would have forbidden him to open his mouth, had chosen the almost exact moment of the General's arrival to adjourn the Court until the next day so that the Government might be given time to decide what attitude to adopt. The face of the Chief of Staff showed no surprise. Just as he had done a little while before, he passed his hand over his ruddy cheek as though stroking or checking a thought. He blinked his eyes, and walked back down the Galerie de Harlay with the same stiff gait, the same pre- occupied expression, and descended the stairs. Disappointed, and suddenly released from nervous strain—since the Chief of Staff's all- powerful words would not be spoken today, and might quite likely, never be spoken at all—the massed crowd on the staircase gave utter- ance to a deafening cheer. The General touched his hat repeatedly but the look on his face was still one of preoccupation and his grey eyes seemed as before to be focused on some inner thought. A number of generals and staff-majors only just apprised of his arrival swarmed behind him, throwing their capes round their shoulders as they pressed forward, and accompanied him to his cab, the driver of which, who had been hailed in the rue Saint-Dominique, had only just learned who his fare had been, and for what purpose—soon to be part of history— the journey had been made. The generals and even the staff-majors after saluting moved closer, and descended the stairs with him in a familiar group. For life on the Staff being less regimental, is less rigid. Its members all work informally together.

6. *Colonel Picquart*

It is a sort of Law of Compensation—a *lex talionis*—in the world of moral values, that those, no matter how intelligent or how sensitive they may be, who as the result of laziness or for some other reason have no inner, no disinterested activity on which to employ their minds, inevitably in their judgments of life attach enormous importance to the merely formal. Very little reflection will serve to show that the workings of this law are inevitable. Take for instance a man like Monsieur Rustinlor who in spite of his intellectual gifts could never, no matter what the reason, bring himself to think seriously about anything, write a single passage of genuine profundity, or withdraw into himself and examine his mental processes in a purely objective manner. This sluggishness however would vanish at once if he were asked to set his name to a manifesto, or to register his vote for this or that candidate. That for him would be an important action, would give him the feeling that he had *done* something, something remarkable, decisive, significant. But such actions are strictly speaking of no importance whatever, since nothing of our true selves goes into them. How is it then that they can seem to do so? Much real kindliness is needed to conquer a disgruntled mood when for instance we are sitting with our mother, to listen to what she is saying, to answer her gently with an air of happy interest which will make the evening bright for her—a small enough matter in all conscience but no less important for her than all the other evenings which go to make up the sum total of her life, because if we speak sharply or merely look bored, our attitude may well produce in her a deep-rooted melancholy as a result of which her passage through life will be marked only by a sad resignation, and should illness come (and perhaps because of it) by a weakening of the will to live. But merely to set one's name to a manifesto, no matter what fine sentiments of justice and pity it may contain, and even if it involves us in the expenditure of a hundred francs (a sum which may mean very little to us, and is not, like kindliness, or profundity of thought, drawn from the deepest part of ourselves) represents no effort, no good-will, nothing in fact that is genuinely personal to ourselves. If such an attitude were to become general throughout mankind, it would soon be apparent that humanity had relapsed into barbarism, that since all impulses of sacrifice or disinterestedness, all searchings of the individual conscience, which as things are we often find pushing, like ivy in the crevices of flagstones, from broken hearts, having ceased to exist, mothers would be abandoned in old age, the dead would be neglected, brother would be at odds with brother, the innocent would be allowed to suffer for the guilty, and the governments of this world would turn harsh and dishonest because harshness and dishonesty would have come to mark the character of the peoples by whom they were kept in power. What real significance would there be, what encouragement to help men to bear the burden of sickness or injustice, in no matter how many thousands of prospectuses and lists of good works, because good hearts as empty of feeling as an abandoned city, stones bearing the names of endless charitable activities with no humanity, nor true effort to second them, would humanly speaking have no value? It would be only too obvious that not on stones, not on papers, could the vanishing human race depend for help, but that stones and papers alike would fall with it into the abyss.

In the fashionable world where there are no inner resources, no objects of disinterested concern, for human hearts and minds to bite upon, it is true to say that all is formality. Among the denizens of the "great world" it is a commonplace that that world judges everything by appearances, a commonplace which certain people in search of pleasing paradox justify by saying, "Of course it does, what else can one judge by *except* appearances?" or in less advanced circles, "Society is compelled to judge by appearances, even though that does often result in one woman being judged more severely than another who may in fact be very much more guilty." In point of fact "Society" is preoccupied by three things which are the epitome of the formal: snobbery or admiration in others of something which has nothing to do with their personal characters or abilities: scandal-mongering, in which for the most part means concentrating (under the colour of criticizing) on nothing but appearances: propriety and etiquette in which formality is made real and actual, more real and more actual than in anything else. Outside "Society" so-called, but where men live in some sort of a community, though with no inner resources, no dis-interested activity on which to employ their powers, it is true to say that the most important things of all are precisely those to which they give nothing of themselves, which demand no personal effort—the "slogans" of the schools, the violent dogmatisms or preferences of the literary "sets", political prejudices and cries of "Long Live so-and-so" "Down with t'other" and votes given in a somewhat irresponsible fashion. In the Chamber, as in the Academy, one will always be sure of seeing Tom, Dick or Harry who has made a point of coming to register his vote. Now it is quite certain that nothing really important in the make-up of Tom, Dick or Harry finds expression in his vote—the impression awakened in him for instance at sight of the sun which is closely associated with his earliest hopes and his mature delights, or the many composite thoughts and feelings which will cease altogether when death puts a full stop to his conscious awareness. Votes, regular attendance at meetings or sessions, indispensable calls on possible supporters, canvassing, party cries—all these are so many refuges in which we shelter from the dread necessity of turning our eyes inwards. It is a common experience to find a man of genuine intelligence settling down to a career of professional criticism, and so conducting it as never to let himself be driven into a corner from which he can escape only by committing himself to a definite opinion. He never states his own attitude clearly, but lets it be mysteriously implied, and ultimately, his work as a critic consists of little more than listing the titles of books, announcing the number of editions they have passed through, describing the reception accorded to them at the time of their publication, etc. They are like persons who, seeing you depressed, will avoid all revelation of their personal feelings, and limit their inquiries to saying "How is your dear mother?"–"Are you sleeping better?"–"What have you been eating?"–"Have you seen so-and-so recently?" And these intelligent men are over-joyed when as editors of magazines they have a ready-made excuse for never writing a line, and can manage to serve the cause of literature in other ways. If such lives—which re-semble those legal documents said to have been "signed in the presence of Madame Y and Madame Z" before the actual text has even been written—may be described as refuges from introspection and respon-sibility, the same may be said of almost all those manifestations in which men of letters and politicians love to indulge, and of the importance they attach to such purely external activities. That is why in assemblies where men of intelligence and feeling can find no deep, no disinterested pursuit on which to expend their energies, you will find them—with a sort of morbid intensity, as though it is essential for them to occupy their minds and hearts with something, if their consciences are to be left in peace—pulling long faces and exhibiting signs of nervous strain when they tell you for instance that the Minister of Public Instruction has acted as Second to a Socialist in a recent duel, and then, as though trying to persuade themselves that the matter is one on which they can worthily expend all the resources of their minds and their sensibility, adding, "It's a very serious matter: quite unprecedented. As I see it, the effects may be very far-reaching."

By another application of the same law, men, even serious-minded men who spend their lives in politics, attach when they are out of office, exaggerated importance to this or that measure put forward by the President of the Council. When Monsieur Rustinlor was a political journalist, there was no end to the emotional thrills in which he could revel. With an air of deep preoccupation, in the tones of someone imparting strange and mysterious news of the highest significance, he would say to Jean, "Something very, very serious has just happened which may well put everything in jeopardy. Méline was overheard in the lobby to say that he was prepared to accord priority to Millerand's motion." – "A person very much in the know has given it as his opinion that de Boisdeffre will declare in open Court that he is determined to stand shoulder to shoulder with the other generals. What we are heading for God only knows! It means revolution!" For those who accord so much importance to *facts* find that they no longer take any account of *laws*. They see the world in a purely romantic light, and believe that things are always on the verge of violent upheaval. "The country's in a terrible state," they say, "poor, poor France. Heaven knows what's coming! Nothing like the present situation has ever been seen before! There'll be big changes soon: this means the end of the Republic!" The fervour, the sensibility which in such men has no genuine outlet, comes into action when they are called upon to make no effort, in a passive way: that is to say it reacts to each item of news as it is made public. These persons emerge from every session of the Chamber in a white heat, convinced that the country is faced with immediate and irremediable disaster, driven by a sort of inner necessity to talk about it, to feel it, because only so can they localize their "sense of anxiety" and, the better to talk of it, indulge in exaggeration. When General Goix spoke in Court of the "trap" which Labori had set for him, Rustinlor and his friends were profoundly shaken and felt their unemployed emotions thrilled as by an electric shock. After this incident they went from group to group in the Galerie de Harlay exclaiming, "Infamous! that's what it is, infamous! One can't say that sort of thing about a barrister—and the Advocate-General didn't utter a word! It's a serious matter, extremely serious, terribly serious . . ." and when Jean with a smile asked him very quietly, "But what's so serious about it?" Rustinlor, deeply offended by his amusement, replied with a superior air, "My dear fellow you must be joking to ask such a question! Isn't it serious enough in all conscience that the most elementary rights of the defence should be at the mercy of a handful of generals? Why, it could quite easily lead to every member of the Bar resigning—and then where would you be supposing you got involved in a law suit? Not that it matters to me, *I'm* not a property owner, but what about people who want to contest a will, eh, what about them? . . ." – "I expect it just slipped out, and wasn't a bit what he meant to say." – "Slipped out! slipped out!—things like that don't 'slip out' when a French general, the Deputy-Chief of the General Staff of the Army is testifying in Court!" By this time the crowd round the two men was growing bigger and bigger. Rustinlor raised his voice, less perhaps as the result of mounting anger than because he wanted what he was saying to be audible to the various groups in the vicinity, and gesticulating, when some perfect stranger addressed a question to him. Excitement was producing an atmosphere of happy fraternization, those in the know exerting authority over the merely curious, and revelling in the knowledge that they could work upon their feelings and at the same time satisfy their hunger for news. As to "resignation", more especially if it concerned a minister, a general, or a member of the *Conseil d'Ordre*, there is no need to point out what a flapping and a cawing it produced among the assembled crows, who felt that by merely making as much noise as possible, they were assuming the role of prophets. As to the resignation of Casimir-Perrier, it was almost too much. Faced by an event of that kind the imagination boggled.

I have known men of letters, too, whose whole capacity for feeling could be exhausted over the admission by the Academy of some particular word to the dictionary, or by the news that Heredia had come out in favour of *vers libre*. "This," they would say, "means the death of the French language!" On the day with which I am here dealing, in the Galerie de Harlay, each new arrival, emerging from the narrow passage reserved for witnesses said, "Colonel Picquart is still

defending himself."–"What's he saying, it's not very easy to hear?"
This remark may have been due to the fact that the Colonel's voice
was very low and did not carry easily, but also to a fact of a quite
different kind, to be gathered from the peaceable and on the whole
happy expression on the newcomer's face, namely that not knowing
precisely what the attitude of his questioners might be, he preferred
not to expose himself to rough treatment at their hands, he being one
of those who say, "It's a matter of opinion: some say one thing, some
another: it's all such a tangle that there's nothing very much one can
take hold of," expressing themselves in this fashion because they realize
that they share the views of a temporary minority which is less violent
than the temporary majority, that they are suspect (that is to say for
the time being at least, supporters of Dreyfus and of Picquart) who
when they make a statement ("I've not the least idea whether he is
guilty or innocent: but you mustn't misunderstand me: I'm not saying
he *isn't* guilty, but only that I have complete confidence in the good
faith of the War Council") know that they are admitting their ad-
hesion to the minority view, and defend themselves on purely intellectual grounds by saying, "That is only *my* opinion: you, of course,
are entitled to yours: a man is free to hold what opinion he likes," a
declaration which makes it quite clear that he does not want to come
to blows, and that whenever tempers look like getting heated he will
reply, "Well, you may be right." But Jean had now made his way into
the Courtroom and was listening to Colonel Picquart.

The Colonel was a friend of Monsieur Beulier, Jean's professor, and
like him a man whose whole life, in spite of his sky-blue uniform, had
been spent in seeking by the light of reason, while he turned his horse
at a corner, or was on his way to the barrack square for an inspection,
the truth of everything which might, with some urgency, involve a
degree of self-examination. But he was as well a cavalry officer just
back from Africa, who knew nothing, except what he could read in the
spite and malice which showed between the lines of the daily papers, of
the world of journalists, adversaries and judges now thronging the
Courtroom, and who having been kept like a horse for some days in
the witnesses' waiting-room, had not yet made acquaintance with that
circus-ring of the Law, into which when his name was called and a door
was opened, he found himself ushered. As though he had only just
dismounted, and still retained even on his feet the quick, light movements of a Spahi, walking quickly straight ahead, with that free and

easy carriage of the body which a man might show who had just
dropped his reins and unbuckled his sword, and with a look of mild
bewilderment upon his face advanced to the President's seat, where he
came to a stop and saluted, not in military fashion, but with a mingled
air of timidity and frankness, as though his every gesture was free of
all formality or merely external significance but was overflowing
like his walk, the sideways carriage of his head and as would soon
be apparent, his well-bred voice, with the elegance and warmth of
his personality.

As the various movements of a man's mind may reflect the uniform,
and to all appearances purely physical repetition of some action, so now
the Colonel's long deposition was accompanied by a swaying of his
body from side to side. All those things which do not form part of
what is generally called a correct attitude, but are personal to those who
are preoccupied not with the world outside but with the world inside
themselves, so that their bodies and their physical behaviour instead of
being controlled by the will, act in obedience to thoughts which are
elsewhere, turn deeply inwards and are concerned with a past that needs
explaining or with an idea that needs to be probed; are at the mercy of
unconscious and involuntary movements which follow instinctively
the processes of the mind and will, expressing them even more accurately
than they would if they were acting in obedience to their deliberate
direction.

For months now it had been said that all the officers would be present
at the trial with the single exception of Colonel Picquart, who was
under arrest at Mont-Valérien. But the very day before the case opened
a well-informed person of whom Jean had inquired whether all the
officers would be there had said, "No, I doubt whether any of them
will except Colonel Picquart: he'll certainly be there." This idea,
overturning as it did all the preconceptions which for a month past
had been firmly rooted in his mind, filled Jean with a pleasing
sense of novelty, and gave to the mysterious Colonel Picquart,
until then confined in prison, and now let out to speak in his own defence in response to the all-powerful summons of the President, something of the charm of a bird released for a moment from his cage.
Things till then wrapped in silence and mystery, though in a few
moments to be expressed in words and established as known fact were
made visible in the person of a youngish, quick-moving man, carrying
with the easy gait of a colonel used to long days on horseback, a

secret which he knew that he possessed, a witness whom everybody even his enemies looked at with interest.

★

Jean therefore had been acquainted with the fact that Colonel Picquart might perhaps put in an appearance. All the same, when on the first day—when witnesses not yet called were allowed to remain in the Courtroom—he could not help being conscious of a thrill when the man next him said, "Take a look down there: that's Colonel Picquart." There was a buzz of conversation in the air; packages of sandwiches were being opened and handed round, and the sunlight which inside the room seemed crude and harsh, though it gave an inkling of what a lovely day it must be in the open air, just at that moment happened to touch Colonel Picquart's hat. A strange sensation came to Jean when he saw there beneath him, free and mingling with the crowd, the man he knew was still a prisoner, a man who looked young with rather too aquiline a nose and a head leaning slightly to one side. There he was in the flesh, one of the general throng. It came to him with something of a shock that he could do nothing to modify that physical fact, each feature of which, the reddish complexion, the easy carriage of the head, made him feel almost embarrassed, such violence did they do to his imagination which so long accustomed to visualize the Colonel in a certain way had now to submit to a reality which it could not alter at will. The resplendent hat was worn at a slight angle and the general impression was that of a man with a far-away but tranquil look, of a head not so much rigid as motionless, even when it turned to right or left, and a carriage of the body which was not straight up and down, but something oblique, and produced in the spectator a feeling of lightness and speed held for the moment in check. Jean had always expected him to look either old, calm and stiff—an embodiment of Duty in its Maturity—or young, ardent, handsome—an incarnation of Duty at the Spring. He felt slightly disappointed, but at the same time fascinated by the man there below him, now and then hidden from his sight by the people round him, now walking slowly about, looking neither young nor old, fair-haired, clean-shaven, with something in his appearance of a Jewish engineer. In the man down below, moving from group to group there was a strange absence of any sign of captivity (nothing to show that the gentleman wearing gloves and a top-hat, with nothing in his appearance to tell of the unhappiness, the enforced idleness, the resignation, which one associates with prisoners, had just left Mont-Valérien to come to the Court), an absence too of anything to show what Jean imagined must be going on in his mind (no indication that he was moved by a feeling of revolt at the thought of the judicial crime which was being committed by the General Staff; nothing to show that he had taken a great decision to do his duty to the end nor any sign of uncertainty, of thought, of a struggle of conscience. There he stood with his elegant gleaming top-hat, gazing at nobody and nothing but with a look of peace in his eyes, seemingly untouched by any mental activity, like a column of thin smoke rising from village hearths on just such a sunshiny day as this, so that one could not tell whether he had come to speak his mind or to say nothing, whether or no he would answer the questions put to him, whether he would come down on the side of the General Staff, or as was being said, would remain steadfast in his support of Dreyfus) a complete absence of anything expressive of his situation (since the mere fact of his presence, of his having been allowed to come, could be taken as implying either that the Minister still regarded him as an officer entitled to his liberty in spite of the sentence he was at present serving, or that like all the other officers he had come here prepared to break with the Ministry and the General Staff and to speak out even though he did so at the risk of being cashiered). It was because of all this, that, seeing him moving freely among the various groups which now and again completely concealed him, one could equally well see in him an officer with an assured future and well aware what he was doing, whom though he was wearing civilian clothes one could far more easily visualize in full uniform at the head of his men—or as a prisoner let out to face what was, in fact a species of torture, because he must be aware of the even worse ordeals that lay before him, who has been allowed by a soft-hearted executioner to give utterance to his last words. Since he was in fact a prisoner one would have liked to know, in spite of the top-hat, in spite of the smart clothes with which he had been issued for the occasion, in spite of the fact that he had been allowed to come at all, whether he was unbearably miserable in his room at Mont-Valérien, and for his sake one rejoiced at this temporary interval of liberty, and could the more easily, for all his civilian get-up, see him as an officer in undress uniform just as he must be in his prison cell. But that was not all. He was not only a prisoner but a prisoner for whose position as something

false and wrong one felt miserably compassionate, miserable at the
thought that he had been allowed out in this manner to play his part in
what for him must be a drama full of nervous strain, a drama meaning
that he must in some sort be holding his future in his own hands, since
what he might say was bound to have an effect upon it, miserable
because one felt that this species of torture, this saying in so many
words, "Well, what about it?—here you are, free: you know now what
freedom is like: it is for you to decide whether you are to go back to
face five years in a fortress," was an additional punishment forbidden
by modern legal standards as being too cruel, too frightful. Standing
there a free man, with his top-hat at an angle, looking like any ordinary
spectator who would go back that evening to his home to return or
not tomorrow as he might feel inclined, he produced the same sort of
painful impression as might a patient roused from his bed to walk to
the operating-theatre, who because of his fully-dressed appearance, as
of one leaving his bed—though in his case, alas! for only too short a
time, because he will later return to it for an indefinite period—
may *look* better, though the look is deceptive, as deceptive as the
brilliant sunlight on this day of anxiety, shining harshly into this
crammed room of bad air and crowded onlookers.

Colonel Picquart was a philosopher whose thoughts, while he moved
ahead of his men, were ceaselessly employed in trying to get a clear
view of the problems with which they were engaged. From this life of
his which was entirely devoted to disinterested search had emerged a
species of cordiality which those who lived with him found distinctly
pleasing. When thought develops along the lines of moral introspection it has the effect of producing in us an extreme form of sensibility, of an attitude to everything around us—when our intellectual
powers are not forced into abeyance by purely egotistical preoccupations—of joyful affection. A poet or a philosopher whose besetting
weakness may perhaps be vanity, is just like any other man when he
finds himself in surroundings which excite that vanity. Consequently
it is impossible for him in, for example, the company of flatterers, to
remain aware of the charms which are to be found in quiet, and in the
strict sense of the word poetic, happiness. Even when he is alone in an
enchanting room, awaiting the coming of some fashionable lady, his
feelings you may be sure are of the most mediocre quality, and when
his hostess at last appears, such words as, "How delightful all this is: I

could gladly spend my life here" really speak themselves. It is not he at that moment who truly forms them.

No, the place in which he would truly have liked to spend his life, which in memory appeared as genuinely enchanting—so much so that having no one with whom to share his thoughts since he was alone, he leaned back in his comfortable armchair, and murmured to himself, 'How delightful all this is: I could gladly spend my life here!' was actually some little garrison town on a day when he was off duty, a small room where he was safe from disturbance, with a fire lit by his landlady with wood borrowed from the tenant on the floor below filling it with a welcoming roar, and producing so dazzling a light that the pictures on the walls seemed as though irradiated by a lamp, though until that moment he had been conscious only of the weak light of early afternoon: a grey day, for it was raining as he could see by looking out of the tiny window with the short red and white checked curtains which obscured it to only half its height. For it was not merely among the rocky wastes of lonely mountain places that this lonely, this truly happy man gave utterance to his cry of love and power and joy. It was not merely with the breeze, when he felt the pulse of its approach in the deep silence, that he felt made one, as though his spirit were its spirit, and held his breath when the short grasses began to tremble. It was each time that the overflowing energy of his inner life moved with divine power through all things, and gave to them a deep reality, feeling itself to be in the presence of, as it were, the humbler and more familiar gods—the god of fire shaking his locks of light and warmth, filling the room with gaiety; the motionless god of the door with its sunken wooden panels, proof of the care such country dwellings took to hide the privacies of the bed-chamber, offering that tutelary service which it rendered to living men who behind that massive guardian, on days rainy as this one, on nights of high wind, when it stood firm and unmoving, came together for friendly talk or slept; where a man and a woman might in solitude take their pleasure of one another after firmly closing the timber emblem of divinity. The painted walls, the furniture, the hearth large enough to accommodate a huge fire of logs in true country fashion, all were things that the freed and flowing spirit could ponder and adore, and sometimes, in a low voice, murmur, 'How gladly could I spend my life here!' and question the silence without waiting for an answer.

Very often in his many billets had Colonel Picquart left happy memories with the landladies who came to light his fire, who stole away so as to leave him to his work, receiving as thanks from that high and crowned intelligence, that character of happy independence which they had acknowledged by entrusting him with the keys of the house, the vague smile, the look of affection which accompany all great up-surgings of thought, which in the stretched movement of our lips, in the dilation of our pupils, we feel still hovering above us as we work, as we write, while the only sign of our body's life is a gentle rhythm, like the quiet breathing of a sleeping child. Look, smile, the child's breathing, give witness by their placid innocence to the withdrawn and hidden life of moments such as those. No matter how different we may be from others, even in things we hold to be of supreme importance, those others, once they have decided that we are decent and intelligent persons, show no disapproval of our ways, or at most permit them-selves only a tolerant smile (what a lunatic you are!) and are prepared to wait until in some moment of crisis those oddities of ours shall dis-appear so completely that they seem never to have existed, and to judge our actions at every moment of our lives, as though they are the expression of some abstract being, though in fact the product of those selfsame oddities. In just such a way will the father of a son with a great talent for poetry exhibit no particular annoyance, so long as all he hears are compliments about the young man's gifts. But should a day ever come when those gifts and his son's temperament combine to prevent the boy from carrying out work he has been given, to lead him into doing nothing at all, or make him refuse an offer of employ-ment, then the father will get angry, and show by the way in which he fires up that in his heart of hearts he has been aware of his son's oddities of character, and has taken pleasure in them without for that reason ceasing to judge him just as he would any "man in the street".

Such oddities of character, should we have them, are apparent in the quite simple answers we may have to make to a series of questions. Standing there, with his head held high before his judges, looking at once free and shy in his blue uniform, Colonel Picquart at each question put to him could not help as formerly, as always, trying to think his way into it, putting himself, according to the rules of what one cannot exactly call a method, since it is a method which a man unconsciously adopts so as to be able to think, as a bird makes use of its wings for the purpose of flying, feeling that it is, at least for him, the best way of going about the business in hand, putting himself into the mental attitude with which he has become familiar in moments when he has been feeling at his best and in some sort inspired, acting in obedience to a highly personal form of sincerity, an instinct that will brook no denial, putting himself in the shoes of the man he has to deal with, ceasing to think of himself as himself, striving to see the other man's actions as he would his own. Such a "method" spreads through the whole of a man's life, and is active even when summoned before a magistrate, or face to face with a threatening antagonist, he feels suddenly that he is quite alone, that the universe has abandoned him, that he has been reduced to the stature of a man in a state of anxiety. At such moments, even though we may feel utterly abandoned, we find at our side—like faithful servants who refuse to be parted from us, or like the gods who stay with us, though not unfortunately always to afford protection—those moral and intellectual impulses which though they are ours are affected by every word addressed to us, so that we cannot prevent them from giving off a sort of continuous electric current. The coward models himself on the fine part he *should* be playing, though under the impact of insults and at the mercy of his fear which he can feel in the beating of his heart, in the rise of blood to his cheeks, and in the false emphasis of his words, he will go on with his play-acting until a moment comes when on some absurd pretext or other he turns on his heel and his natural fearfulness assumes control. In the course of an interrogation, especially when we are in a calmer frame of mind, we suddenly realize that the intellectual habits of a lifetime have not left us but are with us still. We may know perfectly well that what we may say about this or that might just as well not be said at all, because only other philosophers will understand it and rejoice, seeing the man behind the words: we cannot keep ourselves from following the natural bent of our minds. Like those heroes of the Russian campaign who were scrupulous about shaving on the morning of the very day they were to die—though cleanliness and elegance have no meaning in death—the mind even when at grips with persons who are far less capable of reasoning, cannot resist the pleasure of trying to find the precise word for the occasion and expends itself in an effort to distinguish in the question put, two distinct ideas which ought logically to be treated in separation, to get inside the adversary's mental processes so as to follow the emotional current on which he must have been carried forward, and so to arrive quite naturally at the severe judgment he has formed of us and to find it perfectly comprehensible

—as when Colonel Picquart, having been recalled by the President after the archivist Gribelin had accused him of what amounted to criminal activities, was asked, "What is your opinion of the archivist Gribelin?" and replied, at the risk of strengthening the case against himself, "I hold him to be an honest man and, to be precise, wholly incapable of telling a lie."

The truth of the matter is that at the moment of formulating an idea, of answering a question, such men are as much conscious of the authorities in whose presence they are standing as of the processes of their own minds. It is to those processes that they make answer. No matter if their answer sets the Court laughing: they know that it is true and accurate and can do nothing to justify it except by embarking on an argument which will be no better understood than the answer they have already given. Not that what they say is obscure but that in order to make a very simple statement comprehensible to their audience they have expressed themselves according to the logical rules of philosophical discussion. A poet accused of espionage because he has spent two hours looking at the changing colours on a barrack building at sunset, will merely cause his judges to shrug their shoulders if he explains the true reason of his behaviour. "I can't see what there is particularly attractive about a barracks at sunset," says the Judge, "if it had been a cathedral now, that would have been quite a different matter. You're not the only poet in the world, you know. I used to write poetry myself now and again." The poet's only possible reply to such a remark is an equivocal smile expressive of bitter satisfaction which arises in him as the result of an evident contradiction, for he sees the Judge at one and the same time as a real man with the power to do him an injury, and on a different level, the level at which his own gifts of observation operate, as a grotesque figure of fun, as a man who has authority over him, who is stronger than he is, who is much to be feared, whom he must try to influence, and yet as someone definitely his inferior, who is as it were nothing but a caricature. He is well aware that his answer has produced a bad impression and may do him harm, but the Judge's comment, though it hurts him by reason of the unfortunate consequences it may entail, and because it shows how impossible it is for him to make himself understood, produces in him all the same when looked at from a purely intellectual point of view, a lively sense of the mental inferiority of that particular Judge, and of his colleagues on the Bench who at that moment are convulsed with laughter, and convinced that their fellow

Judge has made an extremely apposite remark, and that it is he rather than the accused who is a great poet.

Intelligence of this kind shows to even better advantage when it completely detaches a man from all evil passion—by making him understand the characters of his opponents so well that he is no longer conscious of any resentment against them, opening his eyes to the fact that riches and fame are of no account and that life being of value only in so far as it may be dedicated to a search for truth and to the doing of good to others, can never be worth the sacrifice of those two ends —that every word he speaks and the understanding smile with which he looks on life makes him at every moment prepared to weigh life lightly in the scales against the claims of truth. That was the feeling one had in listening to Colonel Picquart, the same feeling of which we are chiefly conscious, which moves us so deeply, in reading the *Phaedo*, when following Socrates' argument we are suddenly overwhelmed by the realization that we are listening to a process of logical reasoning wholly undebased by any selfish motive, as though nothing, nothing at all, could have any meaning except truth in all its purity: for what dawns on us is that the conclusion of the argument towards which Socrates is working is none other than that it is right and proper for him to die. There is in him at that moment something in comparison with which life is of no value, since it is for that something that he is about to give *his* life. We see that that is precisely what his words mean, and in the moment of seeing it, we are conscious within ourselves of a profound emotional disturbance. So deeply is the trivial human condition intermingled with every potentiality of greatness in us that what we feel matters is not that Socrates will be dead tomorrow, but that at this turning-point in his existence, Socrates is still sufficiently master of himself to remain true to a philosophical outlook which is part and parcel of his being, just as one immediately realizes even at moments of tragedy, by certain gestures, certain professional mannerisms, that the blacksmith remains a blacksmith still, and cannot alter his way of looking at things. All the same there are times when we cannot help but feel saddened by the knowledge that what is most immaterial in us has set its mark upon us as surely as a tool digging a groove, that the mark is indelible, that the old philosopher has his tricks of the trade as surely as the blacksmith has his. We may think it somewhat artificial of Balzac always to put in the mouth of a notary (Grande-Bretèche) odds and ends of legal jargon, yet his doing so is but an allegory which contains a great truth, as Jean came to understand when having one day asked his old professor, Monsieur Beulier, whether he was fond of draughts and chess, he received the same sort of answer that he would have done had he been seeking enlightenment on a problem of metaphysics, and apparently dictated by a similar form of reasoning, "It is not, I fear, very easy for me to give you an answer to that question. But this I can say—within, that is, the limits of my competence, for I am not a great performer at either of those games—so far as draughts are concerned, the truth seems to me to be—and this is how I should put it—that they are a game in which, etc. . . . . so that I am led to the conclusion that they are not a particularly interesting pastime. I don't however think, I am not altogether sure, that I should say the same of chess, which involves a more direct and concentrated use of the intelligence. It is a fine game, etc. . . ."

There is nothing we can do about it. We can think only with our brain, and as we get older, the brain grows tired, so that we gradually come to give our thought the form which we have trained it to assume. It would be wrong, certainly, to say that our thoughts turn endlessly in the same circle: there is an infinite number of different thoughts that we can set turning in that circle. And so in an assembly where Jean, himself a philosopher, found himself surrounded by some two hundred persons with nothing of the philosopher about them, he could not help smiling sympathetically when he recognized the true philosophic note in Colonel Picquart's voice, and heard him answer, "Do you mind if I don't say anything more about that now? I will come back to it later." He recognized those little habits of mind which often accompany the exercise of philosophic thought, though they are not in themselves the essence of that thought—as two eminent men of letters may take pleasure in writing to one another in Latin, or two musicians in transposing what they happen to be playing together—these oddities being the accompaniment of a high degree of culture, and in a sort of playful way, a proof of its existence in the persons concerned, or as good manners in someone we do not know serve to reveal the fact that he has been well brought up. It was with just such a sympathetic smile that he listened to certain peculiarities in Colonel Picquart's manner of speaking (the way for instance in which he said *sécrets* instead of *secrets*) a smile which he would have worn had he been imitating him, as was the case when he imitated Monsieur Beulier— an imitation eloquent of admiration, a smile born of affectionate sympathy, and having nothing whatever in common with irony or mockery.

If we try to discover the precise effect that true grandeur has upon us, it is not enough merely to say that it is respect: it is rather a sort of familiarity. We detect in those who possess grandeur something of our own spiritual essence, what is best and most pleasing in us, and we laugh at them in just the same way that we laugh at ourselves. Even if they are older in years than we are even if they are forty like Colonel Picquart or sixty like Monsieur Beulier, they are not in any real sense our seniors, they may seem even younger, for the richness of their inner life, and the thousand little physical oddities to which it gives rise, imparts to them the charm of children. We think of a colonel as of somebody cold-blooded and solemn, only to find a brother of whom we can make fun at a distance, have as it were a game with him, joking about his failings, about the way he wrinkles up his nose when he talks, but always with an undercurrent of true sympathy, so that should anyone want to do him a hurt, we should be prepared to give our life for him.

7. *From the Opéra-Comique to the Palais De Justice*

Jean was due back in the afternoon at the Palais de Justice, where the Zola case was still proceeding. But the Duc de Réveillon who was confined to his room with the gout, had asked whether he would be so very kind as to do two or three errands for him. The most urgent of these was to look in at the Opéra-Comique and to give the new Director a gratifying message to the effect that the Duke intended to make up a brilliant party for one of his regular evenings, consisting of all that was brightest and best in Parisian Society. He entered the theatre by the door in the Avenue Victoria and found a door-keeper, a staircase, and an immense building seven stories high, honeycombed with innumerable rooms, which constitutes that half of the theatre which the members of the public never see and think of as consisting of a great number of narrow *wings* into which the actors make their exits when the evening's work is done. But every place in which what seems to be a labour one and indivisible has to be built up, involves in fact an enormous number of different employments, confronted with which the author, seeing twenty women busily at work sewing expensive silks for the dresses of the most minor characters who in a moment of whim and fancy he has created, says to himself, 'God in Heaven! All these lovely materials just for Floriette, all this expert labour, all this expenditure of money! Is it really worth it? They tell me that this dress is for Floriette, though when I think of her I never call her Floriette and don't even know why I gave her that name!' This author of ours, making his way through the vast extent of the "wardrobe" which occupies one whole floor of the building, where so many women were working in the interests of Floriette, had thoughts for nothing but his trivial little fancy, his dream of an hour. Another day, feeling how precious that dream of his was, how misunderstood it had been, and sick of hearing everybody praise the costumes and the cast, he told himself how little all that meant, that his play was what really mattered,

345

that it was something which would still be a living reality without all this fuss and bother. But he had gone to the theatre having something to talk over in the wings with the Director, where he heard more than he usually did of the work of that fellow-dramatist whom he was soon to oust from the bills, and stood there humming the music while the stage-hands, eager to know about the new author and to have a good look at him and the actresses, saluted him with no little respect, hoping that he might do something for them, all the more so since they shared the admiration felt by a fraction of the musical world for his score. And so he waited there in a cramped corner, hearing the piece without seeing a thing, in a forest setting, with a top-hat on his head and a favourite book stuffed into the pocket of his overcoat.

Zerlina, who was getting ready for her entrance, and under her black mantilla showed a heavily made-up face, went up to him with a gracious air and started to talk, not in the language befitting Zerlina, but as she spoke in ordinary life, at the risk of missing her entrance and having to be reminded by the prompter, so that she had to push by Doña Anna who had made her exit so quickly that for a second or two after passing behind the "flat" which masked the wings and concealed her fury in which the audience had been so deeply absorbed—whether because she was sincerely wrapped up in her part or because she thought she might still be visible from the front of the house, and ought therefore to remain Doña Anna for a moment longer—plunged into the crowd of stage-hands where the author was standing and the dresser holding a shawl so that she should not catch cold, still crying, "Oh misery! Oh misery!" though nothing there justified such an exclamation, like a mad woman who takes with her into a throng of strangers the personal preoccupations with which they have nothing to do. But as soon as she had stemmed her mad rush and stopped singing, she looked round for her dresser, raised her veil, remarked that her "B" hadn't been as good as it should be, and still no doubt somewhat put out, apologized to the young author for not having noticed him, and started chatting, since in spite of his age he was important to her. She paid more than usual attention to him, because he had not sent her the airs for which she had asked, and used that fact in order to assert herself. The author introduced the friend he had brought with him, who since this was his first experience of "back-stage", and because he was gifted with a certain amount of imagination, decided that it would be just as absurd to expect to attract the attention of the celebrated diva in the very heat and pressure of the part in which all Paris was applauding her, as to ask to see the President of the Republic for an interview at the very moment of the Czar's arrival. Nevertheless she carried on a most amiable conversation with him, and talked a great deal about how much she admired the piece she was playing in, and how deeply interesting she found her part, being extremely anxious to pass for a good judge in such matters and to show that she was only too humbly eager to impress him with the fact that she was just a devoted interpreter and no more, whose sole concern was to understand the author's intentions, and so courageous that she would not allow even illness to keep her from appearing. She actually went so far as to cough as a sign that she was far from well. What joy for the young author's friend, what happiness to have been present on this historic occasion, if this cough did actually turn out to be the one of which the papers would be full next day, and if indeed it were really as bad a cough as rumour said it was—a pleasure scarcely less great than he would have felt had he fetched her for dinner only to be told that he really must forgive her for not coming, because she was feeling unwell, and then seeing on the theatre-bills a statement to the effect that owing to her illness, the piece had had to be "temporarily suspended"—convincing evidence that he "counted" for her because she had just told him with her own lips news sufficiently important to "count" for her public for which she had so great an affection and respect, though not so great as she had for him.

At this moment Don Ottavio and Don Juan made their exit at a run and started to mop their faces as soon as they were out of sight of the audience, and to them she extended her hand with the pert, charming smile of a "good trouper". One of them made a joke to which she responded with a kiss. Then they both shook hands with the young author—who complimented them on their singing—and moved away humming scraps from the music in their next scene. Meanwhile a young Count had managed to get himself introduced to the author. He was a good-looking young fellow in evening dress and white gloves. After the manner of men of his world he exchanged with the singers and the stage-hands the polite greetings, gracious words and impersonal handshakes which he had learned in the ducal home and now brought into action in very different surroundings. But being the lover of the singer who was to create the principal role in the author's new piece, he felt that the latter was a person of importance, and proceeded more than once to ask whether he wouldn't make a few changes in the song she was to sing in the first act. But what, he explained, had chiefly excited his admiration was her intelligence, maintaining that it would be impossible to find its equal in the world of Society, where according to him people did nothing, read nothing, and talked only of clothes. It was all so different, he said, with actors, writers and journalists, who thought, worked, and had more to occupy their minds than the trivialities of dress. His mistress to be sure was superbly turned out, but to that he seemed to attach no importance, and this attitude of his appealed enormously to the shabby but intelligent persons with whom he had to deal, since they could feel comfortably sure that he did not look down on them. It also caused him an occasional disappointment, as when he had been introduced to Loti and heard the great man say that nothing was more important than to be well dressed, that he really cared for nothing but horses, and positively loathed reading. The young Count could not understand how a man of intelligence could talk like that, and had let it be generally known that he thought the writer was much overrated. He almost feared that Loti had been making fun of him. Jean had been told that the Director was "on stage" (the Thursday *matinée* was in progress) and discovered in fact that he was none other than the young author's "friend" (the author's name being Daltozzi). He gave a shake of the hand to the Count, whom he had once met at the Réveillons and was to meet again some years later when that young man, having been married off by his family to a niece of the Rochefoucaulds, had broken finally with the diva, and was constantly to be seen at dinner-parties where he was scarcely recognizable as the same person, since he had renounced (like an advocate who has for a brief moment wanted to be a writer, and wonders how he can possibly have been for almost two years in a state of mind conducive to literary composition) the company of singers and intellectuals, though he seemed not to be unduly depressed by the change.

Daltozzi explained to Jean that the Director was in his office. Jean therefore made his way to the ante-room which looked on to the Place Notre-Dame. Glancing out of the window he could see the Cathedral bathed in golden sunlight, and between its two towers a patch of deep blue sky which seemed to be smiling at him with indescribable sweetness. The floor, too, was getting more than its fair share of the sunlight which reached as far as the door into the office, where an usher was waiting for the Director's summons to show in a man who was pressing hard upon his heels.

But the lovely sun now flooding the Place and ante-room seemed not to have enveloped in its glory the young man in question, who was in attendance with other applicants for an audition on which his whole future depended, and had doubtless spent his last farthing on the purchase of the patent-leather shoes which he was now wearing. Jean remembered how he had once been to a reception given by the Duc de Réveillon without bothering to put on patent-leather shoes, and reflected how tyrannical a power can be wielded by some stranger who holds our destiny in his hands, and how it can completely change our habits. At the very moment when the young singer should have been shown in, the Director, having just received the card brought by Jean from the Duke, came affably forward with a complete disregard of the other waiting visitors and instructed the usher to announce that he would be seeing nobody else that day. Alas! such news meant another sleepless night, and another shilling spent on a barber next morning. The young man, now plunged in gloom, left the theatre and walked across the sun-drenched Place on which he cast a sharp, black shadow unable to think of anything except his own anxieties, for care causes unhappiness, as illness causes bodily discomfort, so that a man with fever finds that his teeth are chattering in the hot sun, and another with a load of misery sheds tears when all around him people are rejoicing, since it is within ourselves that we carry both our joy and wretchedness.

But the sun continued to shine and to penetrate everywhere. Even in Notre-Dame, in that vast and shadowed immensity, after first passing through innumerable panes of azure and blood-red which should have kept it out for ever, a trickle of sun had forced an entry and was now resting gaily on the grey stone of a pillar, while between the pillars of the aisles at this time of the day almost deserted, in the midst of a stretching wilderness of flagstones, here and there a woman could be seen kneeling motionless for minutes on end.

*

It was the month of the year when as the result of a far lovelier miracle than the sweating stones or bleeding statues of Antiquity, little bushes were showing on their black and rugous branches a scented foam of lilac bloom which when Jean sat with a book secluded in a clump of trees within the Park at Etreuilles, where all nature smiled, would spread about him so sweet a fragrance that he stopped reading for a while to breathe it in, feeling so intoxicated that he shook his head, faintly panting, as might one who has tasted a sweet madness on his mistress's lips, while a small and lonely cloud, anchored in mid-heaven, leaving behind it a covey of its fellows, looking for all the world like the white sails of fishing-smacks, changed its position with easy speed, though all the world seemed motionless. In the tiny drawing-room, from which the aged Madame X no longer stirred, at either end of the sideboard in their china vases the stalks of cineraria would be putting forth their stars of a deep and velvety red which, destined to fade each autumn, assumed their buds again when spring came round. Even in Paris, those whose hearts were not closed against the gladness of the sun by dark and gloomy thoughts, could feel its blessed influence. "Lovely weather for the harvest," the footman had said with an enthusiasm in which the harvest—which he never saw—played a far less prominent part than he supposed. "Lovely day for a walk," the barber had said, though his air of happiness, and the way he glanced from time to time through the shop-window at the sunny boulevard, could have owed little to the joys of walking, since he would spend the whole of every day in shaving chins and cutting hair.

Jean, after leaving the Director of the Opéra-Comique, hurried back to the Palais de Justice, where he arrived in time to hear the evidence of Paul Meyer, Giry, and Molinier. Whether it was Monsieur Pinard telling the Court that Doctor Laporte, whom they had been branding as a villain, had performed a remarkable operation, or Monsieur Meyer declaring to the civil and military authorities, who looked on Dreyfus as the worst of traitors, that he could not have written the memorandum on the strength of which he had been convicted, or even Monsieur Chambereaud stating that in his opinion the decree on which the whole political life of France seemed to be resting, ought to be contested, it was with a strong emotion of pleasure that he heard these remarkable and courageous words coming from the lips of men of science who on a point of professional honour had come to the Court to tell the truth, a truth with which they were concerned simply and solely because it was something they had been taught to cherish in the conduct of their art, without bothering about whether they might displease those who saw it in an entirely different light, forming part of a general body of considerations with which they had nothing to do. The doctor who is looking after a young man will not let him go out until he is truly cured, no matter how anxious the Law may be to arrest him, or the

military powers to lay hands on him for service. As soon as his devotion
to the true interests of his profession, which is all that matters to him, is
involved, he sets his face against letting his patient leave his room,
energetically supports the young man's claim to immunity, and feels
nothing but hostility towards the Law, whether civil or military, and
the authorities who, thinking only of their own interest in the matter,
are wholly unconcerned with truth. "His right lung is congested, and
he still has a high degree of fever in spite of the quinine I have given
him." In just such a way did Monsieur Paul Meyer who, till that
moment, had probably never bothered his head about Zola, who
would never have dreamed of going out of his way to do anything for
him, who might even be in private life an intimate friend of the War
Minister, was now prepared to defend Zola with eager sympathy,
once he had realized that the man was in the right and under great
pressure from the Bench, and to all the arguments of the military, was
prepared to oppose a number of assertions about downstrokes and
upstrokes and curves, all leading to a definite statement which took the
form of saying, "I am willing to state on oath that this cannot possibly
be Dreyfus's handwriting." It was thrilling to hear such things said
because one felt that they were simply the outcome of a train of
reasoning conducted on scientific lines, and had nothing to do with
mere opinion about the rights and wrongs of the case, so that one felt
in them the presence of a certain sort of sincerity, the only true sincerity, because where mere opinion is concerned sincerity can never
be anything but artlessness. Here however one could feel with delight
how wide a gap existed between the opinion which the Government,
and the majority of his colleagues expected Monsieur Paul Meyer to
give, and his true opinion, and that truth was really something which
existed in itself and had nothing to do with opinion, that the truth
to which a man of science owes his loyalty is determined by a series of
conditions which are brought about, not by social prejudices—no
matter how fine and noble—but by the very nature of things. Any
man whose profession it is to seek the truth that lies concealed in handwriting or in the human intestines is in some sort ruthless. The
generals, the judges, might be present in all the splendour of uniforms
and robes. No matter, he would speak to them of what he knew, and
one could feel quite certain that he would not go back on his words
because like the doctor who has assumed the role of protector and
friend to his patient—a man suffering from congestion of the lungs

must not be allowed to go out—he would defend Zola to the best of his ability, and all those others about whom he cared very little but was now going to champion with heat and determination, not because he liked them, but because the handwriting produced by the Court was quite certainly *not* Dreyfus's.

We develop a fondness for people like that, who are as a rule rather cheerful folk, because their views are based on accurate reasoning, whereas the opinions of others are influenced by their feelings and can therefore he overborn, while the former cannot, the more cheerful because they are speaking of matters in which they are deeply versed, and know much more about than anybody else, so that should anybody dare to oppose their conclusions they will take the greatest pleasure in arguing with him, which is always an exercise productive of cheerfulness for those who are in the stronger position and better equipped to uphold a discussion. Such men are ready to quarrel with ministers who may up till yesterday have been their friends. The form that their opinion will take cannot be assumed beforehand on the grounds of friendship, social environment, or general outlook. Monsieur Meyer might be the friend of General Billot, but that fact would not lead him to modify his statement by a single word if by so doing he would have to undermine the argument he had built up. No matter whether he detested Zola's books, spoke of him with contempt, or, being deeply religious, regarded him with horror: circumstances being what they were, he would shake him cordially by the hand, fetch him food during the adjournment, laugh and chat with him, and discuss the line he would pursue. And the more such men's opinions may differ from what we had been led to expect, the more delightedly do we feel that Science is something wholly divorced from every other human and political activity. If among the signatories of the protest in *l'Aurore* we see the name of an illustrious advocate, who is known to be a monarchist and a Christian, the emotion we feel is the more intense, because by reason of this deviation in his behaviour, we are made to see what truth really is. It is a pleasure too—and a very great pleasure—to find ourselves confronted by a certain form of courage, a certain air of intellectual freedom, in such men who by a word can justify opinions which we ourselves should have liked to express, but have rejected because, in our constant effort to be sincere (I am talking now of natures like Jean's) we feel that we ought not to rely on our own opinions and range ourselves on the side of those whose opinions are the least favourable to our own attitude. If we happen to be Jews, we make a point of trying to understand the anti-Semite point of view: if believers in Dreyfus, we try to see precisely why it was that the jury found against Zola, and the civil authorities cast a slur on the good name of the Scheurer-Kestners. It comes to us therefore as a pleasurable shock to be able to enthrone henceforward an idea previously expelled and humiliated because we lacked respect for what we genuinely felt, when we read a letter written by Monsieur Boutroux in which he states that anti-Semitism is abominable, and that Jews are just as good as Christians, hear Monsieur Bertrand say that if the juries had had any breadth of vision at all they would have acquitted Zola, or Monsieur Manau publicly pay tribute to the Scheurer-Kestners and the Trarieux.

8. *The Affair and "The Figaro"*

While the *Cour de Cassation* was reaching a decision about allowing a revision of the Dreyfus case, the inquiry instituted by the Criminal Court upon which it would have to pronounce was the subject of daily articles in the *Figaro*. Actually, the only point at issue in this inquiry can be summed up as follows: should Dreyfus be kept on Devil's Island, or should he be condemned a second time—to death? Would General de Boisdeffre find himself obliged to blow out his brains, would Colonel Paty de Clam have to flee abroad and never again see any of the persons whose friendship and consideration had assured him of what is usually described as "an enviable existence"? Was Colonel Picquart, who had already spent a year in confinement, to be brought before a Court-Martial which might sentence him to twenty years hard labour—which would mean that he would never be free again, and would never have any real life before he was sixty-five?

But it was in a quite different mood that the course of the inquiry was followed by all who wished to see Dreyfus set at liberty *if* he were innocent, Picquart freed, and no harm come to Paty de Clam or General de Boisdeffre. This had little, if anything, to do with the practical consequences of the inquiry, the replies made by the witnesses, and the effect they might have upon the President. It was nothing but a deep satisfaction which found expression each evening on thousands of faces when their owners went to bed, wondering happily to themselves whether there would be anything thrilling in the *Figaro* when it was brought up on the morning tray as fresh and crisp as the *croissant* beside it, and no less subtly flavoured. For it was some of the most famous generals in the land who were commenting daily on this most exciting of cases, for which reason what they had to say was just as comforting, just as salutary, as the steaming bowl of *café-au-lait* which must be sipped in leisurely fashion while the day's news was being absorbed during the process, because no one can drink without pausing, or read without a break while nourishment is being taken. What can there be better than a good mouthful of really hot and

generously sugared coffee to give a relish of anticipation to the
reading of the latest instalment of Monsieur Bertulus's revelations,
the sections of which, so far published, had been little more than
introductory to the matter in hand? To be strictly accurate, this
curiosity on the part of the public was never quite so lively on
waking as on going to bed, when there was always the pleasing
prospect of something really interesting next morning. We may
draw the curtains on a star-spangled sky when we go to bed, only
to be roused next day by the sound of rain, and it very often happens
that our moods are as changeable as the weather. We remember
clearly enough how we were thinking of this or that just before drifting
into sleep, but that memory was little more than a catalogue of our
thoughts. The ones we regard as more than usually striking, the ones
which tempt us to take up our pen and write, the ones which seem
urgent enough to keep us from all extraneous pleasures so that we
may remain absorbed in them—those we can no longer recover, nor
is there any especial beauty in what we remember to rejoice our
hearts. Consequently, we have no appetite for our *croissants* nor any
curiosity about what the *Figaro* may contain. But the coming of
coffee renews the curiosity we felt in those days, a curiosity which
stretched itself and awoke again. If anybody came in and took the *Figaro*
from us, we felt distinctly annoyed. We could quite happily read it for
hours on end. "It's really quite frightful how much there is in the
papers just now: it's a positive labour to get through them!" But,
however great the labour, we would not willingly allow anybody else
to take it over. And so conscious were we of the satisfaction which
reading the papers gave us, that for, "I only wish this business could be
settled once and for all: it's getting too much of a good thing!" we
substituted, "When it's all over, what on earth will there be to do?" a
remark which, if it comes to that, was not very much more original.

Reading the papers at that time was all the more entertaining because
the fact that it was entertaining was a little something extra thrown
in for good weight. Those who did the reading were not conscious
of deliberately looking for pleasure—which would have made the
exercise more exacting—but had their minds set on finding the solution
to a puzzle, or embarking on a course of study, even if they did skip the
"more technical parts of the argument". Besides even those who were
not on the side of the Army, found the thoughts and actions of the
military more interesting than anything else could have been. We

know what the skilled orator or the man of letters will have to say, but find in the utterances of an intelligent soldier something quite new, something we have never come across before, so that his revelations have the power to give us a new sort of thrill, which depends less on the mere gifts of words. It is exciting to know too how these men, whose lives are ordered in a hierarchic pattern, behave when they are together, who must at times talk to one another like ordinary mortals, when they are not giving orders, or standing to attention, or saluting. These are, all of them, things that, now and again, we see them doing, but what we want to know is what their opinions may be about the things which we too are called upon to judge, how they speak about them between themselves, whether at times there may be a clash of views between a senior and his subordinates, and, if so, how they are expressed. For in those days we constantly had before our eyes men who, even though they might be disguised as civilians, were actually other than what they seemed and, like the gods who took on human form, were indubitably "soldiers in civvies". The man with the piercing eyes, whom we might see passing by on a Sunday morning, was, we felt sure, in spite of his neat suit, preoccupied with the problems of his military duties: he would walk more quickly, and was not merely somebody in a short jacket, with a tie round his neck and a hat on his head. We were continually conscious of the trained body of the military man beneath the civilian jacket. We saw these men in our daily to and fro. But we knew nothing of what they were thinking, of what they would say. Their intelligence found expression in silent actions about which we could only guess. The lives they lived together was a closed book to us. We are not interested in knowing what just any two generals or two dukes have to say to one another. But to know how General de Boisdeffre spoke to Paty de Clam was to get a glimpse, however partial, into a new and unexplored world of the imagination.

9. *The Truth of the Matter*

After dinner, when by a chance arrangement of chairs, everyone was grouped round General T, and the Comte de T having said, "It really is extraordinary that here in France for four whole years, people could go on thinking that Dreyfus was guilty and Esterhazy innocent— Esterhazy of all men!—but of course, General, you were at the Foreign Office when the Dreyfus affair was being wound up?" And the General replied "I was, and I can tell you this, that though I do not believe that Dreyfus was guilty, I am quite certain that Esterhazy wasn't." All those present turned sharply to look at the individual who had just made so extraordinary a statement. "What on earth do you mean?" broke in the Count, whose conviction was based on reason; and it must be admitted that in comparison with the absurd credulity of those who had held that Dreyfus was a traitor, the guilt of Esterhazy seemed certain, that is to say, a definite and obvious fact, arrived at by men unswayed by prejudice, men of intelligence, who based their conclusions on indubitable evidence. But the essential nature of history, what gives it a special and slightly equivocal charm, what makes it different from the merely topical, is that it never derives its authority from appearances, what makes it differ too from truth—which is an outcome of reasoning—because it is not a deductive process and hovers between truth and appearance, what makes of it something which is never to be found readily to hand, nor in the brain of the man of genius nearly so often as in that of the blear-eyed and experienced diplomat —can always demolish such certainties. This however was not the opinion of the Comte de T, who here interrupted the conversation to say—"But what about the famous memorandum, then?"—"The memorandum was not written by Esterhazy: the handwriting had been copied."

The Count smiled and shrugged. This was precisely the argument which had been advanced by stupid and prejudiced men at the time of the trial. "But if Dreyfus had imitated Esterhazy's writing, he would have accused him at the time of the first trial. The only point in imitating somebody's handwriting is to turn the evidence based upon it to one's own advantage." – "Yes," said the General, "provided one is caught. But suppose one isn't?" – "But Dreyfus was caught." – "I've already told you," said the General, "that I always believed Dreyfus to be innocent" (for those who are used to having importance attached to their words, invariably say—"As I said, my considered opinion was that . . .")–"You mean that the guilty party was neither Dreyfus *nor* Esterhazy, is that it?" said the Count, who had never considered this possibility which in fact made hay of his argument. "Yes," said the General. "Then who was it?" asked the Count. "That's a question which I am afraid I can't answer," said the General. "It was somebody pretty well known," he went on, "and if, in a year or two from now we meet again, I will give you his name. But don't try to find out, because you won't be able to. He has never been mentioned in connexion with the Affair, and only I, and the Duc de X, who was President of the Council in the government under which I served as War Minister, know it. Unfortunately, it came to our knowledge too late for us to do anything."

The moment was charged with interest. An immaterial presence seemed to be hovering about the room which might be described as the truth of historic fact, a something not often noticeable except when two or three persons are gathered round a table talking of matters in which they have been directly concerned. When that happens, the faces of those present assume a serious and definite expression, as though they have, in some sort, become witnesses at the Bar of History. "But what about Picquart?" exclaimed the Count. "There must have been some mistake about him. It is quite impossible that he should have written that express-letter, or that he should, for a single moment, have intended to inculpate Esterhazy on trumped-up evidence, for that would have been a villainous act on his part, and I have always been given to understand that he was a hero. His conduct, when faced by persons prompted by personal interest, was unswervingly dictated by conscientious motives." – "I doubt whether the truth about that letter will ever be known," said the General. "My own feeling is that it *was* written by Picquart. Still, you have every reason to admire him." Then very solemnly he uttered the following words, for he was a highly intelligent and great-hearted man to whom we owe two first-rate novels—*Coeur et Volonté* and *Vers l'Ile des Mouettes*. "If he was chivvied by the soldiers, the public, and the newspapers to the point of becoming something of a martyr, it was not because of his failings, but because with no thought for himself, he was striving to establish something which was contrary to the interests of some and the scheming of others. He really did act simply and solely from a love of truth, and I am quite sure that he felt as sure of Esterhazy's guilt as of Dreyfus's innocence. But having to fight against the forces of calumny, lying, and self-interest, he thought he could support his belief in the eyes of the world by producing a piece of evidence identical with many other pieces of evidence which must have existed. We should remember that his testimony, so far as Esterhazy was concerned, was not damning, but merely set out to prove what he needed to prove—that Esterhazy had been in touch with Schwartzkoppen—a fact of which he was absolutely certain. I would even go so far as to maintain that at a later stage he concocted other pieces of evidence in order to ruin Paty, whom he loathed. He wanted his revenge, for he had his share of human passions, and would often go red in the face and speak very bitterly about certain persons when their names cropped up in conversation. No doubt he was driven to perjure himself when he was asked whether the express-letter was sent by him, and said no, it wasn't. But to have admitted the truth of the charge before a prejudiced crowd out for blood, would have been tantamount to saying, 'Yes, I *am* what everybody believes me to be, a forger. I wanted to ruin Esterhazy, though I was not convinced of his guilt. I am a complete rotter, with only myself to thank for what has happened.' But if he had said that, he would have been guilty of a far worse lie than when he said that he had not sent the letter. Because, don't you see, in going against his own interests, he acted only for the best. He was convinced of Dreyfus's innocence, and it was only when he realized how superior he was to those surrounding him, that he thought he could do what he did do. He had a remarkable intelligence and was proud of it. The vanity of the self-made man was the only egotistical thing about him, and it was naturally enough that vanity which led him to do wrong. He wanted, instead of being taxed with being a dreamer and a muddle-headed fool, to prove the truth of what he had said, to produce evidence of which a man of his quality had no need. But no man is wholly without blemish, and he was a very great man. His behaviour was dictated by disinterested motives, and it is only right that he should have awakened the conscience of a large section of the French people."

Monsieur Xiron glanced at his wife out of the corner of his eye, for he was delighted to think that his house should have been honoured by so many interesting revelations. It was as though he were saying to her, "We really do gather the most fascinating people round us, and there's no denying that we produce the most delicious fare for our guests." At this moment the butler came in with glasses. Madame X, looking distinctly annoyed, motioned to him to leave the room, just to show what a good hostess she was, as when somebody is singing. Then she made as though to take some orangeade to the General, wishing in that way to express her gratitude, so that he might not have to move but could continue to charm her guests. But the General rose from his chair and said, "Please don't put yourself out, Madame: let us all go and drink orangeade in the dining-room," condescending thus to play his part in the affairs of the household, knowing as does every great man how to give pleasure, much as he might have done by taking the children on his knee.

VI

1. *Monsieur and Madame Sauvalgue*

One day Madame Santeuil happened to meet the Sauvalgues, a couple for whom she had always had a great liking, and asked them to dinner for the following week. But they could not accept, having arranged to start on the very date she had fixed for Begmeil, a small seaside place in Brittany of which Madame Santeuil had in fact heard tell. According to the Sauvalgues it was the most enchanting spot imaginable. The general view in their circle was that they had "discovered" it, and they certainly lost no opportunity of recommending all their friends to go there. They had bought a small property in the neighbourhood, of which they spoke to Madame Santeuil with the greatest enthusiasm, maintaining that nowhere in the world could you find a stretch of country to equal it. One felt that their life's happiness—if it comes to that, one's life's happiness does quite often choose for its dwelling a quiet valley running down to a sea which in the evening light looks like a rainbow-tinted mist—one felt that their life's happiness was quite literally to be found in that particular place. Monsieur Sauvalgue had refused a diplomatic post for no better reason than that it would have made it impossible for him to pass long periods at Begmeil. Though he was in receipt of a very good salary, he and his wife still occupied a fifth-floor apartment in Paris, with only one servant, but thought nothing of travelling four hundred miles in order to spend two days at Begmeil—for Monsieur Sauvalgues could count on two free days in each week—where at Bec-dog he kept a boat, a carriage, and a saddle-horse on which he would go riding over the moors where all day long the furze and heather had the colour of a rich sunset.

"Why not come and see it? We'll take you for long walks, you can go fishing, and at night you'll sleep like a log!" Whatever the place in which we live a healthy, happy life, we like to think that it holds the secret of physical fitness and a very special beauty. "Just you wait until you get a sniff of the air! You won't find any difficulty in breathing *there*, you can take my word for that!" But alas breathing depends on more things than air. Nevertheless, Jean felt a very lively desire to be introduced to a stretch of country about which Monsieur Sauvalgue was so eloquent, and was only too ready to believe that at Begmeil he would be rid of all his ailments, that it was a land of beauty quite outside the range of common-or-garden experience. He had often met men for whom happiness resided in one especial countryside whither they returned each year to recover their strength, their gaiety, their inspiration; some place in which they had left these things behind them, to await, but never for too long, the moment of renewal. Such men had often pleased him by reason of a sort of innocence which was the product of detachment from their ordinary ambitions. He felt that the possession of a carriage or a box at the Opera would leave them completely indifferent. Almost certainly they were no less susceptible to the opinion of their neighbours than are most people, and as most people do, enjoyed the feeling that they were pre-eminent in something —as is the lawyer whom important persons go to consult, the workman in his shop, the actor when he is alone upon the stage and knows that many eminent people are in the audience because they have seen his name on the bills, the diplomat who treats as an equal with foreign royalties, or the civil servant who has a respectful staff ready to welcome him when he arrives at his office, to whom the Minister writes twice every week letters, which, though naturally not in his own hand, are delivered by a uniformed messenger, or the author whose work, though he may be completely unrecognized, does express something of his personality.

2. *Jean at Begmeil:*
He Telephones to his Mother

The moment of departure had come. Jean, leaving Réveillon in the hall, kept going back to ask irritably whether his suitcase was ready. "It's really too ridiculous," Madame Santeuil answered in a loud voice "why couldn't you say sooner what time you were leaving?" The door was open, and Jean, feeling quite sure that Réveillon had heard, and seeing his bag all strapped and ready, deposited a casual kiss on his mother's cheek, to which haste and ill-temper had imparted an unpleasant flush. Some hours later, in the Hotel des Roches-Noires at Begmeil, he went upstairs to the room whither his luggage had preceded him. When he reached the strange landing he was suddenly overcome by a feeling that his mother was very far away. In the hollow of his chest a faint but immense palpitation, like the distant incessant pounding of the sea, had begun. Was it produced by thoughts, desires, fears, anxieties, and impulses which till then had grown up in the shelter of his mother's wing, which he had brought with him over this tremendous distance, which now, feeling themselves lost and abandoned, were leaping within him, as though trying to force their way out, frightened and desperate, in a sudden onset of mad terror at finding that they lacked the strength to make good their escape, a tumultuous but feeble host, as childish and tender as a brood of tiny gull-chicks flung into the sea out of sight of land, screaming, flapping their powerless wings in vain, calling to their mother who could not hear them, feeling their hearts leap towards her while they, unable to move quickly enough, could never hope to reach her?

At the far end of the corridor, which was brightly lit by many windows, where there was a strange air of gaiety which made his heart ache, he was brought up short by the hotel servant. This was his room. Hearing the words, he gave a start, suddenly seized by a desire to recoil a step or two, like a condemned prisoner at the very moment that he is being pushed into his cell. In Paris, when he went to his room, no effort was called for. Habit waited for him there upon the threshold, ready to give him a gay welcome. The very spirit of friendship was in the spreading arms of his chair of which the wood, the stuffing and the silken fabric had lost much of their original nature from having become saturated with his weariness, warmed by his jollity, gently stricken by his sorrows. To them he had turned at times of unhappiness, them he had caressed when he had lolled in the self-confidence of joy. Like old family retainers who by long service have earned the right to be made privy to our secrets, and while seeming still as motionless, as sub-servient as ever, have in fact grown into sensitive, warm-hearted and responsive friends, Jean's bed and the curtains of his room had come to be creatures in his own image. The silence floating beneath the ceiling and reflected in the looking-glass, still carried the echo of Madame Santeuil's good-night words, or was on the tip-toe of antici-pation at the sound of her approaching footsteps when she came to pay one of her "little surprise visits", when seeing the ancient objects which still belonged to her, though out of respect for her son's independence she liked to make them feel that she had no further right to them, would say, "These have worn well" or, "Those are getting very shabby and ought to be seen to," giving to all the old and faithful servitors a warm sense of happiness which came of knowing that they were Monsieur Jean's though still to some extent dependent on Madame, a happiness greater than what the soldier feels when he is drawn up with his fellows ready to be inspected by the general, or invalids when the doctor comes to see them, or a young wife listening to the advice of her father who for her now is no more than her husband's father-in-law. And so it was that whenever Jean penetrated into the diffused climate of welcome which was the very essence of his room, he did in fact penetrate deep into himself or it would be truer to say that his room penetrated into him with all the living sympathy and sweetness of a familiar thing. Secure at such times in its solitude, he felt that his heart was richer, calmer and more vast than at others. But now as he opened the door of what had been called, as though in profanation of the past, as though to weigh him down at once with all the burden of a threaten-ing future "his room", when he saw ranged in a strange order, though apparently on nodding terms with one another, two chairs which had no words for him though they seemed to be engaged in mutual inter-course, and a looking-glass with an unresponsive surface which reflected the ironic grin of a marble washstand not yet adorned with towels—he remembered with a pang the towels set by Eugénie in *his* room, towels which came back every week from the laundry, rather more tattered but for that reason softer perhaps, and wiped away the coldness from his body when it was all agog to recover its lost warmth, while his mother from her chair smiled at him silently (he had just stopped her talking, feeling the water trickling in his ears, and saying, "I can't hear a word—just wait a moment")—he could not but feel that he had become diminished, hardened, sharpened to a point, the better to penetrate the world of all these foreign objects that had no fellow-feeling for him, to break the ranks of all these seemingly hostile forces, to cleave a road for himself into this compact, solid, frozen world.

No longer was it a question of going into his own room where friendliness like a river bore him up. On the contrary he had, hurt him though it might, to try to break through the ice, to force an entry. The palpitation of his heart, as it struggled to take wing towards his mother, had increased now, and seemed to be throbbing only just beneath his skin. It was cruel not to release the lost chicks, to keep them thus from running to their mother. But it was he who now endured this torture. He felt stifled in this prison. He went to the window. It was still light but dusk was beginning to fall, and it was impossible to see to any great distance in the street. In front of the grocer's a woman, feeling the coming on of twilight, had just got to her feet, and was carrying into the house the chair on which she had been sitting in the doorway. She vanished into the shop behind the jars of twisted barley-sugar which pressed their pinkish enamel against the glass walls, behind bundles of small brooms, into a smell that was almost certainly combined of paraffin, dried figs, and tablets of soap, the shape of which could be dimly guessed through the grease-paper in which they were wrapped. He was more than ever conscious that the strange, the unknown town, the deepening dark, would soon shut him in like a lamp-shade, far from his mother. His heart was beating violently, and turning from the window, he went towards the door. But, as he did so his eyes fell on the bed which until then he had not noticed, an enormous bed suffocating under a tester with hanging draperies on every side (they could not be opened, being firmly fixed to walls and ceiling) and a pink quilt which gave off a stuffy smell. He imagined himself lying there, unable to sleep, thinking of his mother, separated from her by the unresponsive blankets tucked too tightly round him, feeling the

ceaseless thumping of his heart in the silence of the night, the irrevoca-
bility of absence, the rigid stillness of repose, the agony of solitude and
sleeplessness. If the room was a prison, the bed was a tomb.

He rushed from the room, bumping into the hotel maids who like
gaolers were silently confirming his captivity by unpacking his bags,
hanging towels on the washstand, confronting him with evidences of
despair. For the last five minutes he had been saying to himself, 'I'll
leave: in three hours' time I shall be happy—oh, dear Mamma!' but
no, that would make her miserable, perhaps furious. 'I can't do it:
tomorrow, who knows?—I may feel calmer—tomorrow?—spend a
night here?—that is impossible! I must get away!' His heart was
thudding more and more violently, now with hope, now with
desperation. He felt that it was cruel of him thus to prolong its uncertainty, poised between life and death: but he lacked the courage to have
done with debate, to make the heroic choice. The thudding now had
grown precipitate: it seemed to be driving deep into his being. It made
him feel frightened. He laid a hand upon his heart, and for a moment
stood quite still. Each movement that he made increased the fury of its
wild beating. Then, the thought of escape flooded him with happiness,
and the frightened palpitation of his heart, responsive to this new
mood, changed to a movement of bounding happiness. "At what
time does the next train for Paris leave?" he asked. "There is no train,
Monsieur, until two in the morning."

*

It came over him then that he must send a telegram, must do something, no matter what, which would put him in immediate communication with his mother. "No need for that, Monsieur, we have a
telephone." A call was put through. The answer came at once. He
asked to speak to an upholsterer who lived in the house where their
apartment was. "Would you be so very kind as to have a message sent
to Madame Santeuil, asking her to come down? Her son wishes to
speak to her."—"Certainly." But fifteen minutes passed, and no ring
came. "I am afraid, Monsieur," said the *maître-d'hôtel*, "that there is
only one line to Paris. There has been a mistake, and another call has
been put through instead of yours. You may have to wait for some
considerable time." At once he conjured up a picture of his mother
putting through a call to him, not understanding why he did not

answer (for she must have come downstairs at once, and have been already for some time at the instrument). If only he could explain to her what had happened, say to her, "Mamma, be patient!" If at last he did get through, she would have gone away, tired of waiting, and—this especially—disappointed (she must have gone downstairs in such a hurry to get to the telephone, must have been feeling so happy, as happy almost as if she had been told, "Master Jean has come back," happier, because she would not have had the annoyance of knowing that he had left Begmeil). He began to panic. He felt worn out with waiting, and set himself deliberately to sharpen his feeling of disappointment by letting his mind dwell upon it, to enjoy the bitterness of knowing that he had been deposited here alone without her, four hundred miles away, when all the time she might have been here with him. His anguish was the greater because all hope of speaking to her had vanished: he could not disturb their neighbour twice.

Then suddenly, so suddenly that the sound gave him a shock, the bell started to ring shrilly. It was as though it were running hither and thither in a great hurry. Quickly he put the receiver to his ear. He heard a man's voice, loud and harsh: "Is that Monsieur Santeuil?" Somebody, no doubt, was speaking on his mother's behalf while she was being brought down, all haste and uneasiness, to the instrument. A second voice spoke to him, also a man's, also loud and hard. Then, all of a sudden—as though everyone had left the room, and he were throwing himself into his mother's arms—he was aware, close beside him, gentle, fragile, delicate, so clear, so melting, like a tiny scrap of broken ice—of her voice. "Is that you, darling?" He felt that she was speaking to him for the first time, as he might have felt, after death, hearing her again in Paradise. He always listened attentively to what she said, but never before had he paid attention to the sound of her voice any more than he had paid attention to his own. But suddenly, hearing it in this way, just when he wanted, and least expected, to hear it, being prepared to be spoken to by a man, he was struck with amazement by the vast difference between those loud, hard voices, and this tiny morsel of broken ice, in which from behind a curtain of tears there flowed into his consciousness all the sorrows which had oppressed her over so many years and were still audible in this voice, suppressed sobs and moanings to which she had never given an outlet from a fear of causing pain to those she loved, but which were there all the same, hidden close by, like memories of the dead, in the familiar look of her room, within reach of her hand, in the drawers of her desk. But what chiefly struck, what most amazed, him after the men's voices, was to find in this particular voice, speaking to him over hundreds of miles, something with which, so it seemed to him, he had never come in contact anywhere, something he was now discovering for the first time—sweetness, a tiny scrap of the divine essence he had so often dreamed of, imagining it as quite different from what it was, mild and magnificent, as he heard it now in his ear, close by, like the proffered fragments of a broken heart.

At that moment it was possible to feel what Jean meant to his mother. Ever since he had grown up, ever since he had become some-body almost like his father and had been engaged in studies which she did not share, Madame Santeuil had adopted an attitude of humility towards her son. Compared with him she counted as nothing. In this tiny scrap of splintered voice could be heard the gift of a whole life, a gift which she had made to him, now and always, a tenderness which was meant for him alone, without a single fragment kept for herself. The voice was as pure as a tiny piece of ice, scarcely a voice at all. In it there sounded no strength, no pride, no egotism nor personal desire nor self-interest, nothing but sweetness, a supernatural sweetness which had been close to him, though he had not noticed it, which had seemed in no wise extraordinary, though now, caught suddenly between those other voices, it seemed to be hundreds of miles removed from them, a sweetness which broke and melted gently into his ear, into his heart. But the exigencies of life quickly resumed control of him. What should he say to her? They spoke to one another, and he no longer heard her voice, as, when living in her constant presence, he had ceased to be aware of her physical presence. She was just there. All the while that he was speaking to her of practical matters, he was saying to himself—'Mamma, Mamma, you are there: come closer so that I can give you a kiss: oh, it will be such a long time before I can kiss you again, Mamma darling, darling Mamma!' He realized that his mother was getting tired, and could no longer hear distinctly what it was she was saying to him . . . He rang off. It was over.

3. *Begmeil*

The signal station of Begmeil stands at the extremity of the peninsula. To the left it looks on to the Bay of Concarneau, on the right towards the ocean on the east, to the "Open sea" as it is called locally, to distinguish it from the Bay, though the Glénan Islands which one can see from it, break its full force, so that the waves die away on the beach as do the sleeping waters of the Bay. The peninsula is very fertile. It is covered by a great number of orchards belonging to a few small scattered farms, and the apple-trees with their load of red-cheeked fruit extend to the very edge of the slumbering waters of the Bay. There is a farm converted into a sort of hotel, where one dines in the open air under the apple-trees, through which one catches a glimpse of the sea, but it is frequented almost exclusively by painters who spend their time in boats, or go sketching in the vicinity. It is impossible for Parisians to buy any land, no matter how high a price they are prepared to pay, because the Breton farmers are rich, and since they live on next to nothing, buy frequently, but never sell, either because of a prejudice to which their age-old presence on the land has given the force of a sacrosanct tradition, or because they live in the illusory hope that their holdings may one day acquire a fabulous value. Millionaires have frequently offered five times its value for a small parcel of land, but always just as the contract was on the point of being signed, the owner has changed his mind, and asked double. You will find that a peasant who in the single room which his farm contains, shares with his serving-maid one of those old Breton beds resembling a cupboard, owns three-quarters of the surrounding countryside. In the lanes where at one end you can see the full sweep of the Bay, and at the other, the coastline of Concarneau, you will never meet a soul. The only sounds are those made by the quiet ebbing of the tide in the Bay, or the barking of farm dogs, and these sounds seems to serve as a pedestal for the profound silence, and to intensify it. The sea is always visible between the trees bordering the lane and the woods of the farther coast, cool-looking, and on overcast days, as grey as a fish among the leaves. When evening comes the warm dampness increases, and the smell of seaweed is drowned in the sharper fragrance of green apples on the trees, and of red windfalls at their feet.

*

Jean had spent some time in climbing a hollow road which lay on high ground between steep grass banks at the foot of which great trees thrust upwards. Their foliage was being turned to red by the quiet fires of autumn, which every evening the sinking sun caused to burn brightly. The wind had brought the leaves to the ground which was starred with the spoils of summer, glorious spoils at sight of which Jean was filled with feelings of delight. Here and there the trees ceased and a branch of one of the brambles growing on the banks rose high above the line of encroaching shadow, seemed as though burning gently in the light, like a vine shoot in a winter fire. A wind was blowing but so mildly that it could not drive the clouds across the sky or put the sun to flight. It was not so much a threat as a reminder that the last remnant of fine weather was passing, that the still superb enchanting days were fading in their prime. Through a break in the high bank he could see an orchard where the spaced trees, denuded of their leaves and retaining only a red roof of apples, cast slender shadows across the meadows lying pale in the sunlight. Farther off was the dense mass of a wood, framed within the high line of its tree-tops which had been pruned into the semblance of a bowl, and a ship looking as though it had been brought imperceptibly to a standstill, and was riding hove-to on the vivid blue solid brightness of the sea. The sun was sinking. Jean climbed more quickly and at last reached the church which was as solidly planted on its tract of ground as a country proprietor among his acres. Fine greensward lay on every side of it, and a sow with her young was running round in circles under the ancient oaks whose enormous trunks stood in two rows like the avenue of a park. He entered the vast darkness of the building where in summer it must be as cool and quiet as any woodland glade. Under the branching stonework to the right of the door was a Holy Water stoup, cold as a running stream, and roomy as a feeding-trough. Several small girls, clustered in a corner as though for a game, looked at him with astonished eyes. In the Choir a peasant woman was busy folding a winding-sheet as calmly as though she had been in her own shop. Over the whole of the interior there was an air of rustic elegance. Jean went out again and found himself among the graves behind the church. The pasture-land where cows were grazing side by side in the evening light, the woods, the houses and the roads, fell so steeply that he could see the whole of the horizon. In the distance, the fields looked pink and the woods blue. Above the line of the hills, touched by the same violet colour but in a lighter tone, huge almost pink clouds lay across the sky, crossed by wisps of grey. The sun had sunk and the wide immensity had lost its lovely glow though it still showed blue at the far ends of the woods and on the hills. Between the graves the breeze was ruffling the high grasses. The whole scene reminded him of the stretching distance he had seen a year ago from the terrace of Saint-Germain on a late October afternoon when the sun was veiled. He felt his heart expand like the wide horizon which gleamed where the light touched a tree, and now that the sun had ceased to shine, spread without break or limit its dark and tender melancholy.

*

The narrow peninsula, washed on the west by the open sea, and on the east by a bay with glimpses between apple-trees of the houses and the harbour on the farther coast, was a calm and secure refuge before which ships passed without calling, and boats full of life, which never came so close inshore as to be more than accents in the scene, though close enough to give to the solitary spectator a tremulous, deep-thrusting sense of detachment. In the evenings Jean reached the promontory by a path which led through bracken, furze and heather and circled the whole curve of the Bay, sheer above the cliff edge, like a grassy bank above a hollow lane. So narrow was the sea between the two coastlines that it seemed to stretch at his feet like a charming road along which the fishing-boats moved homewards to the nearby port in single file, looking for all the world like homing cows stopping now and again to take one final mouthful of sweet grass. Like some glorious news which beflagged windows and crowded streets, cheering crowds and solemn silences, all cry aloud in a thousand different yet similar voices at evening, before the dark has fully fallen on the sea where soon the sun will sink, the quivering blue and pink of the wet sands, the lively colours in the sky, the rich and changing tones of mother-of-pearl upon the surface of the bay, a flash of gold or a brilliant miniature of landscape caught in a cottage window, shone bright, and the houses on the opposite shore showed as red now at the day's end as in its dawning when they heralded the sun's fierce reign, trumpeting the muted echoes of the yet invisible but climbing orb, preparing the advent of its power and glory. At such an hour the loiterer quickens his pace and looks about him with delight, happy to see in all these glittering mirrors of the sun the message of its burning mystery. An hour later, blowing on the darkened woodlands' marshy verge, where the last of the daylight touches the rusty colour of burned bracken and dead thistles with a red streak at the entrance to the trees, filling the air with a strong smell of wet leaves, the sea-wind, with its chill fingers and salty tang, awakens in him a longing for home where he will find a bright fire burning, a lamp shining, and fish served for his meal, tasting as salt as the very sea which though shadowed now still gleams blue-grey as a mullet, mackerel or skate. A few slices of pinkish-brown cloud still loitering in the sky have the innocent and healthy colour of smoked ham. Late returned and chilly, a few brown smacks make for the harbour lights, their red sails bellying. Soon will come sleep in cupboard beds; the dark night filled with mysterious dreams, interrupted when the storm rattles the windows, will wake the sleepers, to soft half drowsy kisses, to arms encircling necks and legs held prisoner, kisses that make the silence deeper, when the wind keeps its hold upon the casement, fastens upon the roof-tiles, and sets the damper moaning, when a head is lifted from the pillow, though clasped arms remain unloosed, to listen to the noise which like an enemy is prowling round the house and tearing at the door, then plunges down again under the sheets, there to create a world of warmth and tenderness within, while all outside is cold and hostile.

*

The little church at Begmeil is built in the purest Norman style, though truth to tell its connexion with the Normans could not clearly be defined. It contains a number of admirable paintings by Moreau, including a *Descent from the Cross* (unsigned), which scarcely anybody knows about, for not all a painter's masterpieces stay in the same place. The church of Begmeil is the unknown grave of this particular canvas, which can rest there in its eternal sleep as peacefully as the dead whose names may be read on the flags before the church, catching the sun at the same hours as do they, feeling it flicker and go out at precisely the same moment when a cloud moves across the sky, exposed to the same winds—for the windows are often left open—and looked at occasionally by the same people who show to it the same respect as to the dead, respect in which there is no friendliness, no knowledge of their essential personalities. But a time will come when some enthusiast for Moreau's work will find these pictures out, and come to brood upon their sumptuous and silent tombs, eager to find in them the secret of the dead Master's life. For the works of men, when they have come to rest in one particular spot of nature, eventually grow to be part of it, so that it draws us by the spell of a half human personality, as the works themselves draw us by a sort of local charm, so that we love the pictures the more for having folded their blue and purple wings for ever in the little grey-stone church of Begmeil, where the calm Bay of Concarneau sees reflected in its waters the lovely fourteenth-century ramparts. It seems that the beauty of art can grow roots, can by degrees, become part and parcel of the place where it inhabits, a thing unique, not now dependent upon any man, something that we can never experience again unless we return to that one spot where first it came to us.

4. *Reading on the Beach*

After luncheon, which was a very generous meal, Jean and Henri would go with their books to lie among the low sand dunes which began at the western end of the beach. There they stretched themselves at ease, and sometimes lay for a long time without reading. In order to read without getting in one another's way, they settled down with a wide space between them and occasionally, thanks to the undulations of the dunes, remained out of sight, so that each felt isolated from all human beings, seeing above the sand only the sky, the sea and the ceaselessly flying gulls. When one had finished reading before the other, he would walk away and wander noiselessly, so as not to disturb his companion, though, truth to tell, when somebody has finished reading or working, what he chiefly feels is a desire to talk which makes him careless of another's absorbed attention. It was always the same book that Jean carried with him. Very soon it was the second volume, then the third. He had written to Paris for all the works of this particular author, as well as for information about his life, and Henri, without saying anything about it, had ordered a portrait of the author which would soon arrive.

Numerous are the books which have thus filled our lives with the thrill of pages still unknown, the charm of pages already familiar, concentrating about one single artist all our potentialities of love and interest, so that the succession of these writings gives to our life of the moment the varying aspects to be found in the existence of any energetic and ardent young man, who at first may have been absorbed by horse-riding, then having abandoned horses, by skating and later for a while by dancing and the social whirl, only to give these things up entirely and take to boating and sailing, both of them prominent occupations in the exclusive and rapidly changing enthusiasms of the very young. As life advances, tastes have a way of becoming more definitely fixed. A youth who has developed a liking for literature will be astonished when his mother reminds him that at fifteen he had a passion for mathematics, spent his money on optical instruments, and

wanted to enter the *École polytechnique*. The record of our lives as
grown men is less varied, and so little can we imagine a time when our
tastes were completely out of harmony with our present predilections,
that the earlier period takes on an almost legendary quality. We
cannot understand the enthusiasm we once had for a science which we
afterwards abandoned, for a companion whom we have never seen
since. But when our every interest is absorbed by things of the intellect,
all our most lively impressions, our curiosities and our desires, are
grouped around one single person and one single place. Our mother
smiles when she sees us making for the beach with always a volume of
Stevenson under our arm. She thinks us still a child, and in writing to
Paris for a life of Stevenson, for other books by him, for his portrait,
recaptures as we do the thrill of our childhood's tastes, and the possibility of once again giving us acceptable presents. When we were
young there was always one especial book which we carried with us
to the Park, and read with a passion which no other book could ever
quite supplant. In those days we were never so exclusively absorbed
by what the book had to tell us as to be uninfluenced by the actual feel
of the pages which we turned. Later on no doubt we should be enchanted to find in some manuscript, in some newspaper instalment, a
passage from George Eliot or from Emerson which we had not
previously seen. But in our younger days the book and what it contained made for us a single unity. We had seen little of books, and very
often the one we happened to be reading might be the only one of that
particular format that had come our way, the only one with that
particular soft, brown cover, those square, thin pages with large
margins, the smell which we never grew tired of sniffing. Its physical
enchantment was one with the story that we loved, with the pleasure
it gave us when in the shady arbours of the Park, hidden away so as not
to be interrupted, or on rainy days waiting for lunch beside the fire in the
dining-room, bothered by the cook who, with the excuse of making
us more comfortable, kept on constantly disturbing us, holding it in
our hands and looking at its pages, we never, in our mind, separated
its contents from the softness of its thin pages, from its lovely smell,
from the fine, stiff binding with the gilded corners, which contained it.
The thin pages with their wide margins on which here and there a date
had been scribbled, as in a note-book of the same shape, gave us a
feeling that we were imbibing instruction during those delicious hours,
and that the thrilling objects, from which we would not willingly have

been separated, was the very treasury of truth. I remember that smell as being just as sweet as the smell of the great press in which clean linen and pink biscuits were kept.

But before settling down to read during the long hours of digestion (except when one had all but come to the end of a novel, when one started to read at once so as to finish it before the day was over, and having closed the book, dared not admit the completeness of one's pleasure, either from a sense of shame at being, or from a desire to be, commiserated with, from a wish not to appear too happy, a fear that too close an examination, over-much discussion, might cause that pleasure to evaporate) the two young men would lie for long periods trying to sleep, exchanging remarks at rare intervals, smoking, turning their faces this way and that, looking at the sea or the sky, keeping the sun from their faces with spread handkerchiefs. We envy the boa-constrictor for whom digestion is a matter of long days. We envy the lizard who can spend hours upon a stone, letting the sunshine soak into him. We envy the whale who can go for long and lovely journeys in the Pacific, the seals who frolic in the sunlit ocean, the gulls who play with the storm and let themselves be swept along by the wind. For in the activity of our imagination we love food, sea and wind, since for us they represent sweetness and strength. It is only in the lives of animals that we can think of these things in their pure state filling the whole of life. But our enjoyment is greater than theirs during the hours when we lie in the sun digesting our food, looking at sky and sea, falling asleep with the cries of gulls in our ears, turning over on the sand to sleep again. For our empty minds and satisfied bodies seem, at such times, to be free from all worries. We enjoy them not only physically but in imagination too, the more so if we are persons to whom sleep comes but rarely and no less rarely, a process of digestion which absorbs the whole of our being, and includes the sight of the sea and the sky and the screaming of the gulls.

*

Soon came the moonlit nights. As they walked homewards the dark would be still complete, but in the garden close at hand they could see between the trees an enormous moon being heavily hoisted above the far horizon, spreading already a vague radiance on the tree-tops of the valley's farther side. By the time they went out again after dinner, it would be full moonlight. Then they could lie unseen by anybody, where the sand was all in shadow, and gaze upon the sea, and the moon's silver track. The sweetness and the marvel of such scenes strike even the most simple-minded when confronted by the spread of noon, and when night comes the vast, enormous, sable shadows, phenomena all of them of which Jean without success tried to attain a deeper knowledge, that of those hours he might find something to retain and treasure. He sought too with his bodily sensations to burrow into them. Eagerly we brood on the material realities of life, trying to force belief that they can give us—the sea, its inexhaustible strength, the wind, its force, the air, its purity. In that illusion do ailing folk seek out the wild places of the earth, where Nature's powers are greatest; and men too weary of thought, hoping to find there strength untouched by the weary traffic of the mind, in the blind sea and the deaf wind, in animals who do not think at all. But in the very midst of that unalterable calm, surrounded by the living strength of natural things, death and madness lies in wait and take them at the last. In vain we lean above that source of strength. We find but just sufficient air to breathe, but even that brings to our blood all the impurities of human lungs.

5. *Tempest at Penmarch*

One night—for the past two days there had been terrible tempest of wind and rain, and high seas more violent than had ever before been known in that tranquil bay—one night about three in the morning Jean, who had been fast asleep, lulled by the noise of the wind, though in his half-dreaming state he was conscious of the banging of shutters, the trembling chimney-stacks, and the moaning of trees which seemed every moment to be upon the point of crashing to the ground —was awakened by Ethel. Pierre was downstairs, she said, asking whether Monsieur Jean would like to go with him. He had promised to give him good warning should a great storm be raging at Penmarch, and now the moment had come. He at any rate must go, because men were needed for the lifeboat.

Jean was so snug in bed that he felt very much inclined to let the other go without him. He sent word for him to come up. "Will the storm be really terrific?"–"That it will. It's been a-working of itself up for the last three days. Even here it's blowing fit to bust: over at Penmarch there'll be something worth seeing, I give you *my* word!" Jean was still hesitating, not quite certain that the enterprise would be worth the effort. On the one hand it would be stupid not to see what he could; on the other it would be lovely to go on sleeping. He went to the window. By the light of the lamp which had been lit down-stairs he could see the road in front of the inn. The trees were in a torment, and the ground was littered with great branches which the wind was whirling about like straws. The feeling came to him that something very like the wind was dragging at him too—a craving to do unusual things in this fantastic weather. He hurried into his clothes. Ethel made him take a quantity of blankets. "But I don't feel cold," said Jean. "You just wait until you get there," Ethel replied. "Besides, you'll be drenched to the skin!"–"By the rain?"–"By the sea! This wind'll be blowing it more'n a mile inland. . . ." He wanted to take an umbrella. Ethel laughed: did he really think he'd be able to keep it open? After a while Pierre returned with a rope for lashing Jean should the wind grow too violent. The need for these unusual precautions, and the uselessness of all ordinary ones, made Jean wild with delight and strengthened his conviction that he was about to see unusual sights and do unusual things. It would have been wiser to wait for the dawn, because it was impossible to keep the lanterns from blowing out. But since the plan was to reach Penmarch before breakfast—and it was an eight-hour drive (five in Ethel's trap which went like the wind, but in weather like this they might well be held up by an accident) it was decided that they should start at once. Pierre and the horse knew the way blindfold. "Anyhow," said Pierre, "we shan't meet anything on the road—storm's too bad."–"Won't there be other people going to see it?" asked Jean. " 'Deed and there won't," said Ethel, "they'll be keeping snug between four walls, if only because 'tis mighty dangerous." This information fanned our hero's courage to a white heat, and he was anxious to know what precise danger they were likely to find. He didn't, he said, see how one could be swept away by the sea if one didn't go too near. "I'm sure I hope as *you* won't be," said Ethel, "and I'm sure 'nough you'll be safe: not but what such things *have* been known to happen. You talks of not going too close, as though the sea there is same as here. Don't you make no mistake: a cupful of wind can send a wave a-nosing of you out two hundred yards from the shore, where you'd think as you were safe enough. It could make short work o' you, my lad, and no mistake about it!"

Ethel supplied our hero with this information, not dreaming for a moment that it much increased his pleasure. Not for an empire would he have gone back to bed now! He was filled with pride, and laughed as he looked at himself in the glass, swaddled in all the blankets Ethel had given him. Everyone in the inn was up and about. Not a soul but had been roused by the sound of the trap. The maid-servant came in to ask whether Monsieur would like some hot milk. "Yes, but don't bring it up, Felicité: I'll have it downstairs in the kitchen with Pierre and Ethel."–"Better hurry then, they're down there now."–"D'you mean they've finished?"–"No, they've not started yet: I only said hurry as meaning if you want to have breakfast with 'em." Jean collected his things. "I'm going to Penmarch, you know, Felicité."–"So they just been and told me," she replied. "Say good-bye to me then, I mayn't come back!"–"Mebbe you won't: you'd not be the first as has rested his bones there! Why you wants to go off in weather like this beats me, when honest folk keep warm at home, and turn the key, seeing as the wind makes no bones about opening doors! Why must you choose a day like this'n such as no eye has seen for ten years past?"

'For ten years! and to think I might have stayed in bed!' said Jean to himself. His joy was at its peak. "But it was Pierre who came to fetch me, and he'll stick beside me all the time," said Jean knowing that Felicité entertained hard thoughts of Pierre's adventurous disposition and was for ever saying, "If I was that young man's father or mother, it's not to a fellow like Pierre I'd trust him: both of 'em mad as hatters, if you ask me!" Her only comment on Jean's latest piece of information was to say: "A fine chap to rely on! Why, even the old hands as stop at nothing agree as he'll come to a bad end. A fine thing, I must say, a-coming to fetch you! You'd a been a deal better off in bed. I'd 'ave made you a good breakfast, and you needn't 've got up to it, if so be you didn't feel inclined, and now I can't do nothing of the sort, just along o' you choosing this day for being brave and headstrong. You likes your comforts as well as another—which you won't find at Penmarch, nor food neither! Fine eaters they be, as don't even know how to serve up a fish decent!" Jean could have stayed indefinitely, listening to Felicité's eloquence, which though it might not persuade him, gave him great pleasure to hear: but by this time he had got all his things together and went downstairs to join Pierre and the fisherman who was going with them. He had expected to find them already seated at the table, but instead, ran into them on the stairs. "Have you finished?" he asked. "We ain't begun," replied the fisherman, "seeing as how we was waiting for you." Such consideration on the very threshold of so perilous an adventure, such delicacy on the part of so gallant a sea-dog, seemed to our hero to augur well for the expedition. He felt like flinging his arms round his companions' necks. They drank their piping hot *café-au-lait* in the kitchen, where Jean, seeing the range already lit, began again to wonder whether he might not have done better to stay where he was, eat his midday meal with the landlord, and take a pleasant walk round the Bay, instead of facing the unknown dangers which lay ahead, and renouncing for today—perhaps for ever—the joys of hot lobster for which he had never longed so eagerly as he did now when it was receding into the distance. But self-esteem and a sense of shame at having kept them waiting all for nothing drove him to maintain in the presence of his companions the devil-may-care attitude which he had assumed from the very first moment of the adventure being mooted, which had made him feel so highly pleased with himself.

"I think you ought to be thinking of getting a move on," said Ethel. "It's not far off five." Jean, seeing that the others had finished, made as though to swallow what remained of his coffee at a gulp, but Pierre checked him. "There's not that deal of hurry," he said, "you've plenty of time. But since you *have* finished, and seeing as how you've got all your things, I'll be bringing the horse round." – "Right!" said Jean, to whom these words sounded a solemn note. They packed themselves into the trap. Jean was afraid that he would not get used to the wind. But, "It's not all that strong," he said nonchalantly; less from a motive of pride, as because he wanted to respond to their kindliness with a show of good humour and courage. "Oh, certain sure, 'tis nothing hereabouts: we're sheltered in these parts: but just you wait until we're out upon the road, and, later on, at Penmarch: just you wait!" – "So long and enjoy yourselves," said the landlord, following them with his eyes for as long as the light from the kitchen could still reach them. 'He's staying,' thought Jean, 'perhaps he's made the wiser choice.'

Almost at once the horse was put into a gallop. Frequently the trap bumped over tree trunks in the road, and Jean felt convinced that all was over, that certainly he would be killed stone dead. The fisherman, seeing that there was danger of his falling out, since he did not know the right way of making himself secure, took a grip of his arm, and told him to do exactly as *he* was doing. Noticing too, that his hat would not keep on, he jammed his own beret on his head. From that moment, as ancient warriors, by eating their enemy's entrails and wearing his helmet, felt that his strength had entered into them, so Jean, sharing his companion's strength, was afraid no longer, but put his whole trust in him and in good fortune.

When the wind grew really too violent, they left the trap at Pont-Labbé and took the miniature train which runs between Pont-Labbé and Penmarch. Just as they were on the point of starting, Jean heard the guard telling a young man who had got in with his bicycle, that he must ride on the platform of the train, since it was a rule of the Company that bicycles must not be taken into the carriages. The young man thereupon whisked up his machine and installed himself on the platform.

It needed no more than a single glance to convince Jean that he was a person of high social status and great personal distinction. Though he could not be more than twenty-four or five, the serious expression in his greenish eyes gave to his profile an appearance of remarkable nobility. Jean had prevailed upon the two fishermen to go with him into a first-class compartment. It so happened that though the train was almost completely empty, there were in the carriage with them two ladies who no doubt had been caught by the storm while they were making a tour of Brittany, and were now running for shelter to some town. At once, in the really very beautiful young woman seated opposite to him, whose temperament, almost whose name, he could have described without more ado, in the flashing eyes which first she raised, and then let dwell upon Jean and the fishermen with an affectation of indifference and disdain obviously intended to give the lie to certain assumptions based on her quite obvious interest, and to provoke entirely different ones, in the way that at one moment she kept her lips gloomily puckered, and at others imparted lustre to them with the tip of a pink tongue, in her perfectly audible remarks, her stage whispers and her silences, in her habit of constantly opening her bags without any apparent reason, in the glances that she sent flickering over her fellow-travellers and then, that seeming not to be their chosen destination, moved about the carriage, finally bringing them to rest with an air of self-conscious dignity, in an expression of sulky haughtiness, he recognized a woman of easy virtue or an actress. But if the latter, then one whose name was utterly unknown; the sort of actress who is always being promised a part at the Opéra-Comique, a young woman in short who lives in the provinces with a rich man and when travelling, because she cannot openly explain that she knows Monsieur Carvalho, or has her own carriage in Rouen, makes it obvious by the careful arrogance of her expression, how furious she feels at not being able to deal out these pieces of information, by the care she takes to make it clear that though she is unable to provide such copper-bottomed references, she cares nothing for your opinion which she regards as beneath her notice, though her very effort in this direction makes it abundantly clear that she cares very much about your opinion, and is disappointed at not being able to enlighten you on the subject of herself.

But the person of humbler station by whom she was accompanied served only to increase Jean's bad impression of his *vis-a-vis*. The clown's face daubed with rouge, the hat, none of the feathers, flowers and ribbons of which sufficiently concealed a pair of shifty eyes; the almost criminal cast of countenance, the squalid texture of the reddish, mottled cheeks—all these things forced him to the conclusion that though now in her position of companion she was sharing in her employer's opulence, travelling in a first-class carriage, laughing at the least word the other let drop—even though only Jean was facing her —permitting herself to indulge in familiarities, hoping thereby to produce an impression, that in spite of all these things she could formerly have been no more than an upper servant in the service of a bawd, a trafficker in children, or a murderer's accomplice, unless it were that the extreme vulgarity of her breeding, combined with her appalling taste in clothes, gave a peculiarly repellent air to the comparative innocence of the paid companion who by the very nature of things could not at one time have been above suspicion of having been a tart. But perhaps she was simply an old friend of her actress neighbour, a superannuated professional, no longer able to find work and kept in tow by the other out of sheer kindness of heart, whose features a lifetime spent in playing endless parts in which they had had to show a never ending succession of ugly or meaningless emotions, had wiped clean of all personality, leaving them with nothing but that residue of the bestial, the smudged, the equivocal, which has a way of taking possession of mere faces which have nothing more to express. That often happens with people of the stage. Or perhaps it is fairer to say that a sediment of past expressions still marks them, the flashing eye, the grimacing mouth, and that it is these remnants which, no longer having any connexion with the circumstances of their lives, gives so unpleasant a look of falsity and exaggeration, which is made the more convincing by a mobility of the eyes, an excessive suppleness in the body, which while you are talking to them of quite ordinary things, continue, like a pianist's fingers moving ceaselessly even in sleep, and in some sort caricature that suppleness, that mobility which on the stage is the means of stressing for the audience a great variety of dramatic points.

Bearing all this in mind, Jean found a good deal of amusement in watching his two neighbours, who never missed an opportunity of opening their bags—only to shut them again immediately—of asking each other at what time they were due to reach this or that place, of audibly wondering whether there would be a carriage to meet them, as travellers always seem to be remembering good-byes which they have omitted to say, or some object placed in readiness on the table which is the one thing they have forgotten to pack. But this forgetfulness finds compensation in the relief they feel when on opening their bags, they see the very things they were so much afraid they had forgotten what only serves to bear out what they have always said that, "The one thing one really needs will turn out to be the one thing that has been omitted, you see if it doesn't," in the comfortable feeling that the carelessness is not irreparable, that one can always write to the manager of the hotel at Quimper, who in any case will probably have noticed the mislaid objects and sent them on. . . . They complained that the carriage was dirty, that there was a nasty smell. They were careful to put on their gloves again and to do everything in their power to underline the fact that they were delicately nurtured females. Jean could not resist the temptation to steal an occasional glance at the young bicyclist on the tiny platform, whose solemn gaze was fixed on the horizon, whose fine profile standing out in clear relief against the grey sky, looked chilled to the bone by the icy wind. 'How unfair it is,' he thought, 'that a young soldier so obviously well-born and distinguished, should have to stand out there in the teeth of a biting wind, while these two horrible creatures wrapped in warm furs sit comfortably in here, complaining endlessly about everything. How awful to think that he is probably ranking me with them in his mind, and assuming that I like them am regarding him with contempt.' Once or twice he made a trip to the platform so as to show the bicyclist, by sharing his lot, that he was not really contemptuous at all. Then he returned to his fishermen companions. He was just in time to hear one of the two ladies mention the name of the wife of the Danish ambassador, as though she were one of her friends. It never so much as occurred to him at the moment that this could be true. But suddenly he was so overcome by amazement that they should even know her name, should be aware of the high place she occupied in Society, should, tarts as they were, be so "smart" and so accurately informed as to employ this refined method of enhancing their own importance, that he began to wonder whether in fact he might not have made a mistake about them. 'Perhaps she once took part in a stage performance at the Danish Embassy,' he thought. But no, she couldn't be sufficiently well known to have done that. Those who are well known, no matter in how small a way, show in their manners a vague reflection of the people who know them, in the look that comes into their eyes at mention of the "famous" name, and this at once throws a revealing light on the degree of their reputation. But in this case the complete absence of any such reflection made it perfectly obvious that neither the good-looking lady nor her companion, had ever been regarded as important by anybody.

At Penmarch Jean and the fishermen left the train, and Jean was flabbergasted to see that the bicyclist also got out together with the two ladies. The high opinion which, till now, he had had of him sustained a rude shock. 'No doubt,' he told himself, 'he is the lover of the younger one. Heigho! into what company will sensuality lead a young man of good family! I see how it is. As the young woman's lover he has to play his part in the arrogant, pretentious, vulgar scenes of charlatanry with which she tries to dazzle the company she meets in hotels and railway carriages. If she makes a fool of herself by behaving with impertinence to some man who has snubbed her, he has to call him to account. It is part of his duty to take her part against theatrical managers who don't employ her, to make common cause with her in jealous quarrels with her professional colleagues, to be on terms of friendship with all the ill-bred actors who are in her good books, and entertain them to dinner. He has to laugh at her jokes and give her maid presents. No doubt she is in love with him, and he, from gratitude and habit, which in the long run strips the mask from our most hideous fellows so that we see in them only such purely human qualities as they may possess, has perhaps developed an attachment for her.'

But very soon, pressing with difficulty on the heels of his companions, walking along the road in the teeth of the gale, with blown spindrift stinging his face, he had completely forgotten the three strangers' faces, so that they assumed in his memory that state of immobility in which they had become fixed, in which he would see them again should something occur to recall them to him, though more likely than not he would never see them again. They had already become for him like those faces, whether grotesque or lovely, which we may happen to notice in some public place—a railway carriage or a packed omnibus, those true chariots of Thespis where we find it amusing as Jean had done a while back, to identify Isabella, the Pedant, Zerbinetta, seeing them in imagination with their make-up on, their features fixed in the grimaces of their parts, their tongues repeating the lines, though we know literally nothing about them, neither their true nature, nor even the character they may just have played, or are about to play, but whose costumes and "props"—in this case the furs, the feathered and beribboned hat of the pretty woman's maid—and masks, since nothing about them has any relationship with their true personalities—of which we know nothing, which is powerless to modify the view we have formed of them—occupy the whole of our attention, in which they assume a certain quality of the exaggerated, the detailed, the unchangeable, the opaque. In just such a way, in a corner of Jean's memory, where probably he would never seek them out, there now dwelt the grotesque "maid" with her glittering and shifty eyes under a crown of feathers, the sulky coquette trying so hard to look unconcerned, and farther off the young bicyclist with his fine profile and brooding eyes, standing so calmly in the wind upon his little platform.

*

At Penmarch Pierre and his fisherman friend learned that their journey had been quite unnecessary, because the lifeboat would not be launched —the conditions being such as to make any attempt to get her afloat impossible—and because all the local craft had been safe and sound in harbour since the storm first got up two days earlier. Two of them had foundered, and it was most improbable that any other ship would venture to sail past this stretch of coast until the weather improved. Nevertheless Pierre and the fisherman remained, explaining that they had brought with them a young gentleman who wanted to see the storm. At this moment in the dining-room where they were talking, the sun began to show instant by instant more golden, growing increasingly powerful, hotter, and more brilliant, shining like a lamp that has just been refilled with oil. The plates upon the table glittered.

An enchanting study of sunlight by Harrisson—given to the landlord as a parting present, in which affection and talent had combined to convey the local landscape to those who as yet did not know it, with all that could be revealed only by a continuous process of concentration and an intensity of sympathy which remained in the eye of the spectator as a memory long after he had ceased to look at it—was now touched by this same sun which, playing about the painted image of itself with a bright fondness, gave to the luminosity reproduced upon the canvas a quite indescribable brilliance. Even before the door was opened it was clear from the delicious smell which filled the room that the maid was just about to bring in breakfast. But for the noise of the wind as it set windows rattling, chimneys trembling and doors banging, and whistled ceaselessly about the house with a noise which, now that one no longer had to struggle against the blast, had become a monotonous accompaniment which the ear soon ceased to notice, one might have thought oneself to be, not in a doomed village sooner or

later to be engulfed by an intruding sea which in the meantime took a
monthly toll throughout the winter of human lives, but in some
peaceful refuge, where the charm of art smiled blissfully down on a
scene of good cheer, and the sun was sheltered from the wind. . . . Then
the bright radiance which had filled the room grew pale and vanished.
The sky by now had turned completely black. Jean looked at the
window-panes and saw that they were streaming. "It's raining," he said.
"Yes, and you'd better go down and take a look at the sea at once, if
you want to get back to Pont-Labbé (Begmeil would be quite out of
the question) before it's dark, because you'll have the wind in your
faces, and you'd do well to get under cover before it becomes too
violent."

Jean, Pierre and the fisherman hurried through their meal. It was in
bright sunshine that, linked together in order to offer greater resistance
to the wind, they walked up the street before turning into a path which
climbed to the cliff from which it was possible to get a view of the sea.
The violence of the weather was becoming every moment more
incredible. Objects flew through the air which the eye could not
distinguish so dizzying was their movement. Long before the sea came
in sight, and a good two miles from it, rough gusts of spume dashed
against their faces. It had started to rain again but of this they were not
conscious, because the drops did not fall but were swept forward by
the wind. They reached the summit of the cliff, where suddenly
entering the kingdom of the winds, from which so far they had been
protected by the hills, they were forced to crawl on hands and knees,
for the violence of the gale, far greater than anything they had as yet
experienced or expected, was such that it lifted them from their feet
and flung them to the ground a little farther on, where they clung to
the grass to keep themselves from being blown away, and dared not
raise their heads for fear of having the breath being beaten out of them.
Several minutes passed. Then while the other two remained prone, the
fisherman clambered to his knees, pulled his companions to theirs, and
all three crept and crawled backwards. Sheltered at last, they looked
around them. There, where Jean had thought to find violence and
vertiginous speed at their wildest, he saw as in the childhood of the
world after some battle of the Gods, chain after Alpine chain, a
succession of mountains, each assuming its predestined place, some
fresh peak momentarily rising high above them, all monstrous, all
calm, and between them valleys so deep and wide that from their

white, majestic heights, the figure of a man would have been invisible. At this moment the sun came out and touched with dazzling light the glacier peaks and the formidable cascades dashing down their sides with the noise of thunder. But it was as though all this were happening at the very heart of that deep calm which reigns upon the mountain-tops on the brink of vast crevasses. Like a party of unperturbed young men, the billows surged into the abyss, and climbed the mountain slopes, as a rule to the very top, whence their formidable roaring beat upon the ear.

6. Farewells

Jean went to say good-bye to the sea, after which he said good-bye to the landlord and to the maid, whom he asked to say good-bye for him to the ship's-boy, his so frequent guide who just now was out fishing. To all of them he said that he would return the following year, and perhaps stay longer. He had loved so many things too well, had devoted to their adoration every hour for two whole months, that he could not bear to think of so much fondness as effort wasted, and feel that all was over. Réveillon struggled hard to keep him from giving away all the money he had in his pocket, but could not stop him from leaving with the people of the farm more than a hundred francs. Repeatedly he told them that in less than six months he would be there again, and this he did in order to excuse the smallness of the gift, letting them suppose that the present sum was only a beginning of largess, and that each succeeding year would increase it.

But the same fate awaited these promises of return as so many similar ones. Little by little his affections were diverted to new friends, new places, and for precisely the same reason that at one particular moment they had grown attached to the little Bay of Concarneau, to the fishermen who brought part of their catch to him each morning, to the ship's-boy who took him in his boat at sundown, who knew his fear of jelly-fish and would change direction of his own accord when they ran into a shoal of the creatures, his liking for the sea and, unasked, would get the boat ready when the wind was in the right quarter for the bells, which on calm days could be heard ringing out from Concarneau, and bend to the oars that they might not arrive too late and then, when they had drawn close in to the shore, stop rowing and say nothing, sitting motionless, looking at the sea and perhaps too listening, not only till they ceased but letting his passenger hearken for long moments to the silence that followed all that sound of ringing, letting him look at the sky as the colours slowly faded, and sometimes when night fell, watch the moon rising until Jean gave him the word to row back, handing him unprompted the ink-bottle which was

stowed in the boat in case he might want to write: and next morning
Jean would ask him whether he had slept well after so late a return,
knowing all that he had done till darkness fell, having been with him
all that while, having himself received, if not the same impressions of
things at least an impression of the same things, aware of all his tastes,
of the state of his health, of his character, his pleasures, his appetite, his
successful fishing expeditions and his bad ones, his dreams, his silences.
They could share their thoughts, saying, "The weather is better today
than yesterday. Monsieur had fewer letters today than usual."

Often at the hour when others were sitting down to their evening
meal, Jean would send word to him, and he would get the boat ready.
Almost all the smacks returned to harbour at sunset, and now the sun
had almost vanished. They would start off. The sea far out was pink,
nearer in yellow, over there red, with the smooth and varnished look
of oil. The little waves broke on the beach in a flurry of bluish foam.
The boat as it glided, ruffled the rich colours of the sea, disturbing but
for an instant only the smooth surface which by the time they were a
few yards farther on, had already regained that air of peace it shared
with all the stretch of ocean. As on walks taken in a country where one
has been happy, one could breathe in something of the sweetness and
the thrill of memory. The moon rose white, then turned to gold, while
all the westward sky and sea were pink. Then the full darkness came,
the stars shone, and a track of silver showed upon the waters, widening
as it drew near the shore. They dropped their nets while the boat was
still moving forward. It grew cold. Then the boy covered Jean with a
blanket, and sometimes they would eat a snack. Here and there a
fishing-boat lay motionless in the midst of the sea, having hove-to for
the night. They would pass a late-homing craft which occasionally the
boy would know, though oftener not, and voices would call to Jean,
since it was he who was holding the net, "Good night and good fishing,"
as though he were a real fisherman, as in fact he was becoming. And
then, happy because that "Good night" had been addressed to him as
to a fellow-fisherman, very simply, because there was no one there to
hear him and he would probably never see again the man to whom he
called, there being nothing to ask of him, and all one knew of him was
that like oneself he was engaged in fishing, hearing that, "Good night,
good fishing," Jean would answer in his turn, "Good night, good
fishing," trying to speak the same words in the same tone, concealing
the immense uprush of tenderness they had caused him when carried

on the silence, when his heart was at peace and so full that the least unexpected sensation was enough to awaken many feelings, but in spite of himself, speaking more tenderly than the other, and less simply, because in his heart there was a third who listened to the greeting. Sometimes a few more words would pass from boat to boat in the vast silence which they broke like a gull touching the surface for a moment and then vanishing. Sometimes so true a fisherman had Jean become, he would answer, "Good evening—good night," without thinking, his eyes firmly fixed upon the net. Then a moment later coming to himself again, he would laugh, thinking perhaps that could his mother see him now she would laugh at the serious look upon his face, and that he would not himself be able to refrain from laughter, hearing her say: "What an affected boy you are!"

When on their return he got out of the boat, his feet felt cold. He walked fast, and laughed into the darkness and the wind, when he saw far away through the apple-trees, the flicker of the fire and the gleam of the lamp which told him of the waiting meal. He began to hurry. The landlord would be at the door: "We'd begun to think you weren't coming back." Then he took his place at the table, filled with happiness, rubbing his hands, dazzled by the lamp, hungry for dinner. "Ah! it's you now who'll have to wait a bit; it's not ready yet: you've kept us hanging about a good two hours!" the maid would say. But so great was his happiness that no matter what might come, whether waiting or incident, it at once formed part of his bliss. "Well, if I've got to wait, give me my slippers and my letters." Then the soup would come, and all through dinner he would talk, giving an account of what he had been doing. The maid would know already that he had put in a lot of fishing, having seen the baskets, but while he went on with his eating, in order to keep her there with him, so that he might have a friend on whom to pour out the treasures of his joy, he would tell her all about his prowess, and ask her to see that his bed was got ready.

*

Autumn was drawing on. The rare Parisians who visit the coast, had already left. Jean was alone now in the hotel. It was as though he were its master, more than its master, for did not its master treat him with respect, being socially further beneath him than the servants were beneath the master? But these differences of rank Jean preferred to suppress. He went with his landlord in the trap when the latter had to visit one of the nearby villages, or drove round his land. At such times he sat on the driving-seat and responded to the greetings of the country people whom they passed. Then when the fine days like all good things came to an end, he took his departure. He said good-bye, but added that he would return every year, next summer for certain, and perhaps sooner. For to the people who for the past two months had known him better than his parents had ever done, who had dried him when he came in soaked, who each evening had waited dinner for him while he was out in the boat, who having left him alone to work, had found him hours later working still, who had smiled at his faults, respected his silent reveries, and valued his affection, who had come to know him so well that they could remember, and, should anyone in this remote part of the world happen to mention his name, talk about, all the details of his health and character—to them he would not have known how to bid a final farewell.

Fortunately for our continually changing existence, and so that it may always be surrounded with warm feelings, our potentialities of affection do not stay concentrated on what we have left behind us, but are spread about and embellish, the places and the friends with whom we have to live. And so it was that when next year came round, Jean found he was involved with other places, other people, and for much the same reason that a year earlier his heart had been given to Brittany, the ship's-boy and the landlord—simply because they had been closely associated with his life. The places where he spent his holidays changed. A love of particular places, particular people, becomes so deeply rooted, that when we say good-bye, we feel a strong desire to come back again. But once those roots have been disturbed, the desire perishes, transfers itself to other friends, only to be separated again from them with a sense of regret which does not last. Little by little Jean found in this experience the same melancholy as might have afflicted him when thinking of his loves, finding in the number of those which had preceded the one he thought would last longest, a sad warning of love's fragility.

7. *From Sea to Mountain*

When next year came round, Jean found himself obliged to go with his mother to a watering-place which was situated in a valley surrounded by high mountains. It was a part of the country that he hated, thinking it hideous, and though while there he was conscious of a sense of oppression, he was almost pleased, finding wearisome that necessity which compels us to love the things which we are destined quickly to forget. When the years which we have lived most passionately are gone, they become for us as a novel which we have read to the end: once it is finished we find no pleasure in returning to it. We have the illusion that we have given the best part of ourselves to those among whom we have lived, only to find that we have given them nothing but the veering breezes of our love, the drifting smoke of our senses. For when those transitory feelings have vanished, we realize how little we want to see those persons again.

On the day of his arrival in this particular valley, he learned that Mademoiselle Kossichef was living only two miles away. A month passed, and not for a moment had he felt the slightest wish to go and see her. He sat one day on a rock. Before him he saw the serried ranks of vines sweeping downwards into shadow—for the sun was setting. As he looked it seemed to him that the topmost leaves were rather lighter in colour than they had been a while back, and than, in fact, they should have been at this season of the year. Gradually they appeared to be even lighter, almost as though they were going to turn golden. He realized then that what had happened was that a gleam of sunshine, dimmed by clouds, had reappeared. The vines were still in shadow, but shadow which was already lit by a pale sun. At once he could see himself on a forest road where often a pale sun, trying to break through the mist, had turned the leaves to gold, without ever itself becoming visible, so that the leaves seemed lighter in colour than they actually were at that time, or even later, on those autumn days when he had gone driving with the landlord at Begmeil. The sun at noon turned the golden autumn leaves to red, so that one could no longer be sure

395

whether the lovely colours belonged to the leaves by right, or had been given to them by the sun: perhaps they were really green and only made to seem red by the evening light. In the white sky one could guess the position of the sun by the presence of a paler patch at which the eye could gaze, though not without fatigue. Behind it, not catching its shape, but conscious of its radiance, he could feel the sun's reality, and taking advantage of the thin, disguising veil, could stare at it for quite a long while through half-closed eyes, as on those white afternoons, which grew clear and brilliant only just before sunset, which he had known in Brittany, on the road leading to the forest or lying on his back in the boat with his face turned upwards to the sky.

This resemblance lasted only for a moment. The sky became again completely blue, and the sinking sun brightened the flank of the mountain. But his thoughts were full of Brittany, and, seeing the rays of the setting sun gilding the bright fields, he said to himself, 'This is the moment of the day when if I was not on the sea I used to go and watch the smacks sailing into the harbour. Now, this evening in a very few minutes, they will be doing precisely that. Oh! if only I were there to see them, one behind the other, each with its great sail raised, looking like a gigantic butterfly's wing above the tiny hull, two wings close together sometimes giving the impression that they were one, and all gleaming in the sunset. Yes, this is the moment,' he said to himself, 'and to see that sight I should have to be down at the harbour within five minutes at the latest.' While he imagined those sails gliding by one by one he could see the dazzle on the water slowly dying out and at the same time taking on those rare, enchanting colours, receiving, retaining, vivifying, softening the reflections of the sky on the charmed slope of their surface. He watched with a sense of desperation, the stretch of green fields below him, and the ploughland which so recently flooded by the declining sun, was becoming darker and ever darker, without showing so much as one reflection, without giving back the faintest subtlety of light, holding a single memory of the sun, with the sun becoming a precious memory by reason of the reflected glow from a brilliance which had already disappeared, a sort of enchanted land the dreamlike splendour of which still lingered on and lasted, broken for a single moment by one solitary smack passing across the glow and catching the vanishing but persistent colours, still strange and tender, against an almost now discoloured sky, in the silence and the coolness and the breeze of the oncoming night.

Night fell. He must return to the country which he found so ugly,
and there perforce spend long months under the high, encircling
mountains now weighing again upon his spirits. But it was with joy
in his heart that he hurried home, running down the slopes, feeling his
feet bounding from the earth, so blithely had they touched it. And the
night having hidden all the scene in darkness, and awakened in himself,
no longer the vague reveries of other days, but the thought of other
more material delights, of a good dinner eaten under the lamp whose
comfortable light needed Nature's blackness all around to give it life
and gentleness, he remembered, with his spirits rising, returns to
Réveillon at night, when he could see at the far end of the shadowed
avenue light shining from the dining-room windows, and hastened
up the stairs to change, before hurrying down for dinner, to find
everyone reunited in anticipation of the meal, with the light of the
lamp revealing on every face the silent bliss of well-being, the tiredness
bred of a day passed happily, of appetite soon to be gratified, all filled
with curiosity about the walk he had taken, about news received by
some other member of the party, with the Duke already seated at the
table glancing through the paper, and ready to announce delights planned
for the morrow. Jean now hastened down the slope, and so far from
feeling depressed as he drew near the bottom of the valley, he had a
certainty that once past those mountains his thoughts would encounter
nothing to impede their onward flight. His skull seemed like Jupiter's,
to bear within itself the whole wide world. He met a few late walkers
going home and truth to tell from the happy expression of his face,
the speed of his progress, the feverish motions of his hands which
seemed to impart to every leaf torn loose as he passed and whirled
away the rapidity of his thoughts, it would have been difficult for
anyone to guess what was going on in his heart. But if at this moment
in the little inn from which you had been observing these signs of
happiness, so different from his usual air of melancholy, his slow, discouraged gait, his hand hanging in well-mannered inexpressiveness,
you had set a chair for him at a table lit by a candle, had given him
some sheets of white paper, ink, and a pen to carry it to paper according
to his whim, you might have seen in him the very fire and dash which
you had admired, watching him from the door, making no movement,
no sound, and letting him think that he was all alone and unobserved
—you might, I say, an hour later have seen as in a mirror, as you
watched the characters being inscribed by his feverish fingers which

obeyed the swiftness of his thoughts, upon the sheet of paper, all the ideas which were racing, tripping, proliferating and elbowing one another in his brain, you might have seen what it was that had given him that absent-minded air when the driver of a hay-wain, passing him upon the road, had shouted roughly to "look out", and a moment later had restored to him the blissful look, the easy gait, and had compelled the sheet of paper to endure the monotonous torment of his moving hand.

*

At other times, when weather of a different kind, coming hard on the heels of a fine spell of several days' duration, winter's cold forerunner, stepped ashore one fine day in September, when the sunlight still had the glow of summer though a fierce wind set the leaf-shadows gambolling upon the tables in the sun, it was this that brought back Brittany to his mind. The wind, lashing his face, did more than fill his lungs: it carried a load of memories as well. In still other circumstances, it was the absolute silence and solitude on mountain or in plain that freed his thoughts from all material bonds, making them light and unrestrained as the dried grasses trembling in the passing breeze upon the heights. A long sloping ray of sunlight would be enough to set his mind on fire, a stream encountered on his walk to lead imagination on. He would start to move fast, as we saw him awhile back, would lose his way, and reach home still filled with happiness, carrying more lightly than ever Atlas did, the world upon his shoulders. An irritated complaint from his mother at his lateness, a faintly imperious order from his father, would bring him back to earth suddenly with a thud. Or gradually he would relapse into a state of physical well-being induced by dinner, or into enjoyment of the pleasing prospect of meeting friends, or of spending the evening at the Casino. All through the first part of the meal however it was as though his eyes were fixed, not on his father, not on his mother, nor the servant, but on something else, so that he looked happier than usual. He would talk to his mother then with warm sympathy, and the things he said would stir his feelings so deeply that his voice would tremble, and the tears come into his eyes. But my business is to tell a story, and this is not the place in which to dilate upon the laws of sensibility, or to express regrets for so much wasted energy, or, once the tempest had subsided, to call in question the disturbance it had caused, leaving nothing behind. That could be of interest only to poets and had better be relegated to books dealing with their craft.

All the same for Jean such hours were good. Not perhaps good as they might have been by restoring to him through his power of memory a degree of confidence in himself through months of inaction and mediocrity. He was too heavily oppressed by the immediate sense of his mediocrity for that. What might one day have leaped to life in him, he thought was ended now for ever, being incapable of seeing in it more power than it actually contained. Still, those hours were not entirely lost for him. When, filled with a longing for the sunsets he had known in Brittany, he descended into a valley which was so far from the sea that none of those who dwelt there had ever in their lives set eyes upon a sail or a mast, it dawned upon him that, if the love we feel for things so far resembles the love we feel for persons or for trivialities, in that its object changes, in that all we have loved we needs must leave with feelings of regret which do not last, in order to love other things and other people, we should do wrong to think that in our love of things there is the same nothingness that marks those other loves, or that like those loves it has not kept about it something of ourselves. He realized that though he did not wish again to be in love with Mademoiselle Kossichef, or to take infinite trouble in order to go once more to the house of the Duchesse de Réveillon, it would always be for him a source of blissful happiness to sail with Pierre once more, to sit writing in the sun, despite the wind, while looking at the sea, on the little terrace where the sun shone on the leaves of the vine, some already scarlet, some still green. Maybe he would never again see them. That did not matter, because the yearning he still felt for all those things was a sufficient sign that he had not loved in vain, that he had still kept within himself some part of them. A ray of sunlight, gleaming as it had gleamed there, the wind blowing on a day of sunshine, not only touched his eyes, not only entered into his lungs, but knew the way to his heart, and could bring back memories. For when he had spent long hours writing, breaking off to watch the shadows of the leaves upon the sunlit table, or when, lying in the boat with the pale sea before him, he had gazed at the sun setting behind the clouds, he had given his heart to something that lay deeper than trivialities, something that was more lasting than love of people. It was not only that the sky he had known there he could often see again as immeasurably blue, as profoundly tender, seeming to smile again as of old, and could recognize in it a faithful witness to his happy days upon the sea. It was not the timid fingers of the sun feeling their way through clouds and touching the leaves though not yet fully lighting them, nor yet the chaste caress of the familiar wind, that had not changed. It was that in himself he felt the presence of a something else which had stayed the same, even though he was aware of it only at special times. When those times came he was no longer oppressed by doubts, anxieties or melancholy. His deep tranquillity seemed then, like the blue sky above his head and the rustle of green grass about his feet, to hide a serene delight, a silent joy.

8. Begmeil in Holland

One rainy day, Jean happening to find himself at The Hague, which place he, being uncertain about geography, believed to be well inland, was advised to take a tram which in half an hour would land him at Scheveningen, and did in fact duly arrive upon the shores of the North Sea. Close by was Ostend which he had thought of as lying some distance away, and in a quite different direction. He was conscious of a strange sensation at thus feeling so different a past linking him with the present, thinking that if he followed the grey shore of this immense grey sea on which night was falling, he would reach Ostend, that same Ostend where as a child he had been turned out of the train after a night journey, and had taken to be a seaside beach cut off from all the rest of the world not knowing how he had come there—only to find suddenly that it was connected with places which he had always thought of as being situated in an entirely different part of the earth's surface, that it was in fact a strange and unfamiliar spot, though he would without a doubt most surely recognize it.

It is a curious experience to see in fact places that we have known only in imagination, and even more curious to come on places which we *have* seen, as though they have changed their situation, finding them where we did not expect to find them, realizing that there before us lies the familiar indentation of their coastline under a grey sky of which we think as covering other spots, but not this one. What, if we walk farther, shall we find under the grey moist wing of the misty afternoon? Something that has the nature of a dream, so completely does it seem to exist in and for itself, cut off from the rest of the world, with its own especial sky, having nothing most certainly to do with the scraggy green grass beneath our feet, linked by not very long tree-lined roads with that land of Flanders which, in imagination, seems to be the farthest conceivable from this, a country all cities and inland fields, bounded perhaps by the sea, but at a great distance. Of such a kind was the astonishment which Jean felt at sight of the North Sea. In the course of his journey he pushed still

farther on, as far indeed as the shores of the Baltic which he had
never seen.

He had arrived as dusk was falling, and in spite of the wetting rain
went down to the deserted beach (the time was December) to the very
edge of the sea where little waves were breaking along an infinity of
sand. It was a place where he had never been before, a sea he did not
know, a part of the world where everything gave him an impression of
strangeness. But all the same these wavelets struck him as familiar.
Perhaps at most they had ever so little changed their colour, but had for
all that the cold grey tint which marked them as belonging to the
North. Nevertheless they were beyond a doubt the same that he had
seen hundreds and hundreds of times upon the Channel coast in
numberless seaside places with which he was familiar. Their shape,
their movement, their linked and following run gave to them that
general look which makes us say of certain things that they are "just
the same", that we know them. And so it was that in this evening light
he was oppressed by a feeling of sadness, a more melancholy feeling
perhaps than that which comes to us when we fail to recognize
familiar sights. It comes in part, that feeling, from our recognizing as
familiar things we do not know, but chiefly from our not being
recognized *by* things we *do* know, from an awareness that they have
become strangers. On shores where we have been before, where the
slope of the dunes on which the signal-station stands used to receive
each morning our daily greeting as we stood at the window, and our
friendly glance when, lifting our eyes from our book, we looked
around us, was accustomed to being trodden by our feet gaily or sadly
when we took our evening walk, but for the most part gaily, or rather
happily, because we had ever before our eyes the lovely colours of the
sea which blended so exquisitely, and the homing smacks sailing by on
their way to the evening meal—when on such shores we see the ebb
and flow of familiar tides and recognize the sound, the shape, the
movement of our old friends the waves, it seems that they too know
us. They are like family friends part of a life we love, to which we are
known. But on this Baltic shore which to Jean was all completely
strange, the waves he did not know seemed to have caught from all
the foreign objects the look of those who did not know him, and the
strange land under an unfamiliar, brooding sky, gave to the known
voice of little waves, whose childlike faces, light movement, and
rhythmical, harmonious gesture—all so like what he had often seen

upon the Channel coast—gave even to the sand the appearance of those who say, "I do not know you." At this very moment just such little waves were beating on strange islands, foreign reefs where men have died, where after storm when calm returns, they play with foundered ships whence the bodies of drowned men have not yet been recovered, ships which serve the waves as anything may do, as toys to splash and play with when the days are fine. Other waves too, their very counterparts, which he had known of old, and for that reason seemed to know him, were idling on long lines of beach where human foot had never trod, waves which had never known a man, yet looked the very same as those that he had known, speaking to him with their voices, playing in the old familiar way before his eyes, and after his death, when nothing at all would know him any more, would play the selfsame games, keeping that look we give to all the places that we know, the look we find in them each time we see them afresh. For places change less in appearance than do men, and waves can never change at all, but seem to say to us, "It is no longer ago than yesterday," and cry to us to reassume the life that once was ours. But the lapse of time is long. For those who have eternity before them it may seem nothing, but for us the moment comes too late, for we are old. Let us hope that others may take profit of these things, not perhaps of the waves which to all men are the same but of places which are never quite alike, of which not a few are strange to everyone but us who loved them, keeping that outward show, that unity of look which marks their character. This we have carried with us in our hearts, but others, seeing them, will be conscious only of strange, disparate features.

*

And so it was that Jean, remembering the North Sea and the Baltic and Dieppe while he poked the kitchen fire that he might heat some wine to warm him before he went to bed, recalled the past. His thoughts were swept along by the wind whose first noisy gust had but a while ago caused his heart to beat, and filled him with a sense of joy, distending his wings as though he were a gull responding to the rising storm, carrying him as its force increased to the wave-crests and the shore. Sitting by the fire poker in hand he thus remembered. The wind had carried him to good effect, with speed unparalleled and tireless strength, and that elasticity which had enabled the beloved child

perched on its vast wings, as rubbery and cold as fins, to stay aloft in
air, not caught by the waves, but passing between them, clinging to
their racing backs, hovering above them, skimming the sandy shores
which stretched away under a low black sky; carrying him thus to
every spot where some idea might dwell, some thing might lurk, waiting to be found, some feeling which it was worth troubling to dig for
in the sand, to clutch, to keep, to express, and all this while never ceasing its continuing moan while Jean sat poking the fire in the kitchen,
manifesting its speed by the noise it made in the chimney, in the window-
frames, in the streets, over the guessed-at waves, so as to keep alive, to
fan, the enthusiasm needed for the journey, for the search, for all the
precious thought concealed in the blown sand, while the storm set his
heart now and again beating by reason of the way it caught at the
chimneys and sounded its inimitable moan. So well does Nature know
where what we must express still lies concealed, and carries us thither-
wards unerringly, thus exemplifying a truth which may best be put
by saying that the poet works better in the country than the town,
more inspired by solitude than by the company of his fellows. How
indeed should I have known that whereas all my life, spent in forming
so many friendships, discovering so many pleasures, seeming perpetually to wake in me a host of true ideas, general observations, and facts
of permanent value, all of which drove me on (though drove is too
strong a word, since I never felt that I was driven) to write the most
banal passages imaginable; how should I have known that buried in
the sandy Belgian shore, seen only once for a brief hour and then without much pleasure, there lay concealed a precious truth—had not a
kind wind carried me to the spot, following the only ways that led to
it, those of the imagination, filling me with enthusiasm at sight of it,
revealing signs of all that hidden worth, giving me the strength to stop,
to exert the energies of my mind upon it, and this time setting me,
indeed, to work? Nature knows where that truth lies: and only she can
know it—only she, by making us feel again what once we felt before,
leading us to some point in the fabulous world of memory which has
become the world of truth. You have only to take a handkerchief from
a drawer and smell the subtle fragrance of fresh linen, to know, to feel
again that moment of arriving in the country, that moment when,
dinner done, your mother put you to bed after first dressing you in a
fine white nightshirt, in white sheets, with a white pillow for your
head, in a room where the window gave on to a little garden which

you could not see because you had arrived so late (you had been given a meal after "the others" had finished theirs) though when morning came it would display before your eyes its rich gathering of pansies, and all along its wall hot in the sunlight which beckoned you into the fields, close to the pump, a vision of sweet-peas.

9. *Impressions Regained*

At Begmeil Jean drove through the countryside, sometimes in the carriage with the Duchess, the Duke and Henri, sometimes with Henri in a buggy, sometimes on the box with the coachman. All the time one could catch beyond the fields, sight of the sea held in so deep a peace that it seemed not even to take the trouble to efface the wake left by boats, so that, motionless here and there, they looked as though they had let fall over their sterns a trailing rope, as though perhaps they were attached to some sort of chain, or were lying high and dry in a rutted highway of the sea, which there looked lower, and as though choked with sand. Everything was bright and distinct, no longer confused but separate, here one colour, there another, while the water like a moving stretch of oil looked dry. The eye, held by such spectacles, tries to seek out what makes their beauty, the basic reason of their power to charm. But in vain does the mind grope and the eye stare. Not to them it seems is it given to receive the message of aesthetic joy. Can memory then find out the truth? No. A year later Jean tried to remember those expeditions, and describe them, but found no pleasure in the task. He had to wait for a day which might be long in coming, when seeking out the charm of a garden he gazed intently at roses, zinnias, box and geraniums, or a day when he would have liked to see those flowers and did not. It was then that, his day all spoiled and come to nothing, Madame d'Aleriouvres had the carriage brought round to take him to the railway station near Geneva.

He felt overcome with disappointment. His day had been completely, finally ruined. Meanwhile the carriage started: the horse broke into a trot. It was late afternoon, the time of day when people set off on walks. The horse maintained its trot: there was a sharpness in the air. The villages through which they passed stared through the eyes of their inhabitants seated before their doors, and the chapel looked without seeing, with its sunlit wall. But these things were just ordinarily pleasant. Then when they had got beyond the farmland, the Lake of Geneva in all its length came suddenly into view lying spread in the deep tranquillity of afternoon, with the wakes of boats stretching across its surface and tangled all together like white threads, a skein of life which the sea shows, lovely as the shadowed orbit of an eye, and the pattern of twined curls. Curious too the way in which this picture, all of water made sensitive by the descending sun to every tiniest arabesques of boats which seemed to be standing stock-still, as though followed by something more immaterial than their route, than their itinerary, preserved upon the surface of the lake, as though human life had taught geography to nature which made it visible in lines, employing human memories in a series of notations set down in light and subtle colours. Looking at the sea (at this hour it had almost the appearance of the sea) at the end of the road along which the horse was quickly trotting, Jean suddenly remembered. He saw it there before him as the very sea he once had known, and felt its charm. In a flash, that life in Brittany which he had thought useless and unusable, appeared before his eyes in all its charm and beauty, and his heart swelled within him as he thought of his walks at Begmeil when the sun was setting and the sea stretched out before him.

Between the lake at which he was looking and himself what was it that had come to birth that never had existed between the sea and him, that never would have existed between this lake and him, had not something of the same feeling been present years before at the sea? Could it be that beauty and joy for the poet resides in an invisible substance which may perhaps be called imagination, which cannot work direct on immediate reality, nor yet on past reality deliberately remembered, but hovers only over past reality caught up and enshrined in the reality now present? It is as though before the eye which sees it now and saw it long ago, there floats divine imagination, which is perhaps the source of all our joy, something that we find in books, but only with the utmost difficulty in things around us. The lake before me there is no longer a mere spectacle whose beauty I must try to seek out, but the image of a life I once lived long ago, the charm and beauty of which echoes so loudly in my heart, that there is no need for me to wonder in what it may consist. What has happened is that behind the indifferent spectacle of the present we have found on a sudden a memory of the past revived, the feeling that filled it, a charm of the imagination which attaches us firmly to life and makes us part of it, as though the past, let slip by happiness, not understood by thought, and only vaguely reproduced by memory, had been recaptured once for all by contemplation. Those are the happy hours of the poet's life when chance has set upon his road a sensation which holds within itself a past, which promises the imagination that it shall make contact with a past it never knew, which never came within the range of its vision, which no amount of intelligence, effort, or desire could ever have made it know. What the poet needs is memory, or not strictly speaking memory at all, but the transmutation of memory into a reality directly felt. A smell meets me as I enter a certain house where to be sure I had not come expecting to find beauty—but suddenly it is of beauty that I am conscious. The smell is that of a house where once we spent some time at the seaside, a deplorable wooden villa. Each time I entered it I caught that especial smell. It was a place where I had been sad, where there was nothing to minister to my hunger for the beautiful, but it was precisely that which had wrapped me round in the disguise of a far from pleasant odour. When I pushed the little gate open and walked across the small and ugly garden, that smell had welcomed me. It had followed me as I climbed the creaking wooden stairs. It was with me as I changed my clothes, whenever, by the light of a lamp which our cook who here, quite out of her element and acting as a maid-of-all-work, could never get to burn properly, I sat reading, and, later, ate my dinner alone with my mother. The whole of that period of my life, with its hopes, its worries, its hungers, its hours of sleep or sleeplessness, its effort to find joy in art—which ended in failure—its experiments in sensual gratification, so sharply terminated, its attempts to win the love of someone who had taken my fancy, and my subsequent and absurd disenchantment—all were caught up and made present in that smell. And so it was that when it came to me again I felt a whole life rise up which my imagination had never known, but now after so long a space of time had battened on and savoured. I cannot say whether I felt this recovered life in the smell, or whether my memory gave it me *accompanied by* the smell, but I should like to think that its place of habitation was somewhere common to, somewhere preserving the essence of, both sense and memory, that what it brought to me was bred of the sharp assumption by them of identity, as though that identity is necessary before sensation can lose the immediate and particular quality which it has in the perceived present, which memory alone can never take from it. For what it holds in suspension are the ranged sketches of *a* present which is still the actual present.

The present may be dead but not for that reason less accidental.

When a sensation comes to me in the present though as a sensation belonging to the past, there springs from the impact of that clash something that seems as it were to be a sensation freed from the trammels of the senses, and within the field of the imagination which, having now offered to it an eternal object, can know it, and know it so well that in a flash I find myself confronted by a reality liberated from the temporal circumstances of my life, by a something which I once saw only as a passing show preserved in memory: but preserved in such a way that instead of being conscious of the melancholy that hangs over a collection of pictures drawn from the past, instead of living though not living, I have the feeling not only that I *have* lived, but rather that I have lived something which is living still, which *I* may live again tomorrow. It is thus that I feel beneath the particular species of light-coloured grapes which I used to pick in bunches, and eat one by one in the garden, before starting work; beneath those dark, spiced messes of stewed fruit, reddish, purple, or chestnut, which used to be brought to me in hotel rooms where the furniture smelled of dust, while I was sadly getting ready to catch a train in a bathroom atmosphere of wet soap, eau-de-Cologne and mouth-wash, with the sunlight and the air entering from the garden causing the scent to evaporate—that I seem to touch the very weft and texture of my life of other days—catch the smell of railway carriages, time racing by, the sound of limping, echoing bells; and the fluttering sense of these things within myself is alive on a higher level than memory or than the present, so that they have not the flatness of pictures but the rounded fullness of reality, the imprecision of feeling. That sense of life may well be snatched from me, but without my being conscious of regret, because it comes to me through the medium of something identical with life, something that does not seek prolonged enjoyment, but finds satisfaction whole and complete outside duration. That sense perhaps will not be long preserved, though it does not seem to matter, as though that preservation, no matter how long it may be, exists at a level of Time which is far above the indeterminate zone in which it moves.

And is it not more beautiful we wonder, that the imagination, which neither the present nor the past could put into communication with life and so save from oblivion and the misinterpretation of thought and unhappy memories, the varied, individual essences of life—trains and hotel rooms, the fragrance of roses, the taste of stewed fruit, washrooms and roads from which we can look at the sea while, as it were, travelling elegantly in a carriage—is it not more beautiful that in the sudden leap which follows on the impact between an identical past and present, the imagination should thus be freed from time? For the pleasure of that experience is a sure sign of its superiority, and in it I have always put such trust that I write nothing of what I see, nothing at which I arrive by a process of reasoning, or of what I have remembered in the ordinary sense of remembering, but only of what the past brings suddenly to life in a smell, in a sight, in what has, as it were, exploded within me and set the imagination quivering, so that the accompanying joy stirs me to inspiration. This pleasure which seemed to me sufficient proof of the superiority of that state, is, perhaps, proof of the superiority of a state in which we have as object an eternal essence, and seems to indicate that only so sublime an experience can be captured by the imagination. And this deep-dwelling pleasure, by justifying us in giving to imagination the highest place, since we understand now that it is the organ which serves the eternal, does perhaps raise us too, and shows, because of the happiness we feel when we are freed from the present, that our true nature lies outside of time, and is formed to feed on the eternal, never to be contented with the present nor ever to be saddened by the past. And that is why, living and knowing so many different times, and feeling melancholy in so many different rooms, we should not grieve overmuch at having spent our time in elegant carriages and fashionable salons. So often seeking beauty in a mountain or a sky we find it again in the sound of rubber-tyred wheels or the smell of a scrap of fabric, in the things which have hung about our lives, which chance has brought to hang there once again, though this time we may be better equipped to feel delight, separating their imagined past from their present reality, wrenching ourselves free from the slavery of the *now*, letting ourselves be flooded with the feeling of life everlasting.

❧ VII ❧

Second Stay at Réveillon: the Bad Season

La Marquise de Réveillon · Balzac's Winter Quarters

The Pleasures of Autumn · Le Comte de Saintré

Le Prince de Borodino · A Small Country Town

The Military · Winter · La Comtesse Gaspard

de Réveillon · Army Memories · Fontainebleau

Oysters · Colonel Brenon · The Storm

1. *The Bad Season*

There were very few visitors at any time to Réveillon, for the Duchess had a horror of guests in the country, and nobody in her eyes was considered worthy of an invitation who did not possess such qualities as are rarely found in any one person. The Duke acquiesced in this sort of existence because it was what his wife liked. I need hardly point out however since by this time you know so much about him, that it was not what he himself would have chosen, or that he did not frequently regret, though in silence, his wife's refusal to make of Réveillon a minor Versailles, since there being now no King and the Duke ranking as the Premier Peer of France, it was under his roof that the Court should have gathered. His regrets on this score had grown sharper since the marriage of his cousin, the Marquis de Réveillon, a member of the younger branch, who, having taken to wife a ravishing and enormously rich American woman who adored Society, had bought back the ancient Château of Soubise (his mother being of that family) not far from Réveillon, where he entertained frequently on so lavish a scale that each successive party was accorded ever increasing space in the newspapers. Even when there was no party at Soubise, the unhappy Duke could not open the *Gaulois* or the *Figaro* without seeing that his cousin's horse had won several races, or coming on a description—as long as an article—of what the Marquise de Réveillon had worn at the Horse Show, or when attending private theatricals at a neighbouring Great House. The Duchess's clothes, God knows! were never written about, and that for the very best of reasons.

Gradually the shopkeepers had come to regard as the "real Réveillons" those of the family to whom they sold such quantities of carriages, hats and jewels, while the general public seeing their names figure so prominently in the news made the same mistake. When in middle-class circles somebody mentioned the Duc de Réveillon, somebody else invariably said "You mean the Marquis."—"I thought they were a ducal family."—"I've no idea what they are, but the real Réveillons, the ones who do so much entertaining, are friends of the

Queen, and are so endlessly talked about, go by the name of the
Marquis and his lady." But explanations of that sort demanded a deal
of erudition. For most people the Duc de Réveillon was the Marquis
de Réveillon. Little by little the Marquise came to adopt a style which
would have horrified the Duke had she been his wife, and in any case
caused him no small amount of annoyance by reason of the talk to
which it gave rise in connexion with his cousin. The confusion of
names was never-ending, extremely mortifying, and most unfortunate.
He, who had married a Princesse de Champagne, own cousin to the
Austrian Emperor, and had never in his life willingly ridden a horse,
nor patronized the more obscure theatres, was frequently given the
pleasure of reading in the paper some such paragraph as the following:
"Among the devotees of the bicycle and constantly to be seen at
Longchamps, is the Duc de Réveillon who as is well known married a
charming American, among whose relations may be numbered Miss
Footit, the delicious Clara Timour, Tekita, who has never got over
G—'s defection, Madame Guypper, wife of Israel, the enormously rich
banker, the Duchesse de Réveillon—believe it or believe it not—who
though she was born in the land of the dollar is one of our great ladies,
and a true Parisienne, and Madame Bering-Granval, author of *Vers de
Honte*, etc. . . ." Or . . "Now for a tiny indiscretion about one of our very
great ladies to whom my friend 'Interim' alluded the other day. I can
now reveal the secret, and inform my readers that it is no less a person
than the Duchesse de Réveillon who has been working daily under
the tuition of Mlle Yvette Guilbert at *La Pocharde*. The song *Ah!
laissez moi me tordre!* which our fascinating star has to sing over and
over again each evening at *l'Alcazar* in response to rapturous cries of
encore! will, we have been informed, this summer, at Réveillon, the
Gothic Château where Louis XIV lived and Saint François de Sales lies
buried, be not the least of the suggestive and racy 'attractions'—to
borrow a word from our neighbours across the Channel—of a season
to which the Duchess, a woman of progressive views and a true daughter
of her times and the land of her birth, intends to give a new and quite
distinctive character. The *Gaulois* which is always careful to keep its
readers informed on everything having to do with legends, recently
sent a member of its staff to interview the Duchess on the subject of
this surprise *di primo cartello*. Most unfortunately he did not succeed
in seeing her, since the Duchess whose helpful attitude to all the outstanding persons of the Paris Press is well known, was not to be found

in the exquisite and altogether charming house, with its valuable collection of pictures attributed to Vandore, which is the hereditary home of the Réveillon family. He did, however, manage to get a few words with Mlle Yvette Guilbert, who was only too glad to satisfy his curiosity. Here is his account of what occurred. "You ask for my views on Madame de Réveillon," said the gracious luminary of our theatrical firmanent, "well, the chief thing about her is that she's—if you'll pardon the expression—a dam' good pal. There's nothing of the duchess about her, I can tell you. . . ." The article ended with the words "It is matter of common knowledge that the Duke is the present head of the House of Réveillon. His first wife (deceased) was, before her marriage, Princesse de Champagne." The crowning insult was that the Marquis having rallied to the cause of the Republic, the Duke who had remained so loyal to his king that he refused to serve as Diplomatic representative of a régime headed by the Marshal, at the Court of his cousin the Emperor of Austria, quite frequently saw himself referred to in the public Press as "the Duc de Réveillon whose republican sympathies no one would think of questioning. . . ."

★

But though the Duchess disliked entertaining on a grand scale at Réveillon, she equally disliked being there alone. Consequently, friends were for ever turning up to stay for a few days, and, since very particular qualities were demanded in those she thought worthy of an invitation, very few were asked; but those few had to be at her constant beck and call. They suffered however from the disabilities proper to their age: one would be having a love affair which kept him in Paris, another would be convalescing in Switzerland; one was in duty bound to accompany his mother when she went to take the waters, another had to have his grandchildren to stay in the country. Letters were written calling the faithful to the colours. "The blue room is waiting for you. Boniface has now got a range on which he can concoct *lièvre à l'allemande* just as you like it. Madame de Septcoeurs has just written to say that she will be with us by the end of the week, and Henri is planning with his friend, Monsieur Santeuil—a remarkably intelligent young man whom you will dote on—to produce a little play which I must say is charming. Last but not least the fine weather seems to have come to stay—touch wood!—and you know

how well you always feel in our good air." Not all replied to the
summons. "Any news, my dear?" the Duke would ask at luncheon.
"I noticed that you had a very heavy post this morning."–"Yes, indeed. Sergueux writes to say he doesn't think he'll be able to come.
The poor man sounds quite heartbroken, but he's got his Beauvisage
aunts on his hands."–"Oh, naturally he can't come if he's got his
aunts with him," interrupted the Duke, who did not like having
guests who came to Réveillon under pressure. "He *must* be feeling
terribly disappointed," replied the Duchess, "for there are no greater
bores in the world than the Beauvisage women—though they *are* my
cousins—their mother having been a Montmorency—besides, he's so
fond of Réveillon."–"Oh, a charming fellow, of course," said the Duke
artlessly—for did not being fond of Réveillon prove beyond all doubt
that a man must possess every excellence of heart and mind? But if he
liked having people at Réveillon, he liked still more to be certain that
Réveillon would not be compromised, as it certainly would have been
in his opinion, were guests allowed to come in the "bad season". It
was therefore much against his will that he agreed to Jean's visiting
them in October. He feared that the weather would be uncomfortably
cold—as it always is from September onwards in that part of Champagne, where it frequently rains for days on end. For he made it a
point of honour that his visitors should be able to take long walks,
should be cheered by the sun, and free from all fear of colds, rheumatism and boredom, though his anxiety was dictated less by concern for
their health, and perhaps even for their pleasure, than because he
wanted them to take away with them a pleasant memory of his Château.
But Jean was never happier at Réveillon than at that time of the year.
Not then as in summer need he dread the arrival of the postman with a
telegram, and to hear the Duchess say, "It's from Agénor; he'll be with
us this evening. The victoria must be ordered for five o'clock. We'll
all go to meet him." When that happened, long carriage-drives
would be planned each day, for fear the honoured guest might lack
entertainment, and that meant only that one saw a lot of things without
really enjoying them, and got back just in time for dinner without
having had a moment in which to read or rest. In the evenings,
families from the neighbourhood would come to dine. Sometimes
Henri had to drive them back, with the result that Jean had nobody to
talk to while he was undressing. He had to go for at least the twentieth
time to see the ruins of the Hermitage which the first duke had founded

round about the year 887. But in the "bad season" life was very different. No guests were expected. One could settle into one's habits and make plans or not as one liked without being bothered.

*

In October when the weather was fine, one took a walk before dinner as in summer, about seven o'clock. One passed through the village as the sun was setting. By the time one reached the open country the moon was up. Very soon it was quite dark, the sky filled with innumerable stars, all shining brightly. One took a very narrow path which led through the fields, which made it necessary to walk in single file, or at most two abreast. Everyone would be wearing heavy overcoats to keep out the cold, though Jean always swathed himself in a white blanket with a red stripe lent him by the Duchess, which was so comfortable that he preferred it to any other garment. Once well away in the fields they met nobody. There was something exciting, stimulating, in starting off like that before dinner when it was already dark, and prolonging the walk before returning to dine, in the full light of the moon and under the stars through a sleeping countryside, in a silence so completely hedging one in, that it was almost frightening. In the distant villages everybody was already abed. Sometimes, because the Duchess never liked to go to bed before half past eight, the walk would be still further extended, and one would find oneself in the wilder country, all forest and miniature mountains and sharp declivities, which began about a mile west of Réveillon. One had to climb through tree-shaded solitudes so still that one felt as though one was invading some secret place. The branches which Henri held aside to let his mother pass, sprang back again with a solemn sound, and when the last vibration died away the silence of the enveloping forest sharpened Jean's awareness. At such times he would often find himself alone with the Duchess well in the rear of the others, and then they would talk together of intimate matters, serious, solemn subjects touched on for the first time between persons who up till then had never been together except in a crowd. It was as though these colloquies gave significance to the hour. For the first time on one such occasion, the Duchess told Jean how fond they were of him. She said things he had never supposed she could say. A whole side of her nature, previously unknown, was revealed to him, and the memory of those talks stayed

with him like the recollection of some sweet, dark cavern, enshrined
in a picture of thick woods and darkness. The moon, now high in the
heavens, added its strange illumination to the fantastic scenery of this
strange countryside. Shadows glimpsed in a sudden patch of brightness
had the appearance of solid objects, and once, when Jean trod on what
he took to be a branch, he felt it fall down the slope, bumping away in
the ghostly light which filled the path with imaginary obstacles. The
voices of the Duke and Henri called up to them from below, and they
had to break off their conversation, feeling more closely bound in
friendship than ever before—at least Jean did—for the Duchess often
said quite naturally things which coming from her sounded thrilling,
for she had acquired that habit, which is often to be found in persons of
an older generation, of never talking about feelings as such, though
feeling went into what she did say, so that her remarks, though the
pith of them had been implicit in all her behaviour hitherto, struck the
hearer with astonishment. Then Jean, shouting an answer to the Duke
and Henri, who were calling up to them that the partridges were past
their prime, felt his voice tremble with emotion because he had had to
raise it among the sleeping trees, conscious of being with others in this
solitude, of the reverberations which his words must be setting up in
the sunken road, of not being able to see distinctly those to whom he
was speaking there below him, and also perhaps of the emotional
excitement roused in him by his recent talk with his companion, and
of having heard from her so many affectionate intimacies. When he
found himself again in the company of the others, who were talking
of dinner and shooting, he felt like someone who having been "sent
out of the room" in the course of a guessing game, to wait until "they"
have thought of a word, comes suddenly back into the light blinking
his eyes, and having forgotten what the whole business is about.

But it was lovely all the same just when one was beginning to feel
cold and hungry, to return through the village and to see between the
trees of the Park light streaming from the windows of the drawing-
room and dining-room, and to imagine in anticipation what was
already there awaiting one's arrival, though one would not actually see
it for several more minutes—the glow of the fire, the table under the
lamp, the hot soup in one's plate. They pushed open the gate, and when
the Duchess had not been with them, she would say, "What a time to
come home!"—"I know we're late: we've had a lovely long walk. I
took them round by Montjouvain and back down the hill from

Gelos."–"Oh, in that case, I quite understand why you weren't back earlier," the Duchess would say, laying aside the *Revue des Deux Mondes* preparatory to going into dinner. "Don't bother about changing: we'll go straight in; it's quite late enough as it is, and you all look very nice as you are." The almost dazzling light of the lamp drowned in a flood of well-being, of warmth, of brilliance, of greed, of comfortable laziness, of material things, the vague reveries still floating in Jean's head, all mixed with the smell of the woodland, the dampness of the night, and the cold light of the moon.

*

In the evenings there were parlour games or cards, and the pleasure of being seated by the fire while the wind moaned outside served as a basis to the mingled delights of curiosity, vanity or interest. At eleven o'clock, each took his candle, but this moment of separation was not really sad for Jean, because Henri went upstairs with him to his room, and stayed talking until he began to doze off. And here I must reveal something which many readers will think does not redound to the credit of our hero, which would have caused the Duchess to feel prodigiously amazed had she believed it—though that she would most certainly not have done. The fact is that at Jean's age, to a taste for gormandizing, to a craving for physical exercise and a sense of bodily well-being, is added another form of pleasure, which is much of the same general nature, scarcely less innocent, and on windy nights kept him as pleasantly warm as did the double windows, the fire in the great Gothic hearth, and the snugness of his bed. Close on midnight the tall young woman of twenty-two, so good-natured, so jolly, so strong and so unsophisticated, who was credited by the Duchess with being faultless because she was ignorant of the one particular fault she had, would slip into Jean's room—which she could easily do by reason of the enormous distance which separated it from the other bedrooms of the Château, and because of the noise made by the wind in the chimneys. He would be lying in bed waiting for her, and already enjoying in anticipation the new source of warmth so soon to be provided for him. She would pitch her clothes on to the armchair and lock the door, after first listening for any unusual sound in the corridor, where only the wind was moving, and then, in her turn enter his bed. There they would lie with legs and arms entwined, hugging one another close, mingling their cold, their breath, their desire, their warmth, their tenderness, their abruptness, and their lives. One evening when they had passed one another in the corridor, the desire stirring in each had made discovery of the desire in the other, because desire makes people susceptible, and perhaps most of all because physical entities fore-doomed to be united, unite unhesitatingly. Unfortunately the same law does not hold good in the world of the spirit. They were conscious of no sound but that of the wind, laughed to think what a terrible night it must be in the open, and for that reason found the bed still more delicious. The sound of the wind, the unusual hour, fear, physical contentment, the difference of their daylight moods which kept them from frittering away desire in casual caresses the need for which was not then urgent, this moment of ecstatic happiness which when morning came would seem no less mysterious than the dreams between which it had crept, as she had crept between his sheets (and the dreams were scarcely less voluptuous than she was) would keep alive in each throughout the day, and later during long periods of regret, the thrill of that first moment when in a corridor before ever they had got to know one another, desire had found desire and as happens when sulphur is brought in contact with phosphorous, had burst into flame.

2. Balzac's Winter Quarters

Comfortably installed in the small library at Réveillon, Jean happily renewed acquaintance with the names of those many places—Les Jardies, La Grenadière, Frapesles—where it had been Balzac's habit to go for country peace and quiet. We can imagine him arriving in one of them with a great many things to do. His room looks out on to sun-drenched vineyards and there he works, going downstairs only for meals, intoxicated, possessed by all he has been writing, a fixed look still in his eyes, a slight exaggeration in his movements, infecting others with something of his exaltation and emotional happiness, for from inspiration as from chloroform one awakes only by slow degrees. Later, perhaps, he might find relief in conversation, might gambol in his new-found freedom, might write letters. Maybe long acquired habits of work have the effect of making talk and correspondence take their places as inferior pieces of mechanism drawn onwards in the vast movement of larger, superior organisms, so that a discipline of precision, elegance, and applied intelligence controls with the lightest of light finger-touches, and with no thought involved in the process, both talk and letter-writing. But it may also be that brainwork directed to one specialized end develops its full energy only in solitude, so that the unheard and inner dialogue in the track of which the pen follows may fail to operate in conversation, as happens inversely in the case of great talkers who lose their talent when it comes to writing. That is what happens with those great writers who, concentrating their eyes on reality, work for that only and are not obsessed like Balzac with perfecting a form, or in whom, as in Flaubert, the purely literary reality—a form which fascinates them—lies so deeply buried that it cannot issue in their conversation or their letters, with the result that those letters provide only the raw material from which they can extract beauty, though now and again one may come on a trace of their true selves in a phrase cut free from the mass of that material, much as when a singer is talking to you he may give a momentary musical cadence to something he is especially anxious to stress. Such was the case with Flaubert.

In some such way can we envisage Balzac at La Grenadière or at Frapesles. Winter in a country house is very different from winter in Paris, and being plunged deep in the truth of nature we retain that sharp intuition of reality which keeps the intrusion of human beings at bay, so that we are constantly being overwhelmed by the need to go to our room, with our brain confusedly seething, there to write. We give every scrap of ourselves to our work. The body at such times is chaste, though pricked with desires the gratification of which we postpone till later, though their presence enables us to give a certain gaiety, a greater confidence, to our contemplation of reality. Even when he was old Victor Hugo would follow young servant-girls in the street. I am certain that quite often the urge to visit this or that country house in winter assails a writer because he knows that he will find there a number of pretty young women who will gladly accept his advances, with whom he can let his imagination play for a few moments before he settles down to work, just as he may permit himself to think of the gay and satisfying dinner which he will find waiting for him after those hours of silence and sobriety on which he embarks after first poking the fire, going to the window to have a look at the weather, and making sure that the door is firmly bolted.

A great writer may well be greedy and sensual, especially if he knows how to keep his desires under proper control. Balzac was a snob as well, but his work kept him so much oftener in colloquy with imaginary characters—in other words, with himself—than with persons of flesh and blood, that his snobbery did not much matter. Work over, the denizens of the Great World once more became important to him. He thought nothing of writing to Count Apponyi, begging him with a modesty which sat strangely on him, to accept the gift of his Works, though in the very same letter we find him saying that he has had no time in which to call upon the Countess—and that is the really important point. For books once written can lie on the tables of Countesses. They are finished and complete in themselves: no one can change a word in them. But an author, until the day of his death, never ceases to be capable of modification, and it is essential that the thought which is in him should gradually absorb every scrap of himself so completely that each word shall contribute to the expression of that thought. What he must at all costs avoid is letting others lay hands upon his life and his mind, for when that happens he may find that he is thinking only in terms of what they have said—and by that road comes death

and destruction, whereas the thought of drinking a glass of wine, of
kissing a fresh young cheek, or jumping a girl on his knee, serves to
keep alive that gaiety of heart and sense of life which is so useful where
the work of the mind is concerned, so that very often the absence
of sleep or the lack of food, or an attack of fever, may keep the
mind from functioning, or the phenomenon of inspiration from
emerging.

Sometimes a twinge of conscience may compel him to write a line
to an old friend who has sent him an invitation and will be hurt if it
remains unanswered, just as a great man may lose an hour of inspiration
in order to visit a widow, help in the kitchen, or dine with his publisher's wife. He knows in his heart of hearts that he ought not to be
doing these things, that they are not his job. Whence too comes the
seeming egotism of the literary man, his indifference to the work of
others. The truth of the matter is that it is only on our own work that
we can have any influence. It is a matter of *moral* concern that we should
be occupied with our own work and not with the work of others. We
may be only too anxious to give our attention to it. But it is our duty
to concentrate only on what our preoccupation can influence, that is
to say on the things for which we are ourselves responsible. This
explains those letters of thanks to young authors in which the writer
talks only of himself, though for their benefit he may indulge in a bit
of fine writing, in the expression of a thought which may have come
to him when reading something they have said, as a painter may express
gratitude to a critic or to a hostess from whom he has received frequent
invitations, by sending a sketch. Nevertheless there are moments of
falsity even in the most sincere of lives. It may be that we have to deal
with somebody whom we ought to make a pretence of admiring, in
whom a little intellectual jugglery will easily make it possible for us
to discover excellencies which we do not honestly feel but which we
extol in convincing terms, because we know that even if we have never
read his books it will give him infinite pleasure. A letter of this kind, a
mere line of compliment from a France or a Daudet, provided the
compliment bears the mark of the writer's high intelligence, serves the
purpose of the signed and emblazoned photograph of a Crowned
Head on a Banker's desk. We can find some excuse for such small
dishonesties in reading the letters—even of a man like Flaubert (those
to George Sand, or those on the subject of Renan) which are no whit
more sincere, and this makes us tremble to think what opinion may be

formed of our literary judgments by those who may discover certain
articles of ours after we are dead, or should our correspondence ever
be published, read certain letters.

*

I can quite well see why it was that Balzac's favourites among his own
books were the ones which please us least (*le Lys dans la Vallée,
le Médecin de Campagne*). The fact is that there is a sort of compulsion
upon us to value what we lack at the expense of what we have. Once
let us make the type of effort which we used to fear we never *could*
make, and we are more proud of ourselves than when we have quite
simply made use of the talent which operates in us so naturally that
we give it freely to others to enjoy, while scarcely noticing that it is
ours to give. Our peculiar charm, like that something which makes the
individuality of our face and features in the eyes of others, a something
which no conscious effort can improve upon—either escapes us altogether or seems to us to be of little merit because it has cost us no effort.
We still do not know to what extent effort is necessary, nor whether
it raises us above such small basic originality as we may have, or
debases it. Joubert told Chateaubriand not to sweat blood over the
making of a book, but as often as he could to let his talisman glitter and
earn the thanks of his readers. I once heard Barrès say that the value of
a book is due to the fine passages it contains, and that a very few of
them will have the desired effect. Nevertheless we find ourselves
especially attracted by those efforts of great writers which for them
may have been not efforts at all, whereas Racine makes no bones about
finding high merit in the Port-Royal Elegies, and Balzac preferred
above his other inventions those detestable novels which no one today
even troubles to reprint.

Fundamentally in what concerns the activities of our mind, no less
than in what concerns our bodily well-being, in our search after goodness and happiness, in the confidence we have in friends or mistress,
the belief we have in the goal we have set ourselves to attain, we float
between faith and doubt, or rather we experience both almost simultaneously. We never really know whether we have missed our true
vocation. Especially in matters of work we are all of us to some extent
like Mr Casaubon in *Middlemarch* who devoted the whole of his life to
labours which produced results that were merely trivial and absurd.

Still, our work does produce a few odds and ends of real beauty in which we can find unadulterated enjoyment. True I have known a case in which such odds and ends served to console a man whom I regard as being wholly ineffectual, though he may for all I know conceal beneath his pride as much self-distrust, as much melancholy and heartbreak as ever Mr Casaubon did, who found a similar consolation. Still, some such considerations must also have consoled Chateaubriand (for he too had his moments of depression, which may justify the friend of whom I have just spoken in believing that his own self-doubt may have been as baseless as was Chateaubriand's). What it comes to is that a great man, a beautiful work of art, restores our confidence in life and in the powers of the human mind. It is mediocrity that leaves us without hope. It may be that our faith or our doubt express only the value, the degree of living actuality of our thought: our discouragement or our satisfaction, faced by what we have written, the value of our achievement. In that case it will go hard with the chapter I had just finished when I embarked upon these comments.

But can we be sure even of this? Have there not been men of genius who were discontented with a masterpiece and fools who have been enchanted by a mediocrity? But perhaps in strict truth that has never been known, and a fine work always brings pleasure to its creator, no matter how dark and dense the general atmosphere of melancholy, doubt and hypochondria through which it bursts like a sun ray striking through a cloud, a cloud so black that it may have misled us about the brilliance of the ray. Never again shall I write of the extravagant happiness of earlier years. Is that because I have now less talent than once I had, is it that I have become more blasé? (But I don't really believe that one ever becomes blasé about that sort of happiness.) In a word does pleasure necessarily accompany beauty, as Descartes held that certainty must needs accompany truth, and can it therefore be taken as a criterion? Perhaps.

*

"If I could have *that*," Balzac somewhere remarks, "I should give up writing novels: I should live them!" Yet every time that an artist, instead of seeking happiness in his art, tries to find it in life, he is conscious of a feeling of disappointment, almost of remorse, which is a certain proof that he has been deceived. Whatever one may say, writing a novel is a very different thing from living one. All the same our lives are not wholly separated from our works. All the scenes that I have narrated here, I have lived through. How then can they be of less value in real life than in a book? The answer to that question is that while I was living them, I was doing so consciously, deliberately: I saw them as productive of pleasure or fear, of vanity or of malice. Their true, their inner essence escaped me. It would have escaped me just the same, no matter how hard I stared at them.

3. *The Pleasures of Autumn*

In this way did Jean spend at Réveillon part of the "bad season", a time of the year which has its own peculiar charm, at which one is most happy. Is there not always mingled with the enjoyments which are popularly supposed to be more than usually delightful, a touch of disappointment because they never quite come up to expectation, and is it really worth while to experience something which is not so very much out of the ordinary—though the world at large counts it as pleasure—at the cost of long months of boredom? Is there anything sadder than the ball to which a schoolboy has been allowed to go, so that he may not be deprived of an unusual pleasure, and knowing that when it is over he will be told, "Now you have had your fun, it's high time you got back to the boredom of serious matters"? The secret pleasure, on the other hand, which we savour only so to speak in privacy, which though we have not sought it, is part and parcel of the work we have been putting into the conning of a Latin text, during which time nobody dares to open the door of our room, and being unable to penetrate into our deepest feelings, sympathizes with us, admires us, and thinks, 'We must see to it that he has a bit of amusement after this is over,' is without cloud or blemish. And when after a long day of work, our mother kisses us and says, "*What* a day you've had, my poor lamb! We really must try to make it up to you!" though we allow ourselves to complain, since a good part of the pleasure consists in others not regarding it as a pleasure at all—the happy look on our face, the effusiveness of our affection, the need we feel to take some active exercise, the pleasure with which we overflow when a visitor is announced, or when we are told the name of the play we are to be taken to see, or without any apparent reason expresses itself in the spontaneous smiles which we address to our mother and expect her to return, in gestures which are designed to make obvious our state of weariness, though that very weariness is part of our sense of well-being—all these things serve to show that we really have spent a delightful day.

427

And so it is with the bad season, which since its very name forbids us to look forward to anything pleasurable, and makes it impossible for anyone else to suppose that we should, dresses the pleasure which it actually does give us in an innocence which needs no recompense, an unmixed purity which mankind has never been able to find in pleasure since the First Sin, and can be tasted only in private by those who relish it, though even they suppose it to be a weariness of the flesh. When you who have tasted the pure pleasures of the earthly Paradise come to search your memories, I have an idea that you will dwell with particular affection on the thought of the barrack-room bed where you took your noon siesta during your time in the army, of the roads along which you marched, of some country house where you had to spend a cold and rainy autumn, of the room in an inn where you once took shelter while waiting for the rain to stop, of the carriage met with on the road which stopped at your request, and put you down not far from home in the wind and the lightning.

At Réveillon this year the bad season had set in early. From the beginning of September there were whole days when the sun never appeared at all. The forest, the ploughed fields, the village beneath a sky as soft and grey as the feathers on a bird's breast, seemed to close in upon the countryside as though sheltering it from the noises of the world, in the silence which broods over things which are separated each from each, though it makes of them a single whole—the silence of an empty garden. The striking of a clock in the next village reached one as though it were in the next room. The chimes of the sounding hours came singly to the ear, as in a room no matter how large it may be, one can hear the slightest sound. The note of a bird which alone among its fellows, ventured to sing on so gloomy a day, the rustle of the chestnut leaves when a chance breeze caught them, the noise of a hammer from behind the hill, the indistinct but recognizable barking of a dog out hunting with its master in the woods, perhaps a good four miles off— all these sounds were clearly audible: not one of them was lost. As when in a pond the least ruffle of air sets moving on the enclosed waters ripples which soon cover all its surface, so did the faint barking of the dog far away, awaken the still fainter barking of the dog belonging to the Aigneaux farm, and the murmur of the chestnut leaves was continued by a still more distant murmuring of other chestnut trees, which one heard through the eyes as deaf men do, because of the scarcely perceptible movement of their leaves. No walker now would go for a glass of beer or a mug of milk to the little country inns, to the farms where the tables in their circle of chairs, still standing under the apple-trees as in the summer season, remained unoccupied all day and every day, and had now at their feet fallen apples from the trees, and chestnuts, sometimes their shells only, but sometimes whole branches with their leaves. Often the inn-keeper, instead of waiting unavailingly for the customers who would not come, closed the wooden shutters in front of the door, and with his gun slung on his shoulder, and his two dogs at his heels, went down the short flight of steps— where in the cracks of the stones thistles, dandelions and campanulas were no longer in flower, though the Virginia Creeper which grew there too and was now quite red, fell like a fountain over the whole range of the steps—and set off to shoot. Near by one could hear the barking of his dogs so clearly that now and again though it was impossible to see him, one would say to oneself, 'He can't be far away.' And if for a moment about five o'clock a beam of sunlight fell briefly on the tiled roof of the farm which turned pink as though with pleasure at receiving the reflected light of the fire which must already have been lit in this cold weather, it fled quickly away, having found none of its companions to bear it company.

*

But in the middle of the day, to the church bells striking distantly the exact time and then stopping, but so distinctly that in the following silence, the ploughman who had stopped his work to count the strokes, would say, " 'T'isn't three, 't'is four," there came the answering sound not only of the far-off yapping of a dog, but of the meandering moaning of the wind which untiringly made the circuit of the woods, engaged on its uninterrupted work, scattering the ground with chestnuts already ripe for falling, shaking but only loosening a few leaves on the branches which were still solidly clothed, making all ready for winter. Every now and again there came the echo of gunshots and then the labourer stopped to listen with that gaiety of mind which is bred in us by sympathy when we think of others' pleasures, untouched by envy, or a desire to have, ourselves, a more direct share in them. Sometimes the sun would be obscured by sudden clouds, but far away on the horizon one could see it emerge again and shine upon a hillside under a sky swept clean. The vine swags revealed the bunches of grapes hanging suspended at the root of every leaf, with each pearl-like globe already iridescent with colour. Now and again a hare brought to a sudden standstill between the plants and seemingly incapable of flight appeared to be watching the boys who a few yards farther on were working in the vines, and had not seen him. Then one would grow aware of his proximity, and call to his neighbour, laughingly going through the gesture of aiming, to show that if only he had a gun like the owner of the land, he certainly would not miss. But he could do no more than throw a stone, that being the only means that his sort had of enjoying the pleasure of interfering with the hare's existence. But the creature, perhaps not having heard or not seeing who had thrown the missile, stayed there motionless warming himself in the sun. Then suddenly he would give a couple of leaps and be no more seen, while the boys still laughing would return to their hard task, cheered by the sight of the hare, by the dream of going shooting, by the thought of having indulged in so funny because so incredible a joke as saying, "If only I had a gun!" by having frightened the hare and seeing him run so well.

Dusk came on though one had not seen the sun set, as later, the night would fall without moon or stars. Even when Jean was walking the roads at that late hour the country round Réveillon was beautiful. Time was getting on, and he had to hurry. Regretfully he left behind him the apple-trees, growing raggedly on the verges of the road, bearing stiffly upright the enormous fan of their leaves and fruit, and destined to spend the night there in intimate colloquy with the darkening sky, assuming their night attire, a glitter of bronze which at that hour shows on the sombre foliage of which the bluish-green seems, like all around them, to have reached the moment of its fullest maturity. He left the sterile trees to address the heavens in a language of immense gestures. It seemed as though only their twisted roots could hold them solidly embedded in one patch of earth soon to be sprinkled by their showers of fallen apples. Motionless they let the wind, deprived at this season of vast masses of foliage in which to lose itself, rattle their leaves which could make reply only with a dry sound. The tiny church too, compelled to pass long nights and days in the spot where it was planted and unable to seek a refuge, was doing its best to live in harmony with the common destiny of all things. Its little steeple, getting ready for the night, seemed as though filled with that eager desire to please which new boys show hoping to win a sympathetic treatment from their comrades but failed, for all its small courageous efforts, to force a smile of encouragement from the ancient trees which never for a moment ceased to moan their grievances to the apple-boughs which continued to listen without so much as turning a hair. Now and again when the wind rose higher it tried, by making its weather-cock squeak, to put in a word. But this in spite of all its efforts was recognized at once as a sound that was not of Nature's utterance. Clearly it did not live in intimate relation with the year as they did who were naked in winter, covered with blossom in spring, and at this season still bore their heavy burden of ripe fruit. But in its own way and as far as lay within its power, by presenting the charming yellow colour of its porch, and the embrasure of its door, the church bore witness to the beauty of those laws in obedience to which sunshine and rain changed the colour of the stones, and caused great gaps to show between them. Already, abandoned for a new church at some distance from the village, it had come to share the nearby churchyard with a tangle of Virginia Creeper. At first for a while building and plants had eyed one another with mistrust like cat and dog forced to live in company, but gradually they had become friends and already creeper and ivy were rioting on the church's back, so that all three now mingled so completely into a single whole that in places it was difficult to distinguish each from other. Forced to leap over steps and coil round arches, to leave the windows free since they could get no hold on them, ivy and creeper, playing variations of their own composing on the basic theme supplied by art, their swags and interweavings increasing naturally in density from year to year, had been compelled though without the help of human hand to adapt their pattern to the architect's original design, and now combined a natural wildness with a seemingly decorative intention. It was as though Nature had outdone man in the adornment of the church, and by making use of its own architectural rules and its changing colour range, had produced from between the stones and poured over the walls, while apparently understanding the need to respect the imposed intervals, and to encircle the lines of the vaulting, a rich covering delicately moulded but increasingly intrusive, green in summer, red-green in autumn, and in winter wholly red, of inexhaustible creeper. A few patches of wall had remained uncovered, and they too were beautiful for wind and sun and rain had already as it were, spread them with a scattering of brown and red, and kept them from being wholly swamped by vegetation. Nor, since it was old, did the visitor err in coming to admire this church which once had been ugly, though what had taken its place was the work of an architect of taste. For a beautiful church expresses only the beauty imagined by the architect, whereas an old abandoned church stands as the living evidence of laws in obedience to which rain and sun have given to the stones a golden hue on which the wind has sown innumerable seeds: and these laws are lovelier than the loveliest things in all the world.

By the time Jean reached the village dark had fallen, and sometimes half-way down the street, he could see at ground level, every detail revealed by lamplight, the little button-flowers in vases, the scales, the counter, and looking behind the glass of its window like some exhibit in an aquarium, a tiny shop, or a low-ceilinged room, where the members of the household would soon be busy with their evening meal. Caught in the enchantment of this fiery circle, whose magic glow reached out to touch the pavement, he would stand and contemplate a little world cut off from all outsiders, with its own life of which the stranger could know nothing, displayed to the bewitched eye until such time as darkness should assume its sway over shops, and barns and farms. Not a living soul. He would dearly have liked to see the inhabitants of this strange, small kingdom which had been revealed to him for an instant before he turned back into the cold and darkness of reality. The light within was so intense. Of what kind was the little man, dwarf or gnome, and strange most certainly, who was waiting somewhere to sit down to the chicken cooking on the stove? Why did he not enter that confined stage to play his part in the scene, his every movement visible though he would not know it, Jean being unseen in the darkness, as happens with those fragments of other peoples' lives which a magician conjures up before us in the theatre, where those whose existences we watch never think that they are being spied upon? And Jean, seeing in the darkness that little world of light, not feeling that it had anything to do with the light of day which is more lovely perhaps though more cold, did however recognize in that radiance, which was more human, filled to the brim with well-being, limited, without poetry, aglow with pathos, a useful thing made to serve as a protection, the light that is man's creation, born of an art which he has drawn from his own self, which resembles him in that it brightens a world that is not nature's, being a light which is not Nature's light —fire.

4. Two Officers

The third Fontainebleau regiment of infantry which Henri was to enter in the course of the next year, happened just then to be in barracks at Provins two hours' distant from Réveillon. The men had just been put into their winter uniforms, long great-coats and heavy shakos. When the day's work was over no one felt much inclined to leave barracks. The men brewed punch—the privates in their canteen, the sergeants in their mess—which was drunk in an atmosphere of gaiety. The young recruits, especially those who came from rich families, were at first overcome by the heat and the stench of tobacco, but soon ceased to notice these things, felt themselves to be more truly soldiers by being there, and whenever the door was thrown open, raised their heads with a weary and indifferent air, as though they had been in that particular spot from all eternity, and had no objection to others joining them. Sometimes, one of them would say, "Shut that door quick: it's cold," only to be promptly silenced by one of the older men, who made a point of keeping to themselves the privilege of dressing down newcomers, and would if need be call on the seniors for support—which was invariably forthcoming. All laughed at the youngster's impudence, the other youngsters, who were his friends, and he too not daring to take offence. Sometimes a few sergeants would drop in for a glass of punch on the sly, for the canteen-keeper—like all, whether they be doctors, lawyers, hotel-proprietors, or ladies of easy virtue, who exercise a calling which depends upon the client for remuneration—was interested more in the money than in the number of stripes on the sleeve of the man who paid it. The two groups would exchange mutual salutations and that done each would pretend not to know the other. Sometimes one of the recruits anxious to keep in well with his comrades would stand punch all round. Then the corporal would hand his glass to each in turn, and the recipient of the moment could not refrain from grinning all over his face. Sometimes a sergeant would look in for a few seconds and withdraw again almost at once with a stern expression on his face. Whenever that happened there was a roar of laughter.

But there were several who in spite of the cold hurried off into the town, where they took their mistresses to a *café-concert*, and complained about having to live with boors, none of whom had a thought beyond staying in the canteen, drinking punch, and turning in before eight o'clock. On some days one of the Companies would go out on an exercise in the woods near Réveillon. From the Château one could hear the band, though it was not always possible to make out where it was, which quite often was a good deal farther off than one thought. Twice when the Duke, the Duchess, Jean and Henri were on the terrace, the whole regiment marched past the gate and from time to time an officer of their acquaintance, whose horse moved slowly and with grace alongside the soldiers with their short, quick step, saluted the Duke. This was the Comte de Saintré, the Duke's second cousin, whose father had been *Maître des Requêtes* in the *Conseil d'État* under Napoleon III. Vain and eaten up with a desire to maintain appearances among his Parisian friends, he had soon realized that he was rapidly getting through the family fortune. He had therefore applied for permission to re-enter the army—having sent in his papers almost as soon as he had left Saint-Cyr—thinking that if he spent his life among unimportant people who did not belong to the world of fashion, he would not have to spend much in order to make a show. He so arranged matters as to live in his garrison town and not to return to Paris for some years. But the unexpected happened. The unimportant people became important to him: the people who did not belong to the world of fashion, turned out to be the only world he had. Because his fellow-officers, even those who were rich, had only one horse apiece, he wanted to have two. He flattered himself that his dinners were the best to be had in town, that his parties were the most elegant. He who in the old days had thought that "smartness" was only to be found in the so-called "set of the five duchesses", revelled in his receptions to which he had succeeded in attracting all the petty nobility of the province, and had managed to send out his invitations sufficiently late to make sure that the wife of his Free-Mason commanding officer would not turn up. The commanding officer in question was the leader of a very different group, composed of poor officers with Republican leanings, who asserted that the Saintré gang wanted to deliver the regiment into the hands of priests and aristocrats, though both men for the sake of setting a good example made a point of always going to Mass on Sundays in full uniform with prayer-books under their arms. On the

two or three occasions, however, when Saintré to repay hospitality
received at Réveillon invited Jean and Henri to dine in the officers'
mess, there were always present a few commoners, young lieutenants
who were instinctively recognized—as happens in regiments no less
than at college—as being drawn into the circle of their aristocratic
acquaintances, and could be identified by a certain reserve of manner,
as of men only too anxious to be friendly though not effusive, by the
way their hair was cut, the neatness of their persons, their royalist or
religious opinions. One of these "outsiders" was a man of great
intelligence, the son as a matter of fact of a somewhat pious family,
who though far from being on bad terms with the group which circled
about the Free-Mason commandant, was only too pleased to accept an
invitation to dinner from Saintré who after all was an outstandingly
efficient officer, and intelligent to boot. Saintré for his part thought it
good policy to show that he and his friends were ready to be on
good terms with republicans and commoners, provided they were
neither dirty, stupid nor blasphemous.

*

Madame Santeuil to whom Jean had written to say how much he
enjoyed the company of all these officers who treated him with so much
kindness, replied that she rather thought he would find among them
the Prince de Borodino, nephew of the Duc de Marengo, Desroches's
patron, and the great-grandson of one of Napoleon's illustrious soldiers
whose father had been a Marshal of France and a Minister of War in
the First Empire. Jean who had gone to dine as Saintré's guest, together
with Henri and several officers who were now his friends and sometimes lent him a horse so that he could go riding with them, asked
whether the young Prince de Borodino was, in fact, serving with the
regiment, since he was never to be seen. Noticing however that the
mention of that officer's name seemed to cause Saintré some annoyance,
he did not press the question. Actually the Prince felt that as a man
whose noble lineage was less than a hundred years old, whose grandfather would never have been employed as a game-keeper by Saintré's
ancestors because of his Jewish extraction and revolutionary opinions,
he must amount to very little in the Count's eyes. In his own however
there could be little comparison between somebody like himself
who had inherited a glorious name and was the son of a War Minister

who had been the Emperor's friend—and a descendant of one of the most obscure of *Maîtres des Requêtes* in the Imperial *Conseil d'État.* Mutual contempt had kept the two men apart. The dinner at which this question had been asked was more than usually gay and Jean's pleasure was increased by the fact that he sat next to a young officer named François Lesaule who had already won a reputation in Africa for courage and efficiency. He had so far met Jean only once or twice but the similarity of outlook of the two men and a sense of mutual attraction, rapidly turned them into bosom friends. Jean felt a great liking for Lesaule and was delighted when Saintré told him that the feeling was reciprocated. On this particular evening Lesaule had seemed delighted to see him, and had behaved as though he considered him to be the only person present worth talking to. They conversed with one another all through the meal, and the cordial relationship between them seemed to set a barrier between their talk and the general babble. Extremely curious about every detail of army routine, which had become for him a matter of interest as does anything which touches our lives at all nearly, and eager to learn in what precise way the military mind differs from others, Jean never tired of questioning his new friends, asking them among other matters whom they considered to be the most remarkable of the senior officers, both in the regiment and in the army as a whole. When somebody mentioned the name of some soldier, at present obscure and little known, lauding him at the expense of others, or attributing outstanding merits to some officer who had been unfairly passed over, Jean was overwhelmed by a feeling of enthusiasm, just as formerly—when the theatre had been his passion —he had been conscious of a thrill when some fellow-addict had told him who in his opinion was the best actor living, or later, when he had read some book or other, he immediately wanted to have the view of a man of intelligence who had read it too, seeking in what he loved a reason for loving it still more, an emotion the enjoyment of which he so far had not known. He would not let the subject drop, but bombarded the officer who had answered his questions with endless inquiries —"In what way?—How?—Why?"—and listened enraptured to the detailed replies.

The moment came when they had to leave the gay and friendly company. The carriage sent from Réveillon to take them home was waiting. Saintré, fearing lest they catch cold, lent them a large blanket which smelled faintly of horse and after tucking it round them hurried back into the warmth. They started off and Lesaule from the top of the steps gave Jean a particularly affectionate wave of the hand which seemed to refer like a private password to the subtle and intellectual talk which they had been enjoying together. Jean, just a little intoxicated by the dinner and the gaiety (he had thought it incumbent upon him to drink brandy and indulge in a cigar, holding the smoke for a long time in his mouth before expelling it, so as to persuade himself that he was just like his new acquaintances, was really one of them) sat trembling with happiness at Henri's side under the great blanket which seemed still to hold something of the intimacy of the mess, the smell of horses, and the memory of what in both their imaginations had seemed to be a sort of a bivouac. He was already planning how, when he got back to Paris, he could persuade his mother to let him have a horse so that he might ride out and take part in the winter manœuvres in which Lesaule would be playing a part. He could not imagine the future, the happiness of being always the spoiled friend of all these officers, of becoming more and more adept in things military, following the regiment from place to place, of being a permanent member of the mess. Over and over again he described to the Duke and the Duchess the lovely evening they had spent, and happened in the course of this repetitive narrative to mention the name of Borodino. The Duke pulled him up short, and said to the Duchess, "*That's* what I've been trying to remember ever since yesterday!" – "What?" asked the Duchess. "What you asked me at luncheon whether I had remembered —it was that Borodino had left cards." – "Then we most certainly must ask him over," said the Duchess: "Eugène is always so very attentive to us. If we don't, they'll think we're holding aloof from that side of the family." Eugène was the Duc d'Austerlitz, and Borodino's maternal uncle. He had already been once repulsed when he had wanted to marry into the Réveillon circle. Having however fallen back on an American millionairess who died a short time after the marriage, he had succeeded thanks to his immense fortune and his possession of a ducal title—the full splendour of which the Réveillons had only then realized—in taking as his second wife the Duchess's niece. Jean was delighted to dine with somebody who also knew Saintré and Lesaule, even though he was not on good terms with them. Borodino's manners too were in complete contrast to Saintré's. Whereas a legitimist noble might overwhelm you with an excessive, a deceptive show of friendship, an almost contemptuous familiarity, might find it amusing to play at honouring you with a pretence of intimacy—setting your head swimming with a comradely handshake and an arm laid about your shoulder—might treat you with a warmth so exaggerated as to make you blush; Borodino on the contrary, stately and withdrawn, had a way of bending upon you the majestic brow of a man whose ancestors for two generations had been accustomed to govern, to probe into men's minds and recompense their services, and of fixing you, although in fact he was thinking of nothing, with the vague, preoccupied eye which might have been that of the Emperor himself, and finally of offering you his hand with a politeness expressive of reserve, but, at the same time so dignified that it conveyed to you a feeling that though he did not pretend not to be conferring an honour on you, he was not playing a game with you, that though he was stressing rather than concealing the distance between you and himself, he was doing so in such a way as to let you cross it instead of making it more unbridgeable. Those who today bear the great names of the Empire, which have outlived it because their ancestors like the first Emperor could see into men's hearts, because their fathers who had served in the Council of the second, retained something of his brooding look—still have the piercing glance, though it can see into nobody, and at times a vague something in their expression which conceals a complete vacancy of mind. Theirs is a cast of countenance which is no longer motivated by anything more important than a trick of race which they have inherited, a way of looking which is like a sculptor who may leave behind him the eternal representation of a mere passing thought. Without rhyme or reason, like statues whose fixed stare corresponds to a once genuine reality which it has continued to reflect without understanding its significance or being able to modify it, these heirs of ancient glory, without men to govern or the ability to govern them if they had, still look at what is before them, whether it be a dish just placed upon the table or a friend who is saying something, with a profound and authoritative gaze, or a melancholy and dreamy stare. The Prince de Borodino was one of them. The expression of his face was theirs, and his grave and solemn politeness. The son of a man who like almost all the great nobles of the Empire had occupied a high administrative position, his natural air of command, which even as recently as twelve years ago had still had a solid foundation because his father had been War Minister and he could look forward to a great future in diplomacy, had not had time like that of the aristocrats of the *ancien régime* to grow rusty from disuse, and to become no more than a form of protective armour. It had not yet deteriorated into a mere game to be learned like shooting, or an exercise for which one can train like riding. There was a quality of seriousness about it, a something which seemed to claim a right to pre-eminence, to be the outward manifestation of clear-sightedness and benevolence. A commoner is never, for those whose duties bring them into contact with men who are valued at their true worth, what he is for a noble who for half a century has been accustomed to look upon their like only as so many persons whom he would never treat as his equals, though there may be concealed within him the stuff of true greatness, as in the case of a Rouher or an Ollivier, both of them men whose fathers had been no more than simple rankers. Those whose brevet of nobility is more recent, have a different air, a different form of politeness. They have lived in closer contact with genuine merit, have been familiar with the kind of real superiority which is the source of true nobleness —and they have better manners. They were bred in a Court where they rubbed shoulders with foreign ambassadors whom they had to treat with respect, whereas the scions of the ancient aristocracy, as a result of their noses not being kept to the grindstone, and because they have lived in a world entirely given over to pleasure, have acquired manners to which only the prestige of race can give the name of good, and that only within their own narrow circle. They have been bred for employments of which a very different future than the one they expected has deprived them. With it in view they received an education so complete, at least in externals, that like statues, all booted and spurred which seem to be merely waiting for the moment when they can leap upon their horses, they seem in the government office, the cavalry regiment, or the insurance company with which necessity has compelled them to find employment, where they hover as useless and as charming as porcelain figures in the glass-fronted cabinet of some prosperous farm built on the ruins of a château, all ready for some important embassy, some representative function, in which they would splendidly shine. Their gifts of tact are thrown away on a managing director, their grace and elegance is fated to be seen only by their wives: and so they exist like the mementoes of their grandfathers hung on the drawing-room wall, to be shown only when they entertain those with whom now it is their destiny to live.

And so it was that Borodino, though he had as little to do as possible with the aristocratic officers of the regiment who found his solemnity unjustified and his contempt for the nobility, insufficiently backed by political eminence or the possession of outstanding talent, ridiculous, was reduced to displaying in his dealings with Commandant Soreau —a man ill suited to appreciate such elegant niceties—the manners in which he had been trained when it was intended that he should adopt a diplomatic career. When replying to an invitation sent him by Madame Soreau, he used his letter-paper embossed with a prince's coronet and employed the handwriting which he had been taught in the days when he had hoped to be appointed to an embassy. It was for the Lieutenant-Colonel's niece (a true product of the middle class) who liked Borodino's "naturalness" though declaring roundly that she did not care for "those who used the 'de' . . ." adding, however, that he was not really one of *them* at all, as a certain type of anti-Semite is fond of saying about a Jewish friend, that he told his servant to get out the silver given to his mother by the Empress and—a far more intimate and mysterious delight—assumed the expression of the victor of Borodino and certain tricks of demeanour copied from the second Emperor, and retouched by himself, whenever he played with the child and took her education in hand.

It made him laugh to hear Jean speak of Saintré's friends as officers of distinction. Jean, when that happened, suffered from the particular form of ill-humour which perhaps arises in part from the fact that the opinion of a new acquaintance, whose judgment we have no reason to think is less searching than our own, sets us wondering whether we may not have been wrong. Perhaps what we had previously admired was not worthy of admiration after all. If youth is of all periods in life the one most prone to admiration, it is also the one at which we are least clear-sighted, least inclined to ask ourselves what we *should* admire, the one at which we are not so much sure of our own value as in-toxicated by what we take to be the value of others. And so it was that whenever Jean heard one of his admirations attacked and destroyed by someone with an assured air of "knowing better", he was divided between loyalty to the object of his enthusiasm and self-distrust. He was led by his readiness to admire the critic of his beliefs (often in a worse position to judge, though this he did not know) to accept the verdict and decide that his enthusiasm must be unjustified. Youth is that happy period when it is truer to say that one is full of confidence in life than that one is not plagued by self-doubt. For a young man has strong imagination but poor judgment, so that he imagines others to be as big as he is but considers himself to be very small. He has unbounded trust in the universe but is constantly unsure of himself. Besides Jean was afraid that the Duke and Duchess who had heard him cracking up his new friends, might think that he was entirely lacking in discrimination. Consequently he was distinctly ill at ease. But when Borodino had gone, the Duke and the Duchess, who had treated him with such amiability, had seemed so pleased to see him, and in the dining-room, that holy of holies, had appeared to be treating him as one of the very few persons who might be considered worthy of passing judgment on the human race, now proceeded to declare—with no more marked degree of unkindness than they had shown of kindness to him previously—but does not the mere fact of talking intimately to someone not of one's own circle imply that there is a bond, that he is in a sense one of the elect?—that, "He really was a charming fellow, but as they had always been told not much gifted with intelligence." It was Jean's turn now to be surprised, though on the whole he was delighted to think that he could once again rise in his own self-esteem, and was once more free to admire wholeheartedly Saintré's friends, and in particular Lesaule.

That at least was what he thought. But the fact remained that since encountering Borodino's sceptical smile, though his affection for those friends was still profound, he no longer felt that absolute certainty about their superiority which had once been his, which he had nourished in the secret places of his heart. He had ceased to have that unshaken confidence in their great abilities which goes with unquestioning faith. He felt less eager to see them, and was conscious of feeling a sort of resentment, as one may do for somebody who has put one to a lot of trouble for nothing. All the same he would have felt genuinely amazed had the Duchess told him that he was more intelligent than Borodino. It seemed to him impossible that a young man could be more intelligent than a mature one, and when he laughed at a mature man's foolish comments on poetry or other matters, it was not because he thought *himself* superior, but only those adverse views of his friends and masters which really had nothing to do with him personally. But the main cause of his astonishment would have lain in the fact that a young man is entirely absorbed in what he loves, in the universe which he is trying to embrace, in life. He knows that this or

that book is fine, that this or that man is ridiculous, that someone he
does not know has set his mind on fire—or more precisely he does not
know these things but only that he loves the book, laughs at the man,
revels in life, and armed with this knowledge strides forward into the
unknown. But because he loves, fears, or laughs in this way, does that
mean that he is intelligent? What is he? To that question he can make
no answer: he has never formulated it, being absorbed in *things* and
not in himself. He would be astonished to hear it said that he is intelligent—in a different sense from that meant by the words at college—
meaning that he is just as real as the men with whom life has brought
him in contact, because since he himself is the one thing which his love
has not yet embraced, his desires sought out, his intelligence attempted
to grasp, he would be flabbergasted to discover that he is himself
someone, a man whom others may admire or judge as he admires them,
someone who has a part to play in that universe which he longs to
know but to which he does not yet realize that he belongs. Strange
disillusionment, but a great gain when the immense effort made in an
attempt to know the universe has succeeded in accomplishing the one
thing he did not intend—knowledge of himself. The Duchesse de
Réveillon would have done more than astonish him, would indeed
have caused him serious distress, had she told him that he was more
intelligent than Lesaule. For just because there is in youth an entire
detachment from self, it lacks egotism, and feels instead a tremendous
disinterestedness. Or rather is it not true to say that youth *is* what it
loves, what it admires? It is only through those things that a young
man comes to self-knowledge, to self-love, and thinks that he loves
and admires for reasons infinitely superior to what he *is*. By bringing
down what he admires to what he thinks is the very much lower level
on which his own life is conducted, you will merely cause him to endure the most lacerating pain which he is capable of feeling at an age
when all disappointment has in it something of generosity, because it
is not in himself that a young man's hopes are placed.

5. *A Small Country Town*

For one whole fortnight Henri had to spend each day attending military exercises at Provins. Jean took a room at the Hôtel d'Angleterre. The name meant nothing. The house was a fine example of French eighteenth-century domestic architecture. At one time it had been the Hôtel des Chevreuse, and was situated on the parade ground opposite the Château. In all such public promenades, as silent and magnificent as the *Cours d'honneur* of royal and ancient residences, the houses with their low-set, clear-paned windows have the look of orangeries. At that hour of the day when the moon has already touched with blue the water in the stone basin at one end of the Park, while its fellow at the other end still shows golden in the setting sun, one is always surprised, looking through those lit windows which are handsome enough to belong to a palace, to see within them the postal clerks, or the officials of the local Council at work in a pale aura of gas or electricity. To be sure, when Jean in search of paper or cigarettes before going home went into the town and took his way down the steep streets lined with seemingly endless rows of little houses, it gave him more pleasure to look at jars filled with sweets in the grocer's window, to peer into the cobbler's deep, dark shop, at the bench in the carpenter's workshop, or at some poor family gathered together in the red or yellow glow of a candle.

But in the wide Place where daylight still lingered, the high windows aglow with the golden diffusion of gas or electricity were a more beautiful sight.

Whenever after four in the afternoon he returned "home" feeling thoroughly tired, he could see in the dark façade of the Hôtel d'Angleterre the window of his room alone among others still dark, defying the onset of the night with the rich light of a large lamp already lit, as must be too his fire, both of them awaiting his coming and filling the room with floods of warmth and radiance. His way back led across the handsome parade ground where the cries of children at play ebbed and flowed, keeping the same incessant round as the bats flitting

443

overhead. The staircase, with its low, carpeted treads which were as soft to his feet as grass lawns, was contrived like the staircase of a private house—which once it had been—the walls on either side being hung with pictures and tapestry. Sometimes he would stop in a picture-encumbered gallery furnished with old armchairs which led nowhere. At each step he felt that he was walking on things which though now silent were still brimming with that ancient life which had set them where they were to grow weary with waiting, until when at last their owners greeted them, they had made the place once more a home, summoning silence, warmth, comfort and isolation to serve as a defence against all enemies. As a sculptor's nymphs seem still to be expectant though turned to marble, the carpets, the soft discreet flights of stairs leading straight to where the master wanted to go, seemed to be waiting for him still: as when walking in autumn, one moves through a rustle of leaves, and has the sensation that one is in the very home of beauty, and is treading on a living world. One opens the door of the room that has been on tip-toe for one's coming, disturbing as one passes through it the silence, and as it were the resistant atmosphere of life itself.

On one occasion Jean spent the night at the Hôtel d'Angleterre, and for the first time, in a strange room, was conscious neither of oppression nor of melancholy. When he entered, sick at heart, and laid down what he was carrying, a small armchair received the burden within its arms of white-painted wood, and kept them there beside him with an air of smiling welcome. The double door had swung to behind him, and the curtain, by making silence absolute, had, so it seemed to him, banished the rest of the world to so great a distance that he felt inclined to jump with joy, and to kiss through the hanging folds the little door on which he could count not to open again. Behind the table a fire was burning in a small hearth of carved wood, and to this a chair had been drawn, so low, so wide and so embracing, that he need make no movement in order to approach the blaze. So deeply touched did he feel by the attention to his comfort made manifest in the position of its arms, by the whole air of the charming little object, that he said smiling at his own words, "Good: how nice it is in here—not that I feel the need yet of settling near the fire." And the chair seemed to answer him, "Don't worry: I shall be here when you want me. Do just as you like and make yourself at home." The walls which seemed to be holding the room in a tender hug isolating it from the rest of the world, were close beside him on every side, busy about his interests, watching him, making a sharp turn at the corners, always careful to leave room for the table, the chairs, withdrawing altogether where the little bookcase stood, and opening out at the far end to accommodate the bed, which thus found itself happily enclosed in a sort of alcove which looked neither cramped nor lost nor lone, so careful were the walls not to withdraw too far, and, as it were, saying, "Here, you know, we are," but all the same leaving it well set in the open space of the room and even pressing it closely from behind so as to keep it there. As though to contribute to all the care that was being taken of our friend, columns, but without ornaments, sustained a tester, thrusting upwards, but with no drapery or hangings, so that he could have a clear view of all the things which he might need though not forcing them on his attention. Not far from the fireplace there was a small door almost within reach of his hand when he came to undress. It opened on to three tiny additional rooms in which there was everything in the way of convenience that he could possibly require. But they were each of them so minute that they gave no feeling that one was not still in the bedroom, from which one could shut oneself off by closing the door, though even then one felt oneself to be in it still rather than to have entered a quite different place, since no outer door, no staircase, could bring anyone to it, and one felt that it was the end and limit of this little world which no living soul from outside could approach. When Jean had shut the little door which had revealed to him the sequence of these three small rooms—it stayed there shut discreetly until such time as one might want to pass through it again—he went into the third, and smallest, of them all, which since it gave on to the other two was longer than it was wide. But if he wanted to make it smaller still, and so feel isolated from all that was waiting for him in the main room, he could by shutting the second door, reduce the space to that of two of the small rooms only and by shutting the third to that of the exiguous dimensions of the last. The doors of all these, so to speak, compartments could be opened or shut in a moment, so that with a single gesture he could change the proportions of his room, so that its size could be doubled, trebled or reduced to a half or a third, while still remaining comfortable and charming, as also the field of his vision and the sense of his isolation, alternatively opening on to emptiness, or concentrated. When all the doors were closed the room was like a cell into which he had withdrawn to perform some solitary exercise. He was filled with an excited, an almost unbridled sense of power and isolation. Sometimes he felt shut in because as a result of his seclusion nobody could reach him: sometimes the world seemed to open out because in spite of it nobody could enter. There in that room he could with perfect security have concealed a secret or committed a crime. The walls not too wide apart, the ceiling not too high, were always close to him charming to look at, pleasant to touch, protecting him, silently creating about him silence and isolation. And, since the hotel was next door to an old house dating from the fourteenth century, his window looked down into one of those completely enclosed courtyards where the view is limited to lovely doorways and wide windows. There was nothing anywhere that opened on to a wide expanse of emptiness. What he could see as he looked out was more like one of the tiny rooms which opened out behind the door beside the fireplace, or rather was an additional compartment closing in his retreat, rather than something different for him to look at. But a special sort of life filled it with animation, a life cut off from all the other lives around it, because the four houses which opened on to the courtyard had always been lived in by coachmen of the town—all that remained of its ancient population—who never mingled with its other elements. They were quiet enough as they washed down their cabs, and, besides, three large wooden shutters, obedient to the lightest touch, kept all noise from him while he slept. But if he went to the window one of the coachmen noticing him would sign to his companions not to make a noise. Then they would stop talking, would set their pails down noiselessly, and all that he could hear would be the drip of water from the wheels, and if he called down or seemed to be in need of anything, they would shout from the doorway of the coachhouse, and summon from the kitchen of the Hôtel de Chevreuse which faced the same yard on the opposite side, a servant who would at once go up to his room.

★

One day Jean went with Henri to the office of the Sergeant-Major of the Company commanded by Saint-Gerin. It was there that Saint-Gerin usually arranged to meet him and it was there that Jean would often go to call for his friend. On this particular occasion there was nobody within sight but the Quartermaster Corporal, a tall, thin, sickly young man whose good-natured face Jean had often noticed.

He was the son of one of the local farmers. "Good morning, Monsieur Santeuil," he said with a pleased expression, "has Monsieur de Réveillon brought you, have you brought Monsieur de Réveillon, or has good fortune brought you both at the same moment?" Just then Saint-Gerin arrived and asked Jean and Henri to go with him, but Jean registered a silent vow that he would come back to see the Quartermaster Corporal again, whose natural utterance of so charming a phrase had filled him with amazement. If you found in your innkeeper's room, in a remote part of the country, the poems of Alfred de Vigny, Emerson's *Essays*, and *le Rouge et le Noir*, would you not feel that you were in the presence of a kindred spirit with whom it would be delightful to have a talk?

A few days later when they were all having a meal together, Saint-Gerin mentioned a funeral. "Whose funeral?" asked Jean. "My Quartermaster Corporal's," said Saint-Gerin: "the poor fellow killed himself a few days ago. He was a bit mad." – "He was very intelligent," said Jean remembering the Corporal's words. "You think that because you hadn't seen much of him," said Saint-Gerin, "actually, he was nothing out of the ordinary." Jean quoted the phrase which had so taken his fancy. His companion thought it rather pretentious. That however was not true. "He wanted to impress you," said Saint-Gerin. Jean did not press the point. He knew that the phrase had been a proof of intelligence, though not the sort of intelligence which could grasp the details of a mobilization order quickly, summarize a statement or immediately grasp an instruction issued to him. On the other hand he did not feel altogether sure that intelligence of the kind that the Corporal had shown might not sometimes go with madness. But was it for that reason any the less valuable? Maybe it had delighted him only because, perhaps being predestined himself to madness, he sometimes thought that his own intelligence was to some extent similar.

★

Quite often while Henri was with Saint-Gerin undergoing instruction, Jean would pay a visit to the Promenade where because of an exhibition which had been held that year at Provins, musicians from various cities, engaged for the season, played every afternoon at five o'clock. They lived in cheap hotels, two, three, or sometimes more, messing in together, and knew scarcely a soul in Provins, though not seldom when the concert was over, two old devotees, a husband and wife whose heads could always be seen in the front row beating time like two musical instruments, frequently stayed behind to compliment the performers and to shake hands with the conductor. When their day's work was over, the musicians would all start off for home together. At each street they passed, a group of two or three would break away, until by the time the outskirts of the town were reached, only two remained who were staying at a very inferior inn.

One of these Jean knew by sight. One day when they passed him in the street, Saint-Gerin had pointed him out. His name was Paul Serran, and he was notorious in Provins by reason of an intrigue which he had conducted with a lady who happened to be making a short stay in the town. She had so far compromised herself as to live with him, and when she had departed, had left behind her two massive diamond rings and a promise that she would soon marry him. There was a certain amount of talk in Provins to the effect that nothing would come of it all in spite of Paul Serran's grand airs, his stiff carriage, his carefully cultivated expression of cold disdain, his upturned moustaches, his ruddy cheeks, his impenetrable gaze, his flowing Inverness cape, his cavalryman's walk—all the things in fact which were "him all over" and made him so attractive. Nevertheless, he was fond of displaying his two rings, as well as a few recent letters as evidence that his happiness had merely been put off for a while. He was regarded with admiration by two little violin players who sat behind him and were occasionally regaled with jokes at the expense of the conductor or of the aged performer on the 'cello, which, uttered in a cold, contemptuous voice, made them laugh a good deal, and filled them with a feeling of devoted gratitude. It was clear that for them he was "a character", compared with whom the rest of the orchestra counted for nothing. The many women who had a passion for him, or knowing his reputation came to look at him, could not help being amazed at seeing him always punctually in his place, following the movements of the conductor's baton, and playing the same things as the other musicians —filled with wonder that he should in fact be just one of them. They felt much as one does when knowing that the son of the family is a man well known for talent or worldly pretensions, one finds him at his parents' parties doing the honours along with his brothers, or when one sees a celebrated actor playing a minor role—so difficult is it for us to realize that something which our imagination has isolated, is merely part of some quite different whole.

One of the violins was a young man of seventeen, with long hair hanging over his forehead, and what is generally supposed to be a typical musician's appearance. He had a solemn expression which never altered, remained in his seat during the intervals, or went out by himself and stood apart. He never talked to the others, nor returned with them.

*

Sometimes after he had got home at five o'clock, Jean would go out into the town which, rearing up about him in the night, like a church, set its hundreds of candles and lamps gleaming in the darkness. He brushed against women returning from their work, men on their way to the café, strangers who glanced at him as they passed, never to think about him again, and all hastening to this or that house, where, behind the glazed windows, smoky lamps revealed a life into which he would never penetrate. With the evening wind whistling round the street corners to keep him company, with the smell of cooking food in his nostrils, and the rain blowing in his face while the hour sounding from the church of Saint-Matthieu momentarily reverberated in the silence —the bulk of the building making so dense a blackness that one could tell someone was near only when one touched him—he could feel the life about him, an unknown life, but shared by men like himself who showed as shadows at lighted first-floor windows, visible within their own withdrawn and shut-in world, and, as he was, destined one day to be suddenly precipitated into the measureless black depths of nothingness, men of whom something would for a short while linger on in the framework of the low doors, in the filth of the blackened walls. This life of which because of habit we are not aware in the city where we live, the streets of which are nothing but named thoroughfares, thrilled his imagination, so that he wanted to identify himself with what he saw and to draw profit from his sense of it.

Many were the times when looking at some woman who had caught his eye in the street, or when after getting back to the hotel, taking his dinner in the dining-room in the company of some other woman, at that hour of the evening when relaxed by warmth, enjoying a sense of comfort quite new to him, the stimulating effect of the meal acting upon him without his giving it a thought, the lustres casting an

entrancing light before starting on his return journey to Réveillon, the
waiters more than usually polite and showing an inquisitive respect for
a distinguished stranger—his senses were worked to fever pitch, and
his imagination became over-heated. On a sudden the fancy would
come to him that the woman in question probably liked the look of
him, that in a moment there would be an avowal of mutual attraction,
that she would make an offer to him alone of her beauty and her life.
How delightful those dinners were, when the novelty of the dining-
room and of the guests so completely made him forget that he was
just having dinner, that in a flash all the sadness, all the oppressive
thoughts that had hung so heavy but a short while back, vanished
completely. At such times there is only one pleasure, the pleasure of
doing what you are doing at the moment. Only the people round you
claim your attention. Those you have left at home, at the thought of
leaving whom you were so melancholy, are wiped clean out of your
memory. Nor does the thought of such disloyalty sadden you, so
complete is your happiness. But alas! the head-waiter looks at his
watch, and tells you that the carriage is waiting. But so wholly is your
mind at ease that even so you cannot feel sad, and between your two
journeys through the night is set the bright, warm memory of that
festal dining-room, and all the projects you have formed in connexion
with the desires aroused by each new, charming object seen in the new
strange town, remain in your consciousness like the stirrings of a sweet
and gentle dream.

6. *The Military*

And so it came about that Jean and Henri struck up a friendship with Saint-Gerin, with several lieutenants of his acquaintance, and a number of young men of good family who were doing their military service at Provins and had been to some extent taken under their wing. One of these called Luce, a friend of Madame Marmet, asked Jean whether he would dine with him one evening. Jean chose a day when Henri was the guest of Saint-Gerin and turned up about six o'clock. He found himself in a house each room of which was occupied by one of Luce's friends, since, as they were all together in the same regiment, they had decided to join forces and have a retreat in the town. On the ground-floor there was a common dining-room where they foregathered every evening. They had found a lieutenant already installed in one of the rooms, but the landlord had undertaken to arrange matters satisfactorily. The officer in question was a man of breeding, was careful not to embarrass the young men, and even went so far as to give them a friendly greeting when he passed them on the stairs, behaviour which in view of the fact that the Colonel (brother of a linen-draper) had given strict orders that none of his men were to have rooms in town, was a sort of tacit expression of mockery at his expense, of a sceptical attitude towards discipline, and a way of putting himself on a footing of equality with the other tenants, which delighted them.

Since Luce had to be back in barracks before nine, and Jean was to return early to Réveillon, it had been agreed that dinner should not be late. At six therefore Jean climbed the stairs to Luce's room, where to judge from the glow of half-burned logs the fire had been lit for some time, though being well nursed (there were plenty of extra logs in the hearth) it was still roaring away merrily, was in fact just the sort of blaze which soldiers like to find when they return, thoroughly chilled, to their rooms. The lamp, which had obviously been sent from Paris by an affectionate family with elegant tastes, was of the kind that will light a room for several hours without having to be replenished. Luce came forward to greet his guest. He apologized for his dressing-gown beneath which the red trousers, which he had not yet taken off, were plainly visible. Four or five other young men scrambled to their feet, one of them still wearing uniform, a second in his shirt-sleeves, a third turning round from the washstand where with Luce's permission, he was busy shaving, for, the several rooms all adjoining one another, their occupants had a way of reading their letters and taking their tea in those of their neighbours. From time to time others appeared on the threshold, where they stopped on seeing Jean. One of them wanted to borrow a sheet of writing-paper from Luce, another to scrounge one of his English biscuits, a third to ask what exactly they were supposed to read up in the *Manual of Military Theory*.

"Let me introduce my friends," said Luce: "Monsieur Singlin, Monsieur de La Tour-Hivette, Monsieur Seureau; the Marquis de Poitiers, Monsieur Kahn." Each responded with a friendly greeting. One apologized for his odd get-up, and made a joke about the joys of army life, his frank open face, and intelligent expression, precluding any possible offence in what he was saying; Monsieur de La Tour-Hivette departed with his razor to his own room, there to finish his shaving. Luce couldn't think what had happened to Monsieur Seureau, whereupon Monsieur Kahn and Monsieur de Poitiers explained that he had gone to order some fresh tea for Jean who felt deeply touched by the attention. He wanted to wash his hands, and Luce said he would send for some hot water, but Monsieur de Poitiers, who had just had some brought to his room, insisted on taking him along there and on their way across the landing—which was in darkness, as though to conceal the extreme simplicity of the establishment—Jean could see through the doors left ajar by those who were for the moment with Luce, other brightly lit rooms. One occupant, hearing Poitiers's footsteps, opened his door, but on seeing Jean gave a wave of the hand and shut it again. In a short while Jean and Poitiers went back to Luce's room. A young man called Planteau who had had work to do until half past six, came in. At sight of Jean, he stopped on the threshold, gave a military salute without removing his shako, and looked at the others inquiringly. Luce introduced him to Jean and the others began at once to pull his leg about having more work to do than the rest of them. He kept up a running commentary of complaints and grumbles which the others and especially Poitiers seemed to find highly amusing. It was easy to see that he was treated as an agreeable butt. He for his part went on with his grumbling, though in fact he took his duties very seriously. He was informed of all the fatigues announced for the next day and occasionally one of the company would invent a non-existent one in the hope of producing a still more violent reaction. Since he was a thoroughly good fellow, he shook his head now and again with a broad grin as though to show that he knew the others were pulling his leg. But he hastened all the same to resume his angry attitude, that being what was expected of him, and because he felt obscurely that it was the basis of his popularity. He groused in much the same way that a child will whistle when he is playing the part of a train, and his little friends are the travellers riding in it.

The atmosphere by this time had become very thick because everyone was smoking. Luce asked Jean whether he minded and offered him a cigarette. Seeing that he refused, Poitiers offered one of his which were Russian, of a brand for which Jean happened to have a great liking. Very soon they went down to dinner. One apologized for appearing in full uniform explaining that he'd got to start back to barracks very shortly. Luce on the other hand asked to be forgiven for sitting down in his dressing-gown. Planteau, who had not had time to read up his *Theory*, sent word by the owner of the house that he wouldn't appear until the chicken was on the table and this made everybody laugh. Since he was particularly partial to champagne, they hid the bottles on the floor when they heard him coming, so that he should think it had all been finished. One appeared laughing uproariously, and after carefully shutting the door, announced in a loud voice and still laughing, that he had run into Monsieur Saulces on the stairs who had asked him for a light. At this important item of news silence descended upon the table. Seureau, for it was he who had had this piece of good luck, said that he had sprung to attention and replied "Certainly, sir!" after which when they parted, he had noticed that the Lieutenant—who could see through the open door the party of privates drinking champagne—gave a smile.

"That must have made him sit up!" Poitiers could not help exclaiming with an air of satisfaction which seemed to be shared by the others who were in a mingled condition of uneasiness and happiness. "Then you don't think he'll give us a dose of C.B.?" asked Kahn, in the hope of persuading Seureau to repeat his account of the memorable scene. "Don't be an ass!" replied the latter. "Can you see Saulces giving anybody C.B.? I've told you, he looked jolly envious when he saw the champagne. He'd a dam' sight rather have dinner with us than spend a boring evening with Cotonet and the rest of 'em." – "You ought to have asked him: he'd have been very welcome," said Luce, carrying off with a laugh this harmless little joke which was about on a par with the story of the decent tradesman saying to somebody who had just seen the Emperor of Russia drive past—"Why didn't you bring him along for a bite?—you should have told him I'd be delighted." Planteau obliged with a description of his passing Cotonet in the street, who had returned his salute and then immediately started to scratch his head, in order to make it quite clear that it wasn't out of politeness that he had raised his hand to his *képi* (obviously, these various little peculiarities in returning salutes and addressing the men were matters of the keenest interest, as might be, for a lover of the theatre, Baron's vocal tricks, or the way Sarah Bernhardt has of mumbling whole speeches so that not a word is audible). "You ought to have said 'I'm just off home: rue des Bons-Enfants: have you any objection to that?'—I'm rather afraid he's smelt a rat." But their land-lady who was serving the meal in person said that she knew Monsieur Cotonet well, that he was a nice gentleman and a regular scream, and a good deal politer with her than that Monsieur de Saint-Gerin they all made such a fuss about. "Not with us, he isn't," said Luce.

At this moment Saint-Serves appeared just back off leave. Each of those present began asking him how he had found his family, which reminded Luce to inquire of Planteau about his sister who was ill. But Saint-Serves had more important things to tell. The previous evening at the Paix, he had seen Saint-Gerin with the Duc de Frettes. They had been with a party of ladies. At once the table was all ears. Saint-Serves had been in "civvies" but he felt pretty sure that Saint-Gerin had recognized him, because he had looked more than once in his direction. "What's it matter if he did?" said Luce. "He's a decent chap and wouldn't say anything."–"He was wearing a blue overcoat with a fur collar," said Saint-Serves. This piece of news was intended for Kahn who attached great importance to clothes and though he had not changed for dinner, displayed spotless linen and a tie which matched his socks. He said that the only two times he had run across Saint-Gerin in Paris, the latter had been sporting the most beautifully cut evening suit, adding that even when he was on duty he had four different pairs of fancy pants and was far and away smarter than any cavalry officer.

Jean roused everybody's interest by announcing that he knew Saint-Gerin who as a matter of fact, had asked him to dine that very evening, though he couldn't accept because he was already engaged to Luce.

"So that's what his batman—who sleeps in the same barrack-room as I do, meant," said Kahn, "when he said his boss had company." – "He's asked me again for Thursday," said Jean. "I bet you'll find Lepureau there, and Captain de Traverese, and Toulié," said Kahn. "Toulié?—don't be an ass!" said Luce, "you don't think, do you, that Saint-Gerin asks people like Toulié to dinner?" Jean spoke of Servier, for whom he had a great liking. But he had only recently joined the regiment, and the others knew nothing about him beyond the fact that he had the reputation of being a good sort, though a bit of a stickler. He had given a man who failed to salute him two days in the cells. On the other hand, when his Company was out route marching, he always stood drinks all round, and was free with his money. They described his way of conducting drill movements, and this interested Jean enormously. It appeared that when he said "About turn!" or "Right incline!" instead of dragging the words out as their own captain did, he spoke them sharply raising his sword very high and that this produced an extremely smart effect. Also though when he wore his *képi* tilted to one side he looked as though he had a regulation hair-cut, Poitiers who had seen him the other day in the Company Office signing leave warrants, had noticed that he had a beautiful parting and fair, curly hair. The Commanding Officer thought that his manners were very curt but as the nephew of General de Terrainville who commanded the Division, he had a great deal of influence. He had furnished his Orderly Room in slap-up style and had had stoves put in all the barrack-rooms at his own expense. He was said to be in Cotonet's bad books. All they really knew about him was that he was not yet twenty-seven.

*

When dinner was finished and most of those present sat smoking with their half empty brandy glasses before them, Poitiers took his cigarette and glass over to the piano, and began singing everything that Jean asked of him. The various accompaniments, some soft, some loud, rippled easily under his fingers: he had a charming voice and kept his cigarette in the corner of his mouth all the time he was singing, while his head moved with a sort of nervous twitch, though normally he was a somewhat lymphatic young man. Every word of the songs and musical-comedy numbers with which he entertained them, was clearly audible. He went on endlessly, stressing the rhythm of the accompaniment, singing the woman's part—in the case of a duet—in a light head-voice, and thundering out the choruses so loudly that his listeners, every now and again, were quite transported with enthusiasm, especially when he gave a perfect imitation of some well-known actor. Jean was filled with admiration. Any other singer, any other pianist would have seemed lacking in warmth, would have seemed sadly limited, by comparison with this marvellous *brio*, this charming voice, these touches of humour so completely under control, so exquisitely phrased. They seemed not parodies or imitations at all, but fantasias of his own invention. The piano part was rich and varied. Fixing the keys with an indolent gaze, appearing to hesitate before striking the chords, making it quite clear that here there was a violin passage, that there the trombones came in, giving the effect of both instruments together, loosing all these different sonorities—with a weary and an absent air he filled the room with a combination of delicacy and violence.

It was as though Jean were listening to an incomparable talker. Here was a man for whom subtleties which would have escaped anybody else, presented no difficulty whatever. He could grasp, memorize and reproduce them with extraordinary power and complete ease, could draw from the piano, which many people think of as the mere spelling-book of music, floods of sound in which he effortlessly gambolled, like a gull riding a strong sea-wind, mingling his voice with its crash and tinkle, always unhurried, always at the right moment, and never taking his cigarette from his lips. When he started on his imitations, the essential peculiarity of each was so clearly marked, the quality which Jean had noted when he heard the person imitated performing in the theatre, though he had never defined it to himself, that its hold over him was more powerful than it would otherwise have been, and produced an almost too violent impact (so truly did the voice evoke, reveal, get to the heart of the essential fact, to the basic individuality of another concealed human entity, to the whole truth of the original) because it cast a blinding light on the mystery of something he had once felt, clarifying as it were the precise nature of the pleasure which this or that actor or actress, had once given him. As a result of this performance he at once ranked Poitiers far above anyone he had ever known. Had he wished to let his mother or Réveillon sample and share the most extraordinary experience that had ever come his way, he would have done so not by reading some book aloud to them, not by introducing them to some unusually distinguished man, but by making them listen to Poitiers rendering a chorus from *Lohengrin* or giving an

imitation of Yvette Guilbert. What he most admired about Poitiers
was the way in which quite simply and without ever attempting really
to *sing* a chorus, but merely evoking his listeners' recollections, awakening their somewhat imprecise memories of this or that effect, tune, or
word, he would suddenly say: "It goes, if I remember, something like
this," and, on the spur of the moment, recapturing some piece of
"comic business", bewailing the fact that he could not "get" the exact
manner in which Granier had played a particular scene, or reproduce
the little musical phrase played on the violins, show, even while he was
apologizing for not getting it quite right, that nothing had escaped
him, that he had accurately understood the way in which each point
had been made, that everything—the neatness of the librettist's wit,
the richness of the score, the personality of the singer—was within his
power to reproduce. Then, all of a sudden, he would start describing
something that had happened in barracks, with precisely the same
lightness of touch, as though, abandoning music for the moment, he
was giving rein, in spoken narrative, to the same gift of subtle observation which he had just been revealing in his performance at the piano.
There was nothing, it seemed to Jean, that he could not do.

But the time had come for the party to break up. Already through
the windows of the dining-room, which were on street level, soldiers
could be seen making their way back to barracks. Luce slipped out for
a minute to tidy himself up. The others began collecting their belts
from the various chairs. Planteau had already gone on ahead, grumbling
a good deal, and saying that he didn't want to be deprived of his
Sunday leave. Everyone said good night to Jean, shouting to Luce (for
whom he was waiting) to hurry and Jean thanked them with some
little show of embarrassment, because he was not quite sure whether
they had not in fact been his collective hosts. Finally he left with Luce,
Kahn and Poitiers, asking to be allowed to go with them as far as the
barrack gates. He felt the more awkward with Poitiers, not only
because lacking his gifts he tended to exaggerate their importance, but
because he magnified his own mediocrity, and imagined the contempt
in which Poitiers must hold him, feeling in the presence of a man who
could display with such ease his musical knowledge, his memory, his
voice, and his manual skill, the same sort of inferiority as may oppress
an awkward, shabby student who happens to find himself with a
brilliant man of the world whose clothes and manners are exquisite.
'To all that he adds personal charm, a good-breeding that makes light

of his accomplishments, and other merits beyond counting. I wonder what in his heart of hearts he really thinks of me?'

Poitiers's friends, although somewhat more inclined to take his gifts for granted, and aware of the limits of his repertory, did nevertheless unreservedly admire a facility which made him in their eyes a thoroughly intelligent fellow and an "out and out" musician. Planteau and Seureau on the other hand, having each of them enjoyed a musical education—though they were quite incapable of improvising, giving imitations, or singing—thought that his taste was abominable, his musical intelligence almost completely lacking, his mannerisms tedious, and knew that in other ways and in spite of his amusing manner of telling a story, and the perfect resemblance of his portraits (his skill as a painter was something Jean knew nothing of) and the charm of his manners, he was really far from being clever. But the others thought him so gifted that they were sure he could have turned his hand to anything and gone farther than anybody else. Jean however, having heard nothing but their compliments, never imagined that anyone could see Poitiers in any other way than he did. He was ashamed to think that he had nothing to offer in exchange for what he had been given, and when he thanked him for his evening, noticing that the other merely shrugged his shoulders and thanked *him* with an exquisite grace for listening, felt something of the embarrassment of a man who has been the recipient of princely hospitality which he has no way of returning. Gradually their little group began to be swelled by the addition of other soldiers on their way back to barracks. They all of them walked quickly, because they were late, and because the night was freezing cold.

"After roll-call, tell the canteen to send up some hot wine for the chaps in my room," said Luce to his batman who happened to be passing. "Are you going straight to bed?" asked Jean. "Yes," replied Poitiers. "There's a route march at five-thirty tomorrow morning, and we shall be on the go all day. I doubt whether there'll be time to go to our rooms in town, because there are lectures in the evening. Just ten minutes for a wash and a bite of grub's about all we shall get." The sound of the drum put an end to their farewells. Luce and his friends set off at a run. Jean picked up Réveillon who was waiting for him at the door of Saint-Gerin's billet, and on their way home in the Duke's carriage, gave an exaggerated account to Henri of Poitiers's prowess at the piano, thinking that the only way of conveying an idea—far from adequate though it was—of his gifts and his quite extraordinary intelligence.

7. *Winter at Réveillon*

For the past several days the cold had made occasional appearances. Now it seemed to have settled in for good. As soon as Jean was awake a servant came to set a match to the enormous logs piled in the hearth which occupied one whole side of the room. While hurrying through his toilet in the cold little washroom, he broke off now and again to run back on his bare feet so as to get a moment's warmth at the fire. There was no loitering in galleries and corridors, and in the drawing-room and the dining-room a place was made for each new arrival at the fire. Jean, taking advantage of the blaze while breakfast was being prepared, could not resist looking out of the window at the sun which had come out in spite of the cold, at the yellow poplars now suddenly touched with gold, at the pale, blue surface of the Marne, as brilliant as the cloudless sky, though never once all day would it manage to get warm. It was only just possible for Jean and Henri, who were neither of them chilly persons, to go driving after luncheon in an open carriage. More than once Jean had to stop the horses and run about for a while on the road to get the numbness out of his feet, for though the sky might smile, the woods give off a golden glitter, the water twinkle in the sun, they did not seem to understand what was wanted, and obstinately refused though in the kindliest way, to provide the two young men with the much needed warmth. There was no comfort now to be found in the sun, the open air and the woods. Only in the drawing-room was it present, where the greatest care was taken not to open any of the windows, to sit close in front of the fire on which, to increase the heat, coal was shovelled which gave off a red glow, after overcoats had been shed in the hall. Those entering the room, their faces purple with cold, and taken by surprise at finding it so pleasantly warm could not keep from smiling, from touching their cheeks which were now glowing, from rubbing their hands together, not so much because they were cold but to express their delight, and advancing their feet to the flames at the risk of burning their shoes. Having lost the power, the promise and the warmth which in spring is so pleasing, so titillating to the senses, and in summer has an almost material density, Nature now seemed to have nothing left but charm. Winter was already at hand. The trees, before being reduced to black skeletons, were golden: the sky, before becoming covered for months on end by grey clouds, before growing dark, caressing and sombre, was still unsullied: the river was blue and seemed already decked for a springtime that would never come. It was as though all these things were displaying the fullness of their grace for the first time. The world of the countryside was like a smile which vanishes in the middle of a silence, answering no question, uttering no word, but passing away as someone may disappear of whose grace we have not before had so near a view, leaving behind her only the sense of a delicate and tender presence.

But the cold, after for some days letting the sun appear in the world of Nature which it loves, over which having formerly been its king and its possessor it could no longer exert any influence, sent it too scurrying. There had come a greyness in the weather, and this now drew from the naked landscape different and more virile harmonies of colour. The season of regrets, of useless memories, and dying smiles was over. The woods no longer garnished with the sun's brilliant dyes had lost all poetry. Henri, climbing to the topmost branches of a chestnut tree would shake them hard, and Jean who had been standing with hands outstretched, fearful of the noise the falling nuts would make, ran to collect them from among the rotting leaves. The leaves of the Virginia Creeper had been shed, and their red looked brighter under the iron-grey sky. The last sheaves had been gathered from the fields, and nothing now was to be seen but a couple of horses driven by a ploughman who was busy turning the earth over which birds were flying. From time to time a gunshot could be heard. The cock's crow, seeming to cleave the frost-hard air, took on a vivid quality like the last red berries withering on the hedgerows. Such flowers as still remained along the verges of the roads, such trees as still had kept their foliage, had the unhappy sickly look of the charmless blossoms, of the stunted trees one finds close to the sea. There was scarcely a moment when they had not to bend beneath the wind which seemed determined to uproot the half-faded cornflowers, the yellowed daisies clinging to the earth. Situated like children whose father threatening them with a beating, holds them helpless by the collar, they could not flee from the constant threat of violence, but pressed close to the ground and scarcely ever raised their heads but with a petal the less. The trees

moaned impatiently waving their skinny arms. In the Park in front
of the Château from which the sun, the soft air, the summer warmth
had fled, the two statues no longer dappled with shade had the look of
forgotten things, not knowing how with their sea-bathed faces, their
attitude of frozen flight, to get through the winter now that all the
things that suited them so well had gone.

*

Winter was come indeed bringing with it those pleasures of which
the summer dreamer knows nothing—the delight when the fine and
glittering day shows in the window, though one knows how cold it is
outside; the delight of getting as close as possible to the blazing range
which in the shadowy kitchen throws reflections very different from
the pale gleams of sunlight in the yard, the range we cannot take with
us on our walk, busy with its own activity, growling and grumbling
as it sets to work, for in three hours time luncheon must be ready; the
delight of filling one's bowl with steaming *café-au-lait*—for it is only
eight o'clock—and swallowing it in boiling gulps while servants at
their tasks come in and out with a, "Good morning: up early, aren't
you?" and a kindly, "It's snug enough in here, but cold outside."
accompanying the words with that smile which is to be seen only on
the faces of those who for the moment are thinking of others and not
of themselves, whose expressions, entirely freed from egotism, take
on a quality of vacillating goodness, a smile which completes that
earlier smile of the bright golden sky touching the window-panes, and
crowns our every pleasure as we stand there with the lovely heat of the
range at our backs, the hot and limpid flavour of the *café-au-lait* in our
mouths; the delight of night-time when, having had to get up to go
shiveringly to the icy lavatory in the tower, into which the air creeps
through the ill-fitting window we later return deliciously to our
room, feeling a smile of happiness distend our lips, finding it hard not
to jump for sheer joy at the thought of the big bed already warm with
our warmth, of the still burning fire, the hot-water bottle, the coverlets
and blankets which have imparted their heat to the bed into which we
are about to slip, walled in, embattled, hiding ourselves to the chin as
against enemies thundering at the gates, who will not (and the thought
brings gaiety) get the better of us, since they do not even know where
we have so snugly gone to earth, laughing at the wind which is

roaring outside, climbing up all the chimneys to every floor of the great house, conducting a search on each landing, trying all the locks: the delight of rolling ourselves in the blankets when we feel its icy breath approaching, sliding a little farther down the bed, gripping the hot-water bottle between our feet, working it up too high, and when we push it down again feeling the place where it has been still hot, pulling up the bedclothes to our faces, rolling ourselves into a ball, turning over, thinking—'How good life is!' too gay even to feel melancholy at the thought of the triviality of all this pleasure.

And what wonderful meals Jean had! Madame de Réveillon would say, "We must be punctual this evening because I have ordered a soufflé for you, and it must be eaten *at once*." – "A *soufflé*!—how scrumptious!" Henri would exclaim. "The least I can do is to see that you are properly fed, my poor dears! There's nothing much else I can offer you in this weather. Don't forget now: half past seven sharp! You've got plenty of time between now and then: it's only four, it gets dark so early now." There would be plenty of time indeed, time to read, time to go upstairs and take one's boots off, time to warm oneself by the fire, and when the footman came to take one's dirty boots, to say, "It's cold," because it is so lovely to say, "It's cold," when one has a good fire and the warmth is beginning to spread through one's body.

8. *La Vicomtesse Gaspard de Réveillon*

Among the visitors was a young newly-married couple, the Vicomte and Vicomtesse Gaspard de Réveillon. The bride who before her marriage was a Crispinelli, was nineteen years old and a poet, some of whose remarkable verses the *Revue des Deux Mondes* had recently published. Her whole body, her features, her eyes, radiated so vivid a charm that it would never have occurred to one to wonder whether this detail was better or less good than that, so great a power of attraction did her whole enchanting originality exert, so markedly present was it in everything she did or said. Consequently Jean was as much amazed when he heard somebody say that her nose was rather too prominent as he would have been had somebody reputedly of good taste, remarked of a book to which he was passionately devoted, that this or that character was well drawn, but that the composition was defective—or had made some similar comment. For he was strongly responsive to the essential quality of things but could never clearly define it. The true nature of this great poet (Madame Gaspard de Réveillon)—was never apparent in what she said. On the contrary to judge from the jokes she was continually making, by the way she mocked at people who talked about spring, love, etc.—one would have gathered that she was utterly contemptuous of such matters. If one spoke to her of herself the impression one got was that all she cared about was food, bed and being thoroughly lazy. But it would have been utterly untrue to say that her poems lacked sincerity. On the contrary they expressed something that went so deep in her, that she could not even think, still less speak, of it, or define it, because it was so different from her apparent self that to have revealed it in talk would have seemed to her to be a sort of a sacrilege, as Madame Santeuil would have felt if she had had to mention in conversation how devoted she was to Monsieur Sandré. Listening to Madame Santeuil one was aware only of her constant sly digs at everything—even at her father—

though they were always affectionately phrased. It seemed that the only way she knew of expressing her fondness and her admiration was to talk rather mockingly about his fads and to relate numerous stories about his "little ways". Similarly, all that Madame de Réveillon would say about the winter was that she did not like the cold or that it gave her aches and pains. The pleasure that actually she took in it was an instinctive feeling which she did not feel to be a suitable subject of casual conversation. But the true essence of things about which she never spoke—was all that really mattered to her: by nothing else could she be truly transported and filled with delight as one realized when one noticed that it formed the constant matter of her poetry—poems being precisely the commemoration of our inspired moments which in themselves are often a sort of commemoration of all that our being has left of itself in moments past and gone, the concentrated essence of ourselves which we exude without realizing that we are doing so, which a perfume smelled in that past time, a remembered light shining into our room, will suddenly bring back so vividly, that it fills us with a species of intoxication, so that we become completely indifferent to what is usually called "real life", in which it never visits us unless that life be at the same time a past life, so that freed for a moment from the tyranny of the present, we feel something that spreads out beyond the actual minute.

It was noticeable too that this young woman's poems were consistently sad. Their unalleviated melancholy somehow convinced one that her inner self was genuinely sad, and that this sadness, the essences of things, the memory of herself which she savoured in certain recurring scents—the odour of tangerines in a warm room, the sumptuous festivities of Christmas when we have often brought to the table a heart chock-full of thoughts about somebody who is not there, who never will be there, whose absence gives to the sundering snow without, to the posts that never bring a letter from her, a feeling that is not one so much of absence as of charm—was for her a point of departure for impassioned dreaming, in other words for one of the few activities which she felt as real, a sense of passionate ecstasy being the only sign by which we can recognize the truth of the ideas that flow in upon us. Yet her conversation was unceasingly gay. She was for ever making people laugh by some amusing comparison, by her manner of recounting the least little incident, so that there was never any need for her to tell deliberately funny stories—a funny story would not have been any the funnier for being told by her—by a gift she had for discovering something amusing in all the circumstances of life, in the conversations she had heard, in everything she did—because a sensitive person with the faculty of sympathy which means being able to place oneself in another person's shoes, and not always being locked up in one's own concerns, can see an element of the comic everywhere, whereas those on the contrary who say things intended to sound comic to others, are never thinking of anybody but themselves. Her observation, being free of all concern for self, resulted in her gaiety, since it was so to speak set fairly and squarely at the very centre of her character, being never anything but indulgent and kindly. Without inquiring too deeply into the causes which make it possible to find subjects of gaiety always close at hand, the proof of that possibility can be found in the fact that persons of sensitive intelligence are capable of finding comic potentialities in everything and everybody, thereby demonstrating that if some people hold the belief that there is very little that is laughable in the world, the reason is that they lack the ability to find it. Intelligence shows us that gaiety is a basic element in everything, which we can disengage from all that comes our way, without having to look for it, just as carbon is proved by chemical analysis to be not something which we need go to the moon to find but a quality that is present in all bodies which we find around us, needing only to be freed. Now the wonderful gift of being able to find our own essence in things, or the true essence of those things which we call poetry, an essence the revelation of which is so marvellous that it throws us into a condition of enthusiasm and compels us to take up our pen and write, so that inspiration becomes for the poet the very sign and proof of excellence in what he sees, this condition not being constant but linked with deep sensibilities in ourselves, which may themselves be linked with a certain power of organic response which the changes of the seasons, for instance, may provoke by bringing back memories and modifying things to which we have become so used that we no longer feel them, the poet may in fact sadly reflect that if when he was emerging from adolescence (a period of life when he may already have been inspired though without realizing it, not yet having con-templated the truth of his own nature) and had begun to see that what he had so far believed did not in fact exist, someone had said to him, "Inspiration exists: poets are not like other men," he would have been transfigured with delight, and the world would have become for him again a lovely fairyland, as surely as if he had been told that there really were such things as fairies, or that hypnotism was a fact, though now he feels only too strongly that inspiration is something true and actual. He waits for it and it does not come: he tries to work himself into a state of consciousness in which the surface of material things becomes pervious so that he can see into them, as in sleep for instance, when all he once has felt streams back into his consciousness, and he can in some sort though in vain recover the power he no longer has, and is visited by the knowledge that he really can see into things, is conscious of the deeply moving sensation aroused in him by some vision of the country-side, though on waking he cannot recover it, strive though he may with all the frenzy of the impotent, who cannot achieve his desire (when Goethe lay dying he found in delirium just the words he needed, yet how faded and lifeless are the things he wrote in his old age!) At such times inspiration holds little charm for him. He is like a man dying of love who knows that love is real, but is made no happier by that knowledge, since it is as much part and parcel of himself as life itself, or like a sick man who, compelled to spend all his days in bed, cannot find in that fact the charm that others do. But should inspiration return, though he will no longer find happiness in the thought that the world is once more a fairyland, or that poets are inspired persons, the pleasure it gives him will be genuine.

Now this marvellous gift exists in persons of superior powers, though most of the time no doubt they betray their superiority in the difficulty they find in sleeping, in laziness, in a squandering of their abilities, in unpunctuality, in bursts of temper, in a proneness to neuralgia, in egotism, in passionate tenderness and in abnormal nervous sensibility, but also by an exaggerated working of their intellectual faculties which in conversation gives rise to that perpetual awareness which is evidenced by their feeling for others, so that all poets at moments of intimate converse, show themselves to be charming talkers and always gay, this being no proof of insincerity on their part but rather of a law of co-existence between brilliant intellectual faculties and their marvellous gift which for the time being is in abeyance, and emerges only in solitude. From whence arises the belief that poets would be better employed in writing funny stories about the world around them, or essays in eloquence (for if in the course of con-versation they take sides in an argument, how easily the words come to them, with what fire and passion do they express themselves!) But they are secretly aware that they have quite other things to write, things which alone can awaken in them the true, poetic, enthusiasm. And if at times they do write differently, they feel it is not themselves who are doing so, that they are writing thus only because they need money, or because they want to please the public and at such times the mysterious onrush of delight does not visit them.

It was only natural that Madame de Réveillon, like many other gifted persons, should have about matters which did not at all engage the poet in her, ideas which born of her brilliant intellect, were necessarily so different from those current in her circle, that they were bound to shock and did shock, to such an extent that she was widely regarded as being ill-bred and unbalanced and was thought to exercise a deplorable influence over her husband. She had for instance recently signed a manifesto on behalf of Dreyfus, which action, in view of the name she bore, had aroused a good deal of indignation though not perhaps contempt, and was in fact so much at variance with all that her position in the world implied, that it was held to be completely un-important though tiresome for the family, and a proof of how sadly lacking she was in a sense of her responsibilities. But it was only what might be expected of a woman who trampled the most sacred things underfoot, spoke slightingly of religion and high birth, habitually arrived an hour late for dinner, was a writer, wore the most extra-ordinary clothes—not at all what the Faubourg Saint-Germain was accustomed to—entertained authors of really abominable books, and in the Dreyfus affair had taken sides against the army and hobnobbed with the nastiest type of anarchist (yes, really! one found it hard to believe, didn't one, that a Réveillon could be found in the anarchist camp?)—all of which went to prove that one *couldn't* be too careful in this matter of marriages—for the poor young man was passionately in love with his wife so that he quite naturally shared her opinions, and that in Society one ought to be *very* suspicious of all authors, of women who wrote poetry, etc., etc., because that sort of thing invariably went with every kind of abomination (as the example of Madame de Réveillon showed only too plainly). But what gave more offence than anything else was her intolerable self-assurance. Though frequently silent—which in itself was a sign of ill-breeding—when she *did* start on one of her stories she poured out words at such a rate, interspersed her narrative with so many vivid expressions, stimulating sallies and irresistible touches of humour, that she became intoxicated by the sound of her own voice, sometimes talked for five minutes on end—it might be entertaining but it really was rather exhausting!—and became so completely wrapped up in herself that she frequently interrupted much older persons: in addition to which she sometimes laughed so loudly when she happened to meet an artist at some reception, that the dowagers, though they said nothing, thought the more.

But if it be true that the species of automatism known as good manners destroys all spontaneity, all genuine expression of personality, and all poetry, it is no less true that poetry and the manifestation of intelligence, destroys automatism, and consequently, good manners. If a truly gifted person takes to Society, he will undoubtedly in the long run become a mechanical doll and completely unproductive. When that happens the general view is that he has grown wiser, more settled, generally improved: and, indeed it is true that a man who at the age of twenty could never pass an examination, and was incapable of contributing an article to a daily paper, will at thirty be in a position to pass into the Diplomatic Service and write for the magazines. But with somebody who by birth belongs to the highest circles so that the desire to "climb" is inoperative, and intellectual boredom finds no compensation in gratified vanity, the case is very different. For such a one the denizens of the fashionable world have no prestige, and there can consequently be no wish to imitate them. The young woman will remain herself, and just as her marvellous gift may manifest its presence, physically, in palpitations of the heart and nettle-rash (why not? Summer is characterized as much by its flies and mosquitoes as by roses and star-spangled nights) so in the social organism which she has long outgrown, it will show itself in unpunctual habits, by a look of withdrawn brooding when persons of great experience are speaking, by an inability to stifle fits of nervous laughter, by an exquisite and involuntary choice of adjectives, each more exciting than the last, which flow from her while she talks, as when in a *cotillon* somebody stationed out of sight calls the different figures to the conductor, a choice which seems to be the height of artificiality and little suited to general conversation. A poetess who contributes articles to a magazine may seem to write with affectation as a result of that very self-assurance which leads her to talk so forcefully and to make funny remarks about the very persons she is talking to. But there was another reason for Madame de Réveillon's assurance. Though many criticized her, many admired her, spoiled her, encouraged her sallies. Little by little she had quite won over even her near relations, who now formed a charmed, insatiable public, having come to recognize her superior gifts, not as a result of any definite proof but because she gave play to them in many other circumstances of life—by the happy turn of phrase she could give to letters which were passed round in the family circle, by her more than usually wise and penetrating views on things and people which led to her being considered as a wise counsellor (besides she had such an ingenious way of cutting the ground from under the feet of those who were still critical of her, and knew precisely how best to answer them), by reason even of the spiteful things said about her by the mothers of intelligent daughters, who maintained that her verses were no more than "pretty" and that if she were not a Réveillon, and hadn't got eccentric manners, no one would pay any attention to her, entertaining as she did people who were not only not noble by birth, but were not even like Z, the painter, and X, the poet, ennobled by adoption, both of whom she went so far actually as not to admire. According to these backbiters she was losing her touch, was intimate only with bores, would soon have no "salon" at all, had smirched her good name and was not really so very intelligent when one came to think of it. She infinitely preferred talking with her maid than with so genuinely distinguished a person as Z the painter and scarcely ever read a book. How could a woman like that be called intelligent? All the same Jean found her wholly delightful, and was deeply envious of the husband whom she appeared to love dearly, who was for ever running round to publishers' offices to correct her proofs. But she never said that she loved him and would sometimes look at him with a twinkle in her eye and pull his leg about those visits of his to her publishers. For her love of her husband, like the poetry in which he often figured, was entirely absent from her conversation. But her deep serious eyes, her graceful fragile body seemed to be the outward and visible signs of that profound inner self for which they had been created, which had perhaps over the passing years, given a still greater depth to her eyes, and even more marked fragility to her body.

9. *Memories of the Regiment*

The only beautiful discoveries that a poet can make lie within himself. Give him a moment of inspiration, in other words, so order matters that he can establish communication with himself and you will bring him happiness. By giving him wealth, honours or pleasures, you give him nothing, for you make him come only further out of himself. But this taking possession of himself is not something that can be achieved directly. He has to receive himself from those mysterious hands which have it in their power to bestow that gift. To show him a beautiful woman, an intelligent woman, means nothing. But one there may be who, seen at some earlier period of his life, has left on him an ineffaceable impression. Perhaps if he sees her again he will recover her entirely, and her presence will then give him something truly worth his having, because it will restore to him a portion of himself. Several times a week when Jean was with his regiment, he dined as the guest of his captain, and often on these occasions one of his fellow-guests was a young woman of about thirty, a handsome, smiling creature, who owed to her magnificent singing voice and aristocratic connexions the fact that she was a considerable personage in the city of Orléans. There was something about her reminiscent of a wax figure, as much by reason of the regularity of her features, and by her perpetual quizzical air, as of the rather conventional beauty with which she was blessed, namely full round cheeks and a finely pencilled mouth. She was used to being complimented and had acquired the habit—no less true of her character than suited to her type of good looks, of receiving all appreciative remarks with a certain show of scepticism, "Do you mean that? Is that what you really think?" (indicative of humour in the humorous, of modesty in the well-bred, and, generally a mark of worldliness which life in a country town had frozen into a mannerism): she was fond of repeating such questions *ad nauseam* in an arch tone which was really completely fatuous, because there was nothing particularly funny about seeming to doubt the sincerity of a compliment when its sincerity was perfectly obvious. It is thus that a man's customary responses, his reaction to the ordinary circumstances of life, reveal his true character. The way he looks when walking along the street is the true key to his attitude to life. It may be concealed under a worried expression, an imperturbably solemn outside, a bored look which a smile may, for a moment dissipate, but it will at once resume its sway in the eyes of the casual passer-by.

*

By the time the Sergeant had given his men leave to go out it was very cold and pitch dark. While Jean was getting ready, his batman put the finishing touches to his polishing, and handed him the various objects of his equipment. "Are you sure that's my belt? You know I'm dining out tonight."–"At the lieutenant's?" asked one of the men who were lying on their beds. For it frequently happens that those who never give us an inkling of the fact in their ordinary behaviour, turn out to know—as may later transpire in some casual remark, or in something we are told that they have said—all about our fine friends. "Yes," answered Jean, "aren't you going out, chum?" He liked saying "chum", it gave him a feeling that he was one of them. "Not tonight: I shall trickle down to the canteen for a while, and then turn in."

A chime sounded. Four o'clock! The days were drawing in. "I meant to give the ceiling a wash down . . . but it's too dark now . . . better wait until the days get longer." For we all have plans, projects lying outside ourselves, but for all of us time passes. Jean was ready at last: five o'clock sounded, and he set out with Lachaud who had been waiting for the last five minutes, repeatedly telling him to hurry, threatening to go without him. Together they walked down the faubourg Bannier, and arrived at the little house where they had rented a room. They pushed open the door, collected their letters, and went upstairs. Fortunately the room was warm, and Jean asked Madame Ranvoyzé to bring up some punch for his friends. "Can you manage that?"–"Sure I can manage it: I'll run round to the grocer for two penn'orth of sugar. I expect there's some rum left. I'd better get a couple of ripe oranges while I'm about it—that all right? There'll be plenty for everyone"—and out she went.

When it turned six Jean said, "I must keep an eye on the time: I ought to be getting ready." Hot water was waiting for him on the wash-stand. He took off his belt and his greatcoat and started making himself clean. While doing so, he thought with pleasure of the dinner he was to have when, after walking through Orléans in the dark, he should arrive at last at the café du Loiret and go upstairs to the pleasant little private room with its blazing fire, in which his lieutenant was entertaining. A dinner is a sort of museum of greed, where the different exhibits, about which we have been dreaming in solitude with such intensity that the idea of seeing them actually in front of us, within reach of one's hand, just them and no others, is almost too overpowering.

Yes, there are moments when the thought of Rembrandt, a craving for Rembrandt, sweeps over us. We long for his dark shadows, his especial manner of treating light: we conjure up a vision of his gold-tinted flesh colours. Is not the same thing true of places? An autumn day comes when I should like to see a whole forest, when I am hungry for yellowing leaves, want to be walking beneath them, want material things with which to assuage the cravings of my spirit. But I want more than that—I want not only a forest but Fontainebleau. The more exigent that craving is, the more difficult to satisfy, the greater will be the pleasure, because there is only one thing in all the world which will give me what I need, one single place, one living presence, a personality which can be found nowhere else, compacted of the age of its streets, the way in which they lead into the forest, the shape of the hills, the look of the plain—a unique object, a definite spot, an individuality symbolized by its name which belongs to no other locality. Fontainebleau, a name as soft and golden as a bunch of gathered grapes. That place of which I am thinking so intensely, which I so long to see, actually exists—exists as something clearly defined by its distance from Paris, a product of the life which has yellowed some of its house fronts, has set up new houses in its newer districts, has added fresh trees and brought others down, leaning over one road, lying beside another, the bend of the Seine which here makes a twist and flows on without quays or harbours, sweet and naked, between the encroaching woods. Yes, if I take a train and go there it is Fontainebleau that I shall see, not something else which may be more or less beautiful, but the place itself, the thing that answers to the name which evokes for me such loveliness, which is really called Fontainebleau, which when I walk along its streets, when I touch its houses with my hand, when I move beneath its trees and sit on its rocks, can say to me, "Yes, you are in Fontainebleau: all this is Fontainebleau." Not the wishes of all the sovereigns in the world can so order matters as to turn some other place in which you may happen to be, some place perhaps a hundred times more beautiful or unusual, into Fontainebleau, whereas that officer passing by can say with truth that he is in garrison at Fontainebleau, and the lady who lives there when she invites you to dinner can say that she is inviting you to Fontainebleau: her letters bear across the stamp, like the darkness of the forest's undergrowth, a postmark with inscribed upon it the sweet and glorious name of Fontainebleau: the local chemist can style himself chemist at Fontainebleau—which indeed he is just as the concierge of the lady of your heart is *her* concierge, *her* hairdresser. The pavements are Fontainebleau pavements, and you can say to yourself, 'I am in Fontainebleau.' When you are far from it and let the thought of it come into your mind, it is not of other things as lovely, that you think, not sweeter woods not a more curious town that you desire to see. What you desire to see is that unique something, be it town or place, which by reason of its uniqueness cannot be anything else, over which you can exercise no power, from which you cannot take away one single day of all the days that it has lived, make older or younger what in fact it is—the full-flavoured accumulation of a past existence over which you have no control, in which you can do nothing but rejoice. Nothing else, no matter how beautiful, can ever be "as good as" what it is. What you long to see in order to feel truly that you are close to it, that this *really is* it, that your private imaginings have at last become actual—need not necessarily be any glimpse of great beauty, but merely the way in which the dining-room of the Hôtel de France et d'Angleterre juts out into the street, merely the spectacle of the rank of public cabs, one of which you can hire for a drive in the forest.

*

At other times that of which we dream is not Fontainebleau at all, is not a picture by Rembrandt nor by Watteau: it is the taste of sea-water, it is an oyster, it is the tiny drop of salty liquid drunk from the oyster's iridescent shell which has truly lived in the sea: or perhaps what we long for are Hobbema's avenues, the colour which Hobbema gave them, which has passed from its first fiery brightness and become dimmer until at last it has assumed the indefinable tint which now it holds. It is an oyster that we should like to raise to our lips and swallow while the Sauterne is being poured into a small glass standing there before us, filling it with yellow colour, with its own sweet, sharp taste —colour inimitable and taste which has a depth not to be found anywhere else so that Sauterne has its lovers, as certain canvases have theirs —for it gives a pleasure more fugitive perhaps but not less mysterious or less profound, not less noble even, since as to the master of a dog, as to a lover, it gives to its enthusiasts the feeling that they have attained to something which is the unique product of circumstances which can never be repeated.

How pleasant a museum is dinner, when the flavour of sea-water of which in our far inland town we have dreamed so vividly as almost to have the taste of it within our mouths, is brought to us, is within our easy reach brimming the shallow, silver-tinted, gritty cup; when the colour of the wine gleams like the glow of a picture behind the transparent protection of its glass; when course after course in endless succession is brought in dishes of silver set upon a dazzling cloth, so that in the space of a single hour we receive the full, direct sensation of many masterpieces, of which the desire of one alone suffices to fill with charm the lazy hour when appetite is slowly growing. Here as in a museum as in a library, it is not only our immense desire of something dreamed that makes it real and present to us, that gives us in translation, those judgments made by Ruskin about Rembrandt which we so passionately longed to know that we would willingly have learned English for the purpose, those clouds of Turner to see which we have wanted to cross the Channel, that Fontainebleau which exists in one specific place where, no matter how freely one moves about, one is still in Fontainebleau.

But some book entirely different from the one of which we were dreaming, can awaken other dreams which find in it their satisfaction. We are looking for a George Eliot: we find a Stevenson. By the time we have reached the tenth page Stevenson is all our need, and the eleventh and those that follow it, brings satisfaction, for our dreams have not the form of things accidentally *seen* but the form given to them by a god. And so it comes about that you have not only the oysters for which you were longing, oysters straight from the sea. It is a whole museum that lies open before you, in which each separate masterpiece excites the desire which it alone can satisfy—as for instance the dark, brown-fleshed venison, hot, and soused, over which the red-currant jelly has laid a cool, sweet surface, while as the result of chance, free talk, you feel that the white-jacketed men and the women in low-necked dresses who are your companions at this festival of all the arts, have become more dear to you than anything in that past life which you have shed at the door of this warm, lit room, that each movement made by your arm as you talk, its passivity, even, as you listen to the conversation of your neighbours, gives you a delicious sensation, as though the element through which you are moving, both physically and spiritually, were some quite new element of pleasure, a stimulating, a corrupting, element, so that you feel capable of anything, held back by no scruple, freed completely from all the inhibitions of your previous duties.

*

There was an occasion when Colonel Bresson having asked Henri whether it were not a fact that the Jesuits had recently been trying to get hold of him, Henri had answered, "No", had said, with some show of indignation, that there was not a word of truth in the statements published in *l'Aurore*, seeming genuinely annoyed at having to go on for ever saying "No" and demonstrating his complete evidence. He would have liked to be able to find something to say to his own discredit, just to prove how sincere he was to the Colonel who seemed not to believe him. And because he wanted to be absolutely sincere, he had explained that two years previously Father Z had asked him to find out if he could discover those of his companions who had remained sound in their ideas, and encourage them in that attitude—that was all it had amounted to. "If anything had happened since, why shouldn't I have told you?"

But the Colonel on the contrary had taken his words as a proof that his suspicions were correct—though in fact they were not, and had told Henri that he could go: and later when representations were made by the General of Brigade whom Henri had immediately sought out, who, though a Free Mason, was very fond of the Duc de Réveillon and of Henri, the Colonel had replied, "It's no manner of use trying to exculpate Réveillon: I examined him very thoroughly, and he confessed everything." Tortille, the General of Brigade, did what he could to arrange matters, and Henri went occasionally to see him in order to find out how things stood. When he learned that the Colonel had made use of the word "confess", he protested indignantly, and gave an exact account of what he had actually said. The General though he was

Colonel Bresson's friend, and shared his political opinions, said to
Henri, "Don't bother: everything will sort itself out: all the same, you
shouldn't have told him all that." – "But he said that I was to tell him
everything." – "No matter," said the General, "you were too scrupulous:
there was no need for you to say anything," and he shook his kindly,
ruddy face with the wide-open blue eyes which always seemed to be,
and in fact were, among the most marvellous instruments of precision
to be found (and not only of precision, as was evident from the
flickering light in them, for ever changing, for ever adapting itself,
infinite in its radiance, a light instinct with those moral qualities
which are inseparable from the expression of every genuine human
being) like the eyepieces of a lense which to those looking at them from
the outside, show only their brilliant surface and their size, but for the
man behind them and for him alone (there is never more than one man
behind a pair of eyes, they being a sort of microscope which nobody
else can use) serve as a means of seeing deep into things, and across them
sometimes, after a period of thought, the owner passes the back of his
hand, as one wipes a lense after using it, across those fine, large, blue and
luminous eyes, which for the moment were fixed steadily on the idea
that Henri "should have said nothing", since that was what they were
now seeing.

Yet nobody was more honest, more upright, more the slave of
discipline, than General Tortille. Consequently Henri felt a great deal
happier in his mind when he heard those words, for it was as though
General Tortille, his judge, had become in some sort his accomplice,
and so since he knew him to be so upright, a soldier through and
through, had lifted his fault to a higher level. He was glad to hear
General Tortille say that the Colonel who had behaved so harshly to
him, was in fact somebody whom he should have mistrusted, someone
to whom he should not have unbosomed himself so guilelessly, for
what it was that General Tortille seemed to be saying, though unshaken
in his feeling of respect for the Colonel, was that the latter being a party
man and prejudiced, was quite capable of judging wrongly. We cannot
help feeling warmly towards a man of honour and intelligence who
from a sense of justice and out of a long knowledge of men, says to us
"Don't *overdo* honour"—a magistrate who says, "It's not really for me
to talk to you like this, but if I were in your place I shouldn't admit too
much: you know what the legal mind is like . . . my colleague is an
admirable man, but he is quite capable of, etc. . . ." A general who

rides round daily to take the companies at drill by surprise, who punishes quite senior officers, and stops the men's leave; who at the least expected time comes round to inspect quarters, politely returning the salute of the sentry who immediately has the appropriate call sounded on the bugles, "crimes" anyone he finds to be improperly absent from barracks, but all the same is quite likely to say to you, "You're looking a bit fagged: just you toddle off to Paris without a word to anybody: don't put in for leave, but try not to get caught." We are fond of the man of law who can occasionally laugh at the law; of a man of discipline who can sometimes say, "See if you can't give the regulations a miss."

When that happens we no longer feel too guilty, because we have the impression that a man of honour has taken a good half of our fault on to his own shoulders. Our respect for military justice remains unshaken, but we can't get away from the fact that a general has just been saying, "It mightn't be a bad thing if you weren't brought before that particular Court too often." We feel that for this man who has a profound experience of life and of his fellow-men, including the men who are honest judges, legality, the rules of evidence, truth, are not the sum total of everything—are indeed of not very great importance. He knows that such things as prejudice, and the foregone conclusion do exist, and that by and large it is better to keep out of the net. We like those books, those instances in real life, when wronged innocence throws itself on the mercy of the country's judges, and is treated by them with fairness and humanity, with the result that it wins its case, because that sort of thing makes us feel that men are fundamentally good, that truth is bound to prevail, that life in the social community is conducted precisely as in the bosom of an affectionate family, where a mother no matter how strict believes in her son, and shows her love for him if he deserves it. But when a man of honour says to us, "You shouldn't count too much on your fellow-men's good faith: you acted foolishly in being so frank: I'm a General and I know what I'm talking about: you should have told the Colonel nothing," or, "I am a senior member of the Bench, but if I were you I should get out of the country and not stand trial: honest man though I am I should not attempt to justify myself to the honest judge before whom you will have to appear: I should wait until his anger has had time to cool, as it will do, until the whole business has been forgotten, and time has wiped out the importance which you and the world attach to it." Hearing a man like

that giving us wise counsel, and when our conscience is on tenterhooks
and watchful, saying, "There's nothing you can do, so relax and stop
worrying," we cannot help but have a feeling of relief, of slackened
tension, of satisfaction and repose. Our conscience has no answer to
make, because it knows that a fine, upright general has said to us, "The
important thing is to keep the Colonel in the dark," that it is a magistrate who has told us, "Don't give too much information to the Bench:
the Law never forgets," that it is a man of honour who has said,
"Never believe that the voice of honour is sufficient to convince a man
of honour—just keep quiet."

Henri listened to General Tortille. Life seemed to him less harsh when
he realized that the man who had condemned him so severely was not
Justice Incarnate, but according to the old General who knew him,
someone to whom it might be just as well not to tell the whole truth.

10. *The Storm*

It would be wrong to think that Réveillon lacked charm even in winter. No doubt the sight that met the eyes of a passer-by peeping through the main gate on an afternoon of late summer, was pleasant and gay—tables under the trees, tea set out on one, and at the opposite ends of another Henri and the Duke playing at cards, inconvenienced not so much by flies, as by a level beam of sunlight which forced them continually to shift their chairs, while Jean and the Duchess sauntered slowly beneath the chestnuts, Jean without a hat and wearing round his shoulders an old mantilla belonging to the Duchess, which he found so comfortable that when he went out walking in the fields of an evening, he took it instead of an overcoat. But if the drawing-room tables ventured out into the Park, the warm scented ever-moving air of the Park visited the Château drawing-room too, where the windows were kept wide open and the sun struck deep into the farthest corners so that the Duchess when busy with her correspondence was forced to move her table. Sometimes guests even less discreet would wander in from the garden, butterflies for instance or wasps, and flutter about for quite a long while before making off again straight through the windows and out into the Park. At such times the passer-by could take his fill of the sleek lawns where the Duke's greyhound was sleeping, or pretending to sleep, because if you went near him he could see you perfectly well through his half-closed eyes which did not move at all except to blink in the sunlight, that being the only movement he made, so firmly did he refuse to budge, because where he was lying he had the green sloping pillow which exactly suited his aristocratic head and gently pulsing flank.

But in winter the grass though doubtless shorter now and darker still stretched in front of the Château, and between the bare woodland trees, mile after mile of it, as though all the beauty of the summer, all the life of the countryside had taken refuge there, brought low and driven to seek shelter, but vigorous and persistent still, sole remnant of the colour left over from the season of butterflies to deck the great black chrysalis of winter. The grass was still there as the sea is still there after days of storm with not a fishing-smack to be seen, without a sail, unrolling in the selfsame place the selfsame green of its surface, though there is no sun now to play upon it.

When Jean went out in the morning, the sun was still hidden and the night chill sharp under a white coverlet of frost. The flower-beds were completely empty like a bathing-beach before the season has begun, though a few tulips still showed undisturbed for a few days, there being no other flowers to compete with them, their lovely orange globes rattling in the wind. Not the Park, nor the woods, nor the spreading landscape gave any idea of what the scene was like in summer when every morning one could note among the violets and daffodils, which had already been for months in bloom, the presence of the irises and Bengal roses, could see that the swallows and their fellow-migrants had come back, could watch the passing flicker of butterflies, could greet the arrival of the two owls, those disdainful princes of the neighbourhood, who never showed themselves though they made one aware that their state-progress had been renewed, because at night when honest folk were abed one heard them abroad in the deep woods, lost to each other's sight, but giving call and answer from far away. Nevertheless when Jean started for the village (except for him and Henri and a single keeper there was no one to do anything and he had to go in person to fetch the letters if he did not want to have to wait until the evening and to take those destined for the post, if they were to catch the train) he could at least come on the empty hives ranged under the dead branches, houses which now for many months would not be lived in by their brilliant guests, and in front of them could see the grass stretching away mile after mile, winter and summer alike, green as the sea but darker toned and with never a white sail of a primula to mark it.

People constantly said to Jean, "It must be terribly boring in the country in this cold weather, isn't it?" On the contrary it was lovely to look at all the trees, stripped of their foliage maybe, but showing to greater advantage the beautiful green and gold with which past springs had covered their bark, sole memory of springtime colours in this chrysalis of winter, waiting until they should be effaced and almost forgotten under the intenser verdure of new growth, and the softer colour of the bursting buds—shining bravely bright whenever a quick flicker of sun came in its glory to touch the country scene in which they held their lonely court: flora suited to the rough inclemency of winter, that slow coloration of the trunks, that gleaming sheen of bark, which shows only as the long accumulation of the years, but stays the whole year through and for many years, and is together with the grass the moss, the last remaining sparrows, the only things not human that stay all the year round in country places. Inconveniences there were to be sure: journeys to be made to the village for any purchase that had not been ordered at least two days in advance; letters to be collected, and others posted. But it was these inconveniences which of a morning, should Jean need foolscap paper, drove him out into the cold. Often as he crossed the river he would feel as brisk and active as the icy water, as the urgent clouds, as the tufted grass trembling in the wind, and the hard earth ringing happily beneath his feet. Inconvenience it might be, but it gave him an opportunity of seeing a patch of sunlight alighting on bare hedgerows, creeping across the pale land, sky reflected in the river, scarcely bleaching its surface, already gay with golden radiance catching the village where the tiled roof of the church gave back its glitter in spite of an approaching shower, melting its high good humour into a kind of happiness. But farther off behind the village the clouds were black, though now and again a sudden sunbeam testing its strength upon the fields, laid a bright polish on one side of the houses. But it came too quickly for rain was on the way. Indeed in a moment or two it began to fall but came to nothing, and soon he could put his umbrella down again. It was with a sense of lively satisfaction that he turned the knob of the stationer's-cum-grocer's-cum-chemist's glass-panelled door which set a small bell ringing as it opened, and asked for foolscap. "Would you be needing a quire, sir?" the lame and friendly shopman asked, and hopping away on his crutches brought a fine pack so huge, so smooth, so soft, so shining that Jean felt it to be one of those lovely objects which not to buy would have caused him desolation of the spirit, no matter what it cost. "I think I'll take two," he said with a smile. The shopman was one of those who seem always to ask less for their goods than one expects, who take so little account of the small additional trouble one causes them by asking for this or that "extra", manifesting a nobility of character, a sort of privileged independence in the handling of delicious merchandise, producing so strong an impression of serene contentment, that when you pull the door to and the same little bell sounds again, you are left with the feeling that you have had a glimpse into a more than usually happy existence, compacted of an exquisite substance and subject to none of life's hard laws. You leave the shop with a heart overflowing with a sense of comradeship and gaiety, only quite often to go back again a moment later, having hurried away to buy for the little girl who was with her father behind the counter a doll from the fancy-goods shop which, when Christmas drew near, was supplied with a few toys from Provins.

When Jean turned for home, the road was beginning to dry and a little sunlight was warming the fields. He walked with an even happier sense of relaxation than he had enjoyed during his quick tramp that morning, gay though that had been. Sometimes on these occasions so great was his pleasure in the soft sheen of the sun-touched earth that he took the long way round by the Vervins plateau and reached home only in time for luncheon. At others, the rain having set in for good, he hurried back. There was hail mixed with the rain but he did not care because his overcoat kept him warm. The wind in his face was like an inspiration and he walked quickly, his eyes alight with the ideas which were tumbling over one another in his head while, it must be admitted, the rain trickled down his expressive countenance, though to that he paid scant attention, seeing that very soon now he would be in his room, seated by the fire, there to work with an even lighter heart, until the bell should summon him to luncheon. The sliding and sizzling of butter on the stove could have excited no more delicious quiver of appetite in his empty stomach than did the fretting of rain upon the roof, to which he lent an attentive ear only for an instant, the better to conjure up a picture of the lovely omelette studded with bacon which very soon now he would see being carried into the dining-room. While waiting to go down, he warmed himself at the great hearth. "How cold I am!" he would say to Henri, hopping from foot to foot with excitement and looking out at the desolate countryside under the rain, and at the black sky, while he rubbed his hands in an access of delight. But for the moment all that was in the future: he was not there yet and he redoubled his speed, stiffening his arms like a warrior against the wind to the assaults of which he opposed like a diminutive shield the round disk of his umbrella, taking upon it the darts, which in the form of hard and frozen hailstones the sky unremittingly discharged against him. And so he progressed, doing his best to defend himself but only half succeeding. His mind was tempered by the rain, the wind had blown his courage to a white heat, he had taken the measure of the fanged cold. He loved this hour of drama when he fought against embattled nature. No more unhappy than the chrysalises shaken from the apple-trees, or than the river which all this world of waters caused only to brim its banks, to eddy, and more swiftly flow, longing to feel at one with the great swirl of nature within him and without, he even turned about (had anybody seen him he must have looked like a lunatic!) so as to get a good view, in spite of the hailstones lashing his face, of the little town a few miles off blackened by the great cloud which spread a darkness over all below it, which seemed to be clinging to the slope of the hill, kept in position only by the weight of the church with its pointed steeple, now turned to a deep purple. The wind, the rain, drove furiously at his back, surged over him and in him but without carrying him away, and then rushed on ahead. Already on his left a patch of blue sky was showing above the Vervins plateau and —miracle of miracles—the valley above which he stood opened out to the horizon, though how the change had come he could not say, in a shimmer of returning spring, gleaming and sparkling in the watery sunlight.

*

One day towards the end of December a real storm got up. So topsy-turvy were the elements that lightning flashed and thunder rolled in a flurry of snow, as in a crisis of delirium when we are very ill, the memory of some time now dead and gone comes back to us mixed with the moment's thoughts. The papers had been full of stories about the fierce storms raging over the whole of France. There were hopes at nightfall that the fury of the tempest had been spent but such was far from being the case and all that night the wildness raged unabated. While Jean was undressing, he paused to listen to the howling wind, now roaring in to the attack, holding the Château in a quivering embrace, now retiring with a dwindling whimper which seemed far off. Then the din became more terrible than before. It sounded like the drum-fire of artillery, with no pause in the continuing noise, at times so close that it set the windows rattling, sometimes far off but never ceasing altogether, though it seemed to have weakened, and spreading desolation, for one could hear the dull thud of falling objects. Then the bombardment grew again in force, coming it seemed from quite another direction, creeping closer so that it was as though one were witnessing a battle at no great distance, though where one could not say, nor could one see. But Jean paused all the same, anxious not to miss a moment of the wind's intoxicating uproar, as we gaze for hours on end from the cliff-top at the lovely colours of the sea, when our eyes are spellbound by the sun dissolving on the waters in rich, delicate shades of blue and flickering spangles of light upon the surface, plundering the brilliance of a white sail and gleaming prow, imbibing the one, liquefying the other—so that it seems to be sharing the sea, and like the sea absorbing all the happiness of the glowing day.

In just such a manner did Jean listen to the wind, thrilled by its power, enchanted by its softness, for freed from all foreign elements it is indeed compact of poetry, and seems to rage without a cause, so that it makes us think of nothing human, of no definable activity. And he whom the least murmur of voices, the faintest sound of wheels, the lightest footsteps, the gentlest rustle of a curtain, the lightest breath of music could keep from sleep or waken, had slept profoundly all the preceding night when the storm had started, lulled by the noise which carried no thought of any cause, not trampling the earth nor coming from the roof, being everywhere at the same moment, battering the fields, enveloping the house. Though he could well imagine the Duke's gloom next morning, the paper's tale of desolation, decimated wood-lands, the fury of the tenant-farmer—for whom he had no very kindly feelings—in spite of all this he laughed aloud from sheer happiness, and his heart rose on a great wave of intoxicating pleasure when instead of hearing the wind diminish he knew that its force had now redoubled, that it was blowing itself into a wilder fury, and could catch ever louder the crash of falling trees—as at the seaside in a time of tempest, we want each billow to be higher than the last and so crown the ecstasy with which it fills our heart and herald the arrival of its follow-ing brother. And is there not mingled with our pleasure something of that spirit of revolt which, when a trapped criminal is at the very moment of capture, makes us leap with his leaps and draw his strength into our own bodies so that we long for him to break the fierce circle of his enemies whom he can no longer avoid? For the cheerful com-placency of those superior persons who say, "He'll be taken right enough," exasperates us, admirable citizens though they be, and should he not be caught, should he plunge them into mourning, and show them miserable and less sure of themselves, would have us on their side. It is the same instinct of revolt when a wild boar or a lion which has done much damage, is about to be snared that makes our hearts beat in sympathy with him, and sets us echoing the roaring of the noble beast, so that we silently send forth a cry, 'If only he could escape!' But when the trail of destruction is caused by the wind, then the prudence of the architect, the strength of the farmer is of no avail. One cannot drive away the wind nor encircle it, nor make ourselves its masters. One cannot shoot the waves, nor kill the sea. Suddenly the fury drops and calm returns. . . But until that moment comes something within us swells in sympathy, towers with the waves to their topmost peak. When the wind blows thus with unbelievable violence, if at times it seems to die down, we feel the urge to encourage it, much as those who though they had no knowledge of Picquart, aware only indirectly that he was present in the interests of Justice, wanted to call out to him, "Don't be discouraged! Don't weaken! Don't, when the Esterhazy case comes on, say you have no opinion, or let yourself be shut away!" But in cases such as that, the man in question acts as he does because of some reason private to himself, and threats no more than exhortations can prevail with him. Nor need we fear for what he has done, he has done.

And so it was that if the wind seemed for a moment to have died down, it was only that it might gather itself together for another on-slaught, when Jean, snug under his blankets, as one murmuring words of sympathy for the criminal surrounded by policemen, allowed him-self to whisper very low, "Buck up!" He loved this fine and blustering wind which did not keep him from sleeping as men might do, did not waken him, would have let him sleep on till noon had he wanted to, like the sturdy forester in whose cottage the young man from the city is lodging, lets him sleep on, and tramps the woods until such time as his visitor may call to him. This wind spoke to him of the sea which in weather like this must be a glorious sight. If only he could have set off now for Penmarch or Saint-Malo! He looked with feelings of anger at this stretch of earth which had not so much as a blade of grass to bow and whistle in the wind, thinking of those mountains of water, piling high and crashing down, of that Brittany sea which must at this moment be looking like a world of peaks with valleys between them so deep that one seemed to be looking into the sea-bed on which, had one not been crushed by a mountain tumbling down, and then swept giddily upwards in its rise, one could have walked dry-shod. Each new moaning of the wind gave him the feeling that this spectacle was never-ending, that not yet had it been swept away. He thought now, not of vague tempests in the abstract but of how the beach at Penmarch must be looking, and the Pointe de Raz, those two places which though far from one another, were yet morsels of France, following each on each, for from Penmarch to the right, he had noticed a little headland which marked the Baie des Trepassés, and to the left the Pointe de Raz which, enveloped in the mists of legend, though hidden in winter fog and sea-mist under a watery sun, one still could see from one of the beaches, itself not less desolate than one's idea of it. Beaches, those which we have been amazed to see in very fact, so rapt away had they seemed to be in a world of imagination, and since our seeing them had lapsed once more into the condition of imagined things, because they dwelt in a disturbing memory of a fantastic world where we had left behind something of ourselves, a world no longer abstract but in ourselves, being a spot which stirs and thrills with pleasure when we touch it, a place of beaches lying in the spume of tempests, of foaming reefs misted over at the infinite world's end like legends, though legends now with the power to move us deeply, and sweet in memory. Ah yes! now in this wind that calls to us, how we should love to go there, not to any vaguely thought of place resembling something that we know, but to one specific place marked by a rise of granite on the left, and farther out by a line of rocks, a sheltered stretch of sea where the small smacks sail! For not now is it a question of degrees of resemblances. Places are persons and we know that not the most lovely places of the earth could wake in us as does this wind a desire to go to Penmarch. Places are persons but persons who do not change, whom we find again, often after long years and feel surprised that we do not find ourselves the same as once we were, or, even more surprisingly, that we do, having done nothing since we saw them first to bring us nearer to the happiness whither these wavelets beckoned us, as blue today, as childlike at their games, as they were then. Places are persons to whom what is human in us has given a physiognomy—though not a human one, for their physiognomy is that of places, yet too of a person, a person to be recognized by a cathedral on a cliff, by the indentation of an estuary, by high-pitched fields when, the small town left behind, one emerges into open country. Physiognomies of such a kind that nothing can replace them, so that we think with pleasure of seeing them again, physiognomies which are as much in us as in them, which nothing but they can give us, which nothing but we perhaps can give them, so vividly that they will keep them long after we are dead.

For places change less rapidly than human beings, for whom the screen of willows, the climbing road, the eddying water underneath the bridge between the water-lilies, are like photographs long left in a house, which those who have not known them do not recognize and offer to their eyes a physiognomy from which not only the charm has vanished, but the very meaning, the life, the uniqueness, along with those who loved them, so that they are like family secrets which none can inherit, which cannot be found in a dead man's papers, and perhaps for that very reason are more precious to us, where places are concerned, than anything in all the world because nothing outside of us can restore the impression which once we had; a treasure which can be preserved only in one sort of casket—memory, and cannot be made visible to others save by means of that illusory something—poetry.

Poetry and inspiration, these it was that the wind seemed to wake in Jean for the more he listened to it with a growing pleasure, the more he thought he would discover new ideas, which in their turn would give birth to others—not those mad ideas which turn inwards on our-selves, such as imaginative children have (and in this respect, there are many who remain children all their lives) as they undress for bed, or go walking, ideas which have to do only with ourselves and body forth the things we most desire: 'When I get back I shall find a letter from the girl I love: though as yet I do not know her, and she will tell me of her love, and this is what I shall reply. And we shall go into a room where a man I do not like is sitting, and these are the insulting things that we shall say, and he will have no part in them, and I shall say this or that.' Ideas of this kind are insubstantial things, and call up others no more substantial than themselves. For they imitate reality, and substitute themselves for it: (perhaps in a year's time we shall meet that girl; perhaps she will love us; perhaps we shall be in a position to crush our enemy). Like the vicissitudes of life they give this impression. But later we feel discontented. It is all so useless, all so like what we find in impressionist and naturalistic novels. We shall feel the need of new ones each time that new things happen. Such ideas are in mere competition, and vain at that, with an inexhaustible and unsatisfying reality. Of this kind is all our communing with ourselves, though less exhausting than the day-dreams of vanity in which we never endingly repeat one single name (Madame So-and-so, daughter of . . .), or imagine our own in the intimate diary of an Emperor, but wearisome in the extreme.

*

But the ideas that came to Jean as he listened to the wind were of another kind. They seemed not empty, but packed full, not only of the past—his own past at Penmarch—but of the present, too; ideas that went deeper, and, linking the present and the past, were more real, for they showed the value of the moment past and of the moment present and held a something that in very truth existed, and would not end in the here and now. What he told himself was, 'This is not just another silly dream; I shall no more go back to Penmarch this year than I did last.' No, what he felt was that to go there was no longer necessary, for the desire roused in him by the wind and the memory of Penmarch would not find satisfaction in the self-regarding pleasure he once had had at Penmarch, but in the reality of poetry made from the sense of his own existence, felt in the recovered moments of Penmarch, and so, not speaking to him of a pleasure dead and gone which had lasted for an instant and was meaningless, nor yet of his present pleasure which too was meaningless and in its turn would pass, so that he would not fear a possible return into that past any more than he would fear any other pleasure life might have to offer. He found indeed that he was no longer gulping life down with a sense of anguish at seeing it disappear beneath a surface pleasure, but that he was tasting it with an assured confidence, knowing that a day would come when he would find again the reality contained in these few minutes—provided only that he did not try to—in the sharp reminder of the howling wind, in the smell of firewood burning, in the sight of a drooping sky, sunlit but with a threat of rain, above the line of roofs. For that reality is something of which we are not conscious in the passing moment, connecting it as we do with some self-regarding project. It is something which in the sharp return of disinterested memory sets us floating between the present and the past in an element common to both, which in the present has recalled the past to us, an essence which deeply thrills us, in so far as it is ourself, that self which we do not recognize in the moment when we experience the pleasure, but find again like a hoard of delicious honey deposited by things which have now gone far from us, enchanting us because it *is* those things and giving them an identity across the sundering distance, making of Penmarch a thing so personal, that when we want to see it again nothing can take the place of us ourselves, showing it as a reality which we spread about us as we sit writing pages which are the synthesis of different moments of life.

❧ VIII ❧

Madame Marmet's Evening Party · A Meeting with

Mademoiselle Kossichef · Le Vicomte de Lomperolles

Jean's Room · The School of Political Science

The Guéraud-Houppins · The Duchesse de Réveillon's

Salon: Jacques Bonami · The Duke in Society

Visits · Madame de Thianges and Madame Lawrence

Lieutenant de Brucourt · An Englishwoman

The First Night of Frédégonde *· Daltozzi and*

Women · The Insult · Reparation · Baron Scipio

A Hospital Common-Room · Dining Out

1. *Madame Marmet*

"You *may* be only the fourteenth at table, but, all the same, you are entitled to your ice." This remark uttered with crystal clarity by the lovely Madame Marmet was addressed to a young man at the far end who had just refused the "Bombe". Her charming and characteristic sally was intended less to dazzle her guests than to make it clear to them that only a last-minute crisis had compelled her to include in the company a youth who had neither name nor fame to commend him. He smiled but said nothing. It was immediately obvious that he was sensitive rather than vain, because as soon as he had ceased to smile the expression on his face betokened melancholy rather than annoyance. He made a slight movement of the shoulders as a woman might do who all of a sudden feels chilly. Then his handsome, thoughtful eyes became riveted on those of Madame Marmet—who was not just then looking at him—and seemed very gently to probe her innermost being. When at last he turned away his head the liquid surface of his pupils showed a faint and almost imperceptible glitter which seemed to indicate that the "catch" which he had fished up from the depths was negligible. The diners rose from the table. Next to the young man was the old Comte de Nefforden who being slightly deaf had probably remained in ignorance of the attenuating circumstances which explained the presence of his neighbour. No doubt he would say later to his smart friends, "I dined last night at Madame Marmet's: there were people at her table of whom I had never heard." As they left the room, Madame Marmet said to Jean, "I do hope your father wasn't put out at my spiriting you away just as you were all sitting down?"—which being interpreted meant, "I hope you all of you realize that I asked him at the last minute so that we shouldn't be thirteen. When that sort of thing happens one can't pick and choose, so please don't be angry with me."

"Julien," she went on, turning to her son, "have you introduced your friend to these gentlemen?"—which being interpreted meant, 'You mustn't think he's anything to do with me! He's just one of my son's school-friends. The choice was not deliberate on my part: but I would have you notice that I am showing the same politeness to him as to my other guests, and wish him to be introduced. I may not belong to the Faubourg Saint-Germain set, but I know what's what.' "Your father," she continued, "is always so kind about giving his support to Julien each time he sits for a Foreign Office examination," which being interpreted meant, 'It was a good move on my part to ask him because he has been very useful to Julien and will be still more so in the future. That too is very Faubourg Saint-Germain.' Then aloud, "Your father has some position at the Foreign Office, hasn't he?—though what exactly it is has escaped my memory"—which being interpreted meant, 'Self-respecting persons know nothing about government matters.' At this moment, with a flutter of her fan and a coquettish twist of her ripe figure in its sheath of rose-coloured satin, Madame Marmet turned to her other guests, having just decided that she had now done enough for the fourteenth person at her table. But suddenly visited by one of those momentary inspirations which in the art of snobbery no less than in that of letters is worth whole years of plodding, she let her restless eye come to anchor on a gentleman of about forty and said, "Allow me, dear Marquis, to present Monsieur Jean Santeuil to you. I know that your son Aymar is about to launch out on a diplomatic career, and feel quite sure that Monsieur Santeuil's father will be only too pleased to provide him with a number of useful introductions."–"But dear lady, this young man and I are already old friends. I know his father well, and count it an honour to do so. His father is a very remarkable man with whom it has been my good fortune to serve on more than one committee. I rather gathered from him that this boy of his was somewhat ailing and unsociable when he completed his philosophical studies two years ago. But that, I am glad to see, is no longer the case." With which words the Marquis de Ribeaumont extended a hand to Jean, while Madame Marmet, overjoyed at the turn affairs were taking, delighted at having started off the Marquis and Jean on a long conversation, and encouraged by the new note of animation which was now sounding among her guests, proceeded to apply the warming influence of her beauty and her wit to those of them who still seemed to be in a somewhat too sluggish mood for her liking. Jean smiled his thanks to Monsieur de Ribeaumont and led him into the smaller drawing-room where they could smoke in peace. "What are you doing with yourself these days?" asked the Marquis, lighting a cigarette. "I seem to remember that your father felt you were devoting yourself a little too seriously to philosophy, and that it was affecting your nerves." Jean, being unused to a form of politeness which was entirely unknown in the middle-class circles in which his life had been spent, where each time that he was introduced to a man he did not know, he could be sure of receiving, according to the age of the stranger, a patronizing pat on the cheek (sixty or over), a daunting nod of the head (forty), or a shy bow (twenty), feeling deeply and thrillingly moved by Monsieur de Ribeaumont's show of kindliness, and eager to show his sincere appreciation by entering into a detailed exposé of his views and intentions, began to explain that his health which at the best was somewhat delicate, had been still further undermined by the exhaustion occasioned by his philosophical studies, and that he was now going through Law School which however he found extremely boring. Consequently, since he was lacking in application, and was too lazy to work except when genuine interest in a subject prompted him to do so, he was, he said, devoting most of his time to social activities and was becoming thoroughly stupid, though physically he was feeling a great deal better, was taking exercise and getting stronger.

"It has always seemed strange to me," said Monsieur de Ribeaumont who was no longer listening, "that anyone should really love philosophy. If life were longer it might be a different matter. But life is a great deal too short for studies of that kind."–"Oh, no sir!" replied Jean eagerly, "quite the contrary. What you are saying is true of everything *except* philosophy. Life is too short to work at history, or to give oneself to a merely social existence." Monsieur de Ribeaumont fixed him with that blue and gentle gaze with which he had so often, in a mood of pensive absent-mindedness, followed the projects and the policies of Monsieur le Comte de Paris on those occasions when he had been in attendance on him. "You are young, Monsieur Santeuil," he said, "and to that extent," he added, throwing away his cigarette, "deserving of congratulation. I will say as much to your father when next I see him. Meanwhile it is time you went back into the other room and paid court to the ladies—which is an occupation suited to your age. It is time for you youngsters to take the place of us old 'uns," he said, adjusting his monocle, which in a man of his dignified and exquisite training was the equivalent to the traditional wink common among those of a different social class. "I have heard a great deal about you from someone who is your very dear friend, someone whom you will

soon be seeing again—the son of Madame la Duchesse de Réveillon."
–"Is he really coming back?" asked Jean, going pale with excitement.
"Yes, indeed: I came across them in Vienna where Réveillon invited
me to dine. His charming boy was of the company, and hurried away
for the express purpose of writing to you."–"We write to each other
every week," said Jean in a tone marked by tender emotion and there
upon began to talk at length to Monsieur de Ribeaumont about the
Réveillon family. He was quite overwhelmed with delight at hearing
news of them and eager to hear more. "If you are fond of Society, you
will be pleased to know that Madame de Réveillon intends to do a
great deal of entertaining this winter." This piece of information was
however of little interest to Jean. In fact it rather upset him, because
he feared that he would no longer be able to spend long evenings alone
with Henri as he had so enjoyed doing in the old college days. "She
used to give very delightful parties," said Monsieur de Ribeaumont
with an upward movement of the head. "Of the same sort as this one?"
asked Jean. "Oh, dear me, no" said the Marquis with an almost feline
purr, "they are two such very different persons, don't you think?"
–"Does Madame Marmet visit at her house?"–"I am not at all sure
that they know one another," replied Monsieur de Ribeaumont. Jean
grasped the full meaning of this expressed uncertainty. What Monsieur
de Ribeaumont implied was, "I should be very much surprised to learn
that they so much as exchange cards once a year. But should you ask
me whether there is anything approaching intimacy between them, I
could, though I have no precise knowledge, answer your question with
as much assurance as I would should you say, 'If I went walking in the
Forest of Saint-Germain should I be likely to find oranges growing on
the trees?' " Then did Jean, strong in the thought that he would be
welcomed in a house where Madame Marmet, and all the other
Marmets who asked him at the last moment to "make up" their tables,
knew nobody but the concierge, feel something of that vanity which
he had known at school when asked to dinner by the headmaster, and
feeling himself smile at Monsieur de Ribeaumont's words, was smitten
with shame at the idea that his lips should have parted in an expression
of vulgar delight, that satisfaction should have been audible in his voice,
that his whole person should have been suddenly and ignobly illuminated, when there shone for a moment in his mind a vivid image of his
father's modest self-respect.

"What was that you were saying about the Réveillons?" inquired

Madame Marmet who happened just then to be passing within earshot. "How can you expect Monsieur Santeuil to know anything about them, Ribeaumont?" – "Their son is my friend," said Jean to Madame Marmet. "Oh, yes, of course! You were in the same class with him at school, weren't you? I don't suppose you have ever seen the Duchess, have you?" asked, or rather stated, Madame Marmet. "Indeed I have madame." – "Then I hope, if you ever see her again, that you will let her know that I have feelings of the greatest admiration, what I would almost call a *cult*, for her. If I were a man she would turn my head completely. Yet for all that she is a real saint!" A little way off the Princesse de T—— was chatting with two men seated on stools at either side of her armchair. The Baroness Sheffer, wife of the great financier, said to Madame Marmet, "How lovely the Princess is! I have a strong feeling for her because she is said to be so very intelligent—not that I really know her, but we share a number of women friends"—which meant, "Come on, introduce me!"– "Oh, she is quite exquisite!" replied Madame Marmet, or in other words, "You don't really think I'm going to introduce you and have you steal her from me? I asked her just so as to show that she accepts my invitations, though not at all to imply that she would accept yours!"–"But you haven't got any tea! Are you sure you won't have anything, darling?"–the implied meaning being, "I hope you notice not only that I've got her here, but that I am not at all dazzled by her presence in my house, and am looking after the comfort of you and everybody else. I am, you see, a very great lady." Then she moved across to the Baroness Kuerf, another wife of another great financier, and nodding towards the Princess de T—— said, "How charming she is!"–"I do so agree with you," replied Madame Kuerf, "actually, you know, it was in my house that you first met her," which, being interpreted meant: "I am a Founder Member of your Salon, my dear, and don't you forget it!"

*

Jean heard the names of Madame and Mademoiselle Kossichef announced and recognized Marie in the handsome young woman who at that moment entered the room. But since duty obliged him to go and look at the collection of butterflies in Monsieur Marmet's study, he hurried away. "Santeuil! Santeuil!" Madame Marmet was hard on his heels seeking reinforcements of young men to engage in a little mild flirtation, "Come along with me and pay some attention to the girls. I am going to introduce you to Mademoiselle Kossichef."–"I'd really rather you didn't," said Jean, who knew that the Kossichef establishment was extremely boring. But Madame Marmet had noticed that nobody was talking to Mademoiselle Kossichef, and insisted. "Nonsense!" she said. Jean made no further difficulty and sat down for a moment beside Marie. "I rather think that we used to know one another years ago in the Champs-Elysées," she said to him. "Indeed we did," replied Jean, "is your sister well?—her name, if I am not mistaken was Sonia, wasn't it?"–"Yes," said Marie with a smile. It was now half past ten and Jean very much wanted to go on to a ball. He was on the point of getting up and leaving when Madame Kossichef came towards them. Her daughter introduced him. "Do you mean to say that you two used to know one another? I do hope you'll come to see us. We are always at home on Sundays," said Madame Kossichef, for whom Jean's presence at an evening party in Madame Marmet's house was a sufficient passport, and a recommendation of the highest value. Jean thanked her and left. But on the next few Sundays he had more amusing things to do than to call on the Kossichefs, and later he dared not call, having stayed away so long. Sometimes when he passed their house, he remembered how often on rainy days he had dragged his nursemaid there and forced her to join with him in his amorous pilgrimages. But the memory produced in him none of the melancholy he once had thought he must inevitably feel when the day should come when he knew that he loved her no longer. For that sense of brooding sadness which had oppressed him when he anticipated an indifference still to come, had been part and parcel of his love. But that love no longer existed. A rough finger could now be laid upon what had once been an intolerably sensitive wound, without his feeling a thing, for the aching surface had become as it were an area of dead skin, something we carry about with us, though it is no longer responsive to either pricks or caresses, which is no longer us, having died. Sometimes too as he passed the house he said to himself: 'Why should we feel so terribly despairing because we have not got what we most desire? For as Time's wheel perpetually revolves, sooner or later those things will come to us. Circumstances change and what we once wanted we always get in the long run, but only when we no longer want them.' And he thought that if he were now in love with Mademoiselle Kossichef, this permission to see her in her own home every Sunday would no more

satisfy him than had his daily meetings with her in the Champs-Elysées.
The mere presence of the beloved is powerless to appease desire, being
itself a form of absence, and she whom he adores, by granting to the
poor lover an extra day a week of her company, or an extra hour a day,
can do nothing to lessen his sadness. For he is like a child who longs to
empty the sea drop by drop.

★

Jean noticed an old gentleman buried in an armchair against the back of
which he was resting a curled and greying wig. He sat quite motionless
except for the twitching of his wrists and ankles. Having once met him
at the Réveillons, Jean said good evening. He was the Vicomte de
Lomperolles, one of the Duchess's cousins. To his wife, who was
seated beside him, he was prodigal of those touching attentions which
mark the behaviour of very old and very fond friends (she had been
only twenty at the time of their marriage). She graciously extended a
hand to Jean and her husband politely returned his greeting. But there
was a certain coldness in the way he did so and he did not introduce
him to Madame de Lomperolles. This did not altogether surprise Jean
who had heard the Réveillons say that their kinsman disliked all young
men, whom he considered to be lacking in both intelligence and taste,
indeed without merit of any kind and only too ready to show disrespect
to the merits of others. Not only did he think them uneducated, mannerless, and without tact, but was of the opinion that the whole race was
deceitful to the point of perfidy, insensitive to the point of cruelty, so
malicious and so stupid as to be barely sane. He did occasionally display
rather more indulgence to the young of the past, of that past when he
himself had been young. But youth he said had progressively deteriorated. What he could least forgive in the young men of the present was,
as he never grew tired of saying contemptuously, that they were "no
better than girls". About Santeuil he had once remarked to the
Duchess, "He may be a little less stupid than the rest of 'em, but what's
one to think of a young fellow like that who suffers from insomnia and
cries at the least thing? He's not a man at all, he's no better than a girl!"
Jean was struck by the fact that Monsieur de Lomperolles's wig looked
shorter than when he had last seen him. Monsieur de Lomperolles
guessed what was in his mind. "You think I'm not in looks this evening, eh?" half smirking, half grumbling, "that's because I had my hair

cut yesterday." Jean learned later that he possessed forty wigs each slightly longer than the others. As soon as he had worn the longest, he replaced it without even the briefest of intervals, by the shortest in order to give the impression that his hair had been cut. From that moment, to make believe that his hair was growing again, he appeared each day, for forty days, with a different and slightly longer wig. As Jean moved away Madame de Lomperolles looked at him with an air of timid mistrust. She never spoke about young men but seemed to have no more liking for them than her husband had.

By the time Jean reached home it was late. Madame Santeuil, gratified by the knowledge that her son had dined in brilliant company, seated between an Academician and an Ambassador, but not wishing to express her pleasure, and especially not to let him see it, merely said, "It makes me very happy to know that you move in such intelligent circles."

2. *Waking in Paris*

Jean's bedroom was next door to his father's. Monsieur Santeuil's usual time for getting up was round about seven o'clock. At that hour Jean, having returned from a ball as dawn was breaking, would just be settling into his first sleep, only to be awakened by the sound of his father moving about. Then the swish of his mother's dressing-gown, as she went to her husband's room, would assail his ears like the tormenting buzz of a fly. The two of them would begin to talk, and Jean, abandoning all hope of sleep, his nerves on edge, would leave his bed. Sometimes he settled down to read, and soon, as on a mountain walk, his bodily distress diminished. He began to breathe more easily. Something human, till then buried within his head, emerged and stirred. His eyes grew bright with happiness. At that moment the door would open suddenly, revealing his father who, with that rough and rustic forthrightness which a long life of honours had quite failed to soften, asked him what he was doing, after which he would shout for Augustin to come and shave him in his room. Occasionally it was his mother who appeared. Having opened the door she would move on tip-toe as though in the presence of somebody still soundly sleeping, with the result that the floorboards creaked and all Jean's ill-humour flared up again. Then she would beckon to her husband and point to Jean absorbed in his book as though he were a child amusing itself with some trivial game, with that slightly superior look on her face with which elders contemplate the amusements of the very young. The thought that they should have found him in a happy-seeming mood, that they were smilingly taking notice of the emotions aroused in him by his reading, was more than Jean could stand. He was conscious of a sudden uprush of revolt, as though somebody were urging him on to attack his parents. He pretended to be bored by what he had just been reading, and to revenge himself upon his father and his mother for the happiness he had been feeling before they came in, and now had to conceal for fear that they might see the signs of it in his face, set himself with some violence to contradict everything they said, and to accuse himself falsely of having acted in all the ways most likely to displease them. Though he had registered a silent vow that very morning always to be home by twelve, he now decided to dance every night until dawn. On these occasions he could never bring himself to sit down to meals with his parents, to have them there before his eyes playing the part of adversaries. He turned up late therefore in the dining-room, took his place with a sulky expression, and proceeded silently to chew on his hatred which seemed to have imparted something of its bitterness to the food before him, and unable to hide from himself the immense longing which he felt to strike his father—a longing for which he often found relief by advancing violently upon his table and kicking the walls of his work-room—proceeded to discharge a volley of barbed words. But if even one of them struck home on his parents and seemed to cause them pain, so that though they suffered the attack in silence, the hurt they felt showed in the increasing pallor of his mother's face, or in the appearance on his father's of that look of despondency to which he sometimes fell a prey, then at sight of the blood oozing from a wound he had himself inflicted, the restraining dykes within his heart would burst, and a surge of tenderness would pour out. Only with the greatest difficulty could the fragile and transparent covering of his eyes hold back the tears, or his mouth refuse the kisses with which on a sudden it was filled. He would jump up from his chair and bestow upon his father's cheeks and his mother's those outward signs of all the tenderness he felt.

3. *The School of Political Science*

"If he has got a feeling for literature, then let him read law." In those words had the eminent Professor of Jurisprudence replied, to whom Monsieur Santeuil had gone for advice about his son's future. But what had seemed to be a feeling for literature must have been something quite different, for Jean found in law nothing but boredom and failed in his first examination. His father's immediate reaction had been to fly into a rage. But his mother had put in a word of intercession, with the result that Monsieur Santeuil in gentler tones had said, "Well, what *do* you want to do?" Transported by such a show of benevolence, Jean flung himself on his father's neck, burst into tears, and asked to be allowed to think over his answer in the privacy of his room. He no longer dared to say that "Letters" were his real love, having already had quoted to him the names of many magistrates and doctors with "literary tastes". When however he had tried his hand first at medicine and then at law, he had found both appallingly tedious, and been so it seemed in no way helped by his "natural gifts". This time he said "Philosophy" with the result that Monsieur Santeuil invited the Rector of the University to dinner. The guest declared that both medicine and law were arid fields of study for a young man with literary inclinations, and mentioned in support of this contention the name of a writer who had failed in his law exams. All things considered he said it looked as though diplomacy would provide the best solution. Having been told that Jean had a great feeling for philosophy, he suggested that he should attend the course of lectures being given by one of the professors at the School of Political Science.

On the following day Jean had an interview with the gentleman in question who said to him, "If you have a philosophical turn of mind, I feel sure that our programme of studies will interest you. We have here on the staff among others a man of outstanding philosophical gifts, Monsieur Ralph Savaie of the Académie des Sciences Morales. I won't pretend that he does not sometimes lose himself in somewhat fantastic speculations, but after all are not fantasy and philosophy the same thing

501

in the end? Philosophy today is entirely concerned with physiology and geography . . ." saying which he directed at Jean a sidelong look which was intended to show that in the School of Political Science they were far from being a collection of old fossils, but knew very well what was the proper attitude to take in the matter of philosophy. "It might be just as well if you took a look at some of Savaie's books, before attending his lectures, just to make yourself familiar with his views. In spite of their brilliant metaphysical scope, they are a great deal more solid than might at first appear," and he held out to Jean two or three volumes. The titles were at once so vaguely general and so narrowly precise that the feeling they gave one was that the matters with which the author dealt were at once impalpable and trivial: *The Sense of the Infinite on the Banks of Lake Tchad—The Impulse Towards the Better in The Balkan Peninsula.*

"Monsieur de la Selle-Moutier is possessed of a no less all-embracing intelligence. I have been told that you are imaginative, and perhaps inclined to mysticism. Imagination is not to be sneezed at—far from it! When you have reached my age you will find that you come back to it. You will realize that there is such a thing as prose as well as poetry, though in spite of everything I have remained an impenitent old romantic. Ask my wife if I'm not—for I very much hope that you will give us the pleasure of coming to dinner some evening. She will tell you that when I travel I still carry about with me one of the elder Dumas's volumes: besides I must confess that I have a love of youth, in spite of all its excesses and lunacies. Well if you have a feeling for mysticism—a little of it though not too much is one of life's necessities, as is true of most things. . . ." (Jean felt that a faint smile was expected at this point) . . . "you cannot help but be interested in the course of lectures he is giving on The Religious Claims of the Younger Czechs. I need say nothing about my master Boisset whose fame has spread far beyond the walls of this school. Every young man with an interest in literature should know his *History of German Unity* by heart. Have you never read his *Beyond the Alps?* What *do* you read? That book is literature at the very highest level. Personally I find him no whit inferior to About." Jean stammered out that he was very fond of Anatole France. "Ah yes, a charming mind, a nimble and elegant pen," said Boisard, "but for breadth and grasp not in the same class as Boisset: pleasing enough I don't deny, but when you have said that you have said everything. Besides he lacks virility: there is more of nerves in him than of

muscle if you will forgive the phrase." Jean said nothing. "In addition
to the lectures I have mentioned, there are of course several others less
brilliant and more down-to-earth, but perhaps more practical. Damme
you don't come here just to dream, you know!"

Jean shuddered. Just as he was taking leave of Monsieur Boisard,
Monsieur Ralph Savaie came into the room. He was red in the face,
and said, "I must apologize Boisard, for bursting in on you like this, but
I've just bought an engraving of *Le Vert Galant*, and I don't know
whether I'm standing on my head or my heels. You really must forgive
me, but you know how strongly I feel about art!" He was all of a-
twitter, and Boisard glanced at Jean with a smile as if to say "See what
I meant?—the man's a poet." He looked at Ralph Savaie with the air
of astonished admiration which a nature so different from his own
inspired in him, and the slightly mocking reverence which always plays
a part in the sympathy, even the admiration, felt by a cool-headed man
for an enthusiast. Monsieur Ralph Savaie apologized for not having
noticed Jean. Since he was always in a white heat of excitement, always
suffering from emotional exaltation, always a prey to his enthusiasms,
it was a generally accepted fact that he never recognized anyone, was
always late for appointments and went about with his tie flying loose.
Boisard pulled it straight for him with a smile and a shake of the head.
"I don't suppose I shall ever meet anyone quite like you," he said.
"Thank you dear friend, thank you!" said Savaie with the exaggerated
intonation of an actor. He continued to talk eagerly and without a
pause, as he always did, seemingly unaware of the smiles which his
enthusiasm brought to the lips of his admiring listeners, who often
asked him to dine just in order to serve him up as a particularly
succulent morsel to those who had not yet made his acquaintance.
"We'll get him going on one of his pet subjects: you'll see how remarkably he talks once he gets started!"—and get started he always did. He
was generally regarded as a mad genius, an interesting hysteric, and the
other guests went home as a rule feeling not quite sure whether they
were returning from the Sorbonne or the Salpétrière. On this particular
occasion he suddenly started off on the subject of an opera which he
had heard on the previous evening—"Just a neat bit of contrivance—
that's all you can say about it. Orchestration, cabinet-maker's work,
though not lacking in a certain facility—and that's that!"–"Cabinet-
maker's work," murmured Boisard to himself. "No one else would
have thought of saying just that."

He left as he had come without saying good-bye and still talking. "Well, what do you think of him?" said Boisard. Jean, wishing to be polite, and accompanying his words with an intelligent smile replied, "He certainly is a remarkable person." – "But what you've just heard is nothing!" said Boisard. "He's always trotting out something new. It's worth noting that for all the delightful, the, if I may say so, paradoxical charm of his speech, there is always a shrewd substratum of solid good sense. Take for instance what he said about the orchestration being cabinet-maker's work. The comparison is I must admit somewhat daring—not the sort of thing that could be written down in cold blood, not the sort of thing that you or I would risk saying, or even, if it comes to that, thinking, but see how nearly it pins down the work of some of our modern composers—who do in fact at their best, resemble the old-time master-craftsman." Jean, with the gesture of a connoisseur made it clear that he had taken the point. "Imagination's all right in its way," went on Boisard, "but what really counts is sound critical judgment," and turned on Jean a suspicious look as though he had sensed through the sweet odours of the young man's good manners that he was not really one of the elect. Then he continued, "Please remember that I am always at home on Thursday evenings. I very much hope that you will become one of our regulars, though I should warn you that you will find only young folk. I give them free leave to be as silly as they like. They know whom they're dealing with and don't need much encouragement. Each Thursday we have some new bit of nonsense which sets everybody laughing. I call it my little class. Old though I am they don't hesitate to say anything they like, as you will very soon gather. Not an ounce of respect for my grey hairs! You've no idea how exciting it all is—gloves off and plenty of hard hitting! No mincing of words about one's favourite picture or opera—if someone doesn't happen to like 'em!"

4. *The Guéraud-Houppins*

At the time of Jean's birth Monsieur Santeuil had a younger sister who was married to a financier named Guéraud. This Guéraud, not long after his wife's death, made an enormous fortune as a result of speculating in Turkish railways, which enabled him to marry again, this time a certain Mademoiselle Houppin the daughter of Hector Houppin, one of the Houppin Brothers who were so prominent in the business world as almost to be regarded as the equals of the great Banking Families of France. She had a pronounced limp and for that reason had failed to find a husband. From then on he saw the members of the Santeuil family scarcely more than twice a year, though he continued to use the second person singular when addressing Monsieur Santeuil senior, much as a man may carry about on him a watch which was given to him by somebody with whom he has so completely lost touch that in all probability his children will hear the former friend's name for the first time when they happen to ask their father about his gift. In a short while the Santeuils learned through the medium of the public Press that Mademoiselle Guéraud-Houppin was frequently to be seen in the most elegant houses of the capital. True, when Madame Marmet, though she had no daughters of her own to launch, gave a "hop", Mademoiselle Guéraud-Houppin was not one of those guests to whose "distinction and liveliness" the newspaper columnists drew attention. That however did not stand in the way of her attracting the admiring glances, not only of the young men but of the young women too and even of their mothers who readily forgave her for eclipsing their own offspring, never accused her of behaving badly, and refrained from pointing out that, "When a girl's got as much money as she has, it's easy enough to be a success." Madame Marmet was at pains, when making out the list of guests to be supplied to the Press, only to mention the daughters of such families as the Fontanges, the La Cour des Hardes, the Pistours, Vollancelles and Revailles. But gradually as the name of Monsieur Hanotaux has succeeded in making headway and now figures naturally among those of the really "aristocratic" diplomats who

figure in the accounts given of ambassadorial receptions, so did it come
about that Mademoiselle Guéraud-Houppin's appeared more and more
frequently in the paragraphs issued by the Thianges, the Tourneforts
and the Beyrintes—since those hostesses had not the same reasons as
had Madame Marmet to fear the effect of a bourgeois name in their
lists and were pleased to extend the courtesy of inclusion to so attractive
a young woman. Whenever a journalist in the course of duty had to
supply an account of some great ball about which he had very little
information, after first describing the beauty of the house, the splendour
of the flowers, the zest of the Waldteuffel orchestra, the animation of
the supper tables, the late hour at which the guests had departed—not
without promising their gracious hostess to provide at no distant date a
sequel to so unforgettable an occasion (for no art, however humble, but
has its "commonplaces" and "generalities") he invariably added that
he had noticed among those present "Mesdemoiselles de Vollancelles,
de Revailles, de Pistours, Guéraud-Houppin, de Fontanet, de la Cour
des Hardes" even at the risk of having to state on the following day
that one of these ladies had been mentioned by mistake, being as it
turned out in mourning, absent from Paris, or on her deathbed.

In spite however of her pink tulle dresses, her graceful manner of
dancing the Pavane, the curtsies which she made to the attendant
dowagers—with just sufficient artificiality as to combine charm with
poise—Mademoiselle Guéraud-Houppin found no pleasure in Society.
The world of art and learning, of museums and lecture-rooms, had for
her imagination—she had never experienced it directly—much the
same charm as that of gleaming candle-light, massed flowers and
brilliant jewels, of gentlemen in full evening-dress and countesses
in low-necked gowns for the student who lives immersed in
books. Accompanied by a childhood's friend Mademoiselle Guersnet
who was ugly, poor and soured, she went every morning to the
Louvre where she methodically studied all the great schools of painting
in turn. She had seen in one of the papers that Jean Santeuil had been
present at a dinner-party given by Alphonse Daudet and deplored her
parents' failure to "keep up" with a young cousin who moved freely
among artists and men of letters. Madame Santeuil for her part when
Jean began "going out", fervently but silently hoped that a day might
come when Monsieur and Madame Guéraud-Houppin would meet
him, and would realize that the son of their much-looked-down-upon
brother-in-law occupied a position which was superior to and far more

brilliant than their own. One evening when Monsieur and Madame Guéraud-Houppin were dining with the Baroness de Vieuxbatour the Baron asked whether anyone could tell him about a young man called Santeuil, foolishly omitting to add that he had met him at the Réveillons. At the mention of this name Monsieur and Madame Guéraud-Houppin deliberately held their tongues though their daughter would dearly have liked to exclaim, "Why, he's my first cousin! As a matter of fact, I went to see my Aunt Santeuil only yesterday with my parents." But she held her peace fearing that she might displease her father. "D'you know anything of him, Guéraud?" asked the Baron. "Canteuil?" queried Monsieur Guéraud-Houppin, who appeared to find some difficulty in grasping so unfamiliar a name. "No, Santeuil," replied the Baron, "with an S, like Sainte-Croix." – "Oh, Santeuil!" said Monsieur Guéraud-Houppin, "I believe I *have* heard it. I feel I ought to know it—though I am not quite sure to whom you are referring." – "Why are you asking, Antisthène?" asked the Baroness. "Because the Duchesse de Réveillon has asked whether she might bring him with her this evening." Monsieur and Madame Guéraud-Houppin were at once assailed by a strong desire to go home. As for Mademoiselle Guéraud-Houppin, she shot a furious look at her parents, and was conscious of that mysterious feeling which comes to all of us when we are brought up short by some oddity of behaviour or character in someone we thought we knew intimately.

But Monsieur and Madame Guéraud-Houppin had no time in which to solve by flight the difficult dilemma in which they had landed themselves. At that very moment the door was thrown open, and the Duchesse de Réveillon entered the room with Jean who seeing his uncle immediately went across the floor to greet him. Monsieur Guéraud-Houppin, realizing that he had been seen, hastily turned to the Baron de Berlinges and said: "I should very much like to know what you think of this new piece. ..." – "What piece?" asked the Baron with no little astonishment since he never set foot in a theatre. "What I mean is—I attach the greatest importance to your opinion—and I'll tell you why ..." went on Monsieur Guéraud-Houppin who by this time had not the faintest idea what he was talking about. It was impossible for him to do two things at once, and since he was frantically wondering how he could possibly get out of this frightful situation—what he ought to do next and whether he should pretend not to recognize his own nephew—his tongue was quite incapable of giving any logical sequence to remarks which had nothing to do with his present anxieties. But interlocutors are as a rule so inattentive, so indifferent to what is being said to them, that we often seem most absent-minded when we are most attentive, and the play of our features, our blunders, our mistakes which we think must be only too glaringly obvious actually pass almost unnoticed. The Baron said in the friendliest fashion, "I feel greatly flattered that you should value my opinion——" but without letting him finish the sentence and rudely interrupting him, Monsieur Guéraud-Houppin, almost pushing his face into the Baron's, embarked without a pause for breath, and in the most vehement manner, upon a flow of words which were completely devoid of meaning. The fact was that Jean was at his elbow, bowing and saying, "Good evening." Being apparently engaged in a conversation of great urgency, Monsieur Guéraud-Houppin could hold out his hand to Jean without seeming to notice him, and so be absolved from the necessity of answering. But Jean had quite clearly said, "Good evening, Uncle." This appellation however seemed to the Baron so absurd that he immediately pushed it from his consciousness either assuming that his ears had played him false or accepting the fact as one of those things so patently at variance with reality that they are automatically rejected, deciding that he must be suffering from an hallucination, that what he had heard was so strange that it would be better to pay no attention to it. Our intelligence decides that this or that has been said, yet at the same time not said. The words are like phrases spoken by a character on the stage. The other member of the pair must obviously have heard since he makes a gesture. The first character either tries again or takes refuge behind a piece of furniture, and pretends he is not there at all. Whereupon the other resumes what he himself has been saying, giving the impression that the unexpected remark made by his companion has made so little impression on him, that not the slightest sign of anxiety, curiosity, or doubt is visible.

You will perhaps feel even greater astonishment at the behaviour of the Baron whom Monsieur Guéraud-Houppin, wishing it to appear that he had not returned his nephew's greeting because he was pre-occupied, which would be sufficient explanation to the said nephew why, though the other knew him perfectly well, he had returned his "Good evening" so coldly, and to the rest of the company why he had said good evening at all to somebody he did not know—was treating the Baron to an endless and incoherent flow of talk. For to all this he merely kept on nodding his head, asking no questions, showing not the least surprise. "This," you will say, "is supposed to be a picture of real life, whereas the whole thing is becoming more and more of a stage play. How could the Baron possibly not be surprised? As you present him he is nothing but a stock-figure of farce and completely devoid of life." Dear reader, have you never had the experience of not under-standing a single word of what your neighbour at dinner is saying? Do you think, 'He must be talking like this to cover up something he doesn't want me to notice'? Not a bit of it: assuming you to be a kindly person, what really happens is that you greet the end of his sentence with a polite and interested nod. The Baron de Berlinges—of whom I would dearly like you to know more, though that is im-possible, since he will not appear again in the course of this story for the very good reason that—though there was nothing, on the occasion I am describing, in his pink complexion, short, sturdy legs, and prominent stomach to indicate that a tragedy was hanging over his head, he did in fact a few days later die so suddenly that the other guests were led to remark, "And to think that only a week ago I was at a party with him. He was just as gay as usual, just his usual self——"–"I don't agree at all," interrupted an old lady. "For some time now I have been noticing how tired he looked. He almost always fell asleep after dinner"—the Baron de Berlinges, as I was saying, regarded conversation much as inexperienced players, or persons incapable of mental concen-tration, regard chess, that is to say as a game in which one's adversary's master-stroke is merely an excuse for moving one's pawn, without thinking much about his reasoning, or attempting to foresee his moves. In just such a way, whenever the dissertation of a talkative old man, or an embarrassed young one, showed signs of being too long-drawn-out, and unlikely to provide him with material for an easy reply, his interest lagged and he would sit in his chair staring at the smoke of his cigarette or the tips of his shoes. To which must be added the fact that since he was imperfectly informed on many matters, music for instance and the niceties of verbal wit, he would entirely fail to grasp the point of some reference to the life of Mozart or of some joking remark. But thinking it pointless to make an exhibition of his ignorance he never asked for an explanation, with the result that when for example, some wag, hearing him say that he smoked only hand-made cigarettes said, "In memory no doubt of Tristan and Isolde?"—since he was not shrewd enough to commit himself to either an affirmative or a negative reply, he merely smiled as though to imply that the point of the jest had not been lost on him. His attitude was one of good-natured humility, and this led him to believe rather too easily that everything he did not understand had a humorous intention, so that if anybody started explaining some serious matter in language which he found unintelligible, he at once suspected a witticism, and being too polite to let it be seen that he was not appreciative, would smile broadly, thereby exasperating his interlocutor, resembling in this those foreigners who when they go to see a play by Molière or Musset, keep smiling all the way through the performance, for fear lest the innumerable subtleties with which they have been told the dialogue is thickly strewn may seem to have escaped them. But such misunderstandings were not frequent with the Baron de Berlinges because like deaf persons who being unable to hear what is being said follow the conversation by keeping their eyes fixed on the speaker's lips, as soon as the conversation turned to general matters, in other words as soon as he ceased to hear what was being said, he never once took his eyes from his neighbour's face, and tried to make out from its solemn or sprightly expression whether what he was saying should be taken seriously or in a spirit of fun. Whence no doubt arose his dislike of poker-faced persons, whom he regarded as being in some sort, tricksters in the conversational game, for ever doing something that was not according to the rules.

This having been explained, you will perhaps no longer feel surprised at seeing the Baron de Berlinges listening, without so much as raising an eyebrow, to the incoherent remarks of Monsieur Guéraud-Houppin, meanwhile exhaling the smoke of his cigarette in the direction of the ceiling. To judge from Monsieur Guéraud-Houppin's worried look, there could on this occasion be no humorous intention and when silence fell at last, he looked at him calmly and solemnly, saying nothing, and wearing on his face the expression to be seen there when he was being told about some affair of honour and had not yet been made free of all the details. Then seeing that Monsieur Guéraud-Houppin did not at once continue, he walked across to where there was an ash-tray so as to give himself time. He assumed vaguely that Guéraud-Houppin must be financially involved in some theatrical enterprise, or that he was interested in one of the actresses about whose success he wanted to question him. But he was content to wait placidly until such time as light might be thrown on this hypothesis about which he preferred not to think. Seeing however that Guéraud-Houppin was certainly not going to say any more on the subject, he decided to have a word or two with the Duchesse de Réveillon. But he feared above all things lest Guéraud-Houppin should think that he was avoiding a matter of some delicacy, and making his escape without giving an opinion. Consequently, "I'm just going to say good evening to the Duchesse de Réveillon," he remarked as though to anticipate any protest, adding as proof of his good will, "Come and lunch with me one day at the Club." Then he wandered away, making expressive gestures to the Duchess across the room which were intended to convey with humorous exaggeration how much he admired her new dress.

5. *Madame de Réveillon's Salon*

Whenever Jean went to dine quietly with the Réveillons, he was almost certain to find the Marquise de Tournefort, the Comte de Thianges, and Bonami—an old friend of the Duke's and Vice-President of the Club—Jacques Bonami commonly known as Talondebois. He had lost his left foot in a shooting accident. The Duke explained that he had known him in the days before he had had the elegant wooden appendage which explained his nick-name, and, it must be admitted, added not a little to his vogue. It had to begin with established his identity in Society, and thus set him in the way to becoming a "personality". A Bonami with two feet would have had to work for many wearisome years during which ladies, ready enough to inscribe his name on the list of "smart people" would have been vainly seeking for information about him. "I met a Monsieur Bonami at dinner the other evening: who is he?"–"Oh, I think you must mean Georges Bonami."–"Whether his name's Georges, or what it is, I really don't know: a fair-haired man."–"That may be the chap I'm thinking of, but I really can't be sure." And so the name that might have been treasured in a willing memory, would have been like one of those pieces of floating wreckage which no nail can secure, drifted by the tides of doubt on the sea of the unknown, a prey to innumerable eddies. Bonami however had been spared that stage. If anyone hesitated for a moment—"Jacques Bonami."–"I don't know whether his name's Jacques."–"Well, Talondebois, a fellow with a wooden foot?" –"Yes, that's the man."–"Then it's Jacques Bonami right enough, a great friend of the Réveillons etc. . . ."

Nor was that all. Bonami was a handsome man, plentifully endowed with what is commonly known as "chic", in which a dragging gait (caused, in this case, by a wooden foot) may be an important element. His slight limp, his elegant surgical feature, most certainly did not alienate the women from him. On the contrary, it retained their interest, just as there may be something "rather special", something more interesting in a slight squint and a well managed monocle than in the beauty of a piercing eye and a frank gaze. To have a distinctive appearance, to be not like everybody else, is to be well on the way to achieving a glamorous reputation which no attacks can undermine, and love feeds on glamour. To have projecting from an irreproachable trouser-leg a wooden foot encased in a patent-leather shoe, and not to betray its presence except by a slight hesitancy in walking—which produces an effect of languorous grace and conscious affectation, is to have about one a hint of vice, something infinitely superior to mere distinction—of the sort of vice too which would seem to hold out to the fortunate women who should enjoy the gentleman's intimacy, the intoxicating promise of a passion rich in leisured brutalities and artificial stimulants. And so it came about that when some woman of the world, speaking of Bonami, said, "I simply cannot understand how any woman could fall in love with a man with a wooden foot," the remark was greeted with derisive contempt by those young Society beauties who held the view that in the way of elegant smartness no one could hold a candle to Bonami, and that even if he had two perfectly good feet he could not possibly be more attractive than he was, in much the same way as those who passionately admire the gifts of Sarah Bernhardt would feel their idolatry diminish should a day come when Sarah Bernhardt, though still remaining a great actress, ceased to speak through clenched teeth and a fixed smile in such a way as to make what she says barely audible. The ladies who took the opposite view continued to maintain that there was "something unnatural" about loving a man with a wooden foot, and spoke of it in much the same way as a lover of horseflesh might laughingly comment on a friend who had sold his carriage and pair in order to buy a motor-car which "moves faster, is less comfortable, and looks decidedly ugly".

Bonami had been a married man for some considerable while. After the first year of wedded bliss however Madame Bonami—a niece of the Duc de Réveillon, who at first, had been deeply in love with him seemed, unlike the young women who were habitually thrilled when they saw him limp his way across the paddock at race meetings, no longer to be enthralled by the studied charm of his gait. The power of any oddity to attract us diminishes by degrees, and no man can long remain "smart" in the eyes of a wife who knows all about his ailments, his dislike of being late for an appointment, and the way in which every morning he tints his greying locks. After his wife's death Bonami took to having all his meals at the Club, or in the houses of intimate friends like the Réveillons. It was not long before Jean was introduced to him. As a rule he would have felt annoyed with the Duke for admitting to the circle of his intimates a man who like himself was a commoner. We are delighted when a Minister awards us a decoration, even when we have no claim to be thus honoured, but if he follows this up by awarding the same distinction to others who occupy a position similar to our own, we feel inclined to keep him, if we can, from so foolishly cheapening the mark of esteem which he has bestowed upon us. In just such a way was Bonami deeply attached to the maxim—which he was never tired of enunciating—that there are some people with whom men of rank may properly hob-nob, and others to whom they should give a wide berth, this discrimination being controlled by the position they hold in Society. He had more than once said to the Duc de Breuvas, who liked inviting geographers to his house since he had a passion for travel—"Why you see so much of So-and-so I simply cannot understand. There's no reason for you to behave like that. He's not your sort: nobody else in your set receives him." But he saw nothing improper in the Duc de Réveillon—the simplicity of whose tastes he was fond of applauding, the more so since it was never very obvious, or at least not in his choice of friends—and his wife choosing a hard-working and obscure young student as a suitable companion for their son. He smilingly accepted this intelligent and rather special breach of etiquette, and seemed to find in it a certain satisfaction—almost one might say self-satisfaction, as though faced by the fact that since the Duc de Réveillon had not forced upon his son a titled intimate, it was for him, Bonami, an old friend of the family, and the Duke's social equal, to show an equal condescension. Besides he was not always sparing of critical comments where the Réveillons were concerned. He thought it advisable to maintain his own independence and self-respect in the eyes of Society—his well-known slavish attachment to a ducal family might have produced some tiresome repercussions—by playing the part in his dealings with its head of a plain, blunt man. I am well aware that the generous-minded and indiscreet reader, finding the Duc de Réveillon so very much more sympathetic than Bonami, and feeling surprised that he should have made a close friend of him, might at this point grow indignant about Bonami's falsity, and feel a wish to repeat some of his remarks to the Duke, and so disabuse that over-credulous aristocrat about a man who so shamelessly betrayed his generosity. Perhaps the ill-bred reader who from a sheer love of justice might have committed himself to this delicate manœuvre, only to find that he had no more succeeded in his rash endeavour to interfere than a philanthropist who tries to protect a woman who is being beaten by her husband, or takes sides with the voters whose Deputy is exploiting them, would be shocked to learn that the Duke was already aware, if not of the actual charges levelled against him at any given moment by Bonami, at least of similar ones, and, had his knowledge roused him to a display of ill-temper, it would have been not against Bonami, but rather against the indiscreet informer. We must therefore rest content to admit that, in spite of everything, the Réveillons remained obstinately loyal to Bonami, and suppose that beneath the man's rather too fashionable exterior—the aristocratic limp, the exasperating snobbery, the ill-nature and servility—there did exist certain rare human qualities the precious essence of which, though hidden from ordinary eyes by an unpleasing surface, was known to the Duke who no doubt in circumstances of which we are not aware, had had occasion to see it in its pristine purity.

*

On the not very frequent occasions when the Duke went into Society, he spoke very little. Even when he did open his lips his utterances were confined to somewhat flat commonplaces, as though he were conforming to customary usage, and saying things which could not possibly be understood as expressing his own personal opinions. Perhaps, since in the course of his social duties he found himself more and more thrown into the company of those with whom he could not possibly have ever been intimate, he went out of his way to make it clear that he was engaged in a purely formal activity, and did not wish it to be thought that he would dream of offering to such persons the hospitality—not indeed of his house, such an idea would have occurred to nobody—but of his mind, his tastes, or anything that was his. If some imprudent acquaintance ventured to ask him, "Do you really like *that* sort of music?" he was not only at once upon his guard, but assumed the icy expression with which he would have countered any over-effusive advances from someone whom he might suspect of trying to force a way into his intimacy. If anybody said, "How are you?" using the words in their merely social and formal sense, he would at once reply, "Kind of you to ask: well, thank'ee." If on the other hand somebody, thinking perhaps that he looked tired, inquired with every indication of meaning what he said, "I *do* hope you are feeling all right, Monsieur le Duc"—then, anxious not to appear offensive, but determined to edge the questioner away from the dangerous ground of personalities, he would quickly reply, so as to stop short so tactless an approach, "Charming party, is it not: so nice to see you."

Everything, in this matter of social contacts, caused him acute discomfort, and since he dreaded the necessity of being deliberately rude, he would sometimes blush like a modest woman when a man has ventured, in her presence, to make some rather too daring remark, the effect of which is to convince her that she can never again address even the simplest greeting to him. For this reason he was careful never to commit himself to any statement of an intelligent, sensitive, or even personal nature, such as might seem to display some essential part of himself to those with whom, in the intricacies of social life, he might have been brought in contact, behaving as a man might to a tradesman whose bill he is careful to settle, but with whom there can never be any question of exchanging gifts. But there was another reason, too, for the peculiar attitude he habitually adopted. Like the Head of a State, when making a public pronouncement, he was aware that his least word would be listened to with attention, and made the object of informed comment. Precisely because everything that such a man says is said of deliberate intention, his words at once assume the validity of action, and create an entirely new situation. The Emperor of Russia for instance, making a speech aimed at the French nation, uses perhaps, the word "ally" instead of the more usual "friend". On the very next day France through the medium of millions of vague, anonymous conversations, and the considered comments of newspapers with a world-wide circulation, lets it be known that, "Should there ever be another war, Russia would send five million men to the help of this country." The Duc de Réveillon had only to let fall some casual remark for the man he had deigned to address to be filled with a delicious certainty that he, his wife and his daughter were to receive an invitation to the next Réveillon ball. And so it was that every scrap of that orotund eloquence, no matter how flat, which goes by the name of social chit-chat, and only a fool would take at its face value— when dropped by the Duc de Réveillon, was worth exactly nothing, not so much because of the idea expressed or the turn of phrase employed, or the form in which it was conveyed, but because like a skilled musician who stresses here one note, there another, he could impart to his conversation an infinite number of shades of meaning. The recollection of them at some later date, not so much by those who had been irritated by this or that remark addressed to them, as by those malicious persons who had happened to overhear the exchange, might well alter the opinion of the so-called "intelligent", who till that moment had been inclined to regard him as a nit-wit. No-one excelled him in the concoction of some final variation on a familiar theme which had a way of dashing the hopes aroused in the hearer at an earlier stage. To listen to him was like listening to music where the key can be determined only in the final resolution. Not seldom, some banker with whom he had frequent business dealings in Paris, though the two men had no social contacts, happening to meet him at a "Cure" where he formed one of his party in the evenings, would rejoice when the day of departure came at hearing him say, "It has been delightful having you, here: thanks to you the time has passed very pleasantly. I hope to have the pleasure . . ." of seeing you in my house when we get home was the silent termination given to the phrase by the delighted banker, who felt sure of his ground. But in fact for this version No. 1 was substituted version No. 4, which fell upon his ear like a Judge's sentence from which there is no appeal. . . . "of meeting you here again next year". which meant that in Paris there would be nothing doing. I have said version No. 4, because there was also a version No. 2—which could equally well follow from the same opening—"in Paris"—which was rather better than "here", though less good than "in my own house", and a version No. 3: "I hope to meet you again," which without specifying any definite future, or pinning down the renewed acquaintance to anything so irrevocable as "here", made possible two contrasting states of mind—for the optimist a quiet and pleasing hope, for the pessimist a sense of uncertainty, which to tell the truth was only too often justified by the event. As to the merely unsophisticated, it never occurred to those who were most so to reply, "I shall certainly call," because the Duc de Réveillon's face was eloquent, and in the play of his features one could to some extent read what the nature of his reactions would be in various situations. In this particular one it was not hard to imagine in advance the icy, "That will really be *too* kind of you," followed by the quick suppression of the adumbrated handshake —the very thought of which would for ever discourage the unfortunate victim from carrying out so mad a project.

The Duke's concluding words were therefore always awaited with justifiable impatience, since they might completely alter the sense of those which had preceded them. In the watering-places where the words of farewell were uttered which gave rise to so many hopes, and often to so many disappointments, there were also the formulae of greeting when you happened on him for the first time—having frequently it need hardly be said met him in Paris, though never having been on intimate terms with him. Sometimes he would be friendly for minutes on end, and when that happened you said to yourself: "Obviously, since he is easily bored, he is going to ask me to go and see him. That will get me in well with the hotel staff." Then would come the end of the sentence: "Well, *au revoir*, for I won't say good-bye" (smile of gratified acknowledgment all ready—"But at what hour of the day are you accessible?") "because I very much hope that I shall *run across* you again (what exactly did "again" mean?) some time or other," the inner significance being, "Don't dream of making the first move." Since on these occasions his friendliness was clearly marked, you said to yourself, "This is perfectly splendid. The staff will conclude that I don't go about looking for him because the prospect bores me" (how untrue!). But the look on the face of the polite but impassive Francis set uneasiness stirring. 'That damned fellow, either because his master clearly indicates that one person is negligible, another worth cultivating (not so crudely of course but using a certain tone of voice when speaking of them, accompanied, perhaps by the various subtleties of manœuvre already mentioned) or because he is naturally sharp at putting two and two together, must know perfectly well that he meets, but does not *receive* me.' A servant may be on good terms with a ducal employer, but he is also on good terms with his fellow-servants. He perhaps despises their masters but never them. Very early on they will say to him, "Just fancy, our boss knows your boss!" to which comes the inevitable reply, "Oh, we know him right enough, but we don't *receive* him, not even here!" Finally these casual meetings *may* just conceivably result in an invitation to pay him a visit. You have been counting on the fact that his friends will soon be leaving. You set great store on rainy days. You would like if possible, to starve him into surrender, or so to isolate him as to force his hand. You may go so far as to drop a hint to the effect that you will not be in Paris next winter. Then when winter comes and you are still about, he will sometimes behave in a markedly friendly fashion if you happen to meet him, or will engage you in long conversations at other people's parties. At the conclusion of one of these confabulations, when you have been fortunate enough to arouse his interest, when he has seemed to treat you with more forthrightness than previously, you say to yourself—dreaming of an invitation to the hôtel de Réveillon, 'Is it going to come *now*?' But with an affectionate warmth unusual in him he says, "Good-bye; I *have* enjoyed our talk. It will give me much pleasure to meet you again . . . *here*."

*

When Jean went to see Henri before dinner, several ancient landaus with old-fashioned springs and emblazoned panels, brand-new broughams adorned with heraldic shields no larger than those on fashionable letter-paper, and a hired fly, were standing in single file before the house, extended in either direction beyond its frontage, as though waiting for visitors. On one half of the landau box-seats a coachman was perched high in the air. The other half, momentarily deserted by the footman, remained empty like a pedestal awaiting its statue. The interior of the broughams, fitted with clocks, pencils, and bell-pulls with rubber, pear-shaped grips, were each as crowded and complicated as the inside of a camera, as padded, decked, and soft as a doll's box. From the window of Henri's room Jean could see now and again a footman appear at a door, a carriage disengage itself from the waiting line and manage, somehow or other, to draw up by the curb, and a lady, picking her way between the horses' heads, get into it, gathering up her skirts, taking out her card-case, and issuing instructions to the footman who, running after the vehicle when it was already in movement, clambered to his place beside the coachman on the box. Then another carriage would draw up, the waiting line would grow longer, and a footman, running to the porter's lodge, would return still running, and open the door. Sometimes the lady as she got out would raise her eyes, see Jean, mistake him for Henri, and wave a hand. Often a visitor about to enter the house, and still standing on the pavement, would suddenly recognize a friend emerging and both, as in some wordless colloquy, would exchange distant smiles and silent messages. Sometimes two ladies got out of the same carriage and in a short time got back into it, having agreed to pay their calls in company, and then before moving off, while the footman was still standing at the door, remain deep in consultation before deciding where to go to next.

Often a gentleman wearing white gloves would accompany a lady to her carriage and get in with her. Some of the carriages, having deposited their mistresses, immediately started off at a sharp trot, to keep the horses from catching cold, reappearing from time to time in front of the door in order that their lady should not have to wait.

Since the Duchess was in the habit of asking Jean to dinner several times a week, he sometimes called on her. Ladies would be shown into the drawing-room, loosen their furs, say how cold it was, draw near the fire, remove their furs altogether, express admiration for the tea equipage, confess that they were sadly tempted, accept a cup from a gentleman who would then sit down on a stool beside them, or saying that they would rather choose a cake for themselves, take off their gloves, apologize for eating so little, thank the servant who came to tell them that their carriages were at the door, and meeting on the way out a friend who had just arrived, stay talking with her for as long as ten minutes as though engaged in a serious conversation, and receive a bow from a gentleman who on reaching the drawing-room, proceeded to announce, as though passing on an important piece of news, that he had just met So-and-so. Soon the fresh arrival would be announced. "You ran into Marthe on her way out," said the Duchess. The newcomer expressed astonishment: how *could* she know? A laugh from the informer answered her question and everybody was much amused at having succeeded in mystifying her. As a rule if she had lingered for a while before entering the room, it was to talk about sick friends of whom she wanted news. At once as in a ballet, all the ladies present, even those who did not know of whom she was talking, assumed expressions of the deepest melancholy and if one of them grew bored with the new turn of the conversation, she rose from her chair with a shamefaced air as though she were committing a sin by "carrying off" a friend to whom she was giving a "lift", the said friend not having come in her carriage.

Jean remained with Henri in a corner, for fear that the Duchess might introduce him and he might have to make small-talk and hand round tea. But when he came to dinner he could not avoid being presented to the Duchess's friends. Many in their turn invited him, and at their houses he met several people whom he knew. Consequently he found himself obliged to pay a good many calls. Often, much to his astonishment, some lady to whom he had been introduced, would say that she had heard a great deal about him. "You were dining last week at the Réveillons', weren't you? You sat next to my great friend S——, who found you quite charming. Your father is one of the Heads of Department at the Ministry of the Interior." Jean could not imagine how he had come to be spoken about, why he should have figured as a subject of conversation, or how people who were complete strangers to him should be in a position to know what he had said at the Duchess's table, whereas quite often people who *should* know about this or that failed to do so and he might be ill for a month before his aunt Desroches had word of his indisposition. In just such a way we can be at the theatre on the same evening as a friend, and in a neighbouring box, without having a suspicion of his presence, though a walk we took at midnight in the Bois de Boulogne, in the course of which we met nobody, will be noticed by an Englishman passing through Paris, mentioned by him on his return to London in the hearing of a German whom we have not seen for ten years, and commented on by him when next he comes to France.

*

Though he showed no more than an aptitude for painting, the general view was that he was an artist, not by reason of his aptitude but because he had close ties with Victor Hugo, Leconte de Lisle, Saint-Saëns; because he was shy, because he was wide-eyed, and though not born into Society, was received in the most flattering way by the great. And so it was that when he answered those who asked what he was "working at" by saying that so far he had produced nothing, his questioners, either because they thought him modest, or too much occupied in studying for an examination, admired his simplicity or inveighed against the labours which took up so much of his time. At the first mention of his name, he was said to be an artist: at the second he was credited with having a talent: "He must have judging by the way the Duchesse de Réveillon has taken him under her wing. That'll be a great help to him." People thought they could arouse his interest by asking him to meet men of the Faubourg Saint-Germain who took an interest in literature, or women who knew all about men of letters. Madame de Lavardin expressed surprise when she learned that he had never met Léon de Tinseau. After a moment's reflection, she said, "I'll try to bring you together; nothing would please him more than to give you some advice. He's such a nice, simple creature." Then she asked him about Anatole France and Marcel Prévost. For her, as for all those in her set, a man of letters was somebody who said nothing at big parties, but was charming to meet in the privacy of the fireside. "My dear, would you believe it! Céline Hacqueville once asked Dumas to a great dinner with princes galore, and he never opened his lips. But at midnight when most of the guests had gone, and only a few intimates were left, there was a positive firework display! I wasn't bored for a single moment, as you may well believe. But that didn't comfort Céline who had given the dinner expressly for him. I had told her how it would be, but she wouldn't listen. She knows nothing about entertaining men like that. One should never be more than four."

The general view was that Jean was charming. This made him happy, though not conceited, because he had already seen too many fools admired, and because when he was really making a conversational effort, nobody seemed to respond. On the other hand, sometimes a perfectly simple remark of his would be received with cries of delight, and it irked him to find that when he disclaimed all intention of wit, it should be laid at the door of his "modesty". On one occasion, when he was dining at the house of Madame de Thianges—an admirable but slightly limited hostess—Mademoiselle Nora de Ziewitch, whom Madame de Thianges considered to be the most intelligent woman to be found anywhere, almost a genius in fact, happened to mention the Marquise de Lavardin. Jean was not sure whether he knew her. "Is it she who's got hair like tow?" – "That really is *too* amusing! 'Tow' is quite delightful!" Those present laughed long and loudly and no attention was paid to Jean's protests. When the company rose, Madame de Thianges, who had not heard what he had said, but, encouraged by the approval of Mademoiselle de Ziewitch (who was so difficult to please) felt convinced that she had among her guests one of the wittiest men in Paris, booked Jean for dinner on the two next Thursdays and took the opportunity to find out what his remark had been. "Quite delightful! How *could* you! She has hair. . . ." – "But I assure you, Madame, that I was not trying to be funny. I am dreadfully grieved." – "Tow!" said Madame de Thianges, squirming with delight, "it is certainly straight, but it is very pretty!" – "It is you, Madame, who are turning what I said into a joke," alluding to the way in which she had pronounced "tow". "Now don't pretend to be modest!" exclaimed Madame de Thianges—brushing aside his protest, "what you said was absolutely delicious, Nora told me so," she added artlessly, making no attempt to conceal her criterion of other people's wit. 'Well,' thought Jean, 'after all, if Nora says so, and that seems to be enough for them, it's not for me to make a fuss. All the same it's rather annoying that they should think me just as intelligent as Monsier de Bellièvre, when in fact I'm a thousand times more so. True, if they saw me as I really am, they would probably think me stupid.' "Tow" went the rounds for a week, sharing the honours with the delicious sally made by Monsieur de Bellièvre who, on hearing that Monsieur Faure had offered the Presidency of the Council to Monsieur Bourgeois, remarked that it was "*pas fort*"—like two charming plays which occupy the bills at the same time.

*

At the house of the Princesse de Lunéville, who did not "know her place", Jean met Madame Marmet who immediately called him by his Christian name. The Duchesse de La Tour Acquevive whose salon was the most exclusive in all Paris, was there and Madame Marmet scrutinized her with an attention which only too clearly betrayed her eagerness to be admitted into the charmed circle, though at the same time it was marked by a starchiness which was intended to make it quite clear that she was not the sort of person to fling herself at duchesses' heads, that she was not in fact a snob, but a reserved and dignified person. To be sure, if looks could absorb something of the substance of the object upon which they are riveted, one might have believed that in the course of the ten years during which Madame Marmet had been meeting the Duchess without ever managing to secure an introduction, it was her ardent and impotent stare that had reduced the Duchess to the condition of a shrivelled, dusty skeleton which beneath an old black woollen dress she offered to the contemplation of the snobs, thus stressing the distance between her grandeur of mind and her physical humility, between the wretched appearance of a not very desirable prey and the impossibility of capturing it. Since however she dared not address her directly, Madame Marmet took advantage of such chances as came her way, and, hearing somebody talking to the Duchess about her sons, and the latter's modest rejoinder that they had not got very good marks at school, said very distinctly to her neighbour, without looking at the Duchess, "All the same, I have been told by my son's professor—and indeed it is a matter of common knowledge—that the

Duchess's sons fall little short of being two young geniuses." The
Duchess smiled, but the smile was of a kind to produce a very real fear
that she was about to be sick on the spot. Madame Marmet rose from
her chair, executed a profound curtsey, and sat down again. That was
all. On another occasion, when Jean was at Madame de Lavardin's at
the same time as Madame Marmet, Madame de Thianges came in,
saying: "I've just been at Louise de Ziewitch's." – "Were there a great
many people there?" asked Madame de Lavardin. "No, not many.
Marie Sosthènes arrived just as I was leaving." Madame Marmet thereupon rose from her chair, as though she had just received news of a
victory, for she knew that the lady whom her friends called Marie
Sosthènes was no less a person than the Duchesse de Doudeauville, and
that Mademoiselle de Ziewitch was in the habit of introducing everybody to her. She hurriedly said good-bye, but alas, her carriage, which
did not know that the Duchesse de Doudeauville had gone to call on
Mademoiselle de Ziewitch, and that Madame de Thianges had just
mentioned the fact in the hearing of Madame Marmet, thus playing
the part of the wind which carries the pollen of the male sycamore to
the ovary of the female sycamore, had not yet put in an appearance.
She had to wait at the foot of the stairs, tormented all the time by the
thought of what she was missing. When at last it did arrive, it passed
another carriage entering the courtyard, which happened to be that of
the Duchesse de Doudeauville, who after leaving Mademoiselle de
Ziewitch's house had had herself driven to Madame de Lavardin's.
That very day Madame Marmet dismissed her coachman, and took to
her bed with a fever which lasted for some considerable time.

*

Madame de Thianges, before her marriage a Thierry-Montespan, own
cousin to the Croquemottes, the Puysalé, and the Tour-Espivette
families, a friend at one and the same time of the Duchesse de Réveillon
and of the Escouflac-Le-Gornes (who had quarrelled with the Réveillons), of the Porbois and the Sévinelles (who had quarrelled with the
Porbois), was as well-born and as well connected as anybody could
be. But if our faults seem to us to be less serious than those of others,
so too do our privileges shine less brightly in our own eyes. When
therefore it came to her ears that someone she had known and loved
for a long time, took tea with the Duchess de Réveillon, frequently

dined with the Mirepoix, and was on intimate terms with Madame de Cèbres, the liking shown by these persons, not one of whom was more intelligent or smarter than she was, conferred upon the person in question a superiority and a charm which she by her own unaided efforts and in spite of a feeling of great affection, could never, so it seemed to her, have conferred. The merits which she found in an individual were in proportion to that individual's social contacts. If the number of those contacts increased, the individual in question acquired fresh merits. If after deciding that some young man whom she believed to be without any social position, and not particularly attractive, she learned that he was constantly to be seen in the houses of her friends, her views about him changed, and she had to admit that he "improved on acquaintance". But since in her eyes social relationships developed with mathematical exactness from a major premiss, when they were not implicit in that premiss, she at first refused to believe in their existence, and if someone assured her that they really were as they seemed to be, thought that her informant was in error or had been deceived by some fantastic fairy-tale. When one day Madame Marmet (Madame de Thianges regularly called on her once a year in the interests of a charitable organization of which she was the "zealous President" and Madame Marmet a generous supporter) introduced Jean Santeuil—shy, ill-dressed, and the son of a Republican official, Madame de Thianges decided that he looked very stupid. After he had left, Madame Marmet, wishing to make excuses for him, said, "He's a great friend of the Duchesse de Réveillon, you know," Madame de Thianges replied—"A friend of Marie's, my dear, he *can't* be, that's quite impossible!" in much the same tone that an aristocrat might have used in 1789 on being told that a day would come when a noble and a bourgeois would be equal before the law. But later, when this strange fact had been absorbed into the body of those scientific truths which ruled her life, and by the aid of which she was able to discern truths hitherto concealed from her, she artlessly declared, "He really is a very charming young man, and a great friend of the Réveillons and the Tourneforts—I must say I find him very good company—very intimate, you know, with the La Rochefoucaulds." As she pronounced the words "a great friend of the Réveillons" or "of the Tourneforts" she smiled and puckered up her lips, as though this close connexion with the Réveillons and the Tourneforts was heavy with consequences against which one must be on one's guard, or with delightful possibilities which one must be prepared to recognize. Should a young man or a young woman be under the wing of only *one* great hostess, that single approbation, though it was not sufficient to induce her own, did however prevent her from pronouncing a sentence of absolute condemnation. Her attitude remained in suspense. She would not finally commit herself, and merely observed, "Berthe (Mademoiselle de Tournefort) makes a great fuss of him, but really you know he is almost a complete stranger to me," thus reserving judgment until such time as the newcomer should have found other seconders, or should have been "dropped" even by Berthe. Unlike most people who in their own houses think those "perfectly delicious" whom they would find boring in the houses of their friends, Madame de Thianges reserved all her admiration for what she herself had nothing to do with. When she dined out, guests whom she could quite easily have entertained at her own table, appeared to her to glow with incomparable splendour. She would say, "I am told that the Puyfrettes gave a marvellous party the other evening, the Treflebarbes, the Escouflacs, the Pabaules, were all there," in other words people in whose eyes Madame de Thianges was a power in the land, and all the more impressive for being clothed in mystery.

6. *Madame Lawrence*

One day when Jean turned up at the Réveillon mansion, he ran into Henri at the door who said to him, "What a nuisance! I've got to go calling!" and having made this announcement hurried upstairs to ask his mother whether he might not be "let off", it being she who had arranged his afternoon. But all she said was, "The simplest thing would be for Jean, if he doesn't very much mind, to go with you." Jean would far rather have gone for a walk with Henri. The Duchess however declared that he could really not put off any longer going to see Madame Lawrence and his La Rochefoucauld and Réveillon aunts, who were furious because they had seen nothing of him since the New Year. Jean realized that Madame Santeuil was not alone in her insistence on family visits, and that there was no more amusement to be found in calling on a La Rochefoucauld aunt than on a Friedel aunt. They set off therefore together bound in the first place for Madame Lawrence. Jean had heard a great deal about this lady. He knew that she was an arrant snob, that she had gradually broken with all the members of the American Colony, and now saw only the leaders of the fashionable world of Paris. There had been a time when the Duchesse de Réveillon had greeted her, when they met with an icy politeness which for Madame Lawrence was no more than the flag which she had grown accustomed to see hoisted on her first appearance in any new social group. So far from bearing a grudge against those who displayed it at her approach, she chose to regard it as the very sign and symbol of a glittering prize which mere money could not buy, and continued to move forward slowly, majestically, and bearing gifts, like an Oriental monarch. The Duchesse de Réveillon now thought it incumbent on Henri to thank her in person for the superb sporting gun which she had given him as a New Year present.

Jean had heard, too, more than once about her liaison with Monsieur de Ribeaumont, a liaison so little concealed that it was matter of common knowledge in Parisian circles. Though it had been notorious for something like six years, Monsieur Santeuil had heard about it for the first time only a few days before at the Ministry, and had found as much pleasure in the news as we do in the thought that we are receiving the light of a star which has been on its way to us for perhaps several thousand years. But bourgeois circles get the news of love affairs in the great world only when they are already over, just as it is only when Verlaine's death has been announced that a duke discovers that he was a poet and a talented one at that. This was not perhaps the first time that Jean had been to see a lady when in full possession of the facts, or at least knowing all about them before he had ever been to see her at all. He felt as uneasy therefore as he would have done had he been about to visit somebody suffering from an embarrassing ailment to which he must on no account refer, and from the very first words that they exchanged kept a careful watch upon his tongue. He felt like a man walking with a blind friend who is constantly on his guard so as to avoid bumping into him. He had been careful to empty his mind of three phrases in particular—*snob, loose conduct, Monsieur de Ribeaumont.* But when, having been presented by Henri, he said, "I have heard Madame Marmet talk a lot about you," Madame Lawrence replied, "I can assure you that you will hear me talk a great deal less about her— not because she is said to have been guilty of loose conduct—though I dislike that sort of thing intensely—which I have no reason to believe is true, but because I can't bear women who are such snobs that the only thing they can think about is their own social advancement. I feel sure that the Duchess shares my views," she added smiling at Henri. "All the same," she remarked graciously to Jean, "I quite understand your going to see her," having attributed to his shyness and sense of guilt at being on calling terms with a lady whom *she* looked down upon, the blush which had flared in his cheeks, almost spreading to his eyes, when she had talked about Madame Marmet having been guilty of "loose conduct" and had referred to her as a snob. It never so much as occurred to Madame Lawrence that Jean was feeling embarrassed on *her* account, or that the words had caused him pain as likely to recoil on her, even before he had become fully conscious that it was she who had used them in apparently blissful ignorance of the risks she was running. "I do so understand why you wish to keep in with her," she continued, as though making a concession to her visitor, in the manner of an abbé who says to a Jewess, "After all, there is a deal of good in all religions."–"A young man must find much amusement in her company. Several of my women friends, if it comes to that, think her delightful. One of the men I like most, whose intelligence I deeply appreciate, who is, I really do think, sincerely attached both to my husband and to me—I refer to Monsieur de Ribeaumont" (the purplish haze pulsating about Jean's face prevented his hostess from noticing the fresh wave of scarlet which had just flooded his cheeks and now lay there in a tremulous layer)—"*always* accepts her invitations, and is eloquent in her defence whenever he hears anything derogatory said of her. I myself know her only very slightly, and am not, I confess, particularly anxious to know her better: nor is there any reason why I should, seeing that we have such very different friends."

Jean felt no astonishment at Madame Lawrence's hypocrisy when he heard her speaking thus of loose conduct, snobbery, and Monsieur de Ribeaumont. Ensconced in the delicious intimacy of a fashionable drawing-room, where everything, from the delicate silk upholstery of the chair, to the fragrance of the flowers, and the frank glances of the women, seemed to shed a softening influence on his heart, so that in the warm air it opened as easily as the drooping flowers in the crystal vases, or Madame Lawrence's smiling lips, he was prepared to surrender his heart to anyone who spoke kindly, and with his heart his trust. On this particular occasion it was Madame Lawrence who had gathered from the projecting stamens of his gaze the light pollen of his eager sensibility. Had anybody at that moment told him that Madame Lawrence was a light woman, a snob, and Monsieur de Ribeaumont's mistress, he would have answered, "I know for a fact that is not true! She told me so herself. Or rather she did better than that by speaking in a way that shows the baselessness of those calumnies—making it quite clear on the contrary that what she loves in the Duchess is her kind heart and keen intelligence, and that what leads scandal-mongers to talk maliciously about her relations with Monsieur de Ribeaumont is the fact that she has a warm regard for him which she makes no attempt to conceal. Snobbery? Immorality? One has only to hear her castigating those failings in others to realize how far she is from being guilty of them herself." Had he come to see her another day and spoken not of Madame Marmet, but of some different person, Madame Lawrence would just as certainly have told him that she despised snobs, detested loose conduct, and that Monsieur de Ribeaumont's character was beyond criticism. There had been a time when quite possibly her choice of these subjects of conversation would have had about it a deliberately calculated and rather clumsy intention, though the clumsiness would have been concealed behind success of the same sort as that which her attitude had achieved in the case of Jean. But as the years passed whenever the familiar words began to squeak softly, like the ancient hinges of habit, they fulfilled for her a more disinterested function. No matter what it be that squalid self-interest has made part of our lives, our lives absorb it, and make it serve a more general purpose. The words and phrases to which I have already drawn attention, kept Madame Lawrence's mind continually playing with ideas, which in her case were decidedly unhealthy. But they were dear to her, and had come to constitute one of the dangerous pleasures of life. She took them in such moderate doses, digested them so easily, that it was no longer possible for her to do without them. There is no harm after all, in admiring intelligence in a duchess, or in feeling friendship for a man who fully merits it. If, instead of half a glass of Chartreuse one began by giving a child a whole bottle of Cognac to swallow, the probability is that he would never again, in the whole course of his life, touch liqueurs. Once started on the slippery slope, Madame Lawrence must have known that she was lying when she spoke as she did about the Duchesse de Réveillon and Monsieur de Ribeaumont. But that kind of lying had become sweet to her, for those who love, love to talk of what they love.

Little by little, finding it impossible to think of herself as a liar, she came to believe that what she was saying was the truth. She quite honestly did not think herself a snob because she sought out duchesses, nor guilty of loose conduct because she went to bed with Monsieur de Ribeaumont. The material actions of her life continued to show the imprint of these two vices, though when engaged in them, she no longer gave them a moment's thought. If now and again her mind did turn to them, she saw them in the gay, delightful colours which they wore in her conversation. She had no sense of guilt towards Monsieur Lawrence because she always spoke nicely of him, and the fond and faithful words took precedence in her mind whenever she let it dwell on the way in which she was behaving to him. At such times she was conscious of a warm self-satisfaction, feeling that her affection, her loyalty, and her way of behaving to him, did her credit. The fond and faithful words, which she so frequently told over to herself, were like tiny doses of morphine. Gradually they anaesthetized her conscience, allowing it to live at peace with itself, and stimulated her to commit new faults from which out of sheer habit though it was no longer necessary to do so, she sponged away the rather crude colours which once had been decidedly unpleasing.

*

"Do you mean to say you know Guy de Brucourt, my former lieutenant?" said Jean to Daltozzi. "Do you find him intelligent?—please tell me, I should so much like to know." For those we once knew, whether in the days of our childhood, or when we were living in a world wholly different from the one in which we have grown used to drawing comparisons between the various persons of our acquaintance, still retain, in memory, the charm they once had for us, so that we find it quite impossible to say whether we should have thought them intelligent now, that is to say, more intelligent than Destreu, less intelligent than Luperceaux, or as occupying a position midway between Luperceaux and Le Sisterade.

Lieutenant de Brucourt who in the regiment had had the reputation of possessing more than usual gifts, enjoyed in Jean's eyes all the prestige with which his rank, his exceptional position in Society, his fine appearance on parade, and his kindliness, had endowed him. If Monsieur de Brucourt seemed to miss the point of something Jean said to him, on one of those evenings, for instance, when he had been so flattering as to ask the young man to the big house he was occupying facing the parade ground (on those occasions the batman had put more than usual vigour into his polishing, remarking the while, "If you're dining with the Marquis, you'd better look clean") Jean would tell himself that it had probably been a pretty 'pointless thing to say', or when Monsieur de Brucourt had said something to Jean which didn't sound very sensible, he would decide that he hadn't taken it in properly, and that there must have been more in it than met the eye. For no consideration of manners, tact, or good form ever prevented Monsieur de Brucourt from making stupid or offensive statements, which had he been anybody else would have shaken Jean's faith in his abilities. As it was, his friendliness, the charming way in which he helped Jean to bridge the distance between them, all persuaded our friend that he had to do with a man of unusual gifts, a man whose intelligent outlook must have long ago resolved and dissipated every problem which was interesting Jean at that time. ("I, too, wrote poetry when I was your age."–"I have given up reading novels.") On the other hand he was engrossed in matters to which Jean had not yet aspired, and when at the dinner-table letting his monocle drop he began to explain how fascinating it would be to enter Manchuria from the north, Jean listened to him with absorbed attention. "I mean to write about that to the Queen of Serbia. I am some sort of a relation of hers. In point of fact the relationship is quite a close one though my mother gets furious if I mention it because she won't admit a connexion with any of the noble families of the Empire (her father was created Duc de Moldavie by the first Napoleon)." Jean felt so crushed, so humble, in the presence of this intensely aristocratic person, so ugly compared to anyone so handsome, so ill-dressed beside so smart a member of Society, so foolishly talkative, where the other was so circumspect, that he was filled with what almost amounted to a sense of shame.

One day when he had gone to see him on some matter of importance, Monsieur de Brucourt happened to be starting out in a carriage just as he was approaching the house. He stopped dead and saluted, thinking that he would be asked to join Monsieur de Brucourt, or that at least Monsieur de Brucourt would pull up and make his excuses. The Lieutenant, however, merely returned his salute. Not a muscle of his face moved. It was as though Jean had been some soldier whom he had never seen before, and that the exchange of salutes had been no more than a matter of military discipline. 'He is short-sighted,' thought Jean, 'and he hasn't recognized me.' What was his amazement, therefore, a day or two later, when the Lieutenant said to him, "I was terribly sorry to meet you the other day just when I was starting out on a drive." He remembered the salute which had made him think that the other had not realized that he wanted him to stop. He felt that there was something very like duplicity in Monsieur de Brucourt's politeness. Once when Monsieur de Brucourt had asked him to dinner, his friends in the hope of making him more presentable had twisted his budding moustache into a point and waxed it. It did not occur to Jean that he must be looking slightly ridiculous, and he felt dashed by the way his host had laughed when he introduced him to the company. But so friendly was he, that Jean felt convinced that in spite of the suspicions which Monsieur de Brucourt had aroused in him, should he have left the room at that moment his host would not have made fun of him before the other guests.

After he had finished his military service Jean saw no more of Monsieur de Brucourt, and when some years later he met him in Paris, felt, as one feels at meeting one's old professors, that social convention forbade him to show any sign of recognition. Consequently, he did not greet him. Once or twice, however, Monsieur de Brucourt, having some favour to ask of him, wrote him a letter beginning it with, "My Dear Jean". By a sort of tacit agreement, however, they never recognized one another in the street, but behaved as though they were complete strangers. Once at a party Jean recalled himself to Monsieur de Brucourt, mentioning his name. "Delighted," said the other and moved on with a perfectly blank expression. Jean wanted to say, "But don't you recognize me? I am the Dear Jean whom you used to ask to dinner." Still, remembering the salute with which he had been greeted from the carriage, in the days when he was a simple soldier, he was convinced that Monsieur de Brucourt knew perfectly well who he was, and would merely have replied, "Oh, yes, of course." This incident had the curious effect of making him feel that he knew him intimately, yet scarcely at all.

7. *An Englishwoman in Paris*

Jean now began to feel that Madame Marmet was more and more showing towards him the same sort of inexplicable antipathy of which he had once been conscious in the behaviour of the three "intelligent boys" with whom he had been at school. They had thought him insincere and affected. He had a keen recollection of that experience of long ago, but failed to draw profit from it. He talked to Madame Marmet and wrote her letters. But her behaviour towards him became increasingly spiky, more and more harsh and ironical. She began to resemble a patch of heath in springtime when the gorse is in bloom. Not knowing the reason for this display of prickles, he could do nothing to stop or to slow down its vigorous growth. Madame Marmet's irony arose from the fact that she knew nothing of the sensations, tastes and thoughts from which Jean's opinions had become what they were. There was for example in the circle of her acquaintances, an Englishwoman, a certain Miss Smithson, who was treated as something of a butt. Jean however found as much enjoyment in savouring the peculiar pleasure which he had discovered in this strange poem written by Nature in terms of flesh, hair, accent, a prevailing smell of tea, and the association of ideas to which these things gave rise —which went by the name of An Englishwoman, as he would have done in the spectacle of an Icelandic seal or a Numidian giraffe at the zoo. Many things had contributed to make up a poem which complexion, the colour of the eyes, pronunciation, manner of dressing, a feeling for poetry, and practical common sense, all came together to compose into a whole which was rich with an atmosphere redolent of the banks of the Thames, the parklands of Wales, the paintings of Burne-Jones, and the activities of Temperance Societies. Her very name, with its roots in ancient Welsh, sounded delightful in his ears, especially when she could be prevailed upon to speak it. He never tired of asking her to say such words as *belle, Trouville, Bretagne*, savouring, as he listened to that precious local music, the kind of sophisticated pleasure which sometimes has the charming freshness and

534

vitality more usually associated with simpler delights. To call upon her in her tiny flat, to join with her in a game of *écarté*, using English cards, not only the backs of which were so utterly different from those of French ones, but also the attributes of King, Queen, Knave, and the shape of the Ace, to sip a cup of that tea which was the pervasive flame that gave warmth to her existence and a peculiar flush to her complexion, to look at the photographs hanging on her walls, landscapes of the Home Counties, pictures of parks patterned with white fences —was for Jean a source of far livelier pleasure than he could ever have found in the mediocre satisfaction of taking "the five-o'clock" in sumptuous drawing-rooms belonging to cultivated ladies.

Madame Marmet, ever immune to such impressions, for whom Miss Smithson was just a woman like other women, though less chic, and generally regarded as a bit of a bore, who had no pretty furnishings in her flat, burst out laughing when she heard Jean say that he loved calling on Miss Smithson and looking at her. He could give no reasoned explanation of his preference, and was reduced to saying with a faint blush, "It's such fun to think she's an Englishwoman".—"What a stupid, pretentious creature he is!" murmured Madame Marmet to her neighbour. Jean, who admired in Madame Marmet a gift of facile speech, a glowing eloquence, a gift of concisely summarizing her thoughts, and a neatly poised intelligence—all of them things he lacked himself—had a vague and uncomfortable feeling that he had said something artless, that he had been guilty of a solecism, that he had committed himself to a false judgment, that Madame Marmet must most certainly have felt what he had felt, something so obvious as not to be worth putting into words, namely that a Frenchwoman and an Englishwoman are members of two different species, that so trite a conclusion would have served her merely as a starting-point for ratiocination, and that he had not yet advanced beyond the threshold of intelligence. He was conscious of feeling thoroughly ashamed of himself.

8. *The First Night of Fredégondé*

Madame Marmet had invited Jean to the Opéra. The date she had named was a Monday some weeks ahead. It turned out that this particular evening was to be graced by the first performance of *Frédégonde*, and would be a very brilliant occasion. She felt distinctly annoyed to think that she had not offered the vacant seat to some member of the Union Club or the Agricole, whose presence would have made her box a focus of attention to all the ladies of the Faubourg. The sight of Jean blew the coals of her disappointment to a white heat with the result that she was more than usually unfriendly when he next went to see her. But Monsieur Marmet, more keenly concerned even than she was in the matter of her social success, and using harsher methods in its pursuit—as though in the organism of their twin social existence, it was he who figured as the wielder of the sword, she the patient diplomat—did not so much as look up from his paper when Jean entered the room. After a very short while he said in a whisper to his wife, "The only way of getting rid of him is to have an open quarrel: it won't matter a bit now that Julien has passed his exam." –"It's always better to remain on good terms than to quarrel," replied Madame Marmet who, where expediency was involved, invariably had recourse to the commonplaces of diplomacy. Monsieur Marmet, whose politics were cast in a more realistic mould, shrugged his shoulders. "Tell me," he said to Jean, with a short, sharp bark, and gathering his eyebrows into a frown, "is it your intention, on Monday, to arrive, as you usually do, at eight and to leave at midnight? You are a master of tactlessness in such matters." – "Perhaps it would be better if I did not come at all. I have another invitation for that evening." – "I've heard that sort of thing before," growled Monsieur Marmet— "And since it was sent me by friends whom I have not seen for a long time, I should have asked, in any case, to be excused, were it not that I was afraid of hurting your feelings." – "Hurting our feelings! That's good!" said Monsieur Marmet with a cackle of laughter: "we are deeply obliged by such consideration! Hurt our feelings, indeed! I've never heard anything so fatuous! It will always be a pleasure for us to be without your company!"

Jean took his departure. Madame Marmet lost no time in sending an invitation to Monsieur de Minuls. She already had Monsieur de Mutz and the Prince de T—— in her party. On the Monday in question the Duchesse de Réveillon happened to be lunching with the Duc de Chartres, at whose table she met Monsieur de Mutz, Monsieur de Minuls and the Prince de T——. They all three mentioned that they were going that evening to the first performance of *Frédégonde* as guests of Madame Marmet. She went across to the Duc de Chartres and whispered something in his ear. "I should count it a very great favour," she said to him. The Duc de Chartres approached the three men and said: "Gentlemen, I should be delighted if you would all come with me this evening to the Français."–"But what about Madame Marmet, sir?"–"An invitation from His Highness releases you from any previous engagement. It is a reason that Madame Marmet would be the first to understand. I give you my word that she will resign her claim on you in the interest of His Highness. So that is settled, gentlemen." At five o'clock Madame Marmet received a telegram from Mutz, at six, a telegram from the Prince de T——, and at seven a telegram from Minuls. She hastily got in touch with Ribeaumont, Tourkett, and the Baron Shleier. Not one of them was free. The idea of being seen alone with her husband was intolerable to her. She therefore sent a note to Jean Santeuil, asking whether he could not come after all and so "clear up a misunderstanding" which had not in any way "lessened my affection for you" which was a great deal stronger than "you realize". So tender-hearted was Jean that he felt touched by this appeal, and would have gone had he been free to do so. But he was not and wrote back accordingly. "What an affected ass!" said Monsieur Marmet in high dudgeon when he read the letter, for Jean had been their only hope, "of course he's free! You know as well as I do that he hasn't a single friend who is a regular ticket-holder at the Opéra, and even if he had, he wouldn't have been invited on an occasion like this. I shall ask Shelchtenbourg."–"I forbid you to do anything of the sort!" said Madame Marmet "I'd rather have nobody than him! If Shelchtenbourg were only a Jewish broker who didn't know a soul, people might still think he was somebody of importance. But he has swindled both the Réveillons and the La Rochefoucaulds. They would most certainly recognize him, and I've no wish to see myself shamed in the eyes of the two leading families of France! Thank you for nothing!" – "I'd rather anything than that we should be seen alone together! Think what fools we should look! We should be a positive laughing-stock! Besides, since the Duc de Chartres is to be at the Français, the La Rochefoucaulds will almost certainly be there, too, and this is the evening when the Réveillons are giving a dinner for the King of Portugal, as you may have seen in the *Gaulois*." – "So they are! In that case, let us invite Shelchtenbourg." Shelchtenbourg, being always free, accepted at once. He was already in the box when Monsieur and Madame Marmet arrived. "Wasn't I right?" said Monsieur Marmet, drawing her attention to the auditorium. But at that very moment a crowd of newcomers attracted their eyes, and they saw, coming into the stalls, and taking their places, the Duc and Duchesse de Réveillon, Henri de Réveillon, the Duchesse de La Rochefoucauld, His Majesty the King of Portugal, the Prince d'Aquitaine, the Duchesse de Bretagne, and a young man whose face Monsieur and Madame Marmet could not at first make out because the King of Portugal was just then adjusting his tie, and blocked the view. But the King of Portugal sat down, and, as soon as he did so, Monsieur and Madame Marmet recognized Jean Santeuil. His eyes met those of Monsieur Marmet who made him a deep bow. To be seen in their box with Shelchtenbourg and no one else, was to have ten years of social climbing wiped out in a moment.

Madame Marmet was beside herself with anger. "Let us go home!" she said. "No, the two duchesses have seen us. It would be no good, the harm is done." When the first interval came Jean made as though to leave his seat. The Duchess laid a detaining hand on his shoulder. "I'm sure," she said, "that you're going to see Madame Marmet." – "Yes, Madame," said Jean, already feeling ashamed of his kindly impulse. "My dear Jean, I absolutely forbid you to do any such thing," said the Duchess. "I am as fond of you as I am of my own son, and am entitled to speak to you as your mother would. I am quite sure that when you tell her what has happened, she will approve of my conduct. As soon as I found out the way that woman had behaved to you, I forbade all my friends ever to go and see her again. I don't mean my women friends, for God knows with the possible exception of that silly Eléonore, none of them would ever dream of wandering into that mouse-trap. You really ought not to see any more of those people. You have plenty of friends without them, friends of ours, who adore you already and treat you like Henri's brother, a more intelligent brother who does us much honour by condescending to talk with us. Am I not right, Sire," said the Duchess, turning to the King who during dinner had been told how the Marmets had first invited Jean Santeuil, and then cancelled the invitation. "It would amuse me to take a stroll in the foyer," said the King. "In that case, I will accompany Your Majesty," said the Duc de Bretagne to whom this honour belonged of right, he being the Premier Duke of France. "No, Bretagne," replied the King, "let me take our young friend Jean, who shall finish telling me about the law-case between Ruskin and Whistler, in which I am much interested. Together we will defy Madame Marmet. Since I have a new friend, it is well that the people of Paris should know it, and should see me in his company. I am sure you will not hold it against me, eh?" he said, turning to Bretagne. "How should I, Sire?" said the Duc de Bretagne who since he was fond of Jean and detested the Marmet couple, was enchanted. Then in a low voice so that Jean should not hear, and warmly taking the King's hand in hers, the Duchess said, "I am profoundly grateful to Your Majesty," for she realized that he was acting in this way as much in order to please her as to please Jean.

While Jean was sauntering with the King of Portugal, several persons came to pay their respects to the Duchess, among others, the Comte de Penmarch, and Jules Lemaître, whom many of the older ladies of the Faubourg regarded as one of themselves. He glided into the auditorium with a smile on his lips and a monocle in his eye. "Are you enjoying yourself, Penmarch?" asked the Duchess. "Dear Aunt, does one ever really know when one is enjoying oneself? What more can one ask than an hour of pleasure, and how many things, after all, can give us that?" He smiled at Madame de La Rochefoucauld and took a sweet from the box which the Duchess offered him. The Duchess set it down, and gave her hand to Monsieur de Lomperolles who had just put in an appearance. "Good evening, dear cousin, do please sit down." – "Whom do you think I saw His Majesty with just now?—young Santeuil! Really, the way people spoil young men nowadays. They don't seem to realize what they are capable of! Ah, cousin, if only you knew as much about life as I do! What's that flower Santeuil's wearing in his buttonhole? I wouldn't dare do such a thing, even at my age, and he's only a youngster. But he's not a man at all—no better than a girl!"

he grumbled, taking a *marron glacé*. "I've been hearing the most delicious things about you, from one of your worshippers," said Monsieur de Penmarch—"Madame Ador, who's a perfect pet." He made it a profession to obtain the favours of young women newly arrived in Paris, by promising to ask them to dine in his bachelor establishment with ladies of the Faubourg whom as yet they did not know. Madame de Réveillon said nothing. "Yes, she really does worship you," went on Monsieur de Penmarch. "But how can she do any such thing since she has never met me?" said the Duchess. "What does that matter? One can love people without knowing them. And, after all, what *can* one know? All the same she very much wants to know you." The Duchess began to eat a *marron glacé* with an abstracted air. "Will you come to dinner and meet her?—name your own day." – "Oh, Penmarch, you know that I always enjoy dining with you, you make everything so charming, but if you'll forgive me for saying so, it's a terrible bore to dine with people one does not know." – 'Damme,' thought Penmarch, 'all the women I've promised her are ratting on me. She'll think I've got no influence at all! There's only Jacqueline de La Rochefoucauld left. I only hope she's not overheard us!' – "But Madame Ador gets asked by Madame de Thuringe," he said aloud. "Madame de Thuringe knows her own business," replied Madame de Réveillon, "but you really must leave us free to consult our own tastes." – "I suppose it's no use my talking to you about Madame Marmet then?" – "Certainly not!" said the Duchess: "I would very much rather dine with Madame Ador than shake hands with Madame Marmet after what she has just done to one of my friends, and, God knows, I have no wish to dine with Madame Ador!" – "Do at least tell Madame de La Rochefoucauld that Madame Ador is charming, and quite the sort of person she ought to have in her house." – "Why should I say anything of the sort to Jacqueline? She is perfectly capable of arranging her salon, which is one of the pleasantest in Paris, without any help from me. Besides since I do not know Madame Ador, how can I say that she is charming?" – "Well at any rate don't please say that I asked you to meet her, and that you refused." – "I never repeat conversations," replied the Duchess very sweetly. Penmarch knew that this was true, and felt that he was safe in her hands. At least his request could have no worse result than failure. "Send her an invitation to your Charity Bazaar, then: she is very generous." – "I most certainly shall not. Why should you think I am prepared to take money from people whom I won't ask to my house?" – "That is a very un-Faubourg thing to say, Duchess."

As the audience was leaving the theatre, Madame Marmet made a sign of greeting to the Duchess, who bowed with exaggerated politeness as though to somebody she did not recognize. Madame Marmet felt that there was nothing more that she could do in that direction, though unfortunately for her "that direction" led to the Faubourg Saint-Germain. Shelchtenbourg, realizing that his hosts were in a bad temper, took his leave. "What a boor! He didn't even offer us a lift! That comes of being kind to rich folk!" said Monsieur Marmet. They hailed a cab and saw the Duchess getting into her brougham with Jean. "I suppose she's behaving like this because Santeuil has told her the whole story," said Monsieur Marmet, utterly crushed.

9. *Daltozzi and Women*

When Henri got back from the Opéra he went up to his room. But he did not begin to undress because the Duchess, not wishing to keep her maid who was rather unwell, up, had said, "I'm coming to your room in a few moments to ask you to unfasten my necklace for me." He made a point of never closing his shutters, since he liked to be wakened by the early sun and could now see behind the glass of the window the rain bellying like a bead curtain in the gusty night, and driving down in great squalls from the black sky on to the shining pavement. A hired fly came to a stop in front of the garden railings opposite, at a spot however where there was no gate. A man whose evening tie showed as a white patch above the collar of his overcoat got out, paid the driver, and started to walk down the street. He had no umbrella, and every now and then came to a halt, took his white-gloved hand from his pocket and raised it to his mouth. Henri could see the spasmodic movement of his bent back and realized that he was coughing. As soon as the fit was over, the man resumed his walk in the pelting rain. He was by this time close to the house, and all of a sudden Henri saw that it was Daltozzi. Why if he had come to see him, had he not had himself driven to the front door? But when at last he reached it, instead of stopping, he continued on his way. As he passed beneath a gas-lamp, Henri noticed that he was wearing evening pumps, cut low to reveal the foot. It wouldn't be long before they would be filled with water! Daltozzi went as far as the end of the street, and then retraced his steps. At the Réveillon front door he seemed to pause for a moment, then started off again. Just as once more he reached the end of the street, the door of one of the last houses in it opened and a woman came out. Henri guessed it was Rose, his mother's maid, who must have been spending the evening with her brother-in-law who lived there. Startled by the force of the rain, she put up her umbrella, and started to walk fast, though only a few steps separated her from the mansion. But at this moment Daltozzi turned his head and saw her. He started to run. Henri half opened the window. He heard Daltozzi call out something,

542

as though to attract the attention of the woman ahead to him. She, taking fright, also broke into a run. But he was rapidly gaining on her. There was a mad look about him. When he saw her stop in front of the mansion and ring the door-bell, he sheered off quickly, and resumed his walking.

Daltozzi stopped dead. A woman in evening dress, her head swathed in a shawl tied under the chin, was just paying the coachman. He hurried forward and was already close to her. She must have cried out. Henri could not hear any sound for he had shut the window, but the cabby, who was just about to drive off pulled up, then turned and came back, and while the terrified woman kept on ringing at the carriage entrance, made threatening gestures at Daltozzi, who moved away. As soon as the woman had been admitted the cabby drove away, turning round once more with an expressive shrug of the shoulders as though calling the empty street to witness (there were no pedestrians visible) to the dastardly incident. The rain was falling so hard that Daltozzi made his way back to the front door of the distant house, where sheltered by a projection he halted and looked about him as though to make sure that there was nobody in sight. At that moment seeing a man appear, he pretended to be ringing the bell. The man entered the house. Thinking no doubt that he had not been recognized, and so as to avoid the necessity of going in too, Daltozzi left the doorway and made off. Just then the Duchess came into Henri's room to say that Rose had returned, and that therefore she would not need his help. "What are you doing at the window?–aren't you going to bed?"–"In a moment, Mamma," answered Henri, and, as soon as his mother had left him, started to undress. But before getting into bed he paid one last visit to the window. Daltozzi was still there. At last however seeming to have resigned himself to failure, he looked about him, then went back to the distant front door and rang the bell. He rang once, he rang twice. Just then a working-girl, bare-headed and wearing a woollen dress appeared sheltering under an umbrella at the far side of the Place de la Concorde across which she hurried. The door opened, but Daltozzi turned for a final look and saw the girl. Without a second's hesitation he pulled the door shut, and ran in her direction. Henri, dog-tired, got into bed, and, thinking how cold Daltozzi must be in his water-logged pumps, stretched out his legs and put his feet against the hot-water bottle.

The same thing happened almost every night. Dreading solitude,

obsessed by curiosity, his body too wakeful, or his mind too empty,
Daltozzi, when the time came to go home, rebelled at the thought of
returning to the loneliness of his lodgings, and if he had not found a
woman before reaching them, would hang about sometimes for a
whole hour. There were other occasions when he beat the streets
looking for women, most people would have said, though he called it
pursuing a dream, haunted by the thought of a body to which made
restless by that dream he could cling, of another living creature, driven
on, he fancied by another dream, the brother of his own. Out of the
distance it would come, out of the infinity where he was seeking it, to
greet him. In the desert of streets empty, in the desert of streets full, an
elegant woman, a woman of the world, of the half-world, sometimes
perhaps a working-girl, feeling that he was following her, would half
turn a head. Though knowing nothing of him, she had been conscious
of his desire, and he knowing nothing of her had been caught in awareness of her response, so that each profoundly ignorant of the other's
life had by mute exchange and in a single electric moment, through the
medium of an unspoken avowal of craving at its lowest level, exchanged the inexpressible secret of their two selves, the formless empty
dreams of their two lives. Fleeing at his approach, her face still unre-
vealed, she was the very image of Destiny. She seemed to be beckoning
him onward in pursuit, and he replying was soon hot on the trail, not
of an almost certain pleasure, but of a happiness that was all imaginary.
The idea that it could be other he had renounced, not after the act of
consummation in his bed or in a cab but at the very moment of their
first exchange of words, since a voice immediately suggests the idea of
a person like ourselves who has the power to cause us pain or pleasure,
and, more important still, pain and pleasure that is wholly human. He
often walked the streets with no definite objective in view, not meaning
to look for a companion who might fill the moments of his evening's
loneliness, but like all men in search of happiness and the unknown. Like
all men he was too easily ready to believe in the reality of what he
desired. Sometimes when some woman terrified at the thought that she
was being followed walked more quickly, he interpreted her flight as
invitation. In this way he had had many experiences, had heard the
insulting remarks of passers-by, had seen the raised sticks of affronted
husbands, had felt the wound made in his conscience (worse than
threats or angry words) caused by the knowledge of innocence
affrighted. He feared the insults that he had endured but not the insults

still to come, for when the mind foresees the coming of inevitable dangers, hope so far retards the dreaded moment, as to make them seem no longer frightening, but unreal. There were times too when half blind from having stared so long and hard, he failed to understand the encouragement proffered by some woman who wanted to be picked up and seeing her turn her head, and thinking that she was afraid of being accosted, was suddenly smitten with shame and a desire for flight. Long ago it had been professional prostitutes, who shamelessly outstaring him, had set his desires flaming like dry wood. Though their dirt and squalid paint had told of age and dinginess, their kisses had all the same been sweet, as cider on days when we are very thirsty tastes more than ever delicious when served in the coarse chipped glasses of a wayside inn. Sometimes when driven home by a friend, or having returned on foot after finding no woman to pursue, he had lacked the courage when he reached his door to go inside. At such times he would again set off, no matter what the weather, undaunted by ill-health or the fear of pneumonia. Indeed he was worked into a state of excitement by fog, because it cloaked with mystery the women whom he passed, emerging from it as though they had broken through a veil; by the cold and the rain which awoke in him, the one with a brutal ardour, the other with an enervating softness, a desire to find warmth within a pair of human arms, to hide. The weariness of his heart and the weakness of his already ageing body, drew him to the young and virgin. With them he had the illusory feeling, shared by invalids who seek in the woods the health they cannot find in cities, that by dint of feasting eyes and touch on lovely, glowing flesh, by parting his lips on a kiss, he could make the warm breath captive, and draw it into the channels of his blood.

(*Jean had once seen a photograph of Daltozzi's mother in his office. One day, when Henri had shown him the man thus grovelling in the mire, he had been reminded of that mother's look keeping guard upon her son from high up on the wall. She had known nothing of all this. Then it was that he had taken an oath never to expose his own mother to the sight of so much degradation.*)—M.P.

10. *The Insult*

When next day Jean arrived at Madame Marmet's house and was taking off his coat for the waiting servant to receive, he met the Duchesse de Soria and smiled realizing that Madame Marmet had at last succeeded in getting her to dine, though she was leaving as soon after dinner as possible. He would have liked to feel that he was as important in the eyes of the Duchesse de Soria as she was in Madame Marmet's, high though he stood in the esteem of a Society which regarded her as at most an extremely elegant foreigner. All this he knew. When, therefore, the Duchess passed by without seeing him, he paused in the operation of getting rid of his coat, put himself in her path and with a faint bow, said, "Good evening, Duchess." "Oh, good evening, dear friend" exclaimed the Duchess, in a tone of great animation, "what have you been doing with yourself all this while? One never seems to see you. Will you dine with me tomorrow or the day after?" Hearing these words, Jean smiled. Round him stood Madame Marmet's servants, the Duchess's footman, the footmen of the Marquise de Montfort, of the Vicomtesse de Brieux, of the Princesse de Bonchalon —all of whom knew from the Duchess's man that she moved in more splendid circles than did their own employers, and therefore treated him with respect. "I shall be delighted to dine with you one of these days," he said politely. She held out her hand with a word of thanks. Jean bowed. With a smile he surrendered his coat; with a smile he shook hands with the Marquis de Puybes who happened to be passing at that moment, for with those whose admiration and respect gives us a good idea of ourselves, we are always friendly, just as a woman looking into a mirror which gives back a fascinating reflexion of her face, can never keep from smiling. "*What* a nice young man he is!" exclaimed Madame Marmet and all those present turned to look. On his way into the drawing-room, he bowed to all the ladies, who gave him in return their hands and their smiles. He shook hands with several old gentlemen, military officers, and distinguished authors. He was conscious of his radiant youth, of his gallant air, of his great gifts. Madame

Marmet kept on coming up to present him to some lady who longed to make his acquaintance, and when she spoke to him of the Réveillons, he replied as though he scarcely knew them. Some of the ladies saw in this a proof of modesty, others of pretentiousness. A few, thinking themselves deceived in him, turned to speak to somebody else but could not find anything to say. A number of young men got themselves introduced to him, thinking that one could not afford *not* to know him, others in the hope that later on he would see that they got on to hostesses' lists, would present them to fashionable actresses and to those ladies of the Faubourg Saint-Germain who gave balls. He accepted an ice, joined a foursome at cards, and was soon playing in the boudoir with Monsieur Saylor to whom he had just been introduced. Since Reichenberg was reciting, the other tables were deserted and the room was empty. It opened on to the main staircase, and from time to time, a lady mounting it with her husband wished him good evening or responded to his bow. One even came into the room to greet him. "What on earth are you up to?" she said and looking hard at his hand gave him her advice. Now and again the doors of the drawing-room were thrown open, and gentlemen emerging stopped on the threshold and then passed on, for Madame Marmet did not approve of cards while music or recitations were in action. Once she came in person to fetch him. "You have snatched away my youngest star, and the ladies are all feeling abandoned. They are clamouring for him. You are holding prisoner the first subject in my kingdom. It's all very well for you, you old gambler. Come along, now! this sort of behaviour is not permitted in my house! It's unheard of!" Jean laughed, for impertinence was one of her sanctioned forms of politeness, part and parcel of her "fun", of her authority. But Saylor who was losing, showed signs of obstinacy, and fearing that Jean would not return to the drawing-room unless he were allowed full liberty of action, because she knew that at the Réveillons he was allowed to do exactly as he liked, thinking too that by perpetually changing the tone of her voice and the nature of her opinions she could give a more definite impression of her high spirits and general attitude of detachment, she added, with an assumption of jollity—"Well, stay here if it amuses you. It's natural enough at your age. Besides, you spoilt boy, you know you can always please yourself in my house!–but don't keep us waiting too long"—saying which she trotted off, followed by the majestic sweep of her long train. Jean returned to his game. But all the time he was playing, he could

hear her now and again welcoming new arrivals, and expressing with a
sigh as though somewhat against her will, her admiration of the
Duchesse de Soria's beauty. "Didn't she look lovely this evening?—a
real Titian!—what flesh tints!" (duchesses always seemed to her more
exquisite in her own house)—speaking as though she had just caught
sight of her, as though she had only just passed through the doorway
as though her sweeping train were still in the room. Then she played at
being a scatter-brain, pretended just for fun that she had forgotten the
name of the gentleman who had recently come in, said that she felt quite
worn out and for two pins would wash her hands of the lot of them and
retire into a corner for a quiet chat with one or two of her women
friends (those who happened to be close to her at that moment). Then,
the voice of the accompanist, announcing that Van Zanol was going
to sing reduced her to silence, and if anyone ventured to speak a word,
she cast a reproachful look at the offender, following the silent rebuke
with a smile intended to soften this mark of her disapproval, like a
dancer playing the part of a lieutenant. There was a smile on Jean's
lips as he played, for he was listening to the charming air from *Don
Giovanni*, accompanied when the tempo grew quicker by a faint
murmur from all the charmed and listening ladies, as though a sudden
breeze had turned the pages of the music, and set the fans fluttering.
Suddenly Monsieur Saylor jumped up from his chair. His face was
twitching, his expression inscrutable, and when he spoke it was in a
tone of insulting familiarity. "This has gone quite far enough, sir!"—
"Sir!" said Jean, dumbfounded, and sprang to his feet. The next
moment he was left in no doubt of what the other meant. "Take that
bland look off your face, sir!"—said Monsieur Saylor, dropping the
mask: "you shall play no more with me!—you're a cheat, sir!"—
"Scoundrel!" shouted Jean, and made a rush at his opponent. But
Monsieur Saylor was the taller and stronger man of the two. He seized
Jean's hands and held them in a grip of steel. "Stop it! it's no use
behaving like that! If you send me your seconds I will be so very condescending as to fight with you—which is generous on my part. One
does not as a rule fight duels with men of your sort!"—and he turned
away and went into the drawing-room.

Jean hurried after him, but he knew that the fifty or so persons
seated in the room would not long be left in ignorance of what had
happened, and from stupidity, jealousy, ill-will, and a tendency to
believe the worst, even though they might not pin much faith to

Saylor's imputations, would ever afterwards have doubts about his honour. He waited until the music should have ended before enlisting the services of the Marquis de Trailles and the Vicomte de Boissieux. He sat down beside the Vicomtesse, and, to everything she said replied with an exaggerated smile so that she should think he was listening. Just across the room, Saylor appeared to be laughing with two or three of his friends. The man's laughter struck him as detestable. It was an intolerable outrage, a thing as hideous as some loathsome disease. The Marquis de Trailles and the Vicomte de Boissieux were opposed to the idea of his fighting at all. At last however they gave way to his importunities. The duel took place next day. Saylor was slightly wounded. Already though without mentioning the impending meeting, so as not to frighten her, Jean had related the whole affair to his mother. She was filled with a detestation of Saylor, as she would have been filled with detestation of Jean's illness, had he been ill, of a coachman who had run him down, of anything that might have hurt him. For several days, whenever he spoke to her of what had occurred, she took his face between her hands, and spoke gently to him as she did when he was sick. Just as on those occasions she would say, "It's nothing: you'll be all right tomorrow," when he said, "It was obvious from the way in which Monsieur X—— and Madame Z—— greeted me, that they knew all about it: the X——'s haven't asked me to their party—Saylor must have given them his version of the affair," she raised her shoulders in a shrug, and pretended to laugh the whole thing off as a piece of madness and of no conceivable importance. Then she gently scolded him for making himself ill, which was precisely what that wretched Saylor had hoped he would do. She made much of him, saying, "He's a man of the worst reputation" (which was true) "and nobody's going to believe a word he says." But he knew only too well that a lot of people believed it already. Still, he let his mother talk on, and though the powerlessness of her affection got on his nerves, he found a sweetness in her attempts to comfort him.

11. *Reparation*

Next evening Jean went to a party given by Madame de Thianges, and, just as he was being announced, overheard somebody make so unpleasant a remark that he immediately left the house. When he went downstairs the servants gave him contemptuous glances, and a few laughed rudely as he passed. He had as a matter of fact "a way with" servants which made some of them like him, but as a rule entirely forfeited their consideration. In short he was nice to them. When we are nice to others, we generally lose all claim to their respect. You are perhaps noble, rich, handsome and intelligent. While staying in a hotel you find yourself brought into daily contact with a middle-class visitor who is both ugly and stupid. So long as you keep him at a distance he will be full of consideration for you. He may speak about you to the proprietor and the staff in a contemptuous manner, but that is only because he wants them to think that he is "as good as" you. In his heart of hearts he knows differently. But once you start being nice, really nice, to him, if only for two or three days, all his respect will vanish. From that moment he ceases to look up to you. Indeed his attitude is just the reverse of respectful, because the only persons *he* is nice to are those who are superior to him in the social scale. If you were *really* rich, you would adopt an insolent tone in speaking to him. If you were a genuine aristocrat you wouldn't want to speak to him at all. The words in which Lohengrin told Elsa his name were no more fraught with danger to himself, did not more irrevocably determine the loss of his power, than does your, "I am delighted to see you: I trust that you will give me the pleasure of your company at dinner." If he accepts your advances he will take your words at their face value, and believe that the pleasure is indeed yours. Had you used the word "honour" instead of "pleasure", he would be convinced that he was honouring you. Should you be occupying a whole suite in the hotel where he has only a single room, and should your servant, whom you have brought with you, address you as "Monsieur le Comte", he will all the same take a high line with you.

But if amiability in general is fatal to those who practise it, when shown towards servants it is so exceptional, that those employed in the middle-class house where you sometimes go to dinner, in your dealings with whom you sometimes adopt an air of friendliness, though you have on occasion to tip them (if you didn't, your friendliness would be understood as a deliberate substitute for tipping, and you would, crystal-clear though your motives might appear, be looked down upon) they regard you as a sort of village idiot, a coward, or a man of weak character, with whom they will be gay when they happen to be feeling gay, boorish if they happen to be in a bad temper, and neglectful if they are in a hurry. They may like you more than they do those who are not amiable, but so far as respect is concerned you lag woefully behind and find that you get your food only after they have been served, in other words last of all and about the time that the staff is sitting down in the steward's room. For is not being amiable to them tantamount to expressing your opinion that there is no difference between the servant and his master or his master's friends? That is certainly true where servants are concerned who operate in bourgeois households, and even those belonging to certain rich families. And why after all *should* you wish to be on friendly terms with them? Bourgeois employers pay low wages to their servants, and are constantly having scenes with them. Consequently their servants have no wish to keep their situations, and show as much by the insolent way in which they speak to the son of the house, or reply to the mistress when she addresses them, by their off-hand attitude to visitors—whom they detest as being friends of the house, who *may* be timid, but *do* occasionally complain of the way they are treated by the staff.

On leaving Madame de Thianges, Jean hailed a cab and told the driver to take him home. But when he had stopped crying, he felt the need to do something with a view to organizing revenge, so that he might cease to suffer from the affront he had received, though he could not help thinking about it all the time. He therefore changed his mind and called out, "Go to the Réveillon mansion, rue de Varennes."

He first of all sought out Henri, to whom he said, "I should like a word with your father." – "Is that stupid business still bothering you, dear boy?" said Henri: "why don't you forget it? All the same, Papa will be delighted to see you: come along." As soon as Henri had shown Jean into his father's study, he made as though to withdraw, but Jean said to him: "There's no reason for you to go, in fact, I would much rather you stayed."

He left the house having promised the Duke, after putting up a prolonged resistance, to go that evening to the Lustaud party. He had accepted the invitation a month ago, but had later decided not to put in an appearance there, nor indeed anywhere, in view of what had happened. But the Duke had insisted. He did not wish it to look as though Jean were yielding to calumny. To his mother he said that he was feeling thoroughly upset, and told her how unwelcoming Madame de Thianges and several other ladies had been to him. But he passed over in silence the rudeness of the servants. Either from a wish to spare her pain, knowing that because of her love for him this information would have caused even greater suffering, or because she who knew him so well would doubtless have embarked on one of those discussions which characterize family life, he did not want to reveal the shame he felt, nor to have to keep a tight hold on his pride. It may even be that he did not want to give her an opportunity of triumphing in quarrels still to come, by bringing up the past against him, and to be better armed for the purpose as a result of his admission. This was a hateful feeling on his part, and one to which Madame Santeuil would have been a complete stranger. But doubtless she deserved that her son should credit her with such an attitude no matter how vaguely. It must have been that somewhere in an already forgotten past, or perhaps hidden away in some more recent deposit of his memories, a wound that she had already dealt him was still open, that an occasion when she had made him blush was even now a living reality in his consciousness: something that she had said to the effect that, "When one's as weak as you are, and so incapable of actually taking revenge, one should not allow oneself to be insolent with a friend." There are times when hatred meanders through a vast stretch of love and appears to be lost in it. There are times when the memory of a snub comes between our lips and the dear cheek on which so often we have imprinted a kiss that holds infinities of affection. In eternity those many words we have not spoken to those we loved better than all the world because they have been choked back by some sour memory, words we could not bring ourselves to speak, the sole expression of a tenderness which without them is as nothing, will stay for ever as the cruel counterpart of the wrongs which another's love has allowed itself to wrath on us.

*

Jean went to the Lustaud party like one going to his own execution,
and to torture himself the more, conjured up in advance a picture of the
hands which would be withdrawn at his approach, of the eyes which
would go blank, or self-consciously light up for the benefit of somebody
else, of backs ostentatiously turned, of whispers more terrifying than a
serpent's hiss, of laughter on the lips of those who watched him pass,
more devilish than the laughter of those demons we sometimes hear
in sleep so that we lie with closed eyes and scarcely able to breathe for
fully half an hour after we have been called, of the whole hideous
business of social excommunication which is the worst of all excom-
munications, in which snobbery, stupidity and malevolence artlessly
display for the victim's torment a more excruciating genius than any
talent for mere cruelty is capable of showing, or the instinct bred of
madness when at least the performer has the excuse of no longer being
his real self. He remembered how Madame de Thianges, Madame
Marmet, Madame de Perdan had looked twenty-four hours earlier,
and went beyond the limits of the possible when he tried to imagine
what he would see expressed on the faces of Monsieur and Madame
Lustaud. But he had forgotten the preliminary hell of the entrance hall
where he would have to walk past the groups of servants waiting for
their masters. If he had thought of *that* he would most certainly have
turned tail. But not until he caught sight, through the glass panel of the
front door, of Madame de Thianges's footman, did he realize what lay
in wait for him. He turned pale, but it was too late to retreat. He let
himself be swallowed up in the expanses of the hall. He was like a man
plunging headlong into a furnace. His mind was empty, his eyes could
scarcely see. He did however get the impression that the many servants
in attendance (it was already late, and the party was at its height) were
not laughing. As he moved forward he suddenly became aware that
Madame de Thianges's footman was standing before him in an attitude
of respectful immobility. "I trust sir, that you will forgive the liberty,"
said this functionary, "but Monsieur le Duc de Réveillon, who has
asked Madame la Comtesse to allow him to make use of my services
until his own man arrives, has instructed me to hold myself at your
disposal, sir. His Grace said: Ask Monsieur Santeuil if he will do the
Duchess and myself the honour of letting us drive him home—in
which case, no doubt, he will wish to dismiss his own carriage."
Overwhelmed by respect for the only person to whom the Duc de
Réveillon (in the eyes of the Thianges footman he figured as no less a

person than the King of France) had ever addressed such words (servants who know one another know with great accuracy not only the comparative social position of their respective masters, but also their attitude to other people, their way of behaving, and their particular form of snobbery) the serving-man stood waiting for Jean's reply, surrounded by his astonished fellows. "His Grace," he added, "also gave me this card for you, sir." The card was not enclosed in an envelope, and it was perfectly obvious that all the servants present had read it.

My dear Jean—you must excuse me for sending this message in so incorrect a manner. I have been waiting some time for you to turn up, but my gout has been giving me so much trouble that I don't like standing longer than I need. In any case, I am so fond of you that I naturally behave with you as I would with my wife or my son. You will think this a very complicated way of saying what I have to say, which is simply that I want you to get rid of your carriage without in any way disturbing our hostess or her guests.

"Tell my driver that I shall not be needing him," said Jean. "I will reply to His Grace's message in person," and he mounted the stairs. He no longer felt afraid of anything. Nevertheless, he was somewhat shaken when, arriving at the level of the drawing-room, he found himself confronted by a secondary hedge of domestics who, having been out of touch since the party began with their fellows below, almost certainly did not know what had happened so recently, and were undoubtedly aware of the incident of the previous evening, especially since he noticed among them Madame Marmet's footman whose laugh on that occasion as he stood among the members of Madame de Thianges's staff, had been the loudest. Just then Jean caught sight of Madame de Cygnerolles and Madame de Thianges, who were coming upstairs behind him. When he gave his name to the major-domo, while Madame de Cygnerolles, waiting to give her own, was carefully avoiding his eye, Madame Marmet's servant, far from sniggering as he had done on the previous evening, came up to him and taking no notice whatever of Madame de Cygnerolles or of Madame de Thianges who was with her, said, "Her Grace the Duchesse de Réveillon would be most grateful, sir, if you would go to her as soon as possible in the green drawing-room, and has instructed me sir, to ask you not to accept any invitation for luncheon tomorrow until she has seen you.

Her Grace very much hopes that you will be free to take luncheon with
her."–"Oh, it's you, is it?" said Madame de Cygnerolles, "you were
half turned away from me, and I did not see who it was!"–"I really owe
you an apology," said Madame de Thianges. "I was absolutely furious
with Boissieux about something, last night, and fully intended to tell him
to leave my house. But Delphine (Madame de Cygnerolles) says that I
made a slip of the tongue, and said Santeuil when I meant Boissieux.
You slipped away so suddenly that I had no chance of explaining matters
when I said good night, as I fully intended."–"No need to apologize,
Madame," said Jean with a laugh, for happiness and hope are soon
restored: "why in Heaven's name, should I have taken as intended for
me, who had not exchanged a word with you, what was meant for
Boissieux—who incidentally you must forgive, because he is so very
charming?"

Accompanied by these two ladies as by an involuntary bodyguard,
he paid his respects to his hostess who whispered in his ear "Do, I beg
of you, get hold of the Duke. He's making the most awful fuss, and all
on your account . . . *so* delighted that you could come." Having
bowed to Madame Lustaud, Jean made his entry into the first of the
suite of drawing-rooms. Almost immediately he met Monsieur
Marmet who was deep in conversation with Monsieur de Buest. He
bowed. But Monsieur Marmet looked coldly at him and replied with
the briefest of nods, without offering his hand. Jean heard him growl
something in an angry tone of voice, and caught or thought he caught,
the words—"what infernal cheek!" Then Monsieur Marmet said something in Monsieur de Buest's ear, as a result of which Monsieur de
Tours-en-Langues, and the other two, gave him an appraising look.
Many years later he could still remember the way in which Monsieur
de Tours-en-Langues had stared at him—the amused flicker in his small
dark eyes as he gazed at the man who had been caught cheating. After
this incident Jean proceeded on his way. At his approach, people who
knew him quite well turned away and went on talking with their
neighbours, or moved into one of the other rooms. Monsieur de
Thianges addressed himself with a laugh to the lady at his side, who
took his arm and looked Jean up and down through her lorgnette.
Madame de Cygnerolles was still close to him. Feeling his courage
dwindling, he offered her his arm. But cowardice is slow to learn the
lessons of generosity. 'I expect those servants almost certainly exaggerated the Réveillons' message,' she told herself, 'besides, he doesn't

at all look as though he were *certain* of their support. These people here
will think I've fallen pretty low if I am seen going about with this
absurd creature with whom nobody so far has been willing to shake
hands. Besides, I gather that the Duchess is walking through the rooms
with Monseigneur, and the Duke with the Princess. They've got better
fish to fry this evening than Santeuil.' As a result of this cogitation
she replied to Jean's offer with a gesture which said as plainly as any
words, "I am in no need of an arm." Monsieur Marmet however gave
her his, which she accepted. But at this moment with her hand resting
on the arm of the Duc de Lithuanie, making her way through the
crowd of sniggering men and women who respectfully stepped back
to let her pass, the Duchesse de Réveillon who had been following Jean
at a distance ever since she had heard him announced, approached.
Madame de Cygnerolles made a deep curtsy, and Monsieur Marmet,
hoping perhaps that he might be presented (that *would* be something
to tell his wife when they got home!) bowed so low that his nose very
nearly scraped the floor. But the Duchess, as though not seeing the
lady and the gentleman before her, said to Jean, "In your present weak
state you need the support of a stronger arm than Madame de
Cygnerolles can provide," and taking her hand from the arm of her
companion—whom she had forewarned of her intention—she gave it to
Jean. "I believe that Your Highness has not met Monsieur Santeuil,"
she said. "He is like a second son to me, Monseigneur. I am sure that you
will like him, for all who like me know that they must in duty bound
like him," adding, "he is far too distinguished not to have enemies," with
a laugh, "and far too superior to them to wish to see them punished.
Therefore, it is *I* who have to see to that!—let us sit down." Monsieur de
Thianges, who was with Madame de Buest, rose at her approach. The
Duchess took his chair and made Jean sit down on it. Dumbfounded at
the sight Monsieur Marmet seemed as though rooted to the ground. "I
see, Monseigneur, that you are going to take a drink," said the Duchess
to the Duc de Lithuanie noticing that he had a glass of orangeade in his
hand. "I have changed my mind," said the Duke, "it is rather too cold
for me"–"You, Jean, must certainly have something to drink; it will do
you good," and, turning graciously to the group of gentlemen near
by, "Will somebody," she said, "be so very kind as to fetch Monsieur
Santeuil a glass of orangeade?" Monsieur de Buest, Monsieur de
Thianges, and several others, abandoning the ladies to whom they had
been talking, started to scramble over chairs and elbow their way

through the crowd in their haste to obey her. But Monsieur Marmet outdistanced them all. They were unaware that the Duc de Lithuanie had offered his glass to Jean, saying, "Do please have it," and when Jean refused, "You will probably save me from getting an attack of asthma. It is very bad for me to take cold liquids when I am hot." Meanwhile, well ahead of the other gentlemen, who looked thoroughly put out at having been forestalled, Monsieur Marmet approached with a glass of orangeade in his hand, walking as quickly as he could without spilling it. But Jean indicated with a gesture that he already had one, and there was nothing left for Monsieur Marmet to do but to make himself scarce.

12. *Another Duel*

Having been publicly insulted at the theatre, Jean was determined to send two seconds to call on the offender. Whom should he ask to act for him? Now it so happened that Jean had for some years been on terms of warm friendship with a man called Baron Scipio—when people asked how it was spelled, the answer as a rule was (though it was probably not understood) "Oh like the chap in the Roman History books,"—whom no one would ever have dreamed of mentioning save in terms of grateful affection, for he was the most obliging and the most tactful person in all Paris. What, you will ask, were the services he had rendered?—in what circumstances precisely had he shown his famous tact? His reputation on both counts dated from so far back that those who so to speak worshipped him (and that meant everybody) had long ago decided that it was pointless to undertake researches in the field of Biblical exegesis. When Saint Louis devoted his life, his armies, and his Kingdom to the cause of winning back the Holy Places, he did not think it necessary first of all to examine meticulously all the available evidence in support of the divinity of Christ. Belief in the Baron's "high reputation" was treated in much the same way. To some it seemed a merely Platonic notion, though actually it was of very real importance, as is every belief, and as capable of having useful consequences for the man who enjoyed it, as a bad name is productive of certain positive and tiresome results. It had for instance in the Baron's case, induced Gravier-Bertrand, the richest lawyer in Paris, to give him his daughter's hand in marriage, and the Society for the Assistance of War-Wounded to appoint him its Honorary President. He held no "position" in the precise and practical meaning of that word, which didn't alter the fact that he had more loosely speaking a very great position indeed, and something too that very great positions do not always give to their holders. When somebody from the country or a foreigner asked who he was, the answer was always the same. "It's difficult to give you a simple answer to that question. By and large he is a very, very good man, one of the best who ever trod, always ready to

do you a service, always to be relied upon for his tact." Although he was
a Legitimist, the Municipal Council never failed to include his name
when there was a question of setting up a Commission of Enquiry,
because he was the sort of man in whom all political parties had the most
complete confidence. In the world of Society and in the columns of
the newspapers, people whose reputations were not of the best, showed
themselves to be entirely without rancour towards him, on the ground
that, "you can't expect a man like that not to be a bit squeamish".

He did not often say, "You can count on me," but when he did, you
knew that you could. He had frequently said just that to Jean, and
when as now the question of asking a favour arose, Baron Scipio's
name was the first that occurred to him. He felt the less compunction
in applying to him since at a critical juncture in the Baron's affairs,
Monsieur Santeuil had been able to procure for his mother a licence to
keep a tobacco shop, so that Scipio could as the saying goes refuse him
nothing. But what counted most of all was that for some years now he
had shown for Jean a particularly warm affection. What clinched
the matter was that having already asked one or two very small
favours of the Baron, the latter much to his regret (and a most unusual
occurrence in the case of so obliging a person) had found it impossible
to gratify them. This circumstance had no more discouraged Jean than
would the failure of the Blessed Virgin to answer some particular
prayer discourage a Catholic from praying to Her. But it did remove
any sense of shyness which he might have felt about approaching
Baron Scipio, because he knew that his friend must be feeling that
he really ought to do something for him, and would be delighted at
this opportunity to prove the sincerity of his so often repeated declarations of affection. When he arrived at the flat in the rue de Rivoli, he
was told that the Baron was out. He therefore left a note asking for an
appointment. Being so near the Louvre he could not resist the temptation to take another look at Van Dyck's portrait of the young Duke of
Richmond, and went home fancying that he himself was very like the
Duke, because like him he was thoughtful and handsome, and like him
was about to fight a duel. The concierge handed him a card left by
Baron Scipio, who had been twice to the house in search of him, having
found his message only a few minutes after he had left. Jean was quite
overwhelmed by such evidence of good-will in so important a man
who had broken into a busy day for his sake. He hurried round to the
Baron in a cab, more eager to express his thanks than to make a request.

There were several people waiting in the drawing-room. But at the sound of Jean's name, the butler of the most obliging man in Paris, the very look on whose face inspired confidence, and by anticipation gratitude, just as the sight of a dentist's receptionist produces a mood of anxiety and fear, said—"Monsieur Santeuil, is it not, sir?"–"Yes," replied Jean, whereat the butler, with a quiet deference which caused Jean as much pleasure as the receptionist saying, "You are the gentleman who has an appointment for three o'clock?" causes uneasiness, went on, "My master will see you at once, sir, if you will kindly come this way." After a brief silence during which he led the visitor into a small boudoir, whither he returned a moment later to put a fresh log on the fire, he added, "I am just about to lay the table, sir. My master has asked me to say that he hopes you will take luncheon with him and the Baroness." Jean, feeling the warmth of the fire beginning to spread through the room, had the greatest difficulty in keeping himself from dancing, so delightful was the prospect of a duel for which the preparations were going on so well, and so warm was the sudden gush of affection which he felt for Scipio. At that moment he would gladly have given his fortune and his life for his host, but could find no better outlet for his overflow of emotion than by passing his hand over a terrifying Gorgon's head by Gérome which was writhing and twisting in white marble. But the sight of it no more inspired terror within this sanctuary of certain hope than the perusal of a comic paper in a dentist's waiting-room inspires gaiety, seeming as it does to be redolent not of laughter-provoking jokes, but of the suffering of those victims whom it has already tried to distract. At the sound of a noise in the next room, which at the dentist's would have struck him as sinister, less because it reminded him of the horrible present rather than of the still more horrible, and approaching, future, Jean thought: 'I'm just another person he's going to make happy: what a man!'

He had less than a minute in which to indulge these reflections, for almost at once the Baron ('There are plenty of people with nothing to do,' thought Jean, 'who would not hesitate to keep one waiting an hour') appeared. Filled as he was with a sense of gratitude, which every word spoken by his benefactor had the effect of increasing, Jean felt too shy even to formulate his request, and instead of asking the Baron to act as his second merely inquired whether he could suggest someone who would, and was conscious of no sense of grievance when Scipio proceeded to explain why he could not himself undertake that office, why he could not ask any of his friends to do so, why he felt unable to give Jean an introduction to anybody likely to be willing to represent him. At last however he did suggest that Jean should approach the Duc de Réveillon. "May I say that you have advised me to put that request to him?" the young man asked, feeling too timid to take the initiative unsupported. "Dear me, no: I must beg you not to mention my name in connexion with the matter. I may rely on you, may I not?" When the time for luncheon came, Jean, feeling that so far he had made no progress in his search for seconds, would have liked to make his excuses so that he might still have a chance of finding somebody before the day was over. But he dared not, just when Scipio had found it impossible to accede to a request, leave him in so egotistical a fashion, and stayed to luncheon during which the Baroness behaved charmingly to him and seemed, for her husband was no less discreet than obliging, to know nothing of what had been going on. When the meal was over, he still did not venture to take his departure, and it was the Baron, who said, "I am afraid I have to go out, and must ask you to excuse me. I leave you in my wife's care." – "I must go, too," said Jean. The Baron made him get into his brougham, saying, "I'll drop you." To the coachman he said, "Stop at the Réveillon mansion." Jean did not know how to thank him. When they arrived at their destination, they saw the Duchess just coming out of the house. The Baron retired as far as possible into the recesses of the brougham. "I'd very much rather she didn't see me. It'll be better for you if I remain outside all this." – "Thank you, thank you," said Jean. "Whether it succeeds or not, I shall never forget that this idea came from you, nor the kindness you have shown me in a difficult situation." – "Well, we're two old friends, aren't we?" said the Baron, as though to put him at his ease. Jean bowed very low to show that he was not taken in by this implication of equality, and that he was acutely aware of the other's kindly condescension.

As Jean went upstairs to see the Duke, the immense affection that he felt for him lay heavy on his heart. But when he found himself in his presence he never so much as mentioned that feeling in the few words that he addressed to him. For having so important a favour to ask (he was fully aware that the Duc de Réveillon had only once before acted as a second and that to the King of Hesse) he dared not refer to his affection lest the Duke might think that his words were dictated by self-interest. The Duke accepted at once. After a few moments Jean made as though to withdraw in order to find the remaining second. "Wait," said the Duke: "I rather think that General de Beauvoil is with my wife: would you like me to ask him?" He left the room, and came back with General de Beauvoil, who had accepted the invitation. They went at once to X—— neglecting everything else to do so. Jean felt that the Duke, in spite of his simplicity of manner, was fully conscious how important a service he was rendering. He was somewhat surprised therefore to find that his sense of gratitude was no greater than, no different from, what he had felt in the past when the Duke had shown him kindnesses of a different sort. The Duke would have been much surprised if he had learned that Jean had been grateful on those former occasions. He would however have thought it highly improper if he had not shown that he realized how great a concession had been made on this one. 'Why is it,' thought Jean, 'that I do not feel gratitude proportionate to the service he is now rendering me?'

It was decided that the duel should take place in two days' time. Jean felt that it would be only polite, seeing that Scipio had found it impossible to be of use to him, to let him know how he was faring as the Baron had asked him to do, and thought it not improper to give expression to his feelings of affection, since Scipio could not possibly now suspect that he had any selfish intention. The Baron could not wholly conceal his stupefaction when he was told who Jean's two seconds were to be. He had miscalculated the young man's influence, and would never have thought it possible that the Duc de Réveillon should go to such extremes in order to please him. Since this duel was assuming the proportions of a Social Event, it was of some importance to him to learn when it was to take place, as well as the name of Jean's opponent and seconds. But while they were talking together the electrician arrived to see about the illuminations for a party which the Baron was to give shortly and he lost all interest in Jean's affairs. Jean left almost at once. With his mind still full of candle-problems, Scipio shook hands in a somewhat absent-minded way and because his wife had asked Jean to tell them as soon as he had any news of the impending event, could not repress an irritable gesture at the thought that she was paying insufficient attention to an entertainment which was going to cost no end of money, and had got to be stupendously fine. Jean noticed that in spite of their protestations of affection neither troubled to ask him whether he knew how to use a pistol.

All of a sudden, Jean, who till then had contemplated the forth-coming duel with pleasure, especially since the Duke and the General had undertaken to act for him, because always assuming that he was not killed, he would enjoy reading about it in the papers and the know-ledge that his enemies would be reading about it, too—was conscious of an unpleasant pang of fear. He seemed to remember that the principals were expected to go on horseback to the scene of the combat, and for years now he had had an aversion to, a real nervous fear of that form of exercise which dated from the day when though he had not suffered the slightest injury he had fallen from a horse and been stunned. He knew well enough how to ride, and his seconds were such practised horsemen that he need have no fear that he would fall off a second time. Nevertheless he had such an instinctive dislike of horses that he found himself regretting that it had not been possible to reach a settle-ment without fighting, and began to wonder whether he might not even at the last moment put out feelers. But when next he met his seconds the Duke laughed at the idea that they should all ride to the ground, and said that on the contrary, they would drive. Never had Jean felt fonder of the Duke than when he relieved him of this cruel anxiety. 'To think that I should have tried to avoid this duel for no better reason than that!' he thought. From then on his mind was entirely at ease.

13. *A Hospital Common-Room*

"Are you coming with me tomorrow, Jean?" asked Réveillon of Santeuil. "No, tomorrow I can't. I'm lunching in the common-room at the 'La Pitié' hospital."

When Jean left the room for a moment Madame Santeuil said to Réveillon: "Do please, Monsieur Henri, try to stop Jean from going to that hospital tomorrow. He has been invited by a man called Savone, the brother you know of the Savone who was at school with both of you, and has since died." – "Yes, I know," said Réveillon, "I was at the funeral. His brother made a scene and had to be taken away." – "He was very fond of his brother," said Madame Santeuil, "but he is not the right kind of friend for Jean. He has quarrelled with his father—a most excellent man, and at school, in the regiment, everywhere, he has always got into trouble with his superiors. He once came to dinner here and had a dreadful altercation with my husband on the subject of income tax. Since he is very intelligent, and can talk well, his influence is bad on Jean, who struck up a friendship with him solely on account of his brother."

But Henri had no success with the mission which Madame Santeuil had entrusted to him. Jean had spoken only once or twice to Savone, but had realized in his young enthusiasm a burning sincerity about the man, a luminous awareness of human goodness, which seemed to set him well above Jean and all the other men whom Jean knew (with the exception of Monsieur Beulier). There were moments when feeling how much Savone disliked the worldly sort of life he was leading, the thought of him brought an acute feeling of discomfort. But if he happened to run into him, if Savone made to him one of those meaningful remarks which seemed to be full of deep feeling and profound thought, in the special tone of voice which he used on such occasions, Jean was conscious of a thrill. His sense of admiration for the man was what most enhanced his own moral stature in his own eyes. Often, when he momentarily indulged in a bout of self-criticism, or was

plunged in one of those fits of depression in which we become suddenly
aware of the emptiness of our lives, so that all interest, all purpose,
seems to be drained from the years ahead, as when rain begins
to fall, we lose all desire to go on with the walk on which we have
set out, he would call to mind the moments when Savone had shown
a more than usual esteem for him, and in so doing would recover
not only his own self-confidence, but also his belief in the value
of existence. In spite of all this however during the three years
which Savone had spent as Houseman, he had not yet visited the
hospital even once. Not that Savone would not have welcomed
him as often as he might like to go, but Jean was afraid that he
might become censorious should he get too close a view of the
life that he was leading. So long as Jean's family saw no objection
to that life and much preferred Jean to dine out and go to parties than
be constantly in Savone's company, it was just as well that he did so
feel. But it was only in this that he sided with his mother and father in
their attitude to Savone, and knowing that he would dislike the other's
comments, he had decided that it might be as well not to do anything
that might put Savone in a position to exert a moral influence on him.
In every other way he took up the cudgels on his new friend's behalf
against his parents. He realized that they did not begin to understand
him, and felt intensely irritated when his mother constantly reverted
disapprovingly to the fact that Savone was in the black books of his
superiors, had broken with his father, and quarrelled with Monsieur
Santeuil, because he knew that all these things which they found
blameworthy, proceeded fundamentally from the deep sense of
justice which animated his friend. No doubt Jean felt that if similar
situations had arisen in the course of his own career his lack of moral
backbone and his excess of sensibility would at the last moment have
kept him from taking a stand against his superiors and from breaking
with his father. But he felt too that he would have been utterly incapable of doing any of the fine things he knew Savone to have done,
of being anything like so hard on himself, of giving all his money
to the poor, of devoting all his intelligence, his every day, and often
his nights as well, to the study of social problems. Monsieur Santeuil
clung firmly to the opinion—though he was careful to exclude Savone
from the implied approval—that hospital common-rooms were places
in which the brightest lights of the younger generation indulged in
marvellous discussions about the place of science in the society of the

future. Consequently had it not been that Jean was bound to be brought into close contact with Savone, he would have thoroughly approved of his son's frequenting so intelligent a community. But Daltozzi, though his nervous temperament had made the continued study of medicine impossible for him, had spent a whole year in the company of doctors, and had told Jean that the atmosphere of a hospital was fœtid and squalid, with nothing in it but macabre jocosity and a general attitude of stupid materialism.

But the presence of persons of a type we have, hitherto, not known, has the effect of hypnotizing us. Their individual characters exercise so strong an influence upon us that we forget the abstract questions we might have asked ourselves had we sat down to consider in detachment what it is they stand for. We feel between us and them a new and vital relationship, a spontaneous sympathy, which takes no account of preconceived ideas. At any given moment, of the six or eight young men likely to be present in the common-room to which Jean had been invited, one, or two would almost certainly be engaged in laughing at the blunders committed by a colleague, or otherwise making fun of him. The blunder in question would probably be a matter of common knowledge to the other members of the group, who would straightway join in the laughter, and take sides for or against the victim, his supporters using just as violent language, just as crude a humour, as their opponents. But no matter how loud and violent any one of them might be when it was a question of shouting down the table to make himself heard, he would speak in the gentlest way to a neighbour—addressing him as "poor old chap"—who as the result of an accident had his arm in a sling, and go out of his way several times in the course of the meal to get him something he wanted or to save him from enduring unnecessary discomfort. The loud voices took on a softer note when their owners politely asked Jean whether he would like a second helping, whether he found the draught from the door unpleasant. Among themselves, as the wine went round, there reigned that climate of childlike gaiety, that happy lack of self-consciousness, which we find in those who never have time to think of their own pleasure, since it has no part in their day-to-day existence which, without their noticing it, has become the background to all their activities. Living constantly in one another's company within the walls of an institution where all of them exercised the same authority over nurses and matrons, where they all had the same interests, the same superiors, the same duties, the same colleagues, the same preoccupations, the same problems, the same satisfactions and the same jokes, they were linked in friendship by a thousand different bonds which had become like creepers happily disposed over the surfaces of old walls. Between the most intelligent and the best of these men, a mocking attitude to blunders, but also an awareness of their own weaknesses and a readiness to stand shoulder to shoulder should they be violently attacked, had produced a close, quiet and humorous alliance. Often when one of Savone's friends started to raise a laugh at the expense of Etrat, who did his best never to give a penny when there was a whip-round, who got the house-keeper to polish his boots, and brought in bags of fruit secretly so as to avoid having to share it with the rest of them, Savone, and one or two others would say, "Come on now, pipe down: he's not such a bad chap," or else said nothing at all, which was more than Etrat could reasonably hope, since he knew only too well as the result of old wounds kept constantly sore and open, the dreaded effect of their noisy badinage—but just sat silently smiling. Then he who had started the attack would glance quickly at them, stop talk-ing and smile too. It was at such moments that they all looked like young Gods, confident in their strength, gazing at the golden weapons which they have voluntarily relinquished and now laid aside.

As the result of some peculiarly stupid remark which had provoked a deafening uproar Etrat was sentenced to stand champagne all round. This decision he questioned, and one of Savone's friends, a tall fair young man with a gentle expression called Servais, who was sitting next to Jean, was just setting out to prove in a low voice and with a wealth of ironic argument, that it was his duty to pay up, when an orderly came in. The doctor on call was wanted. "What's up?" asked Servais. "Chap in one of the wards is choking—he's purple in the face," replied the orderly. "All right, I'll be along in a moment, don't bother about disturbing the fellow on call." The orderly went off and Servais proceeded with his unhurried demonstration intended to prove that Etrat had jolly well got to order champagne for the company. In face of the general indignation Etrat's last defences crumbled. After saying to the maid who entered the room at that moment, "Champagne —Monsieur Etrat's paying—so bring the best and most expensive," Servais started downstairs to have a look at the sufferer with a final word to Etrat from the door. "And no sneaking my glass, mind!"

When he returned the diners were busy pulling Etrat's leg about the champagne, declaring that it was no better than herb-tea, and Savone was saying to the maid, "Come on, Félicie, make a clean breast of it, didn't Monsieur Etrat tell you not to bring real champagne?" – "Monsieur Etrat didn't say anything, sir," replied Félicie with a kindly smile which was eloquent of the respect she felt for Savone, and of her realization that everyone else felt as she did! Meanwhile Servais had come back and resumed his place at Jean's side. He took a sip. "Call that champagne! it's water!" he said and threw the contents of his glass in Etrat's face. "Félicie!" he cried, "Monsieur Etrat wants another bottle, and the real stuff this time, or you'll do the paying!" – "How's the man you went down to see?" asked Jean. "Him?—oh, he's croaked," replied Servais. "Really?" – "Did you hear what I said, Félicie? Champagne for Monsieur Etrat, and get a move on. I've not had any yet!"

"Well, what about what you were going to tell Monsieur Santeuil," said Savone. "By Jove! I'd nearly forgotten all about it!" exclaimed Servais. "Not that it's very important. Fact is I know all about your trip to Penmarch on that day of the storm." – "You do? Whoever could have told you," said Jean. "No one told me, I saw you." – "How on earth! I never saw you!" – "You may not have seen me, but I saw you: as a matter of fact, though, you *did* see me. But you didn't know who I was, and therefore you don't remember. I didn't know who *you* were, if it comes to that, but your face struck me." – "Where did all this happen? at Penmarch?" – "No, in the little train." – "In the little train? Then you must have been the man with the bicycle!" exclaimed Jean, who had never thought about his trip in the train since that day, long ago, when it had occurred. But now he saw Servais again as he had seen him then in the light of the setting sun. Indeed though Servais was a few years older he realized that he might indeed have been the young cyclist. "Yes, I was the man with the bicycle, and I'd very much have liked to talk to you. I was bored and dam' cold into the bargain." – "And the two ladies?" Jean's curiosity was now thoroughly aroused. But he flushed scarlet, remembering that one of them had almost certainly been the cyclist's mistress. "Oh, I'm sorry." – "Why should you be sorry? One of them was the Marquise de Lieureux, the daughter of Madame de Miraibout Tournefort: the other was the wife of the Serbian Minister. I've never seen either of them since, as a matter of fact." – "But how can that be? you went off with them."-"Oh no, I didn't: they merely asked me the way when we got out of the train. Actually, I *had* been presented to the Minister's wife," he said with a glance at Henri de Réveillon, "at the Duchess's."-"So that's who they were—I should never have thought it!" said Jean, and the sound of his voice which the surprise and interest of this revelation had caused to rise, the gleam in his eyes which were now concentrated on the suddenly remembered scene, and the deepened colour of his cheeks, made everyone present look at him. Then realizing that he was deep in memories of a trip he had once taken in Brittany, they decided that it was nothing to do with them and resumed their desultory chatter. "It really is extraordinary!" said Jean. "And the old one too: why, I thought . . . no really I daren't tell you what I thought she was, certainly not a lady of distinction! It's true of course that a difference of nationality can produce just as much of an effect as a difference of class. It really is *too* extraordinary: what an unpleasant person you must have thought me!" he said, just to make sure that Servais had noticed him and decided that he was likeable. "You were with two fishermen," said the latter. "Indeed I was: your guess was a good deal better than mine!" And he conjured up a vision of the two ladies, seeing them, now as a tart and her maid, now as the Marquise de Tournefort and the Comtesse Pickitz, now as both these persons simultaneously. The discovery filled him with amazement.

But later seated in the carriage, and remembering the little Pont-Labbé railway which had vanished for ever from his mind, about which but for this conversation, he would never have thought again, dwindling away into a sunset distance, what struck him most was not the identities of the two ladies, but the fact that the young man with the bicycle, whom he had never expected to see again, who had been just a part of the landscape, like the permanent way, like the trees, like everything he had seen on that far distant day without so much as dreaming that they could hold any meaning for him, was now his friend. The whole thing, the two periods of time now brought suddenly into juxtaposition, seemed like the effect produced in some fairy transformation "done" with mirrors. A picture had fluttered before his eyes, and now it was just as in one of those pantomime scenes where the reflection of a person appears, to be replaced almost immediately by a real actor who takes its place, speaks a few words,

and vanishes precisely as the reflection has done, and as Servais himself
would do in a few days, for he would turn out to be only somebody
seen for a few seconds on a station platform.

*

Just as Jean was going downstairs, accompanied by Savone and
Servais, the latter was summoned to another urgent case. They were
just outside the ward, and Jean followed Servais into it, while Savone
went off to fetch his hat and coat. Jean was amazed and delighted by
the gentle, the almost tender way, in which Servais spoke to the patient.
"Things not too good, eh, old chap? That abscess giving you a bad
time? Let me have a look: I won't hurt you." He felt as grateful as
though some kindness had been done to him. Then he saw Servais's
great powerful hands, which, a while back, had been thumping the
table so noisily when the uproar occasioned by Etrat had been at its
height, cautiously approach the dressing, touch it with the most thoughtful care, and undo it so slowly that the sufferer appeared not to feel a
thing. He was moved by admiration for the kindliness of the man
which was not merely passive and blind like most of our vague and
useless acts of consideration, but transformed with precision, with
daring, with gentleness, into suffering spared, into a calculated act of
healing, into a crisis terminated. He watched those hands, sensitive
hands, hands as much informed as though they moved with an intelligence of their own, clever hands, good hands which he felt he could
have kissed as he might have done some sacred object. The feeling of
aversion of which he had been conscious such a short while back, when
Servais had taken the news of the choking man so calmly, had not even
hurried to his side, had drunk his champagne with a show of high
spirits after just seeing a man die, had entirely disappeared. Servais saw
that the abscess would have to be opened. Several incisions would be
necessary. He had completed the first when the patient made a sudden
movement and he received a scratch. Jean, who knew how dangerous
such scratches could be, hurried away to inform Savone, who thought
that Servais ought to have the place dressed at once, and put off making
the other incisions until later. But Servais shrugged and went on with
the operation. Savone got angry. But whether because of a sceptical
attitude to science which every day he saw proved wrong by life and
by death, whether as a result of that same calm in the presence of

danger to which daily repetition had made him indifferent for himself as for others, whether because professional scruple, taking the place of pity, as thought takes the place of sentiment, prevented him from leaving the patient until the dressing had been satisfactorily replaced—whatever the reason, Servais refused.

A few days later (the scratch had had no ill effects) Servais, now quite well again, left the hospital, his period as houseman being ended. Since it had never occurred to him to make a career on the staff of a teaching-hospital, he settled down in Amiens with the intention of building up a practice. He was saddened by the thought of having to leave the friends with whom he had lived in such close contact for so many years, and seemed to have no very certain idea of what the future would hold for him. But anyone seeing him when the first grey hairs were beginning to show among the gold, noting that slight fullness of figure which denotes a man who loves his comforts and is the possessor of a tranquil temperament, conscious of a pair of eyes bright with intelligence, limited though it might be to the nearer reaches of scientific knowledge and practical good sense, anyone seeing him then, as he stood listening to a question put to him by his companion, would have had no difficulty in imagining what he would look like in a few more years—a little older, a little plumper, a little redder in the face, with a few wrinkles just beginning to show, and, later still, just noticeably beginning to wilt like a flower at the moment of its fullest blooming, walking the streets of Amiens where by this time he would have established himself in a good position, being stopped by a passer-by, hat in hand, with a request that Dr Servais (he would be something of a personage in his provincial city) would come and have a look at his little boy who was suffering from the croup, and promising to drop in on his way home to dinner. But gradually the new contacts made at Amiens would fill the gap made by the absence of the old ones and strike deep roots into his still ebullient heart. Little by little in the course of time he would come to forget the ancient friendships, though sometimes, even after he had turned fifty, when bowling along in his gig to the rue Basse where he had a patient to see, he would suddenly find himself thinking of Etrat and the others. Of those of whom he had been fondest he would think with sadness, though without wanting to see them. Indeed, had one of them written to say that he was coming to pay him a visit, he would feel distinctly put out, and be eager for the old friend to take himself off again so that he might sink happily back into the calm little world of neighbours with whom he would now be living as contentedly as he once had done with his former companions. But his backward-ranging thoughts would be filled with affection, for they would carry him to the days of his youth.

14. *Dining Out*

The Duchesse de T——— had invited G——— and the famous Dr M———.
They were meeting each other for the first time at her house. G———
had heard it said that M——— was the most intelligent doctor alive. He
had a vague hope therefore that, if he mentioned his ailments, the other
might be able to cure them. M———, who hád read G———'s books was
pleased to make his acquaintance. He was not especially interested in
the state of G———'s health, but he did want to hear him talk about his
work. For a doctor is a man as well as being a specialist and likes to hear
a good singer and to meet a famous author. The first may be suffering
from influenza, but he will merely say to her, "What does that matter,
since you sing so well?" or the latter may be a victim to insomnia, and
he will remark, "What does that matter, since you write such admirable
books?" He knows that a man who writes admirable books is often a
man who has difficulty in sleeping, who thinks he is ill, who has
attacks of asthma about which nothing can be done, who goes from
doctor to doctor—and that is part and parcel of his talent. All the same,
he likes having a man of that sort for a patient, because though he
knows that he can do little or nothing to alleviate the asthma, the
insomnia, and the general condition of hypochondria—afflictions all of
them that can never be cured, and are in fact the side-products of the
sufferer's genius—his admiration for him, which is something compounded of the writer's fame and of the degree to which the doctor's
own intelligence, having assimilated the more general intelligence of
his period—has assimilated with it the possibility of finding enjoyment
in novels of the naturalist school, and "poems in the grand manner".
He will therefore gladly keep his other patients waiting and see the
writer out of turn, not in order to deal with his insomnia which for
him is a common-or-garden occurrence and as much inseparable from
genius as mosquitoes are tiresomely inseparable from an enjoyable
holiday in Italy, but in order to get him to talk of a thousand and one
matters, so that when G——— is dead, he will in conversation with an
elder colleague be able to enlarge on his memories of him to such good

effect that when the colleague gets home to his wife he will tell her that
M—— knew G—— very well, that he has told him many interesting
anecdotes, and that really they must ask him to dine, and later on these
favourable impressions may quite easily become transformed into votes
when M—— offers himself as a candidate for membership of the
Academy of Medicine. While G—— is still living he asks him to his
house, and G——, who goes nowhere, will accept invitations to dinner
from him on the understanding that they will not do him any harm,
and M—— thinks quite honestly that they won't, for being an extremely
intelligent doctor he knows that writers who suffer from insomnia
dread dining out and can never be convinced that all the dining out
in the world is powerless to have an effect upon the great processes of
Nature. G—— therefore is bound to suffer a great disappointment where
M—— is concerned, who never gives him anything for his asthma,
though his eye beams with silent admiration when he speaks to him of
his books, and discovers that he was one of Flaubert's intimates, with
the result that G——, who weak, ailing and anxious had hoped to find
a solid support in M—— realizes with something approaching terror
that it is the doctor who is seeking support in *him*! Eminent members
of the medical fraternity gladly accept invitations to meet G—— .M——
very graciously asks the whole family of a successful specialist whose
daughter is interested in literature, and is thrilled at the idea of
seeing G—— in the flesh, though her father will remain inflexible
when it comes to recording his vote against M—— at the next election.
No doubt about it, doctors are only too ready to conclude that men of
letters are bad sleepers, suffer from ailments difficult to cure, are tiresome patients who incessantly clamour for drugs, and an easy prey to
hypnotists and charlatans. Business men are only too ready to conclude
that poets are mentally ill-balanced and also susceptible to the allurements of charlatans. Men of learning are only too prone to notice that
poets deliberately say things designed to amaze intelligent folk, and
therefore decide that they are stupid, and will, for instance, quite often
talk with credulity of omens and every sort of superstition: also, that
they are indulgent in their attitude to vice, and even to crimes of a
certain kind, that they encourage young men to be idle, that they set a
high value on lounging about in the country and indulging their
passions, are always down on schoolmasters, education, and hard work
in general: that they poke fun at a great many words and phrases in
this or that newspaper or book which to ordinary sensible folk seem

perfectly reasonable: that they go into raptures over words or incidents which to anybody else would seem to have so purely formal a significance that no thinking person would pay them the slightest attention and are thus led to declare that they have formed a preference, or made a decision for perfectly irrelevant reasons, have travelled to this or that place just because they happen to like its name, and all this in such a way as to make normal persons blush: that they enjoy the company of workmen and peasants, and find men of established reputation stupid and boring: that they are at once generous and egotistical. It is no rare experience too, to find that they are superior to the books they write, for on subjects likely to interest intelligent men, they express superior views, whereas as soon as they take pen in hand they appear to be urged on by some private daemon which seems to find pleasure only in certain places where they once have lived, in over-size beds where once they snuggled down under the blankets in a village where the church bells used to sound the hours at night, where, before going to sleep, they could draw the blind aside and see a blue sky powdered with stars, and houses half in shadow, half in moonlight.

When Jean got home he found the note which his mother left for him every night when she went to bed, in which she asked him to tell her the *exact* time of his return, instead of taking refuge in some such vague generalization as "not very late", and to let him know whether on this occasion he had gone to bed earlier than usual—a matter which was her chief preoccupation. Each evening the question was put in a different way. On this particular one, she had drawn a clock face, and told him to mark on it the time at which he had come in. Whenever we turn our mind to the consideration of ideas which we have not ourselves formulated, which are brought to our attention by circumstances outside our control, and are strictly limited in number, we find in the long run certain connexions between them which seem endlessly new and charming. Just so do imaginative lovers, who give symbolic names to this or that, embellish them as the result of long use with fresh and exquisite features. Just so in this matter of going to bed did Madame Santeuil each evening find some new and enchanting invention. This no doubt is the reason why a writer's most felicitous passages are to be found not seldom in something that has been "commissioned" or asked for as for instance, an article or a preface. The material on which the intelligence is exercised is not the intelligence itself, which is always slipping away out of control, and is never wholly plumbed. It is some fixed and limited subject, over which the intelligence plays, to which it keeps returning, from which it rebounds, each time more forcefully and brilliantly. Those who are amazed by the astonishing invention which I display in a letter, in a piece of duty-writing, in talk, will never find it in this or that book of mine, where the material presented to me to work on is invisible and minute.

❧ IX ❧

About Love · Françoise's Friends · The Agate Marble

Winter in the Tuileries · La Marquise de Valtognes

Monsieur de Villebonne · Madame de Thonnes

Jean and Madame Desroches Visit the Bergotte Exhibition

Madame Cresmeyer's Dinner-Party · Henri Loisel

and Madame Delven · La Duchesse d' Alpes · Presents

Dead-End · The Confession · Wasted Evenings

The Sonata · The Dream

1. *About Love*

Stendhal, who is to so great an extent a materialist, for whom things outside our inner states of mind, and even of our physical sensitivity, seem to have a very real importance—"I am less happy than in . . . even though I have got *punch à la romaine*" (an idealist would have said "an appetite for"): "so-and-so in his talk, did not bring . . ." etc., always set above everything else—love, which for him seems to have been co-extensive with the life of the spirit. What makes us adore solitude, leading us to find in it a thousand various thoughts, what makes Nature comprehensible and eloquent to us—for him is love. He seems never to have known poetry except in the guise of love. I cannot go as far as that. Love does indeed resemble poetry in its power to emancipate us from the tyranny of others, to send us back to solitude, to open our eyes to the charms of Nature. But this subjection of poetry which excludes an individual's total preoccupation *with* an individual, this reduction of Nature's unity to the dimensions of a double individuality, is but a bizarre phase in human life. No individual, however remarkable he may be—and in love generally speaking he is anything but remarkable—has a right to limit the life of the spirit in this way. There is no real, no deep relationship between a face we have found momentarily enchanting, and the life of the spirit. The thoughts into which it intrudes itself so that they come to group themselves about it, do not in any genuine fashion *belong* to it. There is no true reality in it for us. Yet it is nothing less than the whole of our spiritual life which in Stendhal's view is thus systematized in such a way that the universe is seen as a sort of contraption to be for ever driven in double harness. But there can be no manner of doubt that an artist, a philosopher, or a poet, can suddenly—without this momentary change of vision being due to any diminution of his genius, though for the time being it may find itself compelled to work within his own puny personality and be conditioned by considerations occasioned in him by his reaction to another's individuality—see his thought split in two, and systematized in just this bizarre fashion, sometimes for months at a time.

*

It was precisely to Stendhal, whose views I have been quoting, that Jean found his thoughts returning as he sat dreaming of the exquisite profile, with its loosened hair which for the last few weeks had given a new charm to his existence. He could not have gone so far as to say that he was profoundly in love with Madame S——, and perhaps it was for that very reason that he revelled in the pleasure it gave him to *think* that he was in love, to know that instead of going night after night to fashionable parties, he now went to see Madame S—— in the privacy of her home, that he stayed there late and, driving back in the darkness, had before his eyes that pure and smiling countenance, always at the same distance from him, just as on these lovely brilliant nights, seated in his open cab, he could gaze upon the tranquil beauty of the moon whose distance from him never varied. It was happiness for him to feel himself invaded, all the time he was with her, all the time he was being driven away from her, all the time he sat at home thinking of her, by that pleasure which detaches us from other pleasures and give us new ones, the intensity of which he had realized through the predicament of Julien Sorel and Fabrice Del Dongo, and in the pages of *De l'Amour*, though without ever having felt it himself. It had not taken him long to realize that he could not go to bed with this young independent but eminently respectable widow (she received him every night from ten o'clock until two in the morning and more than that he only faintly desired) that he could not even so much as give her a kiss. This quasi-conviction, born of very explicit declarations should have been sufficient to strike a death-blow at love—which seems to reside largely in a waiting to see in what fashion, at present unknown, our possession of the beloved will be fulfilled. The man in love can say with truth that he lives on hope. But certain words, certain letters, something approaching a persuasion that he was for her what she was for him, her way of receiving him each evening—and making no bones about it to a great many people though concealing it from others—managed to keep alive in him for a while longer the love in some sort denuded of its object which still held dominion over him as do many passions of which we shall never experience anything but the idea because we know that their complete realization is wholly impossible, as we still retain within our bodies those primitive organs for which no use can be found in the civilized state. There are many passions which we are condemned to feel only in a reduced form, as one may play a score on the piano when it is impossible for us to hear it played by a full orchestra. But this absence of hope brings to a focus in the mind the satisfaction of knowing that one is "in love", with the result that it is love in the vaguer larger sense, and not the person loved that gives us pleasure. This sensation of "being in love" was perhaps more intoxicating to Jean for this reason, so that he thought of it as a livelier pleasure than any he had so far known. It brought Stendhal to his mind, and led him to consider love as an infinitely agreeable way of savouring life and finding a charm in solitude.

Once we have passed a certain age and our philosophic notions have attained a degree of fixity, we find a greater delight in things, because we are no longer concerned to inquire into their metaphysical basis. We know that the sensations which arise in us with a special and personal vividness, awakening in us a poetical resonance, are to that extent real, and we no longer wish to discuss them, thereby attaining to that condition of tranquillity which is so necessary to our enjoyment. A man who has a passion for the theatre gets more pleasure from a bad performance than does the blasé spectator sitting in a handsome box and watching actors of distinction. But when we love, what we seek in love is the Absolute. When we savour the loved one's every intonation, trying to establish its precise value, the exact degree of its importance for us, pleasure vanishes. It is this torment, to say nothing of others, that love brings to us when we are young. Is not love to some extent like those illnesses which recur from time to time in our lives, but on each occasion are less virulent, and never so violent as they were when they assailed us for the first time? Perhaps we know that we shall never again experience the intensity of first love. It may be too that our subsequent loves are less sincere, because, by the time they come to us, we have learned more about life, and are more self-centred in our search for happiness. If an intelligent man who is naturally prone to jealousy and dreads the possibility of suffering, says to himself, as did Jean, 'Provided she is kind and sweet, and I can see her every day for a fortnight, then by the end of that fortnight I shall have stopped loving her. The great thing is that she should not cause me pain, for if she does I may become bound hand and foot to her.' He will say to his mistress, "When a woman causes me pain, I love her no longer. I love her only for her sweetness and kindness." If he is afraid of loving her for a long time, he will tell her that he fears that his love will last no longer than a fortnight: if he is faithful, he will tell her that he is inconstant. If she says to him, "I shan't be able to see you this evening," he will go pale and reply: "Please don't worry your head about that, it is perfectly natural." For what he wants is her love, and he knows that the best way of obtaining it is not to confess his own. When passions burst into bud on a full-grown branch which has already known the burgeoning of many others, they no more resemble the emotions felt in the dawning years of life, than the hedgerose resembles the cultivated garden species, or rather than flowers native to the soil resemble the same flowers which as a result of being transplanted have lost their pristine vigour. No doubt a first avowal does occur, but the lover fears to renew it, and wraps it about with pretended indifference, pretended threats, pretended inconstancy. And since everything in us becomes adulterated by life—sensibility, sincerity, and even memory, even the clear-cut realization of our own personality and the genuineness of our feelings—we can no longer even be sure whether we are in love or not. Only our actions, being closely knit with instincts of which the brain has ceased to take account, bear witness to the survival of affection. We wonder whether the death of a grandfather has left in us the faintest shadow of regret, but, on approaching his room, we burst into tears. Whether our heart has retained any generous feeling, we do not know: still, we give our purse to an unfortunate. It is as though we had for ever at our side a child who cries and does good, though we have lost the power to read his heart. We do not know whether we still love Madame S——, but we continue to visit her every evening, and, though we may tell ourselves that our going to see her gives *her* pleasure, it is on *our* heart, should she put us off, that the blow strikes. So true is all this that it seems as though our instinctive life continues to unroll in a part of ourselves of which consciousness knows nothing, and this continues till our dying day, just as our blood goes on circulating and our pulses beating.

To return for a moment to love and its lies, it is worth pointing out that life, by accustoming us not to expect too much of others, and by presenting an image of what gives us pleasure, persuades us not to wait until chance shall provide it, but to set about finding it for ourselves. We recognize then that love is more a subjective sensation than anything else, that consequently it is a pleasure of which we know the conditions, and not an object to which we have to subordinate ourselves entirely. And so it is that we deliberately insinuate to the woman we love what it is we want of her, either under the pretext of making our love endure, or of giving her an assurance that what we want will exalt it, so acting that our pleasure may be the greater, and she appear more charming. "Don't put yourself out in any way," said Jean to Madame S——, so as not to seem too tiresomely exacting, "but if I can see you every evening my love will last longer. Speak gently to me, take down your hair, sit in such a way that I can see your profile, be gay." And, indeed, on those evenings when she did what he wanted, sat sideways to him, loosened her hair, was gay, and spoke with an especial tenderness, he felt his love once more fanned to a blaze, and told her so, that thus she might be persuaded to continue. He was careful not to let himself wonder what she had been before she had come into his life, nor what she would be after she had left it, for he saw Time as something closely resembling Space, and it was as though the segment of it which did not come within the radius of his visual beam, but remained hidden behind that vague horizon which the eye, whether looking forward or backward, does not attempt to penetrate, were as nothing. All these things, her gentleness, the particular form of gaiety which seemed to obliterate everything which was not of immediate concern to him, as well as all anxiety, the hair lying loose about her face, because it was thus that she was most herself—that is to say, a mysterious presence interposed between him and happiness, the rays of which could reach him only through her, since a woman, when we come to think of it, is never all of herself, but only that aspect of herself which we associate with our many dreams of her—all these things had the effect of making her more *his*, a condition which he sought in every way to bring about, by giving her pleasure, by doing her little services, by trying to appear in her eyes as someone endowed with every sort of glamour, by endeavouring to make her say openly that he came to see her every evening and stayed late with her, which would be a standing proof, if she did say it, that it was not only something that gave her pleasure, but a fact which she realized should be known to all—these things seemed to establish the truth that she had accorded him a privileged position. If he brought a friend with him, he liked her to say in his presence that she wanted him to stay on when the friend had left; liked her to call him by his Christian name, to praise or to criticize him in such a way as to imply that they had a shared life; liked her to say about him, "If you knew him as well as I do"; liked her to speak of books they had read together, to show that they had the same ideas, that there was something in herself that he had put there; liked her to tell him, "Here's the book you forgot the other day," or "Do write that

letter: I've been asking you to do so for the last ten days"—just to show
how concerned she was that he should be polite, that they had the same
obligations, that they had made plans together; liked her to say, "Are
you going there? If you are, I'll go too, otherwise, if you'd rather come
here, you know that all I care about is seeing you."

One evening, when they came away from a party at which they had
both been, he left her in order to go on to another to which she had
not been invited. Perhaps remembering one of the things which he had
told her gave him so much pleasure, she said, "It's now eleven. You
run along to your party: I'm going home, but I shall wait up for you,
so don't fail to look in at half past twelve." He knew perfectly well
that it would be all one to her whether he did so or not, but he felt
delighted all the same that she should have devised this gentle way of
shutting the door in advance against any possible jealousy on his part,
any uncertainty about how she spent her evenings when she was alone.
His party turned out to be amusing, and it was with a feeling of
considerable reluctance that he left it in order to keep his appointment
with her. It was raining, and the only cab he could find was an open
one, with the result that during the whole of the drive he was in two
minds about the business. Having been assured by her request to him,
that she was not planning to see anybody else, he would very much
rather have gone straight home to sleep secure in that knowledge, than
make an extra journey for no better reason than to say a second good
night to her. Nevertheless, he thought, 'The reason I didn't stay on at
that party was that there is a woman I love whom I am now on my
way to see. She is waiting for me. The friend to whom I waved just
now is perfectly well aware that I am not going home. The fact is there
is something more than social engagements to occupy me now, something much lovelier to which I sacrifice them. It is bliss to know that
one is not the keystone of one's own existence, that there is another in
it who means much, that one no longer feels oneself to be entirely
alone, but one of a pair, so that it is as though one has in oneself a sort
of extra personality who is at one and the same time oneself and somebody else who's reactions one does not know in advance as one knows
one's own.' And though there was not much pleasure to be got out of
going back so late to see her, he felt effusively grateful to her for having
understood so well all the little rites of affection, that one, in particular,
this evening which, by suppressing in advance all suspicion that she
might be spending the time with somebody else, by strangling jealousy

at its birth, ought, as he told her it would, perpetuate his love, though in point of fact as he knew, it would hasten its quiet and gentle death. Truth to tell he could no longer see anything that might interrupt or cast a cloud over his pleasure.

Next evening she told him that having sat up so late on the previous one (he had stayed with her for a long while after leaving his party) had made her very tired and when midnight struck, asked him to leave her so that she might go straight to bed. He said good night—not without having first glanced into the other room—and went away. But no sooner had he got home than he felt a strong desire to go out again, and hailing a cab had himself driven to her street, where he paid it off not far from her house. Suddenly, through the chinks in the shutters of two little windows, he saw a yellow glow in her room.

As a rule when he visited her round about ten, it was that light which told him that she had returned, and he always saw it as a sweet pledge of her presence. But on this occasion, since it was more than two hours since he had left her, it struck him as a detestable proof that she now had with her the man on whose account she had prevailed upon him to go home. He would dearly have liked to know who it was. Moving without a sound he bent down and put his eye to the Venetian blind so as to look between the slats. But they were closed and he could see nothing. The window however was open. They must be feeling hot. He could hear the sound of voices. The first doubt that had come to him when about midnight she had asked him to leave so that she might go to bed, the feeling that some part of himself, estranged from, taken from his heart, might have been given to another, was now when he saw the light in her room, turned almost into certainty, and it came to him that he was deeply involved. No doubt he was suffering, no doubt he was filled with hatred for the light now there before his eyes, in which his enemy twin was moving, no doubt he silently cursed the sound of voices which had revealed to him another's presence, which was the indisputable proof of collusion, of a furtive arrival of another after his own departure, of his lady's falsity, of an outrage done to their quiet and tranquil happiness. But at least, he did have some sort of an advantage over the offenders: he had got them there, pinned down, and if he knocked at the window seeking admission it would be he who would be in the position of victor, because she would be the one who had been caught, who would be dumbfounded, shamed, and compelled to find refuge in lies, the nature of which he could not imagine, because it would be she and her partner, not he, who had been duped and cheated. He was armed now with a piece of factual knowledge in this painful teasing mystery. He thought, 'Well, anyway, I have learned this, I know this.' Her private life might be something about which he was ignorant, something which had slipped through his fingers, but now chance like a net cast at random, had brought part of it to the surface. He felt faintly ashamed at the idea of knocking, of showing that he had returned, but, at the same time, could not help wishing that they should be aware of his presence, should realize that he now knew everything. Besides, though the certainty that all these things were going on without his knowledge, things in which he was not to participate, things in a sense conceived as actions done in hostility to him, troubled him, he felt that, by the mere fact of his having witnessed them, of his having caught the guilty parties by surprise, would, no matter how deeply ashamed he might be, no matter how large a portion of embarrassment he might have to endure, at least have had the effect of stripping away the mystery. He decided that he would knock at the shutter. His heart was thumping as it does when some great change is about to take place in us—and that was precisely what was about to happen to him, because he felt that at the sight of her thus caught in the act, his pain was about to be transformed into confusion, into anger, into self-loathing, into hatred of a life which had suddenly lost all its charm.

He was conscious of a feeling not far removed from pleasure as he thought that he was about to see with his eyes what so far he had only deduced from the light showing through the shutters, from the sound of voices coming from the open window as they talked while no doubt they were undressing. Both light and voices were as painful now to him as when he had first become aware of them because there could be no doubt of their meaning: 'Of course she was expecting somebody, that somebody is there.' But love, which focuses on the person of the beloved so strong a beam of passion, awakens through the medium of jealousy—which is so to speak, love's other face—a wild curiosity as soon as we realize that she is not wholly ours, that maybe she is wholly another's, an irresistible desire to know every detail of what she is doing, and this feeling of curiosity now turned for Jean a fragment of her secret life, a hitherto concealed page of an actuality of which he had been made aware by the sight of a lamplit room, into something of such enormous interest that, though it might cause him pain, it did all

the same give him a certain intellectual satisfaction. He knew perfectly
well that what he was about to do would merely make him an object
of detestation to her, would at most by reason of his shamefaced return,
put her at a disadvantage—but what did that matter? We often rate the
immediate satisfaction of imperative desire, when to procure it depends
only upon ourselves, when, to that end we have not to go through a
complicated series of preparations the need for which has the effect of
making us lose interest—we often rate I say the certainty of immediate
satisfaction above greater and more durable pleasures to which we can
attain only by waiting. We almost all of us, reap untimely in the blade
crops which when ripe would have yielded a splendid harvest. With
beating heart he knocked. He heard someone come to the window and
begin to open the shutters. Then, satisfied by the thought that she would
know he had not been deceived, that she had been caught, and so as to
give the impression that he attached no particular importance to the
discovery, and did not intend to wait even until she had pushed the
shutters open, he said, "Don't bother; don't open the shutters; I just
happened to be passing and seeing your light thought that perhaps you
might not be feeling well." But the shutter was suddenly thrown wide,
and an elderly gentleman appeared in the window. Another elderly
gentleman was with him. For a moment Jean lost his self-assurance.
The first elderly gentleman said, "I'm afraid I have no idea whom I am
speaking to." He realized then what had happened. The room, now
that he could see it plainly, was wholly strange to him. He had chosen
the wrong window! This was not hers at all. Hers was the third
one down, and was completely dark. When he came to visit her at
night the only thing he had to guide him was the lamp she had left
shining to show him that she had come home. Having seen a small lit
window, and prepared by jealousy to believe that he *would* find it lit,
he had not doubted for a moment that the one he had seen was the
window of her room.

He made his apologies and walked away. He returned home in a
somewhat sheepish state of mind. He did not tell her of the incident.
He kept to himself the new mood of doubt and anguish which had
assailed him. It had in fact turned out to be altogether baseless, but
logically, given certain circumstances, it might have been, could still be,
amply justified. Then his natural sweetness where she was concerned
smothered the more recent impression under those quite contrary
feelings which were usual with him. Still whenever she said to him, "I

shan't be able to see you tonight," he was conscious of a small but
painful stab, and though he replied that really it didn't matter, relapsed
into a melancholy and apathetic mood, leaving her to wonder at the
change in him, though never guessing its cause.

There was a charming man whom she had got to know, whose
praises she was never tired of singing, whom she went to see. Jean never
visited her in the afternoons. One afternoon, however, he did go to
her house, rang the bell, heard a sound, then rang again, but nobody
came to the door. She probably had someone with her he thought—
felt a sudden wish to disturb them, and rapped on the glass panel.
There was still no answer. He went away, but came back again two
hours later. She told him that she had been in when he rang, but had
been sleeping. She had run after him she said, but he had vanished; if
she had heard him she would have opened the door. He did not however point out that she was contradicting herself. He felt the pricking
of curiosity, wanted to hear what she would say next, wanted to hear
her, quite probably, lie to him. He felt that it was the truth of all these
details that he in some odd way felt pleasure in, wanted to know, and
could not, though they were there before him clumsily taking shape
under the pressure of his melancholy inquisitiveness. What seemed to
him to be most revealing was her apparent annoyance at not having
been able to admit him on the one occasion when he had come to see
her during the day. She really did seem to be deeply grieved, and spoke
sadly, though there was no sufficient reason for sadness since after all,
he was with her now. It was as though beneath the sadness there lurked
some kind of annoyance, as though she had been guilty of a bad action,
as though she were suffering from the necessity of having to lie to him
about a complicated situation, almost as though she were thinking that
she ought to apologize for what she had done all the while that she was
telling him she had done something quite different. He suggested that
he should come back in an hour's time, but from this she dissuaded
him. He took no particular notice. For when events are concealed
from us, it is only with difficulty that the patently false awakens our
suspicions, that we realize the truth to be precisely what we had
imagined it to be. For the truth is not solely determined by the
possibilities with which our imagination plays, but by an anterior reality
about which we know nothing.

He came back in the evening. But she said that she was feeling less
well than she had done earlier, and gave him some letters to post.

He left her, took a cab, and went home. Just as he got there he remembered the letters. He walked to the nearest box and slipped them in, looking at the addresses on the envelopes as he did so. All but one bore the names of women. The exception was addressed to the charming man whom, just now, she seemed to be seeing so frequently. He kept it in his hand. He thought, 'If I knew what was inside this envelope, I should know how she addresses him, and what she says.' He went home, but he had kept the last letter, and, as soon as he was in his room, held it close to a candle flame. At first he could make out nothing. After a while he succeeded in reading the last few lines through the thin paper of the envelope, and saw with pleasure that the concluding formula was quite ordinary and unemotional. All the same, he would very much have liked to read the whole letter. No matter how insignificant it would have interested him. He had to steady the card, which was slipping about inside the envelope, to move it slightly each time he had read a word, so that the words following should not be made illegible by the double thickness of the flap. But he found this method of reading unproductive. The letter seemed to be about something which had nothing to do with love, something which concerned the writer's father. She had written, in one of the phrases which he could decipher, "It was just as well that I . . ." but he could not quite get the hang of what it was that it was just as well that she had done. Then, all of a sudden two letters which he had not been able to read, showed up distinctly, and the whole sentence made sense. "It was just as well that I opened the door, it was my father."

Opened the door!—then he *had* been there when Jean knocked! She had got rid of him—which explained the sound he had heard. He could now read the whole letter, could understand why she had apologized for behaving in so off-hand a manner to the man she was writing to, why she mentioned the fact that he had left his cigarette-case behind him—which was precisely what she had said to Jean, too, though *then* she had added, "If you had left something of yourself as well, I would have kept and treasured it." Those words did not appear in the letter, nor did it contain any endearment, anything, any allusion which might lead him to suppose that more had occurred than was made clear. Still why had she not opened the door? Why had she written, "It was just as well I did: it was my father"? If nothing had been happening at that moment, how was her not opening the door to be explained? He stood there feeling bewildered and wretched, but holding the truth in his hand, having come on it by chance through the transparent window of an envelope which, because of her belief in him, because of her delicacy (that quality in her of belief, of distinction, was one of her greatest charms) should have protected it, but had in fact made it possible for him to catch a glimpse of one tiny part of her secret life, of that life which remained concealed from him.

The truth of the matter is that what *happens* in a man's life is without interest, and to the scholar and the artist seems merely accidental, so long as it is stripped of those feelings which are the constituents of poetry. But jealousy and love, which subordinate the life of our mind and spirit to a single person, give not only to our dreams, as I have already pointed out, an individual character, but to that also which is the object of our thoughts. Consequently, in the degree to which they have reference to the person who, at any given moment of our inner life, has assumed the position of a ruling influence, events *do* momentarily acquire a certain interest which makes of them things we want to discover and to know, with the result that trust, espionage, curiosity become in some sort the means of knowing her who at that time is the object of our thoughts, and that knowledge being of an individual can only by an individual be acquired. What is to us unknown, that something round which our thoughts prowl and snuffle, is an accident, the individual realization of the events in the life of an individual. At no other moment of a man's inner life is that the case. What *really* she has been doing, compared with what she tells us she has been doing, what those things are *in themselves*, or as they are to the eye of God—her relations for instance with X—— —*that* is the question we endlessly put to ourselves, *that* it is which is truly of interest to our thinking mind which receives light only as it reaches us from that individual. What *is*, what *has been* today, not as she tells it to us, but *in itself*, as it would appear to another, to God, *that* is what we want to know, *that* is the unknown to which the mind cannot attain. This was what to some small extent the letter, like a sort of cross-section of the unknown, had revealed to Jean, laying before his eyes a tiny portion of a real life, the secret of an event which, in all probability, he would never have known otherwise, which she would never have told him, which formed part of that unknown to which it was most unlikely he would ever have obtained access, which chance, and a sure means, had suddenly flooded with light, had brought to his knowledge, had drawn from the darkness of her shuttered room.

Until that moment, even though he had thought it to be within the bounds of possibility that some man had in fact been visiting her, he had been quite unable to say on whom it was that his suspicions rested. He could perfectly well have attributed the fact of his not having been admitted to her house to her wish that he should not meet somebody who perhaps did not like him. All he had noticed was the contradiction implied in her story of having run after him, of having heard him rap on the panel of the door, and the look of sadness in her face (which might well have been due to her having actually been expecting X——, and her dread lest he might turn up at any moment, which had resulted in a nervous anxiety, which, in turn, had caused the sadness of her expression). Actually there had been other contradictions in her version of the affair, and of this she must have been aware, so that the sadness could perfectly well have been accounted for by the difficulty she had been experiencing in inventing a plausible excuse. But how could Jean have known this? We may have full knowledge of a person's character, yet be unable to reconstruct the circumstances so long as the actuality of the event escapes us, so long as what has been differs from hypotheses, no matter how ingenious—from misgivings, no matter how plausible, from calculations based on knowledge, no matter how perfect. Take the case of a thoroughly sensual man who considers all women merely in terms of bed. How can we ever be sure that this or that specific woman is not just a perfectly innocent acquaintance? In the case of another, with whom he spends hours every evening, you may be prepared to swear that there is "more in it than that" as seems clear from the way they behave—though the truth may be that there is *not* more in it than that, that he entertains for her, what you would never have believed of him, a purely Platonic passion. True, the opposite view, that there is "nothing in it" etc. may be no more accurate, since it is impossible to apply the laws of reason to the contingencies of the actual. When Jean knew that the person who had been in the room with her, who had made his escape, was X—— he was plunged into a riot of jealousy, whereas the fact that she might also have been deceiving him when she said "it was my father", and the hope of one day telling her that he knew this, had the effect of diminishing his anger.

Just as all those persons who invited Jean and Madame S—— together, treated them as an accepted couple, and gave him unhoped-for pleasure by asking the two of them to spend the summer months as guests in their country houses, seemed to him to be good and kind, roused his tenderest feelings, and drew from him words of high commendation—so too those who invited Madame S—— and X—— together (at the end of a few weeks the two groups might well turn out to be identical) made him melancholy and malicious, and their gaiety with Madame S——, their pressing invitations to X——, aroused in him the sort of bitterness which makes everything that happens around us seem hateful, so that we become pitiless in stressing all that is ugly and absurd in them. Emotional persons are only too ready to find all the excellencies in those they like, every conceivable fault in those they happen to dislike. For a poet who brings reason to his dealings with life, this state of affairs results in rational panegyrics or diatribes, seemingly based on intellectual observation, though the real flimsiness of this assumption becomes immediately apparent when as the result of a quarrel or a reconciliation the whole pictures changes. But in the lover these feelings are even stronger. At any moment a hostess may raise us to the seventh heaven, or inflict upon us the most intolerable torments by for instance insisting on sending Madame S—— and X—— home together and saying to us, "Good night, I'm afraid you'll have a lonely drive." When that happens, the very same smiles in which we found such pleasure, the easy converse, the daily invitations, which were a source to us of such sweet delight, so that we felt convinced that *her* house, *her* conversation, *her* friends, together went to make up the only small world in which it was possible to live agreeably, and found ourselves growing sentimental on the subject of her goodness of heart, her intelligence, her general niceness—the very same smiles, the very same invitations, when they result in handing over the object of our passion to some hated rival, stab us to the heart and appear in our eyes as antipathetic, odious and false (La Bruyère: Nothing more resembles true friendship than a relationship cultivated in the interests of love). We talk then only in superlatives and decide that such and such a person has behaved to us Nobly—or Ignobly. In actual fact nobility has been entirely absent not only from their behaviour but from our feelings. Behaviour that was *merely* noble would never have aroused in us so ardent an enthusiasm. The prospect of meeting Madame S—— again in some country house to which we too have been invited, or the fact of seeing her carried off to another house where we shall not be present, but X—— will, awakes in us feelings so lively that they can find expression in exaggerated eloquence, with the result that we find ourselves using words like magnanimity and nobility which leave a profound impression on those to whom we happen to be talking. Meanwhile each time that Madame S—— does not want to see us, seems embarrassed by our presence, or preoccupied, we sink into a morass of melancholy, and flog our minds in an attempt to find a way of doing something about it. Anything that could surely bring about the deaths of those she is fond of, or even her own death, would fill us with delight. One day Jean happened to meet a relation of Madame S—— who spoke to him of the true and deep affection she felt for him, how much she loved him. Never before had Jean been conscious of so warm a feeling of friendship for this particular relation. But his sense of happiness was due not only to this welcome piece of news. For a moment his jealousy collapsed, simply because someone had told him how much Madame S—— made of him in his absence and that at a time when he imagined that he counted for nothing with her. Furthermore as when one closes a novel and finds oneself back again in real life, his love had been changed into a feeling of friendship which found emotional satisfaction in this sort of recipro-ity, demanding no more, and instead of delighting in a love which the world at large would have regarded as blameworthy, rejoiced in the knowledge that his friendship with Madame S—— was known, approved and strengthened by the good wishes of other people.

Such a development is but an interruption of love. Sometimes it is the loved one herself who feeling for us not love but a great friendship, melts our hearts by making perfect friendship momentarily take the place of unhappy passion. Sometimes this interruption occurs as the result of a terrible concatenation of circumstances—family rows, ruin, anger on the part of the lady's father and mother, who associate one's love with a number of intensely disagreeable things, declare that the whole business was never more than a baseless fantasy, and state categorically that the truth is something quite different, that it is time to see things in their proper light. It is as though while reading *The Three Musketeers* we had thought we were going to the Elysée only to find that we had on the contrary turned up in a police station. But the truth of the matter is that the life of family rows, debts and loss of temper is no more real than the other, and it is books like *De l'Amour* etc. that show us the true nature of the emotion of love. But the fear which continually haunts us that, by confessing our love we may bore the loved one, by being sincere may lose something of the glamour with which she had endowed us, by admitting our jealousy may make her coquettish, turns the letters we write and the words we speak into a continual lie which creates an abyss between appearance and reality.

There are times when memory takes sides so forcefully against us in this matter of love, that though we can visualize quite clearly any number of persons who mean nothing to us, we cannot *see* the woman we love, as frequently happens in the case of dead persons of whom in life we have been superlatively fond. It is then that, should absence be prolonged, love seems to have come to an absolute and irremediable end. We realize with a feeling of regret that we are no longer in contact with that strange power in Nature which though it may make us suffer, does at least set running through our lives that real, that curious current of emotion which we can never "turn on" by our own unaided efforts. When that has happened and a name read by chance provokes us to sudden jealousy, we are happy in the thought that we still love, just as the last mosquito, or a few days of torrid heat which makes us sweat, give us the delightful feeling that summer is not yet over. But it is sad to think that memory, heart and imagination all function so badly that they can no more let us visualize, except imperfectly, the face of the beloved, than in the letters where we deliberately dress up our feelings in order to prolong her own, we can really show her what they are. We find it impossible to *see* her, impossible to feel any longer the sweet ecstacies of love. It is only in action that they as it were give themselves away to us, as we give ourselves away to her. If we see the name of Monsieur X—— mentioned in such a way as to lead us to suppose that he is in the same place as Madame S—— we are conscious of a stab of pain. If Madame S—— were in Paris and sent word that she would like us to go and see her, at a time when thirty other enticing females were asking the same thing of us, the probability is that Madame S—— would not be the one we should visit. In her letters expressions which coming from anybody else would leave us cold, imply a closeness of relationship between some quite insignificant face and our own, give us a delicious thrill by seeming to brighten her eyes with a look of tenderness meant for us alone, and almost make us feel the constriction about her heart. And so it is that we want to be in the right mood for reading those letters, want to be able to savour them properly, for we know that they will for a while at least seem strangely to change the conditions working within our life, strangely but how sweetly!—and because that experience comes to us so wholly from those deep wells of Nature which we cannot touch, that we feel remembering it, as we feel when we are conscious close to us of something in which Nature is strongly active, as, for example, when at no matter what age, in the darkness we see a wall close at hand showing suffused by moonlight, and a pattern of leaves painted upon it with quite extraordinary vividness, or when, if we have been talking, or are wandering in that silence where light and shadow seem the only speaking things, we see the moon in an unexpected quarter of the sky laying a sheen of silver on the sea where but a moment before the surface was black and lustreless, and the smacks moving from the harbour at an hour when most of the world is going to bed, pass the jetty and are suddenly a moment later bathed in the full radiance of the moon.

Just as in the fantasies of love, be they happy or tinged with sadness, we draw our poetry all from one person, so in the nerve-wracked miseries of jealousy, truth consists for us in events, in actions and in feelings which are one and all bound up with a single individual.

*

Jean's desires, like those of all men in love, were concentrated on the impossible.

We know perfectly well that when we are not loved the working of our imagination in relation to some one person, and our innumerable longings, have no relation to reality. Then, short of being able to give some sort of objective truth to our hopes, as happens when we find our approaches favourably entertained by the woman whom we love, we can at least find happiness when we come on them in poetry and in music. And since we cannot separate the feelings which we there find expressed so forcefully that they make our own love seem more real because poetry and music have the power to assure us that it is more than a mere personal dream, we cannot dissociate them from her who has caused them and come to look on all those lovers' vows, all those passionate outbursts which we find in poetry and in music, as memories of a shared love which may really have existed between our mistress and our self, or which should have existed, so that we play those airs over and over again, and repeat those verses, wiping the tears from our eyes, as when we read over old love letters from the woman who has since betrayed us. At such times love-poetry and the music of love

seem to us to be superior to all other poetry, all other music: or at least
so we maintain, though the assertion may not completely express our
thoughts. But the expression of that judgment gives release to a happiness which underlies the words. Just as somebody who has been clumsily
bumped into, exclaims, "What a dam' fool thing not to look where
you're going!" we more often than not say things which are not so
much the expression of a genuine thought, as pure nervous reaction,
the putting into words of a feeling of pleasure or of pain. When we
are in love we find our chiefest joy in haunting those who can in some
sense bring us closer to the loved one. They talk to us of her, and we
find an infinite happiness in tasting on their lips the charm of our
mistress and the echo of her words. That happiness we express, should
for example her life be spent in the world of medicine, by saying, "I
must say it is a great deal more interesting to live among people like
that than . . . etc." or, should she be ignorant: "Is there any great pleasure
to be got from being educated?—I very much doubt it. I attach more
importance . . . etc." Similarly the poets of love, the musicians of love,
who are also persons who can speak to us of her, make us say, "Those
for me are the finest lines in the whole body of French poetry," when
all we really mean is that we hear them with pleasure because they
provide nourishment for our hopes, and strengthen our love with
proofs drawn, not from the nature of any one loved person, but from
the very nature of love and hope, having been written a hundred
years ago.

     When too we are in love and intent on attaining a purely egotistical
goal, for which purpose we employ all the resources of casuistry, how
often do we not write letters in which we say, "There is nothing more
wholly infamous, nothing which so defaces the creature whom God
has made in His own image, than lying"? which merely means, not
that we think the statement true, but that we are particularly concerned that *she* shall not lie to *us*. Jean did not admit to Madame S——
that he had read a letter of hers through the envelope, and, since he
did not wish to tell her the real manner in which he had learned that a
young man had been to see her, told her that he had been informed of
the occurrence by somebody else. In other words he lied. The fact
however that he had lied did not keep the tears out of his eyes when
he informed her that lying was the only really atrocious crime, any
more than it prevented him from telling a thousand lies, that same
evening, to persons from whom he wished to conceal the fact that he

had been to see the object of his passion. The emotional exaltation which leads us to say fine things for the sole purpose of attaining a purely selfish end, is at the very opposite pole to literary composition which strives to express sincerely what we feel. Thence doubtless arises the antagonism between art and life: and people who write too many letters have too many sentimental interests in their lives (the opposite is true of Flaubert) and consequently less talent, especially those who talk too much. In the case of Musset, when in *Fantasio* (I can never read that play without wanting to be in love with somebody) or in his own person, he says the sort of things in which there is a hint of saintliness, which gives a touch of extra pleasure to his love—that same fault is apparent. But lies of that type, in so far as they faithfully reflect the sentiments of someone who being in love speaks lyingly, have by that very fact a certain truthfulness, a certain charm.

During this particular phase of love, books about love have an enormous interest for us, and novels too, because we feel that the author can show us how we can make ourselves beloved. When we are ill we think that some particular doctor can cure us. In this way do novels appeal to us because we think that they can teach us how to succeed in love, just as we may understand a chapter of history as a lesson in politics. For as soon as we learn that this or that man, who was regarded with suspicion, managed to keep accusation at bay etc., we believe that we can from his case extract some general maxim, as "to keep accusation at bay, etc." But it is not only the poets and musicians who by giving us the impression that some other life is fused with our own, when we understand, by "some other life" that of the woman whom we love, can increase the pressure of our love, it is often the loved one in person who as the result of something she has done, of giving or accepting some object, of using this word or that, of an adventure in common which has brought us closer together, of hearing some piece of music in one another's company, of having a shared secret, of being taken by a casual passer-by for a pair of lovers. Actually our pleasure corresponds to our illusions and not to their intentions. For when one is not loved, the presents one receives or persuades the loved one to accept, the words spoken, the situations with which life confronts us, none of them contain a morsel of real love. Theocritus says that there are no magic powders which can induce love, nor is there anything else which has that property. None the less we become the willing slaves of such illusions, though at any moment they may be withdrawn from us.

For instance one of Madame S——'s former lovers, now an old man, was walking with her one day, and Jean, knowing that she did not now love him the least little bit, was a willing companion in their walk. The lady accidentally used the old gentleman's Christian name, whereupon the old gentleman, with tears in his eyes, said to Jean, "How sweet it is to hear her addressing me like that: it has done me all the good in the world." Then they remembered a tune they once had heard when they were together, and had asked a gipsy band to play again and again. Actually in the words spoken by the lady there *had* been a tiny trace of love. The old gentleman was transported with delight, and Jean realized just how much that was purely subjective, and at the same time hideous, there was in the pleasure he was feeling (hideous perhaps because it had in a flash revealed to him the vanity of love), and that all these things the Christian name, the music etc. contained not a shadow of love's reality, and only in the old gentleman's imagination seemed to constitute a bond between the lady and himself—like the hoarding of old photographs etc., whereas in truth only love can contain love.

2. *Françoise's Friends*

Twice or three times a week about half past nine he would quickly break away from her. The door-bell had just sounded. The new arrival would turn out to be Saint-Géron, or Griffon, or Vésale, usually Vésale, who since he lived alone had more freedom of movement than the others. While he was getting rid of his hat and coat in the hall, Jean would fling himself on Françoise, and hurriedly, carefully, draw from her lips some stored essence of herself, so that while the presence of a third forced them to remain apart, he could have the taste of her skin upon his lips and silently seek it out with an exploring tongue. They would hear the sound of Vésale's steps approaching the door of the boudoir. Françoise would sharply push Jean away but he would suddenly remember that he had forgotten to kiss her on the neck. There it was close to him, but he could not precisely recall its fragrance, and would run to her again, kiss her hastily on the neck, and then as the door began to open, sit down at a safe distance, being careful to say so that the favour of that kiss should not be debited against him, "That was much too quick: I scarcely had time for a sniff."

Sometimes Vésale arrived with Saint-Géron in tow. Dr Potain, saying that he was the best of his house physicians, had recommended him to the Marquise de Saint-Géron, whose wasting sickness needed more careful watching than he could spare sufficient time to supply, and Vésale frequently chose the evening, after dinner was over for his professional visits. Guy de Saint-Géron got ready while the other was with the Marquise, and on these occasions the two men turned up together at Françoise's house. Vésale brought his violin, Saint-Géron his 'cello. Soon Griffon who was always rather late, because worn out by his exhausting labours in a big coal merchant's business he was in the habit of taking a nap after dinner, appeared with his flute. Although the three men were in different employments, and belonged to very different social circles, there existed between them the same harmony as music establishes between their three chosen instruments. Vésale was a full-fleshed Alsatian with a high colour and fair hair, a jovial level-headed doctor. Saint-Géron, whose mother was a Lucinge, had the cold beauty, the melancholy, olive-skinned type of face which gives to all the members of that family an almost Oriental look. Griffon was a southerner, and the feverish excitement of his daily avocations working on a naturally vivacious temperament had usually left him in a condition of nervous tension. Music no less powerfully than race or occupation had given to all three that special expression of high nobility which is to be found on the faces of those who habitually devote themselves to pleasures of a disinterested order. It was more especially in their eyes and in a certain gentleness of intonation when they spoke, that music had so to speak, established its hold and left the traces of its power. Between Vésale's blue and tranquil eyes, Saint-Géron's black disdainful ones, and Griffon's, which were gay and flickering, between the timbre of their voices and the peculiarities of their accent, there perpetually floated as it were something of that life of the spirit which music releases in us. There was in their eyes a trace of that same calm emotion which emanates from those who seated under a bright lamp savour in the intoxication of their music a sadness which is full of joy, a deliberately produced agitation which they maintain by a feverish movement of bows and lips, which for all its restlessness has in it an element of calm, since they seek in it nothing for themselves, and are not at its mercy. This was particularly noticeable in Vésale, whose corpulence, handsome though somewhat coarse features, and slightly lumbering gaiety gave evidence of a life devoted, for the most part, to material concerns. But even when he was drinking beer or playing at dominoes, one could somehow see in his eyes—for nothing of a man's inner life ever proceeds without leaving some trace upon his fleshly envelope—that beauty of expression which told of his efforts to find in the object of his adoration, urged by a sort of faith mingled with anxiety, something over and above mere loveliness, something in which he believed but did not really think he could discover.

Sometimes there were other people present at these evening gatherings. Often there was no music because one of the executants was absent or had come without his instrument, or because the mood of the company was better attuned to conversation. At first Françoise had been in the habit of saying, "I think you all know my friend Monsieur Santeuil," but it was not long before Jean struck up an intimacy with the young men on his own account. In the lives of each of them

Françoise was set on as high a level, occupied as much room, as did music. She played almost as well as they did, seemed to them to be far more intelligent, and, perhaps because though there could be no doubt about her intelligence, had the additional advantage of her glamour as a woman and of a charming and authoritative character. It pleased her to tell them that never in the whole course of her life had she met anyone as clever as Jean, and consequently they had for him a sort of admiring sympathy, and a deep respect which they felt was due to one who though he enjoyed some degree of celebrity in the world of fashion, yet preferred to spend his evenings listening to their playing and applauding their efforts with a friendliness which touched them the more deeply because they knew that there was no lack of objects on which it could exercise itself. Jean was perfectly well aware of what Vésale, Saint-Géron, Griffon and the others felt for him as a man who stood deservedly high in Françoise's esteem. Their company therefore would have been charming on that account alone, even if—quite apart from it—he had not found that it had a stimulating effect upon him for the reasons I have already mentioned, and because their general out-look and their various talents deeply interested him. As soon as he said good evening to them he was conscious of that feeling of untrammelled satisfaction which comes to a naturally friendly man when he has an opportunity to exercise his friendliness freely and undetermined by considerations of intrigue, politeness, or self-interest. He feels at ease in the presence of those with whom he need be at no pains to think about the impression he is making, to "show up" well, or to make himself acceptable to the company, when, at liberty to let his silence, his gaiety, his remarks or his questions, go their own gait, and, in a cordial atmosphere, he is conscious that all that is best in him is naturally coming to the surface. And so it was that lolling in an arm-chair or standing in front of the fireplace, and now and again giving Françoise's fingers a furtive squeeze when the others were not looking, Jean listened to the music, wrote his letters, or exchanged with Françoise, Saint-Géron, Griffon and Vésale, comments on people they all knew and felt much the same about, generally expressed in terms of subtle appreciation. When those of whom they were talking happened to be more than usually stupid, they found consolation in laughter and that pleasurable enjoyment which comes when one knows that the slightest hint will be taken and enjoyed, a state of affairs which is occasionally to be found when an intelligent mother is talking to her

son, or two brothers to each other, so that an indefinable climate of
amusement is at once created. "I used to go every day to see Madame
S——" said Jean on one occasion to Vésale, "for the sole purpose of
discussing with her the idiocy of our contemporaries. But it has
assumed such overwhelming proportions that I find myself compelled
to come here sometimes as often as five times a day." If he said something more than usually amusing, or made some profound comment
on the subject of music, he noticed that Françoise displayed for the
benefit of her friends, as though to let them share in it, that admiring
expression which at those moments showed in her eyes, and seemed to
take possession of all her features. She had a way too, peculiarly her
own, of pretending not to have heard, though indulging in anticipatory
laughter when the remark was amusing, so as to make sure that it
would be repeated and enjoyed still more by the others—a trick which
made Jean's happiness burn with an even brighter flame.

*

Ever since the second of these evenings, Jean had made a point of
always leaving with Vésale, since they both lived in more or less the
same part of Paris. They talked with the shyness, the sincerity of men
who are still to some extent strangers, but feel each in the other a power
of attraction, and would like to know one another better. On either
side there was a display of those little attentions which are never to be
found between men who have been friends for a long while with the
result that their relationship is marked by a sort of rough and ready
comradeship. The words they exchanged, packed full with intimacy
and deep meaning, had even for the one who was speaking an emotional
quality. He felt that in what he had just said he had revealed something
of himself, and his voice trembled like a glass jar which a too hot liquid
has faintly cracked.

Saint-Géron's name was mentioned. "Ah, now, *he's* a good friend
and no mistake: you won't find many men with better hearts. There
is no secret I would not confide to him, and I know that he would
never speak of me in any but the kindliest way." Many years later Jean
was one evening walking home from the house of a dancer with whom
he was much taken, in the company of a friend—the Director of the
Châtelet Theatre, where she was then performing. This friend said how
much Mademoiselle Zita admired Jean and in the cordial atmosphere

thus engendered, they began to chat more freely. Jean asked him what he thought of an actor who had dropped in for a moment that evening at Zita's, and been introduced to him. "Oh!" said the other "I have never come across a more charming and delightful creature: he knows that he can always count on me, just as I know that I can count on him." These words recalled to Jean, as an identical piece of harmony can recall a forgotten air, the evening, already far distant, when he had been walking home with Vésale, of whom, since then, he had entirely lost sight. 'There is scarcely a human being,' he reflected, 'for whom there does not exist some other human being in the security of whose friendship he can install his heart as in a refuge made for it. Each thinks that he has met a unique fellow-mortal, but the grain of pollen which finds its way into the ovary never knows that every grain of pollen is destined to find its ovary. The beauty of these friendships resides, not as those who enjoy them think, in some mysterious and precious gift of Destiny but in a kindly law of Nature.' Then Jean remembered how Saint-Géron used to make fun of certain laughable tricks of Vésale's mother. Once even in the presence of a woman whom both loved, they had mocked at each other not without a note of bitterness. But thinking of their linked lives as a whole, so far as they had been shown to him in the brief moment during which his destiny had like a shooting star shed its light upon them, he felt compelled to admit that Vésale had not been wrong in believing that Saint-Géron was indeed the friend he had believed him to be. Anyone, like every terrestrial body, would sooner or later have given evidence of some weakness or some fault. Thinking now of his own friends, he decided that not one of them was exempt from that law. There were days when it seemed to him that he meant nothing to Daltozzi. Even his mother, his own mother, had once accused him of being a snob.

3. *The Agate Marble*

Jean wanted to send Françoise a tiny pair of opera-glasses. Thinking that he would like to add to the gift, and looking round for something in which he might enclose them, his eye was caught by a pretty bag of light-coloured embroidery which since the days of his childhood had always hung from a corner of the mantelpiece. He loosened the cord which closed its neck without difficulty. But when he held the bag in his hand he felt something rolling about at the bottom of it. It was an agate marble. He at once remembered that it was the very marble which Marie Kossichef had one day given him in the Champs-Elysées. Since no one in that distant past had ever given him money, he could not buy marbles for himself, and if he was ever made a present of marbles they were always stone ones, opaque, and of one colour only, the type of marble which cost no more than a sou. Set apart in a bowl by themselves, in which only the rich and the great dared handle them, compare them, and choose, lay the marbles of agate costing six sous apiece, large, transparent marbles, with light in them as soft as a kindly glance, and these had awakened in Jean admiration, desire, and fear of a marvellous and forbidden beauty. He would never even have dreamed of possessing one. The only boys who had them were those with whom he was never allowed to play, boys in long trousers, who smoked cigarettes. At that tender age, before one has felt the lure of any temptation, it is the most strenuously forbidden vices that loom largest in our imagination, though we know nothing about them. For a very long time the smoking of cigarettes had seemed to Jean to be a form of corruption so repulsive that, during his first year at school, when he was telling his mother what went on there, not with the object of scaring her, but simply in order to give her some idea of the importance of his new life, of the great gulf that separated it from the life he led at home, he once said to her, "Our Professor is most frightfully decent, but he leads a ghastly life. There have been complaints about him, but I don't think he'll be sacked because he's so jolly popular, but his health won't stand the strain for long. He does things

I couldn't speak about, not even to you. Just fancy—there's scarcely a moment when he isn't smoking a cigarette," and fearing that he might have gone too far, he added, "I haven't seen him doing it myself, but all the chaps in my form talk about it."

Though he never aspired to the possession of one of the agate marbles, he could not keep himself from looking at them. In later life —in the windows of jewellers' shops, in the show-cases of museums, on women's necks and in their hair, he saw many diamonds, many rubies, many pearls. But they made little impression on him. Their glitter tired his eyes, but never really attracted his attention. Never did any Crown Jewel cause him even faintly to feel that mysterious craving, that frightened wonder, which had been aroused in him at the booth which stood close to the wooden horses behind the lemonade stall and the playground, by the sight of the blue, the yellow, the smiling agate marbles. Then a day came when Marie Kossichef gave him one. He was for ever kissing it. He talked to it, asking whether Marie loved it. He moistened it with his tears, murmuring: "You're going to be with me for always." At night he took it to bed with him, and, before going to sleep, tucked it away under his pillow, clasped it in his hand, or rolled it to the bottom of the bed, and played with it with his feet. And when he had to go down to dinner, especially if Marie[1] or some other stranger, who did not know *his* Marie and would have laughed at his love for her, was dining with his parents, he took the marble with him, kept it on his knees, in his pocket, or up his sleeve, and as he went through the gesture of putting a piece of bread into his mouth, kissed it secretly. Had it been a scrap of wood that she had picked up and given him, he would have acted in just the same way. But the agate marble was far sweeter in his eyes. In the first place because it was so precious he persuaded himself that Marie must indeed love him to have made him such a present, and in adoring it what he was really doing was sanctifying her kindness to him and his belief in her, the tangible proof of which he tried to lay against his heart. And then so inaccessible till now, so mysterious, so much more beautiful than any marble that he knew, different from all other marbles because of the yellow glint which seemed like a watchful eye deep within it, this particular marble became for him a sort of living creature, at once a thing of this world and a supernatural being for ever linked with Marie's person or rather with his own to which it had become attached

---

[1] Charles Marie, the Minister. (Editor's note.)

as a result of *her* will and wish, given to him to be a slave, a pet animal, a slave to whom he constantly entrusted commissions for her, of whom he ceaselessly asked news of her, questioning him about her love, a slave, who without leaving his pocket could run on messages and reunite the separated lovers. This favourite slave of hers and his was also for him a silent fairy, silent but endowed with power and magic, or at the very least like a star in the sky, a tiny star held prisoner in the marble, a minute gleam of light which he could hold in his hand, but could not touch, as far away as those in the high heavens which seem able to understand the words we speak and carry them to the loved one's ears, one of those stars which seem all smilingly to tell us to be patient, who at that very same moment may perhaps be receiving from her vows of the same nature which they cannot tell to us, though their sweet tranquillity is in some sort a mysterious pledge of her devotion.

And so it was that once again Jean found his agate marble, slipped it into a drawer of his desk, and went off to ask his mother's maid to put a stitch in the neck of the bag so as to keep the opera-glasses from falling out. That done he left the parcel with Françoise's concierge, but on returning home did not open the drawer where he had left the marble. For he had found no pleasure in the sight of it, and because it rolled about making an abominable noise, each time the desk was moved, gave orders that it was to be thrown away. In the far-distant past, on evenings when he was oppressed with doubt, he used to say to himself, 'If a day ever comes when I shall see Marie no longer, if I ever succeed in forgetting her, if she ceases to mean anything to me, all will not be lost. I shall still have my dear little marble. You beautiful thing! I will keep you all my life long, and I shall not have loved for two years in vain.' It was not on the day when he had had the marble thrown away that those lovely dreams were destroyed. Though for many years the marble had reposed within the bag, it had long ceased to have any charm for him, and was as though already lost, since he never troubled to look at it, had even forgotten its existence, and would have got rid of it, without the slightest compunction years ago. When the very body of her whom once we loved has lost, since our feelings no longer see it as a consecrated thing, the magic it used to hold for us, why should we any longer keep an agate marble, a letter, or a ribbon? We live with our eyes turned to the future and when we seem still to find the old sweetness which once upon a time cast a charm upon our past, the reason is that that past still lives for us, that when we think of the future it is as though it is of it that we are thinking. A past like that is never truly old. It is the book given to us last summer by a mistress with whom we think that we shall still be in love next spring. And yet how dead it is compared with the rose she let us take from her but yesterday, though the rose itself is somewhat pale when we think of the words which she will speak to us tomorrow.

*

Jean went out for a breath of air now that the rain had stopped and the sun was rapidly drying the avenues. He felt sad in the knowledge that things which touched us once touch us no longer, that memories die because the past no longer holds a meaning for us. But when he reached the embankment he saw a clump of lovely trees motionless in the shade, with about them an air of infinite joy, but of quietness, too, which kept him from singing and leaping, and made him almost hold his breath and move on tip-toe. Their young tops were close together and wore their scattered coronals of shining leaves, all that remained of the once dense adornment all fresh but fifteen days before, seeming just newly born and so rich in texture that it was as though they had spread above their heads a single and unbroken canopy of lighter stuff over their motionless trunks, quivering gaily in the wind and sun. On the sunlit earth beneath lay the shadows of the leaves dark on the ground, and giving that impression of freshness, of a deep resplendent life which floating water-plants give to the surface of a stream. He walked as far as the parapet. Across the blue, translucent water of the nearer foreground he could see the sloping sand, visible for a little distance, while, farther from the bank, the water, though still blue, showed as murky, so that nothing could be seen but the deep and glittering colour of the surface, with the little waves, sparkling in the sunlight, playing together, running together, and leaning over now and again, blown by the wind. Out in the middle of the stream there lay, like a recess of bright, fair red, the shadow cast by the red prow of a boat at its moorings. The sun-drenched yet cool water lapped on the torrid sand, and it seemed to Jean that he could feel at one and the same moment the charm of this spot on the banks of the Seine, and the charm he had known upon the seashore where the sand was warm and dazzling, and the little rounded waves were clear as crystal, as once in old days he had known them on those blue afternoons when he had dipped his hands and splashed cool water on his forehead, seeming as he had listened to the transparent sea breaking on the shells of the beach, to be drinking down the freshness in great gulps and so quenching his thirst. And the thousands of wavelets driving along the river, playing together and mingling, gave him the same ravished sense of a life that had been innocent, enchanting, alert, gay and indefatigable, but also gentle and light, small as a dimple or a mouth, and infinite, never tiring, always renewed, coming to him in the eternal rustle of the little leaves puffed by the wind or left to droop, but ever shining, brilliant, gilded by the sun, under the sky's unchanging blue, and in the cooing of the pigeons which never ceased even in the shade.

He turned back and stood under the trees. Every so often the sun seemed to slip away like a shadow from his feet, even while the sky showed no less blue, the ground no less drenched in light. It was as though in a lighted room someone had extinguished a lamp close to him, and by this he knew that a cloud had drifted by, but only for a moment, before the sun came out again, growing every instant hotter and more hot, and once again began to warm his face and gaily to compete with the no less piercing radiance which he saw with his eyes. Then did it seem to Jean that he could feel the brilliant and deep-rooted joy of places turned to beauty as by a painter's fancy, drawn from the spreading, silent happiness which quivered all at once so freshly here beneath the trees, and elsewhere, too, over towards the shadowed Cours-la-Reine, and also at this very moment in the woods of Saint-Germain, as once when he was young and had gone to gather violets, if he grew too hot, he had sat down in the shade, and could hear with equal joy the silence and the song of birds which seemed to drift across him leaving him undisturbed, like children fondling a patriarch, both silence and song sweet beyond words. He felt happy, no longer now distressed to think that the past was dead for him, that the objects surviving from that far-off time held no more charm for him, and, in reality, had no more life. And this unreasoning joy was fundamentally reasonable. Of the things that charmed us once, things that we happen on again, it is not true to say that by their very presence they bring back to us, with the same, or perhaps with a still more, dreamlike and quivering delight, the mysterious magic of an earlier day? For what are the small black shadows dappling the ground in the shining pathway of the sun, like water-plants on a river, the early unfolding leaves of lilac drooping their sweet and delicate heads through the railings of suburban gardens, the huge old fruit trees, a witchery of white and red, come suddenly to blossom on the far side of a wall, like the apparition of fresh, intoxicating beauty aureoled in light and dazzling grace— what are all these things if not witnesses of childhood's Springtime, fragments from the memories of our earliest emotions which Nature woke in us, which have lost nothing of their power, which suddenly open our hearts to the coming of the same delicious bliss, letting us escape from the tyranny of the years and give ourselves wholly to Nature's magic, to the mysterious transformation of the seasons which bathe the things and incidents around us in a life that is greater than them, which we recognize from having once already seen them in the long distance of past years, which is no more part of our childhood than it is of our old age, but seems, for a moment, to show us the world in which we live, not as a mediocre thing that soon for us will end, a place of human and familiar life, but as a world eternal in itself, and young eternally, a place of mystery rich with incredible promises? Often above the secret corners of a little garden we see approach, thicken, and grow stationary, great banks of cloud, violet or black with impending storm, soon to be dissipated into vaguely outlined masses, like unknown continents, and starting off on distant voyages, withdrawing, melting into the saffron heaven of high summer, and great white clouds spreading over, melting into the blue zenith, hovering above the busy harvesters or grey clouds keeping pace with walking travellers, moving before them along the roads, skies of violet, yellow skies and blue, gigantic guests, passing Gods of the little garden on which for a moment they shed their brilliant, glittering light or ice-cold shade, blue, violet or yellow, tinted like the pansies which seem to have borrowed from them their colours and misty outlines, pansies which grow bright in the heat of the travelling sun, or tremble in the wind that heralds the rain which soon will come to moisten them.

4. *The Tuileries*

All through luncheon Jean looking out of the window could see the house-front opposite gay with sunlight as though decked for festival, and could guess without difficulty how the other houses in the row must be similarly dressed, with perhaps a little snow turned golden by the light still standing before their doors, like the last scaffoldings, traces of a city's labours, abandoned there because there has been no time left in which to move them and in the confusion of flags and fairy-lamps, they seem to sound an extra note of joy, to make part of the festival display against their will, like old people who have been forced by the young to enjoy themselves. Now and again he was suddenly dazzled by a flash of light which seemed to float about the room, mount to the ceiling and vanish. Someone on the fifth floor of the house opposite had closed a window, and a sunbeam slackly leaning on the window bar, had been seized with panic and was now flickering about the dining-room before running away. But soon Jean tracked it down to where it lay beside the fire whither as though chilled by the still cold air, it had crept for warmth. As on feast days when one cannot bear to stay at home, Jean, though it was not yet time to visit Françoise, left the house, and as though by walking in the sun he had assumed a fine-woven, shining coat of golden mail, strode along with measured steps, head held high, joyful and intrepid, singing like those who follow behind a regiment of soldiers, whom the golden note of trumpets, no less than the long beams of sunlight playing before their feet, thrill with its limpid and uneasy neigh. He made his way towards the scene of festival, choosing the streets most filled with sunlight, seeking, like a beggar who hopes to come upon some lucky find, or like an eager gossip, the highway of the sun. The sight of houses made gorgeous as men in gilded armour, of gay carriages, of strangers with tranquil faces going and coming as on some morning of rejoicing, gave answer with tremendous harmonies to the gaiety which, already and all unconsciously, he had felt waken within him, giving it a new strength. So little empty space was there in all this scene, so solid was this living

quivering mass of humanity, that a shadow might have had time to
move across a wall before Jean could even notice a horseman pass him
by, a shadow of brightness, like two little instruments at opposite ends
of an orchestra, replying to one another for the space of a few moments,
one sufficing to rouse and stimulate and check the other, or like two
birds seemingly engaged in dialogue on separate trees on which they
perch concealed.

When he reached the Place de la Concorde he saw the Madeleine,
and before its colonnade a blue mist as though incense were already
rising before the temple gates. He made a round by the Concorde
Bridge. The very Seine was all aglow with marvellous life, and the boats
cleaving its surface opened up great veins of purple, and in a dazzle of
radiance set hovering in the air a precious dust which, for they could
not catch it as it drifted, settled down as into gulfs of gold. On one of
the banks the snow had still remained, but as sometimes one can see
women climb upon the carcase of a stranded whale which their men
have killed, so children now were laughingly tramping underfoot, as
though it were the inoffensive pelt of a slaughtered monster, these last
soft magnificent remains of winter which need not now be feared.
Jean walked along the river bank, intending to return through the
Tuileries. On the earth still covered by the relics of the conquered
snow, the marble Gods, with at most a patch of it upon their faces,
stood upright there like conquerors in the majestic attitude of victory.
On a small stretch of lawn where snow still deep and covering all the
ground bore witness to a harder and more recent battle, a God still
seemed to be standing in a posture of defiance. Not yet had divine
tranquillity imparted to his taut and eager limbs a noble air of peace.
Farther ahead children were already at play on ground still wet from
recent carnage, and two plaster Hermae with the sun in their eyes
faced one another as though in strife. Round the great basin the
Goddesses swathed only yesterday to their foreheads in thick ice smiled
now triumphant—one holding in her hand a gem that might have been
the trophy of a vanquished foe—while keeping watch beside them a
jetting fountain incessantly at work breaking the icy cover, having
come to their aid in battle, was now permitted to caress their faces
like a tame and much-loved animal. Jean would have liked to meet
Tecmar, Riquet, and all those whose seeming victories had once discouraged him. With what proud and smiling words would he have
shown his joy to them, his confidence in his happiness, his beauty! He

felt happy enough to defy all claims put forth by others to have succeeded more than he had done, to be cleverer or more filled with joy.

He started to run through the Tuileries, as he would have run hatless
through a garden of his own. Then he stopped. The sun creeping to his
feet seemed to be licking them like an animal rejoicing in the happiness
of its master at whose side it has been gambolling. As might a slightly
drunken man who, remembering the most trivial details of the evening
he has passed, and taking note of the most ordinary objects near at hand,
rejoices in them as in messengers of delight, or lavishes endearing
touches on them as on incomparable friends, so now he thought of all the
many assets of his life, almost filled to bursting with a fully conscious,
positive delight, reflecting on his love for Françoise, on his evenings
spent at Réveillon, with the La Rochefoucaulds, or the Tourneforts,
in whose houses he could still appear in all his smiling beauty (as now
he saw it) holding these things to be inestimable advantages. And in
that mood which came upon him always when he thought of those
who had aroused his jealousy, a mood in which he would not admit
defeat, but was urged by a sort of inner necessity to hold his own—at
least in imagination—he now decided that all the things which others
had and he had not, a painter's talent, a brilliant position, a power to
influence the destinies of nations, an unsullied reputation, as things of
no importance, of so little importance that he no longer felt that he
could do without them and not suffer by reason of his deprivation, but
that he could deliberately abandon them to others who not being absorbed in *his* sublime delights (the love of Françoise, the knowledge that
he would put in a handsome appearance at the house of the Réveillons
where Grisard never went) might have the time and the desire to taste
such trivial pleasures. Doubtless he told himself that Grisard too had
known these happy moments when everything looks beautiful, and
that, apart from them, the beneficent illusion which God gives all
of us had made him regard influential connexions as something
insignificant which he would not have wished to have, even if it had
been possible that he should. Then, all of a sudden, remembering that
he had no right to that success in the world of Society which he used,
in imagination, as a defence against Grisard's contempt of him, persuading himself that it gave him an incontestable, because tangible,
superiority, he found himself wondering why Grisard, if he had felt
so inclined, should not have had it too. But we are only too easily
inclined to believe that the things we want are given to us by reason of

some mysterious law which works in our favour, and that the same law brings it about that those we fear shall never have the power to touch us. And so it seemed to him (for no good reason, but as the result of a sort of impression which helps us more than reason can to foresee our future, though it is often proved false, especially when we confuse it with our wishes) that Grisard would never enjoy a great social position. As to himself, so far as political power was concerned, and a reputation which stood high—neither of which he had, though he continually longed for them without admitting to himself that he did so —he was for ever dreaming of these things and had come to see the dream as almost real, setting its coming true, without his having to make the slightest effort to make it actual or even plausible, in a glorious future, indeterminate but close at hand.

But on this particular day these thoughts were but vaguely formulated in Jean's mind; in fact they had risen to the surface of his consciousness only because they were always the form taken by his private reaction whenever he heard of some fresh success achieved by either Grisard or Dubonnet, as though there dwells within us a need when we are touched in our pride, to launch a counter-offensive of hope. Today he was quite sincerely persuaded that what he had not got was not worth having, and grew intoxicated on the thought of all he had, like a man who gets drunk on what he sees around him. Often after a heavy meal and being slightly flown with wine, he would take a cab to some party at which he was due. Then, like one who at the very moment of physical consummation grips with clenched fingers his mistress's hair, the lace trimming of her night-gown, the edge of the sheet—of which they have involuntarily laid hold—so, on such an evening, he could not keep his body under control, could not prevent himself from gripping the door, and, once he had begun a movement, was unable to check it, as though by doing so he would be breaking into, and outraging some tremulous strain of music within him, but would experience incredible delight in letting his shoulder bump against the side of the cab, in speaking aloud, and listening to, the words of gratitude which rose to his lips and were directed at the swiftly moving horse taking him to his party, whose wild magnificent head he could see through the glass bobbing up and down before him. In just such a mood he now walked on, echoing with the full force of his lungs the music of the singing sun which, in its turn, accompanied his progress with all the glinting objects that it shone upon, as though they were sounding instruments a-quiver with the music of the spheres.

Then he grew tired. The sun disappeared behind a cloud. Little by little his confidence and all his dreams drained away, and by the time he got home his legs were aching and he felt as irritable as when some anticipated pleasure has fallen short of expectation, when some hoped-for piece of good news has not arrived, and some great hope has not been realized.

5. *La Marquise de Valtognes*

One day Jean was walking home after leaving Françoise. As he was going down the rue de Rennes he saw emerging from a shabby house at the corner, a woman whom he recognized as his Desroches aunt. She had quite recently invited him to a small reception which she had given in honour of the Emperor and Empress of Russia at her new house in the Avenue du Bois de Boulogne, which had once been the Vanderbilt home, a gigantic stone structure of which the innumerable footmen, horses and equipages were the only mobile elements left by the Prince de —— on his deathbed with the greater part of his fortune, at least sixty million francs, to Desroches. Now at last their intellectual pre-eminence and potential influence had found a fitting background. But since all Jean's evenings were devoted to Françoise, he had not accepted the invitation. He had long given up going anywhere. On the night in question, as he was on his way home, just as he was crossing the Concorde Bridge, he passed the Marquis de C—— who was returning from Madame Desroches's party, a vision of spotless white, from his pleated shirtfront to his tie and the carnation in his buttonhole. He had glanced down at himself, as though taking pleasure in his own less common form of elegance expressed in the simple suit he wore when he went to see Françoise, and with a far greater sense of satisfaction than the Marquis could have found in the thought that he had been present at one of the most brilliant occasions of the Paris season. When he went to bed, he thought as he did almost every evening, 'Another party to which I have *not* gone. All I need do is to leave cards.'

But this he had failed to do. His aunt was not sensitive in such matters. All the same, the knowledge that he had a good excuse made him feel easier in his mind. He now made straight for her. "Well met, dear Jean," she said, "how are you?" They walked on side by side. "Are you going out much these days?" she asked him. "I never go out now: I find it far too much of a bore. There are so many more interesting things to do, and so many more interesting people to see." – "How true that is!" said Madame Desroches with a sudden outburst of intensity, "and yet how little fashionable folk realize it!" – "How strange it is to think that there are people who genuinely believe that you love the great world!" – "There are times when I long to say to them—yes, it is true I loved it once—just so as they could see that I love it no longer. But people are so stupid. Besides, there is great pleasure in concealing from them what it really is that one does love!" – "True enough," said Jean eagerly, "but I wonder why." – "Because as soon as they know, they separate you from it. No one must ever know." There was more violence behind these words than she realized, and it drove her on unconsciously to reveal what she said she wanted to hide. She followed her train of thought for a few moments longer, and said that if she ever loved anybody, she would conceal that fact from everybody, as though the mere fact of saying that she would conceal it enabled her at least to speak of it, and was to that extent pleasurable. Jean enjoyed listening to her, but since already love in general no longer sufficed him, he dashed ahead to the subject of her whom he loved, and said, "But when one is absolutely free, what power has anyone over one?" Since these words however had no bearing on Madame Desroches's own case, they did not interest her. Jean was behaving like a player at Hunt-the-Slipper who, having been almost within sight of the hidden object, suddenly turns away. For those who are in love believe that they take a disinterested pleasure in the company of those who know about love, that they enjoy talking about love. But if they do talk about it, that is only because they hope to turn the talk to the love that concerns them personally. So soon as what is said about love ceases to have any bearing on themselves, they no longer find any pleasure in it. A man in love would find less enjoyment in discussing love with Stendhal than in speaking of his mistress to a street-porter. Madame Desroches replied, "But one never *is* absolutely free," and Jean, thinking of the doctor who might come back any moment, and of all Françoise's many aunts, said, "How true that is!"

Jean again met Madame Desroches next day. She was walking. She had an especial liking for the kind of unostentatious jewellery that can be worn in the daytime, for dresses which, though simple to the eye are lined with precious stuffs, for travelling anonymously second class on trains belonging to the company of which her husband was a director. Finding perhaps a similar satisfaction in setting an excessive value on what was really a common-or-garden love affair, she had little by little abandoned her position in the great world in the interests of a Dutch tenor, engaged at the Opéra-Comique, who lived in squalid lodgings at the corner of the rue de Rennes and the rue de Lamoignon, where every day she had some new picture delivered, or left a jewel. Because of his mother who worked in the day at a tobacco shop, the tenor had forbidden her to call for him in the evenings and drive him to the theatre. She sat beside her fire thinking of him, looking at the odds and ends of theatre announcements which he had given her, newspaper cuttings in which his name was mentioned, and his various photographs. Whenever a friend came to visit her, she talked endlessly about love, about the Opéra-Comique, about Holland, about singing, at regular intervals, as one exhales cigarette smoke which otherwise could choke one. When Jean met her thus for the second time in two successive days, she was on her way to call on the Marquise de Valtognes. She said to him, "Why not come with me? She has often told me how much she would like to meet you." It was three o'clock on one of those January days which seem like hesitant and golden harbingers of spring, caught unawares in the wrong season. In the houses fires were being let out and windows opened for the mild breeze to enter. It was as though comfort, leisure and lazy warmth had abandoned them in favour of the open air and the public gardens. People walked quickly through their rooms in order to get out, though only yesterday they had been walking quickly along the streets in order to get in. It was the moment of the afternoon when schoolboys, compelled to return to their classrooms ask the master for permission to leave the window open. Consequently those inside can hear at some considerable distance the footsteps of their fellows crossing the school yard, who, anxious to snatch at any excuse for prolonging their walk, keep on stopping to stare at their comrades. From his desk the formmaster waves a hand to a colleague hurrying back to his class. A scrap of looking-glass concealed in a boy's satchel catches the sun and sends a tremulous reflection darting over the classroom walls, bouncing up on the master's desk, and quivering in close proximity to his nose. Noone is in the mood for work, and even the school-servants look as happy as though tomorrow were to be the first day of the holidays.

They went through the Tuileries. Men and women were walking slowly, as though they had to make an effort to cleave the enveloping air happily, as though it had touched them as they passed. Many had the smiling, lazy look of those enjoying a warm bath. On the balconies of the houses in the rue de Rivoli a nimbus of light rose to the level of the roof-tops and stood there like some angel of the Annunciation smiling in the Heavens. On one of the windows, a sunbeam striking downwards from the sky had scored the pane with its crimson talon, and showed like a flash of lightning reduced to immobility by the skill of an artist in stained glass. The great basin in the Tuileries Gardens was only half-thawed. But between the blocks of ice the water was as blue as in the spring. They turned into the rue Boissy-d'Anglas which lay in shadow, but when they reached the Faubourg Saint-Honoré they had to fight against the glare of the sun which lay in such profusion on the ground that its reflection was blinding, and Jean was forced to put his hand before his eyes in order to see where he was going. All the florists had set up stalls outside their shops in the open air where none had been the day before, and loaded them with primulas and lilac, hyacinths and wallflowers and daffodils. At twenty paces distant, as though one were already treading on their territory, the scent was so various, so strong, that several women passing by seemed to be almost overcome. They reached the rue de La Rochefoucald, where the Marquise lived. The street rises and falls so steeply that wheeled traffic is scarce. The few sounds that reached their ears soon died away. It was as though they had left Paris behind them. In order to reach the ground-floor apartment occupied by Madame de Valtognes they had to cross a small garden. The path was very narrow and clumps of pansies and of dandelion were already sprouting. Here and there they almost tripped over ragged shoots of box which had encroached upon the footway. The wall was low, and beyond it lay a patch of wasteland, with the result that one could see a great patch of sky at the level of the wall which alone seemed to keep it from flooding over into the garden. The taller trees were bathed to about midway up their trunks in the light of the setting sun, and seemed to have succeeded, as the result of some mysterious chemical process, in dissolving their brown branches and green leaves, into a blurred and golden foliage. The rustic realities of the garden had become, at this height, transformed into a picture of Paradise.

Jean, walking ahead of his aunt, pulled at a small bell which like the bells of houses in the country went on for some considerable time dripping the thin drops of its bright sound. They were shown into the drawing-room where the Marquise was sitting in front of the fire with a number of friends. But the eye went involuntarily to the windows which the sun just now was tinting with the most vivid colours. The blue sky, which seemed to be pressed up against them, and a golden carpet of light spread upon the floor, seemed to spill over into the lives of those present with the ineffable serenity or radiant memory of someone who though close at hand was still invisible, but larger than anybody else, playing a silent part in the company, and imposing with incomparable power his own emotional atmosphere upon the seated circle. Jean, after first paying his respects to the Marquise, hastened to say how-d'you-do to the Comte de Villebonne. Like the Marquise, this latter was gifted with a fine intelligence, a sound knowledge of, and good taste in, curios, and poor health. These peculiarities had according to their friends led to a liaison which had lasted for twenty years, in the course of which time not a day had passed without their lunching either at the Marquise's table or at the house of one of her friends—on such days as she was prepared to accept an invitation to luncheon—and then going off to make the round of the antique shops. At five o'clock (the Marquise was always "at home" from five on-wards) Monsieur de Villebonne was not always present. But he arrived a little later. Not seldom, when they were due to dine together at eight, he reached the house by half past seven, but let half an hour elapse before entering the drawing-room where he greeted her just as they were to go into dinner (for she was never punctual) with the respectful air of a stranger, and the manifest pleasure of someone who had not seen her for a long time. Whenever anybody asked her for advice, she was careful always to give it with a proviso, "Do you agree, Monsieur de Villebonne?" and never failed to submit to his judgment. They held their material goods in common, but kept their characters intact. The Marquise's country house was never open to visitors when Monsieur de Villebonne wanted to be undisturbed, and Monsieur de Villebonne's box at the Opéra, at the Comédie Française and at the Conservatoire, was hers as much as his. But he was insistent that she should not frequent the society of certain ladies who had only recently been admitted into Society, and she after nearly twenty years would never permit him to dine with her unless he was in full evening-dress.

Scarcely had Jean and Madame Desroches sat down in Madame de Valtognes's drawing-room, than Madame Desroches, remembering that she was due home, rose to her feet. "But I thought you were never in to callers at six o'clock nowadays, unless you happened by mere chance to be at home?" said the Marquise. "That is true," replied Madame Desroches, "but it so happens that today someone is coming

who particularly wants to see me: Madame de Thonnes," she added
with a smile. "Since when have you taken to entertaining Madame de
Thonnes?" asked Monsieur de Villebonne. "I seem to remember," said
Jean, "that you were very unwilling for me to present her one day
when she was especially anxious to make your acquaintance." – "That
also is perfectly true," said Madame Desroches, still smiling, "but what
can I do about it?—she is so much more determined than I am. This is
the third time she has asked herself." – "That is excessively flattering,"
remarked Madame de Voltognes. "Not at all," rejoined Madame
Desroches: "it's not, you see, on my account, but because she hopes
to find my drawing-room full of visitors—in which she is much
deceived. She is a woman who has made up her mind to get where she
wants to go. I must say, I envy her for being so young, and for wanting
so ardently what really matters so little." This *matters so little* seemed to
displease Monsieur de Villebonne. He said nothing, and Madame de
Valtognes held her peace in order not to annoy him. He no more liked
her to speak slightingly of their world—as did Madame Desroches, and
some of the younger women—than he would have liked to see her
reading certain books, frequenting certain houses, or using certain
words. She, for her part, respected his prejudices in such matters, but
found a peculiar pleasure in speaking of them, saying with a little
laugh, as though annoyed at her own subservience, "Agénor would
never let me go *there*!"—his pigheadedness seeming to her to be a
pleasing proof of his love.

As Jean and his aunt were going downstairs they met Monsieur de
Valtognes. He was some years younger than his wife, a great deal
better looking, and, in Jean's eyes, more intelligent. But Madame de
Valtognes had succeeded, without difficulty, in imposing upon the
world of fashion—from which she had partially withdrawn as though
the better to dominate it from a distance—her opinions, which were
accepted as truths, and her preferences, which were looked upon as
smart. Monsieur de Valtognes had been eclipsed by Monsieur de
Villebonne, to whom he appeared to be perfectly willing to yield pride
of place. He was for ever running errands, having he explained, to fetch
some powders for Agénor's headaches, buy hangings for his rooms, or
find a publisher for his "slim volumes". Some accused him of being a
willing dupe, others of being a blind one. Madame Desroches said that
he had wanted to leave his wife when he had found out about her
liaison, but had been too fond of her to do so. More than once the

Duchesse de Réveillon had heard him speaking to Villebonne—whom he admired, liked, and was willing to serve—in tones so suddenly brusque and imperative, that she went in continual dread of his doing him some injury, like those caged lions who begin by licking their trainer's face, and end by eating him. Consequently it was often said that if Monsieur de Valtognes was so long-suffering with Monsieur de Villebonne, the reason must be that the latter was privy to certain compromising secrets, and could at any moment, produce damning evidence against his rival. When Monsieur de Valtognes gave utterance to the kind of remarks which are put into the mouths of cuckolded husbands on the stage, those who heard them had the illusion that they were dramatic authors face to face with reality. When, his wife and Villebonne being together in Norway, he pulled out his watch at an afternoon party and said, "At this very moment Villebonne is taking tea with my wife in the New Hotel," nobody could ever be quite sure whether he was indulging in the frightening irony of a man who is soon to be revenged, the comment of a poor fool biting on the bullet, or was giving expression to the simple-mindedness of a gull, or the cynical amusement of a cad.

Since Monsieur de Valtognes did not seem to know who Jean was, Madame Desroches reintroduced him, and Jean bowed with no little embarrassment, as though he knew that Monsieur de Valtognes was secretly thinking, 'Just another young fellow laughing at me.' But if he was he did not show it, but returned the bow, and spoke a few words with that exquisite politeness which when Jean had met him on a previous occasion, had quite disarmed him. Madame Desroches, being in a hurry, cut short the conversation. Monsieur de Valtognes apologized for the parcel he was carrying under his arm. "It's a small Clodion statuette," he explained, "which I am giving Villebonne as a surprise." Then, bowing to Madame Desroches, and giving his hand to Jean with a friendly smile, he disappeared with his parcel.

Jean had it in mind to leave his aunt but she asked him to go back with her. He could feel that because he did not question her about her secrets, but behaved as though he respected them, yet did not talk to her of anything else, as though he knew them, his company was as sweet to her as silence is to burdened hearts. She wanted to keep him with her, perhaps for no better reason than that which makes us seek the company of a young animal which seems to love us better than humans do, and to understand our thoughts before we put them into words; perhaps because he was a young man who had already had experience of love, and would be more likely than ever she would to inspire it in the long years ahead; perhaps because he was as devoted to her as she wished another were, and, she might, perhaps bring herself to speak to him of that other, and even to ask him, with urgency and sadness, to do something for him on some more urgent and sad occasion. "Dear Jean," she said, "do come back with me," and together they returned to her house. She kept him with her in her room while she took off her hat. There was a ring at the front door-bell. Madame de Thonnes had arrived. His aunt sent word that she would be down in a moment. Quickly stripping off her gloves she smiled at her nephew, and went with him to the drawing-room, where she introduced him to Madame de Thonnes, who had a pair of black and smiling eyes in a plump face, and was completely equipped with a chinchilla boa, a card-case, a watch set in the handle of her umbrella, and a deal of conversation about parties, influenza, and death—which had just carried off several young women whom, "I had often seen at my cousin's house." Madames Desroches listened to all this politely, and without showing any signs of irritation. Perhaps she was conscious, not without melancholy, of the illusion which once had been to her as food and drink, now taking fire in another, dazzling her, burning her up, so that Madame de Thonnes, when she had reached her age, and more, would, having attained to her ambition, think of her as one among the brilliant young. Madame de Thonnes spoke of her reading, but confessed that she had not had time to look at the last number of the *Revue de Paris*. Madame Desroches said she had finished it that morning. "But with all you have to do, Madame, how can you find time for reading?" said the other with simple-minded enthusiasm. "But I go out so little," said Madame Desroches. "Oh, Madame!" exclaimed Madame de Thonnes in a tone of protest, as though Madame Desroches had done herself a grave injustice.

The door opened, and the Duchesse de Réveillon was announced. Madame de Thonnes rose to take her leave, feeling that had even a great friend remained in *her* drawing-room when Madame Marmet had called, who was to her what the Duchesse de Réveillon was to Madame Desroches, she would have thought it "very bad form". But Madame Desroches, conscious of the sacrifice which the other was making, said sweetly, "But surely you're not going yet?" – "Well, then, I'll stay just a few moments longer," said Madame de Thonnes. She sounded almost rude, either because she had been caught napping, or because she wanted to seem to be staying only out of friendship. But the emotion she was feeling was too strong to be concealed, and at once she flushed a fiery red. 'How wonderful it must be to feel like that,' thought Madame Desroches, and proceeded to introduce Madame de Thonnes to the Duchess, happy to think that it was in her power to do a kind action. Jean had blushed no less furiously than Madame de Thonnes, for he had not been to see the Duchess for a very long time. But the latter, so that she might not embarrass him, expressed regret that it was so long since she had seen him, speaking in such a way that she seemed rather to be flattering than reproaching him, despite the fact that she had been deeply hurt by his desertion. She could not forget those who had once been of service to her son. At one moment, having ventured on a harmless joke at the expense of Madame de Thianges, the Duchess added, "I wouldn't say a thing like that except among friends." Madame de Thonnes read so much into this phrase that it now seemed to her quite natural for Madame Desroches to have prevailed upon her to stay while the Duchess was there, and could not help feeling that Madame de Réveillon must take a more than ordinary interest in her. The manner however in which the Duchess took leave of her quickly dissipated this dream, and made her see things as they really were. All the same, she wished that others could know that the Duchess had used the words "among friends" when speaking of her, and left the house with a sense of annoyance that they did not, like someone who, having been made privy to an important secret, feels that he would like the passers-by to realize that, at least, he *has* a secret. To console herself for the fact that the friends whom she saw in the street did *not* know, she greeted them more coldly, and in a manner more condescending than usual, in the hope that her remoteness might give them a hint of what had occurred. But what she chiefly felt as a result of her visit, was a sort of exalted admiration for Madame Desroches, whose intelligence, grace, and beauty appeared greater in her eyes by reason of her social position. She had paid her call for purely selfish reasons, but repeated it from motives of pleasure, and in order to satisfy a passion, a sort of a *cult*. "It is easy enough to see why *she* is such a success" was her way of putting it to others—and she put it often.

6. *The Bergotte Exhibition*

Neither Jean nor Madame Desroches had anything to do before dinner. They stayed therefore together for a while, and since nothing occurred to cut, and, so to speak, to garner the pleasure which they took in one another's company, the pleasure itself began gradually to fade, and ended by dropping dead of its own accord. But as Jean was walking home from his aunt's, his eye was caught by a playbill announcing a performance of *Le Cid*, and at once his thoughts turned to Corneille, then to Racine, then to Molière, then to *Les Femmes Savantes*. At that point his imagination, like a peg-top which had been spinning for a long time on itself, seemingly forgetful of the object which, a few moments before, it had been aimed to strike, slowed to a consideration of the character of Philaminte, seemed to draw near to that of Bélise, returned to Philaminte, and then, suddenly resuming its course, made a side shot at Henriette, and immediately bounced back as in obedience to the law of symmetry, to his aunt Henriette. He saw now in retrospect her gentle eyes, though far gentler than when he had been with her, remembered her charming way of treating him, the friendly manner in which she had talked, her rare and gracious ease, her flattering confidences, and instead of merely taking pleasure in something which had been no more than an almost involuntary emanation of natural charm which had been expended upon him today simply because he happened to be conveniently at hand, or from selfishness, because she had felt that nobody was better capable than he was of understanding her—he was suddenly struck by an overwhelming feeling of gratitude. The demon of generosity, the need at once to lay his heart at her feet, to spread its richness like oil upon the tiny flame of liking which had flickered in her eyes, seized hold of him. 'I'll send her some flowers!' It would take him at least a quarter of an hour to reach the florist's, and he was impatient to hear the words of thanks with which his aunt would receive the gift. He took a cab so as to get more quickly to the shop. He had no more than fifty francs in his pocket, and that would have to carry him to the end of the month, for he had spent the rest of his

624

allowance on Françoise. Well it couldn't be helped. He would squander
every penny on the flowers, and take no more cabs until the month was
ended. By eating at home he could, if driven to it, avoid all further
outlay. At the florist's, while he was choosing the finest blooms he
could see, he noticed behind the counter a great flowering shrub which,
like some innocent and lovely captive, was raising its arms to Heaven
and smiling at him with all its load of blossoms. Each was as large and
glowing as a rose, and the saffron colour of the whole seemed as in a
picture to bear witness to the daring inspiration, the sure and perfect
touch, of a subtle colourist. The branches were "put in" with so sure a
touch that like the stroke of a pastel, like the artless, gracious movement
of a child or an animal, it all but drew a swooning cry from the spectator
carried quite out of himself by this sudden consciousness of a human
intention in the whole design. A slight break in the green bark of one of
the branches was evidence of the weariness it felt beneath its load of
blossom, and deep in one of the calices a drop of dew was visible upon
a puffed and bursting bud. A fragrance hung about the shrub like a
caressing breeze. Who owned the shrub would own the perfume too,
as those who buy an animal or a mistress, can feast their eyes on the
instinctive movements of the one, or the flickering thoughts of the
other. Already Jean could see in imagination the surprise which his
aunt would feel at sight of this flowering tree, and could guess how
impossible it would be for her to restrain the gush of gratitude which
would reach him even across dividing distances. Farther back in the
shop he saw a lilac with all its spread of delicate blossoms lying like
violet meal around its springtime twigs, all swarming-sweet and
numberless, like curls upon the head of an antique statue. He said that
he would come back and pay later, gave instructions for the flowering
shrub and the lilac to be delivered to Madame Desroches, and hurried
off to a jeweller's where he sold the diamond which he wore in his tie,
and, with what remained of the money bought a precious stone in
which, blue and misted, sparkling and bright, one hour of an afternoon
seemed to lie imprisoned. This too he sent to his aunt. Next day he
went to see her again.

*

They visited together an Exhibition of the works of Bergotte,
whom both Jean and his aunt held to be the greatest of all French
painters. On the occasion of this Exhibition the Institut had given a

great banquet in his honour, the Government had awarded him the Grand Cross of the Légion d'Honneur—of which for many years he had possessed the ribbon—and all the Sovereigns of Europe had written to him. In one of the rooms they came upon a stout gentleman with a red face and a piercing but wary eye. At his side was an old and ugly lady at whose cloak he plucked from time to time, now and again addressing a word or two to a small boy who was with them. She had upon her head a hat of which the trimmings in imitation gold seemed eloquent of extreme pretentiousness and a somewhat insufficient fortune. The gentleman greeted Madame Desroches with a sort of awkward alacrity. But just as he was doing so the lady, with an imperious air, as though to stress the fact that he was entirely under her thumb, told him to take her arm. "There he is in person! that's Bergotte," said Madame Desroches. "What! do you mean to say you know him!" exclaimed Jean, and turned his head to stare. "I knew him very well at one time," said Madame Desroches, "he even painted an excellent portrait of me. I should very much have liked to give a dinner for him at this time of his jubilee, but his mistress, Madame Delven— that's the woman with him now—never lets him accept invitations unless they are from people she knows." – "I gather that he sometimes goes to the Réveillons." – "Not very often. He refused an invitation to dinner from them which they, too, gave in honour of his jubilee, though as a matter of fact she doesn't so much mind him going to people who are complete strangers to her. My parents knew her once, but gradually ceased seeing anything of her, since when she has for- bidden him to set foot in my house. It gives her great pleasure to have somebody whom we don't, someone I may say who is far more charm- ing than anyone we *do* know. Your mother saw a lot of her in the old days." – "What! Mamma?" – "I'm not sure that I ought to tell you this, but after all you did, didn't you, know the Lepics who used to dine every week with your parents?" – "Of course I did." – "Well then—I don't suppose it matters your knowing—your aunt Clarisse's gover- ness, was the natural daughter, so it was said, of your aunt's father, and Lepic married her. She was always so well-bred that your mother, who at first had qualms about receiving her, later became her best friend. None of us, on the other hand, ever knew her sister who is this same Madame Delven about whom I have been speaking. She first lived with a grocer, then let herself be carried off by a doctor, who kept her—Madame Marmet's father, he was—before she reverted to your uncle Frédéric who ultimately married her."–"My uncle Frédéric!" said Jean, scarcely able to believe his ears. "Yes," said Madame Desroches with a laugh, "that's why your mother gave up having anything to do with him. She was quite pretty up to about ten years ago, after which she rapidly became the horrible creature you now see before you. The only women Bergotte ever had any feelings for were the servant-girls he used as models—he saw them as so many Venuses, employing in the process as much genius as he put into his marbles. Then suddenly he met her and became her lover. By that time she was rich having married, after your uncle's death, a successful wholesale merchant who used to go a great deal to your Crinois aunt's house. As a matter of interest your aunt, just to teach us all a lesson, still receives her."

All this she spoke of while they were moving about the rooms, talking of Bergotte and of his strange love for Madame Delven. "It was she who sat for his *Electra*: if you look at it carefully you will see something of her in it, ugly though she is now. But in his eyes she is still beautiful." Jean was trying his hardest to catch a glimmer of something behind Madame Delven's pendulous and pock-marked cheeks, behind the sharp little eyes through which she peered at those around her, peeling tangerines and feeding sections of them to Bergotte at her side, as though she were nourishing her revenge on a society which had held her in contempt, though she had been rated so high by the great man who seemed to be seeking, as it were like some imprisoned ghost, whether in the profundities of Madame Delven's soul, whether in the physical essence still showing in her type, that look of embittered melancholy which for him had been the outstanding characteristic of *Electra*—a characteristic which he now seemed to be checking in terms of resemblance, so that from being an abstraction it had become a living creature. Jean had left his aunt's side so as to get closer to Bergotte and Madame Delven. She kept constantly addressing the painter by his name in so loud a voice that the saunterers in the Gallery stopped to stare. A mother pointed her out to her son, who hurried away, went towards where Bergotte was standing, and walked past him so as to get a better view by turning and approaching him from the other direction. But when he got close he was too timid to raise his eyes. Jean dogged their footsteps, stopping when Madame Delven stopped to look at a picture. In front of a seascape she said, "That's the one you did from my drawing-room window at Dieppe." In front of a Salome: "Don't you remember? It was my idea that you should place the little black slave just there. It was the day you told me that I had good taste." She pointed to a picture some way off showing a pheasant lying on a table. "That was the bird my husband shot that terribly cold day." She stopped with a proprietary air before a pastel. "You gave me that one for my birth-day." Farther off hung a painting of an avenue, and Madame Delven, plunging suddenly into reminiscence, remarked, "That was the year we went to Fontainebleau," adding with an emotional quiver in her voice, "what a long time ago it seems." A softness crept into her face as she looked at him. But in front of a vase of flowers which bore a more recent date, she said ironically, "That's the one I wanted you to give to my husband. I don't think you'll soon forget painting that, will you, sir?" and there was that in her eye which seemed to lift a veil from the ceremonious "sir". He looked at her with a smile, but dared not answer being embarrassed by the presence of the small boy who was holding his hand. He said: "Poor little Tiennet's getting bored." – "Non-sense! Tiennet's very proud: he's here, don't forget: there's a portrait of him in one of the rooms." But at this precise moment an angry voice spoke close beside them, "So this is how you wait for me at the foot of the main staircase!" It came from a man with an unpleasant Alsatian accent, and was so loud that everyone turned to look. It was Monsieur Delven. His wife told him to speak more quietly. It was clear that all the time they had been moving through the Galleries, Bergotte's mind had been elsewhere and his kindly smile showed that the memory of day-dreams was still strong in him. "If it was because of these you kept me waiting," said Monsieur Delven, pointing to the pastels, "let me compliment you on your taste! never seen a nastier lot of daubs!" – "If that's all you can say, you'd better say nothing at all! You don't know what you're talking about! Those 'daubs' are master-pieces!" – "Worst things he ever did. Trouble with you is you praise all his things equally, whereas I tell the truth!" But seemingly unaf-fected by these insults, and with a gesture of invitation which Jean did not know whether he should attribute to absent-mindedness, gratitude, or irony, Bergotte held out his open cigarette-case to Monsieur Delven. In a few kindly words Monsieur Delven refused the offer. His anger had subsided. They moved on, the little Tiennet still clinging to Bergotte's right arm, while over the other the painter was holding Madame Delven's cloak. Before each work they came to, Madame Delven reminded Bergotte that he had painted it in her part of the country, claimed it for her boudoir, and rubbed with her handker-chief at the frame, saying that it had become slightly tarnished, or commenting on the picture itself, pointing out that an arm ought to be lengthened or a background deepened, all this manifold activity and talkativeness on her part having the desired effect on the bystanders of making the chain by which she held the painter captive shine more brightly. With an occasional sharp reprimand Monsieur Delven seemed to make the prisoner more painfully aware of his fetters. But the absent look on Bergotte's face changed not a jot, and sounds from without seemed to reach his brain only as a confused, vague muttering which concerned him not at all, as the noises of the street form a background to the mental processes of a man absorbed in work. Some-times he stole a glance at Madame Delven, and at such moments his sensual, subtle expression, doubtless discounting the coarse make-up, the pock-marks, the intellectual pretentiousness, and the vulgar smile, seemed to show that he was conscious only of the ideal and determined face of his *Electra*, seen in the light of sweet old memories, or glowing in the glory of his hopes.

7. *Madame Cresmeyer's Dinner-Party*

Though on that evening Bergotte had refused invitations from the Duchesse de Réveillon, Madame Desroches and many others, he had nevertheless to change into his dress-clothes and put in an appearance at a large dinner-party. It was being given by Jean's aunt, Madame Cresmeyer. Madame Delven could not forget that from hatred of Madame Desroches and other members of her family—a motive sweeter to her than any affection for herself—Madame Cresmeyer had twelve years before become her close friend, calling upon her and receiving her in her house at the time when the others had refused her the tribute of the most ordinary politeness. Bergotte who in those days was as yet admired only by a select group of art-lovers, had little by little acquired a wider fame. The promise given by Madame Delven, that he would without fail turn up at this party, was her way of rewarding a long-enduring display of faith and loyalty. Madame Cresmeyer had at first endured several uncomfortable moments when she thought of all the brilliant personages who would have been more than glad to accept an invitation which would have procured them the supreme happiness of meeting Bergotte, a happiness the more desirable for being so difficult of achievement. But she could not ask people she had never met: still she *could* ask Jean, and that would give her the chance of saying, "And do bring your friend Henri de Réveillon: it might amuse him to meet Bergotte." But Madame Delven had declared that if she caught sight of a single Santeuil, she would leave at once, taking Bergotte with her. It was necessary therefore to pick her guests from elsewhere. First and foremost she would have the wife of an ear-specialist, the friend of several ladies of social distinction whom she never invited Madame Cresmeyer to meet. Madame Cresmeyer was prompted to include her by the thought that if she asked Madame Destroyes to so smart an occasion, Madame Destroyes could not very well get out of paying her in kind. The invitation was enthusiastically accepted, and the Doctor promised himself the pleasure of interesting Bergotte with a few stories about Benjamin Constant who had once consulted him about his hearing. The Bliaux too were an obvious choice. Monsieur Bliaux was a stockbroker, and Madame Cresmeyer revelled in the thought that the elegant Bliaux brougham would be trotted out to grace her dinner, that the Bliaux footman would be in attendance in her hall, that should the Deputy-Governor of the Crédit Foncier choose that evening to pay a call on his friend Bliaux, he would not find him at home, and that she, Cécile Cresmeyer would be the cause of his disappointment. She liked to think that the Doctor would remind his wife earlier in the day that, "We're dining at Madame Cresmeyer's this evening, and tomorrow at the Ministry of Finance," as though the two occasions were of equal importance. But that was not all. Madame Delven, seeing the Bliaux, would be comforted by the thought that she had not persuaded Bergotte to come under false pretences. No one, Madame Cresmeyer believed, could fail to be flattered at the thought of dining with a stockbroker. Last but not least, the Bliaux had a box at the Opéra. Perhaps one day they would offer her a seat in it. Not that her immediate hopes went that far, but she saw a golden future opening before her from the moment when thanks to Bergotte the Bliaux would see for themselves that she was on dining terms with the Destroyes, and the Destroyes that one was always likely to meet the Bliaux at her table. The Bliaux would introduce her to their friends as a friend of the Destroyes, and the Destroyes[1] to theirs as a friend of the Bliaux. For they could scarcely do less than express their gratitude for her great kindness by asking her to dinner with the cream of their circle. On an occasion which would have given her an opportunity to show a little friendliness to a number of obscure persons who had once been of service to her, it was not to them that her thoughts turned but rather to those to whom she owed nothing, from whom the benefits she might hope to obtain were still in the future, still to be set in motion. But of this she took no account, nor did she reflect that the Bliaux might well pass her over when next compiling a list of guests, as she now was passing over Flore Simiane, on the ground that, "She is really a terrible bore, and no one knows her." To complete her table she included Monsieur de Blanchefort of the Foreign Office. It was a bitter disappointment to her (God can be very

[1] At this point Proust has changed the name to "Deshais", but, since obviously the Destroyes are meant, I have made the change.—G.H.

unfair!) that she could not even consider asking the most brilliant of all her star-performers, old General d'Apvent, a real aristocrat, who was living with Madame Tournet, Madame Cresmeyer's own aunt. Madame Tournet was at the moment lying gravely ill in Orléans, and the General would not stir from her side unless forced to do so by his military duties.

While Jean was visiting the Bergotte Exhibition with his aunt, Madame Cresmeyer was going through agonies of apprehension. What if the Bliaux should be laid low by sickness! Fortunately, however, her maid told her that she had seen Madame Bliaux out driving, looking the picture of health. Suppose too Bergotte forgot to come! (artists are *so* absent-minded!). Up to the very last moment she had her doubts about Madame Destroyes, whose little boy had got the whooping-cough. Madame Cresmeyer only wished she could find some way of making him better. She included him in her prayers, and waxed indignant against his father for not being able to deal with the ailment—"a doctor, too, and in these days! it's positively disgraceful". Meanwhile she herself refused to leave the house, for fear she might be involved in a carriage accident, might get caught up in a crowd and so prevented from getting home in time etc., or taken off to the police station in error, on a charge of shop-lifting. But even if one keeps to one's room one may still twist one's ankle!—so she remained lying on her bed. A letter was brought to her. It contained the news that Madame Tournet had just had a terrible crisis. She had very nearly died. There was good reason to fear that she would never be able to get on her feet again. The prospect of family mourning which would have compelled her to postpone her dinner, put her into a cold sweat. She thanked God for having spared her this misfortune. But how could she be sure that it wasn't taking place that very moment? She might get a telegram asking her to come at once. The door opened and, "A telegram, Madame," said the maid. "Where from!" – "Orléans, Madame." The blow had fallen! For a long time Madame Cresmeyer stared at the envelope, not daring to open it. All her happiness seemed to have fallen in ruins about her. Then a brilliant idea occurred to her. Why not let it be supposed that she had not received the message until too late? If necessary, and so as to allay any possible doubts in the General's mind, she could complain to the postal authorities. How well the announcement would look in the *Figaro*—where it would have the additional advantage of giving publicity to her dinner:

Scarcely had the distinguished guests named above taken their departure, than a tragedy struck the hostess down—the news that a near and dear member of her family had just died.

Unfortunately it would not be possible to add that the deceased was also near and dear to General d'Apvent. That she might seem less guilty in her own eyes, she decided not to open the telegram until after her guests should have gone, excusing the sophistry by telling herself, 'After all, it may be to say she's better.' But though she was not going to let the telegram disturb her arrangements, its arrival had given her a distinct shock, and put her in a thoroughly bad temper. 'Even if one stays in one room, accidents can still happen,' she kept on thinking. 'Disasters never come singly.' Then she began to feel frightened. If she didn't turn up in Orléans, someone might come to fetch her. She sent down word to the concierge that should any member of the General's staff ask for her, he was to be told that she had gone out, and would not be back until later.

At long last the moment for which she had been waiting all day arrived. The hairdresser had been late in coming, and she was not ready. She could hear the successive peals at the door-bell, and there she was, quite unprepared to greet her guests. But no sooner had she reached the drawing-room than her anger vanished, melted in the warmth of the pleasure she felt in introducing the Bliaux to the Destroyes. Bergotte arrived. Madame Delven who no doubt had come with him was announced a few moments later. Monsieur Delven had turned up before either of them, but Madame Delven had insisted on being last so that the faint uneasiness of the assembled company until she had actually put in an appearance, might give an added lustre to their double presence. She told Madame Cresmeyer that Bergotte had very nearly been kept from coming as a result of a cab accident that morning. He had not, however, been seriously hurt though he looked pale. Madame Cresmeyer had a momentary vision of his being struck down by apoplexy at the end of dinner and dying in her house which as a result would acquire an aureole of glory. Still it is always awkward when a guest dies in one's house. During dinner Madame Delven informed Bergotte that he had had invitations for this same evening from Madame Desroches, from the President of the Republic, from the Duchesse de Réveillon—to whom she referred as the Princesse de Réveillon, perhaps from ignorance or because she wanted to magnify the Duchess's importance by giving her what she believed to be a more glorious title. Madame Cresmeyer, swelling with pride, but at the same time feeling slightly irritated, said, "That makes it all the more charming of you to have come to me." Suddenly, Madame Delven pointed out to Bergotte (whom she addressed as "Monsieur") that he wasn't supposed to eat fish. Madame Cresmeyer asked Bliaux for news of his friend the Governor of the Crédit Foncier, so that the Destroyes should be left in no doubt of the grandeur of their fellow-guests. Next she asked Destroyes about the Comtesse de Pesch's daughter, who had gone deaf at the age of ten—such a terrible thing to happen! Madame Destroyes thought the Comtesse quite charming, and really *so* simple. Why, that very morning she had taken them driving in the Bois. Madame Cresmeyer felt grateful to the Comtesse de Pesch for this kindly attention to Madame Destroyes, since it gave the other guests the impression that she was, if not one of Madame de Pesch's friends, at least a friend of her friends.

Since everyone left before midnight, she decided to take an announcement round to the *Figaro* office at once, though having an uncomfortable feeling of guilt (Bergotte having made a point of nothing being said about his dining out that night) and fearing that she might be caught in the act (she had decided to say that one of the guests had been responsible for supplying the news: after all in this charming Republic of theirs one could never quite be sure of the people one entertained) she made her preparations like a thief, nervously remembering all the clerks she would have to deal with, and having a horrible feeling that Bergotte's eyes would be on her all the time. But suddenly, the thought came back to her of the telegram which in her happiness she had forgotten. It read as follows: "Francine better have to visit ministry can you give me dinner General Apvent." She might have had him all the time! As she went through it again that thought was uppermost in her mind. But annoyance returned with redoubled force as she looked at the drawing-room now empty of guests, at the lamps still burning, at the plates of little cakes almost empty, at the hired butler covered with gold lace and overflowing with subservience . . . all this just for her, the poor remains of her great occasion. The concierge informed her that the General had indeed called, but that acting on instructions, she had told him that Madame Cresmeyer would not be home to dinner. She played for a moment with the idea of including his name in the announcement for the *Figaro* all the same.

But what sort of an explanation could she give him?—or the other guests for that matter who had not seen him? No, a better plan would be to let them all know that they had only just missed dining in the company of General d'Apvent.

Thus brooding and scheming she arrived at the *Figaro* office. Now that she was there she felt frightened. The clerk who dealt with her might ask "Have you got Monsieur Bergotte's authority?" in so loud a voice that Bergotte might well hear him from the next-door room. For she had a fixed idea that artists were always hanging round editorial offices. She went upstairs, and almost fainted dead away at the sight of Delven. He was as much disconcerted as she was. But she interpreted his nervousness as a threat. He had come oppressed by much the same fears, to supply a paragraph to the paper, so that all the world should know that his wife was invited to dinners where she met really smart people. The only precaution he had taken was to suppress Bergotte's name, not from any fear of looking ridiculous (such a thought had never entered his head) but so as not to embarrass the painter who had refused other invitations for the same evening. The whole business had been discussed between the three of them, for Bergotte had gradually lowered himself to the level of those with whom he lived, and no longer saw anything particularly shocking in this way of doing things. They said good night to one another without stopping to talk, which in itself was an admission of guilt. Whenever they thought back to that meeting, it was with a sense of shame. Neither of them slept a wink that night. They lay awake waiting for the delicious moment when the rising sun would awaken the *Figaro's* delivery boys, when they could feast their eyes on the words to which they had been so fondly looking forward, could hear the syllables of their names made glorious, when the paper, neat in its innocent wrapper, would lie waiting until Madame Desroches rang for her chocolate, concealing the wonderful news which would shed a blinding light on the avenging figures of Madame Cresmeyer and Madame Delven.

The sun rose and the sight of it was sweet to Madame Cresmeyer's impatient eyes. The maid was sent out to buy ten copies of the *Figaro*, because her mistress wanted to make quite sure that the words were the same in every one of them. The social column contained a number of paragraphs which even to Madame Cresmeyer shed no particular splendour on those whose dinners were described. But when she reached the most insignificant of all of them, the one which almost certainly no one would read, the characters seemed to have a more appealing look. *Grand dinner given in honour of the great Bergotte by Madame Oresmage.* She sat up with a start. She would have liked to run round at once to the *Figaro* and insist on the issue being withdrawn. Alas, the paper was on the streets already, and every copy was disseminating the fatal error! It was a positive scandal! How could she forewarn her guests of the previous evening? Why, oh why, did she always make her C's so that they looked like O's, her Y's like G's? They would have to be made to publish a correction tomorrow. But between now and tomorrow the damage would have been done. The glory of *her* dinner would go to another! The wording too was so admirable! "The world of high finance was represented by Monsieur and Madame Bliaux. Many notable figures in the ranks of learning were to be seen, such as Doctor Destroyes, as were also those well-known members of fashionable and aristocratic circles, Le Comte de Blanche-fort, Monsieur and Madame Bliaux,[1] Monsieur Delven, etc. The gracious mistress of the house, who a little bird whispers—but hush—has other wonderful surprises planned for us, was wearing a gown of black satin flounced in watered white, which, in every line showed the master hand of Morin-Boissier, and did the honours with all her accustomed charm." No doubt a correction could be published next day "The dinner to which we drew attention in our yesterday's issue, was given by Madame Cresmeyer and not by Madame Oresmage as stated in error . . ." but it would be impossible to reprint all the details, and the reader who in any case had not paid much attention to them (not knowing that they had to do with Madame Cresmeyer) would by that time have forgotten all about them.

But as things turned out Madame Cresmeyer was not wholly to be deprived of her pleasure. Monsieur Delven, seeking to explain for his own satisfaction the reasons that had led Madame Cresmeyer to visit the *Figaro* offices at so late an hour, came to the conclusion that it must have been in order to beg the paper not to print anything about her dinner. He therefore lost no time in diverting his own contribution to the *Gaulois*, though this time he went the whole hog and took a chance by mentioning Bergotte's name (after all, the undertaking given to Bergotte had referred only to the *Figaro*, and nobody therefore could

---

[1] This repetition of names may have been overlooked by Proust. I have thought it best to make no correction.—G.H.

accuse him of a breach of faith) in order to make sure that when confronted by a name so well known to the public, the columnist should have no hesitation about making public the fact of the painter's presence. At the very moment when Madame Cresmeyer was lamenting the fact that fashionable Paris would be kept in ignorance of her party, and had decided to abandon her project of calling upon her friends in order to gauge the effect upon them—whether jealousy or admiration—of the announcement, the lady who lived upstairs sent down her maid with a copy of the *Gaulois*, and a verbal message to the effect that it contained a paragraph which her mistress had thought might be of interest to Madame. She probably was the only person who had paid it the slightest attention. The other readers of the paper glanced at this pale reflection of Madame Cresmeyer's burning emotions, with the same indifference which they gave to the numerous deaths, divorces and suicides which scattered over the newspapers the cold and public ashes of so many secret fires. Much that for us is fraught with happiness or misery, remains almost unnoticed by the rest of the world.

Towards the end of the year Madame Cresmeyer was carried off by that disease of the liver from which she had already begun to suffer at the time of her famous dinner. For her during her last illness as for many others, the question of what her relations with the Bliaux might or might not be, lost all importance. Her funeral was attended by a considerably larger number of guests, though scarcely less indifferent, than her dinner had been, but aroused no interest in the minds of the general public. In that solemn hour her blood connexions resumed their rightful place of priority over the artificial intimates of her social life. All the humble folk who had remained uninvited on the occasion of her party, put in an appearance at the house of death, while Bliaux did not so much as inscribe his name in the visitors' book, "Because," as he told his wife, he had known, "none of the family except her." He did not want it to be made public that his knowledge had gone even that far. On the other hand Madame Desroches, who would not have gone to the dinner had she been asked, and the Santeuils, attended the funeral, because they felt it to be only decent to do so, and because they had a tender spot in their hearts for this cross-grained relative. Since Madame Cresmeyer was in no position to send an announcement to the Press, the ceremony was entirely ignored by the newspapers.

8. *Henri Loisel*

Such incidents, when they became generally known, were no doubt looked upon as comprising the more squalid side of Bergotte's life, the inexplicable complement not only of his genius, but still more of his kindliness, his loyalty, his absence of self-interest. There were others too, which though trivial in themselves caused no little pain to his admirers, and were productive in himself, if not of a sense of shame, at least of that nagging sense of life's mediocrity which inevitably irks all of us when the spiritual level of our existence is too low.

I shall never forget the words spoken by Bergotte to Loisel one evening when the latter had gone to play at Madame Delven's house. Madame Delven had set great store by this occasion because more fashionable persons than those with whom she ordinarily consorted had come to hear him, since they always were careful to put in an appearance whenever, and wherever he was performing. Madame Delven was poor, and Loisel's fee for each appearance was a thousand francs. It was therefore tacitly agreed that he came, not for her, but for the great Bergotte, just as it was for him that on another evening, the actors of the Comédie Française had privately performed a new play for him, and on yet another, that Fauré had given a recital. When the artist had finished, Bergotte's face expressed an enthusiasm deliberately assumed for the occasion. For several minutes he engaged him in talk, and not content to praise his performance said many charming things especially designed to give him pleasure—that being his way of paying him for his trouble. All the time that this conversation was going on Monsieur and Madame Delven stood by with that air of formal politeness which you will see on the faces of the members of a family when papa slips into the hand of the artist who has just completed his programme, the fee agreed upon.

Bergotte was so remarkably intelligent that he had only to listen for a few moments to a pianist or a singer, had only to take in the expressive gestures of an actress, in order to find at once like an old hand at Parliamentary business who need spend no time in studying a motion in order to grasp how best it may be attacked, the words that would most flatter the artist in a very special and personal way, and if not his talent, at least his conceit. He explained so convincingly the reasons for his appreciation that it was as though he were speaking in spite of himself, and bowing to the undeniable evidence of fact. "There is a sense of encroaching dusk in your music, of that precise moment when the light begins to go. One feels a sort of uneasiness, like that which comes to wild animals or children who fear the dark. That is what your playing makes of us . . . just so many small children. Do play that passage again please—the one I mean in which you softly isolate each note, bending your head a little as though you were plucking flowers. And then how wonderful that moment when the music seems to gallop, as though it were carrying you away, though all the time you are in full control, and it is *your* hands that shake the thunder or colour the rainbow. It is all very, very beautiful." Bergotte had a way of making a mental note of certain passages to which he could apply some curious epithet, some charming comparison. Then when he had thus marked down one or two of them, he ceased to listen to the rest of the piece, and relapsed into his brooding mood until the moment when the music had reached a resounding finale. It was in this way that he now addressed Loisel, while the other listeners, silent, and reduced to the role of a Greek Chorus, only when Bergotte had finished speaking, found their tongues again and murmured, "Quite wonderful!"

Rather artlessly, really believing that it would give Bergotte pleasure to hear those particular passages again, Loisel resumed his place at the piano, saying, "This is for Monsieur Bergotte."–"How good of you," Bergotte would say with an air of dreamy enthusiasm, though he was already thinking of something else. "The galloping passage, please!" Then Loisel would laugh. He found the use of that word one of Bergotte's most engaging idiosyncracies and liked to quote it later. He would say, "That's what Bergotte calls the galloping passage," and laugh. "All right, I'll play the galloping passage over again," he would say to Bergotte, whereat Bergotte, like a member of the *claque* instructed when Sarah Bernhardt takes her call to shout, "Let's have it all over again!" would say, "No, all of it, the whole piece!"–"Really!" Loisel with that smile of pity with which we greet any hysterical outburst of applause, though of indulgent pity it is true when we happen to be the cause of the enthusiasm. Then without waiting to be asked twice, he would start again from the beginning. But when this happened, Bergotte like a dramatic critic who never goes to the theatre except when he has to write a notice, made no attempt to listen, having already found precisely the right words with which to express his admiration. The other members of the audience on the contrary, who at the first hearing and before Bergotte had spoken, had not really known what to think (have you ever noticed that when people are listening to a virtuoso, unless somebody has applauded or voiced his opinion, or unless the appearance of the artist has been preceded by an echo of the applause or the catcalls accorded to him by earlier audiences, never seem able to make up their minds, not being sure whether what seems like a break in the voice is a premeditated effect or merely due to a frog in the throat, whether it is to be regarded as superb or ridiculous?) felt now the truth of Bergotte's epithets, as though they had thought them out themselves. So deeply were they conscious of the presence of darkness in the music, that when it was finished, a young poet already assuming the mantle of Bergotte, cried out in the words of the dying Goethe, "Light, more light!" which Loisel considered the best remark of the evening. I have often heard him speak of it as a proof of the physical effect that music can produce. He sympathized with the young man to whom the music had given the feeling of impenetrable darkness as much as he would have done had the experience been something real and oppressive. At this second playing everyone was conscious of a rising tide of enthusiasm, and when in the course of a pianissimo, Madame Cresmeyer who ever since the beginning of the piece, had been swaying her head and her body very quickly to and fro, though scarcely moving either, like a rapidly swinging pendulum which moves so little from its centre of gravity, that it appears to be merely quivering, in the course of the pianissimo, when softer and softer, but quicker and quicker, notes were making themselves heard with perfect equality of tone—an effect which any good Conservatoire pupil can produce without needing for that purpose to possess Loisel's gifts—Madame Cresmeyer who for some moments had scarcely been able to restrain her admiration, and had been murmuring, "Quite, quite wonderful!" when the pianissimo grew even softer, and the balanced rapidity of the notes more marked, could bear no more but laughed affectedly. This manifestation of her enthusiasm at once gave her the clue to the nature of the performance. "So amusing!" she said. Madame Delven having failed to think of any remark to make, was shocked by

Madame Cresmeyer's comment, and instead of showing admiration sat with a wooden face, as though to show Madame Cresmeyer how people should behave who have a genuine love of music.

That evening the footman said to the maid (and to be sure his opinion was not in any way influenced by any praises uttered by Bergotte, but the members of the lower orders enjoy listening to music, no matter what it is, just as they enjoy visiting galleries to see "a bit of painting" displayed in gilded frames): "I must say that chap's a pretty good dab at the piano. I only hope he'll come here often. I've been listening at the door the whole time." – "Oh when anyone plays like that," replied the maid, "I come over all queer. It's a good thing he doesn't visit with us except sometimes" – "Why?" asked the footman. "Because it would make me ever so ill," said the maid hurriedly, as though she were frightened. "The doctor says I'm much too sensitive: you just ask the mistress if he doesn't."

When Loisel had finished playing for the second time Bergotte said nothing. But he acted as though his emotions had been too much for him, and if anybody spoke apologized for seeming to appear absent-minded, saying, "I just can't help it: when that young fellow plays those tricks with my nerves, it takes me at least five minutes to calm down again." – "If I thought that, Master, I would never play another note," said Loisel with a pleased smile. There was another sort of smile on Madame Delven's lips, which nobody noticed, as she looked at Bergotte. But he did not respond to it, either, from prudence, or, because having played a part so often, he no longer felt that he was playing a part at all, and because the artlessness with which Loisel had allowed himself to be taken in made him feel slightly irritated to think that anyone could so fail to understand what after all was only his way of showing friendliness.

I, who had so often heard him talk in just the same way to others, in whom he had ceased to find any sign of talent as soon as Madame Delven no longer needed them for her "evenings", could not help regarding those golden phrases poured out by so divine a genius, and debased to such worldly uses as payment for services rendered, with the same sense of shame as one might feel if one saw a priest haggling with the sellers of temple furniture. All the time that Bergotte was thanking Loisel, and as I heard his voice going all soft and sentimental with false emotion and false gratitude, while Madame Delven who knew so well what those words and that tone meant, because she had been so long accustomed to turn them to her own account, and had grown accustomed to demand them of him as a social necessity, was listening to his performance with an ecstatic look on her face—I felt so deeply humiliated, that I could not bear the sight of either of them. Next day Loisel received from Bergotte a reproduction of his great *Eurydice* picture. Beneath it the Master had written in his own hand— "To Orpheus this Eurydice, from his friend and admirer Bergotte." It was Madame Delven who arranged for its delivery. She had personally superintended its packing. As she gave it to the servant she said to Bergotte, "I don't think there is any need now to ask him to dinner."

★

While Loisel was playing one last waltz which contained a certain phrase, Jean felt a little tremulous movement deep down in himself. Doubtless what he was hearing reminded him of some forgotten melody. Perhaps quite simply it was the same harmonic arrangement which astonished at hearing itself, was struggling up from the deep abyss of forgetfulness, was trying to return to the world of the living, to emerge, to be recognized. For the moment, no recognition came to him: all he knew was that it made him feel sad. Loisel went on playing. But Jean was striving to recapture the phrase which had so suddenly touched a responsive chord in him, to repeat it, in the hope that the multiplication of the impact might finally succeed in awakening his sleeping consciousness. But the air continued to elude him, though all the while, what had started the tremulous movement in himself was rising to the surface of his mind. It was not the tune that was familiar, but the quality of the sound. At last he had it!—at last he recognized it! The sound was the same as the harsh twanging given out by the old piano which used to stand in Monsieur Sandré's room. By a chance movement of his fingers Loisel had drawn from this good instrument the same sound that Monsieur Sandré's ancient piano had made. But for that accident Jean would probably never have thought of it at all, for he had never consciously done so since the day when he had heard it first, often though he had sat before its keyboard. Every evening when he had been dining with his grandfather, he had sat down to play, while his cup of coffee stood on the music-shelf growing cold. It was as though a photograph of the scene had been filed away in the archives of his memory, archives so extensive that into most of them he would never have looked again but for this chance happening, this slight faltering of a pianist's fingers, which had suddenly opened them again before his eyes.

*

Without his having the slightest inkling of what was to happen—for the major changes in our lives occur without any premonitory warnings, and we are only unconsciously their agents—this evening spent by Henri Loisel in Madame Delven's house, where he tasted the, so to speak, impersonal delights of luxurious living—for he enjoyed the whole thing as he might have enjoyed something seen upon the stage, and as though he were completely detached from it—was the last. Later, in theatres and concert halls, he was too intent on being seen by members of the audience, and seen at the precise moment when he was chatting with this person, or forcing from that in reply to a discreet and aloof raising of the hat, a smile of recognition, to have sufficient detachment to let him concentrate his attention on the general scene. He found that to participate in such smart occasions merely as an outsider no longer satisfied him. It so happened that not long afterwards the Duchesse d'Alpes read in the paper that her *Rêverie mystique* had been admirably performed at a Conservatoire examination, by a young pianist, destined to enjoy a great future, a certain Monsieur Loisel, who had studied under Massenet and Marmontel. Like many artists the Duchesse d'Alpes combined a wish for material success with a wholly disinterested devotion to the things of the spirit. This latter feeling was satisfied in an almost romantic fashion by the thought that a young artist, remote from her in space, had recognized in those pages which to so many said nothing at all, something of the mystic emotion which she had put into them, an emotion of which Saint Augustine, more than anybody else, had made her conscious.

With one who among the innumerable works which live out their solitary lives, having to cross infinite distances, comes on a work of ours, a world complete and absolute in which our thought is hidden, but lost among other similar worlds, like a grain of sand among other grains of sand, yet as far removed from all those others as one star from other stars, and greets our soul with a fraternal and a trusting smile, we feel ourselves united by a thread as mysterious, as sacred and as gentle as the beam proceeding from the evening star which has travelled through many hundred centuries, across millions of miles, to touch our welcoming eyes with its soft radiance, as though with head bent from the summit of some infinite height, a sister soul were endlessly, imperishably, watching over our own. But if the sweetness of a responsive heart brought to her from afar, struck a responsive chord in the emotional depths of the Duchesse d'Alpes, success, in other words the admiration of people who could not possibly understand her, but were compelled to admiration because her fame had been noised abroad, because they followed like sheep other people's example, or for a hundred and one snobbish reasons, was no less sweet to her. Now what could better impress upon the denizens of the great world the idea, not yet widely accepted, that she was a composer of quite remarkable talents, than the fact that a genuine artist, guaranteed by an authority which in matters of art, had not its equal anywhere, before an audience of illustrious masters, had actually played as an examination item and without knowing anything about her, something she had herself composed? Already she could look forward to a time when at many a party in the Faubourg Saint-Germain, insipid chit-chat, stale pieces for the harp, or silly monologues, would be replaced by her *Rêverie mystique*, her *King Cophetua*, or her *Assomptions*, all admirably performed by Monsieur Loisel. Given the stamp of authority by a genuine artist, her music in spite of every form of artistic snobbery, would have an immense success in fashionable circles. Following on this thought came another, which sprang naturally from her rich imagination and filled her heart with joy. The vision was to her so solid that she could feel its power and manipulate it for her greater enjoyment, the vision of another form of snobbery which would promise her a long succession of triumphs at parties given by people who would feel flattered to think that they were providing for their guests the same cultural fare as the great folk of the Faubourg. She saw herself in that blessed future obliged to frequent—for every effort would be made to attract her—a considerable number of undistinguished houses, the disadvantages of which would be made up for her by the presence of other artists, and by the fact that she would be better appreciated there than elsewhere. There was something rather daunting about this prospect. But she would go only where she wanted to go. Besides she thought of herself as of somebody with a mission. It was her duty she thought to sacrifice social rank on the altar of art. Just as the battle of Austerlitz—or so the fatalists hold—already existed as a fact in the mind of God when He conceived the world, so too probably Madame Marmet's reception was even now visible to the far-ranging eye of Madame d'Alpes. So happy was she to find that Monsieur Loisel was only too ready to turn himself into a commercial traveller for her music, to spread its fame throughout the world, to multiply its contacts and to gain a high reputation by playing it, only too deeply flattered to turn himself, as it were, into a member of her household, on a par with the doctor who had abandoned the prospect of a large and lucrative practice in order to give all his attention to her health, that she did not suffer unduly from the disappointment of finding that Monsieur Loisel knew a good deal less about Saint Augustine than she had thought he did, and being compelled to conclude that a calculated ambition had more than a little to do with a preference on his part which might, however, be quite naturally explained in other ways.

Since she was an extremely intelligent and energetic woman, the Duchesse d'Alpes automatically fashioned in her own image those who admired her. Certain it is that only after seeing a great deal of her did Madame de Cinq-Cygnes adopt that dying fall of the voice which Madame d'Alpes occasionally assumed, as though she were swooning in ecstasy. If Madame de Lamardin—a fat Flemish woman who was firmly rooted in realities—had not known Madame d'Alpes, Burne-Jones would probably have occupied less wall-space in her drawing-room. But a species of almost complete intellectual inertia, a total ignorance of the ways of Society which led him to accept at their own valuation all women without exception who sought his acquaintance, together with a deal of admiration, snobbery and personal pretentiousness, combined with an utter lack of originality, could alone have produced the strange result that Loisel not only filled his home, including old Madame Loisel's bedroom, with reproductions of Burne-Jones, not only used letter-paper stamped with a design representing Saint Augustine, but also adopted a way of bowing, walking and speaking with an occasional swooning air, precisely like Madame d'Alpes, and exactly as though he were taking part in a game of Dumb Crambo. But copy though he might the ways and mannerisms of Madame d'Alpes, the young Loisel could not turn himself into her. Coming from an almost Royal line—she was a niece of the Comte de Poitou—the Duchesse d'Alpes showed her good manners to each and all by being excessively amiable. She had adopted in her dealings with the world a sort of pantomime which though deliberate was not lacking in charm. When somebody said good evening to her she puckered up her lips as though she were about to kiss him, or so as not to let him see that she was suffering, fixed him with a sweet and absent stare, and said in a sing-song voice, "Good evening, Count, how delightful to see you." Then after a momentary hesitation, as though she were about to offer a gift of such importance that it needed thinking about, she abandoned her hand to her interlocutor who took it with every sign of respect sometimes as though she were offering alms, sometimes with a sort of determined dash, as though she were courageously advancing headlong into a fire. But the sight of Loisel going through the same dumb show, deciding with a smirk to abandon his large hand—which was sensitive only when he was playing—to the grasp of a duchess, produced an extremely odd effect. So too when she was about to enter a drawing-room, no matter how brilliant, having arrived late for dinner, the Duchesse d'Alpes, seeing it as a place filled with painful and vulgar promiscuities, would stop for a moment on the threshold like a frightened bird, as though she were taking in the full horror of what awaited her before plunging blindly into the danger zone. Often on those occasions she merely nodded her greetings, keeping her hands motionless on her bosom, as though fearing to profane herself by offering them. But Loisel, making a similar entry at the house of the Duchesse d'Alpes, went through a series of gestures which appeared to be the result of no comprehensible thought-process, and more like the antics of a madman. The creature, says Malebranche, seems inexplicable to those who do not know that it has its efficient cause in the mind of the creator. The creator in this case was Madame d'Alpes. Loisel had acquired from her many other habits, such as occasionally with a turn of the eyes heavenwards, saying, "God's Grace is indeed beyond our understanding." This phrase exercised upon him a compulsive urge to make it his own, because all the little tricks and foibles of the Duchesse d'Alpes had for him an irresistible prestige, but otherwise it meant nothing to him, and in any case his temperament showed little bent towards philosophical considerations. He would use it, accompanied by a shy smile, at the most unsuitable moments, when for instance he wished to express his thanks to somebody who had congratulated him upon his playing. He also adopted Madame d'Alpes's habit of nibbling the corner of her handkerchief.

Have you ever noticed that we never see something once only, but that having seen it for the first time we invariably see it again almost immediately, as though it had begun to exist at the very moment when it first came within our field of vision? In the course of your reading, you come one day on the name of an author of whom you have previously never heard. What is your amazement to hear him mentioned in conversation that very evening? You discover quite by accident that Madame de Thianges was, before her marriage, a Mademoiselle de Thiolley, only to see in the next morning's papers that Monsieur de Thiolley was present at an Embassy Ball or at the Dieppe Races, or come on the name de Thiolley in a volume of seventeenth-century Memoirs! The reason for this seeming coincidence may be that a name scarcely noticed when we see it first, strikes us more forcibly, advances towards us with an air of familiarity, when next we meet it, as when a young man of whose existence we did not even know, is introduced to us, and that very same evening at the theatre, is the very first person we run into. Perhaps on the other hand a new slant given to our reading or to our social contacts, as a result of which we have come upon a new person or a new fact, continues, so that we are in a prepared state of awareness when the next encounter occurs. Unfortunately the opposite is often equally common, and a first meeting which seems to have been inscribed in the book of Destiny, is never repeated, and leaves in our hearts nothing but the faint and tremulous vibrations of a memory. Try though we may, we can never bring about its repetition, but remain separated from it by no doubt some inexplicable law of Nature.

9. *Presents*

Jean was now spending long hours at home and constantly felt a wish to read and drink tea with his feet stretched to the fire. With the help of Augustin he unearthed from the recesses of various cupboards the tea-services, the flower vases, the drawings of the masters, the ivory boxes, the leather-bound blotters, which, being no longer able to fulfil their delicate and constant functions in a room which he had been leaving every morning, not to return until evening, and abandoned as a result of his social activities, had one by one taken refuge in the silence and oblivion of the attics. But now they had been recalled to his memory by a wish to drink a cup of tea, or to read a new book, with close at hand the fragrance of a flower or the smile of a goddess; and suddenly his love for all these things had become so overwhelming that after having ignored them for years, he was goaded on by a need to have them within reach without a moment's delay, as though only the sight of them, the use of them, could satisfy his craving and calm the turmoil of his impatience. "You mean the drawing which Madame told me to lock away? I must have packed it in moth-balls and put it in the cupboard—I'll get it out tomorrow."–"Oh, but Augustin, I want it *now!*"–"Really, Jean, you must let Augustin get on with his silver. Surely you can't want it as urgently as all that?" said Madame Santeuil, if she happened to come into the room just then, much to Jean's dismay. "I'll get him to look for *l'Education sentimentale* another day. I'm certain you can find something else to read till then: you've got so many books." Jean, incapable of explaining how much greater this platonic desire was than any mere "need", gave as his excuse some piece of research on which he was engaged, or if what he was clamouring for was an object, said that he wanted to show it to somebody. "You're never so active as when you want something," said his mother with a laugh—and gave Augustin permission to start looking at once.

As when in spring new life begins again in all things, and here and there one sees small clumps of jonquils and of violets peeping through the thawed earth, old walls sweating as it were with life, sunshine and moisture, and assuming a garment seemingly woven of silken thread, even water-lilies hoisting their great corolla above floating roots until they reach the surface of the pond—so now in a dead and empty corner of the room a tea-service had once again appeared, to exhale, when evening came, its cloudy perfume, a Louis XV sofa to show its curves before a chimney-piece before the poked and blazing fire, a Tanagra Muse to renew her immortal pose in the little alcove in the wall, so long untenanted, like some divinity, hidden in the cellar for safety while war was raging, but now with the return of peace resuming her place on a refurbished altar. The table once again was covered with books; vases, soon to be filled with flowers, raised their silver stalks at either end of the mantelshelf; photographs of Madame Santeuil and Henri de Réveillon, and a *Salomé* by Gustave Moreau smiled from the walls at eyes, now bright with happiness, which had so longed to see them. Upright before the door, extending to the visitor a branch of welcome, a *Pan* by Clodion upon its marble pedestal stood as of old on guard over this room which had become once more a refuge of the living. When Jean was there the latent life of all these things seemed to show a rich display of bud and blossom, and if when he had left the room, someone else came in, then at every moment in the creaking contraction of a burned-out log, in a shower of sparks given off from the silent convulsions of the fire, in the fall of an iris petal, or the sudden striking of a clock which with a few brief tinkles brought a sense of long periods of time to the listening ear, and in the oil soaking through the lamp's long wick—all these things seemed to be marking the momentary and sounding term of a secret germination, as when in the silence of the noon the ripe fruit bursts its sheath with a faint popping sound, and urgent movement is forced through the hours and days of endless waiting, coming from objects less patient than the white paper, the ink in the ink-well, the sweet wine and all the books which would have lain there motionless for weeks together until such time as it might please their master to make use of all their potencies. For now it seemed that the hour so long postponed had reached the moment when strike it must, when the rose petal could no longer stay immobile on the stalk, and the fire could not refrain from leaping out upon the marble of the hearth.

*

Jean continued to spend hours with Augustin looking for ancient objects, which chosen by his parents with such loving care had been received with no great pleasure, and now lay piled in chests and boxes like those treasures which sailors, soldiers, and all whose lives are spent in endless wandering, cannot keep by them. But scarcely had Augustin after much fruitless searching, succeeded in bringing to light the little silver candlestick for heating sealing-wax, the crystal samovar with golden fittings, and had asked where he should put them, than Jean would answer, "Augustin, will you be an angel and wrap that one up carefully, I want to take it with me." And gradually all these finds, taking the road mapped out for them by his thoughts, would find their way to the rue de Rennes. Jean had them sent to Françoise like those ingredients with which one impregnates the water meant for plants to drink so that they may gain new colours, and become so saturated that new flowers will form, flowers which it is our pleasure to stimulate, flowers which we are amazed never to have seen before. Imagining her joy at the gift, he had the feeling that when he showed them to her, he would gain an entry to her hidden self, would have her in his power, and influence her feelings. And if she sent to him a letter which contained some new phrasing of love and gratitude, he looked at it with pleasure, as at a natural phenomenon, some scrap of herself there, warm and alive, within his hand, and was rewarded for all his ancient pain, as the loving owner of a garden who has spent millions on it, thinks himself rewarded when he plucks at the last some quite new tulip bloom, the infinitely refined quintessence of all tulips, a wonder beyond price. It seemed to him that the little statue of Eros the Conqueror, which he had had put in the boudoir of the rue de Rennes, was his divine ally in that place, that the little ring he had given her kept something of himself present above her bed while she was sleeping, that his love would stay for ever imperishable like the motto engraved over the door of her bathroom: *Semper amores.*

But if each time he sent to her a gift, he was as happy as though a little love had come to him in return, when he received one from her, he was smitten with a great sadness, for it was as though she had tried to repay in some quite other manner the debt of tenderness which he wanted to grow larger day by day, as though it stood for a kiss, a tryst, an avowal, which now sheneed not give. It seemed to him that having spent so much upon a dressing-case for him, or a Delacroix, she needs must love him less, that he could not now demand more of her.

Besides what need was there for her to send him all those lovely things? The humblest object, if it came from her, was just as precious to him, perhaps more precious, as though a flower, a handkerchief, a glove-box which she had used, having no other beauty and no other meaning, could more wholly saturate him with her beauty and the sense of her. A lovely picture might come from her as a gift to him, but it had a life of its own, was not like a handkerchief a thing peculiarly hers. Little by little, as progressively she came to hold less mystery for him, as his earlier turmoil turned to a feeling of mere human tenderness, his ecstasy to a happiness which was of this world, the pleasure grew stronger in his heart which comes from the sense of ownership and from the continuity of habit. A picture which like some lovely stranger, once set us dreaming of a different life, a hidden soul, we still can love though differently, when bought at the cost of a thousand agonies, it stays on night and day within our room, its now familiar look no longer bringing us unease, though ravishing our heart no less with its own peculiar beauties, habitual though they now may be.

10. *The Confession*

They were alone together waiting. He took her face between his hands. For the third time he looked at her, as he had done when they had listened to the Sonata, when they had been at the theatre. Then he drew back a few paces, as though she had pushed him away, stopped dead, and asked, "Françoise, have you ever loved anyone but me?" – "You know I haven't, darling." – "Don't say you know I haven't—say, I have never loved anyone but you." She said like someone repeating a lesson, "I have never loved anyone but you—does that satisfy you?" – "Will you swear it?" Like a drunkard who is being held up by a friend and now and again pulling himself together strikes violently at his companion in a supreme effort to break free, she fixed on him a look of anger, while trying to escape from his questioning. "How long is this going on? What's the matter with you all of a sudden? I can't stand much more." He waited for a few moments to let her fury cool. Then still following the taut string of his thought, went on: "You're quite wrong if you think I should blame you. The only thing I should blame you for would be deceiving me. I won't go on: all I want is just one little word. Give me a frank answer and I'll leave off plaguing you. Françoise, darling." Once more he took her face lovingly between his hands, "All I want is just one word, so as *not* to go on tormenting you, so as to get it all over and done with . . . have you ever . . . you know what I mean . . . before you did with me?" – "That's enough!—what a beastly thing to say. . . . I shall never forgive you for saying that, never, as long as I live!" He lowered his voice. Very quietly, almost beseechingly, so as to soothe her anger, he said, "Answer me." He looked her in the eyes but they avoided his. What he noticed in them was a hint of uneasiness, of caution, of something hidden, as when he had seen her for the first time. He knew already what she was going to say. She said, "I don't know . . . perhaps . . . it didn't mean anything . . . it's all so long ago . . . I don't remember." Something horrible had suddenly happened to both their faces. It was as though the same hideous disease had smitten both at once. There was in his eyes that

652

look which shows in those of the dying, of sick men in the grip of agony, something vague, tormented, something that seems to herald the coming of a great change, while the peace of death or the resignation of the condemned, strives to establish itself, but cannot. Alas! that torment would be with him till his sickness went.

He took her hand and laid it against his heart. He was on the verge of tears: he said, "There is such pain in my heart. Tell me, tell me quickly, for I cannot wait, darling. Listen to my heart. Was it a young man?" – "I don't know, I tell you. I think you must be crazy! You're doing this to me on purpose!" – "No, darling: in a moment all this will be over, and we shall be happy . . . an old man, then?" – "Oh, stop! stop!" – "Then it *was* an old man. I should understand, really I should: I love you enough to understand." – "No, not an old man." – "Who, then?" She begged him not to go on. "Jean, Jean, be kind to me: leave me alone!" Again, he saw in her eyes that look of uneasiness, of caution, that hint of hidden things. Lowering his voice still further, so that it was little more than a hiss: "Women?" he asked. She had hidden her face in his shoulder: she did not answer. He did not pause, but went on: "Forgive me: it's all over now . . . just one, or several?" – "One, I think, yes, one. . . . Oh Jean, please, please, leave me alone!" – "Do I know her?" She started back with a look of terror in her eyes. "No, never! I swear it! I was exaggerating. I was very young. I don't remember!" He did not believe her, but for a moment waited: then "It's a pity I don't know her, because that would make it all the easier to bear, don't you see—if it was some person I could visualize. . . . I should feel so much calmer. . . . The awful thing is not knowing. But you have been too long-suffering with me already. . . . I'm grateful for that, truly I am . . . but if only you could remember . . . one? Just one? But I'm wearing you out. . . . *Only* one?—but there must have been more. Don't say no, don't! As a matter of fact, I'd rather it was that, because love wouldn't have come into it at all. . . . How long ago was the last time?" – "I can't remember . . . fifteen years." – "Not that it matters. But it can't have been fifteen years since the last time. You don't remember. You mustn't wear yourself trying to . You see, it's not *possible*—fifteen years. What about this year? . . . nothing?" – "Jean I swear!" – "Darling, I *do* believe you. But I *should* understand, honestly I should. Something *must* have happened since we first got to know each other: it's not possible there shouldn't." – "I swear I don't remember!" He took a step back like someone who has been hit. "Oh, if only you could remember one occasion, just one, so that I could tell myself, *that's* when it was!" – "Jean, Jean, you're torturing me!" – "Forgive me! I implore you to forgive me!—but just one word—to satisfy my stupid curiosity . . . it isn't important . . . but so's I can be calmer, and not plague you again, *never* again, with tiresome questions—so that we can be happy ever after. Did it happen in your own home? In your own room?" – "I'm no longer sure—perhaps once—but really I don't know." – "In that case you can tell me the name of the other person. Be merciful, Françoise, be kind—I *must* know . . . who was it?" – "I don't remember." – "But you can't *not* remember with whom it was you did this! I promise I won't feel any anger towards her. After all, why should I? You told me yourself it was a long time ago, that it's all over now . . . it's only, you see, that I don't want you to hide anything from me, so that we can feel that our love is complete, that we really do belong to each other." – "I will tell you then, because the whole business is over and done with. I should hate you to think beastly things about her, you mustn't do that. I'm not trying to deny anything. . . . I think I deserve more praise than most for having cured myself, because you see at the time we're speaking of, I was *like that*, naturally, I mean. But it was just chance, just a moment's madness, that it happened with her—actually we've never mentioned it since—so I *will* tell you . . . but you mustn't go reading more into what I say than is there. I've told you it's all over and it is: as a matter of fact it was with Charlotte."

He smiled, but she saw the blood drain from his face. "So it was Charlotte: how very odd: I'd never have thought it. But not now? —you don't do that now?" – "Oh, Jean! I've told you I don't!" – "How many times—*roughly* how many times, did you do it?" – "Oh, how cruel you are, Jean, how horribly cruel! I've told you—just once . . . perhaps twice . . . I really don't know." – "But never since then?" – "Never!" – "Will you swear it?" – "I swear it!" – "Thank you, Françoise. There's nothing else you want to tell me?" – "Nothing. You can't know, Jean, what it did to me. Since all that happened, I've never really had a single happy moment. The consciousness of the awful thing I'd done, the knowledge that I am living a lie, that I'm abusing the trust of those I love, never leaves me. It's between me and everything I look at. Even many years afterwards, when I could have been happy with you, the unhappiness was there all the time. But I've never been so unhappy as I am now!"

He said to her "My poor sweet, my darling, don't torment your-self"—but he was scarcely listening to her, being worried about other things. She said: "I have been wretched ever since I first realized that I had that vice in my blood. At school, when my older friends tried to corrupt me with their stories of young men, and what they did with them, I used to think the cravings I felt were the same as those they described, the same that men always awoke in women. And when I glutted myself on the smouldering or laughing eyes of my companions, crushed them in my arms, embraced them with all the strength in my body, I only thought that I was achieving a sort of communion with willing accomplices, that what was to come would be an equal pleasure for us both. You will never know the full extent of my sufferings. Some of my friends hit me, others wouldn't even say good morning to me. But nothing had any effect. My confessor could find nothing to say to me. The doctor said I was mad. But though that horrible urgency was stronger than me, I have become stronger than it. If now and again in the last ten years, I have had a moment's temptation, a memory, I have always managed to get rid of it." – "Is it Charlotte you remember at those times?" The answer came from her with a sort of violence. "No, Jean: how can you say such a thing? Is that the reward I get for telling you all this?"

11. *Wasted Evenings*

"I'll leave you now," he said. "I shall see you again this evening, shan't I?" – "No, not this evening: I'm going to the theatre with my brother-in-law." – "You didn't tell me about that. Can't I come and kiss you good night after the theatre?" – "It'll be so terribly late." – "All right: but it wouldn't have taken more than a few seconds—just a little kiss to help me get to sleep." – "My dear, it hurts me horribly to see you get into such a state about so little." – "How about tomorrow?" – "I'm going to the theatre all these next few evenings. I have reasons for not wanting my brother-in-law to get suspicious." – "You blame me for never making plans, and all the time while I just go on aimlessly from day to day, you've been making plans of your own. I've always been ready to do as you say. I suppose you mean we must never go out together in the evenings?" – "It's just because I *have* made plans that all this is necessary if they're to work out. Really, you don't seem capable of understanding anything!"

But he, seeing her every day weakly shilly-shallying, hiding all her life from him, and the way she spent her time, though, with such firmness of speech, with such an air of knowing what she was doing, she had made him promises so recently, grew angry, seeing her so sure of herself, pretending that from duty and in spite of herself she was giving to others what she delighted in giving, and quite irrespective of systems. He felt plunged in gloom and suddenly a surge of fury swamped his heart against her brother-in-law, against her, overwhelming all tenderness. He gave her no answer, but said, "So long, then. But there's just one thing: can you tell me whether Charlotte is to be included in these theatre parties of yours?" – "No, I can't. . . ." – "But you should be able to." – "Why? How should I know?" – "You're always making such a to-do about being independent, but actually, you're completely docile. If you weren't, you'd surely be able, knowing how upset it makes me to think of your being with Charlotte when I'm not there, to tell your brother-in-law not to ask her." – "What reason could I give him?"–"There's no need for you to give him any reason at all. You think you can twist your relations round your little finger, yet you daren't even tell him not to invite somebody who after all isn't his friend but yours."–"Oh, how miserable I am, and how beastly you're being!" exclaimed Françoise. "If only you trusted me, if only you believed me when I tell you that I won't ever again let Charlotte say wrong things to me, you wouldn't get in these states. It's because I love you, that I don't want all this to become an obsession with you. If it does, life will be impossible for us. Keep calm, and our love will come to life again. You *enjoy* these tantrums of yours: they're not genuine, and I'm perfectly right not to take any notice of them."

Then remembering his sleepless nights, his despair, his tears, the intolerable anguish of which he had got to get the better, at whatever cost, even if it meant starting to take morphine again, or going away, he grew indignant at her unfairness. She understood so little of what he was feeling, condemned him so thoughtlessly to torment. A curt note came into his voice. "Françoise, I'm asking you only what I can't help asking, what I must ask, if I am to have any sort of a life. If you won't lift a finger to spare me pain, then I must break with you, as I could so easily break with anybody else. Do what you like, and forgive me. No one will ever love you as I do."

They reached the house where she lived and started to go upstairs. She called to the concierge, and sent him off with a message to her brother-in-law. "Tell him I shan't be able to go to the theatre with him this evening," she said. "Say I will write to him explaining why." Then the concierge having gone away and closed the door, she burst into tears and flung herself into Jean's arms. Touched though he was, he could respond to her crying only with a smile. For so great a load of pain had been lifted from him, that he could not share in her grief. Seeing him so gay, she grew angry. "In your heart of hearts," she said, "you'd very much rather never see me again." She was now using the second person singular as naturally as she had previously used the plural. When the sun shines out again, the stream that was dark shows blue and bright. "That would be true enough if I could shut you away in a convent, but perhaps not even then," he replied, and added, "When old agonies are remembered, the fact that you are causing no new ones is not enough. You must charm away what went before by kissing me and letting me kiss you, and by saying 'No' when I ask, 'Was it on this or that evening that you did something you shouldn't have done?'"

By this time she had wiped away her tears, and, with much wheedling, called him, "My darling, my pet." But the new confidence which her outburst of grief had brought to him began once more to evaporate. He was conscious of a certain falsity in her exuberance, of a vague insincerity. With the same earnestness with which she had said, "I won't accept any invitations this winter," she now began to sing a song of Chabrier's, " 'Tis you who make me feel what love can mean, you are my all." She sang with her face turned from him. He took it in his hands and forced her to look at him. To his questioning gaze she responded with a passion which was wholly for the music and not for him. To himself he said, 'It's not I who am making her feel all this. Who is it then? It may be no one in particular now, but it soon will be.' In a sudden spurt of jealousy for the sheet of music which had given her an idea of something which he could never give, he snatched it violently from the piano.

12. *The Sonata*

"Let's go home," Jean had said. "I terribly want to make love to you."
Now they were together in her room, but with a great space between
them. Like one who sits by the bed of a dear friend in sickness, whom
a long illness has weakened before the inevitable end, Jean watched
with uneasy and melancholy intentness their dying love, the progress
of a disease which he had hoped their love would cure, which with
every passing day, was draining his strength without lessening his pain.
Now and again the old love seemed to show its head for a moment
but even when Françoise smiled, he could not see in her smile the least
glint of hope, though he still tried to find in it some unquiet reflection
of the past. He savoured these moments of renewal with the heartbroken, the reverent, sense of fleeting happenings, such as come to
those who hear one, who is already in the shadow of death's wing,
speak, and see him try to walk. But these instants of happiness, fore-
doomed to vanish, became shorter and shorter, more and more rare.
The agonizing quarrels began again, lasted longer, and once appeased
still hurt like gangrenous wounds which will not heal. Like those illnesses from which a young man may emerge with strength increased,
but to which the exhausted resistance of those with a long life behind
them succumbs, quarrels which might have given new stimulus and
ardour to a love still in its early days, led with ever increasing speed to
the end of this love of theirs which had already lasted for so long a
time.

★

He remained there, seated far from her, not daring to move closer, not
knowing whether if he did so, he would awaken love in her or the hate
that seemed to slumber. Suddenly she got up. He thought that she was
coming to him. But she stopped in front of the piano, sat down, and
began to play. At the very first note a sense of extraordinary anguish
gripped him, so that he had to screw up his face to keep himself from
crying. But a glitter of tears showed in his eyes, tears which, looking

out for a moment and seeing the icy bitterness of the unwelcoming world, withdrew and could not flow. He had recognized that phrase from the Saint-Saëns Sonata which almost every evening in the heyday of their happiness he had asked for, and she had played endlessly to him, ten times, twenty times, over, making him sit quite close to her so that she could embrace him while she played, laughing when she pretended to stop, and he would say, "Go on! Go on!" with a laugh which seemed to flow tenderly upon him from eyes and lips, like a warm shower of kisses. Far from her now and all alone, having had this evening not so much as a single kiss, and not daring to ask for one, he listened to the phrase which when they were happy, had seemed to greet them with a smile from heaven, but now had lost its power to enchant. In those old days their love had quickly drowned his melancholy, the sense that love was fragile, in the sweetness of the thought that they were keeping it intact. Their separate tenderness had come together then in a shared feeling that though life was all uncertainty, they were never uncertain of each other and that the pain of hearing that all things pass made ever more profound the happiness they felt in the knowledge that their love would last. Hearing this phrase, they knew it for a passing thing but felt its passing as a sweet caress. In the past, when he could join her at the piano and they could play together, sadness had seemed airy by comparison with love. But now it lay so heavy on them that Jean had to lean against a chair to keep from falling, and tense the nerves of his cheeks, like two strong arms, to stop the tears from spilling over into the infinite abysses of his sobs. Yet in that desolating phrase which told how all things pass, the sadness still was light and airy. Not for a moment was the clear and rapid motion of its flight checked in its passage. If once it had seemed to show their fleeting love caught in a pucker of regret, so now it graced with a shy smile the disenchantment, the irremediable despair towards which it was hastening. Everything had changed, all that had made his life was dead, and he too soon would die, or still continue in a life far worse than death. But the lovely little phrase would still with undiminished speed spread its pure sound abroad, intoxication for those whose love had just begun, poison to infect the wound of those who loved no longer. . . .

Everything around that music too had changed, but it had not. It had lasted longer than their love and would outspan their lives. Long after they were dead, other lovers filled with certainty would wander, like so many of their fellows, seeking by the running stream a

happiness that they would think in league with them, invoking the
mysterious divinity of the sweet waters. Something there was then
more lasting than their love? Could it be that love as they had known
it had never been a true reality? What could that thing be which, once
sad when they had been happy, remained still joyful in their sadness,
and could survive the blows beneath which Jean felt he must succumb?
What was it? The phrase had reached its end. He said: "Play it to me
once again," but she with nerves on edge replied, "No, that's enough."
He begged her. With a sharpness in her voice she said: "But why?
Why?" Then grudgingly at last she played again. But he had caught
the infection of her mood. He heard the little phrase run its appointed
course and draw near to its end, though without once feeling the charm
of that hidden spirit—peaceful, disenchanted, mysterious, and smiling,
which could long outlive men's sorrows and rise superior to them,
which he longed to ask for the secret of survival and the sweet talisman
of rest.

*

Jean was wrong that evening in thinking that the little phrase had often
heard in an earlier year the amorous transports of their silence yet had
not treasured them. He was wrong in his belief that nothing of themselves had stayed with it. Ten years later on a day of summer when he
was walking down one of the narrow streets of the Faubourg Saint-
Germain, he suddenly caught the notes of a piano, and life for him
stopped dead. What he was hearing was the little Saint-Saëns phrase.
At first he did not recognize it, but felt a flood of freshness in himself,
as though suddenly the weight of years had vanished and he was young
again. He breathed once more the warm summer breezes of the days
when he was happy, days of shadow and of sunlight, for though that
music had been a stranger to the sweetness of those distant evenings, it
had kept stored up within itself, intact and fresh, one whole period of
his life which now in a flash came back to him. It rippled on, and now,
as once before, it brought him sweetness. If in the time of his happiness
it had looked ahead and seen a sad time of separation, when the
separation came it had foreseen, it smilingly announced the coming of
forgetfulness.

He had forgotten Françoise. Hearing the music now he felt no grief,
and though it evoked in memory the name of Françoise, it was not of
her that he was chiefly thinking, because the meaning she had had for

him was gone. She was still beautiful in memory, but her beauty now for him was that of a painted portrait. He did not try to think of her. But he did think with intense desire, and a great sense of happiness and love of that now distant summer, of the deep joy of all those hours which they had spent together by the lake in the Bois de Boulogne, on the terrace at Saint-Germain, at Versailles, in all the places where she had played that phrase to him, where he remembered it, where he had longed to be so often when she had played it in her room as they waited for the heat to pass before setting off on an expedition. For Nature, richer far than Françoise, still held preserved a hidden treasure of mystery and life. And he longed on a sudden to set off for the lake in the Bois, for Saint-Germain and Versailles where once he had sought in the mirage of distance the reality of that love which, for so long he had felt within himself, that unquiet craving and painful fantasy. He wanted to recapture the hours when, even before he had known her, walking alone upon the terrace at Saint-Germain, just when the on-coming of night was adding mystery and darkness to the darkness and the mystery of forest glades, and had felt the need of something to love, and an endless curiosity, as sensuous and as sad as the trees and the river, the villages, and the sky stretched there before him. Prey to a vague pain he had walked the roads alone. Of all this he thought but now it was too late. Others would feel those things. Love had made him older than mere age (though age too was threatening), at least too old for love. That he might satisfy a curiosity so suddenly renewed by the little phrase which still could dominate his heart, and held within itself so many of the secrets of his life, he savoured the tranquil charm of innocent and silent things which comes with age, but could no longer find it in that vague desire for love which mingled with the beauty of Nature adds to Nature's grandeur the power it has to inspire us with a wish for love, and to the feelings that we have of sadness, its own powerlessness to bring us satisfaction.

13. *The Dream*

Jean soon became rapidly separated from his love for Françoise, unable to resist the pull of the current which he could feel was carrying him along: for Nature when it wishes to free us from the places where till then we have lived, finds no resistance in us. It is as though we were chained prisoners in the ship of some conqueror, or rather one of those travellers whom we see in passing on a night journey, overcome with sleep and without the strength to open their eyes to take one last look, in the moments that remain, at what they are leaving and will never see again. For the separate periods of our heart's life are like islands which will be swallowed up in the ocean once the traveller takes leave of them, of which, though they may leave fond memories with him, he never more will come upon a trace. In just such a way did Jean travel from his love, and now already could not find again that jealousy which had always lain in wait for him like a patch of sickly, twisted vegetation. It had ceased to grow, and for that reason alone he knew that he had travelled far from Françoise both in thought and feeling. But before she became for ever dissolved into nothingness he was to have once more the feeling of her presence. Françoise, from whom he had parted without a word of farewell, was to come herself and take leave of him. One last time there was to be when he would find himself face to face with the love which already had withdrawn so far from him, which he was leaving behind, though he had never had the strength deliberately to push it from him.

*

Often his dreams would seem to hover about his life, annunciators of that destiny which only later would be his in truth, and sometimes never be his at all. Like a dark night shot through with occasional flashes of lightning, they were filled with signs and portents. The heaviness of circumstance, the weight of passing time, did not lie upon his dreams as on his waking life, and they no doubt were a suitable

setting for that last meeting with a past already distant, so distant that
it could never be resumed into his life. It was in this way that under the
dark portal of a dream, Françoise came back to him for one final
moment, that he felt again when he had lost it for ever the inexpressible
sense at once sweet and cruel of what for years had been driving him
forward, patting him with a soothing hand, or pricking him with a
painful goad. There were several persons in his dream, and they were
all with himself out walking: Madame Saveur, Madame Lavaur,
Monsieur de Guiches, Monsieur du Los, and Françoise. The time was
afternoon but with every passing moment the brightness of the day,
the light that was part of it, in the eyes of Madame Lavaur, in the smile
on the lips of Monsieur de Guiches, in the presence of Monsieur du Los,
and the reality of Françoise, seemed to be hesitating on the very verge of
extinction, as though all those things, the country scene, and the very
day itself, were about to be no more, were about to return into that
nothingness from which in sober truth they would turn out never to
have emerged. But after some seconds of indecision the light grew
brighter, became stationary, and all those there, Madame Saveur,
Madame Lavaur, Monsieur de Guiches, Monsieur du Los, and Françoise
were as solid and actual as in real life. Suddenly Françoise said that she
must leave them, and moved away from the company, including Jean
in her general farewell, not taking him aside, nor arranging with him
for any future meeting. He dared not ask one of her, but suffered
horribly, longing to go with her, but compelled to look contented and
remain behind talking with the others. So great a tenderness did he feel
for Françoise, so deeply did he brood upon her lovely eyes and fair
cheeks, that seeing her leave him thus, he was suddenly seized with
hatred of her, of her eyes, of her cheeks. She took her departure and he
was forced to walk in the opposite direction with the rest, putting so
great a space between himself and her in the short interval of two
minutes, that it was impossible now for him to catch up with her again.
It seemed hours since she had gone. Suddenly Monsieur du Los drew
his attention to the fact that Monsieur de Guiches had left them shortly
after she had done so, and said that doubtless they had joined company
again, though from politeness she had made no mention of this arrangement. Jean felt a stab of agony strike deep into his body, between his
breasts. He kept on saying, "I think she has made a wise decision: it is
what I advised her to do"—that he might not seem at all concerned.
Then in a flash this shadow of the past rejoined a still more distant past

which had, no doubt, been waiting for this final scene, before being swallowed up with it for ever, and Jean sank into a deep, dark sleep unvisited by dreams. But he still felt the pain deep in his breast. Suddenly somebody said, "You may think it a ridiculous suggestion, but to my mind if you want to understand what Françoise has done, you might do worse than ask Monsieur Cornet." His heart gave a violent jump. A day or two before however when he had heard Monsieur Cornet's name linked with Françoise, he had felt not the slightest hint of suffering. But now he suffered as he would have done in the old days, if he had heard it then. For it was his heart of the old days, which, troubled no doubt because he had been cheated of a personal farewell, had come back to him on that particular night, to bring him once again a sense of sweetness, charm, and torment, taking advantage of the darkness, since full daylight had forbidden its approach.

*

Somebody came into Jean's room. A great flood of daylight filled it, and already his old self had taken silent flight, never to return. He opened his eyes. It was as far from him now as though long years had passed, leaving him changed in many ways, since the time when he had begun to forget Françoise. She had gone from him but had left hovering about his ears the name of Monsieur Cornet. He heard it now with no more sadness than had come to him in the last anguish of the dying agitation which had possessed him all night long. With his eyes fixed on the future and his back once more turned to the past out of which he was moving, he set himself with joy to accept the work of life and death and forgetfulness, which nature was accomplishing through others and through him, in him no less than in others.

X

Charlotte Clissette · Meetings · The Game

Dead-End Again · The Dutch Nun · A Dinner at the

Réveillons · Death of the Vicomte de Lomperolles

Madame de Closeterres · Perrotin's Cancer

The Marquis de Réveillon's Monets

Jean Spends a Morning Alone with His Mother

A Winter Evening in Paris

Le Gandare's Portrait · Parents in Old Age

History of a Generation

1. *Charlotte Clissette*

The number of his loves increased. In none did he any longer have the confidence which he had had in the first, but submitted to the influence of his emotions, as the coming of spring seems to restore youth to those on whose way to the tomb it marks a stage. His belief in love was less now, but the mystery and the weight of lovers' vows brought him into closer contact with life. Sensuality brought him into closer contact with his fellows, as did conscious imitation and his taste in aesthetic matters and his love of art. Nevertheless each time that he fell in love, as though he were setting out on a journey, the world he knew seemed to shrink in size, and he left it without regret, his eyes fixed on the unknown.

One afternoon about five o'clock Madame Canut sent him a note asking whether—though she thought it most unlikely—he could possibly dine with her that evening. T—— would be there, B——, and Charlotte Clissette. He at once replied that he would come with pleasure. A moment later it occurred to him that Françoise had not been mentioned among her list of the guests. 'In any case, I shall be seeing her soon . . . besides, perhaps she *has* been invited.' He felt slightly gloomy at the prospect. He would very much rather have seen Madame Clissette without her. The presence of each made it impossible for him to enjoy the company of either. At six o'clock he remembered that he was engaged to dine with the Montfaucons, and wrote at once to say that something had happened which would prevent him from turning up. At this moment, his mother came into the room: "You haven't forgotten, have you, that you're dining with the Montfaucons?" "I've just written to excuse myself." – "But you can't do that!" – "What do you mean—I can't do that?—I've got to do it. It would be very rude to let Madame Canut down." – "How ridiculous! rude not to accept a dinner invitation at such short notice? It's much ruder not to go to a house where they've been counting on you for a month past. That's more than rude; it's impossible! I attach great importance to your going with us." – "And I attach great importance to not going.

I'd very much prefer to go nowhere, but if I must, then I shall go to Madame Canut."–"Well, you must do as you please since you seem to think it so important," said Madame Santeuil, but disappointment sounded in her voice. "Really, I don't know what's come over you: why be so violent about it? You're behaving like a lunatic. I only hope you'll enjoy yourself at Madame Canut's. If you're out to make a conquest, your fair enemy had better keep a sharp look-out. My son seems to be looking quite superb!"–"Am I really?" said Jean. He appeared to be so delighted that his mother could not conceal her surprise. "I shall look even better when I've had a wave put in my hair." He was so happy that he flung his arms round his mother's neck and kissed her affectionately.

Jean remembered all of a sudden that Madame Clissette had said how much she would like to go to the first night of *Les Pêcheurs*. "I don't suppose, Mamma, that by any chance you've got a box for the first night of *Les Pêcheurs* which you could let me have?"–"As a matter of fact I've got two. The Prince has given me one, and Madame Coquard another. You can have Madame Coquard's."–"I'd much rather have the Prince's."–"What's the matter with you, Jean, I really do not know!"—said Madame Santeuil, looking at her son with an expression of seriousness. "For the last few years you have been living the life of a true philosopher. I can say quite honestly that since you started shaving you've not been near a barber, except when I've asked you to get your hair cut. Whenever I happened to say that you were looking very nice, you merely shrugged. You've never, thank heavens, been in the slightest degree conceited about the figure you cut in the fashionable world. And now suddenly you seem to have adopted all its faults in addition to your own. Well, so much the worse: *I* don't mind. At least you're not looking miserable."

Round about half past six Françoise dropped in to see him. "If you were always as you are today," she said, "I should be perfectly happy. You've asked me no tiresome questions, and you don't look miserable. But it won't last: that'd be too much to hope. Will you come and see me after this dinner of yours?" Most days, not daring to give expression to his jealousy, he said: "Quite likely I shan't be able to come." But he always turned up before the clock had struck eleven, just to make sure that no troublesome visitor had put in an appearance, stayed with her until she had gone to bed and locked her front-door, and if Turteuf or anybody else was there, remained in a state of considerable boredom, not leaving until after the other had gone, or going with him, at the risk of not getting any sleep if it was very late, rather than leave him with her. This evening on the contrary thinking that it might be late before the dinner-party was over, after which he might take Madame Clissette home, he replied, not, "I mayn't be able to," but, "Of course I'll come: don't worry if I'm a bit late." Thereupon she left him and he went off to the barber, gave himself a complacent look in the glass, slipped into his pocket the ticket for the Prince's box which he intended to give to Madame Clissette, after first making sure that it had, written on it, "The Prince de Valentinois's box", and set off to look for a cab. He walked so quickly and so carelessly that he was all but knocked down by an approaching vehicle. He got safe away however and was reassured when he caught a glimpse of himself in a shop-window, and noticed that he looked as immaculate and handsome as he had done before the incident had occurred. Thinking back to the accident in which he had so nearly been involved, he said to himself, 'How little good looks matter! I might have broken my leg and not been able to go to my dinner.' He made quite sure that the ticket was still in his pocket. 'I shall be able to give it to Charlotte. That'll please her no end. She's a bit of a snob and will think the more of me for being on intimate terms with Valentinois. I'll give her plenty more. Influential connexions and money are great assets when it's a matter of pleasing a pretty woman who is sensual, snobbish and venal—though of course those epithets don't apply to Charlotte!'

The cab proceeded at a great speed, and Jean felt the same sort of pleasure in being shaken and bounced from side to side as one does when one walks along humming a tune. He suddenly remembered that it was Monday. Monday was one of the days when Herisseux frequently went to see Françoise. This thought however did not give him the same little shock as it would have done once. He would spend the whole evening at Madame Canut's, and not even dream of going back. But might not Clisson too be with Françoise? Well if he were there was nothing he could do about it. The stormy waters of his jealousy had fallen to a calm. In just such a way at times does the climbing moon lay on the surging waves, as it were, a track of silver oil. A god seems to charm with his invisible presence the immensity of heaven. It is as though a delicious mystery, an enchanted calm, were holding all the sea in subjection, and the cloven depths, caught in the radiance of moon and water, show like chiselled silver in opal or in jade, like a bone in jelly. Just so in his new happiness of living was Jean's pride now in being young, in being handsome, powerful and rich.

By this time they had reached the rue Vaneau. Slowly Jean made his way upstairs. He would of course be frank with Françoise, would tell her of his liking for Charlotte, and would not as Charlotte might— assuming that she acquiesced—go one single step beyond simple friendship. He conjured up a vision of that milk-white face with its soft, enchanting skin, of the little pink tongue which flickered now and then between her lips. He thought how pleasant it would be to kiss her. 'I'll tell Françoise that, too.' He paused on the threshold of the drawing-room, shot a hasty glance at the mirror, and remained for a moment quite still, until his breathing grew easier, for he could feel his heart thumping in his breast. The servant opened the door. "This *is* kind of you!" said Madame Canut, coming towards him. "Alas! we have some absentees. Charlotte's not feeling well, and won't be with us."–"How sad you're looking!" was a phrase constantly addressed to Jean while dinner was proceeding. Towards the end of the meal he noticed that one of Charlotte's aunts was among the guests. Happy as a Frenchman coming on another Frenchman in a savage country, he went up to her, astonished to feel how quickly and without her realizing it, the bonds of family were knit between him and Charlotte's relations. Later in the evening this same lady said that she was going to look in on Charlotte. Jean felt a strong desire to leave with her, feared that he might be prevented from doing so, decided that he would go straight down to the hall, reckoned that his hostess would go with Charlotte's aunt as far as the front door, and hurriedly recovering his overcoat, went down the steps, found a cab, and waited.

After a brief interval, Charlotte's aunt appeared. "What, going already?" she said. "Madame, I am going to be guilty of a breach of manners, and ask whether I may go with you and get the latest news of Madame Clissette. I should like to be sure that she is better. Permit me to offer you a seat in my cab." On reaching the house the aunt put a question to the concierge. "It seems that it is nothing, just a slight cold. Good night, Monsieur."–"You don't think," said Jean, "that I might be allowed to go upstairs?"–"Quite out of the question, Monsieur," said the aunt with considerable sternness. Jean felt as though something had been broken, felt that between Charlotte, who was closely bound to so many people, and himself there existed alas! no single bond. He must remedy that and contrive to create a few! But this evening he would not see her, that was certain, whereas her odious aunt, and doubtless others too. . . . "Will you at least give me leave to wait," he said: "I should like to know more precisely how she is."

"There can be no possible point in your waiting, Monsieur," said the aunt with marked reserve "I shall be here until late. Good night, Monsieur." Jean did not insist, but bowed. The aunt went into the house and the door shut ponderously behind her.

★

He had managed to find out the hour at which she left her home, at what time she visited her brother, when she went to church. One o'clock was when she set off. Consequently, luncheon was no sooner over than, after a hurried look in the glass, he took his hat and ran downstairs. No longer was he dyspeptic, no longer lazy. At five he went to see her brother who, being a senior consultant of a clinic at the Necker Hospital, lived near by in the rue de Sèvres. Over were the days when he used to go walking in the Bois. Tea-parties were for him now a thing of the past. He began to take an interest in medicine and hospitals. Meeting at some "crush" one of the professors of the Medical Faculty, he envied him his good fortune in having got Sentleur through his examination, kept bringing the talk back to him, and asked casually whether he had any brothers or sisters. Twice he met doctors who knew him and asked them to his home several times in quick succession, hoping that in this way he might be able to strike up an acquaintance with him. But when he asked to be allowed to meet him he did so only in a vague way, as though he didn't attach much importance to the matter—so as not to give himself away—or better still did not put his request formally but merely dropped a casual hint. But so little attention do people give to what we are saying, that they did not so much as notice what he had asked, but wishing to be polite in their turn, invited him to meet not the man he wanted to meet, but other doctors more celebrated for whom he cared not a rap.

At eight o'clock each morning she went to Sainte-Clotilde. Jean became not only pious but an early-riser, and every time he went out the hope of meeting her made his heart beat. He felt that something thrilling was about to happen, as though he were setting out on an expedition, or was about to begin a new chapter in the novel he was reading. If at the moment of his leaving the house to see her go past, or to meet her, his mother had something to say to him, or if a friend had just come to visit him, he did not even pause but hastened away like a soldier who has just heard the bugle. Though at most times a vague dreamer, when he set out in this way he became a different man, punctual, bustling, unapproachable, in a constant fever, a man whose life seemed eaten up with cares, and regulated by the rules of a strict discipline. If, when he awoke in the morning, he heard the sound of rain, at once he gave way to his fears, thinking that she would not leave the house, or, if she did, only in a closed carriage. Perhaps on the other hand on coming out of church she would walk with him, but in the rain, which was something they had never done as yet. If she asked him to come upstairs until the rain had stopped, and drink a cup of tea in her boudoir from the wide windows of which they could see the rain falling on the Place, or if his opening eyes were greeted by the sun, then all difficulties seemed to be smoothed away. He hoped he might per-suade her to go driving with him in the Bois de Boulogne. Then suddenly he would be overcome by fear that she might have gone off to spend the day in the country. Thus though the rain vaguely threat-ened that he would not see her, it also vaguely promised that he would see her as an almost new person, dressed in a different fashion, observed not in sunlight but on wet pavements running with water, walking more quickly than usual under an umbrella, or vanishing into a carriage to a noisy accompaniment of falling rain, and beneath an unfamiliar sky, a sky so melancholy that in what should have been full daylight it seemed almost night. It was almost as though he had brought her there. And so it was that he saw in the changes of the weather the brutality of fate and the charm he would have found in taking her to new countries. He dreaded them as events and savoured them as a species of travel.

He moved through the well-known streets as though they had been the streets of a city in which he had just arrived for the first time by stage-coach. The houses, the sky, the daylight no longer seem the same to us when we are ruled no longer by our former habits but by feelings that are strange. When out walking, when at a party, when in the company of friends, watching the succession of the hours, the approach of evening, the fading away of darkness, he found in the movement of time a sort of charm, as though it were something that belonged to both of them, something freighted with a part of their two so separated lives, which perhaps it would merge in its own indifferent immensity as the result of some mysterious complicity. To himself he said, 'Now she is sleeping: now she is alone, her secret self standing half ajar: now she is playing her part in the great world: now she is laughing, now undressing, now at her prayers, now going to sleep.' Each separate hour, because it held something disquieting, something sacred, being the receptacle of her essence, of the intimacies of her most hidden being, he breathed in with tremulous emotion, as though it had been a handkerchief to which by the mere act of holding it in her hand she had confided a little of her fragrance. Desiring no longer anything but her, not success, nor power, he had ceased to find a pleasure in Society and preferred to stay shut in upon himself as in some house where everything would speak to him of her. In this way did he live in his love, as when in the country we find in a ray of sunlight or a scattering of rain, the importance of something real, the vague sweetness of something felt: where listening to the striking of the hours we think of them not as the dead measure of our employments, but rather as the very life of time as it passes, compared with which the glories of the world and the goals of our ambition are things strange and foreign, and so live on confined within ourselves.

2. *The Game*

Jean knew that all this was leading him nowhere, yet had he not seen her would have been disappointed. We trust in love as we trust in life, without thinking of the underlying emptiness, without too much believing in it. We go on loving because we are starving for affection. We want to enjoy its sustenance, and leave it at that. Thus we begin again not once but many times.

He did not think of her as being more intelligent or kinder than another, nor tried to prove that she was, as once when he was young and thought that love was something absolute. No, for him she was like a woman in a picture, like a statue which is just itself and resembles nothing else. Her cheeks, her smile, her eyes—it was enough for him to see no more than them when she entered a room. Sometimes he saw her as she looked when bidding him good-bye, with a quick flutter of the hand many times repeated, smiling the while, turning her head again and again to wave to him, and himself looking back at her from the carriage; sometimes trying to explain something to him, with her cheeks moving in and out as though she were sucking some delicious sweetmeat; sometimes saying to him—"I love you very much." He remembered spoken words as a happy lover remembers kisses, for were they not kisses indeed to him?

*

Like someone who having arrived too early at a theatre stands waiting for the doors to open, Jean for the last month had ceased to live, having already reached the moment, from the thought of which nothing could distract him, when he would see her, like a hen, not knowing whether she is hatching a chicken or a snake, but, driven by nature to give life to the egg, he brooded over the unknown future and his doubting hopes with all the untiring warmth of an expectant heart. When evening came, and he reached the rue Madame, he was surprised to find he felt so little joy, so little pain. When he tried to think about his love no image rose before his inner eye. He was conscious only of a dryness and an emptiness. 'The heart is a lesser thing than we believe,' he thought. 'It is imagination that gives it breath, that swells it, inflates it, and makes it overflow. When at the touch of reality it collapses we cease to move forward and are like a ship under reefed sails.' He remembered how he had felt just such a dryness, how he had found himself face to face with the same emptiness, when his grandfather had died. 'So it is not only my goodness of heart which I realize now, as I realized then, is no more than an illusion bred of sensibility: now it is my very love in which I must cease to believe, seeing it as no more than a mirage of the imagination.' There before him was the house where Madame Clissette lived. He wanted to straighten his tie-pin so that the turquoise should show to better advantage. But his groping fingers could not find it, and he had to give up the attempt because his hand was trembling. It could not be the effect of emotion for he was feeling none. 'It must be the cold,' he thought. 'I started too early and walked too slowly.' He turned up his coat-collar, quickened his pace, and soon was under the carriage-entrance. Just as he was opening the door which led to the staircase, the concierge ran after him: "There's nobody at home," he said. His legs seemed to go limp, his heart to swell within his breast, so that he found it difficult to breathe. Its beats were loud and irregular. He leaned against the banisters to keep from falling.

"I beg pardon, sir," the concierge said, seeing who it was. "What Madame told me to say was not intended for you, sir. I didn't make you out in the darkness. I'm afraid I frightened you, calling out like that when you weren't expecting it, sir," said the concierge with a laugh. "Why, you're as white as a sheet." Then, "There's something we want to ask you, sir"—he added shyly: "My son here"—and he pointed to a good-looking young man of about thirty—"is getting married in a fortnight's time, and we should consider it a great honour, sir, if you would come to the wedding." The young man smiled but made no salutation. He was glowing with happiness, and looked as calm and splendid as a tree in full sunlight. "It's a bit sudden," went on the concierge, "he's been going with the young person now for seven years, but she only said yes a couple of weeks ago. Damme! he wants to make up for lost time! Them seven years weren't any too easy for him." His son was listening to him, but not a shadow showed upon his face at the memory of what he had been through. Happiness had wiped away all recollection of his pain as though it had been no more than a dream, and took in all the past and all the future. Jean shook his hand. "You're a happy man," he said, "a very happy man, and I will most certainly be there. Anything I can do for you I will do with pleasure." The tears rose to his eyes, and with a word of farewell he went upstairs.

*

The terrible blow which the concierge's words—"There's nobody at home this evening," had struck at Jean's love, the happiness that flooded in on him now that he was about to see that love emerge fresher and younger than it had been from the threat, like a field after a storm, as new, as delicious as on that day when enumerating the guests someone had said, "Charlotte will be there," revealed to him the sweet and terrifying power of the love which, for a moment, had ceased to touch his feelings without however ceasing to exist. He remembered the long hours of dryness, the vacant mind which had been his on the day of his grandfather's death. 'I was no more lacking in goodness of heart then than I was lacking in love a moment back,' he thought. 'Love is a God who hides himself, and laughs to think we can no longer see him. He plays with us, and his games are cruel. For he does not lay aside his arrows!'

*

He entered the smaller drawing-room. She was not there, but though she was invisible the sound of her voice reached him from the room beyond. She was playing at cards. He stayed where he was, sure that he would see her in a few moments, yet scared of seeing her. At last she came to greet him, but there was an absent look in her eyes. Soon a game of "Hunt the Ring" was organized. Stationed between the two prettiest women of the party, he could not keep his attention from the man who stood beside her, and with only one thought in his mind —that it was not he, that it might have been, that it would not be— could not keep still. He let himself be caught with the ring. Sent into the middle, he saw where the ring was from time to time, but did not move, only followed it with his eyes. There was a general outcry of, "If Jean doesn't take it, that's because he doesn't want to; he *must* have seen it." But nobody guessed what it was he did want. Seeing her so beautiful, so indifferent and so gay, and about to be his next-door neighbour, without having planned to be, and perhaps annoyed at the idea, he thought, 'She has no idea what's coming, and when it does, she won't understand. If she did realize what I am plotting, she'd be angry.' He waited until the ring reached the man at Charlotte's side, made a sudden pounce, forced the other's hand open, and took the ring. The man thus caught had to get up and go into the middle, whereupon Jean took his place next to Charlotte. How filled with envy he had been a moment ago, seeing the hand of Charlotte's neighbour moving along the string and encountering hers. But now too shy to let his hand approach hers, and too excited to enjoy her close proximity, he was conscious only of the quick and painful beating of his heart.

At one moment Charlotte, wanting to make the man in the middle believe that the ring was with her, leaned towards Jean with a little intimate movement. He was not taken in, but began to dream again of how happy he would be should she ever come to love him, should she ever really independently of the quick pretences of the game, be truly intimate with him. Just when, soothed by the impossible hope of such an eventuality, with hanging head and a face pallid with grief, so that it looked like a late autumn afternoon touched by a fleeting ray of sunlight, he felt Charlotte's hand gently stroking his own, her fingers squeezing his. He looked up and saw that her eyes were shining brightly. If in winter you throw a morsel of clear ice into a stream, at once, the ice you had not known was there, rises from the very heart of the swiftly moving current, freezes it to immobility, and in a flash there is no more water. It needed only that to turn it into an expanse of ice. 'That meant she loves me!' "For Heaven's sake take it!" said Charlotte in a furious whisper, at the same time forcing the ring into his hand. "I've been trying to pass it to you for ages!" At once Jean let go of the string. The watcher saw the ring, dashed at him and took it, and at the very moment when Jean felt almost on the point of fainting, he had to get up and take his place again in the middle of the circle, with the laughter of the players ringing in his ears, concentrate his mind on what was happening, and try to find the ring, to talk, to laugh. But Charlotte did not stop abusing him. "That's the last time I ever play with anyone so absent-minded! If you don't mean to pay attention, you shouldn't join in the game! If you ask him to your party, Juliette, don't count on me. I certainly shan't come!"

Giving as an excuse that he had an appointment, Jean left the room. Charlotte said good night to him very sweetly. She was feeling sorry for her recent outburst, he thought, and waited in the street, hoping she might come out. Perhaps she was going to beg his pardon: perhaps she would explain the reason for her indifference. "What, you still here?" said Cachtan, who had just left the house: "is this where your appointment is?" Jean forced a smile and did not refuse Cachtan's offer of a lift. When he reached home, he said to himself, 'At this very moment she is almost certainly in the rue Madame. I shall never see her again. No, whatever happens, it can't be *that*: that's the one thing that couldn't possibly come about. Even if she loved me she wouldn't come here and ring my door-bell. Perhaps she will write to me tomorrow and say she wants to talk to me. If it was only to say she hated me, I could at least tell her of my love, force her to listen, show how idiotic it would be for her to give me up.' He undressed slowly. His every movement had the heaviness of a man who has resigned himself to the fact that he has not yet reached the end of his hopes and sufferings. His restless glance lighted suddenly on the smooth tranquillity of his bed where the straight and narrow fold of the sheet, half turned back, showed like a white wing. "Dear friend who never changes!" he exclaimed aloud. "Who is always soft, cool, deep and protective. Once again you are about to receive my burning, battered body, tireless in self-torture, for ever searching out suffering."

Night after night he climbed the stairs to this selfsame bed in which for so long he had lain in bitter tears, his face buried in the pillows, after the many proofs that Marie Kossichef had given him of her indifference, unable to believe them. 'How many times since then have I known ridiculous sorrows, still more ridiculous hopes! Never shall I know happiness. It's always the same thing. . . .' He had put on his nightshirt which was as white, as short, as clean as in the days of his innocence. 'Oh darling bed! I am still the miserable little boy who used to lie in you long, long ago. I have changed no more than you have done, and you will taste always the same tears till I am dead or you worn out. But no! surely I can at least keep *you* with me till I die? Stay with me, my only friend!' Since the sheet was drawn high, he could pull it over his shoulders to make a pad of softness. His mouth was wholly hidden, and, as in the years of his childhood, he had to disengage it in order to breathe. "You'll suffocate one of these nights," his nurse had always said. He smiled, took one of his hands in the other and kissed it. He wiped away his tears .'After all,' he reflected, 'once when I had ceased to love Marie Kossichef, I had reason to believe that she had loved me a great deal better than I had thought she did, and that had I wished to do so, I could have married her then. The same truth holds in other matters, too. Why then, if all that we love be sooner or later within our grasp, should we make ourselves miserable instead of waiting patiently on the event? They cannot fail one day to be ours—that's true enough, but only when we no longer want them. What we are pleased to call our "power" over those things is perhaps a complete absence of desire where they are concerned. One must love so as to learn one is not loved. When one has ceased to love, it is then that one is loved as much as once one wanted to be.' A button was missing from his nightshirt. His neck felt cold. He got out of bed to look for a knitted shawl belonging to his mother which she had used when he was a child to wrap round his feet when they were cold. It still held something in its meshes of that warming tenderness, of that chilly past. And so it was that, when he put it round his shoulders, a sense of great sweetness came to him. It was as though he were in his mother's arms. He could see himself again, as in the days when he was sick of suffering, leaning his head against her breast, and, having drawn the sheet's white wing over his body, he fell asleep.

3. *Dead-End Again*

So far he had never dared address her as "Charlotte". One day, that he might be able to use the words "my dear", he said, "My dear neighbour," and so tenderly that he could not keep from touching her shoulder. He lacked the courage to suggest that they should address each other in any different way than in the past. They were on their way back from the Louvre. He said to her, "What do you call Réveillon?"—"Just Réveillon."—"And what does he call you?"—"He calls me Charlotte."—"Ah, so he calls you Charlotte! Who else calls you Charlotte?"—"Very few people: in point of fact, nobody."—"Oh, come! surely you must be called Charlotte at home?—but now I come to think of it, you aren't: your father always says 'darling'. And what do I call you? I rather think I say *Madame*, which sounds rather absurd." —"I agree: and I can't very well just say '*vous*' when I'm talking to you: *Bonjour, comment allez-vous?*—it sounds so unfriendly. It would really be very much better if I called you Jean and you called me Charlotte." A few moments later, rather self-consciously, not capable of speaking her name naturally, but seeming to stress it, he said: "Sure you're not tired, Charlotte?"—and, after a while, he having reproached her for not doing the same by him, she at first said nothing, like a child who before uttering a phrase in German carefully considers the placing of each word and then, "Do you think, Jean, that it's five o'clock yet?" He felt as though her mouth, in forming his name, had actually touched him. Then he remembered the many similar scenes in which he had participated, and that this was not the first time that he had endowed such childish tricks with a mysterious charm. He was overcome with sudden shyness like an actor who has played too many parts of the same kind and is beginning to feel old.

*

"I'm afraid that for the next few days I shan't be able to see anything of you." Lying in front of the fire Jean was conscious of a sudden chill, as he repeated her words to himself, the sort of almost pleasant chill which catches one in the pit of the stomach when one has been crying too much, or has been losing too much blood. The mirror told him that he was looking handsomer than usual—on this day of all days when she would not be seeing him! He said to himself, 'For the last six months I have been living in a fool's paradise, always looking forward to the next day, which, when it comes, always turns out to be not what I want it to be, but just as yesterday *was*, and as she no doubt *is*. She doesn't love me.' He felt so cold that he rolled over on to his right side and exposed his stomach to the blaze. Six months. . . . Then suddenly as he spoke the words "six months", he became as it were for the first time conscious of their meaning. It was six months since either had dared to speak jokingly or the other to react with anger. He thought of how these more recent days must have seemed to Charlotte, and the memory of all his little acts of tenderness, his flirtatious approaches, his ironical remarks, his outbursts of anger, his reproaches, his loving glances, his affectionate words, his daily air of concern for her, made him feel ashamed as though he had been guilty of an indiscretion, of a breach of good manners, of a kind of violence (as though trying to take her by storm), which she Charlotte must have endured with feelings of horror, as coming from him a stranger, whom once she had *scarcely known*. He felt that not any longer had he thought of her as once he had known her, so affectionate, yet so reserved, or of himself, shy and timidly docile, but always of what they had said to one another the day before, of the things they would say when tomorrow came, of some friendly smile that had passed between them, of an indifferent silence that had fallen, of the letter he meant to write to her, of the time he would have to wait before she answered. He would have liked to expunge from his memory that half-year of recollections and questions and refusals, of sulks, of plans to please her, of all the things which stood between them now like a wall—he longed to have the sense of her *apart* from all that, to see her again as she had been *before* all that—and could not. Love was slipping from his fevered grasp. He tried to recapture her mysterious essence and could find only a swarm of trivial human actions made for the sole purpose of giving her delight, of being pleasing to her, above all of seeing her, the flicker of feeling that he had caught in her face, the emotions she had made him feel—vague and ordinary feelings, all of them, actions which are the common currency of all mankind and in no way like the love he felt for her, which was something unique and beyond analysis. It was as though his love had been a god fallen from his high estate and forced to speak the language of poor mortals, to take, as the ancient divinities had done, a human shape. Yet there had been moments when like the travellers to Emmaus he had felt his love as a more than human presence.

And though after scouring his memory clean of so many recollected visions of her face—happy, sad, consenting, hurried, indifferent, affectionately angered—of so many hopes too, he could not find again the love which, by these means, he was seeking to recover, though the fact remained that it was love which in his memory gave a unique colouring to so many of his thoughts among other unremarkable ones, to so many circumstances that resembled other circumstances. He could not grasp his love as though it were spirit without body. Was not love a real and actual thing all through that half-year when it had been with him, when every day just to see her was all that he desired, the cruelty of absence, the enchanting moments of meeting, the feverish urgency of his attempts to bring about a meeting with her, the agonies of waiting, the flood of feeling when they had been together, his dreams so ceaselessly haunted by the beauty of a face seen all too rarely, the mysterious personality which had seemed to lurk in the most ordinary of words, the charm that set his imagination aglow, the wound in his heart which would never heal—was it not love that had been the goad to all his thoughts, the stimulus if not the sustenance of his life? But it had always been not her, but his desire of her that he had dwelt upon.

If only he could have kissed her, could have held her a long while upon his knees, he might have been able to feel that she was close to him. But since she was separated from him by her home, her family, her friends, her pleasures, her indifference, her personality—he had a feeling that he could never make contact with her, could never so much as brush against her physical existence otherwise than in dreams. That doubtless was why her least words had the power to hurt him so dreadfully—"No—I am keeping my evenings free for my sister: tomorrow I've got an engagement: in a short while I am starting off on a journey"—because at every moment they reminded him that she existed not for him but for herself, which meant not only herself but all the beings who wrapped her life about with other lives precisely like her own, and for him impenetrable.

*

We often find ourselves in circumstances and in places which *ought* to be the perfect setting for our desires yet nothing happens. There is a moment when the woman we love comes to spend two days beneath the same roof as ourselves, in complete and utter solitude with us. We dine alone with her and when dinner is over, go walking with her, come back with her to her room. There are no witnesses, and nothing to embarrass us. We sit on the end of her bed and speak of unimportant matters. The fruit of our love is nearly in our grasp, since we have gained her friendship, as is proved by her having come. We frequently have occasion to realize how much more Platonic people are than we had thought them. The noble will not sell for money the right of entry to exclusive houses to those who are ready to pay for the privilege, but will give it to those he likes, and to those who pay, if he happens to feel grateful to them, pays in return, but in a currency they do not want, in presents which anyone might give them. And so it is with her. The house where there is no one but our two selves, the moonlit bedroom where none can spy on us, shelters nothing but the most chaste of conversations. At last she is in bed. We say, "Time for good night," hoping that she will take the initiative with a kiss, if she intends that something else shall follow. Then the words of warning spoken, we look about for some way in which we may steal a few more minutes— which pass just as the others have done. "Good night, good night," and we shut the door upon the room that had seemed to offer itself to all sweet delights, having taken no advantage of it.

*

On this third occasion Jean was seated beside her bed. "I'll leave you now to go to sleep: it's midnight. Or would you like me to stay for another five minutes?"–"Stay till five minutes past." The sheets were drawn up to her chin. The brilliant colour of her face was set off by the billows of her loosened hair. He had never felt desire for her, yet longed for tenderness. He said: "I've got a pain in my wrist." She took his hand, and said, "Look, I'll massage it." Then very gently she began to stroke his wrist with her plump, warm, gleaming hand. Suddenly he realized from the look in her eyes that she knew how much pleasure she was giving him, that she did what she was doing for that sole purpose, revealing beneath her indifferent but adored expression a willingness to give him pleasure in yet another way. Desire swelled in him and made him tremble. It was clear that she could feel what he was going through, but continued without giving any visible sign that she was acting thus for that very reason with an apparent hypocrisy which made him mad. Suddenly he was conscious of life renewed. For beneath the surface of the woman who had become indifferent as a result of being loved without desire and without return of that love stripped of desire, he felt the movement of possibilities quite different from those which till then she had kept shut away within herself, and gazed at the face so delicately pink at ordinary times, but now rounded, full-fleshed and flushed against the whiteness of the sheet, under the rumpled hair, at the eyes which seemed to be keenly watching, with an expression of satisfied delight, the pleasure she was giving him. She went on with her stroking movement. She said, "You like that, don't you?—then why do you draw your hand away? Let me go on." Then desire which he felt quite simply as a need and nothing more, came suddenly to birth from deep down in what till then this woman had been for him, an object of craving rather than desire, a craving that had known nothing of collusion or consent, nor even dreamed of such, but a love wholly Platonic, and a lasting charm. Deep down within that feeling desire had suddenly appeared, making him tremble, forcing a way through his nerves and sinews, filling him with a fierce emotion, turning into some new and unfamiliar feeling as though instead of being desire simple and uncomplicated, it was desire working at the centre of a system of older sentiments, of present affection, of a persistent charm, to which it held fast and drew after it. In her too he had become aware on the moment of something which he did not recognize—a woman whom he had never desired, who so it seemed was on the very verge of giving herself to him, an apparent decision, a caprice, or at least an act of consent, something which was not the love he once had asked of her, but, now that he had confessed the pleasure which she was making him feel at once less and more a love which had shown itself capable of giving him pleasure in this manner, which was ready to consent and to come down to earth.

The idea of her which he had had was now completely changed. A sensation of newness had come to him with extreme intensity, because as a result of this chance caress which had revealed to him in relation to this woman something in himself which was utterly strange, and in her whom in this new guise, he had never known, an utterly unfamiliar self, it was as though his whole life had undergone an instantaneous transformation, so that the world had become richer than he had ever thought possible, as though the feelings which he had formerly known, the purely physical delights and desires with which he had grown bored, were not everything, as though the life of reality contained experiences as yet unknown to him, as though having till now presented him with a surface sameness, whether sentimental or brutish, it had now split open in a flash to reveal at its heart something he had never known, had spirited him back to one of those moments of childhood when we believed that life held a promise of the unknown, of the new, of the delicious and intoxicating, or of dreams, when we are convinced that what we have so far felt is not life in the full sense at all, but a mere measure of nothingness, that there is something outside life which is not so much continuing as beginning to be, as though it were some place in which as yet we have never been, into which we are about to enter. And so it was that by passing through a door which mere chance had opened, he was now to repudiate what never yet had been real life at all, those sentimental feelings for her which had got no further than letters, reproaches, adorations, services of homage, pretended coldnesses, to cross, suddenly, the threshold of a magnificent room which might all his life long have remained closed, past which he might have walked without even knowing of its existence. Deep in himself he felt that he was about to enter unsuspected palaces, to tread underfoot with tremulous eagerness all his former ways of behaving with her, to judge her now, to love her now, in a new manner, to feel that what had once been a piece of stage scenery had finally collapsed. The charming, cold appearance which so far had been hers, had collapsed too so that he now discovered in her, as in dreams we see those whom we have known in a new light, a person who would willingly give him pleasure, who would not deliberately turn her back on the possibility, but explore it to its extremist point, and to that end had stroked his wrist with her fingers, and was still doing so, looking at him the while with sweetness in her face, with an expression which seemed to say that she was doing all this only to soothe his hurt, with an hypocrisy which by giving him the notion that she was capable of deception, of caressing him as the result of a calculated trick, made of her someone new and exciting.

And to meet this new situation suddenly created by the chance motion of her stroking fingers, a different self had forced its way into the surface of his being, and another "she" had shown itself because no doubt she had seen the pleasure which she had never known she could give him, and seeing it thus for the first time, had at once made visible that side of her nature which though he had not known it, had always been there, since probably she had been keeping it in reserve for the moment when desire should set it free, and could never have shown it in mere friendship. And so it was that faced by this novelty, faced by this unknown "she", he felt himself to be on the verge of unpremeditated actions, and said contrary to all his anticipations, "Let me kiss you," and took hold of her. Perhaps it was this feeling, this sense of the new, the unknown, which burst from him with his consciousness of a new, true life opening before his eyes, an unknown into which one plunges so surely that one speaks things that one is surprised to find oneself saying, things that owe nothing to conscious thought, that one does things one had never thought of doing, improvisations of the moment, influenced no longer by a mere desire to seem, to please, to explain one's behaviour —the very words are proffered like lips and hands—but solely to achieve satisfaction, seeing that they resolve, minute by minute, one's newborn emotional state. In this way did Jean feel himself striding forward into the unknown, feel himself one with the new life opening, of which her flushed face, thrown into relief by the disordered hair spread on the whiteness of the sheet, symbolized superbly the splendour, the profusion and the life.

Why did she struggle, why push him away before he could kiss her, why threaten to ring for help, to leave the house? Why should he have had to sit down again, sick at heart, with a look of misery on his face, causing her pain, hearing her say, "Oh why did you have to come to my room? why must I take this hateful memory away with me?" She may perhaps in the jumble of her bad instincts and good morals, of her wantonness and her virtue, have held the view that there was nothing "wrong" about "possession" for had she not often joked about it, saying that she would willingly give herself if she thought that she could in any way give others pleasure, though her normal behaviour gave the lie to such an opinion since to give pleasure she would not even surrender her hand into the till now passionless hand of Jean when he had wanted to hold it, and had refused him even a chaste kiss, as though the *idea* of possession were, for her, something quite different from the *fact*, as though while regarding the one with approval, she all the same rejected the slightest thing which in however small a degree, and with no matter what innocence, might come within measurable distance of the other, so that she would embark to please him on a caress so casual that it could not strictly speaking be considered as a caress at all (massage), and then refuse, only a moment later, what were in her eyes the simplest and most innocent of pleasure's acts, whether because she had a special liking for the thing, so that she could perform any act connected with it, so long as for her it was "different" and bore a different name, but as soon as the notion of the thing itself made its appearance, recoiled from it—which doubtless could be explained by the fact that though her indulgent attitude to the "thing" might coincide with her liking for it, either because of the pleasure it gave her, or because though in principle she thought that it was permissible, yet for her it was bad, so that she pulled herself up short as soon as the idea took form in what she happened to be doing, and made her feel that she was about to surrender to something which she felt she ought not to do, or as a result of one of those small and seemingly trivial circumstances which in the conduct of our private lives, as in the battles of opposed and bristling nations, turn out to be decisive. Jean went downstairs, never to return, oppressed by a deep sadness, still heavy with that unknown something which had risen to the surface of his consciousness, which had brought to his imagination, to his sense of those realities for so long left slumbering within him, a new sustenance. The Charlotte whom for the last two years, his eyes had seen was now as in a flash, effaced. Within the four walls of a closed room, with her loosened hair and flushed cheeks more than ever distinct against the background of white sheets, she had become for him a superb, a luxuriant symbol of the pleasure which formerly he had never been able to taste with his body's sense, though now that its being had been revealed to him, his life would evermore be enriched. What had come to him was a sensuality shot through with godlike power, born of feelings already familiar, but at last breaking through them, that sensuality which makes us see a person differently, which gives a new aspect to our hopes of life, to our notions of happiness, to the rooms in which spending our lives, we have found a sweet delight, so that now in imagination we can conjure up an image of what might suddenly take shape in them and come into the light, can in some sort create a past with which the actual past has nothing to do, a past made up of our feelings for one particular person, of her manner of being, of the idea we once had formed of her, with, to which is now added all that we may suddenly find in her, all that may emerge, striking at us from the deep privacies of a bed, from the profundities of two eyes, from the dark truth of her being, in such a way as to make of the room now vainly barred and bolted a place of discoveries which flash out in a sudden glare, discoveries about her whose relations with us we had thought to be for ever fixed, for ever hardened into permanence, a theatre rich with thrills into which we have just entered as into a new room in the house of life, bursting through its appearances, snatching away its mask, so that she seems to be with us we used to think of her with those of whom we thought with jealousy, or rather treating us like some quite different person, no longer saying to us, "You are the one I have deceived," but, "You are no longer the old you, you are my partner to whom I would fain give pleasure, come, let us rejoice in one another," the enclosed, the necessary theatre where at last we live a life never foreseen by us, where we speak words of sincerity to that flushed and lovely face, the very image of splendour and delight richer than all the scarlet hangings which are absent from the bare denuded walls.

4. *The Dutch Nun*

In the year 1866 Henri happened to be passing through Antwerp. The streets through which he walked again were the same as he remembered them, the shop-windows the same, behind which to the same counters, like shell-fish clamped to their rock and visible through a thin screen of water, the same men, animated by the same vices, seemed as though permanently attached, leaving them only for a few hours each day to float as far as the Public Promenade, or to the harbour, and then making their way back; the same old life of the same old human beings, wearing slowly away in the enjoyment of the same old vices which would die only when they died, and every day could give them only the same old pleasure, vices and characters which nature had implanted in them until the moment should come when men and vices alike would wither up and drop to the bottom of the cemetery which boasted more inhabitants than the town. In these same streets which life had built, where life was carried on with its noise and bustle, dirtying the walls, setting lights at the same hour behind the windows, imparting to what lay within an air of mystery, transforming the rooms into secret caverns, secret graves, filling the air with a sense of feverish ferment and a smell of dirt—seeing all this he was conscious in himself of a longing to mingle with this life, to ferret out its privacies, to become, for one brief moment, part of it.

Suddenly as a memory of the Convent came back to him, and with it the old scent of his mistress, his blood began to throb in his veins, to growl like a wild animal in search of its prey. All the accumulated restlessness of this place and day became condensed into the heat of this consuming frenzy.

He asked to be allowed to see Sister Aline. Would he be taken to her room or to her grave?—for destiny had ordained that she should take her everlasting rest close to this town where she had lived. She was there still, they told him. He was shown into the parlour. She would come to him there. She came. She had grown older, but was still the same. When a dog sees its mistress there is no holding it. He could not

restrain his desire, but flung himself upon her, hungry for the taste of
cheeks which would not be pink for much longer, which already had
a faded look about them. There was a hint of crow's-feet at the corners
of her eyes, warning him that her youth had gone. She signalled to him
that they were being watched. They sat down and talked. She had not
much hope now that her passion could give him pleasure, but for
all that she was not changed: only, the discipline which made it no
longer possible for her to find relief for her desires, instead of putting a
keener edge on them, had reduced them to a place of no importance in
her life. She told him that it was five years since last she had slept with
a man. "But what about the soldiers who were billeted in the town last
November?"–"I was afraid," she said, "that they might talk. Nothing
matters to me now but to lead a quiet life and to keep on good terms
with the other Sisters. I have become part and parcel of this place. I
have no wish to change my way of living." Nevertheless, her thoughts
were always of the same thing. When Henri, unable to keep from
touching her, took her hand in his, she changed colour. "Be careful,"
she said, "later on, perhaps—we must see." The watchful Sister was
still at her post. The hour of the Office came. Henri told her that he
would not be leaving until next day, and that he could be found
that evening at his hotel: surely she could get leave of absence from
the Superior? "Oh, I've much too much to do. I haven't even
started my Easter Rosary yet. Perhaps if you come back next year
we might have better luck. It would have made me so happy," she
said with a smile which had in it all the tenderness of a woman who
once had loved. "I often think of it," she said.

*

When Jean went to Holland, Henri having given him the address of
the Convent, he made his way there. 'What if I find I've made a
mistake?' he thought. Suppose he had got the name wrong, suppose
some quite different woman appeared? But, as soon as she came into
the room, believing him to be a friend of her family, or perhaps the
father of one of the Sisters who had come to visit her, wearing on her
face that seemingly peaceful expression which had led the Sisters to
look on her as one of themselves, as perhaps, the most virtuous of them
all—like a policeman who has guessed that the man before him is a
thief, and snatches off the disguising wig without needing to fear that

he may have been misled, Jean at once recognized her for what she was, could have picked her out at once.

Desire is a matter of instinct, as instinctive as the reaction of a dog when it smells desire in the bitch, no matter how well concealed it may be from others. 'This is it,' he said to himself, 'this is she. To all the other Sisters she is just one of themselves, but to me she is precisely like all daughters of pleasure. She may not realize it. She is almost certainly the only one of that species in the Convent, but that does not alter the fact that she bears the mark upon her. And now that the key which was made for her particular door is about to turn, I know what I shall find within.' He looked at her as at a solitary flower growing among wild rocks, where it will stay until it dies, but presenting all the characteristics of the type he knew so well. "Sister," he said, looking her straight in the eyes—but she had no suspicion, did not realize that he had seen her for what she was—"I have come from somebody who still has happy memories of you, an officer called Réveillon, who has asked me to give you his good wishes while passing through this town." She returned his look. Réveillon perhaps, might have told him more about her. "Indeed," she said quite calmly; "I hope that he is well," with which words she gave him a glance from the corner of her eye, believing yet not believing, trying to see into his mind. "And he told me also . . ." said Jean, gazing at her more and more intently, with a smile which tried to awaken in her the sense of, to herald, the words which as yet he had not uttered—and already no doubt she had understood, and her attention was caught and held and imprisoned by the curious expression of his face which seemed to block the way to any further exploration of his thought, an expression of the kind which is always the same, which is not private and special to the individual showing it, but is something common to all men, a dark and clouded look like that of someone who is in danger, or who is jealous, not perhaps because at the moment he is a prey to uncertainty, but because it is not something deeply personal that looks through his eyes, but something profound and dark which is incapable of expressing itself more subtly. When that happens, the eye is like the fleck of quartz in a stone which seems to stare with a blind ardour. Then since the moral character of a person cannot long remain in abeyance, with the vulgarity of those who love pleasure for its own sake, which drives all of them to clutch, as something delightful, what brings them so much trouble and, not seldom, so much remorse—just as he finished what he had been about to say—"that I might perhaps be able to give you again some of those pleasant moments which he once passed with you in the tower, or might be able to put you in touch with certain friends of mine who might come this way...." she smiled and said, "I had caught your meaning already." The smile was indeed vulgar, but perhaps also touching, expressing as it did her happiness at being able for the first time to drop her mask and to breathe freely. And this happiness at finding a brother, at having no longer to dissimulate, at being able to speak of the secret which for so long she had kept hidden, was so great that she made him sit down, so that they might talk together without having to think of what had brought him there, but only of what had caused their mutual recognition.

"Oh, how I envy you men!" she said. "You are the first person with whom for a whole year I have been able to speak freely. For a whole year I have not slept with a man: and there is no-one I can confide in." – "Because there's no one else who...?" he dared not finish. "Yes, the Sister Gate-Keeper," she replied in a low voice, and with a deep blush. "I have sometimes wondered whether perhaps Sister Lélia didn't once carry on a bit with the porter, but I'm not absolutely certain." – 'Two, perhaps three,' thought Jean, struck with wonder at the rich variety to be found in all species of the human family, at the amount of variety concealed by Nature beneath apparent uniformity. He was conscious of a feeling somewhat akin to the anguish with which he had been smitten years ago at sight of the wild digitalis in its remote valley where it was fated to die between two slabs of rock which had known nothing of it. "Three," he repeated, this time aloud. She smiled, prompted by the same vulgarity as before, but also by the same sense of relief at feeling herself no longer alone, at feeling the presence in herself of the characteristics of a particular type which, but a while back, had made him smile. "How did you dare?" she said. "Suppose it hadn't been me at all?" – "I recognized you at once," replied Jean with a self-satisfied smirk. His words wounded her: for two pins she would have said, "Well, you were wrong."

They had been talking for too long. She interested him, but did not stir his senses. She stroked his cheek with her hand, and he felt in duty bound to exaggerate an expression of pleasure which he did not feel. He gave her a grateful, pleased look, to which she responded by an interrogative, modest and coquettish glance. 'Is that really how you feel?' A moment later, he told himself that, in the circumstances, a look was rather less than enough, and, flinging himself on her in an assumed transport of passion, kissed her so violently that he grazed his lips. He was conscious only of an unpleasant sensation of heat in his head, and of a taste in his mouth. He jumped back in pretended fear that someone might come in, and smiled mechanically, noting how handsome she was, but how completely cold she left him. He must be off. She made every excuse to keep him there. When at last she saw him go, tears of disappointment welled up in her eyes.

*

Some years later Jean and Henri made a joint trip to Antwerp. Moved by curiosity they went to the Convent and asked for Sister Aline. She came—a young girl who only too obviously would never know the joys of sexual intercourse. "But this isn't Sister Aline!" they said. The other Sister Aline was dead. They looked sad. The Superior thought that, perhaps, the two visitors might be relatives. She had them taken to the grave, but before doing so showed them a photograph which had been taken during Sister Aline's last illness, and bequeathed by her to the Superior—all that remained of her given to a woman who had never really known her, the visual record of that expression of the face which the Superior still believed to show detachment from the world and the existence within her of a burning fire of piety. It was not difficult to recognize her. There was still so much of her in the portrait: she was visibly the same person. The hair was the hair of an old woman, but across the face under it there still flickered, though less frequent and less vivid, a reminder of the images which had been so constantly present to her inner eye. Then they went to her grave on which the sun was shining with that same look of indulgence which we show to those who are beyond all earthly help. A breeze set the wild grasses quivering. They could imagine beneath the stone that prostrate body still, perhaps, sufficiently untouched by corruption to make it possible to recognize the kind of woman she had been, a woman from whom the last traces of desire would never vanish so long as any vestiges of the living creature remained. They stood for a moment, saying nothing, and about them was unbroken silence. There lay the now useless secret of what it was that God had breathed into that life, of vices which, as day followed day, had given her less and less of pleasure.

5. *Death of the Vicomte de Lomperolles: The story of Madame de Closeterres: Perrotin's Cancer*

"You must have seen the Vicomte de Lomperolles at our house in the old days," said Henri to Jean one evening when they were dining together. "Why yes, the old fellow who hated young men—that's whom you mean, isn't it?"–"Yes: well, our poor cousin was found dead this morning with a couple of bullets in his brain."–"Poor chap!" exclaimed Jean: "but why?"–"I expect you know that my father spoke to yours, only two months ago, about the discoveries he had made, because until then I give you my solemn word that we hadn't had the least little suspicion. To think that for forty years my father——"–"I haven't the faintest idea what you're talking about."–"D'you mean to tell me that your father was all that discreet? The reason why my father took him into his confidence was because he wanted to find out whether something couldn't be done to put a stop to the campaign of blackmail which in fact led to Lomperolles's death this morning." Then Henri told Jean what it was that had lain behind those forty years during which Monsieur de Lomperolles had shown himself to the world as a model of deep devotion and apparent loyalty to his wife.

In a few words he cast a revealing light on that underworld of Lomperolles's existence, once so carefully guarded, and now clear for all to see, lurking beneath his life of every day, which had been like one of those Oriental palaces where in a remote dungeon one lies who only yesterday was thought to be the master of all Turkey, but now is some Janissary's prisoner from whom the merciful release of death has been too long withheld. Jean learned that the two hundred thousand francs which Monsieur de Lomperolles was believed to have lost in one day at the gaming-table had been given in the course of a single night to a Polish violinist, who had vanished the next morning, and thanks to the dowry he had amassed in this way had married a rich young woman with whom he was in love. Then one after the other to say nothing of all those whose identities not even Monsieur de Lomperolles himself had known, a trooper, a priest, a male dancer, and a convict who had had endless opportunities of murdering him as he had murdered others, but had preferred to kill him more slowly and more profitably—had bit by bit extracted from him in two short months the six hundred thousand francs which were all that remained of his fortune. Only then did Jean understand the violence shown by the Vicomte in his condemnation of young men. He had been like an old dotard who having suffered all his life from women, curses a breed which once he has loved so well, but among the members of which, as the result of so many experiences, he has found only cruelty and scoundrelism. He understood too—and the knowledge brought a hot flush of indignation to his cheeks—why it was that Madame de Lomperolles had treated him, and all young men, with such marked reserve, turning on them a look in which distrust of a potential enemy was mingled with a timid melancholy aroused in her by the spectacle of those triumphant rivals who had dispossessed her of her rights, whose hold upon her husband's sensuality had grown daily more complete. Henri told Jean how—the instinct of imitation being stronger than any individual fantasies—this heretic of love had borrowed from love's orthodoxy, not only its language—as had been revealed in many ecstatic letters now discovered—but its peculiar rites and customs, gifts of jewellery and clothes, suppers, theatre-parties and country excursions, trips modelled upon honeymoons, names carved on the trunks of pines in the Black Forest and of the orange trees of Messina.

"But why," asked Jean, with genuine indignation, "did he say about so many young men that they were no better than girls?"–"For a very good reason," Henri replied: "he had been cheated over the quality of the goods he had bought. What worse could he find to say of any young man than that he had the vices of a woman?"

*

Madame de Closeterres came into the room. Overwhelmed by grief after the death of Monsieur de Serves, she had for some time given up going out at all. But gradually she had picked up the threads of her old life again, and was now living on the best of terms with Monsieur de Closeterres. The latter, instead of manifesting that perpetual violence which had caused many people to wonder at her long-suffering sweetness towards him, was now kindly and considerate, so much so, indeed that there were those who held the theory that his former ill-temper, which had appeared to be a permanent expression of his character and his health, might have been in fact due only to a purely temporary situation which had not outlived him. When considering the characters of others it is always difficult to know how much is unchangeable, how much is the product of habits about which we know nothing. We may find ourselves in converse with somebody who without our realizing it was taking morphine but an hour before, with somebody who is going to take his life that very night, yet we have barely noticed if at all that both had their thoughts elsewhere while we were with them. But if deep changes can occur in a man's habits or way of life, changes no less deep often take place in his health. One man with a delicate constitution, who for some years has been showing signs of improvement, may be struck down suddenly round about his thirtieth year, while the stomach trouble of another, which has been growing steadily worse, and looks like leading to a fatal crisis, yields to treatment when he has turned thirty, with the result that he lives happy and cheerful for the rest of his life which resembles one of those lovely late afternoons that usher out a day after a morning filled with the threat of rain and storm. Maybe the death of Monsieur de Serves had had nothing to do with Monsieur de Closeterre's changed attitude to his wife, which may have been caused by his own improved health, his nervous troubles having diminished, without ever having, at least in appearance, sprouted fresh complications.

"I have come to see you because I have wonderful news for you," said Madame de Closeterres to Madame de Réveillon. "Is Marianne engaged?" asked the Duchess. "Yes," replied Madame de Closeterres, "she is going to marry Henri de Serves: they have been in love for the past ten years." This was perfectly true. Throughout the course of the long liaison between Monsieur de Serves and Madame de Closeterres, they had seen one another every day. Madame de Closeterres would have liked her daughter to make a rich marriage. But the young people were in love. Both were shy and unsociable and completely wrapped up in each other.

Madame de Closeterres died very suddenly, of a sudden attack shortly before the official betrothal, and her husband who had loved her to distraction, did not long survive. The wedding of the two children duly took place. Though of a more serious and gentle disposition, Marianne closely resembled her mother, not but what the Duchesse de Réveillon frequently said to Jean, "I wish you could have known the mother when she was *her* age: she was a great deal better looking." Henri de Serves too, resembled his father, though he had not the latter's violent love of pleasure, nor that weakness for style in all its forms which, in a frivolous society, had led Madame de Closeterres to single him out as in a different sort of society, the daughter of a professor, will naturally come to feel a liking for a young man who has passed out first from the *École normale*.

There was something strange, something special about their love. It seemed to be older than they were. It was as though they had never attained to a full knowledge of it, and this impression is often produced by those who have begun to love when very young, and thus make one feel that they are always less old than their destiny. There was also something sad about it, for it borrowed from a past, which it recalled, a certain sense of melancholy, and a feeling that it, too, must pass. Into that wistful smile on her mother's face, which Marianne could see in the photograph which she adored and always kept in her room, she could almost certainly not read what it had meant to another who had been so like her own Henri. It was as though the elder woman knew by divination all her daughter's joys and sorrows, though she could not impart to her the secret knowledge which she now possessed and was filled with regret at the thought that to contemplate them brought her not a jot of consolation. For she had gone to take her rest in that city which looks down upon its greater brother, than which however it is so very much smaller—that city of the dead who take up so little room, who have but one day in our human calendar, a day which as a rule, is so cold that we, the living, spend with them as short a time as possible. We leave behind us nothing but what can live on in the lives of others. Madame de Closeterres, adored by her daughter, then gradually forgotten, had left only the smile which Madame de Réveillon saw so vividly revived in Marianne that she was for ever saying, "How like your mother you are!" and her love for the fair, almost red-haired young man with the finely chiselled features, and a seriousness which she had never had, and was perhaps born of her sorrows.

Jean was fond of Marianne and would have liked very much to see her sometimes. But she went very seldom to the Réveillons. "I was very intimate with her mother," said the Duchess. "My mother and hers—Marianne's grandmother—were childhood friends. I did not know her well, but she was a charming woman. It may be that she died of sorrow as a result of knowing that her daughter was the mistress of Monsieur de Serves. She had been told by Blanche that it was not true, and always swore to her that she did not believe it. I find it very difficult to accept that. There were moments when Blanche had a craving for the truth. Personally, I am convinced that she guessed what was going on, and died as a result. As I have told you already, I remained on the closest terms with Blanche, though, as you may imagine, we had very little in common. But family friendships have a way of loosening. Her daughter occasionally drops a card on me but that is all. I gather that she is out of love with the great world, but it is scarcely for me to make the first move. I asked her to Henri's wedding but she did not come, and her children and Henri's will never meet. Old friendships cease with the passing of the generations, and may do so even in the course of a single lifetime. When as I sometimes do, I rummage about among old letters, I find, it is true, many from friends with whom I am now intimate, though once they addressed me as 'Mademoiselle', but there are plenty of others, full of the most fervent expressions of affection, from women whom I should not recognize today if I saw them, and heaps and heaps from others with whom I am still on excellent terms, who as those letters prove, once saw me several times a day, though now we meet at most perhaps twice a year." All the same the Duchess sent Marianne a wedding present. The two young people spent their honeymoon in Brittany, a part of the country of which Madame de Closeterres had been passionately fond.

We are compelled, alas! to leave our works unfinished, but our ideas are taken over by those who follow us, and when our eyes are closed for ever, old people can see once more the look that lived in them in those of our children, who never knew us, but hold our memory in their features, if not in their hearts.

*

"I found Perrotin greatly changed for the worse," said the Duchess to her husband. "All his old gaiety has gone." – "Well, damme, he's getting on, like the rest of us."–"If he were ill, I could understand it," said the Duchess: "but I couldn't help feeling that he has something on his mind."–"He must be at least sixty-seven."–"How extraordinary!"–"I always thought he was in his early fifties," said Jean.

With his smart appearance and rather common expression, his stocky figure and brownish complexion, Perrotin had the look at once squalid and stylish that one finds in the stub of an expensive cigar. It was said that Perrotin, though he seemed as elegant and talkative as ever, and continued to live as he always had done, was to be seen unfailingly at one o'clock every morning in full evening dress on his way to the club, his face perhaps a little paler, his nose slightly more red (for our physical appearance changes but little, and a touch of powder will disguise any deterioration: for a man's face is himself and always recognizable) was suffering from cancer. The news gave Jean something approaching a shock of astonishment, since it imparted to Perrotin a sort of depth which one had never expected to find in him. It was as though one had suddenly glimpsed in him the existence of an inner life. At night apparently he could not get a wink of sleep, and his daytime cheerfulness was a sham which served to conceal his uneasiness. Somehow one had never imagined that this man, for whom a funeral was something entirely outside his normal preoccupations, one of those tiresome social necessities which he said helped to pass the time pleasantly—"I've got to attend So-and-so's funeral tomorrow"—would one day have to attend his own.

6. *The Marquis de Réveillon's Monets*

The house inhabited by the Marquis de Réveillon was a large modern building with gardens adjoining, in which a succession of great rooms all leading into one another had been contrived in such a way as to realize some of his artistic fantasies, and to express in visible form, the various functions they were designed to serve. There was one entirely of wood. It was like a huge cigar-box. On the sycamore panelling a series of Egyptian hieroglyphs had been drawn. It was the room he used when he was composing music. It led into a Louis XVI "salon" which compared with the bare wooden room, stripped of all furniture, in which every object was designed as part of a severely intellectual conception, seemed a place of greater warmth, thickly carpeted, far more crowded, and a great deal more comfortable, with its numerous armchairs upholstered in light-coloured fabrics, its tapestries, and its wall-mirrors. Here in distinction from the former room all the furniture had been arranged to provide the amenities of life in the idiom of an older tradition. It reflected a period when men had liked to see recorded in paint the pleasures of gallantry, a fashion which has once more come back into favour as expressing, in imaginative terms, the different ideals of a past age.

It was no doubt another imaginative caprice, modern too in a very special sense, which had led the Marquis, who was in love with the past, to accumulate in this room comforts which, two hundred years ago, had been appreciated quite simply as such, but thirty years ago fell out of fashion. For objects which formerly were loved for their own sakes, are enjoyed by a later generation as symbols of the past, and so deflected from their original functions, as in the language of poetry, words which have acquired a figurative meaning, no longer strike upon our ears with the resonance of their original sense. Thus on a table with legs terminating in gilded goat's feet, stood an inkstand which served— not the purposes of writing, for no one ever used the room to write in—but to evoke the days when luxuries of that kind were part and parcel of life, when the years which now belong to history and are regarded as evidence of the changes which have taken place in taste, were lived without any admixture of pretence, were made up of the fleeting and irrecoverable days of those who made merry over the subjects depicted in the tapestries which now served merely to remind the spectator of an outmoded charm, and saw in the portraits and the busts, which have now become just so many pictures of old fellows of a past age, the features of a father or a dearly loved wife. And because they were the likenesses of his ancestors the Marquis displayed them with a feeling of pride, as once had done the sons and husbands of an older time. But what then had been the immediate pride, bred of famous deeds or a great position at Court, was no more now than the charm which the Marquis—being a romantic artist at heart—found in these evocations of a past which had added a sort of poetry to his name.

It was in this room that often of an evening the Marquis assembled a handful of friends to listen, silently seated in the pale-coloured armchairs beneath the portraits, the tapestries and the mirrors, to four musicians playing those quartets of Beethoven, Franck, and d'Indy which were the Marquis's favourites, before retiring when midnight came, leaving his guests to talk for a short while and then to say good night. For though we may come together in the salon of an older day, to sit in chairs which body forth in tapestry the simple-minded entertainments which so much appealed to the eyes, then open, of bygone men, these things do not wholly absorb us: rather is it we who force them to play a part in our modern lives. It is we, who for the space of the sixty years which we are granted to live among these objects, compel them to listen to the life we know. The theatre built for the performance of fairy plays, is filled each Sunday by a concourse of people to whom is offered without scenery, without actors, without action, a wordless music. The tapestries which figured for the men of an earlier time what they quite sincerely, and without the aid of any self-conscious and imaginative twist, found pleasing and gay, now catch the eye of a man seated in a Louis XVI armchair, and listening to what he loves, also sincerely and without any self-conscious and imaginative twist—one of César Franck's quartets.

Thus for the Marquis did the hours pass, in the midst of memories of hours more ancient, and the enjoyment of his pleasures set about with the pictured images of pleasures which had long ceased to be enjoyed.

And when he saw his guests silently seated in chairs of a bygone fashion, and listening to his four musicians, it sometimes seemed to him that this was indeed the life of the past, life as it once had been, life now restored to him, though at other times these playful quirks of life seemed no more than funeral games indulged in by those whose eyes would soon no longer shine save in a portrait which even in that short while would have become the portrait of an ancestor, or in the memory of some young man who seeing them again, would think that he was seeing something he remembered, so inevitably do the scenes of our lives, witnessed at the moment when they are about to vanish into others, appear to us already in the guise of things emerging out of memory. In this way did life pass, and evening follow evening. Yet it was the Marquis's life, the only life he had to live, which thus slipped by.

*

They had reached the door of the Marquis de Réveillon's house, and Jean who had walked home with him, was about to say good night. A feeling of depression came over him at the thought that he must now go home, that he must be careful not to make a noise for fear of waking those who were asleep, when the Marquis said to him, "Why not come, in with me? If you're not feeling sleepy I will show you my Monets, which you have always been so anxious to see. I can promise you all the books you need, many rooms to choose from, quite a good supper, and a comfortable bed when you feel ready for it, in which you can sleep till two o'clock. No one will wake you." They had already entered the house, still talking. The Marquis's voice was loud and they made a good deal of noise as they talked. Already this sense of talking loudly at so late an hour was beginning to evoke a feeling of triumph in one who suffered from his nerves, and dreaded the idea of going home. The spectre of sleep, the absence of which does not trouble us except when we are forced to seek it, is not attracted by the need to move softly so as not to disturb other sleepers in a house, a prelude which leads only too quickly to the moment when we shall be lying motionless in bed, face to face with jangled nerves. Still talking, they entered the first of the long succession of "salons", where the Marquis switched on all the lights the better to display his Monets.

The different places of the earth are living creatures whose personality is so strong that some there are who die if separated from them, and in any case are so markedly individual that many every year seek out the pleasure of their company, and in their absence treasure up the memory of their charm. And each has turn and turn about so many different aspects, that he who loves a place loves it as it is seen at different moments of the day, and at different seasons. For he feels that the life of a place, seem though it may to be so little animated, is a great deal more varied than we think.

When as the first beams of the sun break through, the river still lies sleeping, wrapped in dreams of mist, we no more see it than it sees itself. Here already at our feet is the river, but a little farther on the view is blocked, and we are aware only of nothingness, of a fog through which the eye cannot penetrate. To paint at one spot on the canvas, not what one sees, because one can see nothing, not what one does not see, because one ought never to paint what one has not seen, but the *fact of not seeing*, so that the failure of the eye which cannot pierce the mist, is imparted to the canvas as to the river, is beautiful indeed. And in the case of a cathedral it is beautiful too, for the porch we cannot see is a thing of beauty, but a thing which lives only as a part of Nature. There are certain hours of our life which are beautiful because they are not seen, because they are so wrapped in mist that no one can approach them. We did not know all that there was of reality, of diversity, in the life of the place we love, even at those hours when it is not a place at all, though even then it is not purely negative, since its charm can be rendered. We know that the place is beautiful in autumn, being trans-figured in some sort, but we should love it even better, had it not been at one particular moment of the year a proffered spectacle, if we had loved all the hours of its life because they each and all are a manifesta-tion of its life, a life which in summer brings warmth to the slated roof of the church, and sets beside the old familiar road so many flowering poppies and trusses of bound hay, if on a day of thaw we had not passed it by as though an enemy had swept that way, a stranger to the place but leaving it untouched, if we had seen the sun, the blue of the sky, the broken ice, the mud, and the moving water turning the river to a dazzling mirror, when the eye cannot fix nor recognize the scene, while all around though we know it not the naked trees, glittering with rime, are there still standing about the glade or lining the river bank.

7. Jean's Morning with his Mother

The Minister of Foreign Affairs, having to pay a visit to his opposite number in Belgium, took with him the Counsellor of State and Director of External Affairs who was no other than Monsieur Santeuil. On the evening of his departure, Jean dined with his mother in town, took her home about ten, and then went to spend an hour at the Réveillons. About midnight he returned home in a gloomy state of mind. "How old are you?" the Duchess had asked him in the course of the evening. "Twenty-two." He remained haunted by a sense of irritation and despair. He could not help thinking of all the time that he had wasted during the four years since he had left college, of which each sterile, empty day was in miniature the cheerless, barren image. The years ahead which from the vantage-point of college, he had seen as so fine and glowing, wreathed in the glamour of the happiness and the hard work to which he had been looking forward with such joy, and, especially, of freedom, had produced nothing. This, he thought, brooding on what had happened to his life, was what he had made of them. Life is fair only when seen from a distance. Fundamentally it offers nothing more than is already present in the most boring of all the hours a boy may spend in class. By "getting through that, somehow" he will have lived all life in advance. It is as when, looking at a small pattern of material, we can see the whole piece which after all is no more than the repetition on a larger scale of the same threads similarly woven.

He was careful not to make a noise and so wake his mother. He read for a while, though without succeeding in shaking off his gloomy mood, and then went to bed. As he set down his candle on the bedside table, he saw a slip of paper, on which his mother in her firm but gentle hand, had left the following message for him. "Come and say good night to me, darling. Don't be afraid of waking me: you know how easily I go to sleep again. Tell me what you'd like for lunch tomorrow." Jean laid down the little note, and smiled with happiness. Madame Santeuil never as a rule, let him go into her room at night for fear he might wake her husband, nor, so attentive was she to her husband's preferences, did she ever consult him in the matter of meals.

But now with her husband absent, forgetful of her rest and of her own taste in food, she was thinking only of her son. Jean opened the door of his mother's bedroom and saw her fine, serious profile, her loosened hair and closed eyes. She was breathing through her nose, and her mouth, shut in repose, was like that of a child upon the pillow. Taking off his shoes so as not to disturb her, he tip-toed quietly to the bed and kissed the sheet which was drawn up to her chin and showed the lines of her arms beneath it. Then seeing that she still slept on, he pressed his lips to her hair. She made a slight movement, murmured a few unintelligible words. He started back as though afraid. In a moment or two the easy breathing of one in sleep, and wholly at peace, resumed its sway. He was thirsty. Feeling reassured, and almost disappointed, he went to the pantry in search of beer. There he found a note addressed to the footman: "Julien, I shall not be going out tomorrow morning, nor on any other morning until your master returns. Please call me as soon as Monsieur Jean is awake. Don't bother to light a fire in the boudoir. I shall be in Monsieur Jean's room up to lunch-time. He will tell you at what time he would like luncheon to be served." Jean no longer felt sad, nor feared now to go to sleep. He felt that while he slept his mother would be close to him. He went to the open window of the pantry, saw that the weather had cleared, and felt that the air was milder. The sky was full of stars and the light of the moon, which was hidden by the near-by houses, laid a soft hand upon the window-frame, touching it with a pale radiance. The two notes in his mother's writing, her quiet sleep which he had witnessed, yet had her permission to disturb, the faithful, watching stars which would shine until the morning came, the presence too of the invisible moon guarding his sleep, had a soothing effect upon Jean, giving a sense of enchantment to the night, to the prospect of solitude, to the slumbers which he no longer dreaded. In a mood of deep and silent happiness he got ready for bed, and slept as he used to sleep as a child on New Year's Eve, filled with delicious expectation of his waking and of the morning that would follow it.

How sweet his mother was! Every morning she left the house with his father, thinking only of him from the moment when he rang his bell on waking. And now here she was, all ready for the street, wearing a morning dress, with a hat on her head, and her face fresh for the day. "I wasn't sure whether you would rather go out or stay here. So I prepared for all emergencies. It is for you to decide." But Jean liked to lie late in bed. His mother sat beside him, moving only in order to hurry the cook who was late in bringing up his coffee, and the footman who had not yet lit his fire. Jean told her all about his evening. They joked together about the people he had seen, laughing at the same things. Jean, feeling that his manner of seeing, of judging, was his mother's gift to him, and would long outlive her, was even happier than when he knew that she approved of him. Again and again he made her get up from her chair to give him a kiss. She laughed a little at this display of exaggerated sensibility, but so gently that her sweet gaiety increased his tenderness instead of bruising it. Then she sat down again, and they went on with their talk, exchanging their shared views on people, their intrigues, their absurdities, their intelligence, their kindliness. They brought the same sort of subtlety to others' conduct, though each had a personal contribution to make, finding amusement in what he or she had discovered, especially in the other, sharing childishness and profundity, the pleasures of penetration, spitefulness and affection, of admiration and tenderness, of talk and laughter and kisses. Every now and again Jean felt so happy that he wriggled about in bed and snuggled under the blankets. Then he asked his mother whether it would bore her to be read to. Quite the reverse, she said, she would find it very interesting. He read aloud several pages of Michelet, finding in her an echo of his delight, of his criticisms, of his own especial response. Happiness had widened the field of his awareness, and he was pleased too to know that he was reading well.

She took her turn at reading while he dressed. Then they went out to walk together along the Champs-Elysées in the mild sunshine among the occasional carriages. They walked slowly, but the air was so balmy that Jean was soon too hot. Both sky and earth looked pale in the sunshine. They returned by way of clean and empty streets, and found awaiting them the luncheon Jean had ordered. They ate it with relish, Jean seated in the chair reserved for the master of the house, with his mother opposite, and between them a bunch of snowdrops which they had brought back with them and arranged in a tumbler which the sun, streaming through the windows, touched with an air of laughing gaiety. The sky looked as pale as an hour ago the pathways in the Champs-Elysées with their faint carpet of sunlight. Everything had the charm of convalescence and it was with something of the revived pleasure of a convalescent who has ordered just what he likes for his first meal, that Jean ate his luncheon. He spoke to his mother about his father and his grandfather, conscious of a deep delight in sharing with her his admiration for them,

in feeling them to be so different, yet so like himself, analysing them
without the slightest feeling of embarrassment, dwelling upon their
faults and those comic weaknesses which made them so lovable and so
kind, recapitulating all their known and precious qualities. He felt intelligent and good, and in his mother's goodness and intelligence the con-
firmation and especially, the source of his own. Comparing this happy
day with the years of his imprisoned childhood, when the parental
home had seemed to him a place of slavery, he was conscious both
of the sweetness of his freedom from those bonds, and of his delight
in occasional acts of obedience, though this time dictated by his own
unfettered will, as in response to a brother's tenderness, or to the faults
and merits of a favourite author with whom he had much in common.

His mother left him to get ready for some calls she had to make
while he was away for an hour or two with his friends. He knocked at
her door to say good-bye. "Your way of knocking is exactly like your
father's," she said. "It's really quite extraordinary. If he weren't away I
should have taken your knock for his." It gave Jean a sense of happiness
to feel himself thus bound so closely to his father. He was proud in the
thought that he was something more than a poor, lonely little boy,
that there was in him something more ancient than himself, that he had
an existence outside and beyond his own personality. It was Election
Day. "Who are you going to vote for?" his mother asked. "Denys
Cochin. What about papa?" – "Since your father's not here, he cannot
register his vote. If he had been, he would have voted for Passy." –
"Then so shall I, for I am his son even more than I am myself." Never
had he so much enjoyed the act of voting. In thus attaching greater
importance to his father than to himself, he felt that his own had become enhanced. He would no longer be voting as an isolated individual,
but as proxy for a family which it was an honour to be allowed to
represent. He returned from the *mairie* in a joyful mood, feeling the
same sort of proud and thrilling pleasure as he had done when, for the
first time he had gone to a diplomatic reception with his father, who
had proudly introduced him to his colleagues. On that occasion he had
been conscious of a calm emotion, of that same controlled emotion
which a conservative may feel in his sense of solidarity and tradition.
For he had realized that the warm welcome accorded to him by those
to whom he was presented, had been due not to any merit he might
have as a person, but to the fact that he was his father's son, and as
such had been found worthy of the honour of introduction.

8. *A Winter's Evening in Paris*

That evening Paris was alive with the happy sense of excitement usually associated with Eves and Festivals. A dense fog had blanketed the town, and though every available light was kept blazing, a gas-lamp at the distance of a few paces was so nearly imperceptible as to give the impression that it was on the point of going out and leaving the world to night and black obscurity which would lie as thick and obliterating over the heart of the city as in the fields and forests. It was necessary to know one's way backwards if one was not to get hope-lessly lost. Some pedestrians found themselves going round and round the Place des Invalides in the fixed belief that they were making straight for the Concorde Bridge, and in the Champs-Elysées a cab fondly convinced that it was driving down the Avenue, wandered into a clump of shrubs and could not get out again. Only the huge expanse of brilliantly illuminated café windows in the rue Royale managed to pierce the murk at a distance of more than a few feet, and gave to the mist an iridescent shimmer of softened colours which seemed to hang around the doorways with a welcoming smile, as in great houses the servants in the hall reflect in their faces the pleasure that their master will feel when he receives his guests. The joy of those who made their way into the cafés was the greater by reason of the difficulties they had overcome in getting there, and perhaps of the fear they had felt that they would never succeed in getting there at all. Consequently, the complaints about the weather which each new arrival made to the head-waiter who, not daring to get wet or to leave his customers, but deeply concerned about their more or less comic appearance, had taken up a position close to the door, were uttered, and heard by him, with expressions of unusual jollity. "What an awful night," said one, adding as he removed his overcoat in the damp warmth of the interior, "It's devilish cold outside!" and a moment later, "Impossible to see more than two yards ahead"—his eyes blinking in the bright light—"and everything so quiet—not a sound to be heard"—his hearing, which had been numbed by the silence of which he was speaking, now restored to normal by the gay exchanges going on at the various tables in which the waiters hurrying up in response of repeated summonses, played their part, for unusual events are great bridgers of social distances and it would have seemed so unnatural for two human beings, though one was an elegant client and the other a waiter who would as a rule have maintained a respectful silence, not to have spoken a word or two about this extraordinary physical cataclysm, that the client on the spot gave as it were authority for the putting of those questions which he was burning to answer in some such words, as, "I've just come from the Place de la Concorde, and I give you my word it wasn't all that easy to find the way."–"I can well believe that, sir: one of our gentlemen has come from the Place de la République, and his driver got lost three times."–"Losing one's way would be bad enough; the real trouble is not being able to find it again."–"Yes— sir, that's terrible bad, that is." Thereupon as when after remarkable happenings, life resumes its even tenor, the client ordered a drink and the waiter hurried off to get it. Then, while he waited for it to come, keeping his eyes glued to each fresh arrival, longing to start a con- versation with him as though they had been fellow-travellers on a journey, the head-waiter paused for a moment at his table. "Has Monsieur given his order?"–"Yes, I'm having a grog."–"The very thing for a night like this, if I may say so, sir: a good hot drink." Then the customer relapsed into silence, but the lively yet uneasy eye through which he took in his surroundings, gleamed through the silence which decorum compelled him to maintain unbroken, like the glitter of a loaded rifle which at any moment may be let off. One among the new arrivals but only one, annoyed by the familiar manners of the staff, ordered his drink, very curtly, and replied in a surly way when he was asked whether he wouldn't like to remove his overcoat. In a very short while he took his departure, completely uninfluenced by the general atmosphere of friendly high spirits, and determined to show that he was different from everybody else. Soon the room grew so hot that nobody thought of keeping his coat on his back, or his hat on his head. In a short while those present were drinking and playing and keeping up a continuous flow of gay talk—as happens in military bivouacs, or indeed in any place where careless ease and a general sense of well-being, follows on the heels of uneasiness or discomfort.

*

Monsieur Santeuil—who was highly esteemed in this particular café, though he knew none of the titled individuals who frequented it, because he occupied an important position in the Administration, and had once given the proprietor financial assistance—chatted for a few minutes with the waiter, had a drink, and went out. He was feeling sad because he was thinking of Jean. When he got home he sat down for an instant in the hall to take off his goloshes. Jerked out of its slumbers by the noise, the large dog which was dozing on the mat, fixed him for a moment with its eyes, eyes in which there was all the dignity of sleep from which the lids had just been lifted, all the oblivion which the act of waking had released, so that the animal's expression had in it something of solemnity. You must at some time or another have gone into a child's room at night and seen him suddenly wake up when the light is turned on. He makes no movement, and at first you think that he is still asleep. Then you notice that he is looking at you with wide-open eyes. Perhaps even if you approach the bed, he will express his surprise, his happiness, and the feel of his warm, relaxed body, in a smile, and if you kiss him he will kiss you back. But he does not know what time it is, nor why you are there. You hear a slight sound. He has gone to sleep again, and will have no recollection of your having come into his room. His smile was a sleeper's smile, and he looked at you almost without seeing you, certainly was not thinking of anything, and then dropped off to sleep again. You kiss his little face without waking him. The closed eyes, the quietly breathing mouth, are occupied with that great and serious matter which we call sleeping. For little children, no less than the dog which just now looked at Monsieur Santeuil before dropping off again, employ their small bodies in many serious matters, such as sleeping, such as dying. The child whom you have just awakened, finding himself in his bed and seeing the light, laughs because he does not know how great was his achievement in being asleep. That smile is the true smile of innocence. Then he turns back to sleep.

Monsieur Santeuil went into his room. Sadness, cold, fatigue, had wearied him. He shivered as he took his clothes off, then climbed into bed, felt the hot-water bottle with his feet, worked it into a comfortable position, and pulled up the blankets. He felt terribly inclined to cry though it would be untrue to say that he was conscious of pain or of any kind of suffering. He knew that while he lay there in his bed until the morning, no new worries would come to him, that he would not

be called upon to make any painful effort. He had laid aside his limbs
in the bed as he might have laid aside a set of heavy tools for which,
though he felt a certain fondness for them, he need no longer carry. He
breathed noisily, relieved of the burden of his legs which but a short
while before had been so weary and so cold, but now were stretched
before him in a place of warmth. He could feel against his flank the
hot-water bottle which, like a deflated balloon was gurgling and growing cold. Now and then with a very slight movement, he resumed
control of his resting members, the better to bear on the mattress with
his thighs and so relax completely in the hollow made by his body into
which he fitted exactly, so that the admirable mattress could carry the
whole weight of his loosened limbs, and to bring his feet into renewed
contact with the hot-water bottle. He wanted to cry, and to that extent
still felt cold but with a coldness easy enough to endure within the
general sensation of delicious warmth. Perhaps had the coldness been
complete, he would have felt better, lying on a hard pallet, for the
state of prostration produced by the absence of all hope is more complete when all sense of physical well-being is lacking. The bitterness
that comes over us when we lie freezing in our moments of weeping,
stiff, and aware of our weakness, are loaded with the burden of that
pleasure which resides in human life, and never wholly abandons us
while we live on, but finds refuge in shivering and pain and despair,
a pleasure which it is sheer folly to seek in distant places because it is
always with us, between us and our bed, between us and the hard
ground, between us and our tears, a pleasure which no circumstance
whatever can increase. Then to set the seal on the sense of oblivion
which was already beginning to steal over him, Monsieur Santeuil
flattened with a puff the yellow pyramid of his candle-flame. It
vanished and night's darkness reigned. But Monsieur Santeuil, feeling
his life to be so empty that he would not have been afraid to die, fell
asleep—in other words delivered himself into the hands of those
thoughts which, be they never so poignant, we are forbidden to
remember, of all that part of our life which is absent from our waking
consciousness, and has no influence upon our actions, but through
which we never cease to travel in imagination, so that like our other
life, it produces changes in us, as does everything in which there is a
mingling of pleasure, pain, and thinking. And as when travelling, we
wake up to a countryside quite different from the one in which we
went to sleep, so too our thoughts are in a spot when we awake, which

has no resemblance to the one on which our minds were set when we went to sleep, so that often he who closed his eyes in brilliant light, which gave to all things a look of beauty, wakes to a dull and gloomy day where everything seems difficult, and the life of the spirit seems scarcely to exist at all. He thinks of things which before sleep came to him he told himself he had to do, and then seemed easy. But since that moment and in the darkness of the night, he has made so long a journey that all things in himself have changed, so that the same tasks seem now impossible. He feels harassed, he feels vexed, and it needs the coming of some piece of news or the warmth of the coffee brought to him on waking, to restore to him that savour of life far from which no doubt the vanished spirits of the night just past have been leading him.

9. *Portrait of a Writer*

That year Le Gandare exhibited at the Champ-de-Mars a portrait of Jean Santeuil. His former companions at the Lycée Henri IV would certainly not have recognized the untidy schoolboy—always badly dressed, with tousled hair and stained clothes, his manner either feverishly excited or dejectedly limp, his gestures expressive rather than well-bred, with exaltation in his face when he was alone, though when with other people he was shy and abashed, always pale with tired eyes circled in dark shadow as a result of excitement, sleeplessness, or fever, his nose over-large, his cheeks hollow, and his great brooding eyes, brilliant and tormented, which alone gave a touch of beauty to the irregular and sickly countenance—in the radiant young man self-consciously posing before all Paris, with neither shyness nor bravado in his looks, gazing out from light-coloured elongated eyes, with an air about them of fresh almonds, eyes less expressive of actual thought than seemingly capable of thought, like deep but empty cisterns, with full round cheeks of a faint pink just flushing to red in the ears brushed by the curling ends of his black and silky hair, which showed, shining, undulating, loose, as though he had just emerged from water. A rose in the buttonhole of his green tweed jacket, a tie of some delicate Indian fabric patterned with peacock's eyes seemed to echo looks which were as fresh, as luminous, as a spring morning, beauty not perhaps thoughtful so much as pensive, the very visual sign of a delicate and happy life.

Yet Monsieur and Madame Santeuil, who had at first encouraged Jean to go out and about in Society where he revelled in the position he had made for himself, were irritated now when they saw that he was no longer either working, reading or even thinking, and for the last few months at least had shown no sign of anything approaching regret or shame. "That boy could have done anything he liked, but as things are he will never do anything"—Monsieur Sandré had said to his daughter.

Monsieur Santeuil, whose sturdy common sense was growing less with age and failing health, who had less to occupy him now that he

715

was on the threshold of retirement, and had got into the habit of brooding by the fire in the evening when his son was out dancing, could not help wondering whether after his death his fortune and the high respect which his solid, middle-class name had acquired among his fellows, might not instead of reaching new heights in the person of his son, fall altogether into decay. "There was only too good reason for my anxiety," said Monsieur Sandré, "but you wouldn't listen to me." –"I know now what that rock is on which he'll run aground," said Monsieur Santeuil, who, at this turning-point of his career, saw his son's future in quite a different light, "it is irresponsibility, frivolity, a love of Society. Is there anything we can do to save him? Will God preserve me long enough to keep him from running head-on to disaster? I'd rather anything than this—love, ill-health, even poetry!" – "No," said Monsieur Sandré, "anything's better than poetry! A dude may be more of a cipher than a Bohemian, but he brings less dishonour on his family. I'm positively ashamed when I see his name in the social columns of the gutter-press, but that's not so bad as coming on it at the tail of an article!"

*

The Duc de Réveillon had asked Jean to go and see on his behalf Monsieur Silvain Bastelle, the celebrated author, and a member of the Académie française. He lived in a charming little house in the rue de Berri, and Jean, while his name was being taken up, waited in a large drawing-room. A servant came in to put a log on the fire. There were cards of invitation on the table from the Duc d'Aumale, the Duc de Broglie, and from one of the Rothschild ladies. The sound of a brougham being washed down reached him from the courtyard. The man whom the world calls happy gradually accumulates all the many things which he may have envied in others. Bastelle was a member of the Académie, Bastelle had wealth and a great position in Society, Bastelle had this handsome room in which Jean was waiting. When he went out he drove in the brougham now standing in the courtyard. He dined at the houses of those whose cards littered his table. But in proportion as he took on form and substance of a certain kind in terms of fine carpets, vast rooms, and a rich neighbourhood, happiness departed from his life. He had inherited from his parents a great fortune which they had amassed for him, but they were dead, the only persons whose constant presence since the days of his childhood had been inextricably mingled with his dreams of happiness. There was always a place for him at the tables of those on whom as a young man he had looked as rare and wonderful beings, but the mirage had faded, and he now dined there without the faintest sense of pleasure. He could drive in brougham or Victoria to the Bois, but he had lost the radiant health, the freshness of sensibility which in the old days had set him dreaming at the sight of a simple spray of almond blossom in a florist's window. The spectacle of massed flowers along an avenue now left him cold.

More and more he came to feel it a duty to dedicate himself to the thoughts which, on certain days, flooded into his mind. Or rather he was not quite sure that they were properly speaking thoughts at all: they were something in himself that produced a special feeling of charm, and this he tried not so much to analyse as to conserve. He felt that he must keep them intact until the moment came when, seated in a room where he would be free from all disturbance, he could uncover the thought which so far had come to him only in the form of a vague image—a warm afternoon in a park with irises leaning from the basin of a fountain in the shade—cold rain falling on a town—the freshness of a leafy, shadowed square in a town blazing in the heat of summer. It was as though he kept his thoughts rolled up in some such image, like the fish which an angler lays in the sun which causes him no dis-comfort, under a covering of fresh grass upon the bank, plucked from the borders of the pond in which he has been fishing. And so not yet aware of the nature of the ideas flowing in upon him, he kept them hidden beneath the image which he could see so clearly—the warm afternoon with sunlight playing on the lilac leaves, but with the added sense of some great power within him which would enable him to go beyond the visual image, and bring from it into broad day a thousand different thoughts. He called that "being in the right mood", and when the right mood came, he liked to be alone with plenty of time before him, and paper and ink ready to his hand. The various ideas which then he loved to transcribe seemed to be a great deal more important than himself, so that he brooded upon that consummation, and felt good for nothing when several days went by without their visiting his brain, and, when he had got them more or less written down, saw no particular objection to dying, but was conscious only of resignation. But the word *written* is incapable of suggesting the charm of the precious mould into which he ran them.

*

For some time now his views on the nature of evil had been changing. What in the old days he had fled from; what, when occasionally he had yielded to temptation, had made him feel deeply ashamed, had been snobbery, the pleasure of being made much of by the great, and a concern for his own good looks. For these preoccupations seemed to impart a quality of hardness to his thought, so that the ideas, the images, the sort of liveliness of spirit which served him as a sure guide to the places where he could work, found it impossible any longer to emerge. Little by little, brilliant society and a concern for his own appearance became so much for him a matter of habit, that they ceased to pre-occupy his mind and lost whatever stimulating effect they may once have had upon him. He was no more careful of his smart suits than he would have been of an old working-jacket. He had ceased to pay any attention to them, and they began to show the marks of a casual ill-usage. The same must have been true of Byron, and of many fashionable writers, when having set out to pay a visit to their grand friends, the sight of a flowering lilac or the shock of a sudden thought diverted their attention to poetry. For while one is walking stiff and upright, twirling a cane and looking on the world with an impassive stare, inspiration cannot flow freely, since it needs to come to a point of concentration, to seek out its object, no matter in how fumbling a manner, to move with bent back, to beat a happy wing in a smile of sheer delight. Evil for him became what hardened the spirit by making it a prey to noble names, witty talk, material facts, formulae learned parrot-wise, commonplace desires, aimless to-ings and fro-ings, and idle chit-chat. Laziness on the other hand, so long as it moved freely in response to the charm of the moment, and by that much might be said to earn Baudelaire's qualification of "fecund", came within the category of the "good", of what should deliberately be sought. So, by the same token, he grew to consider sensuality as something good, or at least inoffensive and frequently "fecund", whereas frivolity and in particular facile talkativeness, in so far as its intention was to dazzle an audience, and thereby operated a transposition of the active element so that powers which ought to have been ready to his hand when the moment came for work, were allowed to dribble from a necessary silence, showed to him as the real, the basic, evil. Snobbery had once had the same baleful effect upon him, since its influence had so debased his spirit (even when he was alone) as to fritter away in talk the moments which should have been devoted to listening.

Once seated with paper before him, he wrote of what as yet he did not know, of what lured him on by way of the image under which it lay concealed (which was in no way a symbol), and not what his conscious reason told him was intelligible and lovely. Thoughts of that kind he constantly ignored. It was not of them he felt that he had to write, for they were without the peculiar feeling of delight which for him was the true sign of value in ideas, just as Descartes said that evidence was the touchstone of truth. If conscience warned him that "evil" was what dried-up inspiration (even if it took the form of mere eloquence), and that "good" was what did not weaken it (even the grossest forms of sensuality), it was as though given by Nature the duty of preserving some god dwelling in the marshy places of the spirit and on their borders, he had been endowed before his birth with an instinct to preserve that bodying forth of divinity, and at the same time the better to carry out Nature's instructions—with an excessively keen sensibility and a degree of egotism which kept him from giving himself in any way that might have the effect of killing inspiration, with delicate health, which made him peculiarly susceptible to outside influences and eager to react against everything that might make him ill, with simplicity and a warm heart which found expression in kindness to the humblest of his fellows, with a strong sense of gratitude and a wayward temperament which led others to accuse him of ingratitude and pride. Those who had known him could to some extent when reading him, say, "That's Bastelle to the life," though to tell the truth, whenever he wrote something that was like him, his pleasure ceased and he heard a warning voice telling him that he was no longer writing what he ought to write.

Often at the hour when Jean was setting off on one of his long walks, Bastelle wrapped in a long dressing-gown was on his way to bed where he would remain till noon. For different men find different charms in life. Some soak their spirit in sleep, silence and darkness; others like to feel that it is enveloped, as it were in a napkin, in the golden brilliance of the day, with workers working, and birds singing about them, with nothing between their brains and the outside world but the thickness of a curtain. The first type know nothing of the living gaiety of morning, but the second are unaware of the sweet sensation of thinking through the night hours, of writing in a half-light, of getting up when the sun is already high. Pleasure for some consists in doing the same things every evening, in sleeping always in the same soft bed. But others like to feel the silence of sleep take on form and substance in the infernal din of a railway carriage rocking on the rails, and rest and repose coming to them from the heart of mad and headlong speed of which they soon cease to be conscious.

*

No one could have said that the old master was a very moral man, but that did not seem to worry him, and he behaved with a sort of shamelessness, though at the same time he did not much concern himself about others, and devoted himself to none. It would probably be true however to say that he had not always been like that. There had been a time when fondled by parents who sometimes shed tears over him, his vices had been for him something to which he did not yield without a struggle, nor without a prolonged sense of remorse. During those moments, when he was engaged in performing purely mechanical actions, he thought of all the things he ought to have done, and was conscious of much bitter regret. But it was not, as it was later, of the pages he ought to have completed, of the inspiration which he ought to have received that his mind was gloomily full, but of quite other actions from which he was still hoping passionately that he would be able to abstain. As to his talent, that was a thing he possessed without having to make an effort, and it was only at rare moments when some friend had begged him to contribute to a children's magazine, that he began to write, and then suddenly feeling the ideas flow in on him, the words take on form and beauty, each echoing the other in obedience to his directing hand, experiencing that pleasure which is the writer's only reward, without thinking for a moment that writing might later become a career, and, still less, that this gift of his was, in some sort, a mission. At a still earlier period it was not yet his talent, which so far he had never felt nor exercised, that occupied his thoughts, it was his vices which in the unconsciousness of childhood had not begun to be a cause for remorse or resolution as they later became in adolescence, but had crowded in on him and seemed to him perfectly natural. In those days when he took pleasure in the drinking of wine, he thought of it in terms of being thirsty, of being parched, of being greedy. And in the ancient poets on whom he commented, he clung to the words—"Greeting, Oh wine, gift of the Gods, wine, man's joy and happiness!"—with a sort of passion. He thought that among all the things sung by the poets still unknown to him, this drinking of wine was one of the noblest and most delicious. And, when seated at table, he said, "By Jove, I'm hungry! How lovely to be going to eat!" it did not occur to him that in speaking thus it was wine that he was letting course down his throat with such a sense of delight. For he had not yet defined clearly to himself the objects of his pleasure.

But childhood when one does wrong without knowing it to be wrong, and adolescence when desires and duties are in conflict, and habits already taking shape are known only as tendencies, and are closely knit with remorse and resolution, had long gone by. Little by little the gift of poetry which he carried within him, became the centre of his moral world, so that by then his struggles of conscience had taken on a different form. "Good" now was what favoured inspiration, "evil" what paralysed it. His drinking habits, so long as they did not make him ill and were within his power to control, as well as a certain sensual laziness, in no way hampered his dreaming, nor hindered the rich fecundity of his spirit. Logical reasoning, on the other hand, an exclusive concern with politics, and vanity, would have exercised upon him a dangerous influence. And so it was that gradually, he had formed his art in his own image, had made of it something that had no relation to morality, but was concerned only with thought and beauty.

*

For the only beauties that a poet can find come from inside himself. Give him but one moment of inspiration, in other words, put him into communication with himself, and you will give him pleasure. But give him wealth, honours, worldly delights, and you give him nothing, because by so doing you make him come out of himself. But this possession of himself does not occur directly. He must receive himself from the mysterious hands which hold it. To show him somebody who is beautiful and intelligent is nothing. But there may be somebody whom he first saw at an earlier period of his life, who stamped upon him an ineffaceable impression. Perhaps seeing her again he may recover everything, and *her* presence will have meaning, since it will give him back a fragment of himself. Several times a week, when Jean was doing his military service, he dined with his captain, frequently in the company of a handsome, smiling young woman of about thirty who as the result of possessing a magnificent singing voice, and a number of aristocratic connexions had in spite of poverty made for herself a position of considerable distinction in the city of Orléans. She had somewhat the appearance of a wax figure, as much by reason of the regularity of her features and the perpetual air of roguishness which showed in them, distended her cheeks and gave its peculiar shape to her mouth, as of the rather commonplace expression of her face. Accustomed to compliments, and being temperamentally inclined to receive them with a certain scepticism ("Are you telling the truth? Do you really mean that?"—a trick which might pass for wit in a woman of intelligence, and for modesty in one who had been well brought up—a stamp of worldliness, in short, to which life in the provinces had given a certain fixity) she expressed herself thus with an air of gaiety which at bottom was wholly fatuous. There was nothing particularly funny in seeming to question the sincerity of a compliment merely because it was deserved. It is thus that our habitual expression, our expression in the ordinary circumstances of life, reveals our true character. What a man looks like as he walks along a street gives us the clue to his attitude to life. It may mask itself under a dazed look, an air of imperturbable dignity, a bored expression momentarily lit up by a smile, but almost at once it resumes its sway, and is what the casual passer-by is chiefly aware of.

10. *Parents in Old Age*

Each year now Monsieur Santeuil was giving up yet one more of the numerous duties which hitherto had filled his life. In some cases he had already reached retiring age; in others most of the work was done by his deputy who in due time would succeed him. But to the Ministry he still went every day. This relative lack of occupation, the deterioration in his health, the need to take things easily, and the fact that they were now almost twice as rich as they had been owing to the death of Monsieur Lepic and of Monsieur Santeuil's sister, were the main reasons which had led Jean's parents to lease a small property not far from the Château de Madrid, and having direct access to the lake in the Bois de Boulogne. Every evening Jean went there to dine with them, but because first of Françoise and later of Charlotte, returned to Paris to sleep. Monsieur and Madame Santeuil had greatly changed since the day when we first made their acquaintance in the little garden at Auteuil, on the site of which three or four six-storeyed houses had now been built, several of the apartments in them being already let. Monsieur Santeuil had to a very large extent lost his former ironical harshness of temper. It had gradually become a thing of the past, slowly disappearing along with youth, honours, his arrogant prejudices, and that proud irrational positivism which had lain behind those self-confident and arid illusions which, at one time, had filled his life. Since facts were his god, he had finally after a long interval of astonishment, been forced to add to his collection of them—that there *did* exist great men of science who held religious views, that more than one minister was of the opinion that the title he bore was really rather ridiculous, that there were several high-ranking civil servants, who though they might have had almost anybody to dine with them, preferred to entertain men of letters to whose presence they attached the very greatest importance. Little by little, and in spite of all the official dignities which he had accumulated he found himself turning more and more to those for whom admiration for a poet, the table-talk of a novelist, and fondness for a favourite son meant more than honours and even than their professional work, people for the most part whom he had been accustomed to regard as being "slightly touched". In their presence he could do nothing but laugh and shrug because he did not know what to say to them. That laugh of his could often irritate, because it seemed to be the expression of a crude over-bearingness, though later Jean found in it a somewhat touching quality as his father grew older, for he realized that it was due to increasing weakness. Not seldom exacerbated when it was occasioned by something he was doing, which his father thought was stupid, he did his best to ignore it, only to realize when he saw his father go pale, what pain he had caused him. When that happened, he felt suddenly disarmed, and blamed himself for taking in the wrong way that little laugh which was his father's only weapon against follies and modernisms and an attitude to life which he could not understand: a poor little weapon which a momentary outburst of anger from Jean could so easily shatter. It was then that seeing his father weak and defenceless, he bitterly repented having broken his father's only and very tiny weapon—the laugh which fundamentally expressed a deal of kindliness, surprise in which there was no touch of arrogance, and pity for what he considered to be pure folly, though he was never altogether sure that it might not be a mark of superior abilities.

*

Aware now that he could expect no further honours, no higher position, and having resigned himself to seeing others promoted in his stead, during the long hours when—a quite new thing this—he found himself with nothing to do, walking with his wife at five o'clock beside the lake before the afternoon had lost its brilliance, and often after dinner beneath the stars, his mind filled with quiet happiness in the presence of that high sublimity, he came to know what in earlier days he had known but briefly when travelling, on nights spent at Istanbul or Naples, what his struggling youth and busy, practical maturity had had no time for—the art of dreaming. For him old age was what youth is for others—a time of illusions. What for them is a period filled with sweetness had come to him only when his physical powers were waning. His new idealism was tinged with melancholy, such as, for the too strong-minded, treads on the heels of a disillusionment bred of long contact with realities. His affection for his wife was now more broodingly thoughtful than it once had been, and tended to lose itself in memories. His affection for his son set him often dreaming of a future which he could not hope to see, and, in its sheer disinterestedness, took on a quality of grandeur. His thoughts of that future were touched with sadness only because it seemed only too probable that it would bring misfortune because of his son's temperament, the state of his health, his tendency to gloom, his extravagance, his laziness, his failure to settle down and the way in which he had wasted his intelligence. Otherwise they were tranquil and serene, even though the prospect of his own death was part of them. He developed a new delicacy in his attitude to his wife. He spoke of her father in a way that touched her. The smallest kindness coming from one whom she deeply loved, who had been so little used to showing her consideration, sufficed to stir her feelings. For him however certain sentiments acquired new value, while others seemed to lose what value they had had.

There were things now in his mind at which it seemed extraordinary he should not laugh, seeing them as mere foolishness. He dared not enter his son's room when the boy was day-dreaming, and now, when on their way to Paris from the Bois, as the carriage drove through Auteuil, and would in a moment or two pass the big new building under which not only their old garden, but the happy years of his life and the memory of two persons who were so dear to him, lay for ever buried, a few moments before that happened, punctual to the minute, making use of that knowledge of streets and districts which had always astonished Madame Santeuil and seemed to her one with her husband's gift for geography and skill in reading the barometer—knowing that they would shortly be coming to the houses neighbouring their former home, a few of which had kept something of their remembered look, a flower-decked door, palings through which gardens could still be seen, lawns and paths and overshadowing trees and a glimpse of a garden shed, houses all of them which Madame Santeuil had known, left over now unchanged as though to stress the unrecognizable up-heaval which had carried away the house and garden which had been theirs, like those friends of his parents who still lived on, seeming older than in fact they were—when Monsieur Santeuil knew that they were approaching those signs and portents which would have enabled her to recognize the place where lay what for her was the saddest of all graves, he said, "Shut your eyes." She shut them, while Monsieur Santeuil looked with tranquil curiosity on the new buildings which had so

recently sprung up. He was surprised to note the changes which had
taken place, looked around him to see whether the electric light had
come there, and indulged perhaps in a moment of dreaming. He said,
"Keep your eyes shut." Sometimes she hid them behind her hands.
He had retained from his former role of father, of the man who is
always listened to, of the one practical member of the family, the habit
of giving advice. But formerly he would have said, "There's no need
for you to hide your eyes behind your hands, all you need do is shut
them," and would have accompanied the words with a shrug and
laughed at the ineptitude of a woman who did not know how to shut
her eyes.

Stupidly, one day when he was driving with his parents, accustomed
to hearing his father's way of talking in the old days, perhaps too to
show that he could be practical when he liked, and knowing that his
mother not only would not mind but would be pleased to think how
like his father he was, Jean said, "But, Mamma, there's no need for you
to put your hands in front of your eyes to keep yourself from seeing,
you have only to shut them tight." His father plucked at his sleeve to
stop him, and under cover of the noise made by the horse when it
broke into a canter on the cobbled surface, whispered, "Let her alone:
can't you realize that she doesn't want us to see that she is crying?"—
then at last, "You can open your eyes now," he said, but with his mind
still full of the Auteuil garden, spoke to her of the days gone by and of
her father. She was grateful to him for having spared her the effort she
would have had to make to talk of other things, and for the accuracy
of his memory in all that concerned her parents, feeling that what he
had said had been a special tribute of kindliness to her, and an act of
piety to them. She wondered at his memory, as though it were itself a
form of tenderness, the outward and visible sign of a noble nature, and
felt that it justified her in adopting permanently an attitude of humility
where he was concerned. How she envied him its possession, for she
would often spend whole nights trying to recall the features of her
mother or her father which in the attempt to focus memory were for
ever escaping her by reason of the very intensity of her love. Monsieur
Santeuil said to her, "Do you remember how your father used to go
and fill his glass at the conduit when he wanted to bathe his eyes?" She
was all ears. She would have given much still to have one of those
glasses which her father had always used, hiding them in the little
rockery above the water pipe, so that no one else should find them.

One of Jean's favourite dreams was to revisit at Auteuil the Villa de Montmorency where he had sometimes been in the habit of going to drink the water which tasted so strongly of iron. To such an extent did he let his mind dwell on this that he had acquired once more a liking for the water, and would often take a drink at night from the carafe beside his bed, quite determined to go next morning to the conduit in the garden of the Villa Montmorency where after letting the water run for a while to rinse the cup that hung there on a little chain, he would fill it half-full and drink.

*

In the evening Monsieur and Madame Santeuil went with Jean to the station, and returning by the Bois, walked the full length of the darkening lake where now and again there shone out the whiteness of a swan, sometimes sleeping, sometimes gliding without a sound, giving to the watcher that profoundly poetical feeling of vast and almost unreal movement, such as we are conscious of when from a mountain side we see a train in the valley below, though hearing nothing of its rushing movement, nor being conscious of its smoke. The nearness of the lake, so blue by day, and at night watched over by a sky thick-sown with stars, played no small part in giving to Monsieur Santeuil a lovely sense of pure sublimity. Insensitive though he was to all those charms which we today have come to find in Nature, he could feel deeply moved only when confronted by those beauty spots which in the old days had bred in him a preference for lakes and mountains. Moved by a similar emotion, he would say, "What lovely weather!" using the adjective in precisely the same way as a gardener who dreads the rain, for whom all that threatens it is ugly, who can see no beauty in a day of storm. For him there was nothing lovely in rain, a stormy sky, an overcast day, or low-hanging clouds. But a star-spangled night, a day of sunshine, the freshness which comes at evening after a day of heat, and seems to bring to the listening ear, against a background of silence, the sound of an oar rhythmically striking the water, spoke for him a sublime language which in a very especial way set his thoughts soaring.

Sometimes when Jean had left early, or had not come at all, Monsieur and Madame Santeuil would make their way to the landing-stage where boats for hire were moored. It took them a long time to reach it, for nowadays they both walked slowly. Madame Santeuil's legs were weak, and Monsieur Santeuil's breathing difficult. The movements of each, those at least which were deliberate, for Madame Santeuil had a slight limp, and Monsieur Santeuil was afflicted with a stoop, were a series of precautions, constantly repeated, against the other's disabilities. If the path became difficult, Monsieur Santeuil held his wife's arm more tightly; if a strong wind were blowing Madame Santeuil walked ahead of her husband so that he should not suffer from his breathlessness. Pity for his wife's sorrows, care for her infirmities, their shared tenderness for Jean, and the meaninglessness for them of all happiness in which it did not play a part, had produced in Monsieur Santeuil a tenderness for his wife which was as solicitous and as constant as hers had always been for him. It was a pleasant sight to see them thus moving side by side, mingled, merged, knit one with the other and affording mutual support like two trees which have grown together. They called to the ferryman and asked to be rowed round the lake. The cost of such a trip was three francs, and it is needless to point out that Monsieur Santeuil would never have indulged in such a luxury upon his own account, he being the kind of man who thought it criminal to take a cab unless he were in too much of a hurry to go by bus. These habits of economy to which till then they had remained faithful, but which it was now necessary to modify in order that Madame Santeuil could contrive new pleasures which might soften for her husband the melancholy of old age, had retained for them, like those useless gratifications which can give us only a feeling of wellbeing, or a merely aesthetic delight, a charm which is beyond the comprehension of the blasé young. As they tremblingly set foot upon the moving bottom of the boat, they had the impression that they were doing something dangerous, forbidden, and quite out of the ordinary. A boat hired for a pleasure trip is entirely different from the ferry which carries you from one side of the lake to the other when you happen to want to pay a visit to the island. The absence of all definite goal, the power to choose what the goal shall be, and to change it when the fancy takes you, the feeling that the trip is without objective, the sense that one is floating idly for the sole purpose—as one gives free rein to one's voice when singing—of enjoyment, of feeling the pleasure of passing close by the bank, of skirting the long grasses, of waking the swans, of hearing quite close the ripple of the water, so quiet, so low, that one keeps from speaking loudly for fear of disturbing it, of listening to the silence and being rewarded by the freshness of the air

one breathes—such were the delights which gave to Madame Santeuil's face not the careless happy look of those one often sees spending
an evening afloat, sitting silent or softly singing, but that lively
exaltation bred of delicious sensations which betrays itself in a rapt,
attentive, and tender expression, the concentrated enjoyment of those
who fear to miss a single moment of the experience. Madame Santeuil
would have preferred to seek out the darker parts of the lake, those
narrow passages between wooded banks, which drive deep into the
trees and are overhung by flowering branches, where the boat's forward
movement, always silent, always smooth, is constantly impeded as
though progress were being forced through deep forest country. But
Monsieur Santeuil liked to keep close to the island, to watch its lights
reflected in the water, to see the constant passing of boatloads of
travellers who had just dined there, or were going thither for a drink,
to hear the sound of a piano, and sometimes of a voice singing a tune
he knew. When that happened, he stopped the boat and sat listening.

He had retained the habit which had grown on him as a result of his
love of precision, of the uninspired nature of his own observation, of
the delight he found in exerting his authority, of explaining to his wife
everything they saw. This he would do even while they were being
rowed round the lake "Those lights over there come from the Chinese
Pavilion."–"Those carriages are waiting for people who have been
dining on the island."–"There are two ferries working today instead
of one, because it is Sunday."–"Ah! that's the new café which has been
opened near Armenonville." But though the nature of his conversation
had remained the same, it had acquired a new significance. The words
were no longer, as once they had been, merely a means of exhibiting
his knowledge, or expressing the satisfaction which he felt in making a
new discovery. They had become a system of notation, using the same
old conventional signs, though not now for their own sake, for conveying the soft and almost poetic sensations which he felt, but could
express only by drawing the attention of his listener to what had caused
them. To the reflections in the water, to the voices from passing boats,
to movements in the darkness, he clung as to landmarks, for they were
the facts which produced, though they did not explain, the pleasure
which he found in them, a pleasure which he now increasingly sought
when darkness fell.

From the boat Madame Santeuil threw a scrap of bread, broke off
another, poised it in her hand, threw it. When the bread fell—almost

synchronizing with the oar which touched the water at no less regular intervals—the ducks scurried up, each intent on outstripping its companions, with a great noise of ruffled water, their bodies raised above the surface, then settling on it again, scattering as they swam in pursuit of the vanished morsels. Then as the oar once more rose and fell, as the hand stayed poised in the act of throwing, off they started again. One might have thought, hearing their flight fluttering the water at spaced intervals in time with the rhythmic movement of the oars, that the birds were invisibly attached to the blades, and were putting forth their every effort to drive the boat forward, and pull it along. Now and again too, seeing on its either side, leaping, scattering, spreading, not drops of water but beaks and wings, and hearing shrill cries, one might have concluded that the water had come alive, that the oars in their passage had raised, in a noisy agitation of bright gusts, a spume of swarming life.

*

As the little duck-pond in the Zoological Garden flashed and quivered in the tremulous splendour of the evening light, the band began to play *Estudiantina*. Then did Monsieur Cravant, his wife and his mother-in-law, delighted to come across, in an object which had aroused the fervour of the crowd, a tune which they had long known, with which so to speak, they had been on intimate terms, which of an evening had often gladly let itself be heard on their piano when they were "just by themselves", when Monsieur Cravant treated it so much like an old friend that he listened to it in his dressing-gown—then did Monsieur Cravant, his wife and his mother-in-law, express with little signs of proud, protective joy, the fact that they recognized it. Every now and again, after a moment's uneasy concentration, and as though they feared that the musicians might make a blunder, they nodded approval, seeming to say, "Yes, that's it, right enough, the dear old thing"—mingling with a smile of approbation for the precision of the rendering, an exchange of sentimental glances intended to underline the merits of "their" tune. They set much store on letting others know that they knew it, that even if the name of the piece had not been displayed upon the bandstand, they still would have recognized it, that they had been familiar with it for a very long time, that they had so to speak dandled it on their knees. They made as though to sing, but without producing from their lips any definite sound, their object being to convince their neighbours that they knew the air without however weakening the impact of the message by an inexactitude of interpretation. Thus they waited until the expected note had sounded before nodding a welcome, like people who proud of the fact that they are on terms of friendship with an eminent man are careful to say nothing until, somebody having remarked—"Very light-coloured hair he's got, hasn't he, almost golden"—they answer—"Yes, indeed, almost golden, he's a very intimate friend of ours." In just such a way, at the end of each bar or phrase, they nodded their recognition. Meanwhile, the duck-pond had become quite dark. It was clear by this time that no more boats would cast off their moorings. Side by side they lay, like birds who do not go ashore to sleep, but floating on the water tuck their heads beneath their wings, merged in the gathering darkness of the oncoming night which gradually envelops them.

11. *History of a Generation*

Madame Santeuil as you now realize, was still the same gentle, submissive creature, devoted to others and self-sacrificing, whom you
have come to know over a period of some twenty years. It would however be wrong to conclude that she had not changed at all. By slow
degrees, the son, whose mind and ways and life she had been so eager
to form, had imposed upon her his own conception of mind and ways
and life, and had given a new twist to his mother's outlook. But before
that could happen, it had been necessary that many sorrows should
combine to break the spring which had formerly been so stretched and
taut in her, for her to find, in her hours of desolation an innocent
comfort in listening to that same son, to recognize how intelligent he
was, even when he said things which in the old days she never would
have believed he could say, to realize that he was popular, that he
had successes to his credit, even though they were not always of a kind
that she could have wished for him. For the men who admired him, for
the women who were kind to him, she developed a feeling of tolerance
and liking, though one of them was a journalist who had been mixed
up in somewhat shady transactions, and another, this time a woman,
had had many lovers. The cunning diplomacy which Jean had employed to overcome his mother's aversion to them, found a strong ally
in her secret conviction that, '*She* is a good friend to my son, she speaks
well of him, she will defend him from attack, and so irresponsible a
man will always be attacked by somebody, and one so weak will always
stand in need of somebody to protect him. *He* is kind to my son,
appreciates his intelligence, can be of much assistance to him.' If
twenty years earlier, Madame Marmet had come to ask her about a
maid whose references she was taking up, Madame Santeuil would have
done her best not to see her, would rather have incurred her undying
enmity than have shaken hands with her. The mere presence of that
woman would have caused in her a feeling of physical disgust. But
only two months ago she had been filled with curiosity when Madame
Marmet was pointed out to her at her dressmaker's, and as she looked

at her, had breathed a silent blessing on the woman who was Jean's good friend. Had Jean taken her to call on Madame Marmet, there can be little doubt that her handshake, her smile, and the words she spoke, would have expressed the warm liking for her which for so many years now she had felt in her heart. If she had not sought Madame Marmet's friendship the reason was that she did not wish to draw for her own advantage on that capital of goodwill which Madame Marmet might have felt disposed to employ on behalf of the Santeuil family. She wanted it to be left intact for Jean. The most she would have done would have been to have asked Jean to get his father invited to one of Madame Marmet's parties in the hope that it might have amused him. Not that she did not still believe that Madame Marmet had had many lovers. But she was inclined to think now that the unkindness of her husband, and the promptings of her heart, had been the cause. No matter how lost to shame a person may be, we cannot help seeing in him or her a fellow-creature. That feeling makes us indulgent where failings are concerned. For many years now she had lived in the constant company of her son and for the rest of the time when he was not with her, had followed him, in imagination, into the great world, into the society of tainted women and vicious men whom Monsieur Sandré would have driven from his door. True she knew them only at secondhand, but that in itself was dangerous, because the skill with which Jean described them to her, and her own feeling of tender affection for him, combined to conceal their ugliness and to enhance their charm, so that she saw them as characters in a novel. It was not that Madame Santeuil's moral values had altered, but only her view of the moral values of others.

At the same time as this essentially worldly attitude grew on Madame Santeuil, as her feelings of repulsion for vice grew weaker, and her attitude of indulgence became more marked, other also worldly characteristics began to show in her. For human beings are not changed by the mere addition of isolated and arbitrarily distributed features, as in that English drawing-game where the players can give to a thin man one thick arm while leaving the other meagre. And so it came about that Madame Santeuil, who once would have waxed indignant over an unkind joke at the expense of one of her friends, over some malicious comment on somebody she did not know, was now prepared to laugh at similar comments made by Jean and would go so far—an unheard of thing for her—as to speak maliciously of people, though it must be admitted that from kindness of heart she quickly drew the sting from her words. Now that she no longer regarded vice as tantamount to crime, she had ceased to feel any surprise at hearing it attributed to this person or that. In the early years of her married life, she had been told that a woman whom in fact she did not know very well though she was a close friend of her cousins and belonged to the world she lived in, had a lover. She could not have felt more appalled had she heard that her old butler had been guilty of murder. The mere thought of the woman filled her with horror. Her husband left her. All the husband's familiars hastened to ask him to dine, but nobody was asked to meet him. Madame Santeuil was overwhelmed with feelings of pity when she thought of the woman, but if she had exchanged greetings with her in the street, would have felt that she was being false to her duties. Whenever the husband's name was mentioned, the faces of all the members of the family expressed condolence and deep sympathy. Monsieur Sandré murmured, "Poor fellow." He was now frequently asked to dine in houses where previously he had very rarely been entertained, but always alone. He was treated like a man in deep mourning or whose daughter had been involved in some terrible tragedy. The whole situation was, for Madame Santeuil, so extraordinary, that she could not get used to it, and in the long run had decided that the wife must be mad. Sooner or later they would hear that she had been shut away in an asylum. In those days Madame Santeuil could not have listened unmoved to the news that some woman or other had been guilty of loose conduct: still less could she have treated the matter as a joke, and laughed at it. After all one didn't make amusing small-talk by suggesting that one of one's friends lived off robberies and murders. But when the thought of vice no longer fills one with horror, when one so to speak has rubbed shoulders with it, then talking about vice ceases to be so very terrible, and to live on terms of intimacy with the victims—it may happen to anybody to have vicious friends—no longer makes one feel that one is damned irretrievably. Uncharitable gossip becomes a natural compromise between indignation and friendship.

Her old prejudices against artists and journalists went the same way as her old ideas on the subject of female virtue and human benevolence. That Madame Santeuil still treasured in her heart her old ideal of making her son a great man of action is perfectly possible. But life by degrees had broken her in—even where her demands on her son had been most exacting—to the necessity of resigning herself to something less than perfection. She was fully aware that his sole occupation at present seemed to consist in paying visits and leading a social existence, that meditating, using his imagination, writing—even that—would have represented, in the way of achievement, a great deal more than he had to show. If that was all she could get from him now, then it was her duty to try to get, at least that. Besides the world has a weakness for artists, and, by a slow process of change, her outlook had become worldly. Also—and it is no use blinking the truth—it was her son's defects which gradually she had come to love, even though at first they had shocked her. Love teaches us much, but also it much corrupts us. It both assimilates and estranges us. She had come to be the very image and reflection of her son. It may be true that Madame Santeuil was different from all other women, that nowhere else, no matter how diligently he had sought in all the continents of the world, and through the whole course of its existence, from the creation to the last trump, could her son have found anybody in the least like her. But it is no less true that she still had to some extent the prejudices, the manners and the habits of all the middle-class women of her generation, of all those shut-away social castes the members of which know nothing of self-indulgence and the loosening of moral standards.

It is true, too, that her son resembled all the young persons of his generation, whose effect upon their parents was much the same as his was. Consequently you may decide that this chapter, boring though it may be as part of a novel, is amply instructive regarded as a chapter of social history. Thought is a telescope which enables us to see magnified scenes which are set at a great distance. You know that the actions of a single day can sow the seeds of, can give definition to, the habits of a lifetime which in their turn may prepare or record the changes that occur in the individual. But change in the individual, that revolution which appears to be the greatest of all revolutions, is as nothing to those transformations of the species which you may be witnessing. No matter where your little rut in life may have been traced, whether you have mixed with aristocrats like the Duc de Beauvisage, who had daughters like the Duchesse de Réveillon, and grandsons like Henri, or with members of the bourgeoisie like Monsieur Sandré, who had daughters like Madame Santeuil, and grandsons like Jean, you have seen history in the making, that is to say you have witnessed a transformation in the human species stretching over a period of two generations.

It is impossible to stand at the sea's edge, even for a few minutes, watching the waves form, break, withdraw, and then start the whole process over again, without getting from those waves, which appear to be single, individual waves having connexion only with those that immediately precede and follow them, a seemingly vague, yet fundamentally vast impression of the great movements of the tides. At one point the waves may have conveyed a sense of their irresistible power, at another the rocks may have seemed to shatter each new onslaught of the ocean, but that does not alter the fact that the steady advance of the tide has been neither slowed nor hastened. What your views of mankind may be, I do not know; whether you hold the opinion that the weakness of Madame Santeuil, of the Duchesse de Réveillon, for their sons, is the reason why their own generation has disappeared, or whether you hold it to be the law of generations that each shall let itself be tenderly dominated by its successor, as one wave lovingly submits to the one upon its heels which leaps joyously to overwhelm it—in one case, the weakness of Madame Santeuil, in spite of her intentions, in the other the weakness of the Duchesse de Réveillon, in spite of her prejudices. As when in a gallery looking at a series of portraits all representing men of the seventeenth century, you are struck by the resemblance between them, whether one be a writer of comedies, another a king, you will find less difference between Monsieur Sandré and the Duc de Beauvisage than between Monsieur Sandré and his grandson. Perhaps on the contrary you will find that from the days of ancient Rome to those of nineteenth-century Paris, the patrician type has not changed at all. It may well seem to you that social classes and generations have very little importance, and that what makes truth of character in Jean or in the Duc de Beauvisage consists in a kind of logic of the feelings which is as it were the common essence of humanity across the centuries. You may talk about the aristocrat of 1830, or the journalist of 1880, but like the chemist who knows that sulphur and phosphorous will always combine in the same proportions, you will reach the conclusion that behind and beneath all social differences the only fixed reality is the existence of feelings.

*

Such are the reflections into which I have been tempted to digress while watching Madame Santeuil as she walks back with her husband to their chalet in the Bois, talking of Jean, while Jean ensconced in a swiftly moving carriage is returning to Paris, there to sleep with his mistress. I take another look at Madame Santeuil. In a world where all things become different as they move from the simpler to the more developed forms, but where the same elements are repeated as complication piles on complication, the dejection with which she moves, the heaviness and increasing weakness of her body, is in harmony with the diminution of her moral energy. The changes of which I have been speaking will be realized not in her, but in her son's son, if he have one, or perhaps in the very fact that he will not produce a son at all. The changes in the individual find their consummation in the species. The individual remains attached to his primitive nature, in so far that is as he bears the mark of it in the good or bad features of his face, in the flabby or determined lines of his body, and that body is determined by the pattern laid down by his family, just as the oyster remains attached to its shell, and its shell to the rock. It is possible that the species oyster may as the result of transformism, become the species butterfly, but the individual oyster always ends its life upon the rock to which it is fastened by the shell from which it cannot separate itself and live. Madame Santeuil's shell is her body. The shocks she has experienced in the course of her life may have caused it to deteriorate, to lose the brilliant colouring which once endowed it with charm; but the *form* has remained unchanged.

It is at first perhaps Madame Santeuil's weakness and shapelessness that strikes us most forcibly. Look closer and you will see that what you have before your eyes is her, her father, her mother, her son. But most she is herself. If you are tempted to think that as the result of a long absorption of new ideas, her outlook has widened, let me call your attention to the way in which she matches her steps with those of her husband with the utter devotion bred of love, yet at the same time, undertakes the duties of guide, prompted by a charitable zeal. He has just spoken, "I should like to walk a little farther." Whether she is tired she does not know, but answers: "Let us go on a bit," and looks about for a path which will lead them farther. All her wishes at the moment are concentrated on that. But look again. They have not gone far before they stop. Monsieur Santeuil has over-estimated his strength. They have found a bench, and they sit down. Madame Santeuil says, "We have had a long walk, you know," because she does not want him to guess what she is thinking—that he can't do as much now as he used to, that he is growing old. Then, as he sits there recovering his breath, she, looking at him, is aware (though he does not see her looking) of the body which every day is growing more bent, which can do less and less, of the hair which is whiter now than it was. She bestows upon him a glance of deep affection, in which there is something of despair, shakes her head, and purses her lips to keep the tears from flowing. But she knows that this impotent and passionate regret for what is happening, is only a form of self-indulgence. She is afraid that her husband may be feeling bored and begins to speak of Jean, of how gay he was at dinner: "How sweet he is," she says, thinking that perhaps pride in his son will serve to distract his thoughts. At this moment she is no longer thinking of her father and her mother, both long dead, as she once did during the long afternoons when in his younger years he was away from her. She has a more immediate duty. Sadness can do good only to her. By banishing it she can still be of use.

This woman who is still as she has ever been, whom new ideas have been unable to change in essentials, is not the product of any new ideas. The ideas in which she was bred up were those still lively in the mind of Monsieur Sandré even when he was old, ideas which irritated the growing Jean, too much absorbed in his own, and incapable of sufficiently accepting the different forms which wisdom may assume. In the world which they enclose as the statues of the gods enclosed the Roman hearth, the woman taken in adultery was never more received but driven from the door with stones. No poet would ever have been admitted there, still less it is needless to point out an actor. A son who had taken to the stage would have been thrown out neck and crop. One never went to evening parties, nor came home in a cab, any more than one changed one's clothes several times a day. One spent as little money as possible. Needless expenditure, generous gifts, fanciful indulgences, were looked upon as crimes, to be greeted with anger. A love-match, that is to say a marriage based on love, would have been considered as a proof of vice. Love was something that came after marriage and lasted until death. No woman ever stopped loving her husband any more than she would have stopped loving her mother. Not to consider that one's husband was intelligent—even if he wasn't —would have been looked upon as being as barbarous as not to want to kiss one's mother because she was ugly. Let us take one more look at the house in which Jean was born and grew up, into which he brought so many things, introduced so many people, or, at least gained tolerance for the things, and liking for the people, that it was soon no longer what it once had been. For humanity may put out new shoots but the house is still old. I see many all around me now which are closed and tenantless, because those who once lived there are dead, others which have fallen into ruin because those who lived in them have fallen into second child-hood. Some have been pulled down and will not now be built up again. For what woman, I wonder, whose house will be filled with English furniture, where only those will be admitted who share her aesthetic tastes and have houses like her own, who will entertain nobody who is not a countess or a painter—will husband, father, mother, child be all in all? I cannot yet take my leave of this couple whose union was not a matter of free choice, but the result of middle-class conventions and respectable notions, but who, for all that, will remain together until death breaks the bond. I can hear Madame Santeuil and her husband discussing some item of interest in the morning's paper. I realize that the woman who has just killed herself after her lover's suicide, is the same woman whom Madame Santeuil's cousin once knew, and about whom she felt so indignant. If her views have changed about women who behave badly, they have not changed about her, because she was part of the life she once had known. She judges her by the light of the ideas she held in earlier days. A French-man settled among Mohammedans, grows accustomed to Moham-medan ways, but, if he suddenly comes on another Frenchman he will judge him by French standards. I remember how Madame Santeuil once thought that woman must be mad, and cannot help wondering whether that ancient prejudice may not have been as sensible as the tolerant attitude which she later adopted. When her husband dies, it is most unlikely that she will kill herself, still she will die of sorrow. But no, she will not let herself die if she still has her son. Besides, there is no resemblance between acquiescence in death and the suicide of the little middle-class woman of long ago who left her husband to go with her lover. Ask Jean, who knows that his mother never did anything except from a sense of duty. But there should be no need to ask him. If I have painted her portrait truly, you must know that already.

*

By the time darkness had fallen Monsieur and Madame Santeuil were already settled snug in their home from which they could see nothing of what remained to them of life. If Jean, at the hour of dinner, after crossing the dining-room in the diffused light which the lamp kept on renewing, went into his mother's room to tell her something, then like Thetis visited by her son Aristaeus in the depths of the sea, where seated on a rock she was weaving garlands for her hair, Madame Santeuil would appear to him in the lamplight, writing letters or engaged with her embroidery, letting the soft waves of radiance play about her head and shine upon her handsome face. In front of her, like one of those streams which flow through lakes or ponds, adding to their waters a livelier sense, the lamp emitted wave after wave of pulsating light which softly spread until it filled the farthest corners of the room. He went close to her, and in the glow which did not separate them, gave her a kiss. He knew that in the room next door his father was reading by the fire, or was seated at his desk, enveloped, he too in light, sometimes getting out of his chair, for he could be heard moving about and shifting papers. But he dared not go into that room, scarcely indeed knew what it looked like, having seen it only for a moment when as he was passing his mother had opened the door.

It was a long time before he came to think of it as a room at all. It was called the "tapestry chamber" just as another was known as the "dining-room" and a third as "the library". Each one of them seemed to him to be a thing apart, and it never occurred to him that similar rooms might exist in other houses. Once or twice when he was a child, he had gone to play with his friends in *their* homes, where everything looked larger, richer, more gloomy, and there he had seen rising before him unfamiliar pieces of furniture, like strange animals crouching in the lamplight, and other rooms opening before him like mysterious caverns. In his own home there were many rooms into which he never went, where after dark no lamps were lit, as though they had been abandoned. The hangings in the tapestry chamber, the tall vases and the clock in his mother's room, seemed to him to have a personality of their own, so that when something was changed in them, when in the drawing-room, he saw red hangings on the walls which he had known as white, or when in the dining-room the four velvet chairs were replaced by ten leather-seated Gothic ones, he felt surprised as though these gigantic divinities decked with embroideries, with vases set before them, gods which had rested motionless for ages, which were older far than he was, on which each evening the carried lamp shone with the same light, on which the lamp brought in after dinner, cast only shadows and then night's deep darkness, were powerless, like huge but stationary carven sphinxes, to resist the gleam produced upon them by a fragile human hand.

Dinner was not yet ready. Monsieur Santeuil was in the drawing-room reading the paper. Opposite him sat Madame Santeuil, apparently asleep. "I see they say here that Colonel Picquart is likely to get five years confinement in a fortress," said Monsieur Santeuil. "What's that you say?" exclaimed Madame Santeuil, starting upright in her chair. "Come, come, no need to get worked up," said Monsieur Santeuil with an ironic glance at his wife, whose face, which had suddenly taken on the look of a sick person in pain, was still drawn and anxious. She had raised her hands to her eyes as though to hide from them the sight of something too terrifying to be looked at, as though she were trying to press back beneath their lids the shock which had so violently disturbed her. Looking at the twisted mouth and frowning brow, one might have thought that she had been attacked by some frightful spasm of physical pain. But the misery showing in her eyes left no doubt of the nature of her torment. The sadness she was feeling was of the kind that the soft-hearted can never feel for their own misfortunes which they take on the contrary with gentle resignation. Hers was the sadness which only the misfortunes of others bring, a powerless, suffering tenderness which leaps and spurts in an effort to touch those it cannot reach, on whom, if it could, it would spread happiness, and balm, and consolation. Madame Santeuil's pain was so intense that it was impossible for her to return her husband's smile. "Now, now, take it calmly." In any other circumstance it was precisely those words that she would have addressed to herself, for thinking of herself as wholly unimportant, and much admiring her husband, she would have considered that she ought to have sufficient common sense not to worry about something which had left unmoved the exemplary being whose behaviour it was her duty to copy, would have regarded the sharp pain which she was feeling as an exaggeration deserving of censure. She could not however keep herself from yielding to it, from crying aloud her scorn of those who were torturing a man for whose courage and generosity, though she had never met him, she felt so deep a respect. Monsieur Santeuil shrugged his shoulders. And then because of her affection for him, because she admired his philosophic calm, because in comparison with him, she felt extremely humble, she did manage to smile. "It was foolish of me. I realize now that nothing will stop them, that they know themselves to be the stronger," she said with gentle melancholy.

In none of the archives, no matter how detailed, of this period will you find the slightest mention of anything done by Madame Santeuil, or anything to bear witness to that unceasing tenderness, so vibrant and so true, which the faintest hint of misfortune, the least hope of being able to give consolation, aroused in her, or to that sweet emotion with which she thought of those to whom she felt bound in friendly sympathy. Her name never figured among the lady presidents, vice-presidents, or patronesses of charitable organizations. Never once had she signed any public appeal, nor ever tended the sick in any hospital. Her activities were restricted within the obscure field of family life. But even there, by choosing a husband for herself for instance, or by not marrying at all because she could not find a husband who "thought as she did" she had left no visible evidence of her naturally generous instincts, as have some women who made a choice which became the talk of the town, having picked as husband some man out of a world different from her own, an artist or a humanitarian, the keystone of whose marriage was not the total of the money brought by each to the altar, or the natural affinity of similar social positions, but a shared love for the music of Wagner, a common interest in the emancipation of women, or concern for the care of blind children. Many young women of that kind had shown from an early age omens that their marriages would be thus contracted, omens visible in their eccentric or careless manner of dressing, in the way in which they went out either alone or with women friends who shared their sympathies, who liked the same music as they did, or echoed their contempt for middle-class life, women with whom they made expeditions, not for the purpose of paying social calls, enjoying the conventional cup of tea and listening to illiterate conversation, but to visit the Louvre, the Sorbonne, or even the dissecting room of a hospital. Such young women, whether in their choice of a husband, or in their virginal contempt of marriage as an institution, bore aloft the standard of "emancipation". Their less intelligent friends made jokes about their betrothals, which had taken place at Bayreuth, or about the flats occupied by the young married couples, in which so the story went, there was an organ, but no kitchen, about the manner in which they spent their days in helping the miners, while others were eloquent in their defence, and made no concealment of their admiration of such unions, making it quite clear that, but for their mothers and the conventions of Society, they would have acted in precisely the same way. But Mademoiselle Sandré, when she married Monsieur Santeuil at a time when her eyes more often shone with confident hope and mischievous gaiety than widened sorrowfully at the thought of other people's sufferings, chose him for quite other reasons than those which had inspired Mademoiselle Saintré to pick on Monsieur Maindant—reasons which had been inspired by the thought that in spite of his great fortune he was concerned only to carry sweetness and light into the lives of the workers by playing César Franck to them, or by supplying them with reproductions of Botticelli. Nor later had Madame Santeuil made any attempt to rouse Monsieur Santeuil to the level of her own ideals, but had confined her efforts to being as useful and as sweet to him as possible—giving dinners when he wanted her to, seeing that the strawberry *mousse* was made exactly as his friend Dester liked it, so that he should beg to be invited again, and later when Monsieur Santeuil got easily tired, sitting by him of an evening reading aloud the books he found amusing, and writing letters for him.

*

Death comes to all men, and in death the greatest are made equal with the least—so says the wisdom of the simple. For in death a man journeys into the infinite and into nothingness. No matter how obscure he may be, no matter how limited his intelligence, the thought of death, the coming of death, opens for him a window on the mysteries of eternity.

Jean raised his eyes and saw that his mother was silently gazing at Monsieur Santeuil. For a moment or two, as often after dinner, the old man had let sleep overcome him. His brows were gathered together in a frown, his lips were puckered, but now that he was looking at nothing it was impossible to make out the meaning of what seemed to be going on behind his lowered lids. There was something about his face that was at once arresting and obscure, something that seemed to express a strong but undecipherable intention. The rhythm of his breathing was clearly audible. The sound controlled by no thought, produced by no desire, was neither speech nor song, but just a muffled and unconscious murmur, close at hand, yet mysterious, like the noise of wavelets breaking on the sand, or the soughing of wind in the trees. Jean and his mother continued to watch Monsieur Santeuil in silence.

They dared not look at one another, each fearing no doubt to see in the other's eyes the thought that one day Monsieur Santeuil would never wake again, nor ever again go to sleep. They had a feeling that this sleep had more in it of life than had his waking moments. Just now when the life that one day soon would leave him, still possessed him entirely without his being conscious of it, it seemed a greater thing than wakefulness, because the shut-in life appeared to be something more than an emanation of thought or will. Yes, something great, something powerful, while Monsieur Santeuil seemed but a fragile toy, unaware and worn out, over whom it brooded while he slept. So long as it did not leave him he could surrender himself with confidence into its hands. His arms lay slack and purposeless: his bloodless cheeks sagged beside his loosened mouth, and no expression showed in them. His head drooped farther and farther forward, his breast rose and fell regularly, swinging to and fro like an inert object floating on the waves of life which seemed to be breaking with a rhythmic sound close beside Jean and his mother. They could not turn their eyes away from the spectacle of blind life which, in its very blindness, seemed more than ever to express its power. The even sound of breathing kept on and on. The work of life and death, the work of time, proceeded on its course without a break.